£5=

To Stephen

Love Mum and Dad.
                    March 98.

Gripping, Cunning & Devious –
        Vintage Detective at work
                Dazzling Stuff .

May it give endless hours of pleasure
and enjoyment
                    Your Dad

THE SEXTON BLAKE
DETECTIVE LIBRARY

THE
SEXTON BLAKE
DETECTIVE LIBRARY

INTRODUCTION BY
NORMAN WRIGHT
DESIGNED & COMPILED BY
MIKE HIGGS

HAWK BOOKS

GRATEFUL ACKNOWLEDGEMENTS TO NORMAN WRIGHT
FOR MANY OF THE ITEMS USED AS ILLUSTRATIONS
IN THIS BOOK.

THE SEXTON BLAKE
DETECTIVE LIBRARY

ISBN 0 948248 96 3

PUBLISHED BY
HAWK BOOKS LIMITED
SUITE 309
CANALOT STUDIOS
222 KENSAL ROAD
LONDON W10 5BN
ENGLAND

SEXTON BLAKE COPYRIGHT © 1989 FLEETWAY PUBLICATIONS
THIS ARRANGEMENT COPYRIGHT © 1989 HAWK BOOKS LTD.

DESIGN: MIKE HIGGS GRAPHICS

PRINTED IN FINLAND

CONTENTS

THE ADVENTURES of SEXTON BLAKE DETECTIVE.

by Norman Wright

Sexton Blake is one of a handful of characters who have succeeded in that impossibly difficult task of assuming virtual immortality. The list is short; the odd Greek hero, a couple of Dickensian characters, a fat schoolboy, a number of characters from Shakespeare and a pair of Baker Street detectives.

The genre of detective fiction was nothing new when Arthur Conan Doyle penned his first Sherlock Holmes story for the "Beeton's Christmas Annual" for 1887; but the refinements he wrought proved to be popular with readers and by the time he had consolidated his success with a second Holmes story, and a dozen short Holmes stories in "The Strand Magazine," every magazine editor in the business was jumping on the band waggon. Readers of all ages and classes could not, it seems, get enough of a good thing; and fast thinking, swift acting detectives were a very good thing. Almost overnight a crop of sleuths in the Holmes mould sprang up to satiate the public appetite.

Late 19th century urban teenagers had little in the way of literature on which to spend their hard-earned cash. But all that changed in 1983 when Alfred Harmsworth's "Halfpenny Marvel" radically changed the reading habits of England's youth. His appeal to parents was a masterstroke. If you see your children reading 'penny dreadfuls' take them away and give them the 'Halfpenny Marvel' instead..." Some critics claimed that he killed the penny dreadful by the simple process of producing a halfpenny dreadfuller. But dreadful or not Harmsworth's new paper was popular with readers and flourished. It boasted "original, pure, healthy stories of bravery, mystery and adventure, written by all the best authors..." The first few issues contained a mix of fairly mundane adventure stories set mainly in far-flung corners of the globe. But the editorial of issue five promised readers a real treat the following week. "...See number 6 of the "Halfpenny Marvel" to be issued on Wednesday next, containing a splendid detective story entitled "The Missing Millionaire..." Sexton Blake was on his way!

"The Missing Millionaire" was an unremarkable tale on which to build a legend and that old adage that mighty oaks from little acorns grow was never more appropriate than in the case of Sexton Blake. The Blake acorn was sown by Harry Blythe, a successful writer and journalist, whose articles on true life crime for a Sunday newspaper had landed him a commission to write a series of detective stories for Harmsworth. Blythe was paid nine guineas for his first Sexton Blake story. The fee included payment for the copyright of the character. As things turned out it was an excellent bargain for Harmsworth. Slightly better than that which Ward Lock had obtained six years earlier when Arthur Conan Doyle had sold them the copyright of his first Sherlock Holmes novel for twenty five pounds!

Blythe penned a further six Sexton Blake tales. Three were for the "Halfpenny Marvel" and three were for a new paper entitled "The Union Jack," launched in April 1894. The "Marvel" continued in one form or another until 1922, but "Sexton Blake's Peril" in June 1894 was the detective's farewell to its pages. His first exploit in the pink-covered "Union Jack." appeared in issue 2 and was entitled "Sexton Blake Detective." It was in the pages of "Union Jack" that Blake was to become established as the premier detective of the English pulp magazine, a position he held for more than half a century.

After Blythe's death from typhoid in 1898 it fell to other hands to develop the character. At first Blake's appearances in the halfpenny "Union Jack" were erratic, and when the halfpenny series came to an end in October 1903 the detective had featured in less than a quarter of the paper's 494 issues. Things improved dramatically after the paper's price rise and after an intermittent start, Blake became the paper's resident character. He appeared in every issue of the "Union Jack" from August 1905 until its transformation into "Detective Weekly" in 1933. The Blake of those early tales had a long way to go before he would be recognisable as the character who became so well loved in later years. His office was in New Inn Chambers and several changes of address followed before he finally settled in Baker Street.

It is impossible to say what it is that makes one fictional character a success and another a flop. To know that would make one a millionaire. But whatever it is, it soon became apparent that Harry Blythe's creation had it!

A good detective needs an assistant and Sexton Blake was no exception. In his early days an oriental with the impossible name of We-wee filled the post for a dozen or so cases, but it was in penny "Union Jack" number 53, in a story entitled "Cunning Against Skill," that Blake found a permanent assistant, a bright eyed, street arab with neither kith nor kin. The boy was known as Tinker, a name he retained until the 1950's. Blake found the orphan wandering the streets of London. Here was no burbling Watson, but a wiry lad with wit, natural intelligence and a quick, hard right hook. A handy companion to have in a tight corner. The character appealed to younger readers; he was a character they could emulate. Blake might be hero worshipped but Tinker could be imitated. He became a useful and important character and, as E. S. Turner commented in his book "Boys will be Boys," "Blake (at the time) badly needed someone to prevent him being pompous." Over the years Tinker's character was developed; he became indispensable to the stories. He grew from the "small, bright, cheeky faced boy" of his first meeting with Blake, into a more rugged individual, as capable of piloting a plane or swinging a high-powered car around the back streets of London as his "guv'nor," the title by which he always referred to Blake.

TINKER

It was no lightweight task being Blake's assistant, for when they weren't facing sudden death or chasing the ungodly, Tinker was kept very busy around the Baker Street consulting rooms. A good deal of his time was spent in pasting the daily newspaper clippings into Blake's alphabetical index of everything and everyone worth knowing. When the index was completed there were experiments to be carried out in the well-equipped laboratory; for Blake was a detective of the scientific age and the fate of a man's life often depended upon the colour change in a test tube when a vital chemical was added.

PEDRO

Tinker was also responsible for the third member of the detecting team, a lugubrious-faced bloodhound named Pedro, who arrived on Blake's doorstep in a story appropriately entitled "The Dog Detective," published in "Union Jack" number 100. The massive canine featured in many adventures. He was a dog of great ability and some of his exploits made Lassie and Rin Tin Tin look like dumb mutts. It was all in a day's work for Pedro to track a felon, deliver a message, and save a life or two. His quality was summed up in the story entitled "The Bloodhound's Revenge," published in 1926. "Some dogs can think much better than others, of course, and Sexton Blake's bloodhound, with his inherited instincts and the thorough training that had developed his faculties, possessed canine intelligence to the very highest degree and with it what mankind lacks—an eighth sense which was purely inherent and instinctive." At the end of that particular case the clients expressed their gratitude to Sexton Blake, Tinker, "and his wonderful dog Pedro."

BLAKE & PEDRO IN ACTION

The final permanent member of the Baker Street entourage was Mrs. Martha Bardell, Sexton Blake's stout bustling housekeeper who arrived on the scene in 1905 and remained until the end. She lightened many a story with her ludicrous misuse of the English language. She was a master of the malapropism and her garrulous nature gave her ample opportunity to mutilate the King's English. She was as likely to wish you "...All the condiments of the season" as she was to tell you that she had done for Blake and Tinker "for more years than I can conjugate." But Mrs. B's heart was in the right place and when a distraught client need a meal or a strong cup of tea at three o'clock in the morning, she was there on the spot clucking and fussing over them like a mother hen. Her culinary skills were legendary, a fact greatly appreciated by the appetite of her employer, and on more than one occasion Blake commented that she was, without a doubt one of the finest

MRS. BARDELL

cooks in England. Mrs. Bardell often came into her own during the festive season; not only in preparing a festive board that groaned under its piles of tasty comestibles, but often featuring in the main body of the story in such yuletime favourites as "The Mystery of Mrs Bardell's Xmas Pudding" in the special Xmas issue of the "Union Jack" for 1925 and "Mrs Bardell's Xmas Eve" in the Xmas week issue for 1926. Mrs. Bardell and Pedro were the creations of William Murray Graydon, an author who turned out over two hundred tales of Sexton Blake.

Blake's popularity blossomed during the Edwardian era and soon his exploits were appearing in many papers. In 1905 the "Boys' Friend," a tabloid sized boys' paper, serialised "The Schoolmaster Detective"; three further Blake serials followed in quick succession. Two years later the "Penny Pictorial," an obscure, pocket-sized magazine aimed at older readers, published a series of "The Adventures of Sexton Blake." The detective remained a popular reader-puller with the magazine until the final number in 1913. "Answers," one of Harmsworth's most successful publishing ventures, featured Blake in a series of almost two hundred short stories that ran throughout the latter years of the Edwardian decade.

Even in those early years it was apparent that some readers preferred a longer read than that provided by the weekly "Union Jack" story, and many issues of the "Boys' Friend Library" carried lengthy, sixty thousand word stories of the detective. Some were reprints culled from other publications but many were original stories written for the library. The extra length gave authors scope to develop their plots and characters. The first original Blake tale in the library was published in 1907. It was entitled "Sexton Blake's Honour" and dealt with Blake's pursuit of a criminal who turned out to be his wayward brother, Henry Blake. The "Boys' Friend Library" was fond of titles featuring Blake in different roles—"Sexton Blake Foreman," "Sexton Blake Spy" and "Sexton Blake Clerk" were typical of the titles published in the library. Later came three issues dealing with Blake's exploits at school and at Oxford University. Not to be outdone Tinker's schooldays were also chronicled in issues 229 and 232.

Now that readers were eager to devour stories of Blake and Tinker's schooldays the pair could truly be said to have come of age.

The long Sexton Blake stories in the monthly "Boys' Friend Library" were clearly very successful. Readers were prepared to part with their hard-earned threepencies for a regular long read of their favourite detective. The proprietors of the Fleetway House made a brave decision; they decided to launch a monthly library devoted entirely to Blake. The news was given to readers in the "Union Jack" dated 14th of August 1915. "Advent of a magnificent new publication by your skipper" ran the full page advert, "In response to repeated requests I have decided to issue a new Sexton Blake publication which will make its appearance monthly. It will be called "The Sexton Blake Library" and it will cost 3d. This wonderful new book of Sexton Blake will appear in September, so there is no time to be lost."

The titles of the first issue, published on 20th September 1915, was "The Yellow Tiger." It is now something of a legend amongst collectors, and highly prized by those lucky few who possess an original copy. It was written by G. H. Teed, probably the most popular Blake author of the time. It featured one of his super villains, Prince Wu Ling, a Chinese mandarin bent on world domination, a Fu

YVONNE CARTIER

**THE CHANGING FACE OF SEXTON BLAKE
ILLUSTRATIONS FROM 1913, 1917, 1925 & 1960.**

Manchu type with the human and financial resources to help make his dream a reality. For good measure the story also featured two other Teed characters, Baron Robert de Beauremon and Mlle Yvonne Cartier. 1915 was a risky year in which to launch a new, rather expensive monthly publication, and it says a lot for Blake's popularity not only that it was brought out, but more importantly that it flourished so well. Within two years the number of monthly issues had risen to two. Later came four issues and, for a short time, there were even five issues each month.

The first short Sexton Blake play seems to have been "The Case of Coiners," produced in 1907. In later years it was followed by more substantial dramatic efforts usually based on "Union Jack" and "Sexton Blake Library" stories. The most notable Blake production to face the footlights was "Sexton Blake," a four-act play written by Donald Stuart in 1930. Blake hit the silver screen in 1909 in the Gaumont production "Sexton Blake," C. Douglas Carlile wrote, directed and starred in the twelve-minute epic. A few years later came "Sexton Blake v Baron Kettler." 1914 saw the production of a series of thirty-minute Sexton Blake films issued by The Kinematograph Trading Company. The films were based on published Blake tales and were widely advertised in the periodicals that carried Blake's adventures…"A *real* detective film drama…" declared one advertisement for "The Clue of the Wax Vesta," first in the series of seven. The second film, "The Mystery of the Diamond Belt," was serialised in "The Boys' Journal" and then almost immediately re-

published in the "Boys' Friend Library," where readers who… "had not already had the good fortune to see (it) on the silver screen" were urged to… "get your local picture palace manager to write to the Kinematograph Trading Company Ltd for particulars of bookings." By 1915 Blake had become so well established as a household name that a short spoof film entitled "Sexton Pimple" was produced by Folly Films.

A second series of silent films, produced by British Filmcraft, were released in May 1928. The six films featured Langhorne Burton as Blake and Mickey Brantford as Tinker. A few years ago I had the dubious pleasure of viewing two of the series. "Silken Threads," the first in the series, was ghastly, a sound reminder that detective fiction did not film well in silent days. "The Clue of the Second Goblet" was a little better—just a little.

Sexton Blake was a rattling good name for a character; but readers had to associate that name with rattling good tales, and it was the job of Blake's editors to see that the readers got their moneysworth when they handed over their small change week after week and month after month for the "Union Jack" and the "Sexton Blake Library." Action sold the periodicals and Sexton Blake indulged in plenty of it. Like Holmes he did his share of thinking, and at times probably out-thought his Baker Street rival. But when it came to dealing with the threat of sudden death Sexton Blake was the man to have on hand. His constitution was phenomenal: he could be slugged, gagged and bound, left in a cellar for a week, and still have the energy to dispatch half a dozen thugs in a fist fight after he had succeeded in escaping his bonds. Readers on buses, trams and trains demanded instant excitement in their stories and with Blake their requirements were well catered for. A whistling stiletto streaking towards his heart was mere routine to Blake, for he usually faced adversaries who specialised in the subtle art of dealing death in the most diabolical manner. Circular saws, death rays, packs of starved rats and pits of cobras were all faced with equal equanamity. The villain would smile with satanic pleasure as he relished the thought of Blake, his implacable foe, being slowly done to death in the cellar. But the smile would fade when the detective, grim faced after his ordeal appeared at the study door, a steel blue revolver in his hand. For the arch criminals never seemed to realise that in the time it took for their fiendish schemes to take affect, Blake and Tinker usually had ample time to contrive some equally ingenious method of escape.

It did not take many years for the editors to realise that the calibre of the villains featured in the stories was crucial. Given the right treatment, Blake's adversaries could be developed and gain their own following amongst the readers. Blake and Tinker had to be characterised along strict editorial lines for the sake of continuity; but the villains were another matter and the team of Blake writers were given a virtual free hand to develop their own master criminals. The one stipulation seems to have been that the adversaries were not to upstage the detective!

Blake's first antagonist to receive star grooming was George Marsden Plummer, a crooked detective-sergeant at Scotland Yard who had a taste for high living and luxury. When Plummer discovered that only two people stood between him and a vast fortune he plotted to eliminate the competition and lead a life of ease on the proceeds of his crime. Needless to say Blake foiled his plans. But a good adversary could not languish behind bars for long... "...I congratulate you! Temporarily you are the better man!" Said George Marsden Plummer, coolly and unabashed. Plummer was sent to his cell. He looked round it and resolved he simply would not stay in it..." Like so many others, Plummer escaped to fight again and he became one of Blake's bitterest enemies. Time and again their paths crossed and every time Blake proved to be the better man... "...Frantically Plummer tried to break that terrible grip, but it was useless. He glared in Blake's face in helpless fury. He knew he was beaten once again by the man he hated more than any other man on earth..." Compared with many of Sexton Blake's later adversaries Plummer was fairly run of the mill. He was the creation of Ernest Semphill. After Semphill's death other writers continued chronicling Plummer's exploits against society. Blake and Plummer were still hammering it out on the eve of the Second World War.

An adversary with a lot more muscle was Waldo the Wonderman, created by E. S. Brooks in 1918. Brooks

WALDO IN ACTION

developed the character from an out and out rogue into something approaching a modern day Robin Hood. Waldo had many qualities that would have made Harry Houdini green with envy. He not only possessed super human strength but was also insensitive to pain and capable of contorting his body almost beyond belief. After his reformation Waldo sometimes worked in collaboration with Blake. "..."Waldo has been working splendidly in the cause of justice, Sir Rodney" replied Blake promptly. I only hope that he will continue in this happy strain..."

METROPOLITAN POLICE

WANTED

FOR FORGERY, BLACKMAIL AND ROBBERY WITH VIOLENCE
GEORGE MARSDEN PLUMMER
HEIGHT 6 ft. WEIGHT 12 st. 7 lb. FRESH COMPLEXION BUT EXPERT IN DISGUISE. EYES HAVE A CURIOUS AGATE GLOW. FORMER DETECTIVE SERGEANT, CRIMINAL INVESTIGATION DEPT, SCOTLAND YARD AND NOW ESCAPED CONVICT, BLEAKMOOR PRISON. CARRIES ARMS
THIS MAN IS DANGEROUS

GEORGE MARSDEN PLUMMER

And of course he did—when there was a fat cheque to be had from a satisfied client. If not, well, he kept an eye on the state of his bank balance and topped it up, when necessary, with a healthy percentage of plunder appropriated from the swindlers and blackmailers who were his favourite prey.

The list of Blake's adversaries is long: Zenith, the elegant albino with the crimson eyes; Dr Huxton Rymer; Leon Kestrel, the Master Mummer; and an almost endless host of others. They became almost as important as Blake to the stories and their names usually featured on the covers in

ZENITH THE ALBINO

large print: "A Zenith story complete in this issue," "Sexton Blake versus Waldo!" "Sexton Blake and Leon Kestrel."

Equally important to the tales were Blake's allies who were almost as numerous as his foes! One of the most memorable was Derek 'Splash' Page, the irrepressible crime reporter of the "Daily Radio." Page was created by Gwyn Evans, who also breathed life into another favourite character, the hard boiled American investigator, Ruff Hanson. Blake's work naturally brought him into contact with the official police. Country constables and provincial inspectors usually regarded him with awe. He had only to mention his name to the constable stationed outside the room containing the corpse to gain a smart salute and instant admission. Even the 'big wigs' of Scotland Yard—Chief Detective-Inspector Lennard, Detective Inspector Coutts and Superintendent Venner—welcomed Blake's intervention with something approaching enthusiasm.

In 1920 the "Union Jack" was given a face lift. The rather old-fashioned pink cover it had worn for a quarter of a century was replaced with a two colour wrapper. It would not be an exaggeration to say that during the 1920's the "Union Jack" bore one of the most striking wrappers to be seen on the news-stands. In 1921 there were editorial changes at Fleetway House. Leonard Pratt became editor

of the "Sexton Blake Library" and Harold Twyman became responsible for "Union Jack." Under the guidance of these two men both papers flourished.

In 1922 Twyman introduced a new young artist named Eric Parker to his paper. Up to that time the detective had not had a regular artist illustrating his adventures; his exploits had been depicted by a group of artists familiar to readers of most of the other Fleetway House publications, most notably Arthur Jones, H. M. Lewis and J. H. Valda. Parker's early work for the "Union Jack" was a little stiff but, by the mid 1920's, his distinctive style was immediately recognisable. His covers captured the sinister, brooding mood of the stories. His characters, though speedily drawn with an economy of line, deftly depicted their owner's character. Parker, more than any other artist, was responsible for establishing the visual image of Blake. The "Union Jack" cover for 23rd of May 1925 carried a study of Blake that was used time and again in later issues and in other publications. Parker's illustration depicted Blake the thinker; alert and keen-witted. Two years later the artist drew a similar though more striking study of the detective for the issue dated 25th June 1927. Blake's jaw was a little leaner, his eyes a touch more piercing, his whole poise more lithe and panther-like. He was still a thinker, but above all he was a man of action who could, when necessary bring into play his skills as a boxer, wrestler, swordsman; you name it he could do it! Parker depicted Blake with many Holmesian characteristics and props—the long, hawk-like face, the pipe, the chair by the fire and the worn dressing-gown. But above all his illustrations brought Blake and all the other characters in the stories to life with images that exploded across the page. In 1926

LADY IN DISTRESS (AN ERIC PARKER ILLUSTRATION)

Parker modelled a seven-inch high plaster bust of Blake. Readers could obtain a copy by introducing six new readers to the "Union Jack" and sending the editor the six coupons clipped from page twenty-five. The busts were also given away as competition prizes by cinemas showing the Sexton Blake films. They are now extremely rare with only a dozen or so known to exist in various private collections.

In 1929 Eric Parker began painting the full colour covers for the "Sexton Blake Library." It has been estimated that he produced nearly nine hundred covers over a period of almost thirty years. His work for the library reached its peak during the mid-1930's when, despite his huge output, his work was always exciting and vibrant. Parker's covers had such a compelling and atmospheric quality that it is impossible to glance through a pile of "Sexton Blake Library" issues from the 1930's without an overwhelming desire to dip in, anticipating that the stories will be as good as their covers. More often than not they were, for Blake was as lucky with his authors as he was with his editors and illustrators.

Many of Blake's chroniclers had more than a little experience of life. Men like G. H. Teed, Gwyn Evans and Rex Hardinge had seen much of the world, including a good deal of its seamier side. They used their experiences to instil their stories with first hand colour.

Many of the authors who were busily turning out regular stories of Blake and Tinker were also hammering out crime fiction for Wright and Brown and other publishing houses who specialised in producing detective fiction for the private circulating libraries that were so popular during the first fifty years of the century. With some ingenuity many were able to turn their Sexton Blake stories into non-Blake hardbacked thrillers, deftly adapting Sexton Blake into Double O'Day, Trevor Lowe, or whatever their own particular sleuth was called in their de-Blakenised board-bound manifestations.

Early in 1933 the "Union Jack" changed into "Detective Weekly." The larger format had a more up to date look about it and Eric Parker's splendid cover for the first issue got the new paper off to a flying start. The opening story, "Sexton Blake's Secret" introduced the detective's rascally brother, Nigel, and once again Sexton Blake had to compromise his honour. "This was the ingrate for whom he had sacrificed his code and pride—perjured himself, so that an old friend of the Yard had gone off bristling with suspicion and even his own nephew was in doubt..." Strong stuff indeed!

Blake flourished in the 1930's. Early in the decade he enjoyed the rare distinction of appearing on a 78 rpm gramophone record entitled "Murder on the Portsmouth Road." It was written by Donald Stuart and featured Arthur Wontner as Blake. Seven minutes was not a lot of time for character or plot building, but the cast were enthusiastic. The quality of the thunder, a prominent feature of the opening scene, has to be heard to be believed!

"Sexton Blake and the Bearded Doctor" was the first of three Blake films produced during the 1930's. It was based on a novel by Rex Hardinge and starred George Curzon as Blake and Tony Sympson as Tinker. Second in the series was "Sexton Blake and the Mademoiselle," taken from a story by G. H. Teed. It featured Mlle. Roxanne, one of

ROXANE HARFIELD

the saga's 'femme fatales.' Blake appealed to the ladies and Roxanne was only one of many who would have liked Blake to have taken her to the altar—or at least to her boudoir. The third film, "Sexton Blake and the Hooded Terror," introduced another of Blake's female admirers, the resourceful Mlle. Julie. The film was most notable for Todd Slaughter's gloriously hammy performance as the villain. Curzon and Sympson were adequate as Blake and Tinker and Mrs. Bardell, though less ample than Parker's illustrations depicted her, was appropriately long suffering and lapsed into malapropisms in true Blakian tradition.

The late nineteen thirties were Blake's finest years. His exploits were not only appearing regularly in "Detective Weekly" and the "Sexton Blake Library," but also in the "Sexton Blake Annual," a large, softbacked book of 160 pages that comprised both reprints and specially written stories and articles. The first issue, published in 1938, had an atmospheric cover painted by Arthur Jones. three further annuals appeared in 1939, 1940 and 1941 respectively, each with a full colour cover painted by Parker. The annuals contained a pot-pourri of fact and fiction together with potted biographies of the main villains in the Blake saga.

"You've read the story, now play the game," proclaimed the advertisement for the "Sexton Blake Card Game," produced by Waddy Productions. Unfortunately, the cards were not very well drawn and featured none of the adversaries found in the Sexton Blake stories.

The first Sexton Blake radio serial began on 26th of January 1939. And anyone foolish enough to miss tuning their radio sets into "Enter Sexton Blake" were able to follow the adventure in "Detective Weekly," where it was featured prominently on the cover for several weeks.

1. Sexton Blake and his assistant, Tinker, are in the power of the Hooded Stranger! And Sexton Blake is the one man who can save London from his clutches! The super crook has attacked one of the wealthiest parts of London and overpowered it with his sleep gas. Even now his gang are robbing the houses wholesale, from the cover of armoured tanks. But he has just discovered that in one of his own tanks is Sexton Blake!

2. With the aid of a crane that stands near by, the Hooded Stranger has yanked Blake and Tinker in their tank, sixty feet from the ground. Now he plans to release the crane-grab, and to drop them into the street far below! Luckily Blake and Tinker discovered their peril just in time. Hurriedly they scrambled on to the top of their tank. There was one chance for them—their lives hung by a mere thread!

3. "Jump for the crane-grab, Tinker!" cried Sexton Blake. "This is the Hooded Stranger's doing. I reckon he's going to drop us!" So saying, the great detective leapt for the big steel grab, which was holding the tank up. Tinker leapt a second later, and even as he did so, he felt the tank dropping away beneath his feet. He had jumped too late! Des-

4. The tank crashed into the street below. Built of steel though it was, it smashed to pieces with the fall. There would have been little chance for Sexton Blake and Tinker inside it! Up at the controls of the crane the Hooded Stranger gave a snarl of rage as he saw Blake and Tinker still hanging on to the rope. "They've beaten me again!" he cried. "But

THE EARLY SEXTON BLAKE STRIP FROM 'KNOCKOUT.'

George Curzon reprised his role as Blake, and Tinker was played by Brian Lawrence. A second radio serial, "A Case for Sexton Blake," began a year later on 30th March 1940. The story was adapted for radio by Francis Durbridge, whose own famous creation, Paul Temple, had made his radio debut two years earlier in April 1938.

"Detective Weekly" had looked set for a long run, but several changes of editor helped to bring about its decline. It lost its sense of direction and after featuring in the first 130 issues Blake was suddenly dropped and was absent from the paper for two years. When he did return many of his adventures were re-hashes of old "Union Jack" and "Sexton Blake Library" tales. "Detective Weekly" came to an end in April 1940.

But Blake's versatility knew no bounds and with his usual adaptability he hopped across to the pages of the new "Knock-Out" comic, where he encountered 'The Hooded Stranger,' an adversary worthy of his steel, who spent a lot of his time dreaming up diabolical schemes to do away with Blake and Tinker. The first few Blake strips in

"Knock-Out" were drawn by Jos Walker, but after a few months the artwork was taken over by Alfred Taylor who continued to draw the strip for ten years. The highlight of Blake's comic strip exploits came in 1949, when Eric Parker drew "The Secret of Monte Cristo," his only Blake serial strip.

During the war years Blake battled on in picture strip form and in the "Sexton Blake library." But his exploits in the library were reduced from four to two issues per month, and eventually even those had their page count cut from 96 to 64.

The 1940's were lean years for the "Sexton Blake Library." Many of the best writers joined the Forces and some of those who had been such a driving force during the 1930's had died. The stories became lack-lustre; hardly surprising when they were, for the most part, being churned out month after month by just a handful of writers with the occasional 'guest' author writing the odd story now and again. Even Parker's covers, previously so lively and appealing, became rather dull and uninspired. A new

SEXTON BLAKE AND TINKER IN THE SECRET OF MONTE CRISTO

A GRAND NEW PICTURE MYSTERY STARTING TODAY!

THIS WAS ONE OF THE STRANGEST OF ALL SEXTON BLAKE'S ADVENTURES — IT ALL BEGAN WHEN LITTLE BENNY LEMMING CAME TO ASK HIM A FAVOUR —

THAT'S ALL I ASK, MR. BLAKE. JUST KEEP THIS PARCEL SAFE FOR ME — — ONE OF THESE DAYS, IT'LL MEAN A LOT TO BOTH OF US — WILL YOU DO IT?

I DON'T SEE WHY NOT, BENNY. YOU'VE ALWAYS PLAYED SQUARE WITH ME BEFORE, OFTEN YOU'VE BEEN VERY USEFUL —

BUT I WARN YOU, BENNY, IF THIS PARCEL CONNECTS YOU WITH ANY CRIME, I SHALL USE IT AS EVIDENCE AGAINST YOU AND ANYONE ELSE WHO MAY BE INVOLVED!

IT'S ON THE LEVEL, MR. BLAKE — BUT I CAN'T TELL YOU THE WHOLE STORY — YET — — I'LL BE BACK IN A FEW DAYS, AND THEN, THIS'LL BE A BIG THING FOR BOTH OF US!

1. From the moment that Benny Lemming walked into Sexton Blake's study in Baker Street, the great detective knew that something quite out of the ordinary was afoot. You see, Benny had once been a small-time crook, and Sexton Blake had done a lot to bring him back to an honest life. Benny thought the world of Sexton Blake.

BENNY LEAVES SEXTON BLAKE'S HOUSE — WELL SATISFIED.

THE PARCEL WILL BE SAFE WITH BLAKE — THEY'LL NEVER GET IT AWAY FROM HIM!

BUT IF BENNY'S PARCEL IS SAFE; BENNY ISN'T — — AS HE WALKS DOWN BAKER STREET, A CAR GLIDES AFTER HIM, AND THE DOOR OPENS —

BENNY — — WE WANT YOU! YOU'D BETTER COME QUIETLY!

NO! NO!

2. But now he wanted him to look after a parcel, and he would not say what was in it. Sexton Blake knew that it must be something pretty big to make Benny act that way. And there were evidently other people who thought Benny and his parcel were interesting, for Benny was kidnapped.

ERIC PARKER'S SEXTON BLAKE STRIP FROM 'KNOCKOUT.'

lease of life was required and the transfusion was rather late in coming.

William Howard Baker took over as editor of the "Sexton Blake Library" in 1956. Baker gave Blake a secretary, a suite of offices in Barkeley Square and a touch more sex appeal. He also gave Tinker a name—Edward Carter. Some long-standing readers greeted the changes with about as much enthusiasm as a thunderstorm at a cricket match. They wanted the old Blake of the 30's, but what they failed to understand was that Sexton Blake's survival over the decades had been due to the ability of his chroniclers to change the detective with the times. If Blake was to survive in the 1950's and 60's, he had to be a little more hard-boiled and streetwise.

The covers became more eye catching, often with curvatious females revealing rather more cleavage than Nell Gwyn! A clutch of new authors brought a breath of originality to the stories and revitalised the characters. The "New Order Sexton Blake Library," as it was known during Howard Baker's editorship, ran for seven years,

coming to an end in June 1963 with a story appropriately titled "The Last Tiger." The final few pages carried tributes from many of those who had been associated with the library.

It seemed like the end of Blake, but within two years he was back again; this time in a series of paperbacks issued by Mayflower Books. The series ran to forty-five titles. In 1967 the BBC broadcast a new series of radio plays with William Franklyn making an excellent Blake. At about the same time Lawrence Payne portrayed the detective in a long running T.V. series set in the 1920's. There was new strip in "Valiant" comic and even an annual, "The Valiant Book of T.V's Sexton Blake." Blake's last original appearance to date was in Simon Raven's T.V. serial "Sexton Blake and the Demon God," a period thriller with ancient curses and clill-hanger endings. The villain, as usual, tried time and time again to do away with the detective. But it was to no avail. For Sexton Blake is, of course, indestructible.

OUR ERNIE

MRS. ENTWHISTLE'S LITTLE LAD.

The tales that really take the cake,
Are those about old Sexton Blake;
And Ernie one day thought that he,
This famous man would go and see.

He took a bus to Baker Street,
And found a house, all clean and neat,
Which had Blake's name writ plain and clear,
As Ernie saw as he drew near.

Well, Ernie rang upon the bell,
And out came butler, posh and swell,
Who said "Come in—though Sexton Blake is hout,
'E will be back quite soon, no doubt."

As lad sat waiting patiently,
A man came running in to see
If Sexton Blake could give him aid—
But such a daft mistake he made.

He thought our lad were Sexton Blake,
Which were a proper daft mistake,
Still, man were fussed as fussed could be,
And hardly looked at lad, you see.

With Ernie hanging to his paw,
Man led the way to his front door,
He cried, "I'm proper scared at this—
Each morn some things from here I miss!"

Well, Ernie then took up the chase—
He made a proper muck of place,
He scattered powder all around,
And spread out treacle on the ground.

There in the treacle footprint showed,
And Ernie then with triumph crowed,
"By gum—I've found a clue!" cried he,
"Deee—tecktive number wun—that's me!".

Then Ernie took his little saw,
And then began to saw the floor,
He cried, "If I cut this print out,
I'll catch the crimmy-nal, no doubt."

Just then our Sexton Blake turned up,
And smiling down at our young pup,
Said "Bravo, Ernie—you've done swell,
You've found the swag and the crooks as well."

Up through the floor some mices came,
And it was clear they were to blame,
For there was all the stuff they'd pinched,
Or swiped, or snicked, or just half-inched.

Young Ernie felt a proper lad,
He'd solved a miss-ter-ee, he had,
When he got home, as you will see,
He went and tried to solve his tea.

**EVEN 'OUR ERNIE' GOT TO MEET SEXTON BLAKE
IN 'KNOCKOUT' (JUNE 22, 1940) ART BY HUGH McNEILL.**

THE YELLOW TIGER!

PROLOGUE

Introducing Wu Ling and Baron de Beauremon

The island of Marsey, which lies just off the Welsh coast beneath the frowning cliff of Pembroke, is as lonely a spot as one will find in all the kingdom. It forms a rough triangle in the sea, the legs of which are each about two miles in length. One small bay alone permits a landing, and with that exception the shores are high, rugged cliffs, the haunt of the sea-bird and the home of Neptune's thunder.

The island itself is almost devoid of habitants or habitations. One large bungalow, built by a former owner, gives on to the small cove where a landing-stage has been built; and a second, the only other building, is an ancient farmhouse, fashioned centuries ago from rudely-hewn timbers, and at present the home of the farmer-fisherman, tenant of the present owner of the island.

For the rest, the island is the grazing-ground of sheep and cattle belonging to the owner, and which are looked after on a share basis by the farmer. Beyond that the rabbits hold sway, falling by thousands each year into the traps of the farmer.

A narrow sound of less than two miles in width separates the island from the mainland, yet, narrow as is that sound, it was, in days gone by, the scene of many stirring scenes when smuggler and excise man met and clashed together.

No lighthouse is there to send forth its beacon each night to the ships which pass up and down the wide highway beyond, and for that reason it is a place shunned by the mariner and fisherman alike. For years it formed part of a large estate on the mainland and was seldom favoured by the visits of the landlord.

But lately when that estate was broken up it was bought in by a man who was a stranger to the district, and who, though well-known in certain quarters, was unknown in name or fame to the local inhabitants.

The purchaser was Baron Robert de Beauremon, president of that daring criminal organisation known as the Council of Eleven. Why he had bought it, or to what purpose he intended to put it, none knew.

The farmer tenant was informed by Beauremon's solicitors that the stock on the island had been bought by Beauremon, and that the arrangement which he had with the former owner would continue as usual. To the farmer-fisherman this was satisfactory, and he continued his duties as usual, scarcely troubling himself with thoughts of the new owner.

But a mild feeling of excitement filled him when he received a letter informing him that Baron Robert de Beauremon was coming to the island with some friends, and requesting him to get the bungalow in order. The tenant proceeded to do so, remarking to himself that the owner had neglected to say how he would arrive or by what means he would get across to the island.

Three days later he was enlightened with something of a shock, when, as he stood on the landing-stage in the little cove, he saw what at first appeared to be some strange colossal bird high overhead and winging its way towards the island.

As it approached, it grew larger and larger until, to the startled gaze of the tenant it resolved itself into one of the great air machines of which he had read and seen in pictures, but which he had never witnessed in reality.

Nor was his astonishment any the less when it swooped down towards the island and came to earth on a wide stretch of level field where cattle grazed. The beasts with tails in the air tore off madly towards a distant wood, and the farmer, running towards the spot where the huge biplane had come down, met two men climbing out of the cockpit.

One of them, a tall, fair man of commanding presence, removed his flying helmet as the tenant came up, and, smiling genially, informed him that he was the baron. The other man he indicated as Senor Gonzalez, his friend, following up the statement by asking if the bungalow had been got ready. The tenant, scarcely able to reply from the amazement which filled him, stammered out an affirmative and led the way towards it.

Then he was kept on the move as he had never been before. The new owner wanted this and that attended to, and nothing would do but he must make a complete tour of the island that very day.

For two days he was here, there, and everywhere, and then on the third night there was a new arrival. The farmer-tenant knew not whence he came. His first knowledge of the arrival was when the baron and his friend arranged a strong light on the landing-stage in the cove, and by its beams lighted in a large motor-boat which arrived late at night.

The tenant received a further shock when he saw that the new arrival was a Celestial, and that the one man who formed the crew of the motor-boat was also a Chinaman.

Then the two new arrivals disappeared towards the bungalow with their host, and the tenant saw no more of them for twenty-four hours.

But had he been able to conceal himself beneath the wide balcony of the bungalow he would have heard something which would have given him cause to think.

That same night, when the new arrivals had been refreshed by a plain but plentiful meal, Baron Robert de Beauremon and one of the Celestials went out on to the balcony, and seating themselves in low wicker chairs bent towards each other.

It was the baron who spoke first.

"How do things progress, prince?" he asked in a low tone, though in truth they had only the sea-birds for eavesdroppers.

Prince Wu Ling—for it was he—shrugged slightly.

"My arrangements are complete," he replied. "It is only for you to say the word."

Beauremon was silent for a little, then he said:

"When you first made the proposal to me, prince, I was dubious of its possibilities, but as I told you then I was and am

19

prepared to go ahead with it, providing there was sufficient in it to tempt me. Of course, you know about the Council of Eleven, and will understand that we can only take on propositions which promise a large reward. It takes a lot of money to run such an organisation as the Council of Eleven, and we have been a little unfortunate lately.

"However, I am down here to listen to a definite offer, and if I take it up I am ready to act at once. If not—well, you will be a welcome guest as long as you will honour me with your presence."

"You speak fairly, baron," responded Wu Ling. "I understand the difficulties which are yours, and I understood them before I approached you regarding this affair. But I think the financial reward will be sufficient for you.

"Some time ago—it matters not exactly when—I was in communication with certain sources to whom Britain's power and present policy are inimical. At that time I joined forces with these people, and it was my intention to carry out for them certain operations in return for which they offered me their assistance in affairs which are very near my heart.

"I shall not bore you by a relation of the first step in this agreement. Sufficient is it to say that owing to laxity on the part of someone it was a failure, due principally to the meddling of a man whom you have reason to hate as much as I."

"You mean——" said Beauremon.

"I mean Sexton Blake," replied Wu Ling curtly. "Time and again has that man intruded himself upon my affairs, but one day—one day—ah! my friend! one day he will fall into my power. Then——" And Wu Ling finished with an expressive shrug. "But that is beside the question," continued the prince. "As I said, the first affair was muddled. It is my intention that there shall be no muddling in the second. For that reason I have laid my plans carefully, and have sought you, baron. Together we can do much.

"If we are successful it will take not more than a week of your time. If we are unsuccessful—but I will not consider that possibility. I am determined that we shall be. For the reward I can promise you a substantial sum for our co-operation. I am prepared to offer you ten thousand pounds down and, if success is ours, add to that another ten thousand."

"That would make twenty thousand in all," murmured the baron. "Make it twenty-five thousand in the event of success, prince, and my answer is 'Yes.'"

Wu Ling shrugged.

"As you will," he replied. "It shall be twenty-five thousand. And now to the details. My present allies are, as I have already told you, interested in certain affairs here in England. They have planned a series of coups, all of which lead up to a main coup, the nature of which even I do not know.

"I speak of the Germans. To them I have promised my aid, in return for which they give me theirs, as I have told you. Now I understand, baron, that it is an essential part of the conditions governing the Council of Eleven that there shall be no question of creed or country to influence your operations. Am I right?"

Beauremon nodded.

"That is quite right, Prince Wu Ling. The Council of Eleven is prepared to work for anyone, providing the price is paid."

Wu Ling smoked in silence for a few moments, then continued:

"Do you know the new British Minister of Munitions, baron?"

"I do not know him personally," replied Beauremon. "But I have seen him often."

Wu Ling held up one thin, yellow hand.

"Baron, that man is one of the geniuses of the age. He is probably one of the best-hated and best-loved men who ever lived. When he is spoken of there is no lukewarm sentiment expressed. It is either profound admiration or violent dislike. Yet no man has been watched more closely by the enemies of Britain than he. And it is true that these British pigs owe a vast deal to his brains.

"He has been the strong man at the helm—it is his keen mind which has seen through the muddles created by others, and now when the British have at last awakened, and have begun to realise that only strenuous measures will meet the tremendous demands upon them, they have had the sense to turn to this one man to lead them through the maze.

"With his usual promptitude he has risen to the demands made upon him, and when I say that he is the greatest enemy Germany has, I only speak the truth. Therefore, you will not be surprised to know that Germany is determined to remove him from the scene.

"Without him some muddler will take charge of things, and that will be another step ahead in the German programme which aims to lull this country into a state of security until the Germans are ready for the grand effort. Do you follow me?"

"Perfectly," responded Beauremon. "Proceed, please."

"It is to seek your assistance in removing this man from the scene of affairs that I have sought your aid," went on Wu Ling. "This island is, as it happens, ideally situated for the purpose. Your organisation will complete the circle of conditions necessary to make the situation perfect. Now I have learnt that this Munitions Minister is to leave London to-morrow night by motor-car for North Devon.

"He will visit at Northam, which is near the Westward Ho! golf-links, and on Saturday and Sunday will play golf. Golf is his only relaxation at present, and the only means he has of keeping fit while working at the pressure he is. I have a plan of the golf-links, and will show it to you.

"In a word, my plan is to get possession of the person of the Munitions Minister while he is playing golf at Westward Ho! With your assistance, and the use of your passenger-carrying aeroplane, I am strongly convinced that the thing can be carried out successfully. That is the proposition, baron. Are you prepared to take it up?"

Beauremon did not reply at once, but smoked thoughtfully for some minutes. Finally he roused himself.

"It is a highly dangerous proposal you outline," he said slowly. "If it can be brought off it will be one of the biggest coups on record—to kidnap a British Cabinet Minister! Nor would that be the end of it. The moment his absence was discovered, the best brains in the country would be at work to discover his whereabouts, and it would have to be a lonely place indeed which would suffice to hide him.

"But he wouldn't be kept hidden long," murmured Wu Ling softly. "A few days only would suffice, then he would never more be seen in this life."

"So that is the game, is it?" muttered the baron. "Frankly, prince, I don't like it. But I said I was prepared to enter into any arrangement you proposed, providing the price was sufficient, and I will not draw back. But we shall have to tread very warily indeed. This particular Cabinet Minister is no fool, I assure you."

"He is a dog, and will meet the fate of a dog!" rejoined Wu Ling passionlessly. "And since that is agreed upon, baron, suppose we call the others and discuss the details with them?"

Beauremon rose, and going to the door which led into the living-room of the bungalow, spoke in a low tone to the two men who sat there. One, a stout, powerful-looking Chinaman, rose at once, and bowed politely, waiting until the other man should rise too.

Had it been possible for Sexton Blake, the great London criminologist, to have peeped into that room just then, he would have recognised the Celestial as San, the shrewd and faithful lieutenant of Prince Wu Ling. And it was by this name Beauremon also knew him.

The other man, a small, swarthy-looking individual, whose every movement was as lithe as those of a panther, was Gonzalez, the Spanish member of the Council of Eleven, and the aviator of that organisation. He it was who had driven the great passenger-carrying biplane which had brought Beauremon to the island a few days before.

Both he and San followed the baron out on to the balcony and joined in the discussion. Until far into the night they talked, and when they finally rose to retire, all the details had been settled.

So as they sought their rooms with the distant pounding of the waves, the only sound to break the quietude of the lonely island, they had completed their plans. And at daybreak they began to put them into operation. Beauremon was abroad just as morn mounted out of the East.

The other three appeared on the balcony soon after, and when a hasty breakfast had been consumed, they all made their way to the shed where the biplane had been left. Gonzalez and Beauremon wheeled it out, and for some minutes the Spaniard was busy tuning up. Then he signed to the baron that the machine was ready, and the baron turned to Wu Ling.

"It is ready, prince. Shall we get along?"

Wu Ling nodded, and Beauremon led the way into the hangar. There he and Wu Ling donned flying clothes and fitted helmets on their heads. That done, Beauremon made his way to the biplane and climbed in, followed by the other. When they were settled in their places Gonzalez started the engine, and immediately there sounded a terrific roar as the Gnome barked out and the great propeller whirled.

San and Gonzalez held the machine until Beauremon gave the sign to let go, then the biplane shot ahead quickly, running along over the long stretch of level ground until Beauremon tilted the lifting planes. She answered immediately, and like a great bird shot upwards with incomparable grace.

Setting her to climb in a wide, sweeping circle, Beauremon settled in his seat, and from time to time glanced down at the water below, which was slipping away beneath them at the rate of seventy miles an hour.

Wu Ling, looking like some yellow sphinx from the past, sat motionless in his seat, his eyes fixed straight ahead and his arms crossed. For all the emotion his features displayed he might have been hammering along Piccadilly in a taxi instead of sweeping through the air at a terrific speed.

By the time the biplane had made a complete circle, bringing her nose back to the east, they had climbed to the two thousand foot level, and now, directly below them, the blue water of the Bristol Channel twinkled beneath the morning sun.

Far to the left the rugged line of the Welsh hills showed misty blue and black; to the right stretched the ramparted coast of North Devon; while behind them lay St. George's Channel, which broke on the coasts of Ireland.

The day itself gave promise of being perfect. Not a cloud flecked the unfathomable blue above, and at the two thousand foot level the soft August breeze caught them caressingly. It was an ideal day for flying.

Beauremon set the cloche for a very gradual climb, and picking out two tiny patches of black smoke, which came from steamers far below, steered a course midway between them.

At three thousand feet Beauremon set his right foot forward on the steering-bar, and ever so gradually the huge biplane swung southwards. Still she was climbing, and by the time they were at the four thousand foot level she was heading due south with eighty miles an hour being ticked off on the speed indicator.

Suddenly, far, far below them, a small dark blotch appeared. It looked like nothing so much as a dirty grey chip floating in a wide basin of blue, but when they had drawn almost directly over it, Wu Ling leaned forward, and, cupping his hands, shouted:

"Lundy Island!"

Beauremon nodded, and drew back his foot a little. The biplane swerved eastward again and swung along until Wu Ling again leaned forward and pointed down.

"There!" he called.

Beauremon looked over the side. The distant Welsh coast now only showed as a dark line to the north. The coast of North Devon was immediately beneath them, and where the sea broke against it there showed a long line of white.

Gauging the shore-line with a careful eye, Beauremon tilted the planes and set the biplane to descend in a long volplane. At two thousand feet he shut off the engine, and, shifting the rudder-bar a little, took the descent in a gradual spiral.

Lower and lower they dropped until the beach below seemed to fairly fly to meet them, then as it became still more distinct, Beauremon headed for a wide part which lay glistening white beneath the sun. The nose of the biplane came round slowly as they spiralled, then they slid towards the landing spot; the wheels touched the sand, there was a slight shock as the skids took the ground and they ran along easily to stop just where a tiny sand dune rose. It was a perfect descent and a faultless landing.

For a few moments after the machine came to a stop both Beauremon and Wu Ling kept their seats, gazing up and down the beach. They fully expected some wandering fisherman to come along and gaze with wonder at the strange machine which had dropped from the sky, but at the end of a quarter of an hour there was still no signs of anyone, so they descended and stood on the sand by the biplane.

Beauremon drew out his watch, and, turning to Wu Ling, said:

"We were wise to come early. It is only ten minutes to six now, and it looks as if we had managed to come down without being seen. I was certain the coastguards would see us."

Wu Ling shrugged.

"They may have done so, and even if they have, what care we? I have seen to all that. I have papers in my pocket which will serve to lull the suspicions of any coastguards. But come, let us wheel the machine along to the spot I have chosen in which to conceal it. Your landing has brought us less than a hundred yards from it."

They both took hold of the biplane, and, turning it, began to trundle it along the beach until they came to a thick patch of wood. There Wu Ling made a sign, and after a close scrutiny of the beach, they ran the machine in under the cover of the trees. Nor did they stop until they had succeeded in thrusting it into a deep tangle of cover which would have hidden two machines. And there Wu Ling showed how carefully he had planned things.

"I have been in Cardiff for weeks," he said, as they sat on the ground beneath the machine. "I came over here several times in a motor-boat, and after choosing this spot, set about to prepare it for the reception of an aeroplane, for I knew that if this affair was to be brought off it could only be done so by the air. I'll wager no passing coastguard will discover this spot. It will be uncomfortable remaining in this wood for two days, but the prize is worth it. We have sufficient food and drink, and can manage to amuse ourselves in some way."

Beauremon smiled.

"We shall manage all right," he replied. "Our man comes down to-night, doesn't he?"

Wu Ling nodded.

"Yes. To-morrow he will be playing on the links close by, and we may get a chance then to get him. If not, we shall have to try Sunday. I have here a plan of the links, and in your spare time you can study it."

So Beauremon, with that cool insouciance which was such a deeply-ingrained quality of his nature, lighted a cigarette and proceeded to study the plan of the golf-links which Wu Ling gave him. And the Celestial! What of him? Squatting on the ground he turned his gaze towards the sea, and for hour after hour sat there like a yellow sphinx, calm, all knowing, and inscrutable.

All that day did this oddly-assorted couple sit there in concealment, but in the evening Beauremon slipped off his flying clothes, and making his way to the sea bathed his face and hands in the cool brine.

Then he walked along the beach until he came to the village of Westward Ho! where he struck off across country. He kept on until he reached Northam, and, following Wu Ling's instructions, took the road leading to the residence of Mr. Grindley Morrison, one of the big land holders of the district and a former member of Parliament. It was this place which Wu Ling had said the Munitions Minister would visit.

There Beauremon lay concealed, until late that same evening a powerful motor-car drove along the road and stopped before the main gates of the place. While it waited for the gates to be opened, Beauremon slipped along in the shadow, and by the reflected glow of the powerful road lamps caught a glimpse of the occupants.

Then as it drove up the long approach to the house he started back for Westward Ho! well pleased with the result of his scouting mission. He had seen the Munitions Minister in that car.

The next day Beauremon and Wu Ling lay concealed in the wood close to the golf-links, watching, watching always for the opportunity they sought. Hours went by. During the morning they saw the Munitions Minister and another gentleman playing a round, but on that occasion no opportunity presented itself to put into operation their plan.

In the afternoon the same thing occurred, but so closely guarded was the Minister that they were compelled to return to their place of hiding that evening without having made a move.

Sunday morning they were once more on the spot, but the conditions were even worse than they had been the day before. Instead of two men, four were playing, and when after lunch the same thing occurred, it began to look as if all their efforts were to be crowned by nothing but rank failure. Still they lay there, watching like hawks for their prey to come within reach, and after tea on Sunday afternoon their chance came.

The Munitions Minister came in sight, swinging one of his golf clubs and smiling softly to himself at the result of a particularly fine drive which he had made from the fifteenth hole. Far in the distance the watchers could see another figure topping the rise, which they recognised as the man who had been with the Minister constantly, and who Beauremon knew to be Sir Hector Amworth, the head of Amworth, Strong & Co., the great heavy gun makers.

They watched closely while the Munitions Minister, who was carrying his own bag of clubs, selected another club, and approached the spot where his ball lay.

It brought him less than twenty yards from the spot where Wu Ling and Beauremon lay concealed. From there they could see that it was a brassie which he had chosen, and Beauremon, holding up a cautioning hand, peered out while the Munitions Minister raised the club to strike the ball. Then, half-rising, the baron opened his lips, and, in a somewhat muffled voice, called:

"Help! Help!"

They saw the Munitions Minister pause even as the club was above his shoulder and listen. Again Beauremon called, this time in a tone even more muffled than before, and then they saw the Munitions Minister turn and look towards the wood where they lay.

The next moment he had shouted something at the top of his lungs to his distant companion, and, turning, raced towards the spot from which the cry had come. As he did so, Beauremon and Wu Ling rose, and, as the Munitions Minister dashed into the wood, they both launched themselves at him.

Now, while by no means a powerful man, the Munitions Minister was lithe and active and full of courage. The moment the two men sprang at him, he saw the trap which had been laid for him; but, determined not to be overpowered without a struggle, he raised the brassie which he still carried, and, as Beauremon came at him, struck out with all his force.

There was a cracking sound as the blow got home, and the next moment the club snapped in half as the blood poured from a deep wound in Beauremon's forehead.

The baron staggered, and, had the Munitions Minister taken to his heels, he might even then have escaped. But, instead, he turned to meet Wu Ling's attack, and, as the Celestial struck him, the pair went down together. The Munitions Minister just had time to call for help to the companion whom he knew must be near, and then Wu Ling's fingers closed on his throat.

Beauremon, who had recovered a little from the blow which he been dealt, also took a hand, and, picking up the Minister, they carried him through the wood towards the beach. At that same moment, the Munitions Minister's companion dashed into the wood, and, leaving the Minister to Wu Ling, the baron crouched to wait for him.

Sir Hector Amworth came on at full-speed, and, as he passed the tree where Beauremon crouched, the latter sprang, clubbing a heavy revolver as he did so. The next moment Sir Hector Amworth lay full-length on the ground, unconscious. Taking him by the shoulders, Beauremon dragged him towards the beach, and left him close to the wood while he went along after Wu Ling.

The Chinese prince had carried the Munitions Minister to a spot just opposite, where the biplane lay concealed. There Beauremon lent him a hand, and together they conveyed the now unconscious Minister to the biplane.

They dumped him into the cockpit unceremoniously, and returned for the other. He shared the same fate, and then the two daring men—one the product of the mysterious and inscrutable Orient, the other the child of an effete Occident—trundled the great passenger-carrying biplane out to the beach.

Climbing in, Beauremon turned the rear starter, and Wu Ling, who had clambered in after the baron, had just time to sink down in his seat, when, with a roar, the machine started along the beach. A moment later she was mounting, while the water slipped by underneath at seventy miles an hour.

And the only person who saw the exact spot from which the biplane rose was a single boy, who was idling about some distance along the beach.

END OF PROLOGUE

CHAPTER 1.

The Missing Minister—Blake Called In.

"The Minister of Munitions has disappeared, Blake!"

Sexton Blake gazed thoughtfully out of the window, which looked from the private room of Sir John ———, Chief of the British Secret Service, on to a flagged and cemented courtyard, but vouchsafed no remark.

"The Minister of Munitions has disappeared," repeated Sir John, "and, Blake, he must be found without delay!"

Blake nodded, but still remained silent.

"I have got together the facts which are actually known, and have cut out all the theories, of which there have been plenty," continued the chief. "Listen, and I will tell you what is known. On Friday evening the Minister left town in the company of Sir Hector Amworth, of Amworth, Strong & Co., the big munition people. Their destination was Westward Ho! on the north coast of Devon. As you know, the Munitions Minister is fond of golf, and while he is under such a pressure of work it is practically his only relaxation.

"It was their intention to play golf over the week-end, and to return to town last evening by car. Instead of arriving here Sunday evening, as intended, they have not put in an appearance up to now, and, as you see by the clock, it is half-past eleven. In half an hour it will be midday Monday.

"In ordinary times it would be just possible that the Minister might remain over longer than he intended, but certain extremely important matters demanded his presence in town by midnight Sunday.

"One of his secretaries waited up all night for the car to arrive, but when it did not come he got on the 'phone to the house at Northam, where the Munitions Minister and Sir Hector were staying. The result of that telephone conversation caused him to come hot-foot to me. This is what he told me:

"It seems that the Munitions Minister and Sir Hector Amworth arrived in Northam, which, as you know, is very close to Westward Ho! on Friday night, about ten o'clock. I may say that the Press was not cognisant of their destination when they left town. It was merely given out that the Munitions Minister was leaving town for the week-end, therefore unauthorised persons could hardly have known his intentions.

"At Northam they were guests of Mr. Grindley Morrison, the former member from that district, with whom the Munitions Minister is very friendly. It was he to whom the secretary spoke on the 'phone. The Munitions Minister and Sir Hector retired early Friday night, and breakfasted early Saturday morning.

"They motored through the Westward Ho! golf links a little after nine, played golf till noon, lunched at the hotel at

Westward Ho! and continued their game during the afternoon. They returned to the house in Northam in time for tea, and spent the rest of the day within the grounds of the Morrison place.

"Sunday morning they again motored through to the links, and this time Mr. Grindley Morrison and a neighbour, Major Colin Hart, went with them. They played a foursome during the morning, which the Munitions Minister and Major Hart won. Then they went on to the hotel for lunch, and played another foursome during the afternoon.

"The car had been sent back to the house in Northam for a hamper, and they had tea on the links. After tea, Mr. Grindley Morrison and Major Hart remained at the club-house while the Munitions Minister and Sir Hector Amworth played round for a small wager. After the sixth hole they disappeared from view, and no more was seen of them.

"Time went on, and the two gentlemen who had remained at the club-house thought the game was taking a long time, but never dreamed that anything might be wrong. They attributed the delay to lost balls. I should mention that no caddie accompanied the players, since it was Sunday, and the Munitions Minister would not have one on that day.

At last, however, it got so late that Mr. Grindley Morrison and Major Hart both became slightly worried. They decided to walk out to the eighteenth hole, and work back along the links from there, thinking they would pick up the players about the sixteenth or seventeenth hole. They did so, but worked clear back to the ninth hole without seeing the slightest sign of the players. I believe you know Westward Ho! links, Blake?"

Blake nodded.

"I have played there often, Sir John."

"Then you will know the topography of the golf links there, and will be able to follow intelligently what I have told you. You will remember that the links are situated on Braunton Burrows, on the seashore, and overlook Bideford Bay. You will also be familiar with the position of the different holes, and in your mind can follow the course of Mr. Grindley Morrison and Major Hart as they walked from the eighteenth hole in search of the missing players.

"As I have said, they reached the ninth hole without seeing any signs of them, and not until then did they become really worried at their absence from the scene. They consulted as to what they should do, and Major Hart suggested that they retrace their footsteps to the sixteenth hole, which, it seems, is close to a small wood, which lies between it and the sea.

"They thought the players might have suspended the game for a little to walk through the wood to the seashore in order to admire the view. The two searchers followed this plan, and made their way back to the sixteenth hole. From that green they turned off towards the wood, and, entering it, followed a path which led to the shore.

"About half-way along this path they suddenly came upon a golf-bag containing several clubs, and on the ground beside the bag was the lower half of a driver. The upper half of the handle-shaft they found some distance on. It had been broken, as though under force of a blow, and both bag and clubs they recognised as belonging to the Munitions Minister.

"By now keenly exercised in mind, they followed the path to the sand dunes on the shore, and there found a second bag with all the clubs intact. Mr. Grindley Morrison identified it as the one belonging to Sir Hector Amworth. Close to the bag there seemed to be the marks of several footprints, but so confused were they that nothing could be made of them.

"They went up and down the beach for the best part of an hour, shouting and halloing at the top of their voices, but gained no reply. Thinking, perhaps the two missing men might have returned to the club-house, and anxious to get an explanation of the reason for the two bags of clubs being where they were, they hurried back across the links, carrying the bags with them.

"On their arrival at the club-house, they called the steward and questioned him, but he was positive in his statement that neither of the gentlemen referred to had returned. You can imagine the state of mind in which Mr. Grindley Morrison and Major Hart now were.

"It had dawned upon them that something of a very serious nature had transpired, and, realising the importance to the country of those two gentlemen, set out again to make a thorough search. They went from one end of the links to the other, searching and calling, and not until they reached the tenth green did they hear anything which might by any chance throw any light on the occurrence.

"There they came upon one of the caddies, who had heard their shouts. He said he had spent the afternoon down by the military school, and had seen nothing of the two men for whom his questioners were searching. But he added that late in the afternoon he had seen an aeroplane leave the beach far up past the golf links, and that it had flown in a northerly direction.

"If there had been an aeroplane near the links, it would not be odd that anyone at the club-house should not hear it, for, if you remember, there is a long pebble beach at Westward Ho! which, when the tide is coming in or retreating, makes a loud, booming noise which would effectively drown the noise of an aeroplane engine at that distance.

"As it happened on Sunday, it was high-water at five-thirty, so the booming of the pebbles would continue for the better part of the afternoon, and—so the Munitions Minister's secretary says—Mr. Grindley Morrison informed them it was particularly loud that day.

"Mystified by what the caddie had told them, they walked along the beach to where he had seen the aeroplane rise. There they searched about until they found what may have been marks made by the wheels of a machine as it ran ahead to rise, but they could not make sure. They thought the lad must be romancing, and questioned him closely, but they could not shake his story.

"They sent for Mr. Grindley Morrison's chauffeur, and pressed him into the search. They covered every yard of the links and beach, and made an examination of all the bits of wood which are about there, but the result of all their efforts was nil. There was only a slight hope that the two missing men might have returned to Northam.

"While rather a far-fetched theory, it was always a possibility that a message had come to Northam for the Minister of Munitions, and that his own chauffeur had brought it out to the links. From the road he would follow, he might see them playing and might have taken it direct to the Munitions Minister without the formality of first taking it to the club-house.

"Presuming this, and further presuming that it had been an urgent communication, it is just possible, though, I confess, not probable, that the Munitions Minister and Sir Hector decided to abandon their game, and return at once to Northam without waiting to notify the others of their intention.

"But on the arrival of Mr. Grindley Morrison and Major Hart at Northam, they found that even this hope ended in thin air. No message had come for the Minister of Munitions, nor had anything been seen of either him or Sir Hector. The chauffeur was in the garage with the car, and had heard nothing from his master.

"Mr. Grindly Morrison and Major Hart at once sent word to a few gentlemen in the neighbourhood, men whose discretion they could depend upon. They held a meeting in the library of the Morrison place, where Mr. Grindley Morrison told them what had occurred. Then they formed search-parties and searched the whole night. Mr. Grindley Morrison had just returned to the house, and was deciding that he should notify London of the mysterious disappearance, when the secretary of the Munitions Minister got through to him.

"That is the whole story as I have had it from the secretary, and he gave it to me as he got it from Mr. Grindley Morrison. Of course, you can readily see, Blake, what a serious thing this double disappearance is. To-day, the Minister of Munitions was to meet a very important deputation from several of the producing firms of the country. This evening he was due for a Cabinet conference. To-morrow he had another important conference on, and was on Wednesday to speak in Birmingham on munitions.

"In addition to those engagements, there is much urgent matter in his department which will of necessity be hung up during his absence. He is the brains and driving force of that end of things, and without him business will be almost entirely suspended. A message has been sent to the deputation which was to wait on him to-day, telling them that important business has made it impossible for him to keep the engagement, and postponing it until the end of the week.

"The Prime Minister has been told the truth, and he at once sent for me. He has impressed it upon me that we must find him without delay. His disappearance from the scene of action will cause tremendous complications. The other engagements he had, will, as far as possible, be filled by his assistants, but it is he himself who is necessary. That is all I can tell you, and the rest you must find out for yourself. You can work out the problem in your own way, only find the Munitions Minister as quickly as possible—much depends on it. Will you take up the matter, and push it forward without delay?"

"Of course, I will do what I can." responded Blake, rising. "I shall go to work on the matter at once. You are sure there is nothing further I can learn in London about this affair? Do you think the secretary could give me any further facts?"

"I don't think so," replied Sir John. "I questioned him very closely, and what I have told you is everything I elicited from him."

"Very well, I shall go to the scene of the disappearance and start to work there," said Blake.

With that he picked up his hat and stick, and shaking hands with the Secret Service Chief, strode towards the door. He passed through several corridors, and between several police guards, until he reached the lift, and entering it, was taken down to the ground floor. Passing out into Whitehall, he entered the big car, which, with Tinker at the wheel, was waiting for him.

"Drive to Baker Street at once," he ordered, and Tinker, turning slowly, sent the car along Whitehall at a good pace.

Crossing Trafalgar Square, he drove along Regent Street to Oxford Circus and there headed for Portman Square and Baker Street. He drew up in front of the house in Baker Street, and at a word from Blake followed his master into the house. Once in the consulting-room Blake tossed aside his hat and stick, and lit a cigarette.

"Sit down, my lad. I wish to speak to you," he said.

Tinker threw his cap on a table and sat down.

"Something serious—something very serious has happened, Tinker," began Blake. "The Minister of Munitions and Sir Hector Amworth have both disappeared while playing golf on Westward Ho! golf links. As far as is known, these are the details of the affair."

Forthwith he began and repeated to Tinker the story Sir John had told him. When he had finished, he said:

"It would only be a waste of time to theorise now. We must get to the spot without delay and see what we can. I must confess that, so far, the aeroplane spoken of by the caddie is the most suspicious circumstance, but on investigation that may prove to be nothing of importance. But we shall go prepared for all eventualities.

"In this case speed is the chief requirement. Therefore, you will get a taxi and drive through to Hendon. Telephone the mechanics before you go. Tell them to get the Grey Panther out and get her tuned up.

"When you get to Hendon, you will get into the Grey Panther and start for Devon. Come to earth as near to the Westward Ho! golf links as possible. If you take note of the western end of the golf course, you will find a very decent landing-place close to the beach.

"Myself, I shall drive down in the car and meet you there. Don't wait for lunch, but take some sandwiches and a Thermos flask with you. With luck you should arrive at Westward Ho! before me. If you have to come to earth some distance away, get some reliable men to look after the Grey Panther, and come on to the links. That is all. Now lose no time."

Almost before Blake finished speaking, Tinker was making for the telephone, and, ringing up the hangar at Hendon, spoke to the mechanic, telling him to get the Grey Panther ready at once for a flight. Then replacing the receiver he caught up his cap, and with a nod to Blake hurried out.

Blake, on his part, went into his dressing-room, and threw a few things into a bag. Then opening the door he called to Pedro. With the big fellow trotting at his heels, he made for the street and entered the car. A few moments later, he was thundering along Baker Street, heading for the surburbs and the open country, along the road to the west.

He stopped once on the way long enough to send a wire to Mr. Grindley Morrison, warning him of his coming, and then once he had struck the open country, he let out the throttle and sent the car ahead at a terrific pace.

Through Middlesex he went across a point of Surrey into Berks, and thence he traversed Wilts. until he crossed the border into Somerset. From Somerset he took the direct road to Taunton, and pausing at Taunton long enough for some hasty refreshments, continued his way into Devon, heading for Barnstaple.

At Barnstaple he stopped for five minutes, replenishing his petrol, and seeing to his lights, then on to Northam, only a few miles distant.

At the old sleepy town of Northam, which, in the days of Drake and Hawkins, was, with Appledore and Bideford, a place of bustle and excitement, as the cargoes from Virginia came up the bay and entered the Torridge, Blake paused to ask the way to the Morrison place, then on again to where it lay—a huge black pile of Tudor lines set in the heart of an ancient park, which had gathered vigour from the breath of the sea.

He drew up at the gates, and while waiting for the lodgekeeper to open them, glanced at his watch. It was just on nine o'clock, so that to come from Baker Street to the gates had taken him just under eight hours—not bad, considering the distance was over two hundred miles.

When the gates had been opened he drove up the long, tree-lined driveway which led to the house, and when through the deepening night he was the picturesque house, he noticed that the windows were thrown open to the warm August night, and caught sight of the white gleam of shirtfronts on the verandah in front. He drew up near the side entrance, and leaping from the car, ran up the steps where a man in dinner-jacket stood waiting to receive him.

He put out his hand as Blake reached the top and said:

"You are Mr. Blake, I presume? Ah! Now that I see your features, I recognise you. I am Grindley Morrison. I received your wire early this afternoon, and have been anxiously awaiting your arrival."

"Then there is still no news?" inquired Blake, as he shook hands and removed his motoring-cap to allow the cool night air to refresh him.

Morrison shook his head.

"Not a sign of them. But come along and have some supper. I will tell you all I can then."

Taking Blake by the arm, he led him into the main hall of the place where a footman relieved him of his dusty coat. Then when he had washed, he followed his host to the room where supper had been spread. At a word from Morrison, the servant who was in attendance retired, and when the door had closed after him Morrison said:

"Go ahead, Mr. Blake. You must be famished. I will talk while you eat."

Blake set himself to investigate the merits of the several dishes which had been prepared, for in truth he was hungry, and while he ate the other talked. He repeated, more or less, the story which Blake had already had from the lips of the Secret Service Chief. When he had reached the point where he had received the 'phone message from London, he paused for a moment to take a sip of port, then proceeded:

"Needless to say, we have searched all day. Several of my neighbours have joined in the search, and though our efforts must have aroused some curiosity, I am certain nothing definite is suspected, for the Munitions Minister was here incog., and no one knew he was to be my guest. I was at Westward Ho! when your telegram was brought to me, and as you requested in it, I kept a sharp look-out for an aeroplane. But during this afternoon none appeared."

"That is rather odd," interrupted Blake. "My assistant was to leave London about two this afternoon, and flying at the speed he would, he should have not take more than four hours for the journey. What time did you leave the links?"

"Not until dusk set in. Some of the party have remained at the links, but when I left, no aeroplane had shown up, and although I left word for a message to be sent on to me in case one did, none has come. If there had been any news I should have heard without delay. I came on here to meet you, but was afraid you would not arrive before ten o'clock at the earliest."

Blake tapped the table thoughtfully.

"I cannot understand why Tinker has not arrived. He should have been here. However, he may have had engine trouble on the way, and it may have been necessary for him to come to earth somewhere. If that is the case, he will hardly attempt to finish the journey to-night, but will wait until morning. Now, if you are agreeable, I should like to motor over to Westward Ho! and have a look round."

"Certainly, Mr. Blake. I am entirely at your service. I realise only too well what a serious matter this is, and the fact that both gentlemen were my guests, makes me feel it all the more keenly. But I can't for the life of me imagine what has happened. What could happen to those two in broad daylight on a golf links? I know, of course, that their absence from the helm would complicate matters vastly, and would grant a valuable delay to the enemy, but who would have dared to carry out such a thing? And yet, there must have been foul play."

Blake rose and lighted a cigarette.

"Surmise at present is useless," he said. "When we have had a chance to view what slight evidence there appears to be, and have collected that evidence together, then, and only then, may we attempt to form some theory as to what happened. By the way, where are the two golf-bags?"

"I have them in my study," replied Morrison. "Do you wish to see them?"

"When we return," said Blake. "If you are ready, I think we had better be getting along."

They left the room and passed out to the hall, where a man brought their coats and caps. They made their way outside, where Blake's car still panted at the steps. As they reached the top of the bank which rose from the driveway a man came towards them, and when he had drawn nearer, Blake saw that he was an elderly individual, with the stamp of the retired military man about him. He was therefore not surprised when Morrison introduced him as Major Hart, who had been a member of the golfing party when the mysterious disappearance took place.

He accepted Blake's invitation to join them, and, taking the wheel, Blake turned the car and started down the drive. On reaching the main gates he turned to the left, and with the powerful road-lamps picking out the road which wound like a white ribbon over a mantle of sable, they raced for Westward Ho!

Blake, who had often played on the Westward Ho! links and accounted them among the finest in all Europe, knew the way perfectly, nor did he slacken the pace until the car had passed the hotel and was skirting the links.

Instead of driving on to the club-house he kept on to the beach, from which came the boom, boom, boom of the great pebbles as the receding tide ground them viciously together. Here he drove more slowly until, at a word from Morrison, he drew up and all three descended.

"This is where we started the search," remarked Morrison, when they had alighted. "I suppose you will want to start here, too. We should meet some of the other searchers at any moment."

Blake dug beneath the rear seat of the car and produced a powerful acetylene lamp, which he turned on and lighted. Then he spoke:

"If you will lead the way, Mr. Morrison, I will follow. I do not know that I care to spend much time here. I wish to go chiefly to the spot where the caddie says he saw an aeroplane rise."

Morrison grunted, and, turning, led the way over the sand dunes along the beach until the lights of the village dropped behind, and only the incessant booming of the sea on the pebbles filled the night. To the right shone the light on Bideford Bar, while now and then as they topped a dune they could catch a glimpse of the revolving light on the southern point of Lundy Island, which stands sentinel at the gaping mouth of the channel.

Far up the shore they came upon two men, who were standing close to the water gazing out to sea. They turned as Blake and his two companions appeared, and by the light of the acetylene lamp he carried, Blake could see that they were both rather elderly.

Morrison introduced them as two neighbours, and when they were informed of Blake's name, they gave him an account of the evening's search. They told a tale of woods searched and shore examined foot by foot, without any signs of the two missing men. Blake listened to their report, then, thanking them, requested Morrison to show him the exact spot where the aeroplane had been seen to rise.

Morrison led the way into a near-by wood, and, making a circuitous way to the shore again, paused between two sand dunes.

"It was here," he announced.

Blake, holding the lamp so that the flare would fall on the sand, dropped to his knees and began to make an examination. It was not difficult for him to locate the two lines which Morrison attributed to the wheels of an aeroplane, and at the end of a few minutes Blake was strongly inclined to agree with him.

But to make a detailed investigation of the marks that night was out of the question. Though the acetylene lamp was powerful, still it would not show up the faint marks which might be there and on which Blake might find reason to hang his chief theory.

But now he had located the spot and could gain some idea of it's topography in relation to the lie of the shore and the sweep of the channel, he could apply his intelligence with more certainty to the evidence which had been related to him by Sir John ———— and endorsed by Morrison that same evening.

When he had risen to his feet he closed the mask of the lamp, and addressed the four men who stood close at hand.

"Gentlemen," he said, in low tones, "it must be quite evident to all of you that this affair is of a most serious nature. It must further be plain to you that for the present, at least, the truth must not leak out. Mr. Morrison has vouched for your discretion, and when you understand that matters vital to the safety of the nation are involved, you will see why nothing must be said. Therefore, I want you all to pledge your word of honour that until permission is given you you will say nothing about this."

A deep rumble of voices answered Blake as each one of the quartette gave his word. Then Blake resumed.

"With the gentlemen who live in the district, and who have already been taken into Mr. Morrison's confidence, we should have a sufficient force to keep guard here and watch for any development at this end. The line from here shall be in my own care. But for the present, at least, it will be necessary to preserve every atom of evidence until I can make a thorough examination of it. Therefore I want you to volunteer to take turns guarding the spot. Will you volunteer?"

It was Morrison who answered.

"I can speak for all of us here, as well as the others, who are at present about the links somewhere. We are only too keen to do all we can, and you may consider us, one and all, under orders, Mr. Blake."

Blake bowed his thanks.

"How many of you are there?" he asked.

Morrison thought for a moment, then said:

"Seven."

"Then I think it would be a good idea to divide the force up into watches. If three watches of two each were formed that would take six, and you, Mr. Morrison, could superintend the matter. In that way we could guarantee that this spot and a certain portion of the links would be under continual surveillance for the next few days, which may be critical. On the other hand, if we are successful in our efforts it may only be necessary for me to ask the services of yourself and your friends for a day."

"I shall certainly arrange to do this, Mr. Blake! We will pick up the others and arrange the first watch."

Here Major Hart spoke up.

"If one of you gentlemen," he said, referring to the two whom they had found on the edge of the shore, "will volunteer for the first watch, I will also do duty."

Immediately one of the pair volunteered, and they took up their places by the spot where the aeroplane was supposed to have risen. Then Morrison struck off across the links to acquaint the other three men with the new arrangements, and Blake, well satisfied that the spot would be well guarded until daylight, when he could make a proper examination of any evidence there might be, returned to the car and waited for Morrison to come up. In about ten minutes he appeared, and, climbing in, said:

"I have fixed things up. The others are arranging the watches and will snatch some sleep at the hotel while they are not on duty. I shall return about midnight to see how they are getting along."

Blake nodded, and, starting the car, drove back to Northam. Arriving there he drove to the Morrison garage, where a man took charge of the car, and following his host into the house, went along to the study where the two golf-bags which belonged to the missing men had been taken.

The bag which Sir Hector Amworth had carried presented no particular features of interest. It was a well-made canvas bag, having a hood which protected the clubs. Blake unfastened this hood and examined the clubs one by one, but beyond revealing the ordinary signs of wear, he received no suggestion from them.

Laying this bag aside he picked up the one which had been carried by the Minister of Munitions. It was a very handsome bag of pigskin, well fitted with protecting hood of the same material which fastened by a patent lock, as did the other bag.

In addition, it was provided with all the accessories desired by the inveterate golf player—ball pocket, sponge pocket, umbrella holder, and a multiplicity of leather straps and other fixtures.

On raising the hood Blake saw that it was packed with all sorts of clubs from drivers—of which there were three sorts—to cleeks and putters, the latter represented by two designs.

It was the bag of the enthusiast who knew his game. Taking out the clubs one by one, Blake made a cursory examination of them and laid them aside. At last there was only one left in the bag, a finely-balanced mashie, which he laid beside the others before thrusting his hand into the bag to see what else was there. Then he came upon two broken pieces, one of which Morrison had picked up in the wood and the other on the beach.

Now Blake laid the bag aside, and carrying the broken club closer to the light concentrated his attention first on the shaft. He saw that it had been broken almost exactly midway between the top of the shaft and the tip of the club. It was a brassie, well made and strong, and as he gazed upon the clean break, Blake knew only a heavy blow could have caused it.

He put aside the top part of the shaft and picked up the club end. This he studied for some time, then thrusting his hand in his pocket, drew out a powerful pocket-glass which he applied to the examination.

Along the lower edge of the brassie's face he had seen something which had aroused his curiosity, and now through the glass he made out that the marks which had attracted him were neither the stains made by grass nor yet the remains of mud. They were tiny spots mostly, with one fairly large blotch about the size of a threepenny-bit—dark brown in colour and possessing no lustre.

Blake puzzled over the marks for some little time before suddenly he shot forth his hand and between his fingers carefully grasped something which had been adhering to the lower part of the club. Then as he held his hand up to the light, Morrison, who had been watching closely, saw that he held in his fingers a short hair. Blake laid down the club and placed the hair under the glass.

For some minutes he studied it; then raising his head, he said:

"This is an important discovery, Mr. Morrison. There can be no doubt but that this is a human hair, and unless I am greatly mistaken we shall find when I have made a thorough test that the stain on the lower edge of the face of this brassie is human blood. In my opinion, the club was broken owing to the violence with which a blow was dealt with it."

"Good heavens!" exclaimed Morrison. "Do you think that is the hair and those stains the blood of the Munitions Minister?"

"That is, of course, impossible to say; but hazarding a guess, I should think not. It is more likely to be the trophies of a blow which he dealt his assailants, for that there were assailants seems a certainty now. No, I should much prefer to think that they were the results of a struggle, in which the Munitions Minister had used the first weapon which came to hand and which he was probably holding when the attack came. Though how it came or whence, we cannot guess.

"But to-morrow I shall make certain tests and prove whether or no this is human blood and if this is a human hair, although I am fairly certain on the point already. Whoever wielded this club dealt a fierce blow, and I do not envy the man who received it on his head.

"Now I think that is all we can do to-night, Mr. Morrison, and if you do not mind, I shall retire. I will take this club with me. If anything comes from Westward Ho! please call me at once."

"I will do so," replied Morrison. "I am going out there at midnight to see how things are going on, but unless there is something important to report I shall not wake you."

Blake thanked him, and saying good-night, left the room. He went at once to the room which had been assigned to him, and, carefully laying the broken pieces of the brassie on a table, began to undress. He spent little time in futile theorising, but slipped into bed, and, although worrying a good deal over Tinker's non-appearance, soon drifted into sleep.

It seemed to him that he had scarcely dozed off when he was awakened by a furious pounding on his door, and sitting up in bed with a start, became aware that Morrison was outside the door shouting:

"Wake up Mr. Blake! I have just had a message from the links. There is an aeroplane wheeling round and round overhead, as though looking for a landing-place!"

CHAPTER 2
How Tinker Brought the Grey Panther to Devon

When Blake had counted on four hours as being good flying time for Tinker to get from Hendon to Westward Ho! he had calculated conservatively. With favourable conditions the journey could be made in a machine like the Grey Panther in something under that time. But neither Blake nor Tinker were able to anticipate the trouble which the lad was to have.

When Tinker left Baker Street he hailed a taxi and drove straight through to Hendon. There at the hangar, which Blake used for the Grey Panther, he found that the mechanics had already wheeled out the slim shape of the monoplane.

She stood just without the hangar, shining beneath the warm afternoon sun, her lines as slim as those of any bird, and her silent Gnome engine sufficient in itself to suggest the lure of the boundless azure above. Sexton Blake had designed well when he designed the Grey Panther.

Tinker spent some twenty minutes examining the struts and stays and in tuning up the engine, then, climbing into the cockpit, he gave the word to the two mechanics, and, as the engine roared out and the propellor spun, they released her and she ran ahead in a straight line, throbbing beneath the reserve power of the engine.

A slight lift of the lifting planes and she rose easily; a pressure on the rudder bar and she swung to the left, picking out a spiral course which would take her to the two thousand foot level in a wide swing having a diameter of several miles.

Then Tinker settled back in his seat in full accord with the perfection of movement, which the Grey Panther at all times achieved.

Up, up, up she climbed, until the blunt nose of the Grey Panther pointed west, then, releasing the slight pressure of his foot on the rudder, Tinker let her forge ahead.

Catching the straight bend of the air, the monoplane quivered like a nervous horse at the start of a race, then the ground below was sweeping away beneath with the dark smudge of buildings growing less and less clear as the green country beyond was reached.

Mile after mile was ticked off with swift regularity. Towns were sighted, passed and left behind in a patch of grey and black. Villages and hamlets swept into view and were lost again. A lone farm here and there, the spire of an ivy-covered church, an occasional motor far below on a narrow country road, a slow moving farm cart, a solitary man in one of the fields which formed part of a widely-spread draughtboard—all these and the hundred and one details which the airman sees, passed beneath them as the Grey Panther swept on her way.

Over county after county until he was over Stroud, in Gloucester, went Tinker, then he headed for the wide mouth of the Severn and the Bristol Channel. Away beneath soon glistened and reflected the long line of rocks and sand bars which stetched away to right and left until they broke into the shores of South Wales and North Devon respectively.

As he sighted them, Tinker made a mental calculation. He knew that if he kept straight on down channel, making Lundy Island his point of direction, he would eventually come opposite Westward Ho!—which was his destination. By following a straight line in this fashion he would have the broad line of the channel to guide him, and when opposite Westward Ho! a slight turn to the left would fetch him towards the land.

With this intention, he let the monoplane keep her present direction, and in the ordinary course of events, he would undoubtedly have fetched his landing place. But when the converging upper part of the channel had been left far behind and only the widening sweep of the blue water could be seen, he suddenly sat up in his seat and gazed away to the north, where a dark speck had appeared.

At first it looked like a bird wheeling high up against the blue sky, but as he continued to gaze at it Tinker knew it was no bird, but an aeroplane.

Hastily he swung the chart-stand towards him and gazed at the map of West of England which he had affixed before leaving Hendon. Then, looking to the north, he saw that the other machine was climbing high and heading westward.

"She is from Cardiff way," he muttered; "or, if she is not from Cardiff, she has been flying in that vicinity. I wonder if she is from an air station on the South Wales coast? I'll shift my course a point and see if I can pick her up. Might have a little race down Channel."

Suiting the action to the word, he put his foot on the rudder-bar and gave a slight pressure. The monoplane answered smoothly, and the next moment they were sweeping along on a different course—a course which, while it was still westward, would bring them in gradually until they were closer to the strange machine which Tinker reckoned was now about three thousand feet up. Incidentally, he shifted his lifting-planes a trifle, intending to climb to the level of the other machine.

Slowly the form of the other became more distinct. In another ten minutes Tinker saw that she was a biplane, and then a little later his eyes widened a trifle as he made out the full strength of her lines.

"Thunder!" he muttered. "She is certainly some biplane—a passenger machine, and big at that. I wonder where she is making for? Anyway, the Grey Panther has more speed, and I should be able to overhaul her soon."

During the last few miles Tinker had felt that bane of all airmen—air-sleepiness. On a warm day, with a machine running easily and little wind to strain at the stays, an airman is almost certain to fall under this species of air hypnotism, and in more cases than one it has been the death of those who have yielded to it.

Therefore, the lad more than welcomed the opportunity of a race, for it would rouse all his faculties, keeping him on the alert each moment.

Whether the pilot of the other machine had seen him or not he could not say. In any event he had so far paid no attention to the slim shape of the monoplane which was coming up behind him, and with a superb disdain of the Grey Panther, was forging away westward.

Tinker smiled to himself as he viewed the wide spread of the biplane, then, pressing the accelerator of the monoplane, he sent her leaping ahead. The speed indicator climbed from seventy to eighty miles an hour, from eighty to eighty-five, then to eighty-seven, and, at that Tinker let her hum.

The nearer he drew to the biplane, the more he became impressed with her great size and power, though in a straight-away race she would be no match for the slim and speedy monoplane which Blake had built.

By now the Bristol Channel stretched away on either side until the land was only a dim line north and south, and getting less clear each moment. Then the biplane ahead altered her course a trifle, heading more to the north in a direction which would bring her closer to the Welsh coast.

Tinker gave his rudder-bar a pressure and followed. As the Grey Panther came round he saw that the pilot in the biplane had taken sufficient notice of him to increase his speed, for now the big machine shot ahead at a swifter pace with the monoplane gaining very little.

"At last he has decided to race," chuckled the lad. "It has taken him long enough to make up his mind. Well, we will give him a pretty little run of it until we get opposite Westward Ho! The way he is going now he will drag me across the channel to the Welsh coast, but it won't take long to cross back again."

But Tinker was to find that the big biplane could kick out more speed than he thought, for now she increased her pace again, and for a short time the Grey Panther dropped back. Not until he had sent the speed-indicator up to ninety-five miles an hour did he start to gain again, and then, absorbed in the progress of the race, he did not notice that already he was far down channel.

Not until there suddenly appeared below him a long line of breakers, whose shock was taken by high and jagged cliffs, did he realise that not only had he passed the point which would be opposite Westward Ho! but had got far out towards St. George's Channel.

"Those must be the cliffs of Pembrokeshire," he muttered. "We have certainly come along some. I didn't realise how fast we were eating up space. I guess I had better turn back and call it an unfinished race. Perhaps I'll meet you again Mr. Biplane and give you a better run for your money."

As he pressed his foot against the rudder-bar to make the turning, he leaned over and gazed down at the sea below. He could see the ragged-looking line of coast with a myriad small islets thrown off from it, and in some cases almost hidden by the flying foam as the waves rolled in and broke upon them in a shower of irridescent spray. Between them and the narrow patches of sea which separated from the mainland, Tinker could see the white gleam of low-lying sands and the water glistening on vicious and wicked-looking rocks, bare and gaunt at low tide, but swept by a swirling mass of green and black as the water rose.

Jammed in between them he could, in imagination, see the narrow guts and crevices in which the tossing water sucked and whirled, meaning death to the strongest swimmer were he caught within them. Then, far to the north, away by itself, was one islet larger than those immediately below him. It stuck out, gaunt and bare-looking, from the height at which he viewed it, and for all the world looked like a great solid stone triangle dropped in the sea by one of the mythical giants of old, or a chosen spot on which Neptune or Thetis might rest while viewing the tossing waves which they ruled.

For miles he had scarcely moved the cloche or foot-bar, but now, as he started to turn and while still gazing away at the other machine, his foot suddenly caught in a wire leading to the switch, and in a moment he had pulled the connection loose. The next second the motor stopped, and, after the barest of quivering pauses, the monoplane plunged downwards.

It was fortunate for Tinker in that moment that he was up almost three thousand feet. Had he been only a few hundred feet in the air he would have had extreme difficulty in managing the machine for the drop, but long experience had taught him instinctively what to do, and while getting the Grey Panther into the correct angle for the volplane, he reached down and tried to catch hold of the wire end and replace it on the binding post.

No use!

Try as he would he could not reach it. It waggled aggravatingly just out of reach of his fingers, and straightening up he looked over the side.

"Nothing for it but to let her continue on the volplane and find a place to land," he muttered. "And what a place to have to come down. I haven't the floats on to-day, so can't come down on the water. Nor does there seem to be a square foot of level ground about those cliffs or islets, let alone a flat stretch where I could come to earth with an aeroplane.

At that moment his eyes lit on the triangular-shaped island which lay beyond the small group of islets below him.

With a quick glance he took in the details of the level surface which it presented, and saw that, contrary to what he had thought when at three thousand foot level, there were buildings upon it. Only two houses could he make out to be sure, but that meant people and people meant help in an emergency.

Then his eyes caught the sight of the great biplane dropping earthwards, and to his amazement, he saw that she was volplaning towards the island. Then every atom of his attention was needed for the Grey Panther.

He was about eighteen hundred feet above the sea now, and calculated swiftly that a direct volplane would carry him some distance beyond the island.

Jamming his foot against the rudder bar he changed the course of the machine and sent her into a spiralling volplane which would bring him down on the island. Then, bracing tight, he watched every movement of the Grey Panther, ready for any emergency which might occur.

He was not alarmed at the predicament in which he had managed to get himself. Had there not been a possible landing on the small triangular-shaped island he would have been in a very unenviable positon, but the closer he got to earth the better he liked the look of the landing; and, if he could direct the volplane correctly, he would be little worse off. It would take him very few moments to replace the end of the wire on the binding post and then he could get away again.

Now he saw that the biplane, instead of landing on the island, had started her engine again and was rising in a spiral, but he saw at the same moment something white drop from her and float downwards towards the island.

From one of the houses two men ran out, and Tinker had just time to see that they were making for the spot where the white article must fall, when a patch of wood hid them from view, and all his faculties were taken up with making a landing.

The monoplane came down easily, and, striking the ground with her skids ran ahead and stopped with scarcely a jar.

After the barest look round at his surroundings, which he saw to hold little attraction, Tinker bent down, and, catching the end of the wire, fixed it to the binding post.

Then he screwed up the nut which held in its place, and, straightening up, prepared to get out. He knew just beyond the wood by which he had come down he would find the houses; and it was his intention to seek aid of the two men he had seen run out from one of the buildings.

But scarcely had his foot touched the ground when from somewhere in the wood there came the sound of a rifle, and the next thing a bullet plunked through one wing of the monoplane, just whizzing past Tinker's head.

Tinker whirled quickly and gave a loud "Hallo!"

"Look out there!" he yelled.

For answer the rifle barked out again; and this time a bullet passed through the arm of his coat to strike the Gnome, and ricochet from it to the ground by the lad's feet.

"This is a little too hot for comfort," he muttered, gazing in amazement at the spot from which the shots had come. "Those shots could hardly have come as close to me by mere accident. Hallo!" This as another shot struck the tail of the machine.

With that Tinker leaped into the cockpit, and, bending towards the rear starter, gave it a turn.

Just as the engine roared out, two men burst from the cover of the wood and started to run towards him. One of them stopped after a few yards; and, raising a rifle to his shoulder, fired. The bullet whistled over Tinker's head, and, ducking, he bent low while the Grey Panther tore along the stretch of level ground.

The men who, where they stood, were on his left ran on a little further, then both of them stopped and began firing at him. The bullets tore through the thin wing material of the monoplane and went ripping past the lad's head but no real hit was registered, and a few moments later, when the monoplane had gathered sufficient headway for a rise, Tinker shifted the lifting planes and sent her up.

But not yet did the fusillade of lead stop. All the time he was climbing to the thousand foot level they followed him, nor did they desist until the spiralling course he was following had taken him well out of range.

Then, as he pressed the rudder bar and sent the Grey Panther round to head towards the Bristol Channel, he saw, less than a mile distant, the huge biplane which, in the first instance, had been the cause of his getting so far away from his intended destination.

Tinker reckoned she was about on the two thousand foot level, and as he gazed at her he was puzzled by her movements. She was wheeling round and round in narrow circles, banking at dangerously steep angles as she turned and, seemingly, flying aimlessly.

Putting two and two together, however, it was not difficult for him to guess what was her purpose. He remembered how she had volplaned down towards the island while he himself was dropping. He recalled, too, the white article which had dropped earthwards from her, and which the two men had run from the house to get. Then he called to mind how a vicious and murderous attack upon himself had immediately followed.

Now the biplane was wheeling about watching for him. He was certain of it. Yet it puzzled him, even as he pressed the accelerator, to figure out why this should be so. When he had first sighted the big biplane back Cardiff way he had changed his course a point with the intention of having a friendly race down channel.

Although he did not recognise the machine, he reckoned she was one of the new craft of the extended air service, and, knowing the type of aviator in the ordinary British machine, he did not anticipate for a moment that his challenge would be refused.

Following that, the biplane had increased her speed and they had raced westwards. Then, when the accident had occurred to the Grey Panther, Tinker had found himself over a rocky portion of the Pembrokeshire coast. And yet, in thinking over the race, he recollected that the biplane had always been ahead, thus setting the pace and thus choosing the direction.

It was because he had followed her that he had reached such a lonely spot as he had. But that did not explain the reason for the white article which had been dropped from the biplane to the island, and which, in Tinker's opinion, had caused an unwarranted attack to be made upon him.

Only his own rapidity of action had saved him from being drilled by several bullets. Why? That was the puzzle. Nor was he left long in doubt as to the intentions of the other machine.

As the Grey Panther turned her nose towards the east, Tinker saw the biplane swing after him and drop to the two thousand foot level on which the monoplane was now running.

Had Blake been with him, or had he not been bound under sealed orders, he would have felt strongly inclined to trust to the speed of the Grey Panther in order to circle round and spend more time in the vicinity in an endeavour to discover the reason for what had occurred.

But, realising that he was already well behind time, and that Blake would expect to find him at Westward Ho! when he arrived, Tinker decided to make a run for it and to leave the mystery to the solving of the sea birds.

The biplane, however, evidently had no intention that he should get away, for it now tore after him, and, coming at a sharp angle, made a strong bid to cut him off, while from the cockpit there followed a perfect hail of bullets as someone in the biplane opened fire on him.

Tinker settled in his seat and gazed straight ahead, while the speed of the monoplane gradually climbed from seventy-three to eighty miles and then from eighty miles to ninety.

At that he left it, and, as the sea swept along beneath him, he took the opportunity to turn and look back. The biplane was steadily dropping away behind him, and, when twenty minutes later he looked again, he saw that she had disappeared from view. He was just congratulating himself that he had show a clean pair of heels to the other, when there was a sudden stoppage of the Gnome, followed by a loud explosion as she back-fired. She picked up again a moment later, but before

31

another minute had passed she stopped once more, repeating her back-fire.

Tinker eased his pressure on the accelerator, and, setting her at a slight angle, let her volplane down to the thousand foot level. At the same time he peered anxiously to right and left where the dim line of shore loomed.

He judged he was a trifle nearer the coast of North Devon than that of Wales, and as the Gnome picked up again he pressed the rudder bar with his foot and pointed the nose of the Grey Panther towards the right.

It was only by the most persistent nursing on his part that the Gnome consented to run, and then the action was intermittent and irritating. Still he held on, and, as the line of shore became more and more distinct, he sought anxiously for a landing spot.

A little later he descried a patch of white, which later resolved itself into the village of Clovelly, which nestles in a cut in the cliffs in the lee of Hartland Point.

Then he knew exactly where he was, but seek as he would he could find no spot where he could land. With the engine still running badly he circled out to sea again, the diameter of his sweep taking him in the direction of Lundy Island, which sits bleak and lonely at the mouth of Bristol Channel, sixteen miles from Hartland Point.

Mile after mile was ticked off with the Gnome spluttering and complaining, then, when he had climbed to the two thousand foot level for safety, and when Lundy lay off to the right, the Gnome gave another loud explosion and stopped entirely.

Setting the planes at the angle for a spiralling volplane, Tinker let the monoplane drop in a sweep, which he hoped would fetch the island. He knew that on the flat surface of Lundy there would be little difficulty in finding a landing spot.

Down to the thousand foot level the Grey Panther dropped, then swept in a spiral to the five hundred, and, with a gentle sweep, soared down to a flat stretch close to a wide-mouthed quarry where Tinker could pick out the white patches of upturned faces.

Then the skids touched ground, and Tinker was just about to give a sign of relief at having found a landing place when, for the second time that day, things went wrong; for without the slightest warning, the monoplane heeled over, and as her right wing struck the ground there was an ominous crash.

A strut had smashed. Nor was it until an hour later that Tinker discovered the reason. The spot where he had landed was in a direct line with a deep cut through the quarry which opened straight through to the sea. This cutting formed a vast sort of chimney which caught up the air by the sea and drew it through to the other end of the quarry in a never ending gale of wind.

The monoplane had come athwart this, and as the blast of wind had caught her she had tripped up.

She stopped with the crash, and Tinker leapt to the ground. Immediately several husky looking men ran out of the quarry towards him, and, as they drew near Tinker, who was now suspicious of everything and everybody, saw with relief that their attitude was friendly.

He knew that Lundy Island was owned privately; and that almost the only thing it produced was stone. These men, he thought, must be employed by the owner to quarry the stone, and a few moments later he found that to be so.

They paused by the machine, and in rough but kindly Devon dialect offered to do what they could to help him. Most of them had never seen an aeroplane before, and were lost in wonderment while Tinker good-naturedly explained how it worked.

They had not yet reached the point where they could look on it as anything else but an uncanny creation to be regarded from a safe distance.

When he had gone over the different parts and demonstrated briefly the science of flight of heavier-than-air machines, Tinker set himself to go over the engine and find out what had caused it to behave as it had.

It took him a solid hour to locate the trouble; and when he did he found it was a leakage in one of the valves. That meant the valve must be removed and ground, which, would consume at least another hour.

With the assistance of some of the men from the quarry he set to work, and in the blacksmith's shop attached to the quarry, managed to get the valve into working order again. Then he was compelled to turn his attention to the damaged strut which he found to be a much more serious break than he had at first thought.

Darkness fell and found him still working away at it, and not until the evening was well advanced was he able to assure himself that it was repaired as well as possible.

Then he decided on a thing which only the most daring of aviators would have considered. He determined, in spite of the fact that it was past ten o'clock and full night, to risk flying towards Westward Ho! trusting to the distant light on Bideford Bar to guide his direction and to the revolving light on Lundy, with the small beacon at Clovelly, to assist him in keeping his course.

The quarrymen tried their best to dissuade him, but the lad persisted, and while several of them held the Grey Panther, Tinker started the engine.

The Gnome roared out and then purred smoothly.

Tinker clambered in and gave the word to release her. The monoplane ran ahead, and a few minutes later, with the lifting planes canted, she started to rise.

With his eyes straining ahead through the night Tinker settled down and set the nose of the machine for Bideford Bar Light, knowing that once he had reached that vicinity he would be practically at Westward Ho! And on the chance of finding Blake at that place depended his chances of making a night landing.

So the Grey Panther raced on, with Lundy dropping steadily behind.

CHAPTER 3
Blake Fulfils His Commission

When Blake was awakened by Mr. Grindley Morrison and informed that a message had come through from Westward Ho! saying there was an aeroplane circling overhead, his first thought was of Tinker.

As he slipped into some clothes he puzzled over the circumstances, wondering why, if it were the lad, he was doing dangerous night flying. Then he remembered the other machine, whose traces had been left on the beach by the golf links, and the thought came to him that perhaps it might be that one.

If so, why had she flown over in the night to circle above the spot where the Munitions Minister had been kdnapped?

When he opened the door and went out into the passage he found Morrison standing at the head of the stairs waiting for him.

"Now then!" said Blake briskly, as they went down the stairs together. "Have you any details?"

Morrison shook his head.

"No; only the bare message, saying that there is an aeroplane circling overhead at a considerable height. I took the liberty of telling my man to get your car ready. I took it for granted that you would want to go to Westward Ho! at once."

Blake nodded his thanks, and pausing in the lower hall long enough to get a cap and motoring coat, they hurried outside to the garage. The big grey car was standing just within the door with the engine purring softly and the road-lamps already turned on. Blake climbed in followed by Mr. Morrison, and then the car leaped ahead and started down the drive towards the main gateway.

Once in the road Blake let her out, and they ticked off the few miles to Westward Ho! in record speed. Just as they reached the road by the lower side of the golf links Blake glanced up, and far overhead was able to make out a peculiar yellow and red glow.

He knew at once that it could only come from the exhaust of an aeroplane and as he brought the car to a stop, shutting off the engine, he could distinctly hear the steady drone of an engine up above. By the glow of the exhaust he could follow her course, and, watching her as she flew, he saw that she was going in a wide circle above the links.

He stood rigid for a few moments, listening to every shade of tone of the engine; then turned to Morrison.

"It is my own monoplane," he said briefly. "I could recognise the song of her engine in any place. For some reason my assistant has risked a night flight, and is circling above until we line out a landing place for him. We shall have to work carefully, for a descent to-night will be a risky business."

Morrison glanced upwards and whistled softly.

"He has a nerve!" he muttered. "How will you arrange a landing-place Mr. Blake?"

Blake did not reply for a moment. Instead, he gazed ahead into the gloom which masked the stretch of the beach from view. Finally he said:

"Will you go on and get the two men who are on watch? Have them pull a quantity of the long, dry grass which grows close to the edge of the beach. We shall need a fairly large quantity. In the meantime, I shall be arranging other matters."

Morrison puzzled at Blake's request, but obediently hurried away to carry out the instructions, while Blake returned to the car.

Climbing in, he drove slowly along the beach until he reached a spot which he remembered from the day. He knew that from there the beach stretched away flat and hard for some distance until it broke against a small sand dune just opposite the spot where he had seen the marks left by the aeroplane which they supposed had been used by the kidnappers of the Munitions Minister.

There he stopped, and getting out, switched out the lights of the car. He waited a moment then switched them on again, leaving them thus for a minute. Again he doused them, turning them on again, and for a third time extinguised them for a minute. Then he turned them on and let them burn in all their brilliancy, with their powerful rays sweeping along the straight run of the beach. He had thrown a triple signal to the machine overhead, and if the aviator were on watch he must have seen it.

A moment later Morrison appeared followed by two other figures. All three carried huge armfuls of dry grass, and, under Blake's direction, they placed in several small piles along both sides of the beach, one line following the line of the water and the other following the line of the underbrush.

When the first lot had been placed they returned for more, and then again for a third lot. When it had all been placed as Blake directed the line-out was thus. At the head of the long flat stretch of the beach the car, with the great road-lamps sweeping the full length and lighting it up was a white patch which could be plainly seen from above. Then on either side the piles of dry grass, placed at intervals of about ten yards the whole width of the beach between the lines.

Blake's next move was to tell off the two watchers to one side, while he and Morrison took the other. Then, when Blake gave the word, they started down the lines touching matches to the piles of grass as they ran.

Immediately the dry material flared up, and when all the piles had been lighted, Blake rushed back to the car and masked the lights once. Almost immediately there was a cessation of the drone overhead, and gazing upwards, they could see by following the glare of the exhaust that the aeroplane was volplaning.

Guided by the grass flares on the sides and the lights of the car at one end, the machine dropped swiftly until the watchers could distinctly make out her dark slim lines. Then she grew still more distinct, and a few minutes later had taken the beach at the far end from where the car stood, and was running along the blazing line of flares which Blake had caused to be lighted.

It came on easily until the drag of the skids on the sand gradually brought it to a stop, and at last she came to rest not ten yards from the road-lamps of the car. The next instant the grass flares died down and then became extinguished.

From the aeroplane, which the watchers could now see was a monoplane, a figure clambered out and came along the beach to meet them. Blake, who was in the lead, spoke as the figure approached.

"You made a splendid landing, my lad! But what possessed you to attempt such a risky landing by night?"

"I thought it was necessary, guv'nor," came a clear young voice in reply. "I have had it pretty warm since I left Hendon, and will tell you all about it."

He had reached the group by this time, and when Blake had introduced the lad to the other three gentlemen, he said: "Now then, Tinker, let me hear what has happened."

Tinker leaned against the mudguard of the car, and, beginning with his arrival at Hendon, related all that had occurred until he had decided to leave Lundy Island in spite of the darkness.

When he had finished there was a deep silence for some minutes, broken finally by Blake.

"Peculiar—very peculiar!" he murmured. "You say this big aeroplane had come from Cardiff way, my lad?"

"Yes, sir," replied Tinker—"at least, I should judge so from her direction."

"Do you think her course towards the west was impelled by your appearance?" continued Blake.

"No, sir; I do not. She was headed west when I first sighted her, and I think I saw her before her pilot saw me."

"What followed seems to bear you out," mused Blake aloud. "Following your story, it seems that she flew west until over the Pembrokeshire cliffs. There you had an accident with the wire connection of the motor and were compelled to seek a landing. She also volplaned down towards the one spot where you thought it safe to come to earth, but instead of landing, as you thought she would, she rose again after something had been dropped from her. This article fell on the ground near one of the houses, and just before the Grey Panther touched earth you saw two men run out and pick it up."

"Yes, sir."

"What was it like, my lad?"

"Well, guv'nor, I only caught a glimpse of it, but it looked like a small paper packet."

"Then a few minutes later there was a most murderous attack made upon you," went on Blake. "It would almost seem that it was the receipt of the packet dropped from the biplane which inspired this. Nor does there seem any doubt but that an attempt was made to kill you before you got away from the island. Had the accident to the motor been more serious, and had you been delayed, they would have succeeded in getting you. Then, when you rose you sighted the biplane circling round, and immediately she started in pursuit of you.

"As I remarked before, it is all very peculiar. It is hardly possible that those in the biplane would know your identity. Had any other machine followed them as you did, it seems that a similar attack would have been made upon them. That means it was not you who were attacked, but the one who drove a machine which had followed them. Meaning, I think, that they had some strong reasons for not wishing their movements to be known.

"Now, were it any Government machine they would not have made this attack without first ascertaining whether you were friend or foe. Such a thing would be against all the probabilities. Therefore, we may safely conclude that it was a private machine. But why—why should they have done this?"

"I can't imagine, guv'nor," muttered the lad. "When I sighted the machine I changed my course, in order to have a race down Channel. It was with no intention of following them, though, from my actions, it is possible they thought I was doing so. Anyway, they attacked me, as I have told you, and, if the Gray Panther had not been the faster machine, they would have brought me down even after I got away from the island."

Blake paced off to the edge of the water and stood gazing out to sea, thinking deeply. Five minutes went by and still he stood there, puzzling over the strange adventure the lad had had.

Finally, he turned to the others.

"We can do no more to-night, gentlemen," he said. "If you will continue to keep watch as before, I shall be greatly obliged to you. Mr. Morrison, I shall return to your place. Will you come?"

"I am at your service," responded Morrison.

"Come along, my lad," said Blake, turning to Tinker. "You must be badly in need of some rest. To-morrow we will discuss in detail this adventure of yours."

They climbed back into the car, and, backing her round, Blake started back towards Northam. Arriving there he drove the car into the garage, and, when Tinker had been shown to a room, bade good-night to Morrison.

He ascended to his own room, but not to retire. Instead, he drew up a chair by the open window, and, lighting a cigar, smoked in the darkness for a long time. Not until the east was greying did he rouse himself, and then it was to make his way to the bathroom for a cold plunge.

When he had shaved and dressed again he went along to Tinker's room and knocked up the lad, then descended to the lower hall to discover that Morrison was already abroad.

"I haven't slept a wink all night," he said, when he had greeted Blake. "This affair is nearly driving me crazy. I can't for the life of me think what has happened to the Minister of Munitions. And then there is the strange adventure your assistant had, though I don't suppose that had anything to do with the other. But, at the same time, I am certain the kidnapping was done by aeroplane."

Blake shrugged.

"It would be folly to try to connect the two events while we know so little," he said. "But, at the same time, there is a certain channel of investigation which it might pay to follow. I intend doing so to-day after another examination at Westward Ho! By the way, Mr. Morrison, have you a large scale-map of the Welsh coast?"

The other nodded.

"Yes, in the library. Do you wish to look at it?"

"If you please."

"Then come with me, Mr. Blake. You will have time before breakfast is served, though I have told them to hurry with it."

They went along to the library where Morrison brought out a large map portfolio. In this Blake found the one for which he had asked, and, bending over it, examined it closely. He followed the line of the Pembrokeshire coast until he came to the myriad of small islets which lie near the extreme western point.

There he traced out the different names until he found the name of Marsey. He studied the location of this tiny spot on the map for some time, then finally raised his head.

"Thank you!" he said. "Shall we go to breakfast now? I think I hear the going going."

They went out into the hall where they found Tinker waiting, and then on into the breakfast-room. They ate hurriedly and in silence, for each was busy with his own thoughts. After the meal they climbed into the car, and, with Blake at the wheel, drove to Westward Ho! There they descended and received the report from the two gentlemen who were then on duty.

Nothing else had occurred worth reporting since the arrival of the Grey Panther, and when he had listened to what they had to say Blake turned to Tinker.

"Come with me my lad. There is an examination I want to make."

He and Tinker went along together to the spot where Morrison had located the marks of an aeroplane, and in the clear morning light Blake made a thorough examination of the spot. Here and there he could make out the flat line of what he took to be the impression of a skid, and, following the wheel marks, traced them through the grass and bushes to a secluded spot in the wood beyond.

There he dropped to his knees, and, after a thorough examination of all the surrounding ground, rose, and spoke to Tinker.

"You say this biplane which you followed yesterday was exceptionally large, my lad?"

"Yes, guv'nor," replied the lad eagerly. "She was one of the biggest I have ever seen. I reckon she would carry four or five men easily. She wasn't as large as the 'bus Graham White built to carry six or eight men from London to Paris, but she would have run it a close second."

Blake nodded thoughtfully.

"Tell me, my lad," he said, after a little—"what do you think of these marks?"

"Well, guv'nor, they are pretty wide, and, from the depth of the skid marks, I should say the machine which made them was pretty heavily loaded."

"My opinion exactly, Tinker," replied Blake. "And if you will pace the width of the tire marks you will find that they are nearly a foot farther apart than the ordinary wheel marks of a biplane. What does that tell you?"

Tinker's eyes suddenly widened.

"Great Scott! Guv'nor, do you mean to say that these marks may have been made by the biplane I saw yesterday?"

Blake smiled.

"I would not go so far as to say that, my lad, but they were certainly made by a very large machine, and it was an exceptionally large machine you saw yesterday. We must remember that, as far as we know at present, only one person saw an aeroplane rise from this beach here on Sunday afternoon. That was a lad who was idling about the beach, and who on week days is a caddie at the golf course.

"From what he told Mr. Morrison, it seems that the aeroplane went in a northerly direction, and he would hardly have said that unless he had watched her out of sight. Now, by the time she would have been that distance away, she would be getting well over the Welsh coast, and, my lad, she would be only a short distance away from the triangular-shaped island where you came down, and which I have already identified on the map as Marsey Island off the coast of Pembrokeshire.

"Let us follow that theory a little. From what we have seen here, it seems safe to assume that the machine which left the Westward Ho! beach was of a size larger than ordinary. That, in turn, presupposes that she was a biplane. When she left here she was flying in a direction which would take her not far away from the Island of Marsey.

"Yesterday you met a biplane off the Welsh coast, and it, too, was a machine larger than the ordinary. In addition, the course it took brought it over the island of Marsey where the occupants made a communication of some sort to men on the island—a communication which was followed by an attack upon you.

"It may be only a coincidence, but, in my opinion, it is one worth following. It will be an extraordinary coincidence if we prove that those two over-size machines which were flying along the Welsh coast within a few hours of each other were not one and the same. So tune up the Grey Panther, my lad. We are going to make a flight to the island of Marsey."

Tinker, only too delighted to return to the island in Blake's company, pushed his way through the scrub, and raced along the beach towards the Grey Panther. Blake himself followed more leisurely, and when he appeared Mr. Grindley Morrison and three of the other gentlemen who had been patrolling the spot came to meet him.

To them Blake merely said that he was going off in the monoplane to follow a clue, and that, if all went well, he would return some time during the afternoon. Then they walked on to where the machine lay.

While Tinker tuned up the Gnome, Blake carefully examined the broken strut which the lad had fixed on Lundy Island; then, when the motor was humming soft and regular, Blake opened the locker in the cockpit and took out his flying clothes.

Slipping them on he donned his helmet, and climbed in. Tinker followed suit, and when they were settled in their places with Blake at the throttle, Tinker gave the word, and those who had been holding the Grey Panther released her.

She shot along the beach, then, as Blake tilted the lifting-planes, took the rise easily. Up she went, climbing in a wide spiral until they reached the thousand-foot level.

Blake pointed her blunt nose towards the north, and they shot away swiftly with the speed indicator creeping up from sixty to eighty-five.

Tinker, gazing back, saw the white spots which marked the upturned faces of those on the beach; then they were well out over the sea, with the distant shore rapidly becoming a white-rimmed line blurred and indistinct.

Blake settled in his seat, and not until the Welsh coast loomed up ahead did he alter his course. When the line of breakers grew fairly distinct, he shifted the direction a point, and away they went towards the west.

Mile after mile of the coast on their right passed away beneath them, and here and there a smudge of smoke appeared marking a steamer making her way up or down Channel. Then the jagged point of Pembrokeshire appeared, and a few moments later they came in sight of the tiny islets which lie off it.

Blake glanced once at his chart, then and again changed the direction of the Grey Panther. Just as he did so a small triangular patch appeared ahead, and in the reflecting-mirror Blake saw Tinker raise his hand, signifying that is was the same island where he had come to earth the day before.

Blake drove on only a short distance further before cutting off the motor, then, circling, he started on a steep volplane.

Down, down, down, they went in a long, slanting glide until the island which had been well ahead of them suddenly swept beneath them.

Down still more, until the buildings upon it became distinct, and the formation of the ground showed up plainly. Then the island seemed to leap to meet them, and, with a gentle shock, the Grey Panther touched earth on the same stretch of level ground where Tinker had landed.

No sooner had she run ahead and stopped than Blake rose, and dropped to the ground, followed by Tinker.

"Get your revolver out my lad!" ordered Blake curtly. "I didn't see anybody about as we came down, but our descent must have been witnessed, and, after your experience of yesterday, we can guess what sort of a reception we are likely to have."

Tinker nodded, and, removing his flying-helmet, drew his automatic. Then, when Blake had done likewise, they started off at a run towards the wood which separated them from the buildings which they had seen.

They entered the wood at the nearest point, and, pushing their way through, suddenly came out into another patch of open ground, across which was a low-built farm building. At the moment it seemed untenanted, so quiet was it, nor could they know that the farmer-tenant of the island had been sent to Fishguard by his employer on business, which would take him the best part of a week to get through.

They began to cross the patch of ground, and, as they topped a small rise, they caught sight of another building—a large bungalow which faced on the miniature bay which the island boasted.

No sooner had they done so than they discovered they were not to go ahead without their advance being opposed. They saw a door of the bungalow open, and two men step out on to the verandah.

Though Blake and Tinker were a considerable distance away, they were near enough to make out that both men carried rifles, and, even as they realised this, a bullet whizzed past Tinker's shoulder.

At a word from Blake, they dropped flat, taking their shelter behind the rise.

"They saw us, as I thought they would," said Blake. "We can never rush them from here while they hold rifles. Our revolvers will not carry far enough for that. We shall have to try strategy. But to get there I am determined.

"There is something very queer about this place! They make not the slightest attempt to discover our identity, but the moment we show up fire on us, proving they are determined to keep trespassers off at any price. If they were honest, they would not do such a thing. They would inquire first, and I have yet to know of any British law which permits the occupiers of a place to fire on trespasses without finding out their reasons for being there.

"And, even when you were in distress in the air, and were forced to descend at the first available spot, they fired upon you. We shall have to make a run for the wood, and work our way round through it until we get closer to the house. Then we may be able to slip up on them close enough to use our revolvers. Are you ready, my lad?"

"Yes, guv'nor. But look, guv'nor—look!"

"Where?" asked Blake quickly, as Tinker uttered the exclamation.

"There—in that upper window, guv'nor! Do you see it?"

Blake raised himself a trifle, and, risking the bullets which began to fly close to him the minute he showed himself, he gazed at the upper window of the bungalow which Tinker had indicated. He was just in time to see something white waving from it, then it suddenly disappeared.

"It was a signal of sorts, Tinker," he said. "The more I see of this place, the less I like it. However, we shall know the mystery of the place before we leave it, or my name is not Sexton Blake.

Drawing back under the lip of the rise, behind which they had taken cover, Blake and Tinker crept back for some yards. Then, at a word from Blake, they rose and raced for the cover of the wood.

A perfect hail of bullets followed them, but at the distance the aim was uncertain, and they reached the shelter of the trees in safety. Turning there, they gazed back towards the bungalow, and as they did so saw one of the figures descend the steps and head for the wood.

Blake uttered a low exclamation.

"Do you see their game, my lad? That is proof that there are only two of them at the house. One is remaining there on guard, while the other hunts us out with his rifle. Follow me! We will see if we cannot match our wits against theirs. Easy does it!"

As he finished speaking, Blake turned, and, bending his head, started off through the trees, with Tinker close on his heels. Blake took the direction leading to the right, and, keeping always in mind the location of the bungalow, travelled in a wide circle, which would eventually bring them out near the building.

They were not near enough to the edge of the wood to see what had become of the man who had started out to hunt them down with his rifle, but they were building on the chance that he would think they had returned to the field where the Gray Panther had come down, and make for there. In that case, it would give them a chance to rush the house.

It seemed as long time to Tinker before Blake paused and held up his hand, but he knew from experience how perfect was Blake's woodsman's knowledge, and that his master had a perfect sense of location in the thickest of jungle. To him, therefore, the comparatively open wood in which they were presented no difficulties.

A few minutes later, after creeping along on hands and knees for some distance, they suddenly came out at the edge of the wood nearest the bungalow, and Tinker saw exactly how certain had been Blake's scouting.

The building was now less than a hundred yards away from them, and, instead of being in a line with the front balcony as before, they were now at the back, and as far as they could see there was no one on guard there.

After a cautious surveillance of the situation, Blake rose, and said in a whisper:

"My idea is to rush it, Tinker. If we go gently, we should be able to reach the rear without being seen unless the second man is hanging about the open ground somewhere. Once we have reached the house, we will make for the front, and try to get our man before he can use his rifle to any purpose. Do you get me?"

"Perfectly, guv'nor. When you give the word, I shall be at your heels."

Blake nodded, and, stepping out into the open, began to make for the rear of the house, with Tinker close behind. Yard after yard they covered, until they were over half-away across. Then Blake broke into an easy jog-trot, and Tinker did likewise.

They reached the rear safely, and without pausing Blake continued round the side towards the front. Just as he did so, there was a shout in the distance, and out of the corner of his eye Tinker saw a man burst forth from the wood and, kneeling down, place a rifle to his shoulder. It was the man who had been sent out to hunt them.

The next instant they had burst into view of the front balcony, and came full upon the second man, kneeling down with the muzzle of his rifle sweeping slowly back and forth.

As he heard them, he swung sharply and pulled the trigger. Tinker saw Blake stagger slightly, then recover and go on again. In the same instant Tinker raised his automatic, and, pointing it full at the man who knelt on the balcony, fired point-blank.

At the distance a miss was impossible. The bullet caught the man full in the shoulder, and sent him backwards with the force of the impact, but with an oath he regained his balance, and gain pulled the trigger of the rifle.

The bullet zipped past Blake, struck the barrel of Tinker's automatic, and ricochetted through one of the windows of the bungalow.

Then Blake, firing from the hip as he went, rushed the balcony, and Tinker swarmed over the rail beside him.

Full upon the other man they leaped, all three going down with a crash. In less than a minute, Blake and Tinker had the fellow helpless, and as they straightened up, Blake a low whistle of amazement.

The man's hat had fallen off in the struggle, and now he lay on his back with his face turned upwards to the full light of morning. It was this full view of the prostrate man's features which had inspired Blake's whistle of surprise.

"So," he murmured softly, "it is Gonzalez! Take a look at him, Tinker!"

Tinker was already doing so, and as Blake spoke he turned quickly.

"Gonzalez, of the Council of Eleven, guv'nor!" he exclaimed.

Blake nodded slowly.

"It is he. Secure him well, my lad! It is a little plainer to me now why trespassers upon this land are fired upon without first being challenged."

Scarcely had Blake given the order to Tinker, when from behind them sounded the sharp crack of a rifle, and at almost the same instant a bullet thudded into the railing of the balcony not six inches from the spot where Blake was leaning.

Like a flash Blake ducked, and, seizing the rifle which had been used by Gonzalez, he swung round, placing it to his shoulder as he did so. Across the stretch of open ground, close to the edge of the wood, he saw the figure of a man kneeling with a rifle at his shoulder, and just a puff of smoke came from it.

Blake pulled the trigger of the one he held. He saw the man by the wood fall forward on his face just as the bullet tore its way through the sleeve of his coat. Then, with a word to watch Gonzalez, he vaulted over the rail of the balcony, and carrying the rifle with him, started to run towards the spot where the other had fallen.

As he approached nearer, Blake raised his weapon ready for instant use. The little time he had been on the island had served to make him cautious, and though it looked as if he had registered a full hit, he knew that the prostrate attitude of the man by the wood might only be a blind to draw him on.

As he got still closer, however, he was able to make out the rifle of the fellow lying several feet away, and in the other's attitude there was an odd twist which seemed to indicate a complete prostration of muscular volition.

A few yards farther, and Blake dropped all caution, running forward until he was close beside the other. Then, for the second time within the space of a few minutes, he received a severe shock, for the man who lay sprawling forward on his face was not only not a stranger to Blake, but he was not a whiteman.

In him Blake recognised San, the famous lieutenant of Prince Wu Ling, of the Brotherhood of the Yellow Beetle. He did not pause then to puzzle out why San the Celestial and Gonzalez aviator, of the Council of Eleven, should be together on that tiny island off the Pembrokeshire coast. He saw a splash of deep crimson on the throat of the prostrate Chinaman, and, dropping to his knees, turned him over.

San's eyes were closed, and his breathing was short and laboured. He gave no sign as Blake moved him, and it was plain that he was unconscious, or nearly so. Blake passed his hand over San's throat, and as he wiped away the blood, came upon the wound which the rifle had made.

It had caught San on one side of the throat, just missing the jugular vein, and, ploughing its way along the soft flesh of the neck had finished up by striking the jaw-bone just beneath one ear—the reason, Blake imagined, why San was unconscious from the shock. The tiniest fraction of an inch more, and the bullet would have plunged through his jugular vein as potently as the knife of a pig-sticker.

Blake drew his handkerchief and mopped up the flow of blood, but even as he did so it gushed forth afresh, and he saw that unless San were to bleed to death in a few minutes he must use more efficacious measures. So, heavy though the Celestial was, he threw him over his shoulder, and started back towards the house with him.

Arriving at the balcony, he found Tinker standing guard over the Spaniard, whom he had also taken the precaution to bind securely. His eyes widened as he saw the identity of Blake's burden. He made no remark, but followed his master into the house, where, in a large and well-furnished living-room, Blake laid his captive on a couch.

Then together they found their way to the kitchen, where they procured water and towels, and with these returned to the living-room.

Setting to work, Blake bathed San's wound, and when the flow of blood had been stopped bound it up roughly but well. Then he signed to Tinker to tie the Celestial's hands and ankles, for, though San might be wounded, Blake knew of old the cunning and capability of the Oriental, and had no intention of taking any chances.

After that they dragged Gonzalez into the living-room, and, leaving him in a corner, proceeded to make a thorough search of the place. On the ground floor they found nothing, but neither of them had forgotten that white signal which had been waved from an upper window; so, when they had finished the lower floor, they made for the floor above.

The first room to which they came was a large bedroom which showed signs of recent occupation, but at present held nothing of interest to them. The second door was locked, and pausing before it, Blake knocked sharply. There was no summons in reply, but on the other side of the door they could hear a thumping sound which sounded like nothing so much a boot heel being pounded upon the floor.

That was sufficient for Blake.

Stepping back a pace he turned slightly, then rushed the door, catching it full with his shoulder. It crashed inwards with a rending and splintering of wood, and as they followed it into the room, they brought up to regard a strange sight.

Lying on the floor, bound and gagged, and presenting every sign of woe-begone discomfort, were two men dressed in golfing garb, and one of them—he who lay nearest the wall—Blake recognised as the Minister of Munitions, who had disappeared from Westward Ho! golf links a few days previously.

The trail of the big biplane had led them straight to the spot.

While Blake knelt and loosed the bonds of the man who meant so much to Britain, Tinker released the second man and the two got stiffly to their feet. Then the Munitions Minister, aching though he must have been in every joint, turned to Blake and said, with a faint twinkle in his eyes:

"Our last interview, Mr. Blake, was under somewhat different circumstances. Nevertheless, I am more than pleased to see you. Permit me to introduce you to Sir Hector Amworth."

Blake, catching the spirit of the Munitions Minister's unquenchable courage, smiled and bowed to the big gunmaker, who held out his hand.

Then, in a serious tone, the Munitions Minister went on: "How did you come, Blake? By boat? and have you raked in the rascals who did this?"

Blake shook his head.

"We have captured two of them, sir, but the real authors of the affair are not here. We did not come by boat, but by aeroplane. But come below, and I will see if we can get together something to brace you up. While you have some food, I will tell you all about it."

The Minister nodded, and followed by the others, made his way below. There Tinker exercised his ingenuity in preparing a hasty though nourishing meal for the two released captives, and while they consumed it, Blake related all that had happened since he had been sent for in London by Sir John————

When he had finished the Munitions Minister frowned.

"Then, you think, Blake, that the affair is due to the work of these two organisations of which you speak—the Council of Eleven and the Brotherhood of the Yellow Beetle? I, of course, know of Prince Wu Ling, through the other affair some little time ago, when the Crown Prince of Germany dared to come to England. But I cannot fathom why they should have joined hands for such a purpose as they attempted to carry out. And, certainly, our fate was already sealed. Last night a man came to see us, a tall, well set up fair man, who, from what you have told me, I judge was this Baron de Beauremon. He told us coolly enough that within forty-eight hours we should be killed, and that our bodies would be sunk in the sea. Then all day we heard nor saw nothing of them.

"The first signs we had that there was something afoot in our favour was when we heard the rifle shots. I managed to make my way to the window which I broke by banging my head against it. Then I got my teeth on Amworth's handkerchief and pulled it from his pocket. In this way I managed to wave it from the window, hoping it would be seen. But I was unable to keep it up for long. The attitude was too much of a strain.

"Then we heard more shots, and, as you know, you came soon after to find us. I cannot imagine what has become of the two arch scoundrels."

Blake shrugged his shoulders.

"The big biplane, which was the real clue in the affair, is not on the island," he said. "Undoubtedly they have gone away to arrange the details of their next move. It is probable that they will return some time to-day to put into execution their threat against you; and then we shall try to gather them in.

"But you, sir, I imagine, will want to get away as quickly as possible. The Grey Panther, unfortunately, will not carry more than two—one besides the driver. Therefore, I shall have to take you first, and return for Sir Hector Amworth. Tinker can remain here with him.

"Also, when I have dropped you at Westward Ho! I shall bring back a man with me to go on guard here, and wait for the return of the biplane. Then I can take Sir Hector Amworth to Westward Ho! and when I return for Tinker, bring back another man to go on guard with the first one.

"In the meantime you might arrange, sir, for a gunboat, or T.B.D. to put in here, and take off the two prisoners we already have. If it reaches here before the return of the biplane, it will come in useful in gathering in the pair who are the real authors of the outrage upon you. How does my plan strike you, sir?"

The Minister of Munitions accepted one of Blake's proffered cigarettes, and when he had lit it said: "Like all you do,

Blake, it strikes me as being splendid. I do not think we can improve on those plans. What do you say, Amworth?"

Sir Hector nodded.

"I agree with you," he replied. "I think we had better place ourselves entirely in Mr. Blake's hands."

"Then, if that is agreed upon, we will get away as soon as you are ready, sir," said Blake to the Munitions Minister. "Time will be of value; and besides, London will be wondering what has become of you."

The Munitions Minister smiled as he rose. "It will simply be told that I remained a day or two longer at Westward Ho! than I intended," he said. "Anyway, I had the satisfaction of striking one good blow at the scoundrel who attacked me."

"It was a very powerful blow," remarked Blake, rising also. "It broke the brassie as clean as could be."

The Munitions Minister paused and gazed at Blake in astonishment. "How on earth did you know that?" he exclaimed. It was Blake's turn to smile.

"That was not difficult." he said. And with that enigmatical reply he led the way outside.

On the way through the living-room, the Munitions Minister and Sir Hector paused a moment to regard the two prisoners, then continued on their way. They walked across the patch of open ground to the wood, and pushing through it kept on to the spot where the Grey Panther lay.

While Blake tuned up the engine, Tinker and Sir Hector held the machine, and the Munitions Minister climbed in. When he had shaken hands with Sir Hector, and spoken a few words of thanks to Tinker, promising the lad to thank him properly in London he sat back, and Blake took his place. Then, with the Gnome singing sweetly, they ran ahead and rose easily.

At the two thousand foot level, Blake turned the nose of the Grey Panther south, and away they went at eighty miles an hour towards Westward Ho! Soon, far beneath them, the white line of beach came into view, and Blake shut off the engine and volplaned down, landing with scarcely a shock on the spot where Tinker had come to earth the night before. Then, as Mr. Grindley Morrison and several other gentlemen appeared, the Munitions Minister climbed out and received their congratulations.

Through his influence, a couple of men were sent from the nearest coastguards-station to return to the island, and leaving one of them on the beach to await his return with Sir Hector Amworth, Blake took the other with him.

The Grey Panther rose from the beach in a steep climb and tore away on her return journey to Marsey Island, with Blake giving her every bit she would take.

It seemed no time before the risky islets of Pembrokeshire appeared again, and when he had volplaned down to the triangular shaped island, Blake found Tinker and Sir Hector waiting for them. There the coastguardsman climbed out and Sir Hector took his place. Then, once more, the Grey Panther tore away and shortly after was once again circling over Westward Ho! for the volplane.

When Sir Hector had joined the Munitions Minister and the other gentlemen, who had been waiting at the club house on the golf links, Blake took in the other coastguardsman and started back for Marsey Island on his last journey. There he left the second man to join his mate, and after giving them full instructions as to what to do, he took in Tinker and began the return journey.

When they reached Westward Ho! again, they found that preparations were all completed for the Munitions Minister and Sir Hector Amworth to motor through to London at once. Before departing, the Munitions Minister took Blake aside and said: "Things are too pressing for me to thank you properly for what you have done, Blake. I shall do that in London. I have sent a message which will have a T.B.D. at Marsey Island within an hour. It will land a few men and remain in the vicinity. When the biplane returns, it will endeavour to gather in the two men we are after."

"That will be splendid," rejoined Blake.

Then he gazed thoughtfully out at sea.

"They are cunning, sir—none more cunning in all Europe than they. I have a feeling that I should return there and take a hand."

The Munitions Minister laid a hand on his sholulder. "You will do nothing of the sort, Blake. You have done in one day more than the whole police force of the country could have done in a week. Leave the capture of those two to the men who have been sent to get them. Return to London and rest easy—they must be taken.

"I shall do so, but I have been up against those same two more than once in the past, and I know what they are," said Blake. "However, we shall hope for the best."

So, shaking hands with the Munitions Minister and Sir Hector Amworth, he saw them into their car, and with Tinker at his side walked across to his own. He waited for Mr. Grindley Morrison to join them, and when he had done so, they motored back to Northam where they had a late lunch.

Then Blake got his bag and bidding good-bye to Morrison, they returned to Westward Ho! from where Tinker was to take the Grey Panther back to Hendon.

When the lad had risen and was flying easily at the two thousand foot level, Blake climbed back into the car and started for London. He drove at a stiff pace through Devon and Somerset, for he was anxious to get back to Baker Street to attend to other matters of importance.

He did not make the return journey in as good time as he had come down, but it was very close, and when he walked into the consulting room at Baker Street, he was not surprised to see Tinker sitting at the desk writing busily.

"Well, my lad, did you have a good flight up?" he asked, as he removed his motoring coat and cap.

Tinker sprang to he feet. "Yes, guv'nor," re replied. "But something has happened which will annoy you."

"What is it?" asked Blake sharply.

"A telegram has just come from one of the coastguardsmen whom you took to Marsey Island, saying the the biplane returned before the T.B.D. showed up, and that in the fight that followed they—the two coastguardsmen—were overpowered, and left bound and helpless in the bungalow."

CHAPTER 4
Telling of a Meeting of the Brotherhood of the Yellow Beetle

Blake reached out his hand for the telegram which Tinker held, and hurriedly read the message. Dropping it on the desk with an exclamation of annoyance, he began to pace up and down the room.

"If I had only returned to Marsey Island," he muttered, "this would not have happened. I know how cunning Wu Ling and Beauremon are, and if they have joined forces they will make an ugly pair to fight. But if we had been on the island we should have had a chance in a million of raking the pair of them in. It is too bad—too bad! I—— Answer it, Tinker," This as the telephone on the desk jangled shrilly.

Tinker lifted the receiver, but had said only a few words when he looked towards Blake. "It is the Munitions Minister, guv'nor."

Blake strode across to the desk and took the receiver.

"Hello!" he said.

"Hello! Is that you, Blake?" came a voice which he recognised as that of the Munitions Minister.

"Yes!" replied Blake.

"I have called you up to tell you that those people have got away, Blake." went on the Minister. "It is too bad. I should not have persuaded you to return to London, but should have let you return to the island, as you wished. You knew their capabilities better than I. But it is no use crying over spilt milk. They have got away and have taken with them the two men you caught."

"I know," replied Blake. "A wire has just come in about it. It is unfortunate."

"Still, we must get them, Blake," continued the Minister. "I have just heard from Sir John. He has received a code message from the commander of the T.B.D., which arrived at the island just after the affair was over. He says that he continued on his course up the Bristol Channel, and that not far off Cardiff he came upon a wrecked biplane—a machine far larger than the ordinary. It is not a Government machine, and from the description which Sir John gave me I imagine it is the one of which you spoke.

"At first the commander of the T.B.D. thought there had been an accident, but on examining the wreckage he became of the opinion that it had been deliberately disabled. Therefore, we can only conclude that the occupants had a rendezvous with a boat of some sort, and were picked up by it. The point is, what has become of them? And it is all the more important that we should find out, for Sir John tells me that he has heard vague reports of renewed activity on the part of German agents in England.

"It has occurred to me that these people who gave me their attention might be connected with this new German attempt. What do you think?"

"I think it is more than likely, sir," replied Blake. "When I say they are both capable of anything, I am not exaggerating. It is most unfortunate that they have escaped."

"That is exactly what I think, Blake. And I am glad you agree with me, for I want you take up the matter and run them to earth. Will you do so?"

Blake was silent for a few seconds. Not that he would refuse a definite request to handle a case for the Government, but because he knew it would take longer to run Wu Ling and Beauremon to earth a second time, and already his hands were full of urgent matters. However, he decided that other things must wait for the present, and so he replied:

"Certainly I will take it up, sir. Did Sir John have no further clue whatsoever as to what direction may have been taken by the occupants of the wrecked biplane?"

"I am afraid there is little to go upon," responded the Minister. "He did say that the commander of the T.B.D. had interviewed a fishing boat out of Bideford, and the crew of the smack told him they thought—only thought, mind you—that they had seen a motor boat in the vicinity of the wreckage. This may or may not be so, but it is the only thing in the shape of a clue. The fishermen said this motor boat went off at a high speed in the direction of Cardiff."

Blake pondered this bit of information for a moment, then said:

"Very well, sir, I shall go to work on the matter at once and see what I can discover. I shall make a report to you as soon as I know anything definite."

"Thank you, Blake!" rejoined the Minister. "I shall be greatly obliged to you."

With that he rang off, and Blake, rehanging the receiver, turned to Tinker.

"We shall have to leave London again, my lad. The Government thinks Wu Ling and Beauremon may be connected with some new activity on the part of the Germans, and want them run to earth. We must try to do so. Pack up the bags with some fresh things and see that the car is ready for a run to Cardiff. We shall start our search there, since that seems to be the only spot towards which even the vaguest of clues point. In the meantime, I shall get to work on this pile of letters and attend to anything urgent."

Tinker sprang up at once to obey, and hurried out to see to the preparations while Blake sat down at the desk and took up the huge pile of letters which lay on the blotting-pad. An hour later Blake has completed his task, and when Tinker appeared, carrying two large kit bags, he rose.

Donning their coats and caps, they once more entered the car, and taking the wheel, Blake turned and drove down Baker Street at a smart pace. It was a long and, after the journey they had both just completed, a particularly tiring ride down to Cardiff, and when they finally drew up in front of the Western Hotel, the major part of the inhabitants of the channel port were wrapped in slumber.

Rousing the night porter of the hotel they procured rooms, and when Tinker had driven the car into the hotel garage, they ascended at once to their apartments, knowing nothing could be done that night.

And yet, at the very moment when Blake and Tinker were in the act of retiring, there was a conference afoot in that same town of Cardiff, which, though it was held in secret, was proof sufficient that not all the town was sleeping.

In a house set in a narrow, dingy street, which led off the water front, there was a meeting in progress which, had Blake but known it, was to have a radical effect upon his own immediate fortunes.

In this darkened house, from which not a single chink of light was permitted to escape, there was a room which, like many rooms throughout the world, had been hung with heavy saffron-coloured silken curtains. There were no chairs or tables in the room, but round the sides had been piled great heaps of silken cushions—the prevailing tone of which was the all-pervading yellow.

The floor had been covered by a thick rug of intricate eastern pattern, the colours of which blended harmoniously with the cushions and hangings. From the ceiling hung a huge lamp wrought in copper, and in design not unlike an old Moorish brazier, although a connoisseur would have known that it was of an early Chinese period.

At the upper end of the apartment there had been placed a small dais, upon which had been piled a number of rich-looking cushions, and in front of the dais, within easy reach of it, was a tiny tabourette, upon which rested writing materials. It was a room of the Brotherhood of the Yellow Beetle, and on this night the council of the brotherhood was in session. On the cushions piled upon the dais sat Prince Wu Ling, of Manchu blood, royal legitimate heir to the ancient throne of China, authorised wearer of the sacred yellow and supreme head of that powerful organisation, the Brotherhood of the Yellow Beetle.

On this occasion he was garbed in the garments of his position—loose silken trousers of yellow, and a magnificent saffron-coloured tunic of heavy silk, caught together with a single great yellow topaz. On the breast of his coat glittered a single jewelled order, and one ring only—a massive affair set with a topaz—graced his hands.

He had changed little since his first entry into Europe in his great fight to place the heel of the yellow man on the neck of the white, and since that time in the far-off island of Kaitu, in the China Sea, when Sexton Blake had sent him perilously close to death.

His face was as inscrutably reposeful as ever—the same noble sweep to the brow was there—the hair was perhaps a little thinner, but still black as night, the deep-set oblique eyes, yet slumbrous and reflecting the lore of the ages gone. It was a face which reflected the power of the mind behind those who could see and read.

On this night he was bending forward where he sat, apparently in deep thought, and the members of the council of the brotherhood who were ranged down each side of the room were mutely patient, awaiting the pleasure of their lord.

Ten there were in all—ten sons of the East, who had been gathered from the ranks of the brotherhood and admitted to the sacred inner councils only after Wu Ling himself had tested them by the fire of the inquisition which he knew so well how to apply.

Not all the council of the Brotherhood was present. In Canton or Peking, when a full meeting was held, twenty-four attended, and on those occasions the conferences were affairs glittering with magnificence and lengthened by ceremony after ceremony, for there Wu Ling permitted himself the full sway of his power. But in London or New York, or elsewhere, when a meeting of the brotherhood was usually called to settle some policy of urgency, it was only attended, as on this occasion, by the members of the council who formed part of his personal suite. Yet, even then, the royal saffron was always in evidence.

For the better part of an hour Wu Ling had sat bent forward in thought, but as there was slight rustling sound at the far end of the room and the curtains swayed gently as a Celestial pushed them aside and entered, he raised his head and regarded the newcomer.

It was San, but a different San than usually attended upon his master. To-night his thick throat was swathed in white bandages, and he held his head at an angle as though in constant pain. And he was, for the bullet from Sexton Blake's rifle had been no flesh wound, but, as Blake himself had thought, had ploughed deep in the flesh of the Celestial's thick throat.

Then Wu Ling did a thing which, in all their experience of him, the members of the brotherhood had never seen him do. He rose, and treading with slow dignity, walked down the room to meet San.

As he did so the ten members rose as one man and stood with bent head while Wu Ling took San by the hand and led him back to the dais. There, on his own pile of cushions, he placed his wounded lieutenant, and, turning back to the others, bade them curtly to be seated.

When they were once more squatting on their piles of cushions, Wu Ling thrust his hands inside his tunic and began to address them.

"Members of the Brotherhood of the Yellow Beetle," he said in slow, guttural tones, "you have been summoned to-night to decide matters of urgency. I have waited until San—San, my faithful lieutenant, my tutor when I was but a youth, my substitute when you thought me dead, but when I was in reality in retreat in a Thibetan monastery—could attend before discussing the matters which must be discussed to-night. Before I do so, cast your eyes at San. The bandages which he wears speak for themselves.

"In all our dealing with the cursed white pigs, we have never suffered a greater set-back than we have this day. And members of the sacred brotherhood, it was due to one man who has been our Nemesis during the past, it is due to the man whose fingers were buried in my own throat on the Island of Kaitu, and who nearly succeeded in sending me to the arms of the blessed Confucius—to Sexton Blake—and may the god Mo send him to eternal perdition. And I, Wu Ling, tell you this night that this man must die.

"Listen, members of the Brotherhood of the Yellow Beetle, while I relate to you what has happened.

"At the last meeting of the Council of the Brotherhood, held in this same room, I told you of the arrangement which I had come to with the Germans. To us the German pigs are no more than the British pigs—may the god Mo take them all!—but in the furtherance of our great policy of world empire, in the crushing of the whites and in the placing of the

41

saffron banner over all, it is necessary that we should play off the one against the other.

"For that reason I formed a temporary alliance with the Germans. I promised to lend them our aid in certain things, in return for which they were to give us a free hand in the East. We know how Japan has gone hand-in-hand with the British, and how they have forsaken the call of the East for the lure of the West. But we—we Chinese of the old empire, and the members of the Brotherhood of the Yellow Beetle, will keep the one goal in front of us and strive to reach it with the blessing of Confucius and Buddha—with the aid of the god Mo.

"In fulfilment of our agreement with the Germans, I went to see their prince when he came to England. As you know, our work then ended in failure, due, as in the past, to this dog Sexton Blake. Again, the Germans outlined a plan whereby the man who calls himself the British Minister of Munitions was to be taken and killed.

"On this man depend the present hopes of the British. He it is who holds in his hands the control of Britain and the output of munitions, which is her only hope at present. With him out of the way the Germans would achieve much in a single stroke.

"In order that there might be no miscarriage of plans, I enlisted the aid of a man whose deeds you have all heard of. He is a white man, but a man of decision and resource. I speak of Baron Robert de Beauremon, the head of an organisation known as the Council of Eleven. He accepted the offer I made him, and we set about to get possession of the person of this Minister of whom I have spoken. We succeeded and took him to a safe place of hiding where he was to be despatched.

"Realising how risky such a proceeding would be, we came to Cardiff in the big aeroplane, which is the property of the baron, in order to make arrangements for our escape after the Minister and his friend, whom we had captured with him, had been disposed of. While we were away San-San, my faithful lieutenant, whom you see wounded before you, was attacked, and he and Gonzalez, a Spaniard lieutenant of the baron's, were overpowered, while the prisoners we had taken were released.

"Only our opportune arrival enabled us to release San and the Spaniard before a British boat arrived to take them on board. And, members of the Council of the Brotherhood of the Yellow Beetle, the man who attacked San and released the two prisoners we had taken was this same man Sexton Blake. Therefore, I say to you, this man must die.

"More than once in the past has he been condemned to death, more than once has he been in our power, yet have the fates been with him. He has escaped, and still lives to oppose the will of the brotherhood. But this time he dies. I, Wu Ling, say it, and woe be to him who gets him into his power and allows him to escape. Yet I it must be to visit the death-stroke upon him. See that you do not forget that.

"Let the word go forth through all the Chinese in Cardiff, to all the Celestials, and members of the Brotherhood of the Yellow Beetle in England, that this man Blake must be taken. Not until he is removed from our path may we work successfully.

"Go forth, each one of you, this night, and spread the will of Wu Ling. I, Wu Ling, have spoken."

With that the prince sat down beside San, and for the space of five minutes or more, there was dead silence in the room. Then, slowly and almost noiselessly, the members of the council rose, and after bowing low before Wu Ling retired from the room.

When only Wu Ling and San were left, the prince once more rose, and walking to one corner of the apartment, drew aside the yellow curtains from a small stand which they had concealed. On this stand, which it might have been seen was of black marble, there reposed a small statue of a squatting god. It was of pure gold, which gleamed dully beneath the rays of the great central lamp, and sat upon a base of solid jade.

It was the god Mo, the patron god of Wu Ling—the image which watched over his destinies.

There, before the jade-based idol, he dropped to his knees and bent in submission until his forehead touched the floor. For some minutes he remained thus, then rose to his feet and made a gesture for San to follow him from the room.

He had prayed to the golden god Mo to favour his vendetta against Sexton Blake, and he was certain in his own mind that the god would hear him.

CHAPTER 5
Into the Lion's Den

The morning following their arrival in Cardiff, Blake and Tinker were abroad early. Blake's decision to start investigations at Cardiff was simply the result of a direct assumption that the wrecked biplane, which had been found floating in the Bristol Channel, was the one which had been used in the kidnapping of the Munitions Minister and his friend, Sir Hector Amworth.

If it should prove to be another machine, then he would have to pick up some other line of suggestion. But so far, he was strongly of the opinion that the wreckage was that of the big biplane belonging to the Council of Eleven!

Ever since he had been called down to Westward Ho! in order to trace the Munitions Minister Cardiff had been more or less connected with the affair.

For instance, it will be recalled that when Tinker was flying from Hendon to Westward Ho! and had seen another machine over the Bristol Channel, he had been of the opinion that it had come from Cardiff way.

Then again, the fact that it was able to visit Marsey Island so frequently, and at such short intervals, proved that it had a base not very far distant—that is, not far distant when considering the radius of action of an aeroplane.

Furthermore, the message which had come through from the commander of the T.B.D. had said that the wreckage had been found in the Bristol Channel, not far from Cardiff, and that the fishermen whom he had interviewed had spoken of a motor-boat which they had seen in the vicinity of the wreckage, and which they thought had made off towards Cardiff.

So Blake's quick decision to go to Cardiff and open the new investigation there was not the result of any lengthy deduction, but simply the result of the rapidity with which long experience had enabled him to put his finger on the most likely spot in a case.

He knew, too, that Cardiff possessed a very large Chinese element, and since Prince Wu Ling had climbed into the realm of European diplomatic scheming, Cardiff had more than once been the base of his British operations.

Blake was dead certain in his own mind that Wu Ling had played a leading part in the daring outrage on the Munitions Minister and Sir Hector Amworth. That Baron Robert de Beauremon was also mixed up in the affair he felt confident, but he knew when he found one he would find the other.

The difficulty was to locate them before they shifted their base from Cardiff. They would realise how dangerous that locality would be for them after the rescue of the Munitions Minister, and would use every despatch to make a shift in base.

Therefore, speed was essential if Blake were to track them down before they moved and thus complicated matters. But first he wished to prove one point. He wished to get into touch with the commander of the T.B.D., and to get from that gentleman a detailed description of the wreckage which he had come upon. He wished, also, to find the two coastguards who had been overpowered on Marsey Island, and to receive from them a description of the men who had come to the island. That would take time, but it must be done.

From the Munitions Minister he knew that Cardiff was the base of the T.B.D., and that being so he would have little difficulty in finding the commander. But to speak with the coastguards he must have them across from Westward Ho!

His first duty in the morning, after sending Tinker on a scouting expedition along the water front, was to hire a motor-boat and send it across the channel to Westward Ho! to get the two coastguards. Then he set about to look for the T.B.D.

After a couple of hours about the water front he heard from a certain source that she would be in harbour about noon, so he loitered about until that hour watching for her.

Sure enough midday had just gone when her black nose poked its way into port, and scarcely was she moored when Blake was aboard her.

When the commander was made aware of Blake's identity he invited him down into his cabin, and there, in answer to the detective's questions, gave him a detailed description of the wreckage which he had come upon, and after taking note of, had sunk to prevent it from being a menace to navigation.

From the notes which he had taken Blake got sufficient information to convince him that it was none other than the big biplane used by the Council of Eleven, and when he had thanked the commander for his help took his leave.

He walked back towards the Western Hotel, and just as he reached the portals of that caravanserai met Tinker, who was obviously in a state of excitement.

"I have something important to tell you, guv'nor," he whispered, as they entered the lobby.

Blake nodded slightly.

"Come upstairs at once, Tinker," he replied, scarcely moving his lips.

They ascended in the lift, and walked along the corridor to their sitting-room. There Blake closed and locked the door, and, after a careful search round the room, signed to Tinker.

"Now, go ahead, my lad," he said.

Tinker stood close to his master, and speaking in a low tone said:

"I saw San in Cardiff this morning, guv'nor."

Blake glanced at the lad sharply.

"Are you certain?" he asked quickly.

"Dead certain, guv'nor," responded Tinker. "when I left here to scout about, I made for the docks. I saw you more than once during the morning, but I kept out of sight. I went up in the Chinese part—you remember where we had a mix-up when we were on that Sacred Sphere business?—and scouted about there with some of the crews who were knocking round from pub to pub.

"Well, I had been in half a dozen or more—they took me for a ship's boy—when just as we were leaving one to go to another, the door of a house opened and a Chinaman came out. His neck and the side of face were all in bandages, but I recognised him in a moment as San. I slipped away from the gang a few minutes later and shadowed him. He walked down to the docks and idled about for a little, then he returned to the house from which I had seen him come out.

"He looked pretty bad, guv'nor, and I guess he was only out for a constitutional. Anyway, he disappeared back into the house, and I came straight on here to report.

"Which house do you refer to, Tinker?" asked Blake curtly.

"I mean the one, guv'nor, which you said was an opium joint."

Blake gazed at the carpet thoughtfully.

"I remember the place," he muttered to himself—"a long, low building, with the shutters always closed. It poses as a lodging-house, and in one corner there is a pub. Is that the one?"

"That's it, guv'nor."

"And San is there," went on Blake. "If he is there, it means Wu Ling is not far away. I thought we should strike their trail in Cardiff, and it seems you have done so, my lad. But we must lose no time in getting after them. San is important, but can wait. It is Wu Ling himself we must gather in. This needs some thought, Tinker."

Walking to the window, Blake stood for a long time gazing out at the street below. Tinker, knowing that Blake was revolving in his mind some plan to gain access to the Chinese joint and to follow up the clue he had found, sat down and waited patiently for his master to decide the next step.

Finally Blake turned back from the window.

"Get out my Chinese disguise, my lad—not the mandarin one, but that of a coolie."

"Then you are going there, guv'nor?" asked Tinker.

Blake nodded.

"It is the only way."

"If they get you, guv'nor you will never get out alive!" said the lad earnestly. "You know how hot they are to rope you in after that last brush you had with Wu Ling. It is only a little time since they had us besieged in Baker Street and nearly got us both. If you are suspected in this Chinese joint it will be 'Good-night, nurse' with you pretty quick!"

Blake shrugged his shoulders.

"I am not anxious to go into the place, my lad. I realise as well as you how keen the Brotherhood of the Yellow Beetle is to 'get me,' but I can see no other way. Wu Ling and his crowd are getting altogether too daring in England! They must be stopped, and stopped at once! It was bad enough when they were fighting only for themselves, but now that they have joined up with the Germans, as we know they have, something must be done to clean them out of the place.

"Therefore I shall go to this house. But I shall take all necessary precautions, never fear, and before I go will arrange as far as possible for my safety. There will be work for you to do outside while I am there. Now get my disguise out, and then we shall have some lunch before I change."

Without further protest, Tinker rose, though he did not like Blake's plan. But he knew if his master thought the only thing to do was to enter the camp of the enemy, he would do that thing regardless of the danger it held for him. Nor had the lad forgotten some of his own experiences while in the hands of Wu Ling and his men.

When he had got out the disguise, Tinker returned to the sitting-room and joined Blake. Together they descended to the dining-room, where they ate a hurried lunch. After lunch they went up again to the sitting-room of their suite, and when he had smoked a cigarette Blake prepared to make the change in appearance from that of a keen-looking Londoner to that of a Chinese coolie.

Going into his bedroom, he sat down before the dressing-table and, drawing towards him a large black box of pigments, set to work first on his face.

With a yellowish stain, which he had procured from the Celebes, in the Dutch East Indies, he stained all the skin of the face, neck, and arms. When this had dried, he took up a pencil affair with which he drew hundreds of tiny almost invisible lines, which, although not visible at any great distance, still gave that lined and seamed appearance so typical in the Chinese countenance.

That done, he set to work on his eyebrows, which he blackened carefully. Then he gave his attention to the eyes themselves, working away at them until they presented the oblique appearance of the ordinary Celestial.

Not until he was quite satisfied with this did he pick up the black queued wig which was a tonsorial masterpiece of one of the cleverest West End hairdressers.

Adjusting it carefully, Blake next turned to the garments. On his legs he drew loose trousers of cheap blue cotton, then slipped his feet into the thick-soled slippers so favoured of the coolie. Next he drew on a loose coat which buttoned well up, and, that done, he regarded himself at length in the glass.

He was dissatisfied with one or two points of detail, and proceeded to change them, after which he walked out to the sitting-room where Tinker waited.

The lad rose and cast a critical eye at his master. Over every detail that sharp young gaze went until it had covered Blake from head to foot. Then he nodded.

"It will do, guv'nor. I can't see a single fault."

Blake smiled.

"Then I shall prepare to go along, my lad," he said. "I think you had better accompany me out of the hotel. I don't want to arouse any comment, which might be the case should I go out alone. But before I go I shall post you in what you have to do. Now listen carefully!

"This afternoon you will hang about the docks, and keep an eye out for the arrival of the motorboat which I sent across to Westward Ho! to get the two coastguards. When you have seen them, you will get from them a description of the men who landed on Marsey Island and overpowered them. Get them to sign it. We shall need it in the evidence we shall bring against Wu Ling and Beauremon.

"When you have done that, give them a couple of sovereigns each, and see that they get away again for Westward Ho! If any of Wu Ling's crowd should get on to the fact that they are here, it might go badly with them. The next thing you will do is to go to the police. See the chief of police of the city, and make yourself known to him. Then tell him exactly why we are down here and what we propose doing. Enlist his aid. He will be glad to do all he can to assist you. Have him get a half a dozen men together. I would suggest that they be either plain-clothes men or special constables. If the latter, they can remove their badges, and then there will be little about them to arouse suspicion.

"This force you will hold in readiness until midnight to-night. If by then I have not returned to the Western Hotel, you will know that trouble has arisen, and will start at once for the house to which I am going. There you will raid it, and search it from top to bottom.

"Do not miss a single corner of it! You know as well as I do how cunning the Chinese are in the locating of secret rooms which they do not wish the police to find. Raze the place if necessary, but do not desist from your search until you have found me, because, if I have not returned from there by midnight, it will only be because I have found it impossible to do so. Do you understand exactly what you have to do?"

"Perfectly, guv'nor," replied Tinker, with a worried frown. "But, all the same, I don't like it! I wish you would let me go down there and hang about! These Chinks are out after your blood, and if they dream for a single moment that you are not what you appear to be, they will not rest until they have discovered your identity. Then—well, you know what will happen to you!"

Blake shrugged.

"It can't be helped, my lad. I am going after Wu Ling and Beauremon, and it is the only way I can get on their trail. Do what I have told you, and we will trust to luck and my ingenuity. Come!"

Blake turned as he spoke and, on opening the door, passed out into the corridor, followed by Tinker. Passing along, they avoided the lift and descended by the staircase in order not to arouse too much comment.

Arriving in the lobby, they hastened out on to the street almost before the few persons who loitered there were aware that a Celestial had just gone past. Then, when they were a hundred yards or so down the street, Tinker, with a whispered word to his master, slipped away, and Blake went on alone to enter the den of the Yellow Tiger of the East.

Nor, as he did so, did he dream for a single moment that as they had emerged from the Western Hotel a sleek-looking Chinaman in a shop across the street had seen them come out, and, remembering the order of Wu Ling which had swept through the Chinese element that very morning, and consequently suspicious at seeing a coolie emerge from the hotel in the company of a white lad, had slipped forth from the shop to follow him.

Down the street he went, his slant-eyes half closed, and apparently seeing nothing of his surroundings. Yet from beneath those heavy lids he was watching every step of the two ahead, and then Tinker left Blake, the Celestial trailed the coolie.

On and on went Blake, all unsuspicious of the man who followed him, and away towards the docks went Tinker, equally unsuspicious.

This was by no means the first time Sexton Blake had played the part of a Celestial. Often in the past had it been necessary for him to adopt the role, and, with a perfect command of the different spoken dialects of China, as well as a deep knowledge of the written language of that country, he had carried out the daring project with brilliant success.

Take Sexton Blake, garb him as a Celestial, and drop him into the centre of Canton, and if the Chinese of that ancient city did not know that he was not one of them, they would never find out the truth through any defect in Blake's appearance or slip in his speech.

He had even spoken with Wu Ling as Celestial to Celestial, and the prince had not suspected his identity, and the man who could fool Wu Ling could fool all China.

Arriving at the corner of the street in which was situated the house of which Tinker had spoken, Blake paused for a moment, and gazed sleepily about him, as any other Celestial might have done. Then, turning, he shuffled along the street until he came to the house which was his objective.

Arriving at it, he did not make any attempt to enter it by means of the door, which was apparently for the use of the regular occupants, but, instead, he passed into the saloon part of the place. There, in front of the bar, he saw half a dozen Celestials and seaman of sorts drinking and tossing dice.

Slouching up to the bar, Blake ordered a drink from the Chinaman who was serving, and, with that before him, leaned idly against the bar.

He had not been standing there long when one of the Celestials who had been shaking dice sidled up to him.

"You are a stranger?" he said in low, guttural Chinese.

Blake turned his sleepy eyes upon the other.

"I have come from London," he said.

For a moment the other regarded him impassively, then, bending forward towards the bar, he said, scarcely moving his lips:

"Are you of the East?"

Blake's heart leaped, though his features were as inscrutable as those of the other. The words he had just heard formed the opening phrase of the test of membership of the Brotherhood of the Yellow Beetle, and only too well he remembered the stinking river den in Canton where he had first heard them, and from the memories of the past there came to him the answer.

"Of the East and for the East," he replied slowly.

"Where do you go?" came the next question.

"Into the West," answered Blake readily.

"Do you return?" asked his interlocutor.

"There is no return," responded Blake. "The West will be East."

With that the Celestial sidled still closer, confident from Blake's reply that he was a member of the Brotherhood.

"You will stay in Cardiff long?" he asked.

Blake shrugged, and drew out some yellow cigarette-paper, into which he poured some tobacco.

"Who knows?" he said, as he rolled a cigarette. "Perhaps a day, perhaps a year. It is the will of Buddha. Will the honourable one drink with one so unworthy?"

The Celestial nodded.

"If you will permit one so unworthy to drink in your presence," he replied.

Blake made a sign to the man behind the bar, who filled up two fresh glasses, and pushed them across.

Then Blake and the Celestial pledged each other with the flowery and meaningless compliments of the East.

When they set down their glasses again the Celestial glanced at Blake.

"Do you come in ignorance?" he asked.

Blake puffed slowly at his cigarette.

"I know nothing," he replied.

"The Illustrious One is in Cardiff," went on the Chinaman, in a low tone.

Blake bowed his head reverently.

"My vile ears are unworthy to hear such news?" he said. "Is the great Illustrious One indeed here?"

"He is here, and has made known his will," responded the Celestial. "He does much for the good of the Brotherhood. The Yellow Dragon will yet wave over this country of pigs. The Illustrious One has spoken."

Blake smoked on, waiting for the other to continue. It was evident to him from what he had just heard that Wu Ling was undoubtedly in Cardiff, and that something special was afoot.

Even the stolid Celestial beside him was affected by the importance of it. And he knew by waiting he would hear what it was.

"The order has gone forth," went on the other, after a little. "There is one whom it is the will of the Illustrious One to find, and when he has found him——" And he finished with a shrug. "There is one who is a white pig. He has done much to annoy the Illustrious One, and the Brotherhood is to take revenge for the daring of the contemptible pig. His name is Blake—Sexton Blake—and the Illustrious One has deigned to command that every member of the sacred Brotherhood shall seek him out, and bring him to the seat of judgment. All the members in this cursed country know the will of the Illustrious One."

Blake nodded slowly.

"And this pig, Blake," he said—"what is he like?"

The Celestial beside him laid one hand on the bar.

"He is tall as the sapling in the forest," he said. "He is strong as the oak which bends, but breaks not, beneath the blast. He is neither young nor old. He is cunning—ah, so cunning! Not even in the East are there any more cunning than he. I have heard that in the past he has dared more than once to oppose the will of the Illustrious One. Do you remember when the Illustrious One was not with us for a time?"

"Do I remember that the sun was out?" replied Blake, meaning that the great orb of day had not shone while Wu Ling was absent.

"It was this same pig, Blake, who nearly sent the Illustrious One to the arms of the blessed Confucius," went on the Celestial, referring to the time in the island of Kaitu when Blake had choked Wu Ling into insensibility, and had nearly sent the prince to his death. "The Illustrious One is sending out a picture of the pig, so that all shall know him and watch for him."

Blake nodded again.

"It is well," he responded. "The pig, Blake, will be sought on all sides by the Brotherhood. May I be the one to find him!"

The Celestial bowed in agreement, then said:

"Have you been in the opium-room yet?"

Blake made a gesture of negation.

"No," he replied. "I have but come. I go to seek it now."

"I know it well," went on his companion. "I will take you to it for the price of two pills."

"I will give you the price of one," rejoined Blake, not forgetting to bicker as any other Celestial would have done.

"It is well," said the other. "Come!"

Blake, well pleased at the prospect of gaining admittance to the opium-room under the wing of a regular habitue, turned and followed. His guide kicked open a low door leading into the next room where Blake saw a few Chinamen gaming after the stolid manner of their kind.

Past these, who never once glanced in their direction, they went until they reached a door on the opposite side of the room. Opening this they passed into another corridor.

Like a giant Chinese puzzle-box was that den. Leaving the corridor into which they had just come, they passed through room after room, his guide going ahead with the confidence of one perfectly familiar with his surroundings, and as one who was persona grata in the place. And the nearer they approached to the heart of the place the more mysterious became the subtle air of something concealed which pervaded it.

Here and there in small shadowy rooms sat little groups of Celestials, talking in low tones, and planning Heaven only knew what schemes. In others, too gloomy to be pierced by the eye, Blake could feel the presence of people, whose occupation might almost be anything which skulked under the wing of darkness.

On and on still further through the puzzle-box Blake went, glimpsing scenes which could not be described, and which, if they were, would scarcely be believed, and then at last his guide brought him to the opium-room, where on long mattresses, piled close together, lay the victims of the drug, lying in every attitude of repulsive abandon, saturated with opium—the drug which, as long as it is submerged beneath its thrall, will prevent the Chinese nation from being really great.

There, from out of the shadows a Celestial shuffled up, and with him Blake's guide held a whispered colloquy. Finally, he turned to Blake.

"It is well," he said, in a whisper. "Give me the price of the two pills which you promised."

Blake, who knew the scale of prices in half the opium-dens in the world, held out the price of one shot, and the other, seeing that he would gain nothing by haggling, seized it, and shuffled towards a mattress.

Blake, in reply to an inquiry from the pipe attendant, expressed his wish to smoke, and the latter conducted him to a mattress at the other end of the room. There Blake cast himself down, and while he was waiting for the attendant to prepare his pipe, and to arrange the tiny pill of opium, he gazed about him.

Nearly all the mattresses were occupied, though it was still early in the day. Some were already in the throes of the drug-dreams, muttering and mumbling incoherently, proving that they had been there for some time, possibly since the day before. Others were less advanced in the grip of the drug, and still more were but preparing to take their first shot.

The atmosphere of the place was heavy and fetid, with a nauseating suggestion which affected even Blake, accustomed though he was to such places. Probably not for years had the light of day been permitted to enter the room. What windows there were were heavily shuttered, and inside those hung heavy curtains effectually cutting off all light.

The men on the mattresses were of all sorts and conditions, though Blake could not help but note that in this particular joint they were all Celestials.

When the attendant had affixed the tiny pill of opium to his pipe, Blake put the mouthpiece between his lips, and, settling himself down, prepared to smoke. He knew that he must take some of the drug in order to remain in the place without suspicion, but he had no intention of permitting himself to be overcome by it.

From what he had already discovered he knew that Wu Ling was either in the place at that very moment, or else very close to it. And it was to find Wu Ling he had come there.

But clever though his disguise was, and perfect though his command of the language might be, they were to prove of little assistance to him as he was to find out, for the sleek-looking Celestial who had seen him leave the hotel with Tinker had not by any means had his suspicions allayed.

Even while Blake had stood by the bar talking with the other Chinaman, had he stood outside, peering in idly from time to time, and watching every movement of the man who had aroused his suspicions. Then, when Blake had disappeared from the bar, and had entered the joint proper, he had slipped into the bar, and, standing close to it, had asked the man who was serving what he knew about the Celestial who had just drunk there.

When he was told that Blake was a total stranger to the place, and that by his own words he had but arrived from London, the sleek-looking one had grown more suspicious than ever, and, in his sleepy Chinese fashion, had pondered deeply.

At the end of some ten minutes or so when, as it happened, the bar held very few people, he leaned across to the man who was serving, and, in low, guttural tones, said:

"Is the Illustrious One within?"

The other gazed at him impassively for a few moments before replying.

"Son and grandson of pigs that thou art, why do you speak of the Illustrious One?"

"The open mouth catches the flies," responded Number One slowly. "I have word for the ear of the Illustrious One. Go and beg that he will permit the sun of his countenance to shine upon me."

The serving man bent his head a little lower.

"If you seek to waste the time of the Illustrious One, you will be as the blade before the blast, and will wither before the scorn of his august eye."

"I seek not the presence of the Illustrious One without wheat to bring him," replied Number One. "Go and seek him."

The man behind the bar turned, and, shuffling along, lifted up a dirty curtain which shut off the bar from the room beyond. He passed through and dropped it behind him, and for the space of ten minutes or so the man who stood by the bar waited.

Then the curtain was once more lifted, and the bar-tender reappeared.

Lifting a finger he beckoned to the other, and he, with a slight motion of the hand, walked along to a flap in the counter. Lifting this he passed behind the bar, and joined the bar-tender.

Through a small room the latter led him, and then along a narrow passage lit by a single light. At the end of this passage the guide stopped and knocked thrice. A guttural voice on the other side of the door bade him enter, and, opening the door, he passed through, followed by the other.

The room into which they passed was a small apartment, furnished only with a table and a rough chair. In this chair, writing, sat a Celestial who looked up as the two entered. The bar-tender stepped forward.

"I have brought the presumptuous pig," he said.

The Chinaman at the table regarded the one referred to.

"Why do you seek the Illustrious One?" he asked curtly.

The Celestial, who had followed Blake so closely, spread out his hands.

"I have important word for the ear of the master," he said slowly. "I would speak with him at once. It is about the order which the Illustrious One has sent out to all members of the Brotherhood."

The heavy lids of the man at the table dropped a little lower.

"If you have news, the Illustrious One will be pleased to admit you to his honourable presence, but if you talk as the cuckoo, woe betide you!"

"I have news," replied the other simply.

The man at the table rose, and made a motion to the bar-tender, which caused him to leave the room. Then the former approached a door in the opposite wall, and beckoned to the other.

"Come!" he said. "I will take you to the Illustrious One."

Through a maze of passages and small rooms he now led the newsbringer until at last he stopped before a door, which was almost hidden from view by heavy curtains. Pushing them aside the guide knocked, and a moment later, in answer to a summons from within, opened the door and entered.

The moment he was inside the door he bowed low, and stood waiting until ordered to advance. Then he lifted his head and went forward. The room was the same wherein there had been held a meeting of the Brotherhood the previous evening.

On the cushions before the dais at the upper end sat Wu Ling and beside him, with his throat still swathed in bandages, was San. There was no one else in the room.

"There is one who would speak to you, Illustrious One," said the guide.

Wu Ling, still clad in the saffron tunic of the Brotherhood, made a gesture.

"Let him approach," he said curtly.

The guide again bowed, and, backing out, took the newsbringer by the sleeve.

"Go in," he whispered, "and see that you trifle not with the Illustrious One."

The other nodded, and, pushing between the curtains, stepped into the room. He stood for a full minute with bent head while Wu Ling's all-seeing gaze swept him from head to foot. Finally the prince spoke:

"You are of the Brotherhood?" he asked curtly.

"Oh, Illustrious One, I have been of it long,"

"You bring important word?" went on Wu Ling. "Have you thought well before seeking my presence?"

"Oh Illustrious One," replied the newsbringer, "I sought the sun of your presence because I have word of importance. It is to speak of the Illustrious One's order that I come."

Wu Ling lifted his head a trifle.

"Advance and speak!" he ordered.

The Chinaman walked up the room, until he stood nearer the dais, then he said:

"Oh, Illustrious One, your order went abroad this morning, and we of the Brotherhood hearkened and were glad. It was only when I had heard that I was standing in the shop of Looey Wan Kai. As I talked with the unworthy pig, Illustrious One, I saw two who came forth from the hotel of the white pigs, which is just across the street.

"One, Illustrious One, was a Celestial, but the other was a young white pig. It seemed strange to me, Illustrious One, that one of the East should come forth from the place with a white pig, and, Illustrious One, he was not dressed as one of the elect, but as a coolie.

"I followed them along until the young white pig took leave of the Celestial; then I followed the son of the East. He came even to this place, Illustrious One, and after drinking at the bar with Fan Hei, whom I recognised, they passed into the opium room. Then, Illustrious One, did I enter the bar and make question.

"He who served behind the bar told me that the man whom I followed was a stranger to him, and that he had heard him tell Fan Hei he was but arrived from London. It was strange that he should issue forth from the hotel of the white pigs, Illustrious One. With the order of the Brotherhood in my mind, I pondered, Illustrious One. He may be a traitor, else why should he, a coolie, be with the white pigs? Even now he is in the opium-room. That is the word I would bring you."

As he finished speaking, he again bowed he head submissively, waiting for Wu Ling to speak. At last the prince did so.

"If your word is true, if, with the eye of the eagle, you have seen the gliding snake, then shall your reward be great indeed. You say this dog of a coolie is even now within the place?"

"He is in the opium-room, Illustrious One. Also Fan Hei watches that he passes not out without being followed."

"That is well," said Wu Ling. "I shall see to this dog."

Then he turned to San.

"San," he ordered, "go to the opium-room and have speech with the attendant. See that no one leaves it or enters until he have had our will."

San rose at once, and bowing low, shuffled from the room.

When the curtains had dropped after him Wu Ling rose and made a gesture for the newsbringer to follow him. Lifting up the curtains at one side of the room, Wu Ling pressed a part of the wall, and immediately a wide low panel slid back noiselessly.

Stepping through into a dark passage beyond, he waited for the other to follow him. Then, closing the panel, he walked with slow dignity down the full length of the passage until he came to a door at the end. Opening this he entered a small room, and crossing to the opposite wall, released a panel there.

When they had passed through, the newsbringer saw that they were standing in a tiny apartment completely hung with curtains of heavy black velvet and illuminated by a small copper lamp which hung from the centre of the ceiling.

It was utterly devoid of furniture, and to the uninitiated, it's use would be a mystery. But San could have told that it was the room from which Wu Ling at times inspected the opium-room, and where he listened to the maudlin maunderings of the drug fiends.

More than once had the prince heard the secrets of a man's soul by listening there, and more than once had some poor creature gone forth from that opium-room to an unknown fate—a fate decreed by the prince as a penalty to the indiscreet.

There was never any mercy, any appeal in the Brotherhood of the Yellow Beetle. When a man was once sentenced to death, nothing could alter the decree.

Wu Ling stepped close to the black velvet curtains, and, pushing one of them aside, disclosed a small panel which was scarcely large enough to permit one to place both eyes before it.

Before pushing it back he beckoned to the other to step close, then gently he slid the bit of rosewood to one side.

Bending towards it he peered through at the opium-room beyond, and slowly swept the apartment with his gaze. A gesture brought the newsbringer beside him, and Wu Ling pointed towards the panel.

"Look through and tell me which one is the traitor?" he whispered.

The other did as he was bid, and after peering through for a moment, raised his head.

"It is the dog on the third mattress from this end on the left, Illustrious One," he said.

Wu Ling again bent close, and for a long minute regarded the man who had been pointed out to him. Nor was he in danger of being seen by the coolie, who lay on the mattress sucking at the pipe, for the panel was cunningly concealed from view of anyone in the opium-room by a thin lattice-work screen, which, while it permitted one from the observation-room to see the whole of the opium apartment, still prevented any in that place from seeing the observer.

At last Wu Ling straightened up and softly closed the panel.

"I know not the coolie dog," he said slowly. "But we shall know more of him soon. Wait here until my order comes to you."

With that Wu Ling glided from the room, and the newsbringer squatted on the floor to wait.

. . . . . .

On the mattress in the opium-room, sucking at his third pipe, lay Sexton Blake. Ever since the attendant had prepared his first pill had Blake lain there smoking and peering out from heavy-lidded eyes to see and to hear what he could.

From the broken snatches of maudlin ravings about him he had caught nothing of value, nor in the few new arrivals who had appeared did he see anything of interest. But still he remained there, determined to discover in some way if Wu Ling were really in the place.

As time went on and the life of the den revealed nothing, Blake began to ponder deeply, trying to devise some method for gaining access to even deeper and more secret parts of the joint—parts which he knew must exist.

Once he could run the gauntlet of the outer line of the place he knew that he would come upon things which stopped short at the opium-room.

Yet little did he dream that at that very moment Wu Ling himself was gazing at him through a tiny panel in one end of the room. Nor did he realise how dire was the peril in which he was.

Blake was still smoking his third pipe when the attendant shuffled past him to the upper end of the room. In the shadows there Blake could just see the blue jacket which he wore, and from the fellow's attitude Blake knew he was holding a conversation with some new arrival, though he could not see the person of the latter.

Then, for the barest fraction of a second, the new arrival stepped within Blake's line of vision, and he could have sworn that he had caught a glimpse of a head swathed in bandages. The head was withdrawn so quickly that he could not make sure, but with the suggestion came the thought of San, whom he himself had shot at Marsey Island. And with that same thought a great uneasiness filled Blake.

He lay back with closed eyes as the attendant shuffled back down the room, and could almost feel the gaze of the other upon him as he passed by. Then the footsteps came near again, and upon his ears broke the voice of the attendant.

"Will the honourable one smoke more?" he asked.

"One—one more pipe," he said in the thick voice of the smoker who is falling under the effects of the drug.

The attendant bowed, and, leaning over, laid his hand on the pipe. At the same moment Blake caught another glimpse of a swathed head at the upper end of the apartment, and once more the feeling of uneasiness swept over him.

Through him swept a wave of presentiment. Something within him rang out a clarion call of warning, and, regardless of everything, Blake started to rise, determined to get out of the place while he might.

Then, as he was still half sitting up, the attendant suddenly withdrew his hands from the pipe, and with a hissing sound pushed Blake back. Blake, realising now that for some reason suspicion against him had been aroused, started up again.

There was a sound behind him, and he turned to meet any attack which might come from that direction. But he was too late.

Even as he swung round, a panel in the wall behind him was pushed back, and from the darkness beyond there came a flying yellow cord, which looped and circled over his head, then fell to his shoulders.

A second later it was drawn tight about his throat, and as, choking and gasping, and with senses reeling, he struggled to free himself, Blake became aware that several yellow faces were bearing down upon him.

The Yellow Tiger had struck.

. . . . . .

Once again the meeting of the council of the Brotherhood of the Yellow Beetle was in progress, but far, far different was the spirit which animated it from that of the former meeting which had been held in that same room only the evening before.

No smile lit up those impassive faces, nor was there any relaxation of dignified ceremony in their conduct of the meeting. But yet, from squatting Celestial to squatting Celestial there seemed to pass a feeling of anticipation which held them tense.

On his pile of cushions before the dais sat Wu Ling, with San beside him as usual. And once the members were assembled, Wu Ling wasted no time in getting to business. Rising, he held up his hand.

"Members of the Brotherhood of the Yellow Beetle," he said slowly, "you have been called into council to-night to consider important matters. Last night we met here and I made known my will regarding the white pig, Sexton Blake. This morning the order went out to the members of the Brotherhood throughout the world.

"This afternoon, a humble member of the Brotherhood, who had received word of my will, saw that which aroused his suspicions. From a hotel of the white pigs he saw two men issue—a young white dog and a Celestial. That hotel is the resort of the white pigs who have much wealth, and, members of the council, that Celestial was a coolie. It was not seemly that a coolie should issue forth from such a place in the company of a white pig.

"The faithful member of the Brotherhood followed them and soon the white pig went his way. The member continued on the heels of the coolie and followed him to this place—the headquarters of the Brotherhood in Cardiff. He came into this place and drank at the bar, then he went to the opium-room, where he smoked.

"To me the faithful one came with the word, and I myself looked in upon this coolie, whose actions were as the ways of the snake. Then I gave the order to gather him in and it was done. Before me was the coolie brought, and San saw to it that he was prepared for the inquiry. And, members of the council, when that was done, it was discovered that he was no coolie, but a white pig, and more, he was the white pig which it was the chief aim of the Brotherhood of the Yellow Beetle to find.

"The 'coolie' was Sexton Blake himself. How he managed to get in here you know. But the man himself shall be brought before you, and then the sentence of the Brotherhood shall be passed upon him."

There was a faint stir as Wu Ling finished speaking, but scarcely had his voice died away when the curtains at the far end of the room were pushed aside, and two Celestials entered, dragging a third man with them. Between the rows of squatting Chinese they passed, until they were in front of the dais, then at a gesture from Wu Ling, they stood aside from their

49

prisoner.

And what a woeful-looking object he was. There he stood in the coarse garments of a coolie, but with the queued wig torn from his head, and the yellow pigment all blotchy and streaky.

Yet through it could be seen the clean-cut features and deep-set, grey eyes of Sexton Blake, who when the hands of his captors had dropped away drew himself up and gazed straight into Wu Ling's eyes.

Even had he dared try to escape it would have been useless, for his wrists were bound securely behind him, and about his ankles were two steel cuffs connected by a chain, which, while it gave sufficient freedom to the feet to permit him to shuffle along, forbade a stride of any length.

Wu Ling gave back gaze for gaze; then, raising his hand, spoke to the members of the Brotherhood.

"Behold the man," he said curtly. "Regard him well; you who have not seen him before. There stands the man who has set himself against the Brotherhood of the Yellow Beetle from its inception—the man who has tried time and again to drive us to ruin—the man whose hands sought to encompass my death in our own sacred island of Kaitu.

"He has been in my power more than once in the past, but Destiny was with him, and he escaped. But now he is mine again, and this time he shall meet the fate which is to be his. As well might he try to escape from the yellow dragon as to escape our clutches now. Members of the Brotherhood, he is here to hear your will. He who would speak let him do so."

All during the harangue Blake had stood with a contemptuous smile upon his lips—a smile which must have maddened Wu Ling to see, though the Celestial showed no sign that he noticed it.

When he had finished speaking a stout Celestial, who sat some distance down the line on the right-hand side, rose, and bowing low, said:

"Oh, Illustrious One, with your permission, my unworthy lips would frame a remark?"

Wu Ling inclined his head.

"Speak," he said.

The member stepped forward a little, and raising one hand, pointed full at Blake.

"He is the man, Illustrious One, who would have deprived us of the sun of your presence. Only one fate can be his—death. And it is meant that death should be the death of the Sacred Beetle. He sleeps within his cell, Illustrious One; he hungers for his pleasure, Illustrious One. Let him be brought forth and let him feed upon the throat of this white pig, even as the throat of His Excellency San was seared by the white pig's bullets."

The Chinaman bowed again and withdrew to his place. Then rose up member after member to put forth the same plea that Blake should be at once executed by the poisonous beetle from which the Brotherhood takes its name.

Wu Ling heard them all out, when the last had sat down he turned to San.

"And you San," he said, "what fate think you should be his?"

San rose slowly.

"It is the pleasure of the Illustrious One," he said. "What the Illustrious One says is my will."

Wu Ling then turned back to the members of the council.

"Members of the Brotherhood," he said, "I have heard you, and you speak well. But the death of the beetle is not to be the death of this white pig Blake. I have another fate in store for him. Hark you! To the god Mo I prayed that the dog Blake might be given into my hands. Lo! the god Mo heard me, and this very day delivered my enemy unto me.

"Therefore I, Wu Ling, say to you that his fate shall be this. To the island of Kaitu—the sacred isle in the China Sea—shall he be taken, and there shall he be offered up as a living sacrifice on the jade altar of the great god Mo. I, Wu Ling, priest on earth of the god Mo, shall myself make the sacrifice. Members of the Brotherhood, I have spoken. Take the pig from my presence and see that you keep him well. Let all prepare to leave at once. By night we shall be on our way to Kaitu."

So as Blake was dragged out of the apartment, Wu Ling and San disappeared behind the curtains at the upper end of the room, while the members of the Brotherhood stood with bowed heads in submission to the will of the Illustrious One.

CHAPTER 6
Enter Mdlle. Yvonne. The Raid

When Tinker left Sexton Blake at the corner he strolled down to the docks to await the arrival of the two coastguards from Westward Ho! He had to put in nearly an hour before the motor-boat finally showed up, and when it had drawn in to the wharf Tinker hopped aboard.

From the two coastguards he got a detailed description of the two men who had come to Marsey Island and overpowered them.

From the description he had little difficulty in recognising Wu Ling and Baron Robert de Beauremon; and when the coastguards gave a detailed account of the great biplane by which they had come, Tinker's last doubt vanished.

It was not conclusive evidence, it is true; but in any prosecution which Blake might bring against them would be a very strong card indeed.

When he had got the coastguards to append their signatures to the report, he gave them a couple of sovereigns each, and saw them started back for Westward Ho! then he strolled back up to the town and made his way to the office of the chief of police. He found that gentleman had left for the day, and, finding his address, took a cab out to the house.

It was a fine old place, standing well in from the road, and surrounded by a high hedge, with a wide and airy entrance-hall, decorated with several large game heads. Into a small reception-room off this hall Tinker was shown, and a few minutes later the Chief of Police joined him.

In the first moment Tinker knew he could not have come to a better man. The chief—Featherstone by name—was a well-set-up man, dressed in blue serge, which was set off by white spats. He was tanned to the colour of mahogany, and when at a later date Tinker discovered that he had been in India some years, reorganising the police methods there, he understood why the chief had the air he had.

He greeted Tinker warmly, sat down with smile of interest, when he discovered that he was Sexton Blake's assistant, and had come to see him on important business.

"Well, Master Tinker," he said, good-humouredly, "what can I do for you?"

"I hope a great deal, sir," replied Tinker. "I have come to see you at the order of the guv'nor. He told me to give you all the details of the case, so with your permission, sir, I shall do so."

The chief drew out a cigar.

"Go ahead, my lad!" he said. "I shall be interested to hear what you have to say."

Forthwith Tinker began, and related all the details of the capture and release of the Munitions Minister. When he had finished that he went on to the escape of Wu Ling and Beauremon, and led up to the point where Sexton Blake had taken the daring course of going to the Chinese joint in order to try and get traces of Wu Ling.

"He wouldn't hear of any other course, sir," said the lad. "I tried to persuade him not to go, but he thought if he did not do so, but took ordinary police action instead, the Chinese might get wind of the fact. He wished to find out beyond all doubt if Prince Wu Ling were in Cardiff, or not. But he told me before he went to come and see you, sir, and to talk over with you what he wished done."

"And what is that Tinker?" asked the chief.

"It is this, sir. He wants you to get together some men, he said, either plain-clothes or special constables, and to hold them in readiness for action by midnight to-night. If he is not back at the Western Hotel by midnight, he wants you to raid this place to which he has gone, because he says only some serious complication will keep him later than that."

The Chief of Police smoked thoughtfully for a little, then he said:

"I shall certainly be very glad indeed to do anything I can, Tinker. I shall get together some men. Some of my special constables have been chafing for work lately, so I shall pick out a dozen from that force. I shall tell them to collect without badges or armlets at the Western Hotel at eleven o'clock, and we can wait there for Mr. Blake's return.

"If he hasn't come back by midnight you can lead us to the house and will raid it as he suggests. I have heard of Prince Wu Ling, and also Baron de Beauremon, but I did not dream for a moment that either of them might be in Cardiff. I shall be very pleased if we can rope them in.

"As far as this place you speak of is concerned, I know the house all right, and have had my eye on it for some time. But the occupants are most circumspect in their behaviour, and we have never before been able to get together sufficient evidence to raid it. To-night, with Blake's lead, we have that opportunity, and you can count on us to do all that can be done. Is that satisfactory?"

"It is, sir," replied Tinker, rising. "I shall be at the Western Hotel at eleven to meet you; and at midnight, if the guv'nor hasn't returned, I can lead you straight to the house."

With that Tinker took his leave of the Chief of Police, and made his way back to the Western Hotel. He had done all he could now to guard against things going against Blake, and all he could do until the evening was to possess himself in patience.

Six o'clock drew round, and he went to his room to change into a dark suit. That done, he left the hotel and took a brisk walk. It was nearly eight o'clock when he got back to the hotel, but Blake had not returned, and Tinker cast himself down in the lounge with a heavy heart.

He felt moody and depressed, and seemed to feel a presentiment that things were not going well with Blake. Had it not been for Blake's express orders on the matter, Tinker would have been tempted to make the raid without delay. But orders were orders, and he would obey.

At half-past eight he went in to dinner, but could eat scarcely anything. A bite at this and peck at that, and he rose to seek the lounge again. There he kicked his heels until nine o'clock, and by that time was in a ferment of uneasiness.

As the minutes passed, without Blake putting in an appearance, his uneasiness deepened to a keen anxiety, and finally, unable to contain himself any longer, he got his cap and set off for a walk.

He walked and walked for the best part of half an hour, worrying over Blake and trying to make up his mind that he would be justified in disobeying orders this once.

But always, when he was tempted to do so, Blake's stern countenance rose before his vision, and he knew that he would not do so.

Finally, when night had fallen and the lights of the city were twinkling, he made his way along by the docks, where the bustle of day had given way to the damp mystery of night by the river front.

Unconsciously his footsteps led him to the wharf where he had met the motor-boat that day, and, by walking out to the end, he leaned against a mooring-post, very blue and very worried.

Sunk in reverie, he did not hear the almost noiseless swish, swish of something as it crept towards him out of the darkness, nor was he aware that ever since he had left the hotel the last time his every footstep had been dogged.

But the work of Wu Ling was thorough, and when he discovered that it was Blake, and none other, who had left the Western Hotel with a lad that day, he had lost no time in sending off the same Celestial who had brought the word to him in order to run Tinker to earth and kill him if a chance presented itself.

Foot by foot the creeping shadow drew nearer to the lad, the soft sound of the movements being lost in the guttural lapping of the black water against the wharf. Here and there were the lights of ships moored at the different docks, and in the channel beyond lay several steam craft, as though ready to leave at a moment's notice.

Tinker was idly watching a long, slim, rakish-looking craft which lay moored straight ahead of him when his uneasiness for Blake changed to a sharp feeling of premonition of danger to himself. Some instinct told him that in the darkness behind him a menace lurked, and with a slight shiver he straightened up, intending to return to the hotel.

Just as he did so, he gave a gasp as something came out of the darkness and hurled itself upon him. Tinker had just time to see that it was a Chinaman, with a bared knife in his hand, when they crashed together.

How he managed to elude the vicious thrust which was aimed at him Tinker never knew, but elude he did, and the next moment had sent his fist crashing into the face of the Celestial.

The other gave a grunt as the blow got home, but did not relax his grasp on the lad. On the contrary, he tightened it, and with a panther-like quickness wrapped one of his legs about one of Tinker's.

Tinker strove valiantly to break the hold, and to get his arms free for fist work, but the Celestial anticipated his every move, and held him like a vice while he worked the knife nearer and nearer to the lad's throat.

Some wayward gleam of light from over the water caught the bared steel and revealed the proximity of its menace to the lad.

With fascinated gaze, Tinker watched it come nearer and nearer, while he struggled wildly to get an arm free. He could feel rather than see the exulting gloat of the Celestial as the point of knife grew closer to its intended mark.

Then, just as the cold metal touched Tinker's flesh, he gave a frantic heave, and in the next moment both he and the Celestial went crashing over the edge of the wharf into the black water beneath.

In the fall their holds became broken, and when he came spluttering to the surface, Tinker's first act was to look round for the Chinaman. He saw him close at hand, and even as the lad turned to make for the wharf the other made for him.

Tinker saw that to attempt to climb up the wharf while the Celestial was so near meant certain death. On the spur of the moment, the only thing which presented itself to him was to swim out to the channel and, by outstroking the other, get sufficient lead to make a dash for safety. This plan he followed, and, turning on his side, struck out with a long side-crawl.

The Celestial was not to be thrown off so easily, however, for he made a sharp turn, and, sticking the knife between his teeth, set off after Tinker with a powerful overhand stroke which took him along at a rapid pace.

Tinker changed from his side-crawl to an Australian crawl, and struck out for all he was worth. Once he turned his head and looked.

He caught a glimpse of the Chinaman, with the knife between his teeth, coming hot after him. Then his plans merged into one idea—to find a landing-place as quickly as possible.

Then it was that he saw his present course would take him towards the long, rakish-looking craft at which he had been gazing from the wharf, and as he decided to make for her he began to shout for help.

For a hundred yards or so he kept the Celestial at about the same distance behind him, but then the lad's stroke grew a trifle slower, and from the sounds close in the rear he knew the other was gaining on him.

Again Tinker shouted for help, and this time he saw a white figure appear on the deck of the craft ahead. She was about fifty yards away from him now, and, giving another shout, Tinker put forth every ounce of strength.

The next moment he was almost blinded by a powerful white light which shone full into his face. The craft ahead had turned on her searchlight. It passed over Tinker a moment later, and rested on the Celestial, and there it remained.

So, in the golden path cast by the searchlight, the lad raced on, followed by the determined Chinaman, and just as he thought he must give up after all, a clear voice came from the ship saying:

"Keep it up! You will be all right!"

The following second he was conscious of a sharp crack overhead, and just as he went under, spluttering, a bullet tore through the air and struck the Chinaman full in the mouth, knocking the knife flying, and staining the water in front of him with deep crimson.

Tinker turned, and saw the Celestial throw up his hands and go under. Then he made another effort, and a moment later a rope struck him full in the face. He made a desperate grab at it, and, clinging on for dear life, was dragged through the water over the side of the ship and on to the deck.

To his utter amazement, a lovely face bent over his, and he was aware that Mademoiselle Yvonne was gazing into his eyes in stupefied amazement.

For the space of a minute or so, Tinker was in a fog of stupefaction. Five minutes ago he had been standing on the end of a Cardiff wharf, and had been attacked by a knife-thrusting Chink. Now his mind was telling him that he was lying on his back on the deck of a ship, with Mademoiselle Yvonne standing close to him.

It was unbelievable.

In an effort to come to a clear realisation of what it all meant, he moved his stiff limbs and got to his feet. Then he saw that the girl before him was no chimera of his imagination, but real flesh and blood.

Tinker passed a hand across his brow.

"I suppose it is you," he stammered inanely, "but I can scarcely believe it, Mademoiselle Yvonne."

Yvonne smiled.

"It is indeed I, Tinker," she replied. "But what on earth has happened to you? Why were you in the water at this hour of night, and why was that murderous Chinaman following you?"

At the mention of the hour and the reference to the Celestial everything swept back to Tinker's memory, and as he recognised the face of Hendricks, the mate of the Fleur-de-Lys, who approaching the spot where they stood, he laid a hand on Yvonne's arm.

"You must excuse my stupidity, mademoiselle,' he said. "For a few moment I was a bit dazed. I swallowed some water, I guess. To find you here is a fortunate stroke. I am badly in need of someone with whom to talk over a serious matter.

"Is it about Mr. Blake?" asked Yvonne quickly.

Tinker nodded.

"Then you must get below and get into some dry things," went on Yvonne. "Hendricks, will you take him below and see that he is given some dry clothes? Then bring him to the saloon."

Hendricks came up now, and, after shaking hands with him, Tinker followed him along the deck and down a companion-way to the officers' quarters. In the meantime, Yvonne went down the main companion to the saloon where Graves sat reading.

"What was it?" he asked, as Yvonne entered.

Yvonne lit a cigarette before replying. Then she said:

"It was Tinker."

For a moment Graves regarded her in amazement.

"You are joking!" he said finally.

Yvonne smiled.

"Am I?" she rejoined. "Wait and see!"

"But what is he doing here?" said Graves.

Yvonne shrugged, and shook her head.

"I don't know yet. It is something to do with Mr. Blake. He has gone to put on some dry garments, and will soon be here to tell us all about it. He was in the water, being chased by a Chinaman with a knife between his teeth. I do not know why. But let us wait until he comes.

Forthwith Yvonne strolled along to the small saloon piano, and, sitting down, ran her fingers lightly over the keys.

She was still playing a soft reverie when Tinker came in, nor did she rise until she had finished it. Then, wheeling on the stool, she beckoned Tinker to come and sit near her.

The lad did so, and when he was ensconced in a low easy-chair, Yvonne said:

"Now, Tinker, tell us all about it!"

Tinker began, and related the germane points of the strange case which had brought him and Blake to Cardiff. But when he came to the part where Blake had decided to enter the Chinese joint and find out what he could, Yvonne tossed away the dainty Russian cigarette which she had been smoking, and leant forward tensely.

"Do you mean to say that, after what happened in the case of the Sacred Sphere, Mr. Blake went to this place disguised as a Celestial?" she asked quickly.

Tinker nodded.

"I tried all I could to prevent him," he replied, "but it was useless. You know what the guv'nor is when he has made up his mind to do a thing! One might as well try to move a brick wall with a feather! And it is now past ten o'clock. I have been worrying all the evening about him. I can't get the feeling out of my mind that something serious has happened to him. What do you think about it, mademoiselle? Do you think it would be safe to make the raid before midnight?"

Yvonne frowned thoughtfully.

"It would be the most sensible thing undoubtedly," she said at last. "But on the other hand, you have his clear command to make no move before midnight. Therefore I think the only thing to do is to wait until that hour. Don't you agree with me, uncle?"

Graves nodded his handsome head.

"From what I know of Blake, I should wait until the hour he himself named," he replied. "Undoubtedly it would be the most sensible thing to make the raid now. But still, orders are orders! and if an early raid happened to upset something he was just about to bring to a head, he would be greatly incensed."

Tinker nodded gloomily.

"I suppose that is what must be done," he said. "Any way, it is getting on for eleven now, and the police are to be at the hotel at eleven. At midnight sharp we will be able to make the raid."

"Will you excuse me for a few moments?" said Yvonne, rising suddenly.

Bowing to them, she slipped out of the saloon, and for a quarter of an hour or so Graves and Tinker talked indifferently. All the time the lad's thoughts were running on Blake, and the daring—ay, reckless—mission he had undertaken single-handed, and he had no heart for anything else.

It was just five minutes to eleven, and he was about to ask to be set ashore when Yvonne re-entered the saloon. Both Graves and Tinker gazed at her in surprise. When Tinker had been dragged out of the water, and had looked up to see Yvonne bending over him, she had been clad in a soft, white evening-gown. Now that had been removed, and she wore a dark tweed costume, heavy boots, and a soft felt crush-hat.

She smiled as she saw their looks of surprise.

"Did you think you were going ashore alone, Tinker?" she asked gaily. "Come if you are ready. I am going with you, and the boat is waiting to take us."

Tinker jumped in.

"It is awfully good of you, mademoiselle," he said, "but really you mustn't think of coming with us to-night. It is no place for you."

Yvonne laughed softly, and for a moment her eyes grew tenderly reminiscent.

"Have you forgotten the past so soon, Tinker?" she asked. "Have I never been in difficult positions before?"

And Tinker, remembering the days when Yvonne's name had meant so much to a sensation-seeking Press, grinned, and said no more.

Graves rose and accompanied them as far as the deck where Hendricks and Captain Vaughan were waiting at the head of the ladder. At the foot of it a small boat rocked lightly on the black face of the water, and in it were four seamen ready to row them ashore.

Captain Vaughan greeted Tinker warmly, and. after a few words with his mistress, assisted Yvonne down the ladder. Tinker followed, and when they had taken their places in the boat the sailors pushed off.

It was only a few minutes before they pulled in at the foot of a flight of steps leading to the top of one of the wharves, and, helping Yvonne ashore, Tinker ran up the steps after her.

"You are not really intending to join in the raid, are you?" asked Tinker, as they walked up the wharf together.

Yvonne was non-committal.

"I shall hear what the chief of police says," she responded. "We shall have to hurry. It is past eleven now."

It was nearly twenty minutes past eleven when they finally walked into the lobby of the Western Hotel and approached the Chief of Police, whom Tinker saw sitting in a big easy-chair reading a newspaper. He jumped up as they approached and when Tinker had introduced him to Yvonne, said:

"I have heard nothing of Mr. Blake. Have you seen him?"

Tinker shook his head.

"No sir," he replied. "But, to be on the safe side, I shall just run up to our rooms, and see if he has come in."

He hurried away, and entered the lift. Yvonne sat down, and she and the Chief of Police talked until the lad returned.

"He is not there," said Tinker, as he came up. "Nor has he been. If he had come in while I was out he would have left a note of some sort for me."

Yvonne turned to the chief.

"I suppose you will wait until midnight before making the raid?" she asked.

The chief nodded.

"I suppose so," he said; "but, to tell you the truth, mademoiselle, I do not like it at all. It strikes me that Mr. Blake has tackled a very risky business, and if it were any other man I should be tempted to go along at once."

"I think it is better to follow his instructions to the letter," remarked Yvonne. "At any rate, with your permission, Mr. Featherstone, I am going along with you."

"You!" ejaculated the chief, in astonishment. "Impossible, mademoiselle!"

Yvonne's white teeth came together as she set her chin determinedly.

"Nevertheless, I am going," she rejoined. "I have seen rougher places than this place will prove to be, and I know if Mr. Blake were here he would give his permission for me to go."

The chief raised his hands helplessly.

"If you insist, I suppose you must come," he responded. "Yet, mademoiselle, I can only think it is unwise. But it is twenty-five minutes to twelve. I think I shall gather my men together, and by then it will be time for us to go."

He excused himself then, and Tinker and Yvonne talked in low tones until he returned some ten minutes later. Then they rose and accompanied him out to the street where they saw four motor-cars drawn up at the kerb.

Even as they stood at the top of the steps the cars drew away one by one, and disappeared down the street.

The chief waved his hands towards them.

"There are twenty men altogether," he said, in explanation. "I chose them all from the special constabulary, and I think they are good men. I sent them on ahead, because we don't wish to arouse too much comment. Ah, here is my car now! Let us follow the others."

As a big touring car drove up to the kerb, they descended and climbed in. Then they started, and drove along the silent streets until they finally reached the Chinese district.

At the corner near the joint to which Blake had gone the car drew up, and, as they descended Yvonne and Tinker saw several men standing in the shadow a little farther up. The car in which they had come drove off, and they joined the waiting men in the shadow.

It was then the Chief of Police took charge of proceedings, and in the curt, business-like way in which he disposed of his force, it was plain to Yvonne and Tinker that he was an able tactician. Selecting his men four at a time, he spoke to them in low tones for a few minutes, instructing them what they had to do. Then, as one party disappeared up the street, he turned to the next.

Soon the whole force of twenty men had faded into the shadows, and, pulling out his watch, the chief held it so Tinker and Yvonne could see it.

"It lacks only one minute off midnight," he said. "Come, let us walk up the street! 'it will be just midnight by the time we reach the rendezvous, and then we shall make the raid. It is hopeless for any of the inmates to try to escape, for my men have the whole place completely surrounded. As they dash out we shall rake them in. But I do wish, mademoiselle, that you would stand in a place of safety."

Yvonne laughed softly, and, thrusting her hand beneath her jacket, drew out a small, wicked-looking automatic.

"I can protect myself," she replied. "I wouldn't miss this for worlds, and, besides, Mr. Blake is my friend, and I fear he must be in danger."

Nor did she add that within her was a keen sense of anticipation of excitement which had swept over her the first moment she had set eyes on Tinker, which could not be assuaged until with her own eyes she had seen that Sexton Blake was safe.

For Yvonne was Yvonne, and in yielding her girlish heart to the masterful personality of Blake, had brought that into her life which would never go out of it while she lived and breathed.

He it had been who had loomed up before her in the past like some rock of refuge—like a beacon of hope. Time and again when, during the progress of her vengeance against the eight men who had swindled her mother and herself in Australia, Blake had crossed her path, she had fought out her fight, the while she stared up into the darkness at night trying to put from her mind, and to hurl from the pinnacle which he held in her heart, the man of strength, and yet of unyielding hardness.

Hope had blazed brightly at times, and, lying wide-eyed in her dainty white bed, while the Fleur-de-Lys tossed gently on the ocean swell, or dipped her nose into the caressing waves of the South Pacific, but always the reaction had come.

Then, as Blake had given all but the one thing she desired—his love—she had withdrawn into herself, and, in her girlish pride, has assumed towards him a coldness which her throbbing heart denied vehemently.

And Blake! Even Blake, wrapped up though he might be in his profession, had not failed to realise what had happened. With the sweet radiation of her love he had stood cold and unresponsive; and yet, when it had been withdrawn and locked up within Yvonne's breast, he, man-like, had missed something, and had felt a tugging at his heart-strings which he did not—could not understand.

Something was missing—something which unconsciously he had found very sweet. There were occasions, too, when a very fiend incarnate was roused up in Blake.

In all his life he had never experienced such a feeling of blind rage as sometimes seized him of late. And, strange to say, this feeling came over him only when Yvonne's smiles and Yvonne's sweetness were given to another.

Tinker, shrewdly observant, watched these new moods of his master's and kept his peace; but, young though he was, he read the mystery, and could feel with the master he loved so in the stern fight he was having. It was the age-old struggle between the profession which is all in all to a man and first insidious coming of the tender influence of a good woman.

And Blake, clever though he might be at probing the mysteries of others, and putting his fingers on the weak spot in the armour of the criminal, was strangely obtuse when it came to analysing his own feelings. Something was upon him which he did not understand. It remained to be seen if realisation would come to him. If it did, no man could foresee the result.

So it was with all this memory of the past in her mind, and the present fear in her heart for the man she loved, that Yvonne slipped forward through the shadows towards that dark house of eternal night and mystery. Foot by foot the trio crept forward until they were within a few feet of the door. Then the Chief of Police paused, and, raising a whistle to his lips, blew a triple signal.

Instantly men seemed to swarm from every direction, and, as the cordon drew in the chief made for the door, followed by Tinker and Yvonne. The Chief turned the handle, but, as he expected, the door refused to yield; then, raising his hand, he knocked loudly.

Again and again he knocked, but no reply came. The house was in darkness from top to bottom, even the saloon on the corner being closed and shuttered. The whole atmosphere of the place was brooding and menacing, and, when in response to his summons the chief received only silence, he called two of his men.

Then, standing back, they rushed the door, and burst it in with a crashing and splintering of wood. Into the dark hall the party rushed, lighting the way with electric pocket-torches. Through the hall and into room after room they went, searching here and there for any signs of the occupants of the house, but on all sides there met them only a weird, uncanny emptiness.

At last Tinker and Yvonne, who were together, came to the opium-room, where only that day the besotted figures of the drug fiends had tossed in delirium, but now the mattresses contained not a single human form; the attendant was not to be seen, and only the stale odour of the drug hung all over.

The Chief of Police joined them.

"I have called in all my men," he said curtly. "there doesn't seem to be a soul about the place. They must have received warning of the raid, and made good their escape."

And, though they literally tore the place to pieces, they could find not one skulking Celestial in all that rabbit-warren.

Beaten and disheartened they returned to the opium-room. To say that Tinker was worried was to put it mildly. Blake had come to that place during that afternoon, when, as the lad knew, it was full of habitues. Now, after only a few hours, they found it empty and deserted.

What did it all mean? What could it all mean? There was something very sinister in that desolation about them.

Where was Blake? He had told the lad that if he had not returned to the Western Hotel by midnight a raid should be made, and his absence would mean something had gone wrong. But never such a situation as this had Tinker contemplated.

That Blake was going into the jaws of the Yellow Tiger was certain—that those same jaws might close upon him had been anticipated by both, but that there should be nothing visible by which to follow the fate of his master—there the lad was at a loss.

The Chief of Police was equally at a loss. He stood within the opium-room his keen eyes searching out every hole and corner of the place, the while his men ransacked the house from top to bottom.

Soon they began coming in with their reports. One man had penetrated the upper part, and there had come upon room after room empty of human beings, but littered with all the curious paraphernalia of the place. Others returned from like excursions to the bar, and the rooms off it. But as far as Sexton Blake was concerned they could see not a single thing to offer any suggestion as to what might have become of him. He had apparently vanished into thin air, and each one of those who stood there knew what fate he had gone to.

It was when the last of his men had returned to report that there was no-one about the place, that the Chief of Police turned to Tinker and said:

"Well, my lad, I fancy Mr. Blake has miscalculated this time. We followed his instructions to the letter, and came at the time he said. You have seen what we found. Unless you have some suggestion to offer I am afraid there is nothing to do but to draw off my men. I have had my eye on these people for a long time, as I told you, but they are slick, as they have proved. If I can get my hands on them I shall rope them in quickly enough, but they apparently have some very complete system of underground information, for it is beyond all doubt that they received warning of an intended raid."

Tinker nodded moodily.

"I can think of nothing else just now," he said slowly. "I am much obliged to you for what you have done, sir. But the fact remains that the guv'nor is in their hands, and he must be found. I know Prince Wu Ling, and I know how he hates the guv'nor. If he is in the hands of the Chinks they will kill him as certain as the sun will rise to-morrow. And they will see that he suffers torture before he dies. Wu Ling has had his game queered too often in the past to be lenient. Nor would the guv'nor buy his freedom at any price Wu Ling would ask. No. sir, I shall have to think of something to-night."

With that they turned towards the door with the intention of making their way back to the street. It was not until then that Tinker and the Chief of Police noticed that Yvonne was no longer there.

They turned in some surprise as they noticed her absence, and Tinker, raising his voice, called:

"Mademoiselle! Mademoiselle!"

There was no answer, so, with a word to the chief, Tinker turned back towards the opium-room to seek her.

Just as he did so there was a distant call, and the lad recognised Yvonne's voice. It was full of urgency, and as he dashed back through the opium-room the chief followed him.

Pausing half-way down the room Tinker called:

"Where are you?"

"Here!" came the distant reply. "Follow the opium-room door to the door at the end, and open that. Then come along the passage."

They ran to the door, and, jerking it open, dashed through into a corridor. Along this they sped until suddenly they came to a door of an open room. Inside was Yvonne, and as they appeared she beckoned to them.

"Come at once!" she said. "I have made an important discovery!"

They entered the room, and, standing just within the door, gazed at their surroundings. Lit up by pocket-torches the room looked small and dingy enough, and in no wall was there a window. It was simply a large box, and from the fact that it contained scarcely any furniture they guessed rightly that it might have been used as a room of detention for any fractious habitues of the opium-room. A table, a chair, a rough pallet on the floor, a small mirror, and the most primitive sort of washing utensils comprised the furniture of the room, and as they gazed upon it both the Chief and Tinker wondered what important discovery Yvonne could have come upon in such a place.

A moment later, as they went forward to where she stood by the table, they found out, for she lifted the mirror from the hook on which it had been hanging and held it out to them.

"Read what is written on it," she said, in a low tone.

Tinker took it and held it so they could see the surface plainly. At first they saw only a very dirty surface covered with the dust of months, perhaps years, but as the light of the electric-torch picked out the lines on the surface, they suddenly became aware that in that dust there was a message scratched.

Eagerly they bent to read it, and as they took in its import grew very grave. This is what they read:

"I must have been followed here. Have been discovered and overpowered. Am prisoner in this room. Have been up before B. of Y. B. (which Tinker immediately knew mean the Brotherhood of the Yellow Beetle), and death sentence passed. Will not be killed here. Am being taken to Kaitu as sacrifice. Follow.—B."

Slowly they made their way from the room and walked back to the street. There the Chief of Police told off three men to remain on guard at the joint, and, sending for his car, drove Tinker and Yvonne back to the Western Hotel. As he said good-night to them he laid a hand on Tinker's shoulder.

"Rest assured, my lad, I shall do all in my power to get track of these people, but for the present I see little that can be done beyond watching and waiting."

Tinker said nothing, but, when the Chief had driven off, turned to Yvonne.

"I will not rest in such a state of uncertainty!" he cried. "Something surely can be done—something must be done to find the guv'nor."

Yvonne laid both hands on his shoulders.

"Something will be done," she answered softly. "Come! Let us go to the Fleur-de-Lys and make our plans."

So together those two, who loved Sexton Blake, hurried towards the wharves to form a scheme for his rescue—if they were not already too late.

CHAPTER 7

The Voyage to Kaitu

In order to get a true perspective of the predicament in which Sexton Blake found himself it is necessary to make some attempt to realise the true calibre of Prince Wu Ling. Wu Ling, a man of the East, and one whose whole life had been dedicated to a single great purpose, could in no way be termed an ordinary criminal, if indeed the name criminal might be applied to him at all.

True, in the furthering of his aims, he did not hesitate to apply every known form of pressure, but what he did was at no time done with the spirit of criminality born of a desire for material gain. Of money, of power, of adulation he had more than falls to the share of ordinary man.

Nothing which criminality could yield could swell one iota those material advantages which were his.

The star to which he had hitched the waggon of his ambition was the one which would drag along through its course the great yellow race until it was high over all the races of men, and until the white races, which Wu Ling looked upon as interlopers and arrogant pretenders, were driven into the abyss of annihilation.

Therefore, when he be regarded from this perspective, it can be seen that his hatred of Sexton Blake was not the hatred of the criminal for the enemy of crime, but the hatred of the fanatic for the one man who, more than any other, had continually risen up to stand in the way of the successful prosecution of the plans of the Brotherhood of the Yellow Beetle.

That being so, Wu Ling could conceive of no more fitting fate for Blake than he should go to form a living sacrifice to the golden god Mo, the patron of the Brotherhood of the Yellow Beetle, and the god to whom, more than any other, Wu Ling paid his worship.

Sexton Blake it had been who, in the days when Prince Wu Ling first appeared in Europe to propagate the ideal for which he stood, had always risen to confound the Oriental in his doings. Not only in Europe, but in the whole of the world—ay, even in China itself had Blake come to grips with the yellow man, and on nearly every occasion had his wits proved more inventive than those of the Easterner.

Then had come that awful meeting in the island of Kaitu, when he and Wu Ling had rolled on the sand locked in a deadly embrace, each fighting to encompass the death of the other. It was a fight never to be forgotten by either. When after an eternity of straining Blake had got his fingers on the throat of the yellow man and had exerted all the strength at his command, Wu Ling, too, had got home, and there they lay, each praying that his own power of resistance might last the longer.

Blake's last recollection had been the sinking of his senses into a great gulf of blackness, and as he had passed into oblivion it had been with the thought that Wu Ling had conquered. But he had come out of that eternity of night to find Tinker bending over him and to be told that he had killed Wu Ling. Yet that he had not killed this man Blake was to find out some time after, and the discovery was to be but the prelude to a renewal of the old struggle.

Now, through all the criss-cross paths of the past, he had fallen into the hands of the enemy and from that grip he had little chance of escaping.

After Blake had been before the Council of Brotherhood in the den in Cardiff, he had been thrown into the small room, where some hours later Yvonne was to find the message, which, in his utter desperation, Blake had scrawled upon the dust-laden mirror.

After that two Celestials had come in to him, and before he could prevent them, had shot the point of a hypodermic-syringe into his arm. With the plunger pressed home, Blake knew that nothing he could do would off-set the action of the insidious drug which was in the needle.

Though his natural power of resistance caused him to fight hard, he gradually sank under the influence of the drug until he became comatose.

His next cognisance of life was when he awoke in a dark and stinking hole, to find his legs and face in the runway of scores of rats, and to one of the bites of the filthy rodents was his waking due. Rats—the pests of man, bred in filth and carriers of the worst diseases, dirty and squealing cowards when well fed, vicious and deadly when hungry.

To Blake, coming slowly to his senses, it seemed that there must be millions of the rodents making a rendezvous of his body. Body after body flashed over him, giving off that filthy rodent odour as it passed, and, even in his semi-conscious condition, nauseating him at the thought of the vileness they breathed.

But where was he?

Bit by bit his wits collected and massed into their place, until, with a strong effort of will power, he sat up and stared into the stygian darkness which surrounded him, trying to piece together the broken fabric of memory.

Slowly it came upon him that there was a vile odour which was quite distinct from that of the rodents, which, with his coming to himself, had fled shrieking, to stand off as a safe distance and regard him. Not that he could see them, but he could feel them, which was a thousand times worse.

How long a time had passed since he had been drugged in the room at the Cardiff den he could form no conjecture. It might have been a day or week—he could not guess.

As his thinking machinery began to work more smoothly, he gradually became aware that the strong odour which he had noticed was familiar, and then suddenly if flashed upon him what it was. It was the smell of rotten bilge-water, which meant that he was aboard ship. But where—and bound for what port?

With that came the memory of his sentence at the hands of the Brotherhood and the ruling of Wu Ling that he should be taken to Kaitu as sacrifice to the golden god Mo. Then Wu Ling had had his will, and he was at sea bound for the East, where his fate would be slow, but none the less sure.

There, in the blackness of the hole, Blake thought of Tinker and his last words to the lad before he went into the jaws of the tiger. He had been most emphatic in his instructions, and if the lad had followed his orders, which he knew would be the case, then at midnight of the day when he had gone into the joint, there must have been a police raid.

If that were so, why had he not been found? Had he been spirited away from the place before the raid or had the police come, and had they perhaps passed within a few feet of him? He could not tell.

Next he began to puzzle over the weak spot in his plans which had led to his discovery. That it was nothing to do with his disguise he was certain. It was too perfect for that.

How had it come about? He could not even make a guess, for he did not know of the sleek Celestial who had seen him leave the Western Hotel in the company of Tinker.

Nor was that all which gradually formed in film of fancy as he sat chafing his sore joints and gazing into the darkness. He had a vague recollection of the face and voice of Beauremon—Beauremon, whom he thought had dropped out of the game after the affair of Marsey Island.

Somewhere during the blank of the immediate past Beauremon must have been in evidence before the fog of oblivion seized him, for Blake was certain his memory was not playing him tricks. But where or how he could not place.

As a matter of fact, he was right, for in the small room at the Cardiff joint where he had received his quietus, Beauremon had come in just as Blake was growing unconscious.

What Blake did not know was that there was discord in the camp between Beauremon and Wu Ling—discord, the cause of which was Blake himself. Beauremon had joined with the prince in the kidnapping affair, and when that had failed, had, in accordance with his agreement, stuck to the game.

He had not been present when sentence had been passed on Blake, but when invited by Wu Ling to go with him to the East, and there join in the prosecution of further plans of the prince's, he had consented. Only then did he discover the fate intended for Blake; and whatever his faults, Baron Robert de Beauremon proved for once in his life that he still had some trace of decency left.

Wu Ling had told him coldly and unemotionally that Blake was a prisoner and was bound to the East with them to form a living sacrifice to the golden god Mo. Beauremon had protested vehemently, but what could he do?

There he was alone on a ship, which, while it was disguised as an ordinary tramp, was really the private yacht of Wu Ling, and which was manned by men every one of whom was pledged to the service of the prince.

For once in his life Beauremon was absolutely helpless to do anything, and, realising how dangerous his own position might become did he rouse Wu Ling's antagonism, he said nothing more. Yet he did not forget that he was a white man—one of the inevitable breed.

Even as Blake lay crouched and sore in the hold of that ship were Wu Ling and Beauremon talking in the saloon above, and the result of their conversation was an order from Wu Ling to bring the prisoner on deck.

To Blake a faint square of light showed overhead as the hatch was removed, but he did not shift his position until he saw two dim figures approaching. To save being kicked to his feet he struggled up, and swaying heavily, allowed himself to be dragged along to the ladder.

There he summoned up all his will power for the ascent, and, clutching the iron rungs of the ladder, began to climb.

What a ghastly torture that ascent was! It was no easy feat for a cool-headed, sober man to climb one of those narrow ladders, with a ship swinging and plunging to the dip of a heavy sea, but with a brain reeling to the sheer edge of unconsciousness, with the arteries throbbing with a fierce overcharge of blood, and with every bone and joint aching painfully, such a journey was the quintessence of exquisite torture.

But Blake made it, despite the handicap under which he was struggling, made it because he would undergo anything rather than suffer the indignity of being assisted up by either of the coolies who had been sent down for him.

Once on deck he reeled against the side and almost collapsed. The fresh breeze which was cutting across the port quarter refreshed him like a draught of sparkling wine, and from his brain the fog slowly cleared.

He was not given long, for was not the Illustrious One waiting for him? The two coolies caught him by the arms, and, dragging him along the waist of the deck, hoisted him up the after-companion and along to the companion-way which led down to the main saloon.

There, sitting at the large table which ran almost the full length of the saloon, he saw Wu Ling with Beauremon beside him.

As the hold of his two conductors relaxed, Blake drew himself up and stared coldly at Wu Ling. For a long minute the two stared back at each other, then Blake shifted his gaze to Beauremon.

To the latter he spoke sneeringly. "So you have turned renegade, have you, Beauremon?" he said. "one would have thought you might have done a little better than that."

Beauremon, who was smoking a cigarette and trying to look nonchalant, could not help a flush of anger or shame. He withdrew his cigarette as though to speak, but Wu Ling forestalled him.

"You will reserve your remarks for me," he said curtly. "Baron de Beauremon has nothing to do with you. He is my ally at present, and had I given him his way, you would not be bound for the island of Kaitu. He has the heart of a chicken."

Blake flashed a quick look at Beauremon and saw the latter give an almost imperceptible nod. In a moment it was all clear to Blake. He could reconstruct in imagination the argument Wu Ling and Beauremon must have had regarding him, and if what Wu Ling said was true, then he could only think that Beauremon had put in a plea for leniency.

Undoubtedly the baron had no qualms about Blake being killed, but that he had not consented to the British gentleman being offered up as living sacrifice, caused a glow of respect for Beauremon to rise up in Blake.

He turned back to Wu Ling.

"Well," he said coolly, "why have you sent for me? Have you decided to give me more decent quarters?"

Wu Ling shrugged.

"What matters it where you rest?" he said. "You will soon be beyond caring about such things."

"I have not yet been placed on the altar," replied Blake, "and until then I am very particular about such things. After I have gone as a sacrifice to this god Mo of yours will be time enough for you to talk of other things, and then I shall not be interested. In the meantime I should like some clean linen, a decent bunk, and some food."

Wu Ling made a gesture.

"Silence!" he ordered. "I did not have you brought here to discuss such things. I brought you here because Baron de Beauremon has put forth a suggestion, and which, if you fall in with it, will entitle you to meet death in a different way, and not go as a sacrifice to the blessed god Mo."

"So Beauremon has been bargaining for me as much as he can," thought Blake. "Rather decent of him, at any rate." Aloud he said: "Well, what is your proposition, Wu Ling?"

The prince leaned forward a trifle.

"I have this to offer you, Sexton Blake. Reflect well before you answer. Nor think that anything can save you. That you shall die I am determined, but if you do as I wish, I am willing to concede to you the choice of death you are to meet.

58

"It was you who ruined my plans regarding the Munitions Minister. It is you who can do something towards retrieving that position. I want from you a letter written and signed by you asking the Munitions Minister to meet you at a place where I shall name.

"It will be necessary for that meeting to take place at sea, and an urgent letter from you will cause the Munitions Minister to come. If you agree to that I will return to British waters, and when the Munitions Minister has come will let you choose your form of death. Or, if you are then prepared to swear that never again will you oppose me, no matter what behest you may receive, I may—I say I may consider your release unharmed. What is your reply?"

Blake stared at Wu Ling for a moment, then suddenly he burst into laughter.

"And think you I would listen to any such proposal as this?" he asked.

"You have much to learn, Wu Ling. You will get no letter from me to the Munitions Minister, beyond one telling him where you are and asking him to send a gunboat to blow you out of the water. That is my answer to your proposal, and it is final."

Wu Ling for once showed a gleam of anger in his eyes, but he made no reply to Blake. Instead, he beckoned to the two Celestials who stood by the door waiting.

"Take this man and bind him well," he said curtly. "Throw him back into the place from which you brought him. Leave bread and water there and see that it is given to him once a day. It will be sufficient to keep him alive until we reach Kaitu, and then we shall go to the god Mo as I ordered. You see, Baron de Beauremon, what profit we have found in your proposal."

Beauremon said nothing, but flashed a look of sympathy at Blake, who smiled back, and then, as the two Celestials approached, turned to meet them.

He held up his hands as though in readiness for his bonds, but as they reached out for his wrists, Blake suddenly withdrew them, and, doubling up his fists, struck twice in rapid succession.

Down they went one after the other, and then, before Wu Ling could rise or call out, Blake was upon him.

Like a tiger he leapt across the table, crashing full upon Wu Ling, and they went down together.

Blake realised that he had little time to spare. In a few moments the whole ship's crew would be upon him, and he could not count on Beauremon as an ally. The baron might try to get Wu Ling to be more lenient in his intentions regarding Blake, but he would scarcely take the part of Blake against the man with whom he had thrown in his lot for a consideration.

It was Beauremon's boast that when the Council of Eleven took up a matter they stayed by it until it was finished. Therefore, Blake knew he must play a lone hand.

As he and Wu Ling went down, the prince tried hard to reach something which was beneath his tunic. Blake seeing, or rather feeling, the motion, rolled quickly over, and then shot his own hand beneath the loose jacket of the Celestial.

Almost at once his fingers touched the butt of a heavy automatic, and with a sharp pull he had it out. Without the slightest hesitation he clubbed it and brought it down with all his force full on Wu Ling's head.

No cranium ever owned by man could have withstood the force of that blow. Wu Ling gave a grunt and lay still, and Blake leaped to his feet just as Beauremon jumped for him.

Again raising the automatic, Blake struck hard, catching the baron square in the centre of the forehead. A ridiculous look of surprise appeared for a moment in the Baron's eyes, then his legs collapsed and he dropped to the floor, to lie in a heap across Wu Ling.

Blake now made for the door and raced up the companion-way. Once on deck he stood for a moment to get his bearings. Over on the port side was a boat, and towards this he sprang. That something was amiss was now evident to the crew, for several of them appeared in the waist and started towards the poop.

Blake disregarded them for the time being, and devoted all his energies to the purpose in hand. Reaching the boat he unfastened the falls, and, straining hard, pushed it out. Then he let it go, and it ran down from the davits with a rush.

At the same time one of the Celestials whom he had knocked down in the saloon, rushed up on deck screaming something in Chinese. Whatever it was, it electrified the crew, for as one man they rushed towards Blake, drawing their knives as they came.

Blake turned to meet them, and, levelling the automatic, pulled the trigger time after time.

Man after man went down, but the others kept on, and Blake, who had no extra clip of cartridges for the pistol, saw that he must retreat.

Firing a last shot at the leader, and sending that Celestial to the deck, he sprang for the side, and catching hold of the ropes, slid down to the boat.

Bending, he released both the falls, and, as the boat became free, it dropped swiftly astern.

As the ship passed him, Blake looked up, and saw several of the crew gathered at the side ready to hurl their knives at him.

A moment later the hail of steel started. Blake dodged and ducked. Then the bulging stern of the tramp swept by, and he dropped out of range of the knives. But he knew this respite would not be for long. As soon as Wu Ling recovered, he would issue orders for the chase, and in a little open boat, on a sea of which he knew not even the name, what chance had Blake?

Slender though the chance was, Blake determined to make full use of it. Dropping to a seat, he picked up the oars, and began to pull with all his might. He cared not which way he went or how. His sole idea was to put as much space between himself and the tramp as possible.

Even as he settled down to hard work, he saw her swing round, and Wu Ling standing at the side.

Still he rowed and rowed as he had never rowed before, and he covered the best part of a mile before the tramp came round close enough for him to see what was afoot. Then it was that he saw half a dozen Celestials standing at the side, with rifles trained on him.

"Never mind!" he muttered, as he continued to strain at the oars. "Better to die this way than the way Wu Ling intends, and I swear they will not take me alive! They will have to shoot me full of lead first!"

The next moment the bullets began to fall about him. At first they went beyond him or to one side, falling into the water with sinister little plunks, but when the marksmen had the range, they began to hit the boat.

One struck the bottom in the bow, and as it tore through the wood Blake saw the water spurt in through the hole made. A second struck the starboard oar, and, ricochetting from it, plunged through the bottom. Another hole, through which the water began to bubble, had been made.

Then a perfect hail of lead struck the boat, falling all about him, splintering the sides and the oars, but so far miraculously missing him.

Still Blake pulled at the oars in a race which, if it lasted much longer under those conditions, could only end one way. But the ingrained grit of the white man kept him at it. Then he saw that he must block up the holes some way, or the boat would sink under him.

Drawing in the oars, Blake searched about in the bottom of the boat for something which would serve his purpose, but could find nothing. In desperation he tore the shirt from his body, and, ripping it into strips, rolled them up to form plugs for the holes.

While the bullets still fell about him, he worked strenuously, stuffing the material into first one hole, then the other. It was a poor makeshift at best, but it all was all he could do.

From under the stern sheets he took a battered tin can which he found there, and began to bale furiously. there was still a good deal of water slopping about in the boat when he desisted, but he saw if the plugs held as they were he could keep ahead of the incoming water.

Taking up the oars once more, he started to pull again; but, as he leant back, he suddenly paused and gazed at a great black pillar which was apparently joining sea and sky in the east.

From the appearance of the water and the feel of the air, Blake had formed a shrewd opinion that he was very far indeed from England. He knew that he had probably been kept drugged for days in the hold, and perhaps for weeks, but not until he saw that black pillar before him did the truth flash upon him.

Then he knew that while he lay unconscious in the hold of the tramp it had come many, many leagues. And in truth it had, for they had rounded the Cape days ago, and at the moment when Blake had been dragged to the saloon they were ploughing through the Indian Ocean towards Java and the passage into the China Sea.

The black pillar was the forerunner of a cyclone.

As he realised the full portent of what it meant, Blake drew in the oars again, and bent over the stuffing he had placed in the holes.

He knew, if he were caught by the force of the hurricane, that his little boat would be tossed about like an eggshell, yet he would do what he could.

At the same time, he saw that the tramp had also seen the oncoming menace, for she had sheered off suddenly, and was steaming at full-speed towards the north- east.

It was hard to choose between being in the open sea in a leaking boat while a hurricane approached and on board the tramp in the clutches of Wu Ling, but as Blake saw her drawing farther and farther away, he knew that at least one enemy was out of the way for the present.

How he worked in those next minutes! Frantically he pulled out the stuffing and screwed up the material into balls as tightly as he could make them. Then he pressed them back into the holes, and when he had filled the last, set to work again to bale.

Blacker and blacker grew the pillar in the east. Then came a first ominous puff of wind. It was followed by another, and then there arose a low, booming sound, the meaning of which Blake knew only too well.

Almost before he could catch hold of the seat and cling on for dear life, the hurricane swept upon him, and as the little boat was tossed skywards in a boiling cauldron of foam the fleeing tramp became blotted out from his view.

Of what followed during the next few hours, Blake to this day has only a vague idea. It seemed to him that there was an eternity of tossing and pitching, with a devil's wind catching him by the throat and threatening each moment to crush him to death beneath its weight.

He had a hazy recollection of baling mechanically with one hand while he clung on wildly with the other, of pitching and tossing yellow waves which curled upwards, huge as houses, and came crashing downwards, threatening to swamp the boat each moment, of wild roarings and boomings as the hurricane tore its way across the ocean, and of sheets of rain which came down in pelting, driving, cutting lines.

He was alone, it seemed, of all humanity in a tossing sea of yellow terror. And yet he knew that he must have caught only the tail-end of the hurricane.

How long this went on, he did not know. He only knew that he baled incessantly, and that it seemed that he had been condemned to bale yellow water for eternity.

Then the hurricane subsided and the rain passed, to leave him tossing about helplessly on the sweep of the battered ocean.

Gathering his wits together, Blake stopped baling, and took stock of his condition and that of the boat. The oars had gone in the first wild swoop of the hurricane. One of the seats was smashed, and the stuffing had come out of several of the holes.

Now the water was literally pouring into the boat, and as he again took up the bailing, Blake knew that it was a losing fight. Still he persisted, and as night came down, it found him still at it.

The last thing he did before darkness caught him was to gaze about the horizon. No sign of the tramp nor of any other ship did he see. Then he returned to his bailing.

What a ghastly, fever-haunted night it was! The strain through which he had been had left him constitutionally weakened, and nourishing food had not passed his lips for days.

A man cannot exist on bread and water and stand up under a situation such as Blake was in. It takes solid food basis to stand being pitchforked into such a place, and solid food Blake had not had.

Fever got him about midnight. Delirium followed, and while he baled he sang—sang the wildest, craziest songs which ever came out of forecastle.

Hour after hour he baled and sang, shrieking forth the pirate songs of old to a black and lowering sky.

Morning found him still at it, burning with fever and squatting up to his waist in water. How the boat ever kept afloat was a mystery. She was nearly full of water now, but through the fever of his delirium there came to Blake the idea that he was beating the creeping water. It lent him fresh energy—the energy of delirium, for which his system would pay dearly.

The grey clouds gave way, and the sun came out. Still the crazed man in the boat kept up his exertions, but by noon his fever-stricken brain snapped, the outraged body went with it, and Blake—a shrieking maniac—collapsed into the water which almost filled the boat.

Slowly but surely it crept up and up and up, until it had him by the throat; then the yellow water swept completely over the gunwale, and the man was carried out of the sinking boat into the grip of the waves.

Some instinct impelled the whirling brain to telegraph an imperative message to the limbs of the man. His arms and legs moved, and mechanically he began to swim.

Up to the crest of a roller he went, then down into its lap, tossing aimlessly and without cognisance, but still keeping afloat.

And with the embrace of the water came a change in his condition. The voice broke out once more, cracked and hoarse, but still expressing the madness of the brain. No song went croaking across the waves this time, but the delirious mutterings of the helpless maniac.

Of Tinker he mumbled and gurgled—of Tinker and the case they were on. Somehow his brain conceived the idea that Tinker was lying on the altar to be offered as a sacrifice to the golden god Mo, and that he was bound and helpless to release the lad.

How he cursed and raved as he, in fancy, watched Wu Ling, in the yellow robes of a priest of Mo, approach and lift the gleaming knife which would give the lad's blood to the god.

Then it seemed as if Tinker suddenly changed to Yvonne. It was she who lay on the altar, victim to the god.

As Blake, in fancy, saw her helpless beneath the squatting god, his frenzy redoubled, and, raising his arms, he thrashed the water madly, calling down upon Wu Ling curses which would have frozen the blood of a sea pirate.

In his frenzy he seemed to succeed in breaking his bonds and tearing them from him, rushed for the altar. Wu Ling, with upraised knife, reached for the white pillar which was Yvonne's throat, and, turning to Blake, smiled.

Blake hurled himself forward, and seized upon the bare blade of the knife. Then his tortured brain collapsed entirely, and, with Yvonne's appealing eyes upon him, he dropped into a pit of darkness.

Then the mocking waves seized upon him and bore him onwards—ever onwards!

CHAPTER 8
Yvonne's Rescue

Never had the Fleur-de-Lys had a harder chase than the one she undertook when Yvonne and Tinker boarded her at Cardiff, and set off down the Bristol Channel after the ship which they knew must be somewhere not very far ahead of them. Nor was there any need of a spur to cause everyone on board to do his utmost. Yvonne, to whom, each member of the crew rendered the most implicit obedience—an obedience born of love for the "little missie"—wished it, therefore, it would be done.

From Captain Vaughan, on the bridge, to sour old MacTavish in the engine-room, each man put forth his best, and the high-powered engines of the Fleur-de-Lys pounded mightily as she tore down the Channel, and headed for the Atlantic.

Until the yacht had dropped into Cardiff for supplies she had been doing special work for the Admiralty; but Yvonne arranged a release from these duties, and now the yacht was free to go wherever her mistress willed.

Across the Bay of Biscay they raced, ever on the watch for a tramp steamer, for in Cardiff Mr. Featherstone had discovered that only one ship had cleared for China within the time that Wu Ling must have gone, and that ship was the tramp steamer, Boca Tigris.

Off Finisterre, a British T.B.D. hailed them and released them, but before they tore on again they were in possession of the information that the Boca Tigris was ahead of them.

Not until they were off Gib. did they discover that no ship by that name had attempted to pass through the Straits, which meant that she had gone on past the Canaries, and intended reaching the Indian Ocean by way of the Cape.

Once more the course was changed, and south they raced as fast as the Fleur-de-Lys could take them.

They stopped at Las Palmas long enough to take in coal and fresh provisions then on again, past the Cape Verde Islands, which rise, barren and forbidding, off Cape Verde, and so into warm current which falls down the West Coast of Africa.

No stop was made from Las Palmas till they reached Cape Town, but there they still had no word of the other ship. Yet they knew she had not gone through the Mediterranean, and, since she had been ahead of them as far as the Straits, she must have gone by the Cape.

Even Wu Ling would not take the time necessary to cross the Atlantic and round Magellan, while it was unlikely they had tried the Panama Canal. Therefore, Captain Vaughan reasoned that she had kept well out from the regular track of ships, and for that reason they had not had word of her.

At Durban his reasoning proved correct, for there they passed the word with a small whaling steamer, which worked out from the Durban whaling-station, and she reported that she had signalled a tramp named the Boca Tigris only the day before, and that the tramp was heading under full steam towards the north-east.

That was enough for those on the Fleur-de-Lys. Up the Indian Ocean they raced on the new scent, so to speak, with Tinker, Yvonne, and the crew of the Fleur-de-Lys keeping a sharp look-out.

Nearly four weeks of steady steaming they had done, and still no sign of the quarry. From the grey waters of the north had they come, passing down through the blue of the Tropics round the Cape, and up into the warmth of the Indian Ocean. All zones had they been in, and yet that elusive tramp kept just ahead of them.

Then one evening they held a Council of War, and it was decided to continue on to Java, and to stop at Batavia in order to try and get some further news of the tramp, which they knew must be bearing Sexton Blake to his doom.

The very next day came a terrific hurricane, which threatened to annihilate them, and for ever prevent them from reaching the object of their journey. It was the same storm which swept down upon the tramp and upon Sexton Blake, who was even then tossing about in the small boat which he had taken from the Boca Tigris.

For several hours the barometer had been falling steadily, until Captain Vaughan ascended the bridge wearing a very worried look. He knew the Indian Ocean well, and he knew of old those sudden storms which gather somewhere off Ceylon, and sweep across the ocean to beat themselves out against the shores of far Africa, or, in some instances, at the head of the Persian Gulf. He knew also the absolute necessity of running for it, and abandoning the chase if he would save his ship.

With the coming of the menacing, black cloud in the east, he had not hesitated. The Fleur-de-Lys had been made ready, as far as possible, to meet the shock, and when it came she was sent dashing into the very teeth of it.

Hour after hour the hurricane raged, tossing them this way and that like a cork upon the breast of a giant cauldron, and hour after hour did the staunch little yacht wallow her way through the awful seas.

Then the storm passed on its way west, and, with the lessening of the awful strain to the yacht, those on board began to take stock of their condition. All that evening, and all night they ploughed their way onward towards Java, and at midday the following day took an observation. They found that the storm had blown them nearly a hundred miles out of their track, and that they were well east of the narrow entrance to the Java Sea.

Up on the Bridge another Council of War was held in the afternoon. While Captain Vaughan stood by the man at the wheel, Yvonne and Tinker joined him and together they discussed what should be done. Captain Vaughan and Graves, who had also come up, were for returning to England, and, and in his argument the captain used some convincing words.

"It is this way missie," he said. "The tramp was ahead of us when the hurricane struck. It is just possible that she made the Java Sea before the storm rose. In that case she would have escaped it entirely. If so, she is well on her way up the China Sea by now, and will reach Kaitu before we can get into the China Sea. In that case, we will be too late—well, to put it bluntly, to save Mr. Blake. It is not easy to give up after such a long chase—but what else is there to do?"

"The captain speaks sense," said Graves. "We will never be able to reach Kaitu in time. Wu Ling's tramp had more speed than we reckoned on. They will make Kaitu to-day or to-morrow at the latest, if they missed the storm."

Yvonne held up an imperative hand.

"Wait!" she commanded. "I have no doubt that you, uncle, and you, Captain Vaughan, are speaking with reason, but, at the same time, there are other things to be considered. We must know that Mr. Blake was taken away on the tramp, and that he is to be offered at Kaitu as a sacrifice to the idol Wu Ling worships. Do you think, even if we are late, that I will go back to England, and permit that to be carried out without a fight? If you do you are sadly lacking in proper knowledge of me. We are his only hope. Shall we desert him? Did he ever desert me or you when we depended on him? Did he return to London and say it was useless, when I myself was in the hands of Wu Ling? It is only a short time since you, uncle, appealed to him for his aid when I went down to Kilchester Towers. Did he refuse you? No! He came down himself to Kilchester Towers, and remained there until he had cleared up matters. And will I desert him now? Is that what Yvonne would do? If it were, then I should never again hold up my head.

"Whoever wishes to leave the yacht may do so at Batavia. I have doubt that they can easily get passage back to England from there. But as for me and the Fleur-de-Lys, it continues on to Kaitu, and, if anything has happened to Sexton Blake, then may heaven help Wu Ling and his gang, for I swear I will harry him off the seas and off the earth, if it is the last thing I do! That is my word, and that is what shall be done!"

The two men who were the recipients of Yvonne's anger, stood aghast at her outbreak. She looked very regal and very beautiful in her rage, and Tinker, who had listened eagerly to her words, gave a soft "Bravo!" as she finished.

Graves and Captain Vaughan started to speak in reply, but, with a gesture, Yvonne silenced them, and then suddenly her blue eyes filled with tears. She turned away hastily, and started to descend from the bridge, but Captain Vaughan caught her by the hand.

"That's all right, missie," he said soothingly. "I didn't know you felt that way about it. There ain't no one on this yacht that will go ashore at Batavia, but every hand goes on to Kaitu; and if you want to blow the place out of the water, it shall be done. "I know——" But just then the captain was interrupted by a voice forward.

"Something on the port bow, sir," came the cry.

With the instinct of the seaman, Captain Vaughan turned at once, and, snatching up a pair of glasses, raised them to his eyes.

Yvonne had turned back at the cry, and waited beside him.

"I can't make out what it is," said the captain, lowering the glasses. "If it didn't seem impossible, I would say it was the body of a man or an animal."

Quickly Yvonne took the glasses, and trained them on the object which was being tossed up and down by the waves. For a long minute she looked, then, lowering the glasses, she said:

"Get out a boat at once! It is a man!"

Laying down the glasses, she climbed on to the rail. Captain Vaughan leapt forward to stop her, but he was too late, and a second later Yvonne, placing her hands over her head, had cut the air like an arrow, taking the water cleanly.

They saw her come to the surface, saw her arms rise and fall in a strong overhand stroke, then saw her draw nearer and nearer to the floating object beyond.

Tinker, who had heard her cry, hurried away to have a boat lowered, and as it took the water he was first in it. Half a dozen men tumbled in after, and away they went at top speed towards the swimming girl.

She reached the object on the waves before they reached her, and, as they came up, they saw her arms cradling the thing which Captain Vaughan had said looked like a man or an animal.

Into the boat they dragged first the body of the man whom Yvonne held, and then Yvonne herself, and, as he bent over the wet, sodden, and unconscious man who lay at his feet, Tinker uttered a sharp exclamation.

Unless he had gone stark, staring mad there before him was, or rather was what he had once been, Sexton Blake.

The next moment there was a little gulping sob, as Yvonne, the tears streaming from her eyes, collapsed in a heap, her arms outspread over the body of Blake.

CHAPTER 9
The German Submarine

Sexton Blake was not dead, though he had gone perilously near the valley from which there is no return. Once back on board the Fleur-de-Lys he was put into a steaming bath, then wrapped in warm blankets and put to bed.

Nor would Yvonne hear of even Tinker nursing him. It was she who sat beside him hour after hour—it was she who held his hands while he tossed and raved in a mad delirium—it was she who heard from those loosed lips the full story of his suffering as he raved wildly—it was she who thrilled at the mention of her own name and locked within her breast the secret maunderings of a tortured mind.

And it was Yvonne whose lips shamelessly and softly pressed his and soothed him to rest. To her had come the urgent need to do for Blake.

How her heart, which for months had carried its own sweet secret, thrust aside the bars of restraint and burst forth in a pæan of happiness, only she herself knew.

But those long hours which she spent beside that fever-striken man would remain with her all her life as a bright dazzling stretch of achievement.

It was the need to serve which a woman feels for the man she loved. And Yvonne loved Blake.

Hour after hour she nursed him, watching incessantly while the fever ran its course, and eagerly awaiting the hour when sanity should return. It did return, thanks to Blake's iron constitution, and when, weak and exhausted, he opened his eyes to meet hers, he could only stare feebly at the wonder of it all.

He had gone into darkness while being tossed about by the waves—he had awakened to sanity and warmth to find Yvonne bending over him. And then, with happiness singing in her heart, Yvonne went out and called Tinker.

It is no part of this story to pry into that meeting between Blake and the lad. Sufficient is it to say that when Tinker emerged his eyes were wet, and he sought a quiet corner of the deck, there to give thanks for the great gift which had been theirs.

But hard on Blake's recovery things began to happen which needed the wits of everyone on board to cope with. It had been tentatively decided to change the course of the Fleur-de-Lys, and after putting in at Colombo to make for England. But Fate was determined that they should not do so.

She still had things in store for them which would need all their nerve and courage to handle, and it was perhaps as well that they did not know all that was to happen during the next few hours.

The first intimation that anything was wrong came from the man on look-out, was sighted a steamer on the starboard bow. She was ploughing along at a good speed, and the way she was running would bring her close to them. Then Captain Vaughan, who was on the bridge, made out her name, and with that the excitement arose on deck.

It was the Boca Tigris. That she had seen the Fleur-de-Lys was evident, for she came straight towards them, and after a hurried consultation they decided, in view of Blake's condition to make a run for it.

Captain Vaughan signalled the engine-room for full speed, and while the smoke belched forth from the yacht's funnels he changed her course.

Away they went racing west with the tramp after them, but they soon saw that they were to have no easy escape.

It was then that Wu Ling proved the tramp to be far different from what she seemed. Their first intimation of this was when a dull boom broke out behind them, and a shell whistled overhead, to fall in the water close to them.

To reply was useless. The Fleur-de-Lys, while armed, had no heavy guns, the largest being a Maxim, and what could a Maxim do against a gun which could throw a shell two miles? So they continued to run for it, while the Boca Tigris ploughed along after them, firing from time to time.

It was half an hour before the first hit was registered, and then the funnel of the yacht was struck fair and square. It split asunder with the force of the explosion, tearing loose as it went, and creating havoc on deck.

Another shell struck forward and burst just in front of the forecastle. Three men were struck by the flying bits of shell, and while Tinker went down to keep Blake from worrying, Yvonne went to look after the wounded men.

Captain Vaughan had now adopted a zig-zag course in order to spoil the aim of the gunner on the other ship, but a shell which struck the side of the bridge as it passed showed how well the enemy had the range.

It was a losing race and all hands began to realise it. Then, even as the Fleur-de-Lys shivered beneath the shock of another shell, did a long, slim, grey shape appear on the surface of the water and cut across towards them.

The firing from the Boca Tigris stopped at the same instant, and like those on the yacht, all hands looked to make out the nationality of the submarine which had appeared so suddenly.

From the bridge Yvonne gazed at it through the glasses.

After a few moment she spoke.

"It is German I am certain," she said. "Ah! Someone is coming through the opening in the conning-tower. It is—— I am certain it is German. Hendricks! Get out the British flag and break it out at once."

Yvonne now turned the glasses in the direction of the Boca Tigris and saw that the tramp had come up rapidly, and that already the Yellow Dragon of China was flying from her stern.

The submarine had apparently disregarded the tramp, and was drawing in closer and closer to the yacht. Then the British flag fluttered bravely and defiantly from the stern.

Hard on that the man who had come through the top of the conning-tower on the submarine reached down, and taking a megaphone from someone below, raised it to his lips.

"Ahoy! Fleur-de-Lys!" he shouted, in strongly-accented English. "You are British?"

Captain Vaughan looked at Yvonne, and when she nodded he picked up the yacht megaphone.

"We are British!" he called back. "Who are you, and by what right do you hold us up?"

"We are German," came back the reply. "We give you ten minutes to get out your boats. At the end of ten minutes we blow you out of the water."

To run for it was out of the question. To fight was equally useless. There lay the submarine close to them, and each one on the yacht knew that a torpedo was in her tube ready to be discharged. They could only submit, much as it hurt.

Turning to Captain Vaughan, Yvonne gave the word, and a moment later the old seaman, angry at being humiliated, called out to the crew to lower the boats.

While Hendricks the mate went down to the engine-room, Yvonne hastened to tell Blake, and Tinker superintended the lowering of the boats. Captain Vaughan was busy getting together the papers of the yacht.

At the head of the companion-way Yvonne came upon Blake leaning weakly against the handrail regarding the submarine.

"I heard everything," he said, as she came towards him. "There is nothing else to do. It is too bad. I am ready."

"You shouldn't have come up alone," Yvonne admonished him, her eyes filling as she saw his weakness. Come! Let me help you."

Taking his arms, she assisted him to the side, and there Blake descended into one of the waiting boats. The rest of the yacht's company soon came over the side, filling the other two boats, and when all were in them they pulled away from the side.

Lying off a short distance they lay on the oars waiting to see the last of the Fleur-de-Lys. But for some reason the torpedo did not come, and gazing at the submarine they saw that she was signalling to the tramp.

A moment later a boat put off from the tramp and made for the submarine, and as it danced over the waters the explanation came to Blake. Yvonne was in one boat while Tinker was in the other, and Blake and Hendricks in the third.

Blake bent over to Hendricks and said in a low tone:

"While they are busy watching that boat approach the submarine, tell your men to row round to the other side of the yacht. I want to go aboard."

Hendricks stared at him for a moment and looked as if he would speak, but something in Blake's manner decided him to do as he was requested. He gave the order to his men, and unobserved by the others they pulled round the stern of the yacht.

When the boat had been brought in close to the side Blake got up, and gathering all his strength made his way to the deck of the yacht.

There he paused and leaned over.

"Have them pull back, Hendricks," he said. "We don't want to arouse suspicion. I will manage to reach you somehow."

Hendricks, who was trained to obey, gave the order, and as the boat pulled away again Blake made his way along the deck.

He staggered more than once as he went, for he was still very weak, but sheer will-power held him up and he kept on.

At the foot of the companion, leading to the bridge, he paused to gather his strength together again, then on up to the bridge deck.

There he turned, and making his way along to the wireless room, kicked open the door.

It was only a forlorn hope on which he was bound, but he was determined to try it, and if he went to the bottom with the yacht while doing what he could to save the others, he would not mind.

Seating himself at the instrument he tuned up, then placing the receivers to his ears started to send the S.O.S.

Time after time he tapped it out, waiting at intervals for a call, and hoping against hope that it would come before the enemy discovered what he was about.

Even while the hope flared strongly in him he heard the tramp of feet along the deck, and a few moments later he saw half a dozen vicious-looking Chinese rush for the wireless-room.

Dropping his left hand to his pocket, Blake jerked out his automatic and levelled it. A bullet came crashing towards him and struck the table close to him.

He pulled the trigger of the automatic. It barked out again and again, and two of the Celestials went down.

Then, holding the rest at bay with the weapon, he began again to send. From somewhere across the water came the reply, and Blake discoverd to his joy that he was being answered by a British ship of war.

He sent out an urgent message for help; then, just as he had almost completed it, a bullet struck the key of the instrument and put it out of action.

Staggering to his feet Blake kicked the door to and locked it, then crouched beneath the window to wait for the next rush. And while he crouched there he wondered what had happened since he had come aboard.

Much indeed had taken place, and had he but dreamed what it was he would have thrown open the door and risked death.

The boat which had gone from the tramp to the submarine had borne Wu Ling and Beauremon, and there they had convinced the German commander of the submarine that they were indeed working hand in glove with the Germans.

When Wu Ling showed papers which proved the truth of his statement and requested that certain of the yacht's company be handed over to him, the German commander was only too pleased to do so.

So it was that the boats from the yacht had been surrounded, and with the deck gun of the submarine pointing at them, Yvonne and Tinker had been forced to climb over the gunwale into the boat from the tramp.

A search of all three boats failed to reveal Blake. No one had seen him go aboard the yacht except those in Hendrick's boat, and not twenty submarines would make them tell.

Wu Ling, shrewd as always, speedily guessed the truth, and rushing his two prisoners aboard the tramp, sent his men back to drag Blake off the yacht.

But Blake's message had gone and not even Wu Ling guessed that the answer had come from a blunt-nosed British T.B.D., whose smoke was at that very moment rimming the horizon.

She was coming up hand over hand, and while Blake held the wireless room against the attacking Celestials, succour was nearer than he thought.

He emptied his pistol once, hurriedly thrust in a fresh clip and emptied it again, just as the enemy made a fierce rush.

Though Blake got several of them, they succeeded in reaching the door of the wireless room, and it strained inwards as their weight was thrown against it. Then across the water there came the low wail of a siren—once, twice, thrice.

Almost immediately Blake heard the rush of feet as the attacking party raced down the deck. At first he thought it was only a ruse, but as no further attack came, he risked a peep out, and saw that the deck was clear.

Opening the door, he stepped out on to the deck, and, going to the side, was just in time to see the German submarine sink below the surface.

Turning, he gazed in amazement at the tramp. She was already under way, heading north as fast as she could go, and then, looking south, Blake saw the reason.

Scarcely a mile away was the British T.B.D., coming on the scene as quickly as her powerful engines could drive her. Tossing about on the waves were the three boats from the yacht, and as he saw them Blake essayed a feeble cheer.

Little did he dream that Yvonne and Tinker were not in them, but instead were prisoners on the tramp which was racing north at top speed.

As he appeared at the side, Hendricks gave an order to his men, and they pulled in close to the yacht.

Blake swarmed down to the small boat and tumbled in. Then, while they pulled towards the other boats, Hendricks told him what had happened.

Blake's eyes grew sombre as he listened, and his hands clenched fiercely.

"If I had only dreamed it!" he muttered, when the mate had finished. "Wu Ling has played a winning card, and Heaven only knows what fiendish fate he will think out for them! Nor will it be any the less because he has lost me. But the T.B.D. will be able to overtake them, and then—wait until I get my hands on Wu Ling!"

By this time the T.B.D. had come close, and the boats pulled in to them. In a few words, Captain Vaughan recounted what had occurred, and then he and Blake were invited to come aboard.

There Blake related the whole story, even from the time the Munitions Minister was kidnapped, and as he listened the young commander of the T.B.D. set his jaw grimly.

"So that is the game—is it?" he said, when Blake had finished. "Well, I'll tell you what I will do, Mr. Blake. I will go after that tramp, and if she refuses to heave to, I will let her have a shot or two. Do you care to come with me?"

"I should be very glad indeed to do so," replied Blake. "The Fleur-de-Lys could follow as quickly as possible."

So it was arranged, and soon the crew of the yacht were back on board, with MacTavish and the stokers in the engine-room, getting ready to give the Fleur-de-Lys all she would take.

Captain Vaughan was on the bridge, and as the T.B.D. raced away north after the tramp, Blake waved his hand to the gallant old seaman.

An hour passed—two hours—and they began to gain perceptibly on the tramp. Then Fate gave them another blow, for, as the afternoon waned and the commander of the T.B.D. expressed his hope of overtaking the other ship before night fell, a thick bank of cloud came down from the Java Sea and swallowed all the visible world within its damp maw.

CHAPTER 10
Rogues Fall Out

It was a hot night on the Island of Kaitu, as steaming day, with the jungle sweating hard, and not a breath of wind in from the sea, had presaged the night which had come. For once the night breeze had not come down from the hinterland, and over the lagoon and village which lay close to it the heat pall of the day still clung.

On the narrow, fringing coral reef beyond the lagoon, the surf rolled in lazily, murmuring incessantly, and rousing thoughts of cool depths. In the lagoon itself, the water lay still and limpid, its glassy surface broken only by the glow of phosphorescence as a school of fish struck the medusa and spread it apart.

Through the paw-paw trees and cocoanut palms, which lined the edge of the lagoon, lay the village, and from it came a low constant hum as of many voices. Now and then the wail of the temple bell broke out, calling through the night to those who would hear. Then its jangle would die away and silence reign once more.

In the lagoon lay a single ship—a small tramp steamer—and on her stern was painted the name Boca Tigris. For the Boca Tigris had made Kaitu safely, and on this night—the same night of the day which had seen her arrival—there was much to be done. The Illustrious One had come back to his own, which was a great event in itself, but rumour had it that he had brought two prisoners.

It was said by some of the priests that the blessed god Mo would receive a human sacrifice before the night was over, that the sacrifice would be a white man, and that the Illustrious One himself would perform the sacrificial rites. Hence the constant murmur of voices which came through the trees.

From the jungle near the edge of the lagoon appeared a man. He stood for some time gazing out at the tramp which rode at anchor in the best holding ground of the lagoon. Then he turned and made for the trees.

As a slanting beam of moonlight struck his face, it might have been seen that he was no Celestial, but a white man, and some would have recognised him as Baron Robert de Beauremon, of Paris and New York and London. But what a different Beauremon from the usual suave and nonchalant man who was well-known at the International Club of London!

On this occasion his eyes were filled with trouble; his usually immaculate dress was all awry; his hands twitched nervously as he swung them at his side.

He looked as if he had gazed into the mirror of his own soul, and had not liked what he saw there.

For be it known Beauremon and Wu Ling had arrived that day in Kaitu by the Boca Tigris, bringing with them the prisoners which by the grace of the commander of the German submarine they had been permitted to take—Mademoiselle Yvonne and Tinker.

With Blake lying in the hold of the tramp, Beauremon had made a protest; with Tinker in the grip of the Yellow Tiger, he would have been content with a similar objection. But from the moment he had laid eyes on Mademoiselle Yvonne, things had assumed a far different perspective.

Not that the Baron Robert de Beauremon was any sentimentalist. Far from it! He was the head of the Council of Eleven, which organisation had carried out many daring and conscienceless affairs since its inception. He was not so much immoral as simply unmoral. He didn't know what morals were.

When he had formed the Council of Eleven, he had been world-weary. He had tasted of the sweets and bitters of life, and found them not satisfying. In the Council of Eleven, he found the constant excitement which his blase nature craved. Nor had he flinched from any deed in the carrying out of his purpose.

That type of nature, combined with the wealth which was his, had made him all the more dangerous. But never before had he been up against exactly this type of proposition.

He had joined in with Wu Ling in the Island of Marsey, off Pembrokeshire, for a certain consideration. He had done his part in bringing things to a successful issue.

When Sexton Blake had outwitted them, he had still stuck to Wu Ling. He had sailed with him for the East, and, to do him credit, had objected strenuously to the offering of Sexton Blake as a sacrifice to the god Mo. But, as is already known, he had been ruled down, and for the time being had submitted.

But when Yvonne had been brought aboard the tramp, Beauremon had looked once into her eyes, and his fate was sealed. It had come home to him exactly what he was doing, and with that realisation had come the decision to have an understanding with Wu Ling.

When they had gone ashore in Kaitu, he had sought the prince in his quarters behind the temple, and there had stated his case.

"It is no good, Wu Ling!" he had said bluntly. "I will not stand for this sort of game! I am pretty bad, I know, but I cannot bring myself to lending a hand to any such thing as you contemplate. With all due respect to you and your Royal blood, you are yellow and your prisoners are white. Therefore I wish to know your exact intentions regarding them."

Wu Ling shrugged and said:

"I saw you when you looked at the white girl this morning, baron. I have been expecting some such objection on your part. It is strange that you should have these scruples after seeing the girl. But you will be unwise to attempt to baulk me in my plans. I gave you an opportunity of leaving me before we sailed from Cardiff. You elected to remain."

"That was because I felt I had not fulfilled my contract with you," broke in Beauremon.

"That is neither here nor there," resumed Wu Ling. "I tell you now that I will brook no interference from you. As to what my intentions are, I will tell you. To-night, at the moment when the moon has reached its zenith, the boy shall go to the altar in sacrifice for the golden moon god Mo. The girl—the girl, baron, goes to my harem."

"And I say these things shall not be done!" burst out the baron.

"So?" had replied Wu Ling softly. "And who, pray, will prevent me?"

"I will!" the baron had replied, and therein he had made a great mistake.

Wu Ling had shrugged, and, with a wave of the hand, had dismissed him, and Beauremon, wishing to think, had gone out from the temple to plan against the prince.

But Wu Ling was not the man to have an avowed enemy loose on the sacred island of Kaitu, and when Beauremon had gone forth from his presence, two Celestials had slipped along after him.

Into the jungle had the baron gone, carrying with him the memory of the two eyes of morning blue into which he had gazed, and after him had gone two yellow executioners.

A hundred yards from the temple they came upon him and attacked him. Beauremon had been taken by surprise, and had he attempted to fight would have been cut to pieces in a few seconds.

The orders of the assassins had been to see that he did not return. But Beauremon, knowing something of Wu Ling and his methods, had taken to his heels, and had dashed on blindly through the jungle, with the two Celestials after him.

Without any sense of direction had Beauremon run, and it was probably this which saved him, for at the end of half an hour, when he had staggered out on to the edge of a high bluff overlooking the sea, he had shaken off his pursuers.

All that afternoon he had lain there, gazing out to sea, and trying to think of some way by which he could save the girl who was in the grip of Wu Ling.

With the coming of evening he had ventured to leave his retreat and make his way down to the edge of the lagoon, and so it was that, while Kaitu panted and gasped beneath the lingering heat of the day. Beauremon ventured forth from the concealment of the trees.

It would be some time before the moon reached its zenith. As yet it had only come up above the gaunt peak which rose in the centre of the island, striking the water of the lagoon slantingly, and causing a path of gold which stretched clear out to the narrow entrance, which lay between dank bunches of stinking mangroves.

Though he had thought and thought for hours, Beauremon had been able to hit on no plan whereby he, single-handed, might overcome the forces against him. Yet was he determined to release Yvonne, and if possible Tinker, before Wu Ling should have had his will with them.

So much to his credit.

It was with this aim in view that he started for the village, where he knew must by now be gathered every inhabitant of the island, to witness the sacred ceremony which preceded the offering of human sacrifice to the god Mo.

At the very edge of the paw-paw trees, he paused and gazed out across the lagoon at something which was stealing in through the mangrove-lined passage.

For a few moments he stood there thus, scarcely daring to believe what his eyes told him he saw; then, turning, he stole back down the beach to the very edge of the water.

Again he paused, watching the grey shape which had come through the passage resolve itself into the blunt lines of a ship of war. And then, as she dropped across the path cast by the moonlight, Beauremon saw that she was the same T.B.D. which had put the tramp and the submarine to flight the day before.

What did it mean? Before he had time to answer his own question, his attention was attracted by a noise in the direction of the tramp. He, himself, knew that only one man had been left aboard on watch, and now as he saw a boat being lowered he knew that one man had also seen the sinister, grey shape steal into the lagoon, and was off to warn Wu Ling.

Beauremon screwed up his eyes, and watched the progress of the small boat as it came shorewards; then, when it was still halfway between the tramp and silvery beach of the lagoon, he stepped into the water and plunged, cutting the surface with scarcely a sound.

Swimming easily, he headed for the small boat, and, as he drew nearer, saw the Chinese watchman, who had been left aboard the tramp, rowing with short, powerful strokes.

It was evident that a severe panic had seized upon him. Yet he could have no suspicion of Beauremon, for he knew nothing of the split between the baron and Wu Ling. Nor did he have any suspicion for when Beauremon drew near the Celestial eased up, and in Chinese said:

"There is danger, Excellency. The Illustrious One must know."

Beauremon laid a hand on the gunwale of the boat, and drew himself over the side.

"The Illustrious One will know," he said shortly. "I myself will tell him."

While he was speaking, he was drawing nearer and nearer to the unsuspecting Celestial, who was still resting on the oars. Then suddenly Beauremon sprang on him, and the startled Chink went down with his mouth open ready to yell.

But the baron jammed his clenched fist into the aperture, and the cry died off with a choking gurgle. Beauremon followed up the jab with whole weight of his body, and, getting one knee in the pit of the Celestial's stomach, he began to exert a gruelling pressure.

The Chink gasped and wriggled and fought like a tiger; but Beauremon was out for quick work, and, using his left, sent in blow after blow to the other's face.

There could be only one result—there was only one result. Under the hail of blows the Chink doubled up and collapsed, and Beauremon, jamming him into the stern of the boat where he could watch him, sat down and took to the oars. Then, turning the boat, he sent her skimming across the lagoon towards the grey shape of the T.B.D.

As he drew near he saw several forms at the side, and, pausing in his rowing, he called softly:

"Are you there, Sexton Blake?"

Immediately came the reply:

"Yes. Who is it?"

"Beauremon," replied the baron. "Throw over a ladder. I want to come aboard."

Instantly a ladder was thrown over the side, and, pulling in the oars, Beauremon clutched it, running up easily.

Once on deck he saw by the light of the moon that four men had gathered at the top to receive him, and that foremost among them was Sexton Blake. Yet there was something concerted in the way that quartette of hard-bitten men stood which made Beauremon smile.

It was evident that they were taking no chances of treachery. And when Blake spoke, it was plain that he was decidedly suspicious of the baron's coming.

"Why have you come here?" asked Blake curtly.

The baron leaned against the side.

"I suppose on the face of it my visit must look decidedly suspicious," he replied coolly. "But I shall be as brief as possible in my explanation. To jump all that happened in England, let me begin at the point where you were sent for by Wu Ling on board the Boca Tigris. Wu Ling himself told you, I think, that I had interceded for you, Blake?"

Blake nodded.

"That is true," he said coolly. "Proceed, please."

"Then your attack on Wu Ling came, and you almost brained him. If you will remember, I did not lift a hand to help him, though you next attacked me, and nearly finished me. Is that true?"

"Is it true," said Blake.

"You succeeded in getting away," went on Beauremon. "You know what happened after that. I have spoken of the other things in order that you may try to appreciate the position I was in. I was trying to keep my contract with Wu Ling, and yet I would not consent to some of the programme he had outlined. The appearance of the German submarine was a great surprise to me as to you. I knew nothing of its coming—neither did Wu Ling. Then, while Wu Ling went across to the submarine to explain matters, you managed to get aboard the yacht, and send a wireless message for aid. The crew of the tramp, which had been sent to recapture you, were held off by you at the point of the revolver, and the appearance of this T.B.D. on the scene forced Wu Ling to recall them before they had effected your capture.

"But he managed to get possession of Tinker and Mademoiselle Yvonne, and managed also to drive through the Sunda Straits into the Java Sea, and on up the China Sea to Kaitu without being overtaken. Nor does he dream yet that you are here. There are great doings in Kaitu to-night, and it is for that reason you see me here an apparent traitor to Wu Ling. To-day I thrashed out matters with him. I would not consent to the programme he had outlined, particularly regarding Mademoiselle Yvonne."

"And what is that programme?" asked Blake tensely.

"It is that Tinker shall go to the altar as a sacrifice to the god Mo, and that mademoiselle shall go to join Wu Ling's harem. That is what brings me here. I informed Wu Ling that it must not be. He insisted on it, and I left his presence. But I did not go alone. Two of his henchmen followed me, and tried to knife me in the bush. I escaped from them, and made my way through the jungle. I lay hidden all day, and this evening I ventured down to the beach in order to devise some plan for rescuing the two prisoners. It was then I saw your boat steal into the lagoon, and that I realised that you had come in the nick of time. While I stood there I saw the watchman put off from the tramp to warn Wu Ling. I swam out to meet him. He did not suspect me, and I overpowered him. He lies below in the boat at this moment. That is my story, and that is why I am here. After all, I am a white man, and I cannot bring myself to countenance what Wu Ling intends this night. You can believe me or not."

Blake stepped forward, and, bending his head, gazed deeply into Beauremon's eyes.

"If I thought you were laying some trap for us, I would kill you where you stand!" he said tensely. "But if you are telling the truth, then, Beauremon, you are more of a man than I thought you were. Look me in the eyes and answer me!"

The baron lifted his head, and gave back look for look.

"I swear by the eyes of Mademoiselle Yvonne that I speak the truth!" he said, in a low tone.

Blake's hand shot out, and they gripped.

"I believe you," he said. "If you could take that oath and perjure yourself, you would be a skunk!" Then Blake stepped back. "Gentlemen," he said, turning to the three officers who had stood close by, "now that I am satisfied as to the intentions of our friend here, let me present him to you. Baron Robert de Beauremon—Commander Porter—Lieutenant Trepwitt, and Midshipman Fortescue."

When the three had shaken hands with Beauremon, Blake turned back to the baron.

"You said, baron, that there were great doings afoot in Kaitu to-night. Do you know at what hour Wu Ling has planned them?"

Beauremon looked across the limpid waters of the lagoon, which was being stirred ever so gently by the first caress of the coming night breeze, then his gaze travelled upwards to where the great stars rode supremely beautiful.

Raising his hand, he pointed towards the moon.

"They take place when the moon reaches zenith," he said, in a low tone.

Immediately all eyes were riveted on the great disc which hung like a glorious golden globe over the jagged summit of Hani-Ku, the towering peak which rose from the centre of Kaitu.

When the moon reaches the zenith," they murmured, one by one, "and that will be inside an hour."

CHAPTER 11
The Last of the Temple

Beauremon had made no mistake when he said that there were great doings afoot on Kaitu that night. Up in the temple the priests had been busy all day, feeding the flames of the fire which burned at the foot of the great statue of the god Mo, and preparing the ceremony which would take place that evening.

In the room at the rear of the temple Wu Ling had spent the entire afternoon in prayer and meditation. Outside, the people of the village moved about restlessly, waiting for the word to come forth that the Illustrious One was ready.

What a barbaric scene it was. The temple—a miniature of the great one in Peking—standing with its front to the east, facing the eternal coming of Morn. Within the huge statue of the Buddha, which rose at the rear, its outlines silhouetted against a tracery of palm-branches which could be seen through a large semi-circular opening which looked to the west.

All round the temple the beautifully carved scenes of the life of Confucius and the Buddha stood out clear and distinct, even in the mellowed light of the temple.

The floor was antique mosaic of the finest, and the panels of the walls themselves were covered entirely by goldleaf.

To one side was the alcove where stood the altar to the god Mo. It was a richly-decorated place, covered with mosaic and goldleaf, and lit up ruddily by the light of the censers, which burned night and day.

On a jade base sat the god, a huge figure of pure gold, whose eyes were blazing emeralds. At the foot of the figure was the great block of porphyry hewn, and polished by hand, on which the sacrifices were made.

Usually these sacrifices composed the bodies of white kids—young goats—specially bred for the purpose, and once a month when special invocations were made to the god was a white bullock slain. Be it noted that always the sacrifice was white.

Those who have read the classics of the ancients, those who have enjoyed the beautiful poetry of Homer in the "Iliad" and the "Odyssey," or followed the adventurous voyage of Aeneas, when after the fall of ancient Troy he took his father Anchises and his little son Ascanius to seek a new home for the remnants of the Trojan race, will recall the consistency with which the ancients made sacrifices to their gods. Then the gods were Jupiter—Juno, Neptune, Venus, Mercury, and Minerva, and a host of others.

They will recall, too, when Aeneas, after passing through many stirring adventures, after leaving the shores of Ilium, and passing the Cyclades as well as the terrible Harpies, to be finally shipwrecked on the shores of Africa, made his prayer to the gods, and later on, when, after his sad dallying in the new city of Carthage, he finally reached Italy, he made sacrifice of white bullocks.

In some way the sacrifice of white animals to the god Mo must have descended from those ancient times, or in the past have been contemporaneous with them. Perhaps the idea travelled from China to ancient Troy. Who knows?

At any rate, it still persisted in the worship of the god Mo, but with the difference that on occasion a human sacrifice—if white—was also demanded by the ritual. Therefore, it will be understood how great was the excitement on Kaitu, when it became known that a living sacrifice would be made to the god.

At the very moment when the moon rose over the jagged edge of Hani-Ku, Wu Ling emerged from the room of meditation at the rear of the Buddha.

After making a short prayer there, he rose and passed on to the alcove where squatted the god Mo. Once more he prostrated himself, and for a long half-hour remained motionless, while six priests of the order, in robes of yellow and white, knelt behind the altar awaiting the pleasure of the great high priest.

Finally, Wu Ling rose, and, approaching the sacrificial altar, gazed upon the fire which burned there. Then he turned, and spoke in low, deep tones.

"Let the people enter." he said.

Forthwith the six priests rose from their kneeling posture, and passing out of the alcove, made their way to the main entrance of the temple.

In the meantime, Wu Ling passed across to the foot of the Buddha, and waited there for the people to come in. They came at the summons of the priests—one by one with bowed heads. The temple was scarcely large enough to hold them, but there was no pushing—no unseemly hurry.

Each one took his place, and when all were there, Wu Ling held up his hand.

"My people," he said solemnly, "You are gathered here to-night for the great ceremony. I have let it be known that to-night, when the moon reaches its zenith, there shall be made to the god Mo"—here Wu Ling bent his head, while the rest followed his example—"a sacrifice such as delights the heart of the blessed one. Here in the island of Kaitu we have reared to the God a temple, which in truth is poor enough, but which is the best our feeble efforts can fashion. To him the glory of the heavens we bow in submission this night, and to him we make sacrifice."

"Before casting upon the altar the food which the god craves, I shall tell you why the sacrifice will be particularly welcome to him. Listen, my people! I have but come from a far country—a stronghold of the hated whites. While there I saw many things, and did many things. Also I formed a temporary alliance with one of the whites, in which I was to help him in certain things for his aid out here. I kept my word to him, but even at the moment of victory was the prize snatched from me."

"And, my people, whom think you was the cause? Remember you the days of old, when on the ground in front of this very temple I was cast down, and the hands of the white dog went to my throat. Remember you the man who, as you all thought, sent me to the arms of the blessed Confucius."

"It was he, and he it was who fell into my hands. But again he escaped, and that even while I was near to Kaitu. He it was whom I intended to be the sacrifice to the blessed god Mo. But he escaped. Yet there fell into my hands one who will also please the god. I speak of the one who will form the sacrifice this night."

"He is the heart of the man whom I lost. He is with him at all times. He is to him what the faithful San is to me. It is the lad whom the man Blake always has with him. Ah! Indeed will the god Mo be pleased this night. And on that altar will this white one feed the flames. Now you will see him prepared for that altar."

Wu Ling's voice died away, and he stood motionless while two of the priests slipped away to the room at the rear of the temple. They returned a few minutes later, leading between them a figure garbed in white—a figure whose hands were bound, but whose head was proudly erect.

The two priests conducted him along to the feet of the Buddha, and stood him so he could be seen by the whole assembly.

It was Tinker—Tinker, white as a sheet, with the strain and his whiteness enhanced by the white garments in which he had been clad, but a Tinker whose head was held proudly, and whose eyes never faltered as they gazed out at the hostile crowd before him.

At the sight of him a low murmur rose from the assembly, and this soon resolved itself into a sort of chant which Wu Ling took up and beat time to. It was the chant to the god Mo.

When it was finished, Wu Ling raised his hand and again spoke.

"There is more to tell you, my people," he said. "Into my hands there fell another—a woman. She it is who is the apple of the man Blake's eye. She it is who loves the man Blake, though she strives hard to hide it. But think you the secrets of the stupid white pigs are hid from the gaze of the East? They are transparent as the water in yonder lagoon.

"She goes not to the sacrificial altar, since it is forbidden to make sacrifice of that sex. But she goes to grace my house, and thus for ever will be hidden from the gaze of man. No vengeance against the man Blake could be greater than that. You shall see her my people."

Again Wu Lings's voice died away, and two more of the priests disappeared towards the room at the rear. A minute or more passed, during which all eyes were turned expectantly in the direction of the rear room, then slowly the great stone door swung wide, and the two priests entered, leading between another white-clad figure.

It was Yvonne.

Fancy, if you can, the scene. A barbaric Eastern temple, redolent of mystery and incense—a hot tropic night, with the land breeze just floating down from the jungle-clad hinterland—the sickly odour of the mangroves from the swamp by the lagoon—the sweet smell of the paw-paw blossoms, and the soft rustling of the palms—over all the great bowl of night, with its thousands of stars riding supremely beautiful, and reflected in the limpid waters of the lagoon.

Then the wild, savage-looking crew which was gathered in the temple—yellow and seamed Chinese, brown and nearly naked Malays, Alfours, Cingalese, not a few Japs who had given up their own country. Javanese, Sumatrese, Kanakas, Polynesians from the outer islands. Dayaks from Borneo, and the Celebes and Melanesians from as far south as New Guinea and the Solomons.

There they stood, wildly clad and wild-souled, held under the spell of the man they looked upon as a demi-god, and swayed utterly by his every word—standing in hungry regard of the two whites whom the Illustrious One had brought home with him—the one to go as a living sacrifice to the god Mo—the other to share as awful a fate.

As for Tinker, who stood with head held high, only he himself knew what he was suffering, and had suffered. From the moment when he and Yvonne had been dragged out of the boats and taken aboard the tramp, it had not been hard for him to guess that Wu Ling would have little mercy on him.

But though he realised the danger of his own position, Tinker was glad that at least Blake was free. Yet his heart bled for Yvonne. He understood enough of the rough dialect which Wu Ling had used in speaking to his motley crew to gather what the prince's intentions were regarding Yvonne. She would go to be his wife—to be the wife of a Celestial.

When he thought of Yvonne, in her winsome loveliness, being forced to become the wife of a Celestial, prince though he might be, all the control which he had guarded so well threatened to break its bounds and send him dashing in among the crew about him in a mad and a futile endeavour to wreak vengeance upon them.

Mad and futile it would have been, for what could one lad, however valiant he might be, do against that mob?

As Yvonne was led forward, Tinker's eyes met hers. What did those two so very much alone there say to each other in those glances? It was a mutual message of courage and trust.

Yvonne, garbed in a long, white gown which had been provided for her, stood proudly erect, with her glorious bronze-gold hair rippling over her shoulders like a stream of molten copper. Her skin looked even whiter than usual, and her throat gleamed like a beautiful pillar of pure alabaster. Her feet were clad in sandals—her hands hung loosely by her side. She looked like the incarnation of some goddess of old.

As the eyes of the savage assembly looked upon the white captive who would go to grace the house of their chief, a low murmur of admiration broke out. It was forgotten in that moment that she was of the hated whites. Her beauty conquered them as it had conquered others. But even her beauty would not save her from the fate which was to be hers.

Yet her eyes, heavy with fatigue, and large and shadowy from the effects of the strain under which she had been, again looked into Tinker's.

"Don't give up," she whispered, so he could hear. "He is doing all he can, you may be sure"—"he" meaning Blake, as both knew.

Tinker smiled bravely. "I am not afraid," he replied. "I am worrying for you."

The next moment a heavy hand was swept across his mouth, cutting off all further speech.

Then, Wu Ling spoke again.

"My people," he said, "behold the woman. Behold the one who goes to the house of your chief. Behold the illustrious pearl which I plucked from the lap of the whites. It is indeed fitting that the one of all who is precious to the man Blake should become the property of Prince Wu Ling.

"Now, before she is to be taken away, never more to see the world from the outside, she will witness the sacrifice to the blessed god Mo. Let the altar be prepared."

With that, the low chant to the god Mo broke out again, and as it rose and swelled on the tropic night Wu Ling turned towards the alcove wherein squatted the golden god, now looking grim and hideous under the slanting rays of the moon, which came in through an opening at the rear of the alcove.

When those rays struck the god full on the top of the head, the moon would be at the zenith. Then would the sacrifice be made according to the ancient rites.

Two priests shuffled across to the great porphyry altar, where burned the fire of sacrifice. Two more dragged Tinker along to the altar while the other two forced Yvonne to walk nearer to it.

The whole assembly strained forward, still chanting the barbaric wail, and waiting eagerly for what was to come.

70

Tinker was held upright before the altar, then, with a single sweep of the hand, his white garment was torn from him revealing him clad only in a white loincloth. Beneath the ruddy reflection of the altar flames, he looked like a young Adonis, standing white and slim and erect, his limbs clean cut and straight, his head and features like an old cameo.

Verily the god Mo was out to receive a worthy sacrifice, which would appease even his Molochian appetite.

Wu Ling approached the altar, and, bending his head before the god, chanted a prayer which was echoed by the assembly behind him. Then, the prince stood aside, and the two priests who held Tinker dragged him slowly forward towards the altar on which the fire burned.

Yvonne stood like a statue, her hands pressed against her breast, her eyes full of a nameless terror, and her limbs frozen with horror.

As the lad was dragged nearer and nearer, her breast rose and fell in an increasing agony of suffocation, until finally her suffering broke all bounds, and her lips opened.

Then, on the tropic night, there rang out a passionate cry for succour—a cry which was caught by the vaulted roof of the temple, and echoed and re-echoed throughout the place, to go wailing with rising cadence through the palms which stretched to the lagoon.

In her desperation she had called upon the man she loved—she had called upon Sexton Blake.

· · · · · ·

When he was quite convinced that Beauremon was telling the truth and that his visit to the T.B.D. was no scheme to catch them in ambush, Blake lost no time in preparing for the rescue party to go ashore.

He knew that if Wu Ling said he would carry out certain intentions regarding Tinker and Yvonne he would do so, unless some power stronger than himself prevented him.

Whatever way he looked at it, one had to acknowledge that Yvonne and Tinker were in an extremely hazardous position. In the hands of a savage crew, whose law was the word of their chief, they stood little show of leniency. And if what Beauremon said was true, then when the moon reached its zenith, rescue of any kind would be out of the question.

In a few minutes Blake lived years. His mind leaped back to the years which Tinker had been with him. He recollected the first early days of their friendship when the young street urchin had been of great value to him.

Then he recalled the time which had followed when the lad had developed from the urchin into a fine specimen of youth, and how by diligent study and application he had made of himself not only a charming, but a cultured young fellow such as one rarely met with.

Then came the memory of the dangers through which they had passed together—of struggles and triumphs, of sicknesses and recoveries, of joys and sorrows which they had shared together.

And, thinking, a lump rose in his throat, and the limpid waters of the lagoon became suddenly obscured by the mist which filled his eyes. Was the end of it all to be such as this night seemed to promise? Was the lad, so fine and stalwart and clean, to go to form the living sacrifice to a barbaric golden god?

Not while Sexton Blake lived and breathed and was able to fight. And if he were too late then he would wreak such a vengeance upon the despoilers of the lad as the deepest mind in China could not conceive.

Then his thoughts went to Yvonne—Yvonne whom he had first met when she was a wayward, whimsical girl—Yvonne who had been to him what no other woman had been. He remembered how with her wilfulness she had at times made him sad, and then how, with her sweet surrender, she would relent and try to make up for it all.

There were times—ah! he scarcely dared think of them. And one thing stood out clear and distinct as a star shining to a man in the void. That was the warm pressure of her lips on his when he lay weak and exhausted in the bunk on board the Fleur-de-Lys. His pulse throbbed at the memory, and the cords in his wrists stood out as he thought of the yellow hands of Wu Ling laid upon her.

With that thought his anger broke bounds. With a savage exclamation he turned to the commander of the T.B.D.

"Commander Porter," he said, "will you authorise a landing-party to rescue the two British subjects who have fallen into the clutches of these Celestials?"

The commander looked back at Blake with sympathy in his eyes. He had seen something of what the stern-looking Englishman was suffering.

He nodded briefly.

"The resources of the ship are at your disposal, Mr. Blake. I shall give orders at once to have a landing-party got ready and then we shall go ashore. Before we have finished with these people we shall teach them a lesson they will remember for many a long day. I shall also send a party aboard that tramp to take possession of her.

"Fortunately I sent a wireless to the commander-in-chief of this station asking his permission to act as I thought best in this emergency, and he has instructed me to do so."

Blake nodded his thanks, and then the low voices of the officers rang out as they went to muster the landing-party.

Blake turned to Beauremon.

"Will you come?" he asked curtly.

The baron shrugged.

"I have no particular score to settle with Wu Ling," he said, with all his old sang froid. "But still it was a bit crude of him to order me to be cut up in the jungle to-day, so, with your permission, I think I will join you, Mr. Blake."

As the boats were lowered and brought round, the crews tumbled in, and while one of them rowed across to take possession of the tramp, two more made for the shore.

Blake, who had been at Kaitu in the past, took the lead when they had tumbled out on to the beach, and with drawn cutlasses, they started through the trees.

On they went, foot by foot, with the utmost caution and striving to anticipate any possible ambush.

Half-way through the grove of palms and paw-paw trees Blake paused and held up a warning hand. They heard a low murmur which rose and fell and rose again as a chant—and chant it was to the savage god Mo, as Blake well knew.

Then it stopped, and they were about to go ahead again when loud and clear in the ringing urgency there came a cry for succour—a cry full of terror and laden with horror—a cry in a voice which sent Blake's pulses hammering madly.

It was Yvonne's voice.

That was the last thing needed to make Blake fling all caution to the winds.

With an exclamation he turned to those behind him.

"Follow!" he cried. "Follow to the temple!"

Drawing his revolver, he dashed on through the grove with the others tearing after him. Into the opening where stood the village they burst, and racing down between the palm-thatched huts which rested on piles they made for the temple which Blake knew stood at the other end of the village.

Again he heard Yvonne's voice raised in a cry of frantic appeal, then it was cut off suddenly. Blake was several strides in advance, with Commander Porter and Beauremon next, and the panting crew of the T.B.D. tumbling along after with their cutlasses drawn and their eyes alight with the joy of battle.

Whatever may have been Beauremon's attitude in the past when he was for the nonce an ally. There were old scores to settle between him and Blake which no attitude of the present could wipe out. But the call of the white had clutched him, and in the final test he had, as many more, answered the call.

Blake had always had a certain respect for the baron, for he had always fought according to the creed of the gentleman until his recent alliance with Wu Ling. There had been a little affair in South America not long before when Beauremon and Rymer had tried to steal a republic, and in which, by keen strategy, Blake had outwitted the pair.

In that affair, as in others, Beauremon had remained cool and nonchalant, while undoubtedly Rymer had sadly lost his temper. And a man who could command the sang froid which was Beauremon's, always roused Blake's admiration.

Nor could he ever forget that it was Beauremon who had swum out to warn him of what was afoot in Kaitu that night.

As the party dashed towards the temple, a wandering pig crossed from beneath one of the huts, and seeing the advancing horde racing towards it had raced off with a startled squeal. An old woman, too old to attend the assembly at the temple, saw them go by and gave vent to a shrill scream.

But they were beyond caution now, and when the temple finally came in sight they raised a mighty cheer as they raced for the steps.

Up them dashed Blake, followed by Beauremon and Commander Porter, and in to the sacred precincts of the temple went Blake, his automatic held ready for action.

As they broke through the main entrance into the crowd of savages which was gathered there, a strange sight met their eyes. Over the heads of the assembly they could see Wu Ling in his yellow robes of priesthood standing by the altar on which burned a fierce fire.

Beside him, and in the very act of lifting a bound figure upon the altar, were two priests clad in yellow and white. Near at hand was a figure in white—a woman clutching her heaving breast and gazing with eyes of horror at the altar to which the slim figure of the lad was being dragged.

Behind the altar two other priests were standing ready to attend to the sacrifice when it should be laid upon the block of porphyry. And over all sounded the barbaric sacrificial chant of the assembly.

It was a weird scene. And into that scene tore Sexton Blake, followed by Commander Porter and a crew of British bluejackets eager for a fight.

How to describe the pandemonium which followed. The chant of those nearest the door changed into a startled squeal as the party entered, and there were wild reaching for cutlasses and knives.

Blake, who had eyes for only one thing, the lad who was being hoisted to the altar, levelled his revolver and pulled the trigger twice in rapid succession.

First one then the other of the two priests who were lifting the lad to the altar threw up their hands and fell forward, one of them striking the altar fairly and dropping into the flames—an unwilling sacrifice to the god he professed to worship.

The other went tumbling to the floor at the foot of the altar, while the lad in the white loincloth stumbled to his knees, safe but still bound.

With a loud cheer the bluejackets now took a hand, and as they dashed into the thick of the yellow crew Blake fought and shot his way through to the front of the temple where Yvonne was held by two priests.

They, in panic and at the command of Wu Ling, started to drag her towards the room at the rear of the temple, but Blake shot over the heads of the crowd and sent her captors reeling back.

He next turned his weapon on Wu Ling, who he saw making for the spot where squatted the god Mo, but at that moment a struggling party of Celestial and bluejackets crashed into him and his bullet went wild.

The next moment Wu Ling disappeared. The very floor seemed to have swallowed him up.

Blake kept on until he came to Yvonne, who had stumbled to her knees. Catching her in his arms he lifted her up and held her tight, and as her white face became upturned to to his, Blake saw that the strain had been too much for her—she had fainted—which was well.

Laying her down in a safe place he loosened her bonds and made for Tinker.

"I'm all right, guv'nor," whispered the lad weakly, as Blake picked him up like a baby and carried him across to where he had left Yvonne. "Bit of a strain, but you came in time."

"You plucky lad," muttered Blake with choking utterance. "If they had done that thing to you I should have followed Wu Ling to the ends of the earth. But, thank Heaven, I was in time. One moment, my lad, and I will have you free."

All this time the fight in the main part of the temple was raging fiercely. Commander Porter, Lieutenant Trepwitt—

Midshipman Fortescue had been sent to take charge of the party which had boarded the tramp—and Beauremon were leading the bluejackets and were fighting with a will.

Caught like rats in a trap, there was nothing for the Celestials to do but to fight. There was no way of escape but by the main entrance to the temple, and between them and that entrance were the British bluejackets, just getting warmed up to their work.

It was, in the words of one of them, a glorious scrap. Back and forth the fighting, cursing crowd swayed, cutlasses rising and falling, knives flashing and men going down in all directions.

Methodically the bluejackets were driving their men towards the altar, and if they succeeded in getting them there they would literally cut them to pieces.

Blake, who had been busy with the two who meant so much to him, watched the progress of the fight, even as he strove to revive Yvonne, and as the crowd came nearer and nearer to him he lifted her up again to carry her to a place of greater safety.

Then, as he held her to his breast, her eyes opened and the fear in them died out as she saw whom it was who held her. "Oh, it is you!" she breathed.

Blake looked down at her. She seemed very small and very sweet, and very helpless in that moment, and as he bent his head her lips came perilously close to his.

A strand of her soft hair floated across his face and the sweet perfume of it filled him. Then his head went lower, his eyes gazed deeply into hers, her lips parted ever so little, and with a red mist suffusing his eyes Blake pressed her to him, kissing her warm lips fiercely.

The next moment, shaken and trembling from head to foot with a strange, exquisite feeling, he forced his way through to the open air. Tinker followed, and as they got outside they could tell by the sounds within that the bluejackets were forcing the enemy back to the altar.

Just as victory was within their grasp there sounded a sudden rumbling, and the walls of the temple split asunder. They fell to the ground with a roar, and as the stone and dust flew in all directions, bluejackets and Celestials staggered into the open air, coughing and spluttering.

In a moment Blake had grasped what had happened. Wu Ling, who had so strangely disappeared, had not been unprepared for some such contingency as this. Blake's previous visit to the island had taught the prince something.

When he disappeared by the god Mo, he had left the temple by a secret passage and had touched a switch which had blown the walls asunder.

How that struggling horde managed to reach the open air without more casualties was a mystery, but on both sides there were few left within the ruins. Then with the true spirit of the fight which had gripped them, they renewed the struggle. But here the bluejackets redoubled their efforts, and after a sharp struggle the Celestials broke and fled for the safety of the jungle.

The bluejackets went in pursuit, but once the Celestials spread out in the almost impenetrable jungle, it was useless to persist. So Commander Porter whistled for his dogs of war to return, and they gathered by the temple to take toll of the casualties.

They were far less than they had thought would be the case. Two men had gone down in the fight in the temple, while two more had been caught beneath the falling walls. Four deaths in all, with a good many minor wounds.

Of the Celestials they found nine dead and half a dozen cases with severe wounds. So far the honours were with the landing-party.

Now the island of Kaitu is not large as islands go. It rises abruptly from the yellow waters of the China Sea, being the submerged fragment of part of that once great stretch of continent which, in ages past, linked up the Dutch East Indies with Papua and Australia.

It is not an atoll, as one sees in the Polynesian Islands of the South Pacific, but a mountain-top of the old continental shelf, and, like all those peaks which now form the Solomons, New Guinea, and the Dutch East Indies, it possesses a high, jungle-clad, and almost impenetrable hinterland.

Only too well did Sexton Blake know how difficult it would be to follow Wu Ling and his men into those dank, humid depths. Once in the past had he and Tinker attempted to force their way into the country where the hill men held sway, and he still retained the memory of that disastrous affair.

Yet the chase for Wu Ling had been a long one. Was he to leave Kaitu, knowing that Wu Ling was still on the island and unharmed? Every inclination of Blake's nature rebelled against such an idea.

Yvonne and Tinker had been in the grip of the Yellow Tiger, and had the torpedo-boat destroyer arrived only a little later, their fate would have been a terrible one. By now Tinker would have gone into the brazen maw of the god Mo. And Yvonne—ah, Heaven only knew what her fate would have been!

Gazing at the white, drawn face of the girl, whose lips had clung to his such a short time before, Blake vowed that he would go after Wu Ling, and stay on his trail until he had captured him, or killed him.

Once and for all he would wipe from the face of the earth the man who was such a menace to society at large. Wu Ling must be scotched.

With this determination in his mind Blake approached Commander Porter, and, drawing him aside, said:

"I have been thinking over things. I know this island pretty well, and I know exactly how difficult it will be to follow the fugitives into the bush. They may go in as deeply as possible, or they may lurk near the lagoon—we can't tell. But I am much mistaken in my estimate of Wu Ling, if he has not prepared a retreat in the jungle.

"We razed this place once before, and the very perfection of his arrangements here leads me to think that he was not unprepared for any contingency. At the same time I am strongly in favour of hunting him out and ending his career, once and for all. What do you think?"

Commander Porter stroked his beard thoughtfully.

"I am quite prepared to base all calculations on your statements, Blake. You have already proved that you know the island and the man. If you think it advisable to follow them up and make a final settlement with them, I am ready to give you the men with which to do so, but you can understand that I don't want to lose any of my men unnecessarily."

"I realise that, Commander Porter. I will be quite frank with you. The jungle is thick, and if Wu Ling had made some sort of treaty with the hill men who live in the hinterland, then the advance into the jungle will be fraught with extreme danger.

"We are bound to have some casualties—they may be light, or, on the other hand, if the hill men make a strong effort to oppose our advance, then they may be heavy. All the same, I am inclined to think that the object is worth the risk."

"I'll tell you what I will do, Blake," responded the commander, after a moment or two. "I will call my men together, and put the proposal to them. All those who volunteer may go, and I myself will accompany you as well."

Commander Porter spoke to one of his men who stood near, instructing him to call together in front of the ruins of the temple, and, taking up his stand in front of them, the commander addressed them:

"My men," he said. "you have done splendidly to-day. We have achieved part of our purpose on coming here, and before we leave we shall raze this place to the ground. But the man whom we hoped to capture has escaped into the jungle. This man—the arch-mind who rules the Celestial Brotherhood, which is such a menace to the white races of the earth—still goes free.

"Mr. Sexton Blake, who stands beside me, knows the island as well as any white man living. He does not underestimate the dangers and difficulties of penetrating into the jungle in pursuit of the man we want, but he thinks it can be done, and, if possible, to get sufficient volunteers to go, he will undertake it. I may say that I shall accompany him.

"Do any of you wish to volunteer for the attempt? Bear in mind I do not ask you to go. If you do so, it will only be your own free will. All those who wish to do so will take one step forward."

The commander broke off then and waited. There was a restless sort of rustling along the ranks of the men, then, as one big bluejacket at the end of the front rank stepped forward, every bluejacket on the semi-circle followed his suit.

The commander smiled as he saw the result of his words.

"I thought I knew my men," he said with satisfaction, as he turned back to Blake.

Blake nodded.

"They didn't need to be asked," he replied. "Men who fight as they fought to-day are not the men to hang back for all the hill men in the China Sea. I think, Commander Porter, that the sooner we start the better."

Scarcely had Blake uttered the words, when a man suddenly burst through from the cover of the grove between the village and the lagoon. As he ran up they saw it was one of the bluejackets, who had gone aboard the tramp with Midshipman Fortescue. He paused when he reached Commander Porter, and, saluting, said:

"Mr. Fortescue's compliments, sir, and he begs to inform you that the yacht, Fleur-de-Lys, has just come into the lagoon. He wishes to know, sir, if he may permit Mr. Graves to land?"

Commander Porter nodded his head.

"My compliments to Mr. Fortescue, and tell him to permit Mr. Graves to come ashore."

Saluting, the bluejacket turned, and made off. A little later they saw Graves coming through the trees.

It was a strange reunion which he and Yvonne had there before the ruins of the temple, but in that moment they showed how truly deep was the affection which existed between them.

When it had been arranged that Yvonne should go on board the yacht at once, Blake prepared to start for the jungle. He himself took the lead, with Tinker directly behind him, followed by Commander Porter.

Then came the long file of bluejackets, with Lieutenant Trepwitt bringing up the rear.

Slowly, and with infinite caution Blake advanced. He knew he could not get far until morning came, but he was determined to accomplish as much as possible in order to anticipate any counter-move which Wu Ling might attempt.

He knew, too, that during the first part of the journey they would meet with less danger than when they go further along. It would be when they were climbing the trail to the hinterland that they would need every ounce of caution.

The hill men of those islands have some nice little traps for the unwary, one pleasant diversion is to bend down a sapling in the thickest part of the jungle, and to fasten it so that one passing along the faint track, which is known as the trail, must strike it.

The veriest touch releases a poisoned spear, which has been carefully arranged at the height of a man's heart, and before he can save himself he is lying on the ground in the throes of violent convulsions.

Again they find particular pleasure in concealing beneath the thick mulch which has gathered on the trail a small poisoned bar, which the unwary may walk upon. Result—sudden death.

To add to these diversions the hill men have a faculty of loitering along close to the trail screened by the almost impenetrable jungle on either side, and from the safety of this retreat to wing forth poisoned arrows against the unwary. In fact, they are quite a pleasant people those hill men.

Sexton Blake had had more than one sample of their pleasantry in the past, and for this reason he exercised a caution which struck the bluejackets as somewhat unnecessary.

But before that small band got out of the jungle again they thanked their stars that it had been Sexton Blake who had led them into the jungle-clad hinterland.

The roseate hues of dawn were just suffusing the sky when Blake halted at the end of the swampy lowland, at the spot where the upward climb to the hinterland began.

There he reapportioned the loads of arms and ammunition, saw that his party was all right, sent back two men who showed signs of fever, and, lining them up, once more began the climb.

As the hours passed a dim twilight spread through the forest, but never for a single moment did they get a glimpse of the sun. In the heart of those great jungle aisles, twilight, and the dank humidity of the tropics, held perpetual sway.

It was ten o'clock by Blake's watch before they came upon anything which seemed to indicate that their progress would be disputed.

It was one of those spear traps which, cautiously though he was advancing, Blake sprang. As the sapling flew upwards the poisoned spear shot forth from the screen of thick leaves, behind which it had been hidden, flying with a vicious swish past Blake's shoulder, butted itself in a great bank of ferns on the other side of the trail.

Blake paused for a moment, then, watching carefully for a second trap, started on again.

Another hour went by, and though the air was still intensely heavy, there was still a fresher feeling in it than there had been farther back, proving that they were steadily climbing higher.

It was broad noon when, as he suddenly came out upon a wide opening in the forest, the first definite attack came. Then it burst upon them with fierce suddeness.

From the cover of the trees opposite them, a perfect hail of poisoned spears and arrows came flying across the tiny glade.

Blake sprang back quickly, and sharply ordered his men to take cover. Like clumsy elephants, the seamen plunged into the thick screen on either side of the trail, with Blake, Tinker and Commander Porter following closely.

But even then one of the poisoned arrows struck a bluejacket in the breast, and even as he plunged for cover dropped in convulsions of death.

Blake rapped out his orders sharp and clear.

"Make ready to fire!" he ordered. "Ready—fire!"

He himself had snatched up a rifle, and, aiming it at the trees on the other side of the open space, began to fire as rapidly as possible.

A fusillade broke out on all sides, as the bluejackets followed suit, and from the cover of the trees across the glade there came the sound of shrill screams, as the bullets found a mark.

The shower of spears and arrows suddenly stopped, and when Blake gave the order to stop firing, there regained a silence strangely at variance with the pandemonium which only a few moments before had filled the surrounding jungle.

Springing out into the open, Blake called upon his men to follow.

"They will have taken to the jungle," he said rapidly to Commander Porter, who had joined him. "We shall have to be on our watch for the next move."

Going forward, Blake made boldly for the trees across the glade, and plunging into the forest again, started along a trail which was far more distinct than that by which they had travelled during the morning.

A few hundred yards or so he went, before he received the second surprise. Once more he saw that the forest opened up, and as he came out into the open he saw a sight that held him breathless with wonder.

Before him was a sheer descent of open country, which dropped away for a half mile or more. Here and there rose giant trees, which gave it almost the appearance of an English park.

At the foot of the first drop there lay a wide lake, limpid and black in its mysterious beauty.

Suddenly there flashed upon Blake a strange rumour he had heard from the salt-water men of the lagoon. They had told him, in times gone past, of a sacred lake in the interior of the island.

Until then Blake had thought the whole story but a myth. But now he knew that he had come upon the very lake which had been spoken of, and in some way he knew that it was connected with the worship of the golden god Mo.

In a flash he knew that it was here Wu Ling had fled from the temple, and it would be here that they must meet again.

He approached the edge of the drop, and standing easily, gazed down at the expanse of park-like country which stretched before him.

Commander Porter and the bluejackets followed him, and stood about him, waiting for the next word.

Even as they waited, there came to them across the black waters of the lake of a great voice, which droned, sweeping up in deep cadences to the brink on which stood the small body of white men.

"Go back! Go back!" said the voice. "You who desecrate this sacred spot of the god Mo will suffer as man never suffered!"

Then the voice died away, and Blake shaking himself free from the uncanny feeling which threatened to sweep over him, and which he could see had already gripped some of the bluejackets, drew his revolver and dashed down the incline.

"Come on, men!" he cried. "Let us clean out this hole!"

The calm confidence of his voice jerked them out of the spell which was sweeping over them, and, with a loud cheer, the bluejackets tore down the incline after him.

At the same moment a horde of Malays and Celestials appeared close to the edge of the lake, and, screaming with rage, charged up the hill.

They were armed with knives, cutlasses, and rifles, but now that they actually saw that which menaced them, the bluejackets steadied down wonderfully, spreading out to take cover whenever possible, started firing as the went.

Still the savages came on, though many of them went down beneath the hail of lead which the bluejackets poured into them.

Then, when scarcely a hundred yards separated the two forces, Blake gave the order to charge.

With a loud yell the bluejackets sprang from cover and raced forward. They crashed into the front rank of the enemy a few moments later, and in the park which sloped to the edge of that sacred lake there ensued a fight which for savagery and fierceness could scarcely be excelled.

Through the press of the struggle Blake caught a fleeting glimpse of Wu Ling urging on his men to destroy the white men. But, back at the temple, the bluejackets had got the measure of the foe, and now, fighting with cool confidence, they steadily drove them back.

Foot by foot, yard by yard, they retreated, until they stood at the very edge of the black waters of the lake. There the Celestials and Malays made another desperate stand; but Commander Porter cried to his men to strike and strike hard, and, led by Blake and the commander, the whites dashed forward with renewed vigour.

Under the intense onslaught the yellow men wavered, broke, tried to recover, broke again, and dashing down their weapons fled.

Springing out of the crush of the fight, Blake singled out Wu Ling, and keeping his eyes on the yellow tunic of the flying prince, tore along the bank of the lake in pursuit.

A hundred yards or more the prince fled, until ahead there appeared a wide shelf of stone.

There he drew up, and standing at the very edge of the shelf, turned back and faced Blake.

Blake saw Wu Ling raise both hands over his head, saw his eyes flash eternal hatred, saw in them the promise of vengeance, then the prince dived down into the black waters of the lake, which ripped under the impact of his body and closed over his head.

Blake stopped, panting, at the edge of the shelf of stone, and leaning over, gazed down at the lake, waiting for the head of Wu Ling to reappear.

Before he would let the prince escape he, too, would dive into the lake and finish the fight there.

A minute passed, and still Wu Ling did not come to the surface. Two minutes went by, and the black waters of the lake remained limpid as ever.

Three, four, five minutes crawled passed, and then Blake straightened up.

"Suicide," he muttered. "Still, I can scarcely believe that Wu Ling would give in so easily. However, that settles it, and there is nothing to do but to get back to the lagoon as quickly as possible. If the hill men make a fresh attack, things may turn out badly for us."

So it was that a little over an hour later the small party of white men started back along the trail for the coast. It was full evening when they finally came out again to the village, for their return had been retarded owing to the wounded, whom they had been compelled to carry.

In front of the temple, the exhausted party drew to answer the roll call. Then, in charge of Lieutenant Trepwitt, the bluejackets prepared to return to the T.B.D.

When the wounded had been attended to, a party was told to look after the dead.

Sexton Blake stayed behind in order to make a thorough search of the temple. In what had been the alcove devoted to the god Mo he found the golden figure of the god lying on its face, its jade base still intact and beautiful. Blake had it hoisted up and carried down to the beach, the one trophy he wished to take away with him. Then with a party of men he started in and razed the village to the ground, burning it from end to end.

In the blanket of the smoke they retreated to the lagoon and went aboard the yacht, leaving the island to its ruins, its jungle, and what that jungle hid.

As red morn flaunted upwards in the east, the blunt nose of the T.B.D. led the way out to set through the mangrove-lined passage, followed by the slim and rakish-looking Fleur-de-Lys with the tramp bringing up the rear. Dipping a curtsey to the soft caress of the China Sea they sailed away, leaving Wu Ling to brood in his jungle.

Beauremon came with them as far as Batavia, and there they left him. The T.B.D. had gone off with her prize to report, and with its own happy party on board the Fleur-de-Lys sailed through the tropic seas for England.

So ended the strange chase which grew out of the kidnapping of the Munitions Minister by the Yellow Tiger.

. . . . . .

Nor did Sexton Blake dream that as they slipped out to sea from the purple lagoon, which had been their anchorage, a tall Celestial stood on the stone shelf, back at the edge of the sacred lake, with his hands stretched high to Heaven, cursing the whites who had desecrated the retreat of the god Mo, and vowing vengeance on the one man who had led them to that retreat. The waters of the sacred lake had closed over the head of Wu Ling, but in their limpid depths he had not found his grave. Beneath that stone shelf was a cunningly constructed tunnel leading to an underground chamber, where Wu Ling, as High Priest on Earth of the god Mo made worship of his deity. Well was the sacred lake called in Chinese the Lake of Concealment.

THE END

ILL-GOTTEN GAINS;
or, The Secret of Salcoth Island.

CHAPTER 1.
Hector MacLeod—The Rescue.

Big Ben had just struck the hour of midnight when a slender, well-built youngster, with a great hound at his heels, turned out of Bayswater Road through one of the entrances of Hyde Park.

He made his way along the drive, which moves in graceful sweeps down towards the Serpentine and on past the magazine, over the bridge, finally passing out through Alexandra Gate into Knightsbridge.

The lad was moving along at a leisurely pace. The night was rather cold and chilly, and there were very few people about the Park.

Here and there on a seat one could make out the shadowy figure of some belated individual, and now and again a smooth-moving motor would rustle past, the rubber-tyred wheels crunching on the hard gravel.

Once a solitary policeman passed the lad and hound, just as the two came beneath a lamp-post. The constable came to a halt and touched his helmet.

"Good-evening, Mr. Tinker."

The youth smiled and nodded.

"Good-evening," he returned.

The constable stooped and patted the broad flanks of the dog.

"How is old Pedro, eh?"

The hound snuffled his muzzle into the thick palm, then he and his young master went on into the shadows.

Hyde Park was a favourite place for Tinker and the dog to stroll in at night-time. One could always get a breath of fresh air and a clean pair of lungs in that vast breathing space of London.

"Better than being cooped up in a rotten old kennel, eh boy?" Tinker murmured to the animal by his side.

Pedro wagged his broad tail in complete agreement with that remark. They passed the Magazine and began to climb the slight rise that leads to the dimly-lighted bridge.

They were half-way up the rise when suddenly the vast silence was broken. Tinker heard a quick call, more of a sigh than a call, followed by a splash. Then a moment later another voice rang out:

'Help! Help!"

Tinker made a grab at Pedro, but he was too late. He had ventured to unleash the hound, and Pedro was off at a tearing gallop up the slopes.

The lad broke into a run, and, reaching the bridge, darted off along its paved side. He saw a dark figure scramble on to the low parapet, and as soon as it was erect it turned towards him.

"A woman in the water!" he called.

Then the next moment the hands had wedged themselves above the head and the figure had vanished in a long, beautiful dive into the dark waters below.

Tinker fumbled in his pocket and drew out a police-whistle, sending several sharp, clear calls out into the night. He heard an answering call from the drive beyond, and knew that it was his friend the constable who had heard his signal.

He was now quite close to where the stranger had leapt from the parapet, and he leaned forward, peering down into the Serpentine, listening intently.

Presently from beneath he heard a splash, then another, and his eyes growing accustomed to the drakness, he saw a round, wet object appear close to one of the arches of the bridge.

"Come along, Pedro, well have to take a hand in this," Tinker shouted.

He whipped round and darted off along the bridge, almost colliding with the blue-clad policeman who had answered his call.

"Hallo, Mr. Tinker—is it you? What's the matter?"

"Someone in the water," said the lad. "Quick! Let's get a boat!"

They rushed off along the shore, leaping on to one of the landing-stages where a number of boats were tethered. Pedro was the first to leap into the boat, making himself comfortable in the bow, while Tinker scrambled into the stern and the constable dropped in the thwarts, grabbing at the oars.

A strong push saw the boat driven out from the landing-stage, and, pulling with a lusty strength, the policeman urged the boat through the water at a swift rate.

Tinker in the stern grabbed at the tiller-ropes, and he steered the boat towards the arches of the bridge.

Suddenly Pedro, in the bow, threw back his head and gave vent to a low-toned wouff!

"Steady on!" Tinker called, dropping the tiller-ropes and rising to his feet.

The policeman backed water just in the nick of time. A round wet head appeared close to the bow with another by its side. The constable quickly shipped one oar and the boat glided forward, then Tinker, leaning out, grabbed at the swimmer as he passed.

The boat tilted, and there was a brief tussle, then finally Tinker's strong arm prevailed, and the swimmer and his burden were brought close to the side of the little craft.

"Right-o! Hang on!" said Tinker.

There was a gasp from the man in the water.

"Take her first!" came a clear voice; and the policeman reached out and caught at the wet, sodden garments of the woman in the swimmer's arms.

She was drawn up out of the water and laid across the thwarts where she lay still and silent, her wet faced turned up towards the sky, her lips moving, little broken moans coming from them.

"That's all right," said Tinker. "In you get."

He hooked his arm beneath a pair of broad shoulders, and tugged, the rescuer came up over the side of the boat to roll into the stern along with Tinker. The constable slipped the oars out again, and the boat was rowed back to the shore.

The rescue had been carried out with an extraordinary celerity, and a few minutes later the woman and her rescuer were landed on the bank.

"I am all right," the man said. "Don't trouble about me. Look after that poor creature."

One or two casual stragglers had gathered, and presently a hand-ambulance came along. The woman was placed on it, then the policeman, with a nod to Tinker, turned away.

"You will get this gentleman's name and address, Mr. Tinker," he said. "I know you'll look after him all right."

The ambulance moved off, and Tinker slipped out of his coat, holding it towards the rescuer.

"Better get into this, old chap," he said, "then we will find a taxi, and I'll take you home."

The stranger's teeth were chattering slightly, and he was glad of the extra wrap. He and Tinker pressed through the little knot of people, with Pedro at their heels, and they were fortunate enough to find a taxi moving through the drive.

"Where to?" Tinker asked, as he entered the vehicle.

The stranger shook his head.

"I have got no place to go to particularly," he said; "but you needn't trouble about me. I shall be all right."

"Nonsense," said the young detective, and, leaning out of the open window, he told the driver to take them to Baker Street.

About twenty minutes later they were in Sexton Blake's quiet chambers, and Tinker led his companion into his own bedroom and insisted on him changing.

He saw now that the plucky fellow was a youngster of about his own age. He had a pleasant, tanned face, and his speech, despite a slight Northern accent, was that of an educated individual.

"It's awfully good of you," the stranger began.

Tinker shook his head.

"Rubbish!" he said. "I am only lending you an old suit of clothes. If there is any credit to be got out of tonight's affair, you are entitled to it."

He insisted on giving his companion a rub down before the change was effected, and by the time that the stranger had completed his dressing, Tinker had managed to slip down and have a word with the old landlady, with the result that there was a steaming hot cup of beef-tea and a round of toast waiting, when they entered the quiet sitting-room.

Tinker drew a comfortable chair up to the fire and made the stranger seat himself in it and sip at the hot fluid.

"It was jolly lucky for that woman that you were so handy," Tinker said. "What happened?"

"Oh I was resting on a seat close to the bridge," the stranger explained. "I saw that unfortunate woman go past. I don't know how it was, but it seemed to me as though she was thinking of—of finishing everything."

His eyes went hard, and he looked into the fire.

"As a matter of fact," he said, in a strained tone, "I—I had somewhat similar thoughts myself."

"You! Get out!" Tinker put in.

His guest turned towards him, smiling, revealing a set of white perfect teeth.

"Sounds a bit strange, doesn't it?" he said. "Still, it's true. Only, when I saw that poor creature clamber on to the parapet and throw herself into the water, everything seemed to change, somehow."

"And so, instead of committing suicide yourself you rescued another would-be suicide?" said Tinker.

"That's about it."

"You are not a Londoner?"

"Oh, no. I am from the North—Grangepool," the stranger returned.

"What brings you down here?"

"Bad luck."

"How long have you been here?"

"Fortnight."

"Where have you been staying?"

"I stayed at one of the Rowton Houses for the first six or seven days. But even sixpence for a bed was a bit too much for me at last. I've been sleeping in the Park since then."

"But, I say, that's pretty rotten. Couldn't you find something to do?"

The stranger leaned forward, and in his hazel eyes a sudden fire burned.

"Have you ever tried to get a job in London without a—without a character?"

"Can't say I have," said Tinker.

"Then you're lucky," the stranger returned, "for I can tell you it's a hopeless task."

Tinker had had a great deal of experience of men, and he was able to make a pretty accurate guess at a person's character. The strong young features in front of him were pinched with hunger, but the eyes were wide and fearless, and the chin was strong. There was no suggestion of the criminal about the handsome countenance.

"Look here," Tinker said, "I don't want to interfere in your affairs, but perhaps I might be able to help you. In the first place, I am a sort of detective—that is to say, I help my guv'nor. His name is Sexton Blake."

"I think I've heard of him," the stranger replied.

"The guv'nor is known all over the world," said Tinker, "not only as a detective, but as one of the best."

He leaned forward slightly.

"And if you are in trouble, old chap, we might be able to help you," he went on. "You did a jolly plucky thing to-night—just the sort of thing that the guv'nor loves to hear about. You risked your life to save that woman—"

"Oh, I didn't think of it in that way," the stranger broke in. "My life is not of much use to anyone."

"Nonsense! Why, hang it, you are only about a couple of years older than me. What is your age?"

"Just twenty-one."

"You don't look as old as that," Tinker returned. "Anyhow, twenty-one isn't a very extraordinary age. Certainly, you ought not to be fed-up with life yet."

The stranger finished the beef-tea and laid the cup aside. He leaned forward, stretching his hands out towards the fire. Tinker noted that they were well-shaped and smooth, the hands of a man who had never done much rough work.

"You couldn't help me," his guest said at last. "Mine is a case that no one can interfere in, I'm afraid."

"Well, anyhow, it might do you good to tell someone else about it," said Tinker, "and anything you might tell me will be quite confidential."

His keen, alert countenance inspired confidence in everyone. The stranger, with another glance at it, nodded his head.

"Perhaps you're right," he said. "Anyhow, if you really wish to hear my story, I'll tell it you."

He leaned back in the chair, looking musingly into the fire for a few moments.

"My name is Hector MacLeod," he began. "My father was once one of the most prosperous men in Grangepool. It was in the old days, when they used to send out whalers and sealers from Grangepool, and dad owned one of the finest vessels of the lot. They still talk about the Sea Foam in the old town. It had once been one of the fleet that had gone to the Arctic regions on an expedition."

"What happened?" Tinker put in.

"I'm not quite sure," Hector MacLeod continued. "I was only about a year old when dad was ruined. From what I can make out, it was his skipper, a man called Nat Marle, who defrauded him. Marle sailed for the Seal Island, and never came back. I believe that the Sea Foam made an immense catch of seals, worth a tremendous amount of money, but it never returned to Grangepool. Dad lost everything, vessel and property, and it absolutely ruined him. He died about two years later. My mother never got over it, and she soon followed dad. I hardly remember her, for I was brought up by strangers."

"Beastly rough luck!" said Tinker, who, himself an orphan, knew what it was to be alone in the world.

"Oh, I was fairly well treated," said MacLoed. "It was a man named James Phillips, a bank manager, who took me in. I have lived with him ever since, and when I was old enough he gave me a position in the bank. He is one of the directors now, and is quite a wealthy man in Grangepool."

"And you have been employed in his bank, have you?"

"Yes."

Tinker hesitated.

Hector MacLeod noted the hesitation, and smiled.

"I see what's at the back of your mind," he went on, "but you need have no fear. You think I have done something, but it's not true."

His brown fists clenched, and he turned towards his companion.

"All I have been guilty of is falling in love with Ruth Phillips, the daughter of my employer," he said fiercely. "At first her father did not seem to object. He even encouraged it. But about three months ago a big change came over him. He suddenly seemed to hate me, and he did his best to drive me out of Grangepool. I was not living in his home then. I'd taken lodgings for myself. But I used to see Ruth every day, and about a month ago her father told me I was not to see her again. I asked him why, but he would give no reason. He urged me to get another situation, and I refused to do so. At last it came to an open row, and he sacked me."

Tinker watched the strong chin, and saw that it was set and grim, and he realised that perhaps some of Hector MacLeod's trouble had been brought about by his own obstinacy.

"He wouldn't give you a character, then?"

"I wouldn't ask him for one," said Hector. "He treated me so badly that I would not be indebted to him for a thing! As it is, I owe him a lot, for he brought me up; but I'll pay it back some day!"

He stretched his arms above his head. Then his face changed, and a quiet smile crossed it.

"That's really the whole of my story," said MacLeod. "It's not a very exciting one, is it?"

He hesitated for a moment, then suddenly he arose to his feet.

"There is something else," he said. "I received a letter from—from Ruth a week ago. I wrote to her from the Rowton House that I was staying at, and she answered me. There is something in her letter that I can't quite understand."

"Have you got it with you?"

"It's in my other clothes," said Hector.

He left the room, and returned a few moments later with a sodden pocket-book in his hand, out of which he drew a bulky envelope. The envelope was grimed, and the letter inside gave many indications that it had been read and re-read over and over again.

Hector glanced at the letter for a moment, then, with a slight flush, removed the first two pages.

"They—they really concern me," he said.

Tinker half smiled to himself, for he saw the tell-tale flush on the tanned cheeks.

"You can read the others," Hector went on, handing the rest of the letter over.

The handwriting was neat and clear, obviously feminine. It ran as follows:

"Dad seems to be getting worse. He hardly ever stirs out of the house now, and he spends long hours alone at night walking up and down his room. I am sure that he has something on his mind, and his changed appearance frightens me. Last Sunday he dropped asleep in his chair in the study, and I went in with a cup of tea. I didn't dare to wake him, and while I stood there he began to speak in his sleep. I do not remember all he said, but it was something about 'prison gates opening and the dead past returning.'

"Have you ever heard of a place called Salcoth Island, dear? Dad mentioned that name twice, and something about a secret it contained.

"It is all very dreadful, dear Hector, and I miss you so much! I am almost afraid to live in the house with dad now! You ought not to have left Grangepool, for I miss you dreadfully."

The rest of the letter was obviously private, and Tinker only glanced at it before he returned the sheets.

"Where is Salcoth Island?" he asked.

Hector shook his head.

"I don't know," he returned. "Never heard of the place!"

The clock on the mantelpiece chimed the hour of two, and Tinker arose with a start.

"Well, we've had enough jawing for one night, I think," he said. "The guv'nor is away, and will not be back for a couple of days. He's gone down to see a friend of his, the governor of Laidstone Prison. His room is empty, so you might as well use it."

"Oh, no; I—I——"

"Don't be an ass!" said Tinker. "The guv'nor won't object. Besides, you have no place to go to, and I'm hanged if I'm going to turn you out to-night! You have just got to stay!"

He bundled his guest into Blake's quietly-furnished room, and waited there until he saw Hector MacLeod safely between the sheets. When Tinker found himself in his own bedroom again, he began to undress slowly.

"I wonder what's at the back of all this?" the lad thought. "That chap isn't the sort of fellow that a man would turn away without cause. I believe he's as straight as a die, too, and if anyone is in the wrong it's the other party."

It was Hector MacLeod's loneliness and destitution that really attracted Tinker to him, for in Tinker's memory was a period when, he too, had been lonely and destitute in London until that wonderful hour had come when he had first come in contact with his great-hearted, kindly master.

Tinker never forgot the hours when he was a waif, and he had always a soft corner in his heart for anyone in a similar plight.

"You are not the sort of chap that one could help very easily," the lad thought, remembering the stubborn chin and wide eyes, "but I'm going to do it, whether you like it or not."

And so, on the following morning, after breakfast, Tinker took Hector MacLeod's affairs in hand.

"You might as well go down to your Rowton house first," he said.

'There might be another letter waiting for you. I suppose you never thought of going to see?"

Hector hesitated.

"Well, I—I owe one of the attendants a—a shilling," he said. "I didn't want to take it, but the man insisted, and I—I've never been able to repay him yet. I couldn't go there until I had the money to pay back."

They went off to the Rowton house, which was situated in Hammersmith, and Tinker duly paid the kind-hearted attendant. There was a letter waiting for Hector, with the post-mark dated six days previous. As soon as he had broken the seal and read the contents, Hector turned to Tinker.

"There—there's trouble at Grangepool," he broke out. "I think I—I shall have to go back."

"What it is?"

"Ruth's father has—has vanished," said Hector. "But here! Read the letter!"

It was written in a trembling hand, and was very short:

"Dear Hector,—You must come back at once! Dad has gone, and I am distracted. He came home on Tuesday night as usual, and had dinner with me. He seemed to be in a better humour, but the nine o'clock post brought him a letter which altered everything. He went out at ten o'clock, and has never been seen since. I found the enclosed letter in his study, and sent it on to you, for you are the only one I can thrust now. Do come back at once!"

There was another note enclosed, and as Tinker glanced at the heading his eyes lighted up suddenly, for it was the official paper which the prison authorities issue to the convicts in their charge.

It was headed "Laidstone Prison," and ran as follows:

"Dear Sir,—The man from Salcoth Island will be calling on you by the end of the month. He hopes to hear good news.
"No. 72,053—JOSEPH SMITH."

"But how extraordinary!" Tinker broke out. "Laidstone Prison! Why, that's where the guv'nor has been staying for a few days!"

They looked at each other in silence.

"I can't make head or tail of it," said Hector MacLeod, "but I think I shall have to go back to Grangepool."

"How far is it?"

"Oh, I should think the best part of three hundred miles! I can do it in ten days."

Tinker looked at his companion for a moment, then burst into a laugh, and caught at MacLeod's arm.

"Going to walk it, are you, by Jove! You've got a nerve! You'll do it in less than ten days, old chap; on fact, you'll come along with me now, and I'll advance you the fare, and a bit over. And if you say a word against it, I'll give you a punch on the nose!"

80

This pugnacious threat was made in such a quaint manner that, after the briefest hestitation, Hector MacLeod laughed and held out his hand.

"You are a brick, Tinker!" he said. "I met a friend indeed when I met you, but some day I shall make it up to you all right."

And that day was soon to dawn, for out of that strange meeting was to arise a curious and complex case. It was the beginning of an intricate problem, with many ramifications, for behind it all, and working secretly, were two great personalities. Who those two were the ensuing chapter will reveal.

CHAPTER 2.

A Secret of Long Ago.

A deep-toned bell was rolling out its steady summons, the long notes echoing and re-echoing over the great expanse of moorland, and along the roadways and cart-tracks little squads of men were marching like so many gangs of ants heading for the nest.

They were the convicts returning at nightfall to Laidstone Prison. The grey bulk of the gaol stood stark, isolate, and remote on the edge of a long, rolling Yorkshire plain.

All around the prison the scene was fair enough. Great swaithes of gorse bushes, long leagues of heather, and stretches of green turf. In the summer one could catch glimpses of browsing rabbits in the emerald grass, and here and there a lark would soar up into the blue sky singing its song of freedom.

The peace of a contented world hung like a cloud around the grey melancholy pile, but inside the high walls a stern, harsh discipline ruled, and the fettered souls of lawless men fretted in the silence.

In October, however, the mists began to gather around Laidstone, and on this evening the tolling of the bell sent little fugitive echoes twisting and turning in the hollows and byways of the moor.

The great gate of the prison was open, and two armed warders stood, one on either side, watching the gangs of convicts as they came striding through, each with an armed guard marching in front and rear.

They filed on through the half-mist like vague shadows, passing into the yard and wheeling to right or left into the great gloomy buildings.

Close to the gates of the prison there stood a low-roofed structure, and at one of the windows a man was standing, watching the gangs file in. He was dressed in the prison clothes, and on his undersized, shrivelled body the loose-fitting garments hung in a shapeless way.

There was nothing to distinguish him form the herd outside except his face. It was an extraordinary one—a large, dome-shaped forehead, thick, beetling brows, beneath which two hard black eyes shone. There was a suggestion of the vulture in the visage—the small, pointed chin, the hooked nose, and the thin, expressionless lips.

His head was craning forward slightly, giving him a bird-like aspect, and he was staring at the groups of convicts as they passed.

Presently there came swinging on through the gate another gang. The man at the window peered out, and his eyes rested on a massive figure marching in the front rank. A giant of a man, he was, in his convict clothes, with bull-like throat, strong, merciless countenance.

Just for a moment the huge figure turned its head towards the low-roofed building. Raising a claw-like hand, the man behind the window tapped on the pane. The tall convict nodded a quick return to the signal; then the gang passed on, and the man at the window turned his head and glanced into the interior of the long chamber.

It was the hospital of the prison. On either side were arranged long rows of narrow cots. At one end of the ward was a cubicle marked "Dispensary," and a fire was glowing at the top.

The little figure at the window turned and began to pace along the chamber.

A convict's life is necessarily a hard one, and a man has to be really ill before the authorities will allow him the privilege of rest.

At that moment there was only one other man in the ward. He was lying on the cot nearest to the fire, and as the wizened little man came closer, the patient stirred uneasily and raised his head.

"That you, matey?"

"Yes."

"My head's bad. Give me summat."

The man on the bed raised himself slightly and looked up into the vulture-like counternance.

"Go on," he cried; "they won't know. Give me summat for my head."

Across the features of the man above him there stole a slow smile.

"It's against orders," he returned; "but I'll give you something presently."

"You're a good 'un—better than the doctor here. He doesn't know nothing, he doesn't." The patient laughed weakly. "Anyone can see how he looks up to you in this sort of game," he went on.

The attendant shrugged his shoulders.

"The doctor is in rather a difficult position," he returned. "Years ago, many years ago, he was a student in the hospital that I was head of."

The man on the bed gave vent to a chuckling laugh.

"Blow me, that's funny, that is! I thought there was summat like that in it," he said.

Then a sudden idea seemed to come to him. He reached out a weak hand and caught at his companion's sleeve.

"What about me?" he said. "You ought to know. What's goin' to happen to me?"

The vulture face twitched for a moment.

"If you want to know the truth, my friend," the attendant returned, "you are going to die!"

81

"No, no! For Heaven's sake, don't say that!"

"You asked for the truth, and I have given it to you."

The feeble hand on the attendant's arm tightened its grip.

"But I tell you I must not die—I ain't goin' to die! They were goin' to let me out they were. I only 'ad another two or three days to go; then—then——"

The voice broke off into a wailing cry.

"It's not a bit of use," came the cold voice. "If you don't believe me, ask the doctor."

There was a long silence then.

"How long—how long do you give me to—to live?"

The lean-visaged attendant bent down, and the long, thin hands moved over the patient's face for a moment, raising the eyelids and peering into the dimmed pupils.

"You may last another day," came the reply; "certainly not longer."

The figure dropped back on the bed and tossed to and fro, the chest rising and falling, thin, broken sobs coming from between the parted lips.

"Come, come!" the cold-voiced attendant said. "After all, it means release for you doesn't it? You have been here long enough, Heaven knows. You were a 'lifer', weren't you?"

"Yes, yes; I've been in here the best part of twenty years."

The attendant sat down on the side of the cot and looked at the huddled figure.

"I think you ought to be glad to die."

"No, no; I heard they were going to let me out for good conduct. I was expecting to go this month, and I—I was looking forward to—to revenge."

A sudden change come over the patient. The weak, childish expression on his face died away, and he turned towards his companion.

"What's your name?" he asked.

"I am not a name, I'm a number."

"But you had a name once. Quick! Tell me! Mebbe it'll be worth you while."

There was a moments's silence, then the vulture-like man leaned forward slightly.

"In London I was known as Professor Kew," came the reply; "But I doubt very much if you ever heard of me, my friend. You have been in prison nearly twenty years, and that's a long time."

There was another silence, then the man on the cot turned his head again.

"Look here," he said, "if I've got to die, I've got to; but there's summat that's got to be done, and as I can't do it myself you'll have to do it for me."

"What is it?"

"I want to square a little account of mine. Twenty years ago I did a man a bad turn, and I didn't reap any benefit of it either. It seems to me now that someone else has reaped that benefit, and I want to put things square."

The sunken eyes were fixed on Kew's face.

"There's a matter of twenty thousand pounds in this," the dying man went on, "and that's a big sum of money."

"What is your story?" Kew asked.

"In here I am known as Joseph Smith, but my right name is Nat Marle. Years ago I held a master's certificate, and I was captain of a sealer that sailed from Grangepool. The Seafoam was her name, and she was just as stout a boat as ever tackled the Arctic seas."

His head dropped back on the pillow, and his voice took on a softer note.

"Ah, but these were the good days. Hard work it was, and cold—lumme, yes, it was cold. But we got money. I can hear the roar of 'em now. I bet there used to be thousands and thousands of 'em—the mother seals and the young 'uns and the bachelors—all fightin' together. It used to be clubs in those days—hit among 'em with the clubs, laying' 'em out right an' left—thud, thud, thud! I tell yer, there was money to be made then."

It seemed as though the man would go on for an indefinite period in his half trance-like musings. Kew leaned forward and touched him on the shoulder.

"What about your story?" he asked.

The dying man aroused himself with a start.

"Yes, yes; I was forgetting. Well, one season I was in charge o' the Seafoam, and we struck it rich, we did. Inside of a month we was absolutely packed up wi' pelts, the best haul that a sealer ever made. It was when we were just about to start for home that the thought came to me of all the money that was down there in the hold. I knew I could find a free market for the goods anywhere, and I went for'ard and talked it over with the men. They was all agreeable, and, to cut a long story short, I sold the Seafoam and its cargo to an American skipper. I gave a fair share to the crew, and kept the rest for myself."

"How much was that?"

The man on the bed leaned forward.

"The best part of twenty thousand pounds," he said.

"What did you do then?"

"I went back to Grangepool," the patient went on. "I'd grown a beard and wore specs, so nobody recognised me. I slipped into a bank there, an' deposited the twenty thousand with the manager. His name was James Philips. He gave me a receipt for the money, and I cleared out o' Grangepool that same night."

He drew a deep breath.

"I did another voyage, and this time went to the Russian parts. There's an island called Salcoth, and on it there's a hut where a half-caste Eskimo always lives, year in and year out. I had the Seafoam's papers and the deposit note with me, and just to make things sure I left them in the hut. They are in a little steel box buried in the floor."

"Yes; go on."

"I was unlucky that trip. Two days before we got back to England there was a row on board."

The man's voice became stronger suddenly.

"I swear it was an accident, but I was among the mob, and in the fight the first-mate was killed. I struck the blow; but how was I to know that his skull was like a piece of tissue-paper? Anyhow, I was brought up to the Hull Assizes, and it was touch-an² go wi' me. They might have hanged me, but instead of that they gave me the long stretch."

"And so there's twenty thousand pounds in your name in the bank at Grangepool?"

"Yes. It's called the Grangepool and District Bank," said the dying convict.

"What about the manager—James Phillips? Does he know what's happened to you?"

"Yes. I wrote to him twice while I was waiting for trial, but he never answered my letters. But I saw him at the court—oh, yes, I saw him! He thought I didn't twig him there, but he was wrong. I wrote to him asking him for some money, but he never replied."

A fierce look came into the man's face.

"I believe that if I had been able to use some of the money, I'd have got off," he went on; "but I hadn't the cash to get any tip-top man to look after me."

"Then this bank-manager knows that you are a 'lifer'. What has he done with the money?"

"Stuck to it, I'll swear," came the hoarse whisper. "It really belongs to my owner, Malcom MacLeod. I swindled him out of it and it practically ruined him. Phillips knew me—knew who I was, but he kept that to himself. He stuck to the twenty thousand, and all these years I've waited."

"What were you going to do?"

"I wrote to him only a few days ago—last Tuesday," came the grim reply. "I had heard that they were going to let me out soon and I warned Phillips that I was on his track. Then this thing happened, and you tell me I'm going to die."

Kew was looking at the man intently. He lay on his back, a huge figure, almost filling the cot. The long confinement in prison had tinged the hair with grey, the cheeks were hollow, and the eyes sunken, but at one time Nat Marle, must have been a heavily-built, powerful-looking man.

"Yes, you are going to die," said Kew. "No one in the world can save you, not even I."

"I—I must put things straight," the man on the bed murmured. "I know that my old master MacLeod had a boy, a baby he was when I left. The money ought to be his, it ought to be his. I'd like to give it back to him."

He looked up into Kew's face.

"Couldn't I manage that?" he said. "If I was to tell the governor here couldn't he—couldn't he arrange it?"

Into the black eyes of the attendant there leapt a sudden malicious light. The story he had heard had caught at his keen intellect. Already Kew had planned one great move, and now the news that Marle had given him made his scheme take another shape.

"I think I will tell the governor. He would arrange it."

The man on the cot was talking half to himself, and Kew arose to his feet, glaring, down at the muttering patient.

"Do you hear me matey?" Marle's voice range out. "Tell the doctor that I want to see the governor. He will be coming round presently."

It was getting close to the hour when the surgeon made his evening visit. Kew glanced at the clock on the mantelpiece.

"Go on, matey; you'll tell the doctor, won't you?"

It seemed as though Marle, now that he had reached the end of his wasted life, was desirous of making restitution. It was certainly a belated penitence, but it was obvious from the anxiety in the voice that it was sincere enough.

"All right, I'll tell him."

Kew slipped away from the cot and shuffled down towards the dispensary. He disappeared inside, and as soon as the door closed behind him, his clothful manner vanished. He darted across to where a number of bottles stood on a shelf, and, with quick, certain fingers, took out one or two phials.

Bending down, Kew picked up a piece of cotton-wool. He had measured out several drops of the fluids from the various bottles into a test-tube, then lighting a spirit lamp, he held the test-tube in the blue flame. The liquid in the tube began to splutter, and from it there came up a yellow, pungent smoke.

Kew held the cotton-wool in the smoke for a few moments, then extinguishing the flame, he emptied the test-tube into the sink and rinsed it out.

He had just completed this task when the clock began to chime the hour of six. Kew hurried out of the little cubicle and walked towards the cot.

The sound of voices came to his ears, and he recognised the clear one of the surgeon. Darting to the bedside Kew lunged forward suddenly and placed the cotton-wool over the patient's mouth and nostrils. There was a feeble struggle, a choking gasp or two, then the heavy figure of Marle went limp and his hands relaxed, falling to his sides.

Kew withdrew the cotton-wool, and, keeping it at arm's-length, ran to the fireplace, dropping it in the flames. There spurted up yellow light for a moment, then the wadding consumed.

The door at the end of the ward opened and Kew saw the surgeon appear. He was accompanied by a man in quiet blue-serge. They came up the ward together, and Kew, leaning in the shadows of the fireplace, watched them.

The surgeon bent over the patient. Marle was breathing thickly, heavily, with an ominous rattle in the throat.

"Orderly!"

There was a certain deference in the surgeon's voice as he called. Kew's mis-shapen figure straightened up, and he came forward slowly to the side of the cot. The surgeon pointed to the patient.

"I think he is nearly finished, don't you?"

The vulture-like man leaned forward and pretended to examine the convict on the bed. The lips were parted and the breath was coming and going in thin gasps.

"He may linger for an hour or two," said Kew; "but I don't think he will recover conciousness."

At the sound of his voice, the man who had been standing beside the surgeon started slightly, and took a pace forward. Kew, still bending over his patient, turned his bird-like face, and looked up. Into the hawk-like eyes there flashed for a moment a look of utter hatred, which was answered by a stare from the steel-blue ones above him.

"You have met this—this man before then?" said the surgeon, turning to his companion.

The clean-shaven face was set and grim.

"Yes," said Sexton Blake. "I have met him before."

Kew had moved away from the cot now, and was standing in a sullen attitude at the window. His face was set in its usual expressionless manner. Only his eyes, quick and vivid, moved restlessly, first searching Blakes face, then lingering for a moment on the pallid one of the patient on the cot.

"All right, orderly. You had better call me when any change takes place."

Kew bowed with a quick, sardonic smile, and the surgeon turned away, pacing off down the ward, accompanied by Blake.

"An extraordinary man that," said the doctor. "I have no doubt he is a criminal, but, well—he was one of the cleverest physicians in London."

He was speaking in a half apologetic tone, and Blake smiled.

"I know Professor Kew very well," he said. "In fact, I, personally, am responsible for his present position. He was a clever doctor, but he was also a clever criminal, and the world is better for his absence."

He looked at the prison surgeon.

"Personally," he said, "I would not trust him in there."

"Oh, but what harm can he do?" the surgeon asked. "He is very useful in the ward, and he certainly would be no good outside. He is physically unfitted for the hard work on the moors, but his long hospital experience makes him valuable where he is now."

"Perhaps so," said the detective. 'Still, I wouldn't trust him!"

They made their way across the wide yard, and, from the window of the hospital, Kew watched them go. His claw-like hands were folded until the knuckles gleamed dully through the white flesh.

"Blake!" he murmured beneath his breath. "So fate has sent that man across my path again, and just at the moment when I have practically completed my plans!"

His eyes fell on the man on the cot, and he laughed sullenly.

"That was a near thing!" he muttered. "Had you spoken, it would have spoiled everything. As it is, I made you dumb—just in the nick of time!"

In the governor's house that evening, Blake sat down to his last meal there. At about nine o'clock the surgeon joined them and, before seating himself, he made his report.

"Convict No. 72,053 is dying sir," he said. "I thought the poor beggar was doomed."

"Yes, It's very hard lines on him," the governor returned. "He was a good-conduct man, and was going to be released very soon."

"Is that the man I saw in the hospital this evening?" Blake asked.

"Yes," the surgeon returned, smiling at Blake. "Mr Blake doesn't like the idea of Kew being in the hospital, sir," he said to the governor. "He doesn't trust him."

The head of the prison, a blond giant, laughed.

"There are two of Mr. Blake's particular enemies at Laidstone just now, doctor," he said—"the man Kew and that huge fellow, who is a recent arrival, No. 24,750. In the outer world he was known as Count Ivor Carlac."

"I don't think I know him," said the surgeon. "At least, he has never come under my care."

Blake laughed.

"Oh no!" he returned. "Ivor Carlac is hardly the man to be put in a hospital ward. He's a strong as a bull!"

The governor puffed at his cigar.

"Yes, doctor. Mr. Blake has been trying to make me feel anxious. He doesn't like the idea of those two men being under the same roof, but I think I can trust my staff to keep their eyes on 'em."

"I certainly hope so," said Blake quietly, "for in my opinion those two men are the most dangerous criminals in the world. Both Kew and Carlac had long runs, and it cost me a great deal of time and trouble before I finally settled them."

"Oh, well, you can leave it to me, Blake, my dear chap," said the governor. "Carlac and Kew are in Laidstone, and in Laidstone they'll remain! There has only been one attempt at escape made in this prison during the last ten years, and he was shot before he got a hundred yards away."

He leaned back in his chair.

"It's impossible for anyone to escape at night," the head of the prison went on. "The walls are lighted up—a little idea of my own. A fly couldn't creep over the wall without being observed. Then, of course, during the daytime the work gangs are under a close guard. We are not so bad as Dartmoor, you know. There's not so many mists here, and I've made it a rule that when the fogs do come all work stops, and we use chains."

He laughed—a rollicking, jovial sound.

"In fact," he added, "I can assure you that everything is just as it should be at Laidstone, and if Carlac and Kew can escape from here, then they will have to do so by some superhuman method."

The worthy gentleman had every reason to be proud of his arrangements, but he had not reckoned with the cunning of the dwarf-like man in the hospital ward.

When Blake entered the train that evening at the quiet railway-station, he had a foreboding in his heart that he could not quench. He leaned out of the carriage window to catch a last glimpse of the huge pile of Laidstone Prison.

"There is something in the wind," he told himself. "Kew is plotting. I'm sure of it. I saw fear in his eyes when looked up at me, and that could only have been inspired by one thing. He must have some scheme afoot, and I am the only man that has ever checked him. By Jove, I'd give anything to prevent him from getting into the world again! The man is ruthless and merciless, and behind prison walls is the only place for him."

Sexton Blake was soon to find out how correct his judgment had been.

Link by link a chain was being formed that was to encircle for a brief spell the lives of those two criminals with that of Blake and Tinker, young Hector MacLeod, and the other characters in Grangepool.

CHAPTER 3.

The Escape.

At about nine o'clock in the morning of the day following, Blake's visit to Laidstone prison, the bell in the chapel began to toll, and its mournful notes came to the ears of the gang working on the lonely moor.

There were only a few chimes, then silence, but the hard-featured men glanced at each other, and the whisper passed round: "No. 72,053 was dead!"

Rigid silence is enforced in all our prisons, yet by some mystic means the happenings in the prison pass from soul to soul, nor have the authorities ever been able to check that practice.

No. 10 gang, the one in which Count Ivor Carlac worked, were engaged in making a road—a broad, smooth track from the main highway to the prison.

Carlac was one of the barrow men, and the strength of the convict was visible in the way in which he handled the heavy loads on the barrow.

He worked, as a rule, in a sullen, aloof silence, and, as the warders observed, even the men in his own gang seemed to treat him as a superior being.

It was rather grotesque this deference, but it was, nevertheless, very real. Carlac's magnetic personality, that had brought him to the forefront of European criminals, could not be quenched even in the drab life behind prison walls.

That morning, however, as the bell tolled in the chapel he paused to exchange a whisper to the man by his side.

"That's Smith, isn't it?"

"Yes; he's gone."

A glint came into Carlac's eyes, and for the rest of the day he seemed as though he had found a new strength. He was indefatigable, and the grim-jowled warder in charge of the gang spoke to him at last.

"You needn't overdo it," the man said; "you'll kill yourself if you go on at that rate."

Carlac straightened his broad shoulders and glanced at the man. The warder had meant the remark kindly enough, but there was a sardonic smile on Carlac's face.

"It pleases me to work hard," he said.

At dusk, when the work was over for the day, the gang fell in to be marched back to the prison. Carlac placed himself as usual in the leading file, the warder gave the gruff word of command, and the gang began to trudge wearily towards the prison gates.

Just as they entered Carlac shot a quick glance to the right. The door of the hospital was open, and standing in it was the wizened figure of Kew. An imperceptible signal passed between the two; then Kew nodded towards a rough gravel path.

There was a round white pebble lying directly in Carlac's track. The big convict stumbled, apparently tripped, and fell on his face. The gang came to a halt, and the warder whipped round with an angry word.

He was just in time to see Carlac pick himself to his feet again. There was a faint trickle of blood on the man's check, and the warder stepped up to him.

"What's the matter with you?"

Carlac lifted a hand and brushed it across his face.

"All right," he said; "I felt a little faint, but I'm all right now."

The warder looked at him doubtfully, but Carlac straightened his shoulders.

"All right!" he repeated; and, apparently satisfied, the warder marched the gang on up the yard and into the prison.

Before the men were dismissed to their cells they were searched as usual, but this was a somewhat perfunctory ordeal. Carlac, with a little white pebble in his mouth, did not allow a muscle to relax as the warder ran his hands over the convict's clothes.

The gang was marched up to the second floor and along the iron corridor. Carlac's cell was an end one, and he passed into it, while the door clanged to behind him.

Stepping over to the hard wooden bed, the master criminal seated himself on it, then extracted the pebble from between his lips and looked at it.

To an ordinary observer it appeared just a common piece of flint, with the usual coating of chalk. Carlac began to scrape the chalk away with his fingers until at last he had a heap of white powder, just about as much as would cover a sixpence, in the palm of his hand.

He placed the powder carefully on one side, then thrust the bit of flint into a corner of his cell.

Half an hour later the clang of a heavy handle indicated that the final meal of the day was being brought round. Carlac leapt to his feet and scraped the white powder into his hand, glancing at it for a moment.

"I must take the risk," he thought. "Kew is no fool. Here goes!"

A moment later the powder was placed on his tongue and swallowed. Carlac sat upright in his cell waiting.

A sudden icy thrill ran through his bones from head to toe; he felt the cell swing round, and staggering to the door, he beat on it with clenched fists.

A half-strangled cry came from his lips that carried to the ears of the warder in the passage. The man came hurrying down, and opened the door of the cell.

Carlac was lying on his face, his fists clenched, his eyes closed. For a moment the warder thought the convict was dead. He dropped on one knee and leaned forward. Heavy laboured breathing came to him, and he leapt to his feet again.

Four minutes later a couple of convicts, carrying a creaking stretcher, came swinging across the yard, and entered the hospital ward.

Carlac's heavy body was lifted on to one of the cots, and the surgeon was hastily summoned. The unconscious man's appearance suggested a touch of apoplexy, and Kew, standing on the other side of the cot, nodded his head as the surgeon gave his verdict.

"It's only a temporary collapse," the doctor said. "Whose gang does he belong to?"

"To mine, sir," said the warder.

"Has he been taken like this before?"

The warder shook his head.

"No, sir; but he was working rather hard to-day. In fact, I told him not to overdo it. Then he had a bit of a collapse as he entered the gates."

"Oh, well; that's all right! Twenty-four hours will see him on his feet again."

The doctor wrote out a prescription and handed it to Kew, who took the paper without a word. During the two years that Kew had served in that prison he had been of exemplary character, and, little by little, the young medical officer had commenced to trust the man.

"You know what to do, orderly," the surgeon said, as he turned away. "You can let me know if his condition changes for the worse."

He left the hospital, followed by the warder. As soon as they were gone a swift change came over Kew's attitude. His meek manner vanished, and he darted up the ward into the dispensary, returning a moment later with a tiny glass of amber-coloured liquid.

Raising Carlac's head he poured the liquid between the lips, then held him steady for a moment. There was a tremor and movement from the massive convict, and Carlac opened his eyes, staring round him dazedly for a moment.

Gradually his eyes fixed themselves on Kew's face, and dawning intelligence entered them.

"All right, my friend," said Kew. "We arranged that very nicely."

Carlac caught at the claw-like hand.

"I thought you—you had tricked me," he broke out. "That drug was lightning-like in its effect."

"I meant it to be," said Kew, with a sardonic smile. "Our worthy doctor was assured that it was apoplexy. You are safe for twenty-four hours. Get up!"

Carlac swung himself round and stood up. He had to clutch at Kew for a moment, but gradually his reeling brain righted itself, and he raised his arms above his head.

"Wonderful!" he said. "I feel as fit as ever. All trace of the drug seems to have gone."

"The antidote was as strong as the drug," said Kew. 'Besides, I want you to have all your strength; you'll need it."

The master-criminal dropped back on the cot again, glancing into Kew's eyes.

"We must come to some sort of understanding," he said. 'So far, I have trusted implicity to you. I received your message and agreed to come in with you; but I want to know more now."

Each of the criminals were of strong personality, and Kew realised that he had a man of his own calibre to deal with.

"Right!" he said. "I have put all my cards into it. Listen to me!"

He pointed towards a door at the end of the ward.

"Convict Smith died last night," said Kew. "He was unconscious to the end. Had he not been unconscious, what I am about to suggest would not have been worth while."

"Go on."

Very briefly Kew told Carlac the strange history that the man Marle had revealed to him. Suddenly the vulture-like man arose to his feet.

"It gives me a reason for escape," he said, in a thin voice. "For over a year I have been planning this—waiting for someone like yourself to come and help me. Marle's story simply makes the scheme I have worth while. If you and I can get out of here, I promise you that we shall be rich men."

He looked into Carlac's face.

"You are very like Marle," he said, "and with very little alteration I can make you to exactly resemble him as he appeared here. Anyhow, this bank manager, Phillips, has already been warned that Marle was coming back for his money. I think that Phillips must have gone crook and stuck to the money himself. But even if he hasn't that doesn't matter. In a hut on Salcoth Island there is hidden the ship's papers of the Seafoam, and also the deposit note given to Marle by Phillips twenty years ago. When we escape from here we will go to Grangepool first, and tackle Phillips. Then twenty thousand pounds will be ours."

He threw back his head and laughed, his yellow teeth gleaming.

"Twenty thousand pounds is quite a decent little sum to start into business with again—eh, Count Carlac?"

The massively-built criminal nodded his head.

"Yes," he returned; "twenty thousand pounds is a tidy sum. But you haven't yet told me how we are going to escape."

He glanced around the ward.

"Don't you know that Laidstone Prison has a reputation of never allowing a single soul to get away from it? The governor prides himself on that."

Kew's face lifted up into a slow smile.

"The governor's pride has to have a fall," he returned. "You and I will be able to clear out of this place to-night."

"What do you mean?"

"Listen to me!" said Kew. "At about nine o'clock this evening the big laundry-van comes in to take away the soiled linen. It is a motor-van."

"Yes—go on!"

"After the man has collected all the washing from the staff quarters, he comes to the hospital here. I have usually a couple of baskets for him. Of course there's a warder, but he waits outside watching the van."

"Yes?"

"The vanman comes in here, takes the baskets out, and puts them into the van; then drives off. The hospital is the last place that he calls at."

Kew stepped into the centre of the ward and beckoned to Carlac.

"Come along," he said, "and I'll show you what I mean."

He led the way down the ward into an ante-room. There were a couple of huge laundry-baskets standing in one corner. Kew raised the lid of one, revealing the fact that it was full of soiled linen. Then he stepped up to the other and opened it.

It was empty.

"Watch!" he said.

A moment later the professor had stepped into the basket and dropped the lid over him. His small monkey frame was easily concealed in the capacious basket.

Presently he pushed the lid up again and stepped out.

"This is my plan," he said. "The van comes to a halt at the door there. The warder usually lounges outside. He does so because he is afraid that someone may slip into the van while the driver's back is turned. The vanman comes in here and takes the baskets away. Now this is my plan. I am going to let him take out the first basket; then as he comes in here again to take out the second one, I'm going to attack him. You must be waiting just inside the ward, and as soon as I signal to you, you must come and change into the driver's clothes. It will have to be quick work, Carlac—only just time to put on the long coat, and with the peaked cap drawn down over your eyes you will be safe from detection. I'll get into the basket and you must carry me in the basket and place it in the van."

"What sort of motor is it?" Carlac asked.

"A Daimler," Kew returned.

Carlac nodded his head.

"That's all right, then!" he returned. "I have driven a Daimler many times before."

Kew seated himself on one of the baskets, and glanced at the man who was to be his confederate.

"What do you think of the plan?" he asked.

"It has every chance of success," the count returned.

It was ten minutes past nine before the heavily-laden laundry van, having completed its round of the dismal prison, came to a halt outside the door of the waiting room of the hospital.

The armed warder who had stolidly trudged round behind the van lowered his carbine, and nodded to the vanman as he passed.

"Thank goodness that's the last call, my man," he said. "I shall be glad to get back to my supper."

"So shall I," said the vanman, as he stepped up to the door and turned the knob.

He entered the anti-room, to find Kew waiting for him.

"How many to-night?" the man asked.

Kew pointed to the two baskets, and the laundryman, a hefty fellow, tilted one of them up and, swinging it on to his broad shoulder, stalked through the doorway to his van. He slid the basket into its place, pushing it well into the interior, so as to leave room for the second one.

Kew had stepped aside as the man left the room, and from his pocket the criminal drew out a small tube. There was a plunger at the end of the tube, fully drawn. Kew, leaning against the wall, waited.

The vanman entered again, and as he passed through the door Kew slid his foot forward and pushed the door to. It swung into its place noiselessly, and the vanman was just leaning over the second basket as Kew turned.

Two quick, cat-like paces brought the professor to where the laundryman was bending forward. The tube was aimed and, with a quick thrust of his palm, Kew pressed the plunger forward.

A little, feathery spume of yellow smoke shot out from the tube, enveloping the head of the vanman. There was a choking gasp, the man's hold relaxed, and he rolled over on to the basket, then to the floor.

"Quick, Carlac!"

The door leading to the ward opened, and Carlac leapt through it. Kew was already bending over the inanimate form, tugging at the buttons of the coat.

In less time than it takes to tell, Carlac had dressed himself in the long overcoat, and had drawn the peaked cap over his eyes.

"Lift him up! Come along!"

Kew reached for the man's feet, and Carlac took the shoulders. Then, at a run, they carried the unconscious laundryman into the ward, and laid him on the cot that Carlac had recently vacated, drawing the sheet over the head.

They rushed for the small room again, and Kew leapt into the basket, drawing the lid down, while Carlac turned the key in the little padlock.

A moment later the powerful criminal had slung the heavy basket on to his shoulder, and was stalking out through the door. He went round to the back of the van, placing the basket on the tilt and pushing it into the interior. Then, leisurely he raised the tilt, adjusting it into its place and lowering the flap of the canvas.

The warder lifted his carbine and slung it over his shoulder.

"All right now?" he said.

"Yes," Carlac returned, with a nod of his head as he made towards the front of the motor.

The warder stood aside, watching Carlac at work. It was just as well for the master criminal that he knew the engine. He found the magnetic switch, turned it on, then adjusted the throttle. Passing round to the front of the bonnet, he gave a swing to the starting-handle and the powerful engine commenced to hum.

A moment later Carlac had swung into his place, slipped the first gear into position, and the heavy laundry-van lumbered slowly forward, out through the prison gates, turning to the left of the broad highway.

Carlac heard the clang of the iron gates as they closed behind him, and the heavy van, gethering speed at every turn of its wheels, went thundering on down the dark road.

The man at the wheel was smiling to himself as he steered. The tang of the fresh night air on his face was like a breath of freedom, and the peace of the moors was like the cold joy in his heart.

For seven miles he drove the van forward; then coming to a halt at a lonely part of the road, where a thin growth of trees stood, he leapt from his seat and went round to the rear of the van.

He lowered the back, then, clambering inside the vehicle, he unloosed the padlock, and lifted the lid of one of the baskets. Kew rose up out of the darkness like a wraith.

There were one or two beads of sweat on the vulture face, and he raised a hand and brushed them aside.

"Very warm inside there!" said Kew. "But you have done quite right. How far have you come?"

"About seven miles," said Carlac.

"Good!"

Kew stepped out of the basket, and turned towards the other one that had been taken from the hospital. With a quick wrench, he undid the lock and lifted the lid. Then, rummaging through the soiled linen, he produced a couple of clothes.

"Where did you get these?" Carlac asked with surprise.

Kew smiled grimly.

"One suit belongs to the governor of Laidstone, and the other to my friend the doctor," he said. "I told the doctor a few days ago that I had found a new fluid that was very useful for renovating old clothes, and I cleaned one or two suits for him. He was so pleased with the result that he told the governor about it, and they sent these two suits to me to be cleaned."

He dropped from the van into the road and, selecting one suit of clothes, tossed the other to Carlac.

"We could not have gone very far with the broad arrow on us," he said, "but with these we are safe. We had better change now."

He slipped into the woods, and Carlac did the same. A few moments later they emerged again, dressed in the stolen clothes. Kew was carrying his convict garments over his arm, and he told Carlac to bring his discarded suit with him.

"There is a bridge about four miles farther on," the professor explained—"a bridge that has a very low parapet. We are going to enact a small tragedy there."

Carlac gathered his clothes and placed them on the seat of the van. Then he and Kew climbed into their positions, and Carlac took the wheel once more.

About twenty minutes later they reached the bridge and, just as they gained the centre of it, Kew held up his hand.

"I get out here," he said, "and I want you to just fix it up so that the van will go over there into the river. Can you manage it?"

A deep laugh broke from Carlac's lips.

"Yes, I can manage it."

Kew slipped from his seat, and Carlac engaged the first speed again; then, allowing the engine to race for a moment, he slipped in the clutch and swung the steering wheel round hard to the left. The heavy vehicle barged forward, and Carlac swung from his seat, hung on to the wheel until the front of the bonnet was only a yard away form the low parapet, then, opening the throttle to the full extent, Carlac leapt for safety.

The huge Daimler van went butting at the parapet full tilt. There was a crash and a jar, then the low wall gave way, and the heavy motor went hurtling into the stream below.

Kew was leaning over the edge of the parapet lower down, and as the black mass went headlong into the river, the lean head nodded and a claw-like hand was waved in a mocking farewell.

"It'll make quite a startling headline!" he said, as he came towards Carlac.

"THRILLING ATTEMPT TO ESCAPE."

"TWO CONVICTS MEET TERRIBLE DEATH."

Carlac laughed.

"All the better for us if that does happen, for it will give us a clear run," he said.

They went on across the bridge, trudging along the dark roadway until they reached a point where the road splayed out in three different tracks.

"We will go north," said Kew. "Grangepool lies north, and that is our happy hunting-ground for the moment."

Side by side in the darkness they went on, to vanish at last into the silence of the night.

CHAPTER 4.

A Guilty Conscience.

Grangepool is a seaport town, with a splendid history, although modern commerce has chosen now to ignore its quiet little haven. In the good old days of the past, Grangepool owned a vast fleet of whalers and sealers, vying even with Dundee in that respect.

It has still a fair coast trade, and many of the coal-grimed vessels that ply in and out were at one time used on the old whaling expeditions.

88

The town itself is a straggling collection of houses around the harbour. There is the old town and the new town, a more modern division placed somewhat higher up the cliffs.

The house of James Phillips was in the new portion of the town—a handsome red-brick structure, standing in its own shaded grounds.

One afternoon, about two days following the escape of Carlace and Kew from Laidstone Prison, Hector MacLeod was seated in the drawing-room of the house, while Ruth Phillips poured out tea.

She was a strikingly beautiful girl—tall, slender, and, despite the pallor and the anxious expression in her eyes, her face was a most attractive one.

"I don't know what I should do without you, Hector," Ruth sighed. "It was so good of you to come back at once!"

The young man flung a quick, loving glance at his companion.

"Why I'd come back across the world in answer to a word from you darling," he said. "You know that!"

He caught at the tiny hand that was holding the teacup and pressed it. Ruth drew her chair a little closer and sat down.

"You haven't heard anything, I suppose?" she began.

"Not a word! I have been down to the bank again this morning and made inquiries. Fortunately they haven't missed him yet. The note that he sent has made everything all right for the time being."

James Phillips was now the managing director of the big bank, and at first Ruth had had a vague fear that all might not be well with the concern. But, beyond a few courteous inquiries, the bank had not troubled about their head man, chiefly because a letter had been slipped in the letter-box on the Tuesday night, in Phillips's handwriting, which had stated that urgent private business was calling him away, and he might be absent for some time.

It was this fiction that Ruth had to keep up among her many friends and acquaintances in Grangepool. It was a difficult position for the young girl to fill, but so far she had carried it out faithfully enough.

No hint of her suspicions or fears had been allowed to escape her red lips, and Hector MacLeod was the only one who shared her confidences.

Half-way through the tea the electric bell on the front door whirred, and a few minutes later a trim maid-servant entered, bearing a silver salver.

"Doctor Kay," Ruth read, glancing at the card. "What does he want, Mary? Who is he?"

"I don't know, Miss Ruth," the maid returned. "The gentleman said he wanted to see Mr. Phillips. I told him he was not at home but that you were in, and he said he would like to have a few words with you."

Ruth arose to her feet.

"I think you had better see him in here, dear," said Hector.

Ruth turned and nodded to the girl, and a few moments later the door of the drawing-room opened again and two men appeared. They were Professor Kew and Count Ivor Carlac.

Kew was dressed in a well-made frock-coat and was wearing a pair of dark glasses. He had made but very little attempt to disguise himself, for his features were not of the type that could be easily altered.

The man behind him, however, would hardly have been recognised as the huge convict that had marched at the head of gang 10.

Kew's disguising of Carlac was a masterpiece of ingenuity. The hair had been tinted to a slight iron grey at the temples; the hawk-nose had been broadened, the eyebrows altered, for they were now heavy and pendulous.

Kew had studied the face of the man Marle, and Carlac's countenance was now almost an exact duplicate.

The vulture-like man came across the room with his little bird-like steps and bowed to Ruth.

"Good-afternoon, Miss Philips," he said in his chirping voice. "I hope I do not disturb you. Let me introduce my friend, Mr. Free."

Carlac bowed to Ruth, and the girl indicated two chairs.

"Pray be seated," she said. "I understand you have called to see my father. He is not at home just now."

Then, turning towards Hector, she introduced him.

"This is Mr. Hector MacLeod."

It might only have been imagination on Hector's part, but he fancied that Kew started slightly and the thin face was turned in his direction, while a pair of hard eyes peered at him from behind the smoked glasses.

"Mr. Hector MacLeod," Kew reported. "I wonder if you are any relation of Mr. Malcolm MacLeod?"

"I am his son."

"Ah!"

"Did you know my father?" Hector put in.

"I never met him," said Kew slowly, "but I have heard about him. He was a well-known man in Grangepool once, I believe?"

"Yes," the youngster returned.

Kew's lips twitched for a moment. To him there was a certain grim humour in this meeting, for here was the boy who, if Marle's story was correct, had been defrauded out of the very money that Kew and Carlac were now in search of.

"And your father, Miss Phillips," Kew went on. "I understood you to say he is not at home. Will he be back soon?"

Ruth caught a warning glance from Hector.

"I don't know," the girl returned. "He has been called away on very important business."

Again Kew's lips twitched. He knew that Marle had sent off the letter of warning to Phillips immediately he had heard that he was about to be released.

"When did he go?"

"He left Grangepool last Tuesday week," said Ruth. And Carlac and the professor exchanged glances.

So far they had had no proof of the truth of Marle's statement, but now the fact of Philips's sudden flight seemed to indicate that the dying convict's story was true enough.

"And you have no idea when he will be back?"

"I'm afraid not," said Ruth.

She was half frightened of the lean face that was staring into hers. She looked at it now, noting the cold curve of the chin, the long, curiously shaped head. A criminal, evil visage.

"Oh, well, in that case we might as well go," said Kew, rising to his feet. "Our business was not very important and can wait."

He bowed politely to Ruth, an action followed by Carlac; then after a nod to Hector MacLeod, Kew and his companion left the drawing-room.

As soon as they had vanished Hector rose to his feet and went to the window. He was just in time to catch a glimpse of the two men as they passed down the gravel path.

They were a strangely-assorted pair. Carlac, broad-shouldered, burly, masterful; Kew, slim, delicate, tripping along, trying to keep pace with the strides of his companion.

"Who on earth are they, Ruth?"

"I don't know, Hector," the girl said, coming to his side. "I have never seen them in my life before."

"I don't like the look of them."

"Neither do I. That little man is a—a terrible creature. I felt his eyes on my face all the time and he—he seemed to almost hypnotise me."

"I wonder what the dickens they are after here?" Hector went on. "They are not Grangepool men, although they seemed to know about my father."

"Yes; so they did. That was rather strange, wasn't it?"

"I can't make it out," the youngster returned. "Dad was well known in Grangepool, but he has been dead so long. Why should two strangers know about him?"

It was certainly rather curious that these two men should have known of his father, and after he left the house and made his way back to his humble lodgings, Hector found his brain returning to that question again and again.

"They were evil-looking beggars," Hector thought. "of course, they were polite enough, but, by Jove, I think what they are is stamped on their faces clearly enough. The big fellow looked like an ex-convict—by Jove!"

A sudden inspiration had flashed into his mind. He remembered the mysterious message that Phillips had received, the letter that Ruth sent on to him whilst in London.

"Can it be possible?" the lad thought. "By Jove, I think I'm right. They are in search of Ruth's father and he is hiding himself from them."

He made up his mind that he would call on Ruth the following morning and let her know his suspicions. It would have been wiser had he gone back the same night, but he did not want to be seen at Phillip's house too often.

The servants knew that there had been a quarrel between Hector and Mr. Phillips, and the former did not want them to think he was taking advantage of the owner's absence.

Yet it would have been better had he pocketed his pride that evening. For about ten o'clock Ruth, seated in her father's study, heard the clatter of the letter-box, followed by a double knock on the door.

She knew that the servants had retired for the night, and, rising to her feet, she went to the hall. In the letter-box she could see the outlines of an envelope, and she hurried to the door and opened it.

There was no one in the porch and although she went to the top of the steps and looked down the avenue, she found it was quite deserted.

Ruth went into the hall again, and, closing the front door, she opened the letter-box and withdrew the envelope. It was thumb-marked and dirty, but the handwriting brought a quick thrill into the girl's heart.

It was that of her father. Standing in the dim light of the hall Ruth hurriedly tore the envelope open and drew out the sheet of paper.

"My dear Ruth," the letter ran,—"I want you to open the second drawer of my desk and take out a note-book and a little bag of gold that you will find there.

"Do not a let a single soul know that you have heard from me. I am in great danger and have to leave Grangepool at once. I am staying at present at 23a, Ravell's Alley! If you take a tram down to the Old Town and get off at the terminus, Ravell's Alley is the third turning on the right. No. 23a is quite close to the docks. It's a very low neighbourhood, but I don't think there is any fear of you being molested. Anyhow, you are a brave girl and I know you will help your father. Bring me the money and note-book to-night. As soon as you have read this letter destroy it."

Ruth crushed the paper in her fist and looked about her. Her face was bloodless, and in her eyes the gathering fear had deepened. What could it mean? Why was it that her father, the respected managing director of the local bank, had to hide in a dirty slum? The girl's heart was beating painfully, but her father had not been mistaken when he had chosen her as his confidante.

The old town, especially that quarter in which Ravell's Alley was situated, was seldom visited by any of the better-class residents. It was really given up to rough polyglot sailors that came and went from the harbour.

There were tales of dark crimes, of awful deeds having been committed in the ill-kept, badly-lighted slumways there.

"Second drawer in the desk," Ruth repeated. "I must go and get the things at once."

She darted off into the study again, and, finding the bunch of keys in the desk, she drew out the second drawer. A little canvas bag was the first object that met her eyes, and as she lifted it up the chink of gold came to her ears.

Below the bag was a note-book, just as her father had said. It was old and rather faded, but Ruth did not stop to do more than glance at it.

She closed the drawer again and left the study, hurrying upstairs, to return a few moments later wearing a dark cloak.

The pocket-book and bag were safely tucked away in the bodice of her dress, then, pinning a little motor cap over her tresses, Ruth went out of the house and turned into the quiet street.

As she emerged on to the edge of the pavement, she halted for a moment, glancing to right and left. The street was deserted, so far as she was aware, and she began to walk swiftly down the hill towards the main thoroughfare.

As soon as her back was turned a figure detached itself from a gateway belonging to a house opposite and began to move along the wall. As it passed the third house another figure, a taller one this time, emerged.

"She lied to us," said Kew in a thin voice. "I thought as much. She is going to see her father now."

"Perhaps you're right," said Carlac, "although I did not think so at the time."

From that moment that they had left the house, these two men had hung about. They had seen Hector MacLeod depart, and, at last, their long vigil had been rewarded by the sight of Ruth in her dark cloak.

The main throughfare was reached at last and they saw the girl step on a tram. It happened that there was another car running close behind the one that Ruth had entered, and Kew and Carlac boarded it.

The second tram was almost empty and the two men went up to the top, where, by looking through the window, Kew could keep his eye on the clanging tram ahead.

He saw that the electric sign above the foremost car proclaimed the fact that it was the Old Town they were heading for.

The long run down the steep slopes was completed and the terminus reached at last. Ruth stepped out of the front car and Carlac saw her glance around for a moment before going on into the dimmer-lighted streets beyond.

They were old hands at tracking, were these two, and the unsuspecting girl had no idea that she was being followed. She turned down into Ravell's Alley shuddering slightly as she plunged into its narrow, evil-smelling depths.

The unmistakable tang of the sea came to her, and at the end of the alley, she could see the high mast of some ship moored to the quay.

The girl crossed the passage, and, coming to a halt beneath a lamp-post, peered at the doorway opposite. It was No. 22, and hurrying on, Ruth stopped again in front of 23a.

Her knock on the door was answered by a figure in blue. It was dirty, dishevelled, with a growth of stubble on its chin. For a moment Ruth stared at it, not recognising her father, then Phillips put his hand out, and caught his daughter's arm.

"Ruth," he whispered, "good girl. Come in!"

She was drawn in through the narrow doorway, and the door was closed behind her. The two fugitive figures drew closer and waited in a dark doorway opposite. They had not long to wait. Three or four minutes later Ruth emerged, and now her father, in his dingy blue serge, accompanied her.

The girl was silent, her small hand resting in her father's arm, and they walked up to end of the alley. Carlac and Kew, watching from the darkness, saw a quick farewell take place.

Ruth flung one arm round her father's neck and clung to him for a moment, and the sound of a smothered sob came to the ears of the watchers. Then, disengaging herself gently, the man pushed the slender girl away and Ruth, with bowed head, hand over her eyes, tottered towards the lighted thoroughfare.

For a long moment Phillips stood in the shadow of the alley, looking after his daughter; then wheeling he began to retrace his steps.

He reached 23a, and found that the door was still open. He entered, closing it behind him, then turning in the narrow hall he stepped into the room on the left.

It was in darkness, and, fumbling in his pockets, Phillips struck a match. As he did so he saw two faces looming in the darkness in front of him.

With a muttered cry of fear, the man staggered back, the match slipping from his fingers. He turned and made a blind rush for the door; but he was too late. Before he could reach it, two powerful hands shot out, gripping at him, and he was hurled aside.

Another match spluttered, and the gas-jet above the fireplace was lighted, revealing the shabby interior of the room.

The man who had hurled him aside was now standing at the door, a massive figure he was, while underneath the gas-jet stood Kew. Phillips, drawing back a few paces, turned his head from side to side, eyeing the two men.

"What's the game?" he asked in a thick, trembling voice. "What are you after?"

Carlac took up his part then. With a quick movement he turned the key in the lock, then advanced across the room towards Phillips, at the same time removing his cap so that the light would fall on his close-cropped head.

"Don't you know me?" he said. "Twenty years in gaol makes a lot of difference to a man, but you ought to recognise me again."

It was the crucial moment of their scheme, and Kew leaned forward slightly, his eyes fixed on the face of James Phillips. The bank manager stood stock still, staring into the hard face in front of him.

Carlac's nose had been broadened by the careful injection of hot wax beneath the skin, then it had been moulded and fashioned until it exactly resembled the squat nose of the dead man. There was also the mark of a scar on the left cheek, an old one. It was these marks that really brought success to the nefarious men.

Phillips drew a deep sigh, then spoke.

"You—you are Marle?"

"Yes," said Carlac; "Nat Marle, alias Joseph Smith. I've come to have a reckoning with you."

The wretched man tottered to a chair and collapsed on it. Had either of the two men been capable of a spark of pity, they would have been moved at the sight of the terrible anguish in Phillips's face. The cheeks were hollow and the eyes sunken, the whole aspect that of a man in the depths of despair.

'You got my note?" said Carlac.

"Yes." With a sudden energy Phillips drew himself to his feet. "Yes, I got your note," he said. "I have been waiting for you, expecting you. All these years I have been haunted by that one crime."

Carlac laughed.

"And all these years I have been thinking of it," he said, playing his part to perfection. "You haven't been so badly off, after all. It is I who have had to suffer. I've had twenty years in gaol. Now, what about it?"

He leaned forward, his heavy face set in a grim look.

'Twenty thousand pounds.' Carlac went on, "that's what I want from you. Twenty thousand pounds and interest—interest for twenty years. That makes a tidy sum, Mr. Bank-manager Phillips, and you've got to hand it over."

"I tell you—it's impossible, man," the distracted managing director returned. "I haven't got such a sum of money in the world."

"What have you done with it, then?"

"It—it saved me from ruin," said Phillips. "The very time when you came and deposited your money, I was on the verge of being found out. As it was, your twenty thousand saved me. I paid off everything, and the bank never discovered my defalcations."

"But the money—I want the money!"

"I have not got it to give you."

"But you can get it. You are managing director of the bank, and have the handling of all the cash."

Carlac glowered at the figure opposite him.

"If you were able to swindle twenty years ago, you are able to swindle now," he said. "That twenty thousand pounds is mine, and, by heavens, I mean to have it—do you hear?"

The harsh, metallic voice rang out in the little room and Phillips looked fearfully around him.

"Not so loud, man—not so loud. Someone might hear you," he said.

"I don't care if they do," Carlac returned. "All Grangepool will if you do not pay."

Kew, who had been a silent observer of the scene, came forward now. He was rubbing his thin hands together, and he glanced at Phillips.

"You must not mind my friend, Smith," he said. "He is rather inclined to lose his temper."

"I am entitled to," said Carlac. "I want my money."

"Oh, quite so—quite so!" Kew agreed, in his cackling voice. "But you will have to give Mr. Phillips time. I have no doubt he will be able to arrange something. Say, a little advance?"

He was eyeing Phillips with his hawk-like stare. There were beads of sweat on the hunted man's brows, and he was trembling visibly.

"Just a little advance on the capital," Kew went on. "Perhaps two or three thousand pounds. You might manage that—eh, Mr. Phillips?"

"I must have time—time to think," the wretched bank manager broke out. "I am not a rich man. I never have been; and this crime has haunted me like an evil dream always."

He flung one hand above his head and turned his twitching features towards Carlac.

"I wish to heaven I had never seen you or handled your dirty gold," he broke out, dropping into the chair and covering his face with his hands.

There was a long silence in the room. Carlac, looking round it, saw a black bottle and a couple of glasses on a table near the wall. He went across to it and measured out a stiff peg, which he carried and handed to Phillips.

"Drink this," he said. "it's no good crying over spilt milk. You've had a good time of it, and I have only come to claim my due."

Phillips caught at the glass eagerly and drained it. It was rum, strong and potent, and it brought back some of the wretched man's courage.

"Who lives in this house?" asked Kew.

"Nobody," Phillips returned. "It is my property. I am here alone."

Kew crooked a finger, and he and Carlac went across to one corner and whispered together for a moment. Then Carlac returned and spoke to Phillips.

"Look here," he said, "we are going to stay here to-night, and you will have to do the same. Have you any money?"

Feverishly Phillips slipped his hand into his pocket and drew out the bag of gold.

"This is all I possess," he said, handing the bag over. Carlac cut the string and titled the contents of the bag on to the table. There was sixty pounds in gold.

"We will give you till to-morrow night," he said. "By that time you will have to hand over at least a couple of thousand. Your name is good enough for that amount in Grangepool, I know, and it will keep me quiet for a little while. You understand?"

He leaned towards his victim.

"Beg, borrow, or steal it," he said. "Only get it."

Kew had left the room now, and with a candle which he had found he made a quick tour of the house. He found that it was a small cottage affair, with two rooms on the ground floor and two upstairs.

It was arranged then that Phillips should occupy one of the rooms, while Carlac and Kew slept in the other, and when Phillips entered the back room Carlac turned the key in the lock—a grim hint that the bank manager was a prisoner.

"It works," said Carlac, when he and Kew found themselves alone. "We will make that man fork out to the last farthing."

Kew had seated himself on the edge of a bed in the little room.

"You won't find it so easy," he returned. "I think his story is right; he evidently hasn't got the money himself."

Carlac laughed grimly.

"But the bank is rich enough," he returned, "and he is the managing director. We will bleed him to death. If he was dishonest once he can be so again."

He drew out the bag of gold, and counting out thirty sovereigns dropped them into the claw-like hand of his companion.

"That's the first," Carlac said—"the first I have earned for many a day. Let's hope it will not be the last."

In the other chamber James Phillips had removed his boots, and now he was walking up and down in the darkness with long, nervous strides.

He felt like a caged beast, and his heart was like lead within him.

From the moment the temptation had come to him, and he had made use of Marle's ill-gotten gains, James Phillips had vowed that never again would he allow himself to tamper with the funds of the bank.

For the first few years his crime had haunted him, but gradually, as the time went on, and he found himself rising, comfortable and respected, the crime ceased to trouble him.

Malcom MacLeod had died, and Phillips had seen to the wants of his boy. It was the only way in which the wretched bank manager could make a return, and, in his way, he had carried out his compact faithfully enough.

It was only when that first intimation from Laidstone Prison had come that fear had entered his heart, and he had turned on Hector.

For the twenty thousand pounds that Phillips had used was really the property of the youngster, and, in his terror, Phillips had thought that it would be better if he were to get Hector MacLeod out of the way.

Then another note had arrived, and finally that dreadful one hinting of the nearness of Marle's release. Phillips had fled from his house at once, and had sought sanctuary in the little place in Revells Alley. He had remained hidden during the day, and had only ventured out at night-time.

He had gone down to the docks, and, that very day, had arranged to join an out-going tramp. The vessel was due to sail with the turn of the tide at two a.m., and Phillips knew that it was now riding at anchor in the harbour, with the little tug waiting to draw it out into the Channel.

That was the reason that had made him write to his daughter for the sum of money, and the note-book which contained his story of his crime.

And now all his plans had collapsed about him, and he was in the hands of his enemies.

From somewhere in the distance a clock chimed, and he listened to the solitary boom of one o'clock. Within the next hour the cargo steamer would be sailing.

It was bound for San Francisco, and Phillips knew that it was from the city of the Golden Horn that the sealers sailed for the Russian islands.

His plan had been a desperate one. He had meant to make his way to San Fracisco, and there ship on board a sealer in the hope of reaching Salcoth Island.

He knew that Marle had desposited all evidence against himself in the little hut, and if he could only reach the hut in time, and possess himself of the Seafoam's papers, and also the deposit note, he could deny all knowledge of the old crime.

He paced on, up and down, finally halting in front of the narrow window. He could see the square yard beneath and, beyond it, a glimmer of the dark waters of the harbour.

He stood for a long moment staring into the dusk, then into his brain there leapt a desperate plot.

The Kittywake, the tramp vessel on which he had agreed to sail as common seaman, was lying in the centre of the harbour, a good mile from the quay. In his youthful days Phillips had been a fairly strong swimmer, but he had given up that pastime years ago.

But now, as he listened to the sluggish swish of the slow-moving waters, it came to him that this was his only chance. There was no other means of escape from these grim-jawed, merciless captors of his.

He realised what their game was—blackmail. Little by little they would bleed him, drive him into fresh crime, make him a fugitive and a criminal.

He saw the ruin of his home, and the disgrace of his daughter—the daughter whom he loved better than anything else in the world. It was really for the sake of the sweet-faced girl that Phillips had determined to be tempted no more. He loved Ruth with a passionate worship that was capable of the greatest sacrifices.

Leaning forward, Phillips drew the rusty catch aside and, inch by inch, lifted the lower half of the window. He saw that the low wall which divided the narrow courtyard of 23a from that of the next door, was some five or six feet below the level of the window and a little to the left.

He felt in his pocket to make sure that the notebook was there. Then, slipping through the window, he lowered himself out until he was hanging on the sill. A swift move of his body saw him swing out to the right, and his feet came in contact with the top of the wall.

He released his hold and his body swung on. It was touch and go whether he would fall into the yard below, but he managed to keep his balance and, doubling up his body, Phillips ran along the top of the crazy wall, reaching the end one.

The tide was rising now, and the water was lapping against the foot of the wall. He knew that it was fairly deep there, and he measured the distance.

As he did so, he heard a quick click from behind him. Turning round he looked at the house. The window of the other room was flung up, and he saw the shadowy outlines of a man's head and shoulders. An arm was outstretched and a hoarse voice sounded.

"Stop, or I'll fire!"

Only for the briefest of seconds did Phillips hesitate. Then, with a swift movement, he stretched his hands above his head, and his body poised in an arch. Crack!

Carlac pressed the trigger and the revolver barked. Quite clearly he heard the thud of the bullet as it found its mark. Then Phillips's body shot out from the wall, and they heard the splash of the water below.

Carlac darted across the room and opened the door, and he and Kew rushed down the stairs, making their way to the back of the house. They stumbled across the garbage-filled yard, finally reaching the end wall.

Carlac, with a cat-like spring, was on top of the wall in an instant, and, craning his bull-like head forward, the criminal listened.

Plainly to his ears there came the sound of steady breathing, and the splash of moving hands.

"I must have missed him," the criminal whispered, leaning down and stretching an arm towards his confederate.

Kew caught at the powerful fist, and, with an easy swing, Carlac drew his companion on to the wall by his side.

From the dark harbour they could still hear the steady progress of the swimmer as he made his way out into the darkness. They listend until it died away. Then Kew turned to his companion.

"We must get a boat and try to follow him," he said. "There's sure to be one about here. Come along."

The two were out in the alley by now, and a few moments later they turned towards the quay. The passed the vessel that Ruth had noticed, and, finding a flight of steps, saw a heavy skiff moored to the weed-covered side.

Carlac dropped into the thwarts, and Kew seated himself in the stern, releasing the painter. Carlac unshipped the heavy oars and began to pull steadily.

For half an hour they moved to and fro, and, at last, they found themselves close to a buoy in the middle of the harbour.

Suddenly there came to their ears the long shrill whistle of a siren, and the beating of heavy paddles. A panting tug-boat, sending a shower of sparks up from its squat smoke-stack, was moving down through the shipping, dragging behind it the huge black hull of a cargo steamer.

It was heading almost directly for the little skiff, and Carlac had to take to his oars to get out of the track.

Just as the tramp steamer passed, another skiff that had been dragged along behind the thrashing wake, was released, and it danced up and down on the foaming waters.

Five or six strokes brought Carlac close to the little boat, and he hailed it. It proved to be the skiff that had taken the pilot on board the tramp, and the figure in it swathed in oilskins, glanced rather doubtfully at Carlac, as the latter ran his boat against the side of the pilot.

"What are you after, mate?" the sailor asked. "Funny time o' the morning to be having a row, ain't it?"

"We are looking for a friend," said Carlac; "fell off the quay and was carried away into the harbour. We're afraid he must have been drowned."

It was only a chance shot, but it brought an unexpected reply.

"Oh, that's it is it? Well, I can tell you he ain't drowned. He's on board the Kittywake. It was just touch an' go with him, but we managed to pick the beggar up."

"Was that the Kittywake that passed just now?"

"Yes."

"Where is she bound?"

"San Francisco is the first port it touches at," the sailor returned; "so it strikes me your friend will have a long time to wait before he sees you again."

Carlac released his hold on the boat and they drifted apart, then the massive criminal took to the oars again, and rowed towards the docks in silence.

For the moment James Phillips had escaped from the toils, but only for the moment.

CHAPTER 5.

The Head of the Bank Meets Blake.

"What can I do for you, Sir Donald?"

Blake had looked up as the elderly, sprucely attired gentleman entered his consulting-room.

The card which the landlady had handed to Blake bore the name of Sir Donald Bardale.

"I have come to consult you professionally, Mr. Blake," the baronet said. "In the first place I went to Scotland Yard, but they pointed out that the matter was hardly of sufficient public interest for the moment, and they advised me to come to you."

Blake bowed and remained silent. Sir Donald seated himself on the chair, and placed his silk hat and gloves on the desk.

"I am chairman of the Grangepool and District Bank," he went on, "and my business with you is to ask you to try and help me to discover the whereabouts of our managing director, Mr. James Phillips."

Blake drew forward a paper, and poised a pencil between his fingers.

"You say that Mr. Phillips has disappeared?"

"Yes," the baronet replied. "As a matter of fact, there is a little mystery attached to the matter. He was last seen at the bank some six or seven days ago. It might be a week or a little over, I'm not quite certain. He left a note, however, saying that he had been called away on important business, and we did not pay any particular notice to it at the time. Mr. Phillips had the handling of a great deal of the business at the bank, and we have every faith in him."

"Then, when did you make up your mind that he really had disappeared?"

"Only yesterday morning," said Sir Donald. "I was rung up at about ten o'clock, and the chief cashier at the bank asked me if I would go down to the premises at once. I found Miss Ruth Phillips awaiting me there. She seemed very much distressed, and she told me that she feared some harm had come to her father."

The portly gentleman fidgeted for a moment.

"Of course, anything you may say to me now, Sir Donald, will be treated with strict confidence," said Blake, with a slight nod.

"Yes, yes; I quite understand," the chairman of the Grangepool and District Bank returned, "But, well—my position is rather a difficult one. You understand that I do not for one moment cast any sort of doubts on the conduct of Mr Phillips. As a matter of fact, the books at the bank have been carefully gone through, and we find everything exactly as it should be."

He drew an envelope from his pocket and handed it to Blake. The detective unfolded the note it contained. It was from a firm of auditors, and it stated that the work of checking the books of the bank had been completed, and everything was found correct.

"That must be very satisfactory to you, Sir Donald?" said Blake.

"It is, and yet it isn't," the baronet returned. "Mr. Phillips's daughter seemed to imagine that her father had been murdered, or got at in some way. She inclines to the belief that it was blackmail, and that it has something to do with Mr. Phillips's position at the bank."

He glanced across at Blake.

"I am anxious to preserve the dignity of my bank," Sir Donald put in, "and that is the reason that I don't wish the matter to go into the papers. In fact, that is why I have accepted Scotland Yard's hint and have come to you."

He placed one hand on the desk and looked into the detective's face.

"I have been authorised by my board of directors to expend a considerable sum of money in clearing up this affair," he went on; "so any expenses you incur will be readily met. The question is, will you accept the case?"

The baronet's story was not a very exciting one, and under ordinary circumstances Blake might have refused to have taken up the affair. But the fact of Scotland Yard having sent Sir Donald to him put a different complexion on the matter.

Blake was always ready to help the 'Yard' men, and so he bowed to his client.

"I am quite ready to do what I can, Sir Donald," he said.

"Good! Then if you are disengaged I should like you to come to Grangepool with me this afternoon."

The chairman of the bank drew out a gold watch and glanced at it.

"There is a train which starts at four o'clock," he said. "I have to make one or two calls in the City, but I will meet you at the station if you are prepared to join me at that hour?"

'Very well, I will be there,' said Blake.

A few moments later Sir Donald left the consulting-room, and Blake went into his quiet dining-room, where Tinker was awaiting him. The youngster glanced up as his master entered.

"I can see you have got something on, guv'nor," the lad said. "What was the old gent after?"

"That 'old gent', as you call him, is Sir Donald Bardale," said Blake, with a qaint smile. "He is a very important person in his own way. He's the chairman of the Grangepool & District Bank."

Tinker leaned forward in his chair, and his lips pursed into a whistle.

"The Grangepool & District Bank!" the lad repeated. "By Jove, that's funny!"

"I can't quite see the humour in it," said Blake.

"Oh well, it is rather strange, guv'nor," Tinker went on. "As a matter of fact, the name has brought back an incident to me that I had almost forgotten about."

"And what was the incident?"

"It happened while you were visiting Laidstone, guv'nor," Tinker explained. "I meant to tell you about it. As you know, however, you did not come straight back to Baker Street, but went down on to Portsmouth for a few days."

This was perfectly true, for Blake had only returned to his chambers on the previous day.

"Well, what about the Grangepool Bank?" Blake asked.

Tinker told him all that had happened in Hyde Park, and the ensuing adventure. The detective was in a brown study by the time that Tinker came to the end of his report.

"I think it is very curious, guv'nor, don't you?" the lad said. "For, you see, this Hector MacLeod worked in the very bank that you mention."

"It's more than curious, Tinker," said Blake; "It's a most singular coincidence. Sir Donald has come to me now and has asked me to try and trace James Phillips, the managing director of the bank."

"Hasn't he turned up yet?"

"Apparently not."

Tinker leaned back in his chair.

"By Jove, guv'nor, it is a bit of coincidence," he repeated. "I haven't heard a word from MacLeod since he went back to Grangepool, and I think it is rather strange. But perhaps he has been too busy to write."

He looked at his master eagerly.

"I don't think you can leave me behind this time, guv'nor," Tinker said insinuatingly. "You see, I know quite a lot about the affair already."

Blake smiled.

"All right, Tinker; that's quite true," he said. "And you can come along with me."

He gave the lad a warning nod.

"But I shouldn't say anything to Sir Donald about Hector MacLeod's story," added Blake. "That can keep."

Over the meal Blake discussed the various points in the case. More particularly did the letter which James Phillips had received from Laidstone interest him. To Blake that letter was really the big clue, and was worth following up.

"I must find out who this Joseph Smith was," Blake said. "Fortunately, that won't be a difficult matter. I have only to drop a line to the governor of Laidstone."

Tinker arose to his feet suddenly, and vanished into the study, to return a few moments later bearing a bulky volume. It was an atlas of the world—one of the latest of its type.

"I've never thought of looking it up before, guv'nor," said Tinker; "but I am going to see if there is such a place as Salcoth Island."

The front part of the atlas was devoted to an index, and after a long search Tinker discovered the situation of the island.

"Why, it's right away up off the coast of Alaska," he said; "Miles and miles away from anywhere apparently."

He had placed his pencil on the little dot that represented the island, and Blake studied that atlas for a moment.

"Salcoth Island must belong to Russia," he said presently. "It's in the sealing-ground."

Tinker looked at the atlas with his head one side.

"But what the dickens had a man from Salcoth Island to do with Mr. Phillips?" he asked.

"That's a question we have got to decide later," Blake returned.

95

At half-past three they left Baker Street, reaching the station a few minutes before the train was due to leave. Sir Donald had engaged a first-class compartment. He eyed Tinker rather doubtfully until Blake introduced the youngster as his assistant.

The journey to Grangepool was a long one, and it was getting on to nine o'clock before the train finally ran into the station of the old town.

Sir Donald invited Blake and Tinker to be his guests at his house, but Blake refused.

"I don't think that would do, Sir Donald," he said. "My assistant and I will take rooms at the Station Hotel here. If we have to make inquiries we must do so cautiously, and we don't want anyone to know what we are up to."

It was arranged then that Blake and Tinker would call at the bank on the following morning at ten o'clock, when Sir Donald and the board of directors would be ready to see them.

The baronet entered his limousine and was driven off, while Blake and the youngster sought rooms at the hotel. When they had washed and changed and had a light meal, Blake arose.

"It's fairly early yet," he said, glancing at his watch—"only a quarter to ten. I think that we might as well stroll up and see if we can have a word with Miss Phillips."

Blake had received the bank manager's address from Sir Donald, and, after receiving instructions from a porter of the hotel, they boarded a tram and were carried up the High Street to the new town.

It was a few minutes after ten when Blake rang the bell of James Phillips's house. The maid-servant answered his summons, and he and Tinker were ushered into the quiet study.

The had only to wait a few moments, for suddenly the door was swung open, and Hector MacLeod pushed into the room and darted across to Tinker with extended hand.

"By Jove, old chap, I am pleased to see you!" the youngster cried. "You must have thought it beastly of me not writing to you, but I have been worried to death."

When his impulsive greeting was over Tinker introduced Hector to Blake. The youngster shook hands heartily with the great detective.

"I am very pleased to meet you, Mr. Blake," he said. "It seems to me something like a miracle that you should have turned up here. You're just the very man that I would have most wished to see."

"The guv'nor has been employed by Sir Donald Bardale to find Mr. Phillips," Tinker explained. 'That's why we have come down here."

"By Jove, is that so?"

A troubled expression crossed Hector MacLeod's face.

"So Sir Donald has gone to the police, has he?" he said, half to himself. "I thought he would."

He looked at Blake.

"But I must not keep you talking here," he said. "Ruth—I mean, Miss Phillips—has sent me for you. Come along!"

He crossed the hall and entered the quiet drawing-room. Ruth Phillips, a white-faced ghost of her usual happy self, arose to her feet and bowed as Hector introduced the visitors.

"I have heard about you, Mr. Tinker," said the girl, giving the lad a warm greeting. "You—you were very kind to Mr. MacLeod when he was in London."

In a few brief words Tinker explained what had brought his master and himself to Grangepool, and Ruth seated herself while the others followed her example.

"I am going to meet Sir Donald and the board of directors in the morning," said Blake, "but I thought it might be worth while to come and see you first."

It was a quick, grateful glance that the girl shot him.

"That was very kind of you, Mr. Blake," said Ruth, clasping her fingers nervously. "Hector told me that he had made a confidant of Mr. Tinker, and perhaps you will know just how we stand in the affair."

"On the face of it, I should think that your father is the victim of blackmailers," said Blake.

"Yes, that's it, I'm sure," Ruth put in. "But I had better tell you what has happened."

She gave Blake a brief account of the letter that she had received, and of her visit to the squalid house in the little alley, then went on:

"I didn't sleep a wink all that night, Mr. Blake," the girl said. "You see, in the few moments that I had had with dad he told me something about himself. He said that he had to leave the the country at once; that a—a man he had known in the past was about to be released from prison and—and had threatened to ruin him."

"Did he give you any idea of what he was going to do?"

The girl was silent for a moment.

"He—he said that his only hope of salvation lay in him getting to Salcoth Island first. He said he was leaving Grangepool that same night, and told me to—to wait here for him until he returned."

"Then in all probability he had gone on his journey."

The girl raised her handkerchief to her lips and Hector MacLeod interrupted.

"Ruth has forgotten to mention to you. Mr. Blake , that a couple of men called here earlier on the same afternoon as she received the letter from her father. I was here when they called, and I did not like the look of them. They were just like two ex-convicts. The next morning, when I came round here to see Ruth, she asked me to accompany her to Ravell's Alley."

"I—I felt that something terrible had happened," the girl broke in. "I simply had to go down there."

"We got to Ravell's Alley about eleven o'clock," Hector went on. "We went to the house and found the door ajar. The back door was also open, and on the end wall, which is on the edge of the harbour, we—we found bloodstains."

"And this!"

Ruth slipped her hand into her dress and drew out a handkerchief. It was smeared with blood. Lifting one corner of it, she indicated the initials—"J.P."

"This belongs to my—my father," the girl said; "and I am sure that it is his blood that has stained it."

Blake examined the handkerchief a moment, then handed it back to the girl.

"About these two men who called here to see Mr. Phillips," he began. "What were they like?"

"One was a hideous creature." Ruth said, with a shiver. "I never saw such a face in my life before. It looked to me like the face of man dead to all human feelings."

She leaned back, closing here eyes.

"It was an old face," she went on, "but yet the eyes were as bright and as cunning as those of a fox. The nose was long and thin, and the ears were pressed back into the skull."

She leaped to her feet suddenly.

"I can draw it!" she said, hurrying across to a little desk.

The girl picked up a sheet of paper and a pencil; then, in few quick lines, she drew a portrait, which she brought over to Blake.

"That is it," she said, "to the very life!"

Hector MacLeod leaned forward.

"By Jove, you're right, Ruth!" he said. "It's splendid!"

Blake's eyes were fixed on the sketch for a long moment; then, without a word, he handed it over to Tinker.

"Have you ever seen anyone like that, old chap?" he asked.

Tinker stared for a minute, then leapt to his feet.

"Jiminy, guv'nor, it—it's Kew!"

"Kew—Kew!" Ruth repeated quickly. "Coming to think of it now, he gave his name as Dr. Kay."

"Can you remember what the other man was like?" he asked.

The girl gave her description, which was correct enough, but the reader will remember that Kew had altered Carlac's face.

"A broad nose, heavy ears, narrow, arched eyebrows." Neither Tinker nor his master could recognise that description.

"There's one curious point about it," said Hector; "they seemed to know me. Dr. Kay, as he called himself, spoke to me, mentioning the name of my father. I could not make head or tail of it then, and can't do so now, for my father has been dead for the best part of eighteen years."

They chatted together for nearly an hour, and Blake said a few words of comfort to Ruth when they arose to leave.

"You will try to save my dad, won't you, Mr. Blake?" she said. "I mean if anything is—is proved against him, you will—will help him if you can?"

"I believe your father is the victim of a clever scoundrel," said the detective. "I must say that there are a great number of points in the case which baffle me for the moment, but the mere presence of one particular man in it proves to me that your father, dead or alive, has been victimised."

He glanced down at her white face.

"You haven't told the bank about your last interview with your father, I suppose?"

The girl shook her head.

"No," she said, "I dared not do that."

"Perhaps it's just as well," said the detective; "and you have really nothing to fear from the bank. From what I have heard from Sir Donald, everything there is in perfect order, and they have no sort of charge to bring against Mr. Phillips at all."

Ruth's hands clasped together quickly.

"Thank Heaven for that!" she broke out. "I—I was really half afraid that he me might have done something wrong."

"No; I have been assured on that point," Blake returned, "so you need not be alarmed. If your father has vanished it is not because of any defalcations on his part."

His quiet words and the assurance that he gave brought something like a ray of comfort into the heart of the girl. She went out to the front door with her guests, and when Blake and Tinker reached the gate and looked around they saw her slim figure silhouetted against the lighted hall.

Hector MacLeod had also taken his departure along with the others, and the youngster fell into pace by Blake's side.

"I shall be glad if I can help you in any way, Mr. Blake," he said. "Before we quarrelled, Mr. Phillips was very good to me, and I'd like to make some sort of return. Won't you give me the chance?"

"Yes; I think I can promise you that," said the detective; "in fact, I need someone who knows Grangepool fairly well."

He arranged an appointment with MacLeod for the following morning. The lad had to be down at the railway-station hotel by eleven o'clock. This would give Blake and Tinker time to get their interview at the bank over.

When they were alone in the hotel together, Tinker turned to his master.

"I don't understand it, guv'nor," he said. "How on earth can Kew turn up here in Grangepool? I thought he was safe under lock and key at Laidstone Prison?"

Blake went across to his gladstone, and, opening it, drew out a notebook, from which he extracted a buff-coloured envelope.

"This came to me at Portsmouth," he said. "The governor of the prison sent it on to me. Read it."

Tinker glanced at the message. It was laconic enough in all conscience.

"Your prophecy was correct. Carlac and Kew vanished!"

"By Jove, guv'nor!"

Blake's face was like a steel trap, and his blue eyes were set and stern.

"I warned the governor, and I said it was a mistake in the first place to allow Carlac to be in the same prison as Kew. They were two of the most dangerous criminals in the world!"

97

CHAPTER 6.

Mother Shipton's Boarders.

Ravell's Alley in the daytime was even more hovel-like than when the friendly shades of darkness covered its drab houses. One or two gangs of grubby-faced mites played in the gutters, and now and again a hawker would pull his barrow up the narrow space, shouting his wares.

Immediately opposite No. 23a was a shop. Outside the shop there hung various garments—thick, blue jerseys, rubber boots, sou'westers, and oilskins.

The shop had really once been a house, and the window had been widened to allow for the display of the miscellaneous collection of goods that the owner, a withered-looking old dame, had gathered together.

Mother Shipton, as the old creature was called, was well known to the sailors who came and went in that quarter. She had the reputation for driving a hard bargain, but there was also a streak of kindness in her complex character.

Many a time a destitute sailor had gone there, and the old woman had lent him a few shillings, sufficient to tide him over until he had got a ship.

The old dame was in the shop attending to a customer, when suddenly, a double knock sounded on the ceiling, and she looked up.

"If that's all yer want to-day, my lad," she said, "I'll 'ave ter be goin'."

The man paid for his purchases, and Mother Shipton wrapped them up in a piece of dirty brown paper. Then, as soon as her customer had left the shop, the old dame hobbled along the side of the counter and vanished through a glass door, to climb a rickety flight of stairs on to the first landing.

She entered a room on the left, and stopped at the doorway. In a truckle bed a huge figure was lying, while beside it, on a chair, sat a stunted shrivelled man.

"What do yer want?" Mother Shipton asked.

"Only a little news," the man on the chair said. "Have you heard anything this morning?"

Mother Shipton came across the room.

"There was a young sailor in a little while ago," she said, "an' he told me that he had got a berth on the Anastor, bound for San Francisco. I remembered what you had asked me, and I put a few questions to him. He says that she is lying in the south basin now, and is due to sail to-morrow morning."

"The Anastor?" the figure on the chair repeated.

"Yes; that's the name."

The woman glanced at the figure on the bed.

"But I don't think you'll be able to get your friend well enough to go," she said. "How is he this mornin'?"

A dry smile crossed the hard mask of her lodger.

"Oh, I think he will be all right," came his reply. "he seems much better this morning."

"Well, I'll go an' make him a cup of beef-tea; that's the stuff for invalids."

She nodded her head, and went off across the room, closing the door behind her. As soon as she had gone, Carlac arose to a sitting position and smiled.

"We are very fortunate in finding this old fool," he said. "It was a stroke of luck for us."

And, as a matter of fact, it certainly was extremely lucky for Carlac and Kew to have found a safe sanctuary in the second-hand clothes shop.

For they knew that a hue-and-cry had been raised, and their descriptions flashed around the whole of England. Every port and railway-station would be on the watch for them, and they had had to lie low.

They had spent three days as Mother Shipton's boarders, and in order to hoodwink the old creature Carlac had pretended to be ill, while Kew had sent the old dame out now and again with prescriptions which he had made up.

"You had better be careful," Kew said. "She might be back at any moment, and if she sees you sitting up she might suspect something."

The kindly old dame returned a few minutes later bearing a bowl of steaming beef-tea, which Carlac received from her shrivelled hands with a grunt of thanks.

"How do you feel this mornin', mister?" she asked.

"Better," said Carlac. "I think I shall be able to have a stroll out this evening."

"We are going round to the Anastor," Kew explained, "and you had better let us have your bill. We've got a few shillings left; we'll see that you are paid all right."

"Oh, you needn't worry about that," said the old dame. 'You will be wantin' your kits, mebbe, and if you ain't got enough money—well, I'll trust yer till yer comes back again."

She left the room once more, and Kew, rising to his feet, went across to the window. It gave him a view of Ravell's Alley with its dirty pavements and cobbled stones.

The clouds had cleared away now, and, above, the blue sky smiled down on Grangepool.

The lean figure of Kew remained for a long moment at the window, head forward, eyes fixed and gleaming. Carlac finished the beef-tea had swung his body out of the cot, revealing the fact that he was fully dressed.

Rising to his feet, Carlac began to pace up and down the room, now and again flinging a word to Kew, which was answered by a monosyllable. They were both of an impatient nature, and the forced inaction was beginning to tell on them.

"By hook or by crook we must get on board the Anastor," Carlac said. "San Francisco is the very place we want to get at."

"It will mean that we will have to go round the Horn," Kew put in, "and that's a very long journey."

"That't won't matter," Carlac growled. "Better a long journey and a safe one than a short journey and dangerous."

He had halted and glanced at Kew for a moment.

"Neither you nor I can risk landing at New York and going across by rail," he said. "I, for one, do not care to run up against the American police."

He resumed his striding up and down; then, suddenly, a quick call from the window brought him to Kew's side.

"Look! Look!" the professor whispered.

He had drawn away from the window, and extended a claw-like hand. Pacing down the opposite pavement were three figures, two of them youthful and slender, while the third was an athletic-looking man in a suit of blue, well-fitting serge.

Carlac glanced for a moment at the third figure, then his teeth set, and he drew a deep breath between them.

"Blake!'

Kew's hand went out and caught him by the arm in a quick, nervous clutch.

"Keep back!" he said. "They must not see us!"

They drew away from the window, watching the figures. Blake and his companions came down and halted outside No. 23a. They saw one of the youngsters produce a key from his pocket and open the door. As he stepped aside allowing the others to enter, he turned his head slightly, and Kew recognised the face.

"That's young Hector MacLeod," he said. "Don't you remember? We saw him that afternoon when we called to see Phillips."

"And I recognise the other," Carlac put it. 'It's Tinker.'

Kew's face was drawn into a mask of thought. He watched the three figures vanish into the little house, then turned towards Carlac.

"I don't like this," he said. "What has brought Blake down here?"

"He is searching for Phillips," Carlac returned.

A sudden inspiration came to Kew, and, hurrying across the room, he opened the door and called. An aswer came to him, and Mother Shipton shuffled up the stairs. Carlac had, at a warning look from Kew, slipped back into the bed and drawn the coverings over him.

Kew took the old dame by the arm and walked her across to the window, then pointed to the house opposite.

"There's a detective just gone in there," Kew said, "and he is searching for—for my friend and I."

"Bless my soul!" said Mother Shipton, "Then you be wrong 'uns—eh?"

"No, no; nothing of that kind!" said Kew. "We are two deeply-injured men. We are trying to get away from England to start on a new life. But the hounds of the law are hunting us down. We want another chance, just to make good, and we can't get it in this cursed country!"

Kew's quick intuition had told him that this attitude of his was the best to adopt. In Slumland the representatives of law and order are always looked at askance, and Mother Shipton was no exception to this rule.

"They're after yer—eh?'

"Yes," said Kew; "and unless you save us we are lost."

"What can I do?"

"Oh, perhaps you won't have to do anything," the ex-convict went on; "But I am afraid one of them may come across here and question you. If so, you must say you haven't seen anything of us—that you don't know us at all."

He caught at the old woman's hand.

"You wouldn't like to see two poor sailormen dragged away and thrown into prison, would you?"

His appeal was framed exactly in the right words. Mother Shipton returned his pressure, and her wizened old face lighted up in a quick smile.

"Trust to me, boys," she said, nodding to Kew and then turning and nodding to the figure on the cot; "I'll see that they don't get yer! Drat all the 'tecs, say I! I suppose yer got into trouble with jumpin' a ship, or something?"

"That's it!" said Kew quickly. "We had a row with the skipper, and we both got away. They caught us though, and shoved us in prison."

"It's a shame, that' wot it is!" Mother Shipton put in. "You leave it to me, though; I'll send this Mr. 'Tec right about if he does come anywhere near me!"

She squared her frail old shoulders, and, with another reassuring smile that revealed her teethless gums, the old dame went off down into the shop again.

"You took a big risk then," Carlac said, when they were alone.

"I had to," Kew returned; "but I think we are all right. We can trust to the old fool. She has a soft corner in her heart for sailors, and I think she will prove useful."

His prophecy was to be amply fulfilled, for about half an hour later the little bell above the shop door tinkled, and Mother Shipton, entering the shop from the room, saw a man in blue serge, with an alter-eyed youngster by his side, standing at the counter.

"Good-morning, sir! Wot can I do for yer?" said the old dame, eyeing Blake steadily.

Tinker's quick eye noted that there was a certain antagonism about the attitude of the woman, and he smiled inwardly.

"I just want to make a few enquiries," said Blake. "Your shop is immediately opposite No. 23a, and I want to know if you have seen anything of a couple of men who were in there quite recently?"

"I ain't seen nobody in there," said Mother Shipton—"at least, not this last week or two. It used to be occupied by a family o' the name o' Hodson, but they went away, and it's been empty ever since."

There was every possibility that James Phillips had kept his presence in the house a secret, as Blake did not doubt the old dame's report.

"I have reason to believe that there were a couple of men in the place a few nights ago," he said. "Perhaps if I were to describe them to you you might recognise them."

He gave a brief description of the two men, and Mother Shipton's eye did not waver, although Blake had described one of her lodgers upstairs exactly.

"They must have been a queer couple, sir," she said; "but I ain't clapped eyes on'em. There's all sorts pass up an' down Ravell's Alley, and if they have been here I ain't noticed them."

In her way the old woman was loyal enough. She was not to know that her loyalty was utterly wasted, and that her words now were helping to shelter two unscrupulous rogues who were really entitled to no man's sympathy.

"Oh, well, that settles it!" said Blake. "I am very much obliged to you. Good-morning!"

Mother Shipton put her lean hands on the counter and watched Blake and his companion leave the shop. The wizened face lighted up into a smile, and she nodded her head.

"That's one against yer, yer dratted 'tec!" she said. "Huntin' honest men round an' frightenin' the life out of 'em! Yer didn't get nothin' out o' me."

Yet although Blake had got little out of Mother Shipton, the house opposite had afforded him ample proofs that Carlac and Kew had been there.

When Hector MacLeod had stepped aside, allowing Blake and Tinker to enter the dingy house, the young bank clerk had followed the two inside and had spent an interesting half-hour watching the great detective at work.

There was a certain systematic method about Blake's movements that fascinated the lad.

Blake had searched the lower rooms first, finding many tell-tale proofs that the house had been occupied—fragments of food, a litter of dirty crockery, tobacco ash, and one of two stumps of a good-class Egyptian cigarette.

He had shown one of these stumps to MacLeod, and the lad had recognised it.

"Yes," said Hector, "that's the brand that Mr. Phillips used to smoke."

Under the table of the second room on the ground floor, lying close to the leg of the table, Blake had found a round piece of sealing-wax. Embedded in this wax was a piece of string, and a seal had been stamped into the wax.

Again Hector MacLeod had been able to help the detective.

"That's the seal of the bank, Mr. Blake," he said. "The Grangepool and District is rather an old fashioned bank, and that piece of wax has come off a bag that must have contained over fifty sovereigns. We always used to seal the bags like that before putting them into the safe."

"You are probably right," said Blake, "and this seal must have come off the bag that Miss Phillips brought to her father."

He was standing close to the table, when suddenly he knelt down, and drawing a magnifying-glass from his pocket, bent over the boards.

Hector came to the table and looked down. On the dirty boards was a faded imprint where a wet boot had rested for a moment. Blake measured the mark and then arose to his feet.

"It is too large and broad for Miss Phillips, and much too small for her father, I should think," he said.

Hector examined the footmark on the floor.

"Yes, it is much too large for Ruth," he admitted, "and I know that her father's foot is no bigger than mine."

The footprint was quite clearly defined, and, although small had the broad heel-mark of a man's boot.

"There has been another person in this room," said Blake, his eyes travelling round slowly. "But we will leave it now. I want to look upstairs."

He went up the rickety stairs and turned first to the room that had been occupied by James Phillips, to discover that the door was locked.

"We found it like this when we came down," said Hector. "I came up and tried the door, while Ruth waited for me downstairs. It was only then that Ruth discovered the back door was open, so we both went out into the yard and found the wall where the bloodstains were."

Blake stooped and peeped through the keyhole.

"The key is not in the inside," he said. "I think we shall have to break it open."

He stepped back to the wall, raised his foot, and drove it hard against the door. There was a crash, and the door swung open. Hector's eyes widened, and he gave a quick glance at Tinker.

"By Jove, he is thundering strong!" he whispered.

Tinker smiled.

"That's quite easy when you know how to do it," he returned.

Blake had stepped into the room, and the open window attracted him at once. He went across to the window, and his voice called the two lad's to him.

On the dust of the window-sill were the clear imprints of fingers. Bending over, Blake looked down at the brickwork. Here and there were fresh scratches on the wall.

"If James Phillips was in this room," said Blake, "he must have been a prisoner, and he escaped by getting out of the window. Look, you can see the footprints on the side wall!"

The top of the wall was flat and grimy. Quite plainly they could see the feet marks.

"He had evidently taken off his boots," said Blake, "you can see the shape of the foot if you look closely."

'But why should he do that, Mr. Blake?" Hector MecLeod said. "What made him risk breaking his neck in getting out of the house through the window?"

Blake turned towards the lad.

"He was a prisoner here," he said—"Or, at least, someone had locked him up in this room so that he should not escape."

The detective withdrew his head and began to examine inside the room. It bore evidence that it had been made much use of. The bed was ruffled, and there were numerous cigarette ends on the floor and also in a tin that stood on the table close to the bedside. There was a handful of candle ends in the fireplace.

"He must have been hiding here all the time," said Hector. "What a rotten place for a man like him to live in!"

Tinker had been standing close to the bed, and he suddenly caught sight of a corner of a paper sticking out from beneath the pillow. He reached out a hand and drew the paper forward. Disclosing it to be a half-sheet of note-paper.

Someone had been attempting to draw a map, and presently the lines became familiar to Tinker. It was the coast of Alaska, and a pencil mark had been made at a certain spot.

Tinker turned and held the paper across to his master.

"Look here, guv'nor," he said, "the man that was in this room has been hunting up Salcoth Island!"

At the top of the map the longtitude and latitude had been written, and below the map someone had scrawled a few lines in shorthand.

"I think I can read that," said Hector. "It is Mr. Phillips who wrote it, He had an abbreviated shorthand of his own."

"All right," said Blake; "transcribe it, please."

Hector bent over the sheet for a moment, then wrote a few lines.

"That is roughly what it is," he said, holding out the sheet to Blake.

"Papers and deposit note in Eskimo hut, above south beach."

Blake folded the paper and slipped it into his pocket.

"I can't make head or tail of it," said Hector MacLeod.

"There is a great deal here that I can't make much out of at the moment," the detective returned; "but they will all have their uses, and sooner or later we will find the key to the puzzle."

He left the room, and, crossing the landing, went into the other one. The first thing that caught his eye was a key on the window-sill.

"You might try this in the lock of the other room, Tinker," he said.

The young assistant slipped away to obey the order, and returned a few moments later.

"That's the correct key, guv'nor," he said, as he re-entered the room.

He found Blake bending over the fireplace, and presently the dective stood up and extended his hand. There was a small canvas bag in it.

"Is that one of the Grangepool Bank bags?" he said, turning to young MacLeod.

Hector nodded.

"Yes, sir. That's right!'

In one corner of the bag someone had written the figures "£60" in indelible pencil.

"I think this is the same bag as Ruth brought to her father," said Hector.

Blake had now crossed the room, and was standing before the open window that looked out into the yard. Suddenly his eye was attracted to something on the faded paintwork. He reached out his finger and drew it across the surface. A little smudge of black appeared on his finger.

"Gunpowder!" he said. "There is no mistaking the smell of it!"

"And quite fresh too!" said Tinker.

The detective measured the distance where the gunpowder had appeared on the paint.

"It was a tall man who fired," he said. "The average man invariably levels his weapon before shotting. This man must have been close on six feet, for you will notice that the mark on the paint is five feet above the level of the floor."

Carlac had steadied his arm against the side of the window when he had fired at the poised figure of Phillips. It was only a small slip, but it had not escaped the observation of the lynx-eyed detective.

"Then if he was a tall man, guv'nor, all I can say is he had jolly small feet!" Tinker put in.

Blake turned towards his young assistant and smiled.

"Can't you see it yet, Tinker?" he said. "Just think for a moment!"

The youngster's alert brain worked swiftly.

"By Jove, I see it!" he broke out suddenly. "Those two visitors—they——"

"Exactly!"

A cry of enlightenment came from MacLeod's lips.

"By Jove, sir, they fit in exactly!" he broke out. "I remember noticing the wizened man's feet; they were very small. And the other chap was well over six feet—a huge giant of a man."

He looked at Blake perplexedly.

"But how could they have found—they didn't know that Mr. Phillips was——"

"They might not have known," said Blake, "but it was not difficult for them to find out. They may even have waited, watching the house, and they would no doubt see Miss Ruth leave the house at night and follow her."

"Then you think they have murdered Mr. Phillips?"

Blake was silent for a moment.

"That was my first impression," he admitted, 'but I am rather beginning to doubt it now."

"But the blood-stains?" said Hector.

"The blood-marks prove very little," said Blake. "they are on the back wall, and it is a good thirty yards from the wall to the house. The man who fired at Mr. Phillips did so from this window and in the dark. It is more than probable that he wounded him, but that would be all."

He looked at Hector with a quick smile.

"The very fact of Mr. Phillips using his handkerchief to temporarily stanch the wound," Blake went on, "proves that he was not mortally injured."

"Of course! You're quite right, sir," Hector said, with a sigh of relief. "I never thought of that."

Yet it was certainly a very simple explanation. A man mortally hit would hardly have found strength to staunch his wound with a handerchief.

"I am inclined to believe that it was merely a scratch," said Blake, "and Mr. Phillips succeeded in getting away."

He nodded towards the wall.

"I think that at high tide the water is close up to that wall," he went on.

"Oh, yes. In fact it would be quite easy to dive into it from there."

"Then that is just what Mr. Phillips has done," said Blake. "But whether he came out alive or not is a question we have yet to decide."

Tinker had been walking leisurely round the room, and suddenly he turned and called to his master.

"I think this might interest you, guv'nor," the sharp-eyed youngster said, pointing to the panel of the door.

Blake came across the room and looked at the mark indicated by Tinker. It was the imprint of a thumb, clearly and well defined.

"By Jove, that is a discovery!" said Blake. "The man who put his thumb on the door here must have rested his hand, quite unconsciously, against the patch of gunpowder smoke, with the result thast he has left his mark just as clearly as though it had been taken by the police authorities."

The paint on the door was old, and Blake drew out a sharp penknife. Hector MacLeod drew near to watch the detective at work. Very carefully and skilfully Blake cut away the portion of paint to which the thumb-print adhered. The paint came off in a huge flake, and the detective, folding the precious clue in a piece of cotton-wool, slipped it into his pocket-book.

He spent another ten minutes examining the room, but no further clues were found, and the trio went down into the narrow hall again.

It was when they emerged into the alley that Blake noted the ship-chandler's shop across the way, and while Hector remained behind to lock the door Tinker and Blake went into the shop together.

When they emerged again, Hector was waiting for them, and they walked up the alley and turned into the main thoroughfare.

"Queer sort of woman that, guv'nor!" Tinker said at last.

Hector MacLeod looked up.

"Do you mean Mother Shipton?" the bank clerk said with a smile. "She is a well-known character in Grangepool. A great friend to stranded sailors, I understand."

"Oh!"

It was only a monosyilable from Blake, but it contained as world of meaning. Blake turned to Hector.

"I suppose you have a harbour-master here?" he asked.

"Oh, yes," the lad returned. "He has a little office at the south basin."

"I think I'd like to have a word with him."

The day was young, and presently they found themselves on a tram, which deposited them close to the south basin at last. Hector led the way through the sheds, and came to a halt at a little office.

"How do you do, Mr. Marshley?" the youngster said to a portly man in blue reefer with brass buttons who was smoking contentedly at the door of the hut.

It was the harbour-master, and Hector presently introduced Blake as a friend of his. Blake chatted with the man for a few minutes, then presently he put the question that had arisen in his mind.

"Any vessel sailed on Tuesday night or Wednesday morning?" the harbour-master repeated. "Yes, there was one. The Kittywake went out on the high tide. Must have been about two o'clock in the morning. We don't have so many sailings now as we used to."

Blake looked out across the south basin. It certainly did present a rather deserted appearance, but he noted that there was a fair-sized steamer drawn up close to the quay, not far away from the little hut.

There was a feather of smoke rising from the vessel's funnel, and the Blue Peter moved at her peak.

"That ones clearing out shortly, I see."

"Yes. That's the Anastor, bound for Frisco," said the harbour-master. "She clears the quay at twelve to-night, and I expect she will sail at dawn to-morrow."

"Do you have pilots?"

"Oh, yes. We have two or three of the old hands. But the Anastor won't carry a pilot. Old Captain Turner knows the way out was well as any of us here."

"Did the Kittywake have a pilot?"

"Yes, sir. she did."

The harbour-master straightened up and, glancing along the quay, pointed towards a stout man who was seated on a bale of goods.

"Old Jack Timmins is the pilot who took the Kittywake out," he said.

At that moment the telephone bell rang, and the harbour-master, with nod to Blake, turned and entered his little room. The detective sauntered up the quay and spoke to the weather-beaten old fellow seated on the bale.

By passing the old chap his tobacco-pouch, Blake brought a smile on the pilot's face.

"Yes, sir, I did take the Kittywake out. I don't suppose I'll have another job like it for three or four weeks. Things ain't what they used to be."

"I am rather interested in the Kittywake," said Blake. 'I wonder whether you could tell me if a passenger arrived there late at night?"

Old Timmins's eyes wavered for a moment, and Blake caught the doubtful expression that came on to the features.

"I didn t see any passenger, sir," the pilot began hesitatingly.

"It's rather important," said Blake, "and, as a matter of fact, whatever you tell me will be in strict confidence."

The pilot lowered his voice.

"Well, sir, to tell you the truth, there was someone did come on board the Kittywake. It was just as I took the bridge. The vessel was due to sail when I saw one of the sailors rushing aft to the port companion-way. We heard him give a hail, and he went down the companion-way, and presently we saw him come up carrying a man over his shoulders. Half-dead the fellow were too, with a nasty bullet-wound in his arm."

"You don't know who he was, I suppose?"

Timmins shook his head.

"No, sir," he returned; "I don't. But it seemed to me as though the skipper was expecting him, for the man was bundled below at once. When I was leaving the boat I asked after the man, and the skipper told me he was doing all right."

"I'm glad to hear that," said Blake. "Is that all the information you have concerning him?"

Again Timmins scratched his stubble-chin.

"Well, sir, to tell you the truth it ain't," he said. "Of course a pilot has got to keep his own counsel in most things, and it had nothin' to do wi' me. But my mate, that put me aboard the Kittywake, said as how he came across another boat with a couple o' men in it. Just rowing about the harbour they was."

"Indeed? What were they after?"

"They was also inquiring about a man," said Timmins, with a dry smile. "But they didn't get much change out of my mate. They said as how they were looking for a friend o' theirs who had fallen into the water. But my mate didn't believe that yarn. It was pitch-dark, and he couldn't see 'em very well; but he didn't like the sound of their voices."

"Did he describe them to you!"

"Well, all he could see of 'em was that the fellow at the oars was a big, hefty-looking chap, while the other seemed a little feller—more like a monkey than a man."

Blake slipped his hand into his pocket, and drew out a sovereign, which he extended towards the old pilot.

"Thanks very much!" he said.

"I hope I ain't gettin' no one into—into trouble, sir!" Timmins said.

"I can assure you on that point," Blake returned. "As a matter of fact, your information will only be used for the purpose of helping an innocent man."

The pilot drew a quick breath of relief.

"Then that's all right!" he said. "I've kept the story to myself, for I wasn't quite sure how things stood; but I'm glad I've been able to tell it to someone at last! It's been worrying me ever since."

Tinker and Hector MacLeod found Blake strangely silent when they made their way back from the south basin to the hotel. Blake insisted on Hector remaining for lunch, and after the meal was over, the detective turned to his young assistant.

"I am going out this afternoon," he said. "No, you can't come with me. I have one or two little things to see to which must be done alone."

"Where are you going, guv'nor?" Tinker asked.

Blake had a time-table in his hand, and was glancing through the columns.

"As a matter of fact," he said, I'm going to Laidstone. I find I can get a train at a quarter-past one, and by changing at the junction, I can reach Laidstone at about four o'clock. There's another train starts back at five, and I ought to be here by nine at the outside."

"Then you'll be away practically all day?"

"Yes," Blake returned. "But, in the meantime, I can make use of both of you."

Hector leaned forward.

"Only too glad to help," he said eagerly.

Blake smiled at the lad.

"Oh, it's not a very big job," he said. "I simply want you to go to the south basin and keep an eye on the Anastor."

He looked at the young bank clerk.

"You saw Dr. Kay, as he called himself, and his companion?"

"Yes."

"Well, I want you to watch for them."

"Then you think they are still in Grangepool?" said Hector.

"I am almost certain of it." Blake returned; "and I am half-inclined to believe that they will try to get away from Grangepool on board the Anastor."

He turned to his young assistant.

"Your job will be to hang round Ravell's Alley," he said, "and I would suggest that you disguise yourself. You know who to look out for, and you also know just how clever they are. You must take no risks."

He left the quiet dining-room and went to his bedroom, Tinker following.

"Then you really think that is Kew and Carlac, guv'nor?"

"I haven't the slightest doubt about it," said Blake grimly, "and I am also sure that they are hiding somewhere in Grangepool. I know that the police have got the descriptions of them, and every port and railway station is being watched. They can only escape from England by some trick and sleepy old Grangepool is just the ideal place for their purpose."

Tinker seated himself on the edge of the bed, watching his master while Blake prepared for his journey.

"I can't get to the bottom of it guv'nor," the young assistant said. "Why should Kew and Carlac come here and tackle this man Phillips? What can they know about him, anyhow? And what good will it do them?"

"I think I shall be able to answer those questions when I return from Laidstone," said Blake. "Anyhow, I am convinced beyond doubt that it is Kew and Carlac who are hiding in this town."

"But the face of the big man, guv'nor, it isn't a bit like Carlac. Both you and I know him too well to be mistaken."

"Yes; we could never be mistaken in Carlac's features," said Blake; 'but I always reckoned that Kew was the greater criminal of those two—greater because of his surgical skill."

He stopped and looked at Tinker for a moment.

"You and I are both fairly good at disguising ourselves, old chap," he said; "but, if you remember, Kew was cleverer than either of us. A man of Kew's ability is quite capable of altering another person's face so that it would be completely changed. There are many little tricks of the trade that make a permanent alteration in a man's appearance."

He slipped into his travelling cloak and picked up his hat.

"The whole point of the case lies in the fact that this man who is accompanying Kew is of the same build as Carlac, heavy and burly. We know Kew and Carlac escaped together from Laidstone prison, and I shall no doubt hear how they accomplished that to-day. But, to my mind, there can be little doubt but what they did so by a clever trick, and they had evidently a preconceived object in their minds, for they must have practically headed at once for Grangepool."

"Yes, it looks like it, guv'nor."

"And what their object was is the point that I want to get at now," said Sexton Blake, as he left the room.

CHAPTER 7.

Blake Visits Laidstone Gaol Again.

It was exactly five minutes to four when Blake stepped out of the train at the quiet station of Laidstone, to find the governor's private motor-car awaiting him. Blake had telegraphed from Grangepool to Major Crofton, telling him of his intended visit, and the major was seated in the car, waiting for the detective.

Sexton Blake entered the vehicle, and the short journey across the moor road began. Major Crofton had lost some of his healthy colour. his eyes were weary-looking and depressed. He turned to the subject nearest to his heart at once.

"Not a sign of those rascals yet Blake," he said. "By Jove, I tell you I havent slept a wink this last week!"

He tugged at his tawny moustache, glancing moodily along the road. It was evident that the man was feeling his position keenly. The governor of a prison has a personal responsibility for all the men under his charge, and the escape of two notorious criminals such as Kew and Carlac, was calculated to do Major Crofton a certain amount of harm at the Home Office.

"How did they work it?" Blake asked.

The governor's face set tightly.

"It was one of the most cunning schemes that has ever been carried out," he said. "They knew well enough that it was impossible to break out of prison in the ordinary way. As a matter of fact, Blake, I am rather inclined to blame Dr. Manton."

"Indeed!"

"Yes," the governor went on. "You see, it happened that he had been a student in the London Hospital where Kew was head, and he had always had a rather sneaking regard for the rascally professor. Of course, Kew was physically unfitted for the heavy work of the gang, and he certainly was useful as hospital attendant. But it was through him being in that position that the escape was effected."

The governor gave a brief account of how the clever ruse had been carried out.

"It was an hour before we found out anything about them," Major Crofton said, "and then it was only through the van-man recovering consciousness and staggering out of the hospital. Kew had chosen the time very well, for it was just when the usual rounds were being made to see that all lights were out and the convicts asleep."

He contined to give an account of the search that had taken place all over the moorland, and finally of the discovery of the wrecked Daimler in the river.

"At first I was half inclined to share the warder's belief that the two ruffians had met their doom," the governor said, "More especially as part of their clothing was found in the river. But afterwards, when I heard that my suit of clothes was missing and also a suit of the doctor's I relaised that whole affair was only a trick."

The major brought his fist down on the side of the car with a thud.

"The impertinence of the blackguards!" he roared. "Just fancy, Kew got my suit under the pretext of cleaning it. By Jove, Blake, if ever they come into my hands again, I'll see that I make them both smart for this."

It was obvious that the major was highly indignant at the use that had been made of his clothing. He was still harping on the subject when the car swung through the prison gates, and came to a halt at his residence.

He and Blake entered the study, and presently the thumb-mark which the detective had carried with him was compared with the registers.

It was the exact copy of Carlac's left thumb print.

"That settles the only doubt that I had," said Blake. "I was assured in my own mind that it was Carlac who was accompanying Kew: but the description I had of him did not tally with my recollections of his face."

"You mean that it was altered?"

"Quite," said Blake. "I have had descriptions from two independent witnesses, and they both agree. Carlac, as we know him, had small ears, heavy, bushy eyebrows, and a thin nose. Now, it appears, that his ears are thick, and heavy, and his eyebrows are thin, arched ones, while his nose is broad and quite changed."

"Melted wax would change his nose," said the major.

Blake nodded.

"Yes," he said; "and I have no doubt that Kew has been at work on the other features."

"But what is the object of their going to Grangepool?" the governor asked. "It is not by any means the nearest port."

They were alone in the study, and Blake drew out his note-book.

"I have one or two questions to ask you," he said, "which I think might have a bearing on the case."

He turned over the leaves for moment in silence.

"In the first place," he went on, "is there a convict here named Joseph Smith—a man who expected to be released shortly?"

The governor looked at him.

"There was a convict here named Joseph Smith," he said. "By Jove, you ought to remember him, Blake! He was in the hospital when you visited it and recognised Kew."

Blake leaned back in his chair for a moment, then a bright, illuminating light flashed into his face.

"I remember now," he said; "and I believe I have got it."

He looked at the governor.

"Don't you remember what the man was like?" said the detective. "I have a distinct recollection of the thin eyebrows, and he had a thick nose, and his ears were puffed and swollen. He was a big man, heavily built."

"Great Scott, Blake! What are you driving at?"

"I mean that Kew has altered Carlacs features so that they would resemble this Joseph Smith."

The revelation came like a thunder-clap, and Blake and the governor stared at each other for a moment in silence.

"I believe you are right," Major Crofton said at last. "Coming to think of it, Smith was almost of the same build as Carlac; of course, he was a much older man."

He leaned back in his chair.

"But Smith is dead," the governor went on. "He died shortly after you left. As a matter of fact, he died on the morning of the dame day as Kew and Carlac made their escape."

Blake's eyes were steely and hard.

"The puzzle begins to fit together," he said. "There can be little doubt but what Smith's death was the signal that Kew and Carlac were waiting for."

"But why—why should that be so?"

Blake glanced again at his note-book.

"Some five or six days before Smith died, he sent a letter from here. I dont know whether it passed through your hands or not?"

"I have no recollection of him sending a letter," said the governor, "and we always keep a record of these things."

"Then in that case, Smith must have smuggled the letter out by a another channel," said Blake. "It would not be the first time that such a thing has happened."

"But not in my prison," the major broke out angrily.

Blake smiled.

"Well, I am afraid he did manage it."

"Well, go on."

"That letter was addressed to a Mr. James Phillips, of the Grangepool and District Bank, Grangepool," Blake continued, "and it had the effect of making this Mr. Phillips hide himself immediately on its receipt."

He repeated to the governor the story that Ruth Phillips had told him, continuing his report stage by stage, until the whole of his discoveries, including the sailing of the Kittywake, were told.

"Then you think that this man Phillips has fled in order to escape from Kew and Carlac?"

"There is no doubt about that," said Blake. "You see, they called on him and must have followed the girl down to Ravell's Alley. They had some sinister object in view in doing so."

The governor tugged at his moustache.

"I am not going to doubt your theory, Blake," he said, "but I simply can't understand it. Smith, you know, was a 'lifer.' he came to Laidstone prison nearly ten years ago and then he had done ten years elsewhere. That means that for going on twenty years almost he had not been outside prison walls. What possible connection could Kew and Carlac have with Smith?"

"None in the world," said Blake; 'but you forget that Kew was attendant in the hospital where Smith lay dying. How are you to know but that Smith, realising he was so near to the end, made a confidante of Kew, telling him of some old crime in which perhaps Phillips of Grangepool was mixed up?"

"Well, I can easily get on to that," said the Governor. "I have still got Smith's record here. I'll look it up for you in a moment."

He went across the study and opened the safe, taking out a huge portfolio. There was a sheaf of papers on the top.

"I haven't returned these yet," he said. "Smith, of course, is dead, and I meant to return the papers to the Home Office as soon as possible."

He spread out the chests and read the contents. It was a summary of Smith's trial for manslaughter and gave the whole details.

"I see that it was on board one of the old sealers that the fight took place," said Blake.

"Yes; apparently the vessel was just returning from the Russian Islands of the coast of Alaska."

"Then my theory is still sound," said the detective, "for in the letter that Joseph Smith sent to Phillips, he mentioned Salcoth Island. In fact, his letter ran as follows:

"The man from Salcoth Island will be calling on you by the end of the month. He hopes you will be ready for him."

"But the case seemed clear enough," the Major put in. "What on earth could this man Phillips have to do with it? It was simply a fight on board ship and a murder by one of the crew."

Blake nodded.

"That's quite true," he returned, "but Hull is only some thirty or forty miles away from Grangepool, and in those days, I believe, most of the sealing vessels sailed from Grangepool."

"Well, it's all a pretty tangle," said the governor, "and if you can see daylight through it, it's more than I can."

He glanced across at Blake.

"But I shall be jolly grateful to you if you can lay these two scoundrels by the heels, Blake," he added. "I've had a stinging letter from the Home Office."

He arose to his feet and began to pace up and down the study.

"I rather prided myself on the way in which I looked after those rascals," he went on, "but I have been beaten and that's the long and the short of it."

The interview had taken longer than Blake had anticipated, and it was five minutes to five before the motor car came up to the governor's house to carry him to the station. The chauffeur did his best, but something went wrong with the engine and a precious ten minutes was wasted, with the result that when they did arrive at the railway station it was to learn that the train had gone.

Inquiries revealed that the next train did not start till seven o'clock, and two hours delay made Blake chafe inwardly. He and the governor had a light meal at the little hotel close to the station, and at the appointed hour Blake boarded the train.

It proved to be a slow one, stopping at practically every station up the line, and it was a quarter to ten before they reached the junction of the main line of Grangepool.

Blake had to rush over the bridge and dart across the platform to leap into the main line train. A porter opened a door of a third-class compartment, and Blake managed to leap inside just as the train started.

He found himself in the atmosphere redolent of tobacco smoke, and a burly, grey-haired man reached out a hand and caught at Blake's sleeve.

"Steady on, mate," came a deep, rumbling voice. "There's plenty of ways o' breaking your neck without doing it like that."

The detective seated himself in the corner opposite his companion. He saw that he was a stumpy, tremendously stout man, grey-whiskered and clear-eyed, bearing on him the unmistakable stamp of the sea.

Above the man's head was a battered sea kit-bag and next to the bag was a cage, covered with a linen cloth. A tapping on the wires of the cage sounded, and the man, reaching up a long arm, brought the cage down to the seat by his side, lifting up the cloth and displaying a green parrot.

"What's the matter wi' you, Polly?" he asked; and the bird shrieked at him, raising its wings and displaying it's red tongue.

"Got him on the west coast, sir," said the sailorman. "My little nephew'll be pleased wi' him, I bet."

"Are you going to Grangepool?" Blake asked.

"Yes, sir. Born an' bred at Grangepool, I was."

The old sailor dived his hand into a capacious pocket and produced a piece of biscuit which he pushed through the cage. The bird grabbed at it quickly and, making itself comfortable on one corner of the perch, lapsed into silence.

"Ever been on the west coast, sir?" the sailor asked.

Blake nodded.

"Yes," he said; "Sierra Leone, Port Kalabar, the Cameroons."

The sailor's eye widened.

"Bless me 'eart, I've been all along that part o' the coast, too," he said.

They chatted together for a few minutes and it was evident that Blake's knowledge of the "White Man's Grave" made a big impression on the old sailor.

"I can't say as I like that part o' the world at all," he said. "Give me the ice and a good old Greenland whale puffing in the distance."

He leaned back in his seat, swelling his broad chest.

"Them were the days, sir," he said. "My word, Grangepool was a prosperous town in them days. I've seen as many as twenty whalers and sealers set off the little harbour, sir. There was money to go in they days."

"Yes; we have lost that part of the trade, havent we," said Blake.

"Oh, yes; still there's a few go out from Dundee even now, sir," the old sailor went on, "but there ain't any money in it. The Yankees have collared it all. From Vancouver and 'Frisco out to the islands."

Here was a man who evidently might be useful to Blake.

"Did you ever hear of a place called Salcoth Island?" asked the detective.

The broad visage in front of him smiled.

"Rather," the old tar said. "Why, its one of the best sealing spots in the world."

He leaned forward and wagged a fat forefinger.

"You mayn't believe me, sir," he said, "but I tell you we've run a boat ashore on the south beach of Salcoth Island and there's been as many as ten thousand seals there. Lor'! what a chorus they did make, with their roaring and champing!"

His eyes smiled at the remembered vision.

"We used to club 'em, sir—the bachelors, you know. It was a dirty job and a man had to get hardened to it before he could do the work. Just swing the club over the head and down they went. But there was money in it, heaps o' money—and allus a chance o' havin' a fight with the Russians, too. Them were the days."

"And you used to sail from Grangepool, did you?"

"Yes, sir. I was second mate o' the Seafoam."

The name conveyed nothing to Blake, yet it had been a wonderful turn of chance that had brought this weather-beaten old sailor across the detective's path.

"She was one o' the best, sir," the old chap went on, "and she come to her end in a dirty way. I never forgave the man for it."

To the old sailor it was simply a piece of ancient history and a story that he must have recounted a hundred times.

"She belonged to Mr. Malcom MacLeod," he went on.

Blake interrupted.

"MacLeod! I know someone in Grangepool of the name of MacLeod. Hector MacLeod his name is."

"Hector! That's my old master's son," the sailor broke out. "My name is Ben Wade, sir, and if you know Mr. Hector he'll tell you that story is true."

He lighted a pipe and drew a couple of puffs at it.

"It's a long time ago," he went on, "the best part of twenty years. Mr. MacLeod had not been doing very well, and the Seafoam was all that he had left. It was a good boat, worth a power o' money, and if it hadn't been for the treachery of the skipper, Nat Marle, Mr. MacLeod would ha' been all right."

"What happened?" Blake asked.

"I wasn't on board at the time, or it never would have happened," Ben went on. "I got a bad touch o' rheumatics and they put me ashore at 'Frisco. They thought I was a going to die, but I was a bit too tough for that. The Seafoam went on to the island, and from all accounts she made a bumper catch, the biggest haul of seals that was ever known. They tell me that the holds were filled up with 'em, and that means that there must have been the best part of twenty or thirty thousand pounds worth."

"Well, what happened?"

The old fellow brought down his first with a crash.

"Marle was a dog and a traitor, sir," he said. "I heard the whole story later in 'Frisco. One day I went down to the docks and, lo and behold, what should I see comin' sailin' into the harbour but the old Seafoam. I would have knowed her a mile off, although she was flying the American colours and was under another name. I tried to get on board, but they wouldnt let me, but after a bit I tumbled across one o' the crew. Ravin' drunk he was, in Chinatown, slobbering and throwing his sovereigns about as though they was dirt."

The old fellow's face was aglow now and he breathed heavily.

"I got the truth out o' the skunk," he said. "Marle had turned traitor and had sold the Seafoam and the whole catch to a rascally American skipper. Every man of the crew got a share of the swag and the drunken beast that told me about it, got the best part o' three hundred pounds."

"What a scoundrelly thing to do," Blake put in.

"It wur worse than that, sir," said Ben. "No honest sailorman would ever have done it."

"What happened to Marle?"

"Dunno," said the old man. "He never showed his face again in Grangepool as I heard on, so I expect he is all right. He must have collared the bigger part o' the swag and no doubt he's a rich man now, livin' in every comfort. But it killed MacLeod, sir, an it made a beggar o' his son."

The old sailor's face was stern and his fist clenched again.

"I've often hoped to come across Marle," he said. The world ain't a very big place, an' mebbe I'll do so some day."

He little dreamed that never in this life would he meet the traitor Marle. An unmarked grave within prison walls held all the mortal remains of his one-time skipper.

The little bit of ancient history had served to while away the journey very pleasantly, and at a quarter to eleven when the train came to a halt at Grangepool Station, Blake was quite loath to leave his talkative companion.

"I should like to see you again," he said. "I'm staying at the Railway Hotel, and if you care to drop in, say, some time to-morrow morning, you would meet your old master's son."

"Young Mr. Hector, sir?" said Ben. 'I'd like to see him again, I ain't been back to Grangepool for many years. He was only a nipper when I left."

Blake saw the old fellow comfortably installed in a cab with his kit-bag and parrot, and when they shook hands Ben promised to turn up on the following morning.

Blake made his way to the hotel, and as soon as he entered the hall a slim girlish figure arose and came towards him. It was Ruth Phillips, and there was an anxious expression on her face.

"I have been waiting for hours," she said. "I wondered what had become of you all."

"Hasn't Tinker or Hector turned up yet?" Blake asked.

"No," the girl said with a shake of her head. "I have asked the manager and he says they haven't been in since this afternoon." She caught at Blake's arm impulsively.

"I hope that—that nothing has happened to Hector," she said. "I've had a foreboding all this afternoon and evening that he was in—in danger of some sort."

Blake looked at the anxious face, then took the slim hand in his own.

"I don't think you need have any fears, Miss Phillips," he said. "If you will just wait a few moments I'll change, and then we'll go and look for them."

The hour was very late, and it was almost midnight before the two left the hotel. Blake hesitated for a moment before turning to his companion.

"Don't you think it would be better for you to go home?" he said. "I'm quite sure that Hector MacLeod and Tinker are all right, and it is rather late."

The little, firm chin tightened, and the girl shook her head.

"I will not go home, Mr. Blake," she said. "I must find out what has happened to Hector."

She slipped her hand under Blake's arm.

"Besides," she went on, "I know that I shall be quite safe with you."

There was a certain appeal in her voice that Blake could not withstand, so they made their way through the old town together, catching a belated tram that landed them close to Ravell's Alley.

"Tinker should be somewhere about here," said Blake. "I told him to stay on guard."

The girl shivered, and drew a little closer to her companion.

"This dreadful place again!" she said. "I hate it! It brings back memories to me—memories of my dear dad!"

The alley was in pitch darkness save here and there in the upper windows of some of the wretched houses, where a feeble light glimmered.

Blake and his companion went down until they came opposite 23A. It was in darkness, but in the ship chandler's establishment a light was burning from one of the first floor windows.

The detective gave a low whistle, and waited. It was a signal that was often used by himself and Tinker. There was no reply, but sudddenly the girl's hand tightened on his arm.

"There is someone watching us up there," she said. "I saw the blind move just a little."

Blake stepped up to the door of 23A and knocked on it sharply, then turned his head quickly towards the opposite house. He saw the curtain of the first floor window move, and just for a moment a face appeared in the gap. It was that of Mother Shipton, and she was peering out into the dark alley.

A moment later the curtain dropped, and the light in the room vanished. Blake tried the door of 23A, and found it was locked, just as Hector Macleod had left it.

"They are not here," Ruth said, pressing Blake's arm. "Oh, do come away; the place frightens me!"

"I'm afraid we must wait a moment or two longer," said the detective grimly, "and you will have to be a brave girl."

He was watching the other house intently, and presently he saw the flash of light in the ground floor window. It was only a momentary flash, evidently coming from the inner room.

"Mother Shipton seems to be rather alarmed," the detective muttered. "I must find out why."

He took Ruth by the arm, and, crossing the road, rapped loudly on the door of the shop. There was no response to his first summons, and he rapped again, louder and more persistently this time. They heard an inner door rattle, then footfalls came to them, and presently the clang of a bolt as it was drawn.

The door of the shop opened, and Mother Shipton's wizened figure appeared in the gap. She was holding a candle above her head, and she blinked her eyes as she stared at Blake and his companion.

"Wot's the matter with you?" she asked. "Wot do yer want comin' 'ere disturbin' folks at this hour o' night?"

Blake saw at once that the old dame had recognised him, and he stepped into the doorway, followed by Ruth. Mother Shipton fell back a pace.

"Wot do yer want—wot do yer want?" the old dame croaked.

Blake closed the door behind him, and put his back against it.

"I want a word with you," he said, in a stern tone. "I don't know what your motives are, but it appears to me that you are not going straight."

He slipped his hand into his pocket and drew out an object which he held forward. It was a badge.

"I am a detective," he said.

The old woman nodded her head.

"Yes, I know that—I know that," she said. "You're a 'tec, you are. I knows all about yer."

Quick as a flash Blake pounced on this admission.

"Indeed! Who told you that?"

For a moment the eyes of the old dame wavered, then she drew her withered body up.

"I ain't goin' to tell yer, mister," she said. "I'm an honest woman, I am, and I ain't going to——'

At that moment Ruth Phillips moved forward so that the light from the candle fell on her face. Mother Shipton's eyes turned towards the girl, then the hard, frightened look vanished from her face.

"Why, bless my soul, it's—it's Miss Phillips! 'Ow do ye do, my dear?"

The change in the tone was so marked that Blake stepped back, and a fleeting smile crossed his lips. The old dame had gone up to Ruth, and was holding her hand in a close grip.

"How are you, mother" Ruth said. "I haven't seen you for quite a long time."

"Oh, I'm all right, my dear," the old dame returned. "I don't forget my kind friends. How's your father?"

It was obvious from the question that Mother Shipton had very little interest in the more important game that Blake was following. The detective, however, saw in her question a sudden chance of winning the old woman over.

"It is on Mr. Phillips's behalf that we have come here" he said. quietly. "His life has been in danger, and Miss Phillips has asked me to help her."

Mother Shipton turned towards Blake.

"Mr Phillips in danger!" she repeated. "Why, he be a kind, good man, he be. Who would think o' hurtin' the likes of him?"

"There are two men in Grangepool who are his enemies" said Blake. "One of them is a tall big man, while the other is a thin, clean-shaven, short individual, with a face like a hawk."

He saw the old dame's lips drop, and a frightened look come into her eyes. She moved nearer.

"You have seen these two men, Mother Shipton," Blake said. "Come, admit it. I have no doubt but what they tricked you. The smaller man has a very plausible tongue, and I may as well tell you now they are escaped convicts."

"Convicts! Bless my soul!" The old dame staggered back against a heap of miscellaneous clothing. "Comin' to think of it, their hair was mighty short!"

"Then they have been here?" Blake put in. "They were here when I came in this morning?"

Mother Shipton's defiance had vanished now. Her companions saw her lips twitch, and Ruth suddenly slipped up the old woman's side and put her arm around the thin shoulders.

"It's all right, mother," she said. "Mr. Blake is a friend of mine, and he will be a friend of yours, also."

"I—I didn't know, sir—I didn't know," the kindly hearted woman began. "They told me that they was two pore sailormen who had deserted their ships, and were afraid o' being locked up by the perlice. I allus had a soft corner in my heart for sailors, and that's why I told yer a lie. I wouldn't have let 'em go if I'd knowed."

"Then they have gone?"

The old dame cleared a space for herself on an upturned case, and sat down.

"I'll tell yer all about it." she said. "About half an hour ago they called me upstairs, and said that they was being watched. They pointed out o' the window, and showed me someone standing by the house oposite."

"What was he like?"

"A young sailor he looked like, sir," said mother Shipton. "I'd seen him walking up and down the lane during the evening. They told me he was a 'tec, and they would have to get away. They asked me to watch until the sailor had gone up the street, then give them a call. I did so. As soon as his back was turned I called to them, and they both went out o' the shop and into the house across the way."

"How did they get in?"

"They 'ad a key, sir." And any doubts that Blake might have had as to the identity of Mother Shipton's guests vanished.

"What happened then?"

The old dame began to tremble.

"I don't quite know, sir," she said. "I left the door and went upstairs to tidy up a bit. I glanced out o' the window, and I—I think I saw the young sailor go into the house."

"Yes; go on!"

"I cleaned up the room, and came down to the shop again, and I heard the door opposite bang, and my two lodgers went off up the alley."

With a quick movement, Ruth turned to Blake.

"Come, we must go into the house" she said. "Who was it? Was it Hector who was watching?"

Blake shook his head.

"No" he returned; "it was Tinker."

They rushed out of the shop across to 23A. There was no time to be wasted, and Blake, bunching his shoulders, went at the door like a bull. It gave way at the impact, and he leapt into the dingy hall.

An electric torch was drawn from his pocket, and he searched the lower rooms, but found them empty. Then, darting upstairs, he leapt into the room on the right.

A huddled figure on the bed caught his eye, and, with a rush, Blake was across the room.

Tinker, bound hand feet, and gagged, lay quite unconscious on the dirty mattress. Lifting the lad in his arms, the detective carried his burden across the floor and down the stairs out of 23A, crossing the road to the ship chandler's shop.

A knife quickly severed the bonds, and the gag was removed, then Mother Shipton and Ruth began to attend to the youngster, and, at last, Tinker opened his eyes and sat up.

He looked very sick and dazed, and for a few moments seemed lost to his surroundings. then, suddenly, his eyes cleared, and he nodded up to Blake.

"I thought I was done for that time, guv'nor" the lad said, in a weak voice. "The beggars tricked me."

Mother Shipton had brought a little pannikin of rum and water, and she made Tinker sip the fluid.

"I was at the head of the alley," said Tinker, "and saw them come out of the shop. I recognised them at once. They went into 23A, and I followed them. They must have done it to trap me, for as soon as I stepped inside the door, I received this."

He raised his hand to his head, and disclosed a huge wound. But his smile was as bright as ever as he turned his eyes towards Ruth.

"I don't remember much what happened after that," the lad said, with a dry smile. "It was really a score to them."

Blake had already made up his mind what he was going to do, and he turned to Mother Shipton.

"You must try to get a cab for us," he said. "Tinker will have to go back to the hotel, and Miss Phillips will go and look after him?"

"But what are you going to do, guv'nor?" said the youngster.

"I must get down to the south basin," Blake returned. "I feel sure that these two rascals are going to try and get on board the Anastor; and, besides, I want to find MacLeod."

"But mayn't I come as well, Mr. Blake?" Ruth began.

"No," Blake said, pointing to Tinker. "You will have to go back to the hotel and look after Tinker."

"But I—I am quite all right, guv'nor," the lad said. But even as he spoke the words, he swayed and had to clutch at the counter to support himself.

"You are anything but all right, old chap," the detective said; "and, in any case, you can't come with me just now. Get back to the hotel and wait for me there."

He nodded to them both, and in another moment had vanished. Tinker leaning against the counter, turned a sorrowful face towards Ruth.

"That's done it," the lad said disgustedly. "There's going to be no end of a dust-up at the south basin, and I shall jolly well be out of it all. It's just my luck!"

CHAPTER 6.

On Board the Anastor.

Hector MacLeod had taken up his task of watching the Anastor, with a keen zest. The young bank clerk felt that it was no small honour for him to be favoured by the great Sexton Blake, and apart from that, there was also the fact that he was helping to clear up the tragedy that hung over Ruth Phillips's life.

As he made his way down to the quay, a slight drizzling rain began to fall, and Hector, diving into one of the numerous little shops in that region, emerged presently wearing a second-hand oilskin coat and a blue peaked cap.

He left his bowler hat and light coat behind him in the shop, little dreaming that many months would pass before he would return there to claim his garments.

He went down to the south basin, and presently found himself on the quay to which the Anastor was moored. It was evident that the lading of the vessel had been completed, for the hatches were down and the tarpaulins tight over them.

One or two of the crew were hanging about on the deck, and, after watching a few moments, Hector saw a thick-set man emerge from one of the companions and come to the end of the gangway. The man was in his shirt-sleeves, but the fact that he was wearing a collar and tie hinted that he had some sort of rank on board.

As a matter of fact, he was chief engineer of the Anastor. The man looked right and left, the apparently enraged about something, came down the gangway and stepped on to the quay, close to where Hector MacLeod was lounging against the capstan.

"What are ye hangin' aboot here for?"

The voice was distinctly Scotch, and Hector straightened up sharply, making as though to move away. The chief engineer thrust out a broad fist and closed his fingers on the lad's oilskin sleeve.

"A'reet, ma son, dinna get scared. What I want to know is, do ye want a job?"

"Do you mean on board?" Hector asked.

The chief engineer nodded.

"I've been waiting all day for a young scamp to turn up," he said. "but he hasn't come yet. He's my cabin-boy. If ye want a job ye can hae his."

It's not by any means unusual for one or two of a crew to fail to put in an appearance prior to a vessel's departure, and there are always one or two men hanging round the quays in the hope of getting what is called a "jump" job.

The chief engineer had evidently mistaken Hector for one of this type, and instantly, the lad saw his opportunity.

"When do you sail, sir?" he asked.

"Midnight," came the reply. "I'll tell ye what I'll do. Come on board now an' set my cabins to rights, and if that young scoundrel doesn't turn up before the ship sails, ye can take his place. If he does turn up, why, I'll pay ye well for what you do."

This exactly suited Hector's rôle, and, a few moments later, he was striding up the gangway behind old Thomson. He was led along a narrow galleyway and shown into a small cabin on the right.

"There ye are," said the chief engineer, "jest put this place to rights. I haven't time to bother aboot my kit now. I must look after the engines."

He stopped for a moment to point out the various articles to Hector, then with a nod to the lad, the chief engineer turned and stalked away, his iron-shod shoes clanging on the steel steps of the alleyway.

Hector crossed the cabin and looked out of the porthole. He saw that it was just level with the quay and close to the gangway that ran up at a sharp angle. If anyone came or went by way of the gangway, Hector was bound to see them.

He slipped off his oilskin coat, removed his jacket and waistcoat, then, rolling up his shirt-sleeves, set to work.

His task was quite an easy one. He made the bed in the little bunk, opened a couple of old portmanteaux that belonged to the chief engineer, and set to work to arrange the various garments in a couple of lockers.

It was quite dusk now, and one of the sailors came round lighting the lamps. A lamp was also hung above the gangway, its yellow gleams shimmering on the wet boards.

At the end of an hour Hector was summoned by a man in greasy dungarees to "come and have a bite o' food." He followed his guide along the deck and into the fo'castle, where he found a gang of men seated in the stuffy quarters. A pannikin of tea was issued to him with a generous chunk of bread and jam, and Hector set to work.

There was very little conversation, the men were tired and were content to munch away in silence. They were practically new hands, and not made each other's acquaintance yet.

The young bank clerk hurried through his meal slipped back to the cabin where he could keep his watch.

Somewhere about ten o'clock he saw two or three men come on board, and one of them, a sturdy individual, was wearing the regulation captain's cap. Hector had seen Captain Turner before, and he recognised the old skipper.

The other men were civilians, evidently clerks from the shipping office, for they chatted for a moment with Turner, then, shaking hands with him, went off down the gangway and disappeared.

The coming of the skipper seemed to be a signal for fresh bustle on board the Anastor. Hector heard one or two sharp commands ring out, followed by the clatter of feet on the deck above. A whimsical expression crossed the lad's face and he drew back from the porthole.

"By Jove, it looks to me as if I shall be carried off in this old tramp unless I am careful," he mused.

He dressed himself again, slipping into his oilskin, and stepped out of the cabin, hurrying along the alleyway and gaining the upper deck. He had no desire to find himself a member of the crew and he made up his mind to slip ashore at the first convenient moment.

Just as he reached the upper deck one of the seamen sounded the bell, six times. It was eleven o'clock.

The echoes of the bell had hardly died away when Hector, standing close to the rails, heard hurrying feet sound on the quay. He turned and peered into the darkness. A little undersized figure was just looming up the gangway, and behind him came a huge, broad-shouldered man.

As the two came higher the lamp swinging above the gangway shone on their faces. Hector drew back and turned the collar of his oilskin coat over his ears.

He had recognised them at once. They were the man he knew as Doctor Kay and his huge companion.

As soon as Kew reached the deck he halted for a moment. The captain's cabin lay aft, and there was little light in the doorway.

The young clerk waited until he saw the door of the cabin open and the two figures pass inside, then, with a quick rush, he was across the deck, and, passing round to the back of the cabin, he raised his head and gazed through the porthole.

Kew and Carlac were standing in front of a table at which Captain Turner was seated.

"The matter can be settled here and now," Kew's voice was saying. "There's a hundred pounds for you for a passage for myself and friend to San Franciso."

"This is not a passenger vessel," Turner's voice replied.

"No, I quite understand that. We are ready to rough it."

Hector had a good view of Kew's hawk-like face, and he saw in it a strained anxiety.

"Come," he went on, "a hundred pounds is a lot of money. I have it here and ready."

He thrust his hand into his inner pocket and drew out a bulky package. Hector saw the captain lean forward, and into the man's eyes there came a look of greed.

The skipper of a tramp steamer such as the Anastor is only very poorly paid by the owners, and a hundred pounds means a small fortune to the struggling man.

Turner realised, of course, that there was something shady in these two characters in front of him. But then, within the hour, the Anastor would have sailed and Turner knew that once he was clear of England he would be safe.

"I can only give you a small cabin," the captain said. "there will just be room for the two of you, but there won't be any space left for your kits."

Kew's lips parted in a quiet smile.

"We haven't any kit," he said in his harsh voice. "We are travelling as we are."

He had unfolded the package and drew out a heap of gold with several crinkling banknotes. He counted out the notes, then the gold, placing the sovereigns in heaps of ten on top of the notes, which he pushed forward.

"There you are," he said, "one hundred pounds. That settles it."

The captains's fingers closed over the little piles of gold and notes, and Kew knew that he had succeeded in gaining his point. He removed his heavy coat, revealing the fact that he was dressed in a suit of good blue serge with clean collar and shirt, and new tie. It was evident that both he and Carlac had made a swift change in their wardrobe. There was nothing of the down-at-heel sailor about them now.

Kew drew out a gold watch and glanced at it. The obvious value of the article seemed to impress Captain Turner.

"You sail at twelve I believe?" said Kew.

"About that time," Turner went on. "And now, if you wait a moment, I'll send for the steward."

Hector slipped away from the porthole, and from a safe hiding-place behind one of the boats, he watched until the steward had entered the cabin and emerged again, followed by Carlac and Kew.

The trio went along the deck towards the stern, and Hector, moving noiselessly, saw them vanish at last into a little cabin, from which, a few moments later the steward returned alone.

Hector ventured up to the cabin and cast one glance inside. Carlac had flung himself on to one of the bunks and was puffing contentedly at a cigarette, while Kew, perched like a bird on the opposite bunk, was speaking in low tones to his companion.

Hector drew back, a grim ex pression on his young face.

"You've managed to do the trick after all," he thought. "By Jove, what am I going to do now?"

It was rather a difficult position for the youngster to find himself in. Sexton Blake had asked him to keep a look out for these two men, and here they were on board! But the minutes were swiftly winging past and Hector knew that within the next hour or so, the Anastor would be on its way out of the harbour on the first stage of its long journey.

"What the dickens am I to to?" the young clerk repeated, cudgelling his brains.

It was impossible for him to find a messenger to go up to the hotel and tell Blake of what had happened, and he felt that if he himself undertook that task there was every possibility of the Anastor sailing before he could return.

Deep down in his heart Hector MacLeod felt that it was absolutely imperative for him to keep in close touch with these two ruffians. He would have found it hard to explain why this opinion dominated everything else, but it was so, and, at last, he shaped his course on it.

"I'll wait here," he decided. "It's the only thing I can do. These fellows are on board and I can watch them while they are here. When they go on shore, wherever it may be, I can follow. It won't do to lose touch with them."

It was certainly the best thing he could have done, under the circumstances, and he slipped off along the main deck and went down into the galleyway in which the chief engineer's cabin was situated.

He entered the cabin to find old Thomson seated at the little table with a big tumbler of whisky-and-soda in front of him.

"Hallo, you young scamp! Where've you been?" the chief engineer broke out.

Hector came to a halt in the doorway.

"I did everything, sir," he said, "and I wasn't quite sure whether you wanted me to stay on or not."

Thomson cast an approving glance round the cabin.

"Yes, you're quite right," he said, somewhat mollified. "Ye've put everything in ship-shape order. But what do ye mean by me not wanting ye?"

"Well, sir, I thought the other lad might have turned up."

"He did, dang him, but I sent him aboot his business!" the chief engineer barked out. "Ye'll do for me all right, and as soon as I've finished this tumbler I'll take ye along and sign ye on."

He pointed to the oilskin coat.

"But ye can't knock about the ship in togs like those" he went on. "I'll show ye where my boy used to sleep. It's not very decent quarters, but he liked it all right."

The old chap finished his drink, then led Hector along the galley and opened a door. It was really a store-room, filled with kegs and bales of waste. In one corner a hammock had been slung, and there was small locker close to it.

"There ye are." said Thomson; "ye can either sleep here or for'ard with the crew, jest as ye like."

"I'd rather sleep here, thanks," said Hector.

"Right; you'll find some blue togs in the corner there. Jest git into them, and come down to the engine-room when ye're ready. Mebbe I'll find ye a job down there."

Hector would rather have remained on deck, but he realised that it would be foolish of him to go against his new master's orders.

Thomson swung along the galley, and Hector made a swift change of garments. The lad grinned to himself as he slipped into the blue dungarees.

"I wonder what Ruth would say if she saw me now! he thought, glancing down at the oil-stained, ragged suit.

He managed to make his way down the steel ladder into the bowels of the vessel, and Thomson beckoned to him. The engineer was standing on a little iron bridge that spanned the engines. Despite the fact that he was chief engineer, Thomson had a piece of oil waste in his hand and also a huge oil-can. He had evidently been giving the last finishing touches to his beloved machinery.

"Everything's tight and trim, lad," the old Scotsman said to Hector. "In as few more minutes ye'll hear the bell clang, and these long pistons will begin to rise an' fall and they won't stop again, mind ye, until we are the other side o' the world. Here, take hold o' this!"

He pushed the oil-can into Hector's hand, and indicated a small steel-runged ladder.

"Jest ye shin up there and fill up that tap," he said, indicating the oil-gauge.

Hector was nimble, and he quickly climbed the little ladder and reached out, tilting the oil-can until the cup above the gauge was filled. When he came back to the bridge Thomson gave him an approving nod.

"That's good!" he said. "I see ye've got a steady hand. Boy, we'll mak' an engineer o' ye yet!"

All this time Hector was on tenderhooks, for his mind was constantly returning to the deck above. He was, however, forced to remain beside his master, and presently the sharp clang of a bell sounded.

Thomson's voice roared out an order, there was a rush of steam, a sharp throb, and the huge piston-rods began to rise and fall. The Anastor was under way.

Another clang, and then for the space of half an hour or so a series of orders rang out, and then gradually the ship got clear of the quay and moving like a grey wraith down through the silent harbour out to sea.

The first long swell of the ocean lifted the tramp, and Hector caught at the rail of the little bridge to steady himself.

"Ye'd better get up on deck now," Thomson said, with a nod to him. "The smell o' the oil might upset ye for a bit, but ye'll soon find ye're sea legs. Go on, up ye' get!"

He gave the lad a slight push, and Hector was only too glad to escape from the oil-laden atmosphere, climbing the steel ladders and emerging on to the deck.

The rain had passed away, and there was a starlit sky above. The fresh sea wind was whistling through the riggings of the tramp, and the Anastor was thrashing her way out into the grey Atlantic.

To port and starboard there were still tiny lights, revealing the nearness of the coast. Hector turned and glanced back to where a little cluster of lights glittered in the darkness behind. He knew that was Grangepool, and just for a moment a feeling of depression swept over the lad.

"Perhaps I have been a confounded idiot," he told himself. "I've gone off on a wild goose chase, without a soul knowing about me."

The feeling only lasted a moment, however, and he remembered again the presence of the two evil men on board the tramp steamer. He decided to have another look at them, and he made his way towards the stern, slipping past the captain's cabin and going down the deck until he reached the little cabin at the end.

There was no light showing, and he stepped up to the porthole and listened for a moment. But there was no sign of any occupants inside.

Again a doubt arose in the lad's mind.

Was it possible that these two after all, had changed their plans and had not sailed?

He moved away from the cabin and halted for a moment beside one of the lifeboats, leaning against its side. Five or six minutes passed, then presently Hector saw the two figures emerge from the lighted companion-way that led to the salon.

With a quick movement Hector drew himself up into the lifeboat. He found that the canvas which usually covers these boats had not been placed in position, and he knelt down in the centre, his fingers coming in contact with a lifebuoy.

He had recognised the two figures at once, and he waited. He heard their footfalls sound, and to his nostrils there came the scent of cigar smoke.

Raising himself cautiously, Hector peered over the side of the boat. Kew and Carlac were just turning the corner to enter their cabin. He heard the metallic click of the door as it was opened; then suddenly Kew's harsh voice sounded:

"Quick! Get him!"

There was a scuffle and a rush, and three figures came swaying out from the cabin doorway to reel across the deck locked in a fierce embrace.

Hector leaned forward to watch the struggle. He saw that Carlac had wound his arms round the shoulders of the centre man, while Kew was struggling furiously to release his arms from the grip of the stranger.

They thudded against the lifeboat, making it sway to and fro, then went down on the deck in a sprawling heap.

There was no sound, only the heavy, gasping breathing of the men as they fought. It seemed to Hector as though the unknown man was putting up a wonderful battle. Twice Carlac's bulky figure had almost pinned the man to the deck, and yet with a superhuman effort the terrible grip of the ex-convict had been broken, and the bold-hearted stranger escaped.

Once Kew, with an agility that astounded Hector, leapt across the deck and swung a thin arm round his antagonist's throat. At the same time wedging his knee into the unknown man's back.

They went down on the deck together, and Carlac, gasping for breath, flung himself headlong, trying to take advantage of his nefarious comrade's attack.

But the man they fought with seemed to have the strength of ten. Kew's arms were plucked away, and a fierce thrust saw the monkey-liked professor flung aside, to roll over spluttering and snarling like a wild beast.

For ten long minutes the silent contest went on, and at last the end came. The unknown man had staggered to his feet and had evaded one wild rush from Carlac, but in doing so he had flung himself against the heavy iron stancheon that supported the lifeboat.

Hector heard the impact of the head against the iron, and it fairly sickened him.

"Now, Carlac—quick! We've got him!"

With a snarlish cry of triumph Kew leapt forward, with Carlac by his side. Hector, shifting his position to the other side of the lifeboat, peered over.

He was just in the nick of time. He saw the body of the unknown man being pressed slowly over the rails. Carlac, his long arms clutching at the man's throat, was pushing out and out, and finally Kew, raising his clenched fist, struck at the face of the man in front of him.

It was a fiendish blow, and it brought about the collapse of the gallant fighter. Hector heard a muffled groan, then the tense body tilted forward and went headlong into the sea.

Quick as a flash Kew and Carlac turned and darted back to their cabin. Hector, aghast with horror, stumbled across the boat; his foot came in contact with the lifebuoy, and a moment later the lad had lifted it and, swinging it clear above his head, tossed it out into the waters.

As he did so his feet slipped, and, unable to check himself, he went sprawling over the side of the boat to fall with a thud on the hard deck. His head came in contact with an iron bolt, and for a few moments he was knocked senseless.

How long he lay like that he was never able to say, but he recovered consciousness to find himself still alone on the dark deck, with the lifeboat above him.

He sat up, pressing his hands to his forehead. There was a huge lump above his left temple, and for a moment the lad sat, still waiting for his reeling brain to clear.

Then with a half-groan, he drew himself to his feet. The memory of the tragedy that he had witnessed came back to him, and with a sickening sensation, Hector MacLeod glanced at the cabin at the end of the deck.

There was a light there now, and the young bank clerk stole forward, raising himself until he reached the porthole, and peered inside for a moment.

Carlac was lying on his bunk, while Kew, bending over the huge fellow, was bandaging his left wrist. The big ex-convict groaned once during the ordeal, and Kew cast a quick glance around him.

"A twisted wrist is nothing, my friend," the harsh voice said; "if you had broken your neck it would have been worth while. This is the best night's work we have ever done, for it has freed us of the man we had most to fear."

A cackling laugh sounded in the cabin—a laugh so cold and callous that it sent a shiver through the listener's body.

"You and I have been in at the death, Carlac," said Kew. "Sexton Blake will trouble us no more."

"Sexton Blake!"

Hector MacLeod staggered back from the porthole, his hands pressed against his temples.

So it was the great detective that had struggled with these two vile ruffians; it was Sexton Blake who had been cast over the rails into the seething sea!

For a moment Hector felt inclined to blame himself for the part he had played. He had remained silent in the lifeboat, watching that struggle, without lifting a hand to help.

"If I'd only known—if I'd only known!"

He was still weak from the effects of the heavy fall, and at last he turned and reeled off down the deck, his heart as heavy as lead within him.

Sexton Blake was dead! The grey seas had closed over him and it seemed to Hector as though all his efforts had been wasted. Just for a moment a fleeting hope entered his heart.

Not more than a second could have elapsed from the time that the detective had been flung into the sea to the period when Hector had flung the lifebuoy out.

Yet the hope was such a flimsy one that the lad had to dismiss it at last.

"No; it's not much good relying on that," he muttered. "I've got to see this thing through myself. Those two brutes have won out so far, but I'll hang on to them to the bitter end!"

It was a plucky decision to come to, for Hector MacLeod was well aware of the type of men he was up against. It spoke volumes for his splendid courage that he did not falter.

Wherever they went he would follow, and when it came to the final test he would be there to try his youthful strength against their combined villainy.

He found his way to the little store-room, and, wearied out, flung himself into the hammock, and, in a few minutes, was fast asleep, while the Anastor went on its way breasting the grey waters of the great Atlantic, heading for the west.

CHAPTER 9.

A Fight For Life.

Hector MacLeod had not been mistaken. It really was Sexton Blake who had made such a dramatic appearance on board the Anastor. And, yet the mystery of his being there had a very simple solution.

The reader will remember that Blake had left Tinker and Ruth Phillips, telling them that he was going to the south basin to find Hector MacLeod.

It was about a quarter to twelve when Blake had found himself at the quayside, and a search revealed to him the fact that the young bank clerk had vanished. He was at a loss to account for the disappearance of the lad, but before he had time to study it out very clearly, a man came down the gangway from the Anastor and crossed the quay towards the sheds.

Blake, who had been in the shadows of the sheds, took a pace forward, and the man, turning his head, went up to him.

"Want to earn a shilling, mate?" he said.

"Don't mind if I do," Blake returned.

The detective was wearing a long overcoat and cap. It was the steward of the Anastor who had accosted him, and the fellow jerked his thumb towards the sheds.

"All right, come on," he said. "We ain't got much time to waste. I've got to get another couple o' cases o' whisky for the old man."

Blake fell into step by the steward's side, and presently they cleared the sheds and turned towards a line of houses that stood just outside the south basin dock.

"Can't make out why the skipper didn't get his store o' whisky at the proper time," the steward grumbled. "I tell yer, it ain't no cop being steward on board the Anastor. Ye're just like a bally messenger boy, running here an' there, an' attending to anyone an' everyone that likes to shout to yer."

He was evidently in a bad humour over something, and Blake smiled to himself.

"Still, you'd be worse off if you were on board a passenger boat," he said.

The steward snorted.

"Oh, I dunno," he returned, "a steward on board a passenger ship gets a lot o' tips. Besides, our skipper's gone an' turned the Anastor into a bloomin' passenger vessel—goodness knows why."

"Carrying passengers are you?"

"Yus; two came on board about half an hour ago, and between you an' me, mate, I don't like the looks of 'em."

Blake was on the alert at once.

"Two passengers, eh!"

"Yus; sneaked on board they did. But I guess they've squared the skipper all right, so it ain't got nothin' to do wi' me."

"What are they like?"

"Why ye never saw such a funny lookin' couple in ye're life," said the steward. "One of 'em is a great hulking feller, looks as strong as a bull, while the other is a little monkey of a man."

Crude though the descriptions were, they fitted the personalities of Carlac and Kew exactly, and Blake felt a quick thrill of contentment run through him.

His reasoning had not been at fault. There was no doubt but what Kew and Carlac were escaping from Grangepool by making use of the Anastor.

"I expect the whisky is really for them," the steward went on, as he came to a halt outside one of the dark houses in the row. "Jest wait for me here, mate, I won't be a minute."

He knocked on the door and was admitted, to emerge a few moments later carrying two cases, one of which he indicated to Blake, then the return journey began.

Blake put a few questions to the man, and soon discovered where Carlac and Kew had taken up their quarters.

They reached the Anastor and mounted the gangway, the steward leading the way across the deck and down the companion-way to the saloon.

"Jest put it down here, mate," he said, as they entered the saloon, "I'll look after it now."

Blake swung the case from his shoulder, and the steward slipping his hand into his pocket, produced a shilling which he put into Blake's hand.

The detective took the tip with a word of thanks, then, turning, went up the stairs and on to the deck again. But, instead of crossing to the gang-way, Blake moved along the deck past the skippers quarters, and finally found himself close to the end cabin in which Kew and Carlac had taken up their abode.

Blake looked around him and saw the lifeboat, the very same one in which Hector had later on found shelter. A swift leap saw the detective over the boat's side, and he made himself comfortable between the wide thwarts.

Presently he heard a commanding voice ring out, and one or two sailors appeared. There also emerged on to the quay a little knot of officials, and the gangway was moved from the Anastor, while the cables that had bound it to the quay were drawn in.

As the clang of the engine bell sounded, Blake heard a click! and a moment later, two figures emerged from the aft cabin. As they passed into the shaft of light, Blake cast a quick glance at them, and all doubts that might have been in his mind vanished.

For the first figure was that of Kew, and behind him came the massive-shouldered Carlac. They stepped across the deck, passing quite close to the boat in which Blake had hidden himself. They reached the rails and stood there watching, while the bows of the Anastor sagged out from the quay.

The beat of the propeller sounded, and the vessel began to move away into the darkness.

For the best part of half an hour Blake crouched in his hiding-place, then someone came along the deck, and, after glancing in the end cabin, came up to where Kew and Carlac were standing.

"Supper's ready, gentlemen," said the steward's voice, "the skipper would like you to join him."

Carlac grunted in acknowledgment, and the two went off along the deck. The steward moved towards the cabin and vanished inside.

As soon as the deck was cleared. Blake slipped out of the boat and stepped across towards the end cabin. He saw the steward at work arranging the bunks. The man had brought a bundle of blankets with him, and he was making everything ship-shape for the night.

Blake watched the man for ten minutes. The steward was evidently in no hurry, for he went about his work in a leisurely way that made Blake fume inwardly.

"Why the dickens don't you finish and clear out?" the detective thought to himself.

A moment or so later, however, his impatience was rewarded. The steward extinguished the lamp in the cabin, stepped out of the door and closed it behind him. Blake darted back into the darkness behind the boat, then waited till the steward had vanished. Then, after a momentary hesitation, the detective went back to the door and opened it, stepping inside.

Producing his pocket-torch Blake touched the switch, and a little white bulb of light flashed out. There was a heap of clothes on one of the lockers, and Blake, going to up to it, began to examine the pile.

They were two suits, one of them evidently belonging to Kew, while the other was Carlac's property. Presently, the long frock coat that Kew had worn came between Blake's fingers, and in the deep breast-pocket Blake's hand came in contact with a bulky notebook.

Dropping the garment on to the floor, Blake seated himself on the side of one of the bunks, and, fixing the electric torch so that its light fell on the book, he began to turn the pages.

Suddenly his eyes gleamed, and his head fell forward. It was an address that had caught his eye: Mr. James Phillips, the Grangepool and District Bank, Grangepool. Beneath it were a number of other entries, and Blake read them swiftly.

"Joseph Smith, alias Nat Marle, one time captain of the Seafoam."

A quick, indrawn breath sounded in the cabin.

Kew, always a methodical man, had taken care to note down all necessary particulars concerning the strange story that the dying convict had revealed to him.

"Deposit of twenty thousand pounds made in Marle's name at Grangepool and District Bank. James Phillips signed receipt for money. Ship's papers and deposit-note hidden in Eskimo hut, Salcoth Island."

Then underneath this note there came what was obviously a fresher entry.

"Phillips got away but no matter. He was convinced that Carlac was Marle."

The entries were all contained in two leaves of the book, and Blake, withdrawing a sharp penknife from his pocket, carefully cut the leaves out, then taking his own notebook from his pocket, folded the precious slips and placed them inside.

The search had taken him longer the he had thought. He stooped to pick up the frock-coat and replace the book, when suddenly there came a metallic click! and the door of the cabin opened.

Swift as a flash, the detective had extinguished the torch, but the keen eyes of the man in the doorway had caught sight of the strong, clean-shaven face in the glow of the little bulb.

A muttered word sounded, then Carlac, with a spring, had reached his man, and one mighty tug saw the detective drawn out through the door of the cabin, to stagger across the deck, with Carlac and Kew clinging to him.

There is no need to repeat the scene of the deadly struggle. Blake put up a splendid fight, but the odds were against him, and, at last, the end came. Kew's vicious blows brought Blake's tough resistance to a close, and the detective went down into the deep sea.

The cold waters closing over his head roused Blake, and madly, furiously, he began to swim down, deeper and deeper into the sea. He knew the the suction of the water would drag him towards the keen blades of the propeller, and it was to battle against this tremendous force that he fought.

He went down and down, striking out madly, powerfully, until at last there came to his ears the churning beat of the propeller as it passed over his head.

In the welter of water that followed the wake, Blake came struggling to the surface gasping for breath. He was tossed hither and thither for a moment, like a cork, then to his ears there came a faint splash.

He began to tread water, and peered through the darkness. He saw the broad hull of the Anastor vanishing into the distance. The lights from the tramp were sending little shafts of yellow gold over the troubled surface.

From the portholes in the stern came a great beam of light which flashed over the foam-flecked wake. Blake fancied he caught sight of a white gleam in the beams of light, and he struck out towards it.

Twenty strokes saw his fingers come in contact with the wet, round edge of the lifebuoy, and, with a gasp of relief, the detective dived to come up in the wide circle of the life-saving buoy.

By this time the Anastor had vanished into the darkness, and Blake was alone in the grey sea. He had made himself comfortable in the buoyant circle, his hands outstretched on either side of him.

The lifebuoy was a big one, capable of keeping a couple of men afloat, and Blake rode high in the water. A feeling of thankfulness came down on him; and he drew a deep breath.

"I wonder what the solution of this problem?" he thought. "It was neither Kew nor Carlac who threw this lifbuoy overboard, and yet, it almost seemed to follow me into the sea."

A swift intuition came to him.

"By Jove! is it possible it could have been young MacLeod?" he went on, his quick wit leaping to the truth at once. "That must be it. No doubt the lad is on board, and in all probability he witnessed our struggle."

If his conclusions were correct, Blake knew that it meant that Carlac and Kew were not yet safe. Hector MacLeod was on board the Anastor with them, and the incident of the lifebuoy told Blake that the lad was quite able to use his wits in moments of stress.

"Good luck to him, anyhow," said Blake. "He certainly did his best for me."

He began to tread water to keep the blood circulating through his body. The sea was bitterly cold, and although it was smooth enough, there was chill wind blowing.

The struggle which he had gone through had weakened the detective somewhat, and had it not been for the buoyant circle around him there is little doubt but what Blake would have paid the penalty of his temerity with his life.

Through the long hours of darkness he floated, sometimes resting in the buoy, at others swimming inside it. Fatigue began to claim him, and he felt the deadly coming of sleep.

Blake knew that were he to sleep it would be the end of everything; his unconscious body would slip through the circle and he would drown.

Yet the powerful influence of sleep began to grow on him, and he had to fight furiously against its numbing, insinuating touch.

From the east the grey dawn came slowly, revealing a barren sea. The sun came up at last, and the tired, plucky man turned his face towards it.

An hour passed, then another, and Blake began to weaken visibly. Once he almost slipped from the circle of the buoy, and the effort he had to make to reach it again warned him that his strength was fast leaving him.

Another such slip as that and there was every probability of him not being able to regain his balance.

He began to tread water again, languidly, slowly. He felt that he was in a current of some sort, for the buoy was floating at a steady rate.

Suddenly, ahead of him, Blake saw a thin, white flicker of foam appear for a moment on the surface, then vanish. He watched it wearily. It appeared again, vanished, appeared and vanished; then a moment later the meaning of it dawned on him. He was close to a sunken reef, and the foam he saw was the waves breaking over the half-submerged rock.

He began to swim towards it, putting out all his strength. Nearer and nearer he drew, until at last a scurrying wave carried him forward a couple of yards, and his trailing feet came in contact with the jagged rocks over which the sea was breaking.

He saw now that there was another rock some twenty yards ahead. It was higher out of the water, and, although the waves broke over it, Blake saw that the surface appeared always above the sea.

"I suppose I must try," the wearied man told himself. "Twenty yards isn't much, but it seems a long way just now."

He set his teeth hard, and drew a deep breath. He knew that the lifebuoy, although it served to support him, was a drag on his arms as he swam. He came to a quick decision, and, raising his hands above his head, dropped through the circle, allowing the buoy to float away from him.

Then, taking his chance, Blake struck off from the submerged reef, heading for the more solid rock in front.

The memory of that swim was never to leave him. Twice he went under the surface, and only his indomitable courage, his immense determination, brought him above the sea again. He was at the end of his strength when his fingers clawed feebly at the wet rock, and he had to cling there for long moment before he found sufficient strength to drag himself up slowly, laboriously, to the weed-covered ledge.

He had to lie flat on his face in the weeds for a while until his strength returned, then he sat up and looked around him. The ledge he was on was only some thirty or forty yards square—a desolate perch in the midst of a lonely sea.

He was wet and hungry and tired, and it seemed to him as though his struggle had been a useless one. He arose slowly to his feet and stumbled forward through the slimy seaweed. Now and again a wave, higher than the others, would shake up through the weed and fall for a moment on the ledge.

In stormy weather there could be little doubt but what this perch would be absolutely covered with sea and foam, and it was only the fact that it was a calm sea that made it secure.

Right through the long hours of the day Blake remained on the little platform of rocks; then at last, in the waning light, came rescue.

The brown sails of a fishing-boat appeared westward. Blake caught sight of it silhouetted against the setting sun, and rising, to his feet, the plucky man drew off his coat and began to wave in languidly round his head.

At first he was afraid that his signal had not been observed, for the fishing-smack kept on its way as though it would pass him. Then, just as he was beginning to despair, he saw the brown sails swing round, waver for a moment in the breeze, then the broad bow of the smack was pointed towards him, and, with a double spume of foam rising from its sides, the boat came nearer to the reef.

A small skiff was put out, and a man jumped into it, thrusting an oar into the stern and sculling with vigorous strokes.

Blake waited until the bow touched the weed-covered reef; then, with a staggering rush, he flung himself into the little craft.

He was saved!

At seven o'clock that evening Ruth Phillips, a prey to a thousand fears and doubts, heard a knock sound on the door of the little sitting-room of the Railways Hotel, and she leapt to her feet.

The door was opened, and a burly man in blue clothes came into the room holding another man by the arm.

A shriek of joy broke from Ruth's lips, and she rushed forward.

"Mr. Blake—Mr. Blake!" she cried.

"All right, missy," a deep voice said. "Jest give him a chance."

Blake was weak and tired, and his burly companion helped him across the room and made him sit down on a chair. Ruth saw then that the detective was dressed in ragged blue trousers, and a thick blue jersey which was redolent of the unmistakable odour of fish.

His face was white, but the eyes were as clear and courageous as ever.

"How is—is Tinker?" Blake asked.

Ruth dropped on her knee by his side with a little smothered sob.

"He is quite all right, Mr. Blake," she returned; "but we have been—been so anxious. What has happened? You look so—so ill."

The deep-chested man who had accompanied Blake turned to the girl and laughed.

"He's all right, miss," said Ben Wade, in his booming voice. "The sea don't make no difference to a man like him. Jest you run along and get something hot—beef-tea, if you like, or a tot o' rum with sugar an' hot water. That's the stuff for a man that's been fighting with Davy Jones."

Ben Wade had been lounging on the quayside when the fishing-smack had arrived, and the old fellow had recognised Blake at once as he was being helped ashore. The kindly fishermen had done their best for the detective, taking off his sodden garments and dressing him in some of their own kit.

Exhausted though he had been, Blake had remembered about the notebook, and he had insisted on the sodden case being handed over to him.

When Ruth slipped away, at Ben's suggestion, Blake drew the notebook from his pocket and examined it carefully. Thanks to the fact of it being waterproof leather, the contents were practically uninjured, and Blake, opening the case, found the two slips that had come so near to costing him his life.

"I am glad it was you who met me, Ben," Blake said at last, "for I have got something here that ought to interest you."

"There ain't going to be anything interest me until you've had something hot to drink an' a bit o' food," said Ben. Nor would he listen to a word until Ruth had returned with a steaming bowl of beef-tea.

Blake had almost finished the strengthening food when Tinker burst into the room. The lad had been out all day searching for his beloved master, and the way in which the young detective ran across the floor and caught at Blake's hand made Ruth's red lips quiver with sympathy.

"Oh, guv'nor—guv'nor!" Tinker broke out. "You gave me the scare of my life this time?"

Blake's wonderful vitality was already revealing itself. The colour was returning to his face, and his laugh was a quiet, reassuring one as he patted the youngster on the shoulder.

"That's all right, old chap," he said. "I have had a close shave; but—well, it isn't the first time."

He introduced Ben to Tinker, then motioned him to be seated.

"I might as well tell you what has happened," he began. And they listened, spellbound, to his stirring narrative.

Dismissing Ruth on a small errand, Blake nodded to Wade.

"I didn't want Miss Phillips to hear the rest of the story," he went on; "but it concerns you, Ben."

"What's it got to do wi' me?" the old sailor asked.

"It is news of your old skipper—Nat Marle," said the detective quietly. "You told me once that you would like to meet him again. I'm afraid you will never have that opportunity. Nat Marle has paid the penalty that all criminals do, sooner or later. He died recently, at Laidstone Prison, under the name of Joseph Smith.

The slips of paper were produced, and Blake read them aloud. Ben Wade's brows wrinkled in perplexity as he shook his head.

"Can't make head or tail of it, mister," the old salt said; "but then I never wur a good hand at that sort o' job."

"Oh, I see it all right," Tinker broke out—"everything fits in. Kew was looking after Marle in the hospital at Laidstone, and Marle must have told him his life story."

Blake pointed to the last entry on the slips of paper.

"It's a diabolical scheme," he said. "Kew has altered Carlac's face so that he resembles the dead man, and it is evident that Phillips has been deceived by it. The bank manager believes that Marle reappeared, from the very grave almost, to claim the return of his money. I can understand now why Phillips has gone away."

"Why?" Tinker asked.

Blake leaned forward.

"He has gone to Salcoth Island," he said. "There is no doubt about that. The papers of the Seafoam and the deposit note are hidden in a hut on the south beach."

"Yes, yes; I know it. I know the very hut," Ben Wade broke out.

"Phillips has had a good start," Blake went on, "but Kew and Carlac are on his track now. If Phillips succeeds in getting to Salcoth Island first, and gaining possession of the deposit note and papers, those two rascals will be beaten; but, knowing them as I do, I am afraid that Phillips will not be successful."

He dropped back in his chair, and turned his eyes towards Ben Wade.

"That means that there is a job for all of us," said Blake. "and you will have to help, Ben."

"I'm ready to do anything," said the old tar. "What do you want me to do?"

"I want you to come with us to Salcoth Island," the detective returned, "for that is the next scene of this drama. Will you come?"

The old salt leapt to his feet and squared his shoulders.

"Will I come?" he repeated. "Rather! Why, love yer, mister, don't you know that 'once a sealer, always a sealer'? I'd give anything to be back on board one o' the old boats again, and Salcoth Island is the very place I'd like to sail to."

"It'll be 'Frisco first," said Blake. "We ought to reach there before the Anastor. We will travel by one of the swift liners to New York, then across America by rail. By the time the Anastor reaches the Golden Horn we ought to be there waiting for it."

"By jiminy, that's the ticket, guv'nor," Tinker cried.

There was a footfall at the door, and Ruth appeared.

"What is the ticket?" she asked.

Blake and Tinker exchanged glances.

"Come along, you must tell me," the girl cried. "I know you have been planning something. What is is?"

Ben Wade stretched out a thick hand and picked up the two slips of paper, folding them in his palm. It was only a small action, but it proved that the old fellow's heart was in the right place.

The old salt did not want the daughter of James Phillips to know of her father's crime.

Ruth came towards the trio, a little flush on her beautiful face.

"It's not fair," she broke out. "You are hiding something from me, and I think you are very unkind."

"Oh, we are not really hiding anything from you, Miss Ruth," Tinker put in, "only we have just decided to go on a journey."

"Where to?"

"To San Francisco, missy," said Ben Wade.

"You—you are going to find my father?"

"Yes; we hope so."

"Then I'll come too," Ruth Phillips cried.

She saw the look of blank amazement cross the features of her companions, and she laughed aloud.

"Oh, I know—I know," she said. "You think that a woman is no good, that I shall get in the way. But you are wrong. I am strong and healthy. Beside, I have as much rights to as—as any of you."

117

She looked at Blake.

"What about Hector?" he went on. "You say that you think he is on board the Anastor, and it is bound for San Francisco?"

"Yes I do believe he is on board," said Blake.

"then if you don't let me go with you to 'Frisco, I shall go by myself."

She ran forward and perched herself on the arm of Blake's chair, putting her warm young hand over the detective's shoulder.

"Come, Mr. Blake," she said in a little wheedling voice, "you wouldn't be so unkind as to leave me behind when everybody else, my father and Hector, have deserted me?"

Tinker, watching his master, turned his head away suddenly, and grinned to himself. Ruth's beautiful head was close to Blake's shoulder now, and she pressed her cheek against that of the detective.

"You wouldn't be unkind, Mr. Blake?" she cooed.

Blake laughed.

"I am afraid you are a little witch, Miss Ruth," he said; "but, well—perhaps you are right."

"Then you will really take me with you?" the girl broke out.

"We are going on a long and very hazardous journey," Blake said. "It would be far better for you to stay here. But if you really insist on it, I won't refuse."

"I do insist," Ruth cried. "I should die if you were to leave me behind. I should do nothing else but think, think, think all day. It would drive me mad."

Ben Wade brought his fist down on the table with a crash.

"She's quite right, Mr. Blake," the old tar said. "Let her come. Bless her heart, she'll cheer us up."

And thus it was arranged that these people who had been thrown into each other's society in such a curious way, should travel together.

On the following day Blake had cast aside all traces of his grim experience. He visited Sir Donald and had a short interview with the baronet, then sat down and wrote a long report to Major Crofton at Laidstone Prison.

"I am following your men," the letter ran. "It is going to take me to the other side of the world, but I am on their track, and I think you will have news of them before very long."

Blake had left the securing of the berths to Tinker, and the youngster managed to fix up everything by Friday. And so, on the Saturday morning when the Mauritania sailed from Liverpool, Ruth Phillips, Sexton Blake, Tinker, and Ben Wade were among her many passengers.

The fast Atlantic liner made the trip in its usual smooth manner, and the long journey across the American continent was also safely accomplished.

It was Ben Wade who took charge of the party at 'Frisco, for the old fellow knew the city from end to end. He took them to a quiet hotel on the heights, from where they had a fine view of the bay and the vast shipping, and there they settled down to wait for the arrival of the Anastor.

CHAPTER 10.

A Surprise Meeting.

All great cities of the world have their evil places, and San Francisco is no exception to the rule. Although the great earthquake and fire had done much to clear the city of the "Golden Horn" of its slumlands, there are still portions of it where honest citizens do not care to enter.

Chinatown, in particular, is the haunt of the unsavoury criminal class.

Yet, outwardly, the streets seem to be respectable enough. They are fairly wide and well-kept, and the little restaurants, shops, and laundries that one pass do not seem to differ in any great detail from others of their type.

But the police, and more particularly the sailors who come and go, know well the manner of life that is hidden behind the apparently innocent walls.

It was getting dusk on the Saturday evening when two men turned out of one of the wider thoroughfares and made their way along the narrow street. They were Kew and Carlac, and the contrast between the two men was more marked than ever.

It was Carlac who was leading the way, and it seemed as though the master criminal knew the place well enough, for presently he stopped outside a restaurant, above the door of which hung a sign in Chinese.

"This is the place," he said; "come along."

They passed through the doorway to find themselves in a long room arranged in a number of alcoves, each with a table and a couple of chairs.

A few moments after they had entered the restaurant, the door opened again and another figure appeared, a young sailor in blue serge and dirty greasy dungarees. He walked into the room, passing down the line of alcoves, finally entering the one next to that in which Kew and Carlac had seated themselves.

It was Hector MacLeod, tanned and weather-beaten from the long sea voyage that he had undertaken.

The Anastor had had a rough passage, and had only reached port on the previous evening. Hector Macleod had not neglected his task of watching the two men, and about midnight, when the Anastor had been moored to the quay, he had noticed Kew and Carlac enter the captain's cabin, and a few moments later, the skipper had appeared and ordered a boat to be lowered.

Hector had swiftly divined what was going to happen, and he joined the sailors who were at work lowering the boat. When it was swung clear from the side he was the first to enter it, taking his place at the oar.

Kew and Carlac had appeared, and a few moments later the boat, under that charge of the third mate, set off shorewards. When they touched at the quay it was Hector who was first ashore, and when Kew and Carlac went off together, the lad, watching his opportunity, slipped away from the quay and followed them.

They had gone to a hotel quite close to the docks and had spent the night and the greater part of the following day there, then at dusk they had set off for Chinatown, and Hector, still sticking to his task, had dogged their steps.

He was rather at a loss as to what to do, but he knew that it was absolutely essential for him to watch these two men as long as possible. He was alone and friendless in a strange land, and he realised the magnitude of his task.

The young bank clerk had very little money in his possession, certainly not enough to pay for a cable to England. He had not been able to make a confidant of anyone on board the Anastor, and he was well aware of the fact that his position was anything but a secure one.

It spoke volumes for the lad's pluck that he still stuck to his guns, hanging on to the two criminals with a bull-dog tenacity.

He took his seat in the alcove, and a moment or so later a Chinaman in short robe and wide trousers came in for his order. The bill of fare was printed in English as well as Chinese, and Hector ordered a cup of coffee and roll and butter.

There were only a few diners in the restaurant, most of them of the sailor type, with here and there a Chinaman.

From the next alcove there came a murmur of voices, but although Hector strained his ears to listen, he was unable to catch any of the conversation.

He was seated close to the opening of the alcove, and presently he saw the Chinese waiter emerge from the one that Kew and Carlac had entered, with an envelope in his hand. The waiter went up to the counter on the left, exchanged a word with the seated figure there, evidently the proprietor, then a moment later he went out through the door into the street.

A half hour passed before the door opened again, and when it did so the waiter appeared, accompanied by another individual. Hector caught a glimpse of the waiter's companion as he came down the room. He was a lean, tough-looking fellow with a strong, cruel jaw.

The man was dressed in the exaggerated style of the American, and sported a quantity of jewellery. Hector drew back as the man came nearer, and he heard him enter the adjoining alcove.

"Gee! count, this is a surprise!"

A deep voice said something in warning, and the raucous Yankee drawl died into a whisper.

But the American crook could not quite control his voice, and now and again Hector could pick up a word or two. It was evident from the trend of his talk that Carlac was asking the Yankee to do something for him, and the crook was doing his best to oblige one whom he termed a "pal."

Presently the conversation came to an end, and Hector heard the scraping of feet. He also arose, and, picking up the bill that the waiter had handed to him, went up to the counter and paid, passing out of the restaurant into the street.

A moment or two later Carlac and Kew and the flashily-dressed Yankee emerged. Hector was on the opposite side of the street, looking into a shop window. There was a mirror in the shop front, so that he could watch the movements of the men opposite.

He saw them turn and go on down the street, and the lad followed. It was dark now, and the street was rather badly lighted, but the young bank clerk's eyes were keen, and he was able to follow the trio. They plunged into a labyrinth of narrow lanes and alleys, the houses became more and more squalid, until at last Hector found himself down a narrow street in which a solitary lamp stood.

He watched the three men ahead and saw them come to a halt at a gloomy-looking house. Hector drew back into the shadows and pressed himself flat against the wall.

"Tap! tap-tap!"

It was the crook who rapped on the door, one long and two short taps. There was a long pause, then a heavy bolt was moved, and the door opened cautiously. The faint light from the street lamp rested for a moment on an evil Mongolian countenance that came round the edge of the door.

"Alright, Tao. We have come to have a smoke."

The door was opened a trifle, and the crook with his two companions vanished.

"An opium-den," Hector thought.

The young clerk remained for a moment in the darkness, his brain studying out the problem in front of him. Plucky though he was, Hector MacLeod realised that there was a great danger ahead of him if he dared to venture into that vile-looking place.

But, at last, his grim courage overcame his misgivings.

"I don't care," the lad told himself, slipping down and touching a bulky object in his pocket. "I am armed, and if it comes to a fight, well, by jingo! it'll be a good 'un."

He walked across the dirty street, and, after drawing one deep breath, he raised his knuckles and knocked on the door.

"Tap! tap-tap!"

It was an exact repetition of the signal that the Yankee crook had given. To Hector's ears there came the sound of the heavy bolt being drawn, and again the door creaked, and the ugly face came round the corner of it.

"What you wantee?" a sleek voice asked.

Hector came a pace nearer.

"You don't remember me, then, Tao?" he said, assuming a half drawl.

The Mongolian's eyes narrowed as they peered at the young figure. Hector's sailor garb and tanned face seemed to reassure the Chinaman.

"Me forget."

Hector laughed.

"It's a long, long time since I was here," he said, "and I have been looking for the place all the evening."

"You wantee smoke, eh?"

"That's it."

"Velly well."

The door was opened a little further, and Hector entered. He hvard Tao's shuffling footfalls as the man reached forward, pushing the door to, and bolting it. Then a lean, clawlike hand fell over the lad's wrist, sending a quick shudder of disgust through his veins.

"Come this way."

The attendant drew him forward down a dark, evil-smelling passage, down a flight of steps. Tao brushed aside a heavy curtain, and Hector came to a halt in the doorway of what was obviously an underground chamber.

The place was thick with smoke. It was lighted by three or four oil lamps. Along the walls were ranged bunks, each with a discreet curtain over it. In the bunk nearest to him the curtain was pulled back slightly, and Hector saw the half-clothed figure of a man lying prone on the cushions inside.

The man's head was back, and one arm was lying listlessly over the edge of the bunk, the fingers crooked.

On the other side of the chamber, near to where one of the lamps was hanging, a group of squatting men were gathered round a bowl. Hector watched for a moment, and saw one of the men lift the bowl and begin to fill it with various coloured beans.

It was fan-tan that they were playing, but the youngster had never seen it before. Presently a touch on the arm made him look round. Tao was at his elbow once more.

"You likee somet'ing to drink first?"

The atmosphere of the place almost stifled the youngster.

"Yes," he said.

"What you likee—whisky?"

"Yes."

"All right; come along."

Tao led the way down the half-lighted saloon, and Hector, remembering who he was in search of, kept a sharp look-out. Presently Tao turned to the left and drew aside a curtain, revealing an empty bunk. It was close to the end of the saloon, and Hector seated himself on the edge of the bunk, while the sleek Mongolian vanished once again.

There had been no sign of Kew or Carlac, but Hector noted that there was another curtain over what was obviously a doorway on the left. It was through this doorway that Tao had just disappeared.

"They have probably gone in there," the young bank clerk thought. "I might as well have a look."

He arose to his feet, and went to the other curtain, drawing it aside. There was narrow passage, and beyond it a glimmer of light. Hector went down the passage, and came to a halt in the darkness.

He found himself looking into a smaller chamber in which there were only a couple of bunks. In the bunk on the left he saw a broad-shouldered, black-bearded man lying. Carlac was leaning over the bunk, while the Yankee crook was standing by the man's head, shaking the shoulders and trying to rouse him. Kew stood apart, his arms folded, a grim look on his vulture face.

"It ain't any good," said the crook. "You'll have to give him time. He'll waken up presently."

"We have no time to waste," Kew's voice broke out.

Carlac turned towards him.

"You must have patience," he said.

"Oh, I guess it won't take long," came the drawling voice of the Yankee. "Old Captain Baydoe here is jest the man for you. I have been up to the island with him before to-day, and I tell you that the Paul S. Modie is the very ship you are lookin' for."

"But this man won't be fit to sail by to-morrow," Kew said.

The Yankee grinned.

"You don't know old Sam," he said. "He's jest the toughest thing in the world. He told me he was going to sail to-morrow, and he will be there to time. Perhaps a bit shaky an' mebbe feelin' liverish, but that will work off."

He looked down at the black-bearded man with a smile on his ugly countenance.

"It's the 'smoke' that's done it," he went on. "He'd have made his fortune years ago, honest, too, if it hadn't been for the dope. But you say you want to get to Salcoth Island, and this is the man to take you there."

The youngster hiding in the dark passage drank in the scene. He memorised every word that was said. He saw now why it was that Carlac had sought out this unsavoury quarter. They were trying to arrange to be taken to Salcoth Island.

He would——

A sudden click from behind made him whip round. A concealed door in the passage opened, and in a flood of subdued light he saw the figure of the Mongolian.

Tao was bearing a black bottle and a tumbler with him, but as soon as he caught sight of the young sailor in the passage down went the bottle and glass, and the man leapt forward.

"What do you want here?" he cried.

Hector made a quick effort to evade the clutching fingers, but they closed round his throat, and, with a fierce lunge, Tao forced Hector down the passage and into the inner chamber.

The lad heard Carlac's quick shout of alarm, then, with a fierce effort, he succeeded in releasing himself from the Chinaman's grip. He swung round on his heel and made a dash for the door, but the curtain tripped him up, and he went sprawling on his face.

He heard a scuffle and a rush, and someone flung himself headlong on him. Hector thrust his hand into his pocket, and his fingers closed round the butt of the revolver. But even as he withdrew it a powerful grip closed round his wrist and tightened until the bones cracked with the strain.

Carlac, with one twist of his hand, drew the lad's arm up into a lock and, winding his other arm round Hector's body, the master criminal lifted him to his feet and jerked him into the middle of the room.

"Who's this?" the American cried, as he leapt to Carlac's side. "Is he a 'tec?"

Kew's slender body came to a halt in front of Hector. The vulture face was thrust forward, and the professor peered for a long moment into the tanned countenance of the young clerk. Then, with a chuckle of satisfaction, Kew turned to his companions.

"What did I tell you, Carlac?" he said. "I never forget a face. This is the youngster who was on board the Anastor."

Carlac slipped his hand down, and drew the revolver away from Hector's fingers; then, releasing the lad, he stepped back.

"What are you doing here?" he asked.

For a moment Hector tried to bluff it out.

"Much right to be here as you have," he said. "Just going to have a 'smoke' when that confounded Chinaman barged at me."

"One minute!" Kew's face was thin and cutting.

Again he peered into the young, tanned face.

"Ah!" The thin lips were rubbed together, and a cruel smile lifted the bloodless lips. "I think we have met before," the professor went on. "Come, my young friend, your memory is not so short as all that, I'm sure. We had the pleasure of making your acquaintance in the house of our dear friend Mr. Phillips, of Grangepool!"

"What! By heavens, is that true?"

Carlac stared as the defiant young face, then gave vent to a great oath.

"You are right, Kew," he broke out. "I remember the face now,"

Kew's baleful eyes had never moved themselves from those of the plucky youngster in front of him.

"You are Hector Macleod, aren't you?"

Hector saw that it was useless to go on with his attempt to bluff. He drew himself up to his full height, and squared his shoulders.

"Yes," he said, "I am Hector Macleod."

The evil eyes of Kew narrowed into little pin points of light, and over the pallid face there came a terrible look.

"From Grangepool! This is very interesting. You were on board the Anastor and have come here?"

He stepped forward and bent his head until it was within an inch of Hector's face.

"What's you game?" he hissed. "You have been following us. Why?"

"That's my business," the plucky youngster returned, "and if you want to find out you will have to do so by yourselves."

It was three to one, and he knew that he was absolutely helpless in his enemies hands. But his eyes did not lose their fine courage, and he faced the rage of Kew's countenance smilingly.

"I know a great deal about you," the lad went on, "and I know that the police are after you both."

"Gee! You're a plucked 'un!" the Yankee crook broke out; but I guess you've signed your death warrant this time."

He looked at Carlac, and the latter nodded. It was a signal that settled Hector MacLeod's fate.

In an instant the three men had flung themselves on the lad. Hector half-expected that rush, and as the Yankee reached out for him the young bank clerk ducked swiftly. In another moment his young arms had wrapped themselves round the Yankee's thigh, and with a quick Rugger heave, Hector has tossed the lean body clean over his head.

There was a howl of pain followed by a thud as the crook's head drove against the wall. Then the next instant the man had collapsed in groaning heap in the corner of the room.

"Quick! Collar the cub!" Kew snarled, making a vicious swing at Hector.

Carlac flung himself at the lad, and his immense weight sent the youngster off his feet. They crashed to the floor together, the big criminal on top. Kew glanced around the room, and caught sight of a pewter candlestick standing on a table close to the bunk. He ran across to it and picked it up, then darted to where Carlac and Hector were locked in each other's arms.

Unequal though the struggle was, Hector was putting up a great fight. He had always been a fairly good athlete, and the long sea voyage had served to toughen his muscles. Carlac, powerful though he was, found it impossible to pin the lad down.

Again and again Hector wriggled out of the strangling embrace, and they rolled over and over together on the dirty floor of the room. Kew, leaping here and there for all the world like a grotesque bird, was snarling out commands to his big confederate.

The vulture face was set, and the small eyes were gleaming with deadly hatred, while the lean fist, clutched around the candlestick, was waiting for an opportunity to strike.

It came at last from the result of another fierce effort on Hector's part, which saw Carlac rolled over on to his back. Hector flung himself on to the broad chest of his antagonist. and drove his fist hard into the heavy face.

But in doing so he had to raise himself slightly, and this was Kew's opportunity. A couple of quick paces saw the shrivelled figure close to Hector's side, then the heavy weapon was raised and brought down with all the power of the lean arm.

It landed full on Hector's head, and, without a groan, the lad collapsed, falling in a loose heap over the gasping body of his opponent.

"Quick! Come along; bind him up!"

Kew leapt towards the bunk, and dragging the thin coverlet from the recumbent figure of Captain Baydoe, he tore it into strips, then he and Carlac pinioned Hector's arms and legs, finally stuffing a corner of the material between the lips of the lad.

By this time the Yankee crook was seated up against the wall, holding his reeling head. Tao, the Mongolian, had a glass of whisky in his hand, and the crook, reaching out for it, allowed the fiery stuff to run down his throat.

"Gee! That was some fight!" the lean man said, drawing himself to his feet with a grunt. "That cub made a mighty big effort for it."

"Oh, we've settled him," said Kew. "The point is now, how are we to get rid of him?"

They exchanged glances, then the Yankee turned and nodded to the Chinaman.

"We can leave that to Tao here," he said. "Take him away!"

He nodded to the man.

"Don't forget he hasn't got to see the light of day again! You savvy?"

The Mongolian's face was expressionless as he stepped forward and lifted Hector, slinging him over his shoulder like a sack of coals.

"I savvy," he said, as he shuffled across the room and out into the narrow passage.

The clang of a door followed, and few moments later everything was quiet again.

"Is he quite safe?" said Kew. "If I thought there was any risk I'd make it doubly sure."

"Oh, you ain't got anything to fear," the Yankee returned. "By to-morrow night the harbour police will have found your young friend, and no one on earth will be able to recognise him."

He nodded across to Carlac.

"We have a lot of dogfish in the harbour," he said, and——"

He did not complete the sentence, but the expression on his face was sufficient.

There was a moment's silence, then another idea came into the Yankee's mind.

"There's only one thing you have got to be skeered about," he said. "Does anyone know that he came here? That's the point. You see this den is pretty well known, and if anyone found out that he had been here there might be a raid."

"I don't think there is any fear of that," said Kew. "He was on board the Anastor, and he must have followed us when we came ashore yesterday."

He looked across at Carlac.

"I told you that I thought I recognised him last night at the hotel," the wizened professor put in, "but you would not believe me at the time."

Carlac nodded.

"That's true; I admit my mistake now."

Kew drew him aside.

"He must have been working with Blake," he said. "There can be no doubt that."

"It doesn't matter much who he was working with," Carlac returned. "I think we can trust to Tao."

They went across to the bunk, and this time Kew took charge of the operations of restoring the opium-sodden man to life. At the end of half an hour the black-bearded figure did recover sufficiently to rise to its feet.

The eyes were still half-hazed and heavy with the tope, and the breath was coming and going in fluttering gasps.

"Do you know where his vessel is?" Kew asked, turning to the American crook.

"Oh, yes!" the man returned.

"Then we will get him down there. Once he gets into the clearer atmosphere he will come round quicker."

They found Captain Baydoe's clothes lying in an orderly heap at the foot of the bunk, and they dressed the man. Tao came shuffling back into the room, and led by him, the party made their way along the narrow passage, through the big saloon and up the stairs, finally reaching the street.

Kew dropped behind to slip a gold coin into the Chinaman's hand.

"You know what that is for?" he said; and Tao's face lighted up with an avaricious smile as the lean fingers closed round the coin.

"I know," he said.

Then the heavy door was closed, and Kew hurried off after his companions.

Carlac and the Yankee crook, with the tottering figure of Captain Baydoe between them, went on through the labyrinth of dirty alleys until at last they came across a crawling cab, into which the drugged skipper was lifted.

It was the Yankee who took charge of the party then, and an hour later Kew and Carlac found themselves seated in a stuffy cabin on board the Paul S. Modie.

The drive had revived the skipper to a certain extent, and he was able to listen to the plan. The Yankee crook had taken his departure now, and it was Kew who made his terms with the sealer.

"Want to get to Salcoth Island, do yer?" said the captain, in a slow, drawling voice. "Yes, I know it well, but it's gettin' durned risky round there now! There's allus a few Russian gunboats knockin' about, and we've been warned off the place."

"I'd make it worth your while," said Kew.

"What's your figure?"

Kew and Carlac exchanged a whisper together, then the former turned towards the master of the Paul S. Modie.

"I'll give you five hundred pounds to land myself and friend at the south beach, Salcoth Island. You need not come ashore with us, but you will remain until we return. You can take us back to Vancouver if you like, and as soon as we arrive there you will receive your money."

"Two thousand five hundred dollars!"

Captain Baydoe's drug-laden eyes raised themselves and stared at Kew.

"That's a lot o' money for a pleasure trip. Wot's in the wind?"

"That's our business!" said the professor curtly. "The question is—will you do it?"

"If I am going to Salcoth Island, I ain't comin' back empty-handed," said the skipper. "It'll just be about the right time for the seals. I'll carry you there all right, but you will have to give me a day among 'em. If that suits you, then I'm game."

Kew and Carlac argued with the skipper, but the old fellow stuck to his guns. Salcoith Island was a risk in any case, and the old sealer was not going there without taking his toll of the seals.

"You give me a day there," the obstinate skipper went on. "Whatever business you have got to do must take you about that time, and I ain't goin' to waste the opportunity."

"All right. We agree to that," Kew said at last; and so the bargain was made.

When they had shaken hands on the compact, Kew arose to his feet.

"But you will have to sail at once," he added. "San Francisco is dangerous, so far as we are concerned."

"I can sail as quick as you like," came the reply. "I've got everything ready, and I meant to go to-morrow, anyhow. We will be off as soon as it gets daybreak.

He was as good as his word, for as the grey dawn broke over the vast harbour the Paul S. Modie put out to sea, bearing with it the two master-criminals.

Kew and Carlac were seated in the bow of the taut little vessel watching the panorama of 'Frisco as it faded away behind them.

"I think we have got through the worst part of it now," Carlac said presently. "First Blake and then that young cub have gone under. I don't think that there is anyone else to fear."

Kew's face was expressionless.

"There's one man ahead," he said—"James Phillips. He's bound to turn up sooner or later, and I think we shall find him at the island."

Carlac laughed.

"We can handle him all right," he returned. "There is only one man I ever did fear, and that was Sexton Blake. But he's gone, and, by Heavens, Kew, you and I will set a new pace in this humdrum world when we get back to civilisation again!"

There was a long silence, the monkey figure of Kew did not move; but at last his head was turned towards his companion.

"You think Blake has gone, then?"

"Why not?" Carlac broke out. "What could have saved him?"

Kew stretched out his lean arm.

"Fate," he returned. "It appears to me that you have never calculated with that indefinite article. I tell you, Carlac, neither you nor I can ever get the better of Blake!"

"But he's drowned—drowned!"

"I doubt it. There is a quaint Providence that looks after a man of his type. He is on the right side of the law, and we are on the wrong. Somehow or other the right side has always Providence with it."

He laughed sharply.

"I know that we are going to win in this case," he continued, "because we have a weak man in the person of James Phillips to deal with now. There is nothing to prevent us from getting hold of the deposit note, and with that we can force Phillips to pay up. But the future is not so easy, for sooner or later you and I will fall foul of Sexton Blake, and——"

He snapped his fingers.

"I can see Major Crofton's welcome waiting for us at Laidstone Prison," he ended.

Carlac leapt to he feet with an oath.

"Confound you for a croaker!" he broke out. "What's the matter with you? There's going to be no more prison for me, I've had enough of it. If Blake and I get to face again, I tell you one of us will go under for good!"

His massive features twisted, and his powerful fists clenched.

"If I go into prison again," said Count Ivor Carlac, "it will be feet first!"

"That's very likely," returned Professor Kew.

CHAPTER 11.

In 'Frisco Slums.

"I am yours to command, Mr. Blake," said Lieutenant MacCradel. "I have heard a lot about you, and I am very pleased indeed to make your acquaintance!"

Blake was seated in the austerely-furnished room of the lieutenant of police. The San Franciscan police is perhaps one of the best organised bodies in the world and MacCradel was head of the detective force.

He was a square-shouldered, massive-looking individual, with a strong, clean-shaven chin and grey eyes. He had been smoking a cigar when Sexton Blake entered, and his smoke was still smouldering in the ash-tray.

MacCradel slipped his hand into his pocket and produced a well-filled cigar-case.

"Have a smoke?" he said, holding the case out to Blake.

"Thanks!"

Sexton Blake selected a weed and lighted it; then MacCradel dropped back in his chair and turned to his visitor.

"I guess it's business that has brought you to see me," he said; "you are not the sort of man to come across to 'Frisco for mere pleasure."

"It is business," Blake returned. "I have had a long hunt, but just for the moment I'm at a loss."

"What's the trouble?" MacCradel asked.

"I'm afraid I am partly to blame myself," Blake resumed. "I and my party came to 'Frisco four or five days ago. We were waiting for the arrival of a steamer the Anastor——"

"The Anastor came in yesterday," said MacCradel.

"That's quite correct," he returned. "But we were not here at the time. As a matter of fact," the London detective went on. "there is a young lady with our party, and several days ago we heard the the Anastor had had to put into port to do some engine repairs. We were informed by the shipping company that there would be very little chance of her turning up for another week, and as the young lady who is accompanying us had never been in America before, we thought it a good opportunity of seeing the Yosemite Valley."

"I don't blame you," said MacCradel. "it's one of the show places in the world."

"Oh, yes, we thoroughly enjoyed it!" Blake returned; "but on coming back to 'Frisco last night I discovered that the Anastor had beaten us by twenty-four hours."

Blake leaned back in his chair.

"There were two men on board the Anastor," he went on, "that I particularly wanted to keep in touch with. There was also a youngster on the vessel who was working for me."

"What's happened to him?"

"I went down to the Anastor last night and I tackled the skipper," said Blake, a quiet smile crossing his lips at the memory that came to him. "At first he was inclined to be rather aggressive, but he listened to reason afterwards."

MacCradel, looking at the steel-blue eyes in front of him, nodded his head.

"Yes, I guess you're right, Mr. Blake," he said. "I don't think there are many men who could stand out against those eyes of yours for long."

"Oh, Captain Turner did all he could for me afterwards," Blake admitted. "He owned up to the fact that he had taken two individuals as passengers, and he told me that a member of his crew was missing—the engineer's cabin-boy. From the description that he gave me of the boy I am convinced that it is the youngster who is missing from my group. His name is Hector MacLeod."

"What have you done since?" asked MacCradel.

"Oh, I have not been idle," said Blake, drawing out a notebook from his pocket. "I succeeded in finding the hotel in which my two men spent the night. They left there yesterday afternoon, and the boots at the hotel, who was rather an intelligent chap, remembered that a young sailor who had also put up at the hotel followed them out."

"Any idea where they went?"

"No. But after a long search I did discover something concerning them."

Blake glanced at his book again.

"There was a sealing vessel called the Paul S. Modie that was due to sail to-day," he went on; "but I find it sailed last night."

"Yes."

"The skipper—Captain Baydoe—was brought down to the quay by a couple of men who answer identically with the descriptions of the men I am after. They all went on board together, and, shortly after, the Paul S. Modie sailed."

A genuine look of admiration came into MacCradel's eyes, and he leaned forward.

"Say, have you found all that out single-handed, and in a strange city?"

Blake nodded.

"It's very little," he said, "but it satisfied me on one point. I know where the men are bound. What I want to discover now is the whereabouts of the young sailor."

MacCradel thrust the black cheroot into his mouth and rolled it between his lips.

"You've done a heap, Mr. Blake," he said. "Believe me, 'Frisco is just about the worst place in the world to trace men who don't want to be traced. Still, I think I can help you now, and I can only do so because I happen to know something about that Captain Baydoe."

"Indeed?"

"Yes; he's a dope fiend."

"In what way?"

"Mind you, Captain Baydoe ain't a bad sort at all, but he's absolutely under the influence of opium. He's gone through one or two fortunes in his time, and he spends every cent of his money in Chinatown."

"The man who saw the skipper go on board told me that he was pretty tottery," said Blake; "but I took it to mean that he was drunk."

"Oh no, Skipper Baydoe doesn't drink. He must have been under the influence of the drug."

MacCradel leaned back in his chair and put his feet up on the desk. He was silent for a moment. Blake saw that the keen brain was studying out the various points of the case.

"The Paul S. Modie was not due to sail until noon to-day," said MacCradel at last, "and knowing Captain Baydoe as I do, I can't understand how they managed to get him on board by twelve o'clock last night. It would be his last opportunity of drugging himself with that rotten stuff, and you can bet your boots that he would go in for an extra dose and wait in the opium den until the very last minute."

"I see your point," said Blake. "You mean that those two men went to find him and roused him out of his sleep?"

"An opium smoker wants some rousing," MacCradel returned.

Blake nodded his head.

"One of the men is the cleverest chemist in the world," Blake said.; "If anyone could rouse Captain Baydoe, that man was the person."

"Well, I'll grant you that point," said MacCradel. "And now we are getting nearer to the root of the affair. Just wait a minute."

He touched a bell, and presently a clerk entered.

"I want to see Detective O'Donnel," said the lieutenant of police. Two or three minutes later a heavily-built man strode into the office. He looked as though he were a sailor, with his rough, hairy hands and little black moustache.

"O'Donnel, this is Mr. Sexton Blake," said MacCradel, introducing the detective. "You've heard of him, I should think?"

O'Donnel and Blake shook hands.

"Yes, we have all heard of Mr. Blake," he returned. "Proud to meet you, sir."

MacCradel leaned forward.

"We want to find out where Captain Baydoe had his usual dose of dope last night, O'Donnel," he went on. "Can you help us?"

"Sure! I saw him about five o'clock. He turned down into the Yokomar Street, and that, of course, meant Tao's."

"Tao still in the business?"

"Yes. We have never troubled to run him yet, but we know his game all right."

MacCradel turned to Blake.

"If the men you are after followed Captain Baydoe they must have gone to Tao's den, and if your assistant was on their track there is no doubt but what he went after them there. It strikes me that it would pay you to go along with O'Donnel and have a look round, Mr. Blake."

"I think it would," said the London detective, rising to his feet. "And I'm very much obliged to you."

He shook hands with MacCradel, promising to look up the lieutenant later on; then he and O'Donnnel left the offices to find themselves in one of the main streets of the beautiful city.

It was ten o'clock in the morning, and O'Donnel, chartering a taxi, beckoned to his companion to enter, and the two men were driven through 'Frisco into the grimy, over-populated quarter known as Chinatown.

O'Donnel dismissed the taxi and they continued the journey on foot. Blake noted that every now and again a Chinaman shuffling past would turn as pair of almond eyes towards the black-bearded man and give a furtive salute.

O'Donnel, however never acknowledged any of these greetings; but at last he turned to Blake with a grin.

"They know me, these yellow devils," he said. "There's not a man among 'em who wouldn't like to drive a knife into me if he dared."

He turned into an alley, then, halfway down it, swung sharply to his left and darted into a laundry, followed by Blake. The latter had noted that the street was deserted at the moment, and O'Donnel, without pausing to say a word to the man standing at the counter, pressed on right through the laundry and into a chamber behind.

There were four or five Chinamen hard at work, starching and ironing. At O'Donnel's entry a wizened figure arose and came a shuffling forward.

"Please to see you, Mister O'Donnel," a cackling voice said. "You wantee go downstairs?"

"Yes."

The old Chinaman—he must have been eighty if he was a day—tottered ahead, opening a door, and passed down a dingy flight of stairs.

Blake found himself in a little lighted chamber, and he noted that O'Donnel had already removed his coat and waistcoat.

"We've got to dress up for this, Mr. Blake," said the 'Frisco detective. "We are going into rather rummy quarters, and a dark robe and a pigtail may help us through."

It was evident that O'Donnel had used this place before. The old Chinaman fished out a couple of dark robes and wide, native trousers which the two men donned.

With a round black skull-cap drawn over his head, and a black pigtail attached beneath it, O'Donnel wrapped a shawl round his head, so that his bearded chin was completely hidden.

Blake was supplied with a wig and pigtail, and O'Donnel grinned at his companion when the transformation was complete.

"I guess you'll do," he said. "You've been at this game before."

He turned to the old Chinaman.

"We may not be back for a little while," he said. "You had better wait here until we return."

He went off across the room, and Blake saw him fumble with a projecting piece of stone; then suddenly the whole slab slid aside, revealing a dark passage beyond.

O'Donnel drew aside, allowing Blake to step through the gap, then followed him, and the heavy slab dropped into its place again. There was a click, and a shaft of light shot out from a powerful electric-lamp that O'Donnel was carrying.

"We have got about a hundred yards to go," he said. "Tao's den is at the end of the street. But we could never have got into it if we had kept above the ground. You had better be careful; you'll find it rather tricky going."

He led the way out through a bricked archway, and Blake saw now that he was in one of the main sewers that ran below the vast city. There was a ledge running along the side of the sewer, just wide enough for a man to move along.

O'Donnel, with his lamp shining on the moist sides of the huge iron sewer, moved on, and Blake kept close to his heels. Once the 'Frisco detective came to a halt and pointed upwards.

"Manhole," he said. And Blake, looking up through the arched brickway, saw, far above him, the iron grating that covered the manhole in the street.

O'Donnel seemed to know his way about, for the sewer twisted and curved, breaking off at every nine or ten yards into various cross sections.

For over twenty minutes Blake followed his guide, and at last, O'Donnel came to a halt.

"This is about the place," he said; "but there is something happened here that I don't quite understand."

He was standing at a branch of the sewer and was peering down a narrow track.

"Don't understand it," said O'Donnel. "This sewer is a flush one, and ought to be pretty well filled up."

He turned into the dark gap, and Blake found now that he had to move more cautiously. The sewer, a bricked one, was about two feet wide, and there was a narrow ledge only some five or six inches broad on either side.

O'Donnel, straddling the gap, moved on ahead, and Blake had to follow by the same awkward method. They went up the ever-narrowing channel for about ten yards, the Blake heard O'Donnel give vent to a low murmur of surprise.

"What's this?"

Sexton Blake moved on until he was standing close behind the detective. O'Donnel's way up the sewer was barred by what appeared to be a solid steel plate. It fitted into a double groove in the masonry, and ran right down from top to bottom of the channel.

"This is new," he said, eyeing the thing closely. "I haven't been along here for a year or so, but I guess it wasn't like this when I came down before."

"What do you make of it?"

"Can't say. But I know that we ought to be immediately below Tao's place. I guess that this steel plate is blocking up a mighty lot o' water."

He turned to Blake and handed him the electric-torch.

"Just hold on to this for a moment," he said. "I'm just going to see if this can be moved."

Blake caught the torch, and O'Donnel dropped into the dry channel of the sewer, bending down and examining the plate. There was a projecting flange on it some four or five inches from the bottom, and around this O'Donnel curled his powerful fingers.

Blake saw the stout shoulders of the 'Frisco 'tec twitch and heave, the muscles on his neck swelled and throbbed; then at last the steel plate lifted slightly and there came gushing out from beneath a great spout of water.

It came up with such terrific force that it almost swept O'Donnel off his feet. The man lost his balance, and Blake, with a quick snatch, caught at the detective's coat.

It was touch and go with O'Donnel, but Blake's powerful grip never released its hold, and at last, while the water roared and foamed down the narrow sewer, Blake drew his man up into safety.

O'Donnel leaned against the wall gasping for breath, then, with a quick movement, he thrust out his hand.

"That's one to you, Mr. Blake," he said. "Gee! I never thought that the water was as strong as that. If you hadn't caught me I'd have been carried away and they would have probably found me in the bay later on."

They glanced at the rushing, swirling flood beneath them. A terrible death for any man to die, indeed!

They stood in silence for a long moment, watching the water tear out through the narrow gap. There seemed to be a tremendous force behind it, and Blake watched it, fascinated.

"It'll be all right presently," said O'Donnel; "the water has been heaped up somewhere, but it'll soon quieten down to the proper level, then we'll be able to move that plate and see more."

But they had to wait for the best part of half an hour before the force of the flood died away to a steadier flow. Then Blake and his companion dropped into the knee-deep water, and, gripping at the bottom of the steel plate, they tugged together.

The plate shot upwards, noiselessly, testifying to the fact that the grooves were well made. Soon the plate was breast high and another heave saw it up to their shoulders.

"That'll do," said O'Donnel, "we can see what's ahead now."

He had placed the torch on the little ledge of the sewer, and now, reaching out for it, he drew the light forward and ducked beneath the steel plate.

Blake followed and come to a halt with a word of amazement. They were in a square, bricked space, and in the centre of the space, sitting on a chair, its hands and feet tied tightly with lengths of cord, was a wet, collapsed figure.

"Gee! What does this mean?"

O'Donnel darted forward through the foot of water that was still left, and reached the chair. The head of the figure was resting on its breast, and the detective, raising his chin, allowed the light of the electric torch to fall on the white, tense face.

"By Jove! It—it's Hector MacLeod!" Blake broke out.

O'Donnel slipped his hand into his pocket and drew out a small flask containing brandy. Unscrewing the cork he forced the lips of the youngster apart and allowed a few drops of the strong fluid to run into the mouth.

Blake had already severed the bonds that tied the lad to the heavy chair, and presently, with a low moan, Hector MacLeod came back to life.

He stared about him for a moment, then his eyes fixed themselves on the two figures in front of him and his lips moved.

"All right, Hector," said Blake, putting his hand on the lad's shoulder, "you are quite safe now."

A look of terror leapt into MacLeod's face and he swayed away.

"You—you!" the lad broke out.

Just for a moment the young bank clerk thought that his wits were playing a trick with him, for the voice was the voice of Sexton Blake, and the face looking down into his own was that of the detective.

Yet Hector MacLeod knew that Blake had been cast headlong into the sea off the coast of England!

"Don't get skeered, youngster," O'Donnel's voice went on, "you are all right now, though I dare say gone through a durned rough time of it."

The water had now fallen to its ordinary trickle, and Blake saw that it was issuing from a sewer pipe which was embedded in the wall of the opposite side of the chamber.

"Gee! This is some death trap!" said O'Donnel, with a grim frown. "That sewer pipe should have come straight through into the open drain there. It's a fresh-water sewer that they use for flushing out the big pipes into the main drain."

He looked around the walls, and his lips tightened.

I guess Tao has got to answer for this," he said. "Running an opium den is bad enough, but I didn't know he added a death trap to his other devices."

He looked across at Blake.

"We'll get your friend out of this first," he said, "then Lieutenant MacCradel and I can settle what's to be done."

With the assistance of O'Donnel, Blake was able to get Hector Macleod below the steel plate and out into the side channel. As soon as they had cleared the plate, O'Donnel turned and forced it down into its position again.

"I reckon you don't need me to tell you why I've done that," he said, turning to Blake with a smile.

The detective nodded.

"No, I quite understand," he said. "You want to make the scoundrel who fixed this up believe that his victim is drowned?"

"That's so," said the man. "There must be some mechanism on the other floor that works this steel plate, and I guess Tao will come back sooner or later to raise it again."

The journey back was an uneventful one, and they soon found themselves in the underground room of the little laundry. Blake changed into his ordinary clothes, and the Chinaman was able to produce a suit of dry things that fitted Hector fairly well.

O'Donnel accompanied them to the shop above, then came to a halt.

"I don't think you'll need me any more," he said; "besides I am not going to leave here. I'm going to get on the 'phone to MacCradel in a few minutes. This Tao business has got to be put a stop to, and I want to get on to it at once. Old Lo Chang here will send for a taxi for you, and you'll be safe enough."

Blake held out his hand.

"I'm very much obliged to you, old chap," he said. "You've been of great assistance to me."

The rugged hand of O'Donnel closed round Blake's strong palm.

"It's been a pleasure to me to do anything for you, Mr. Blake," the 'Frisco 'tec returned; "your reputation stands good for you in any part of the world."

Lo Chang sent one of his young laundry-hands in search of a taxi, and presently a vehicle drove up to the door, into which Blake and Hector stepped. The lad looked at the detective again.

"I can hardly believe my eyes, sir," he said. "I was a witness to your struggle on the board the Anastor. I had hidden myself in the lifeboat."

"Then it was you?" said Blake. "I thought there must have been some friendly hand behind it."

He stretched out his arm and laid it round Hector's shoulder.

"You saved my life, Hector," he went on. "That lifebuoy that you threw overboard was found by me, and it kept me afloat."

"Well, it's tit for tat, sir." Hector returned; "for, by Jove, you saved my life just now, and from a far worse fate than yours."

He shivered at the thought of it, then little by little Blake heard Hector's story. The lad told of all that had happened to him, right up to when he had been knocked senseless and gagged and bound.

"I don't know what happened to me afterwards," he went on, "but when I awoke I found myself in that awful place with the horrible face of Tao watching me. The brute never moved or spoke, but I knew what he was up to. I saw him open the grating above the drainpipe, then he drew himself up through the trap-door and closed the door after him. Even then I didn't know what was going to happen until I heard the first swish of water and felt it lapping my feet."

He leaned back in the vehicle and shivered.

"I shall never forget it," Hector MacLeod resumed; "to feel it creeping up, inch by inch, sitting there, not even able to shout."

The young bank clerk was obviously unstrung and unnerved, and Sexton Blake set his teeth as he thought of the terrible ordeal through which this youngster had gone.

"Never mind, old man," the detective said grimly, "the people who were responsible for your position will have to pay."

"Have you found them?" Hector asked.

"No; unfortunately they stole a march on me," said Blake, "but I know where they are going and I know the vessel they are on, and with a little bit of luck we may arrive at the place they are bound for before they do."

He looked at Hector MacLeod for a moment.

"We have found out several things concerning this affair," he went on, "and you, now, have a larger interest in it."

"What do you mean?"

"I mean that the man Carlac has made himself out to be a certain Nat Marle——" Blake began.

The lad looked up quickly.

"Marle, sir, but that's the name of the man who swindled my father."

"The man Marle is dead," Sexton Blake said, "but Carlac is masquerading as him."

He leaned forward and laid a hand on Hector's shoulder.

"I am afraid you are going to make a very painful discovery," he went on, "and that is that James Phillips, the man we are going to try and find now, was in a measure responsible for your father's failure."

He gave Hector a brief account of the discovery that he had made on board the Anastor. The young bank clerk leaned back in the taxi and was silent.

"And what are you going to do now, sir?" he said, after a long pause.

"My duty is to guard James Phillips against these blackmailers," Blake said, "but what happens to Phillips afterwards depends on you. If the story is true, and Phillips knew who Marle was, then he has been guilty of a crime. It was his duty to notify the police that he had recognised Marle, and the money that Marle deposited at the Grangepool and District Bank should have been claimed by your father."

"And as my father is dead that money is mine?"

"Yes."

The lad smiled.

"Then I shall never claim it, sir," he said. "In many ways Mr. Phillips was good to me, and, besides, I—I love Ruth.

He turned to Blake.

"If you can save Ruth's father from these brutes, sir, that's all I want. The rest we can settle between ourselves."

Blake gripped the lad by the hand.

"Well said," the detective broke out; "that's what I wanted to hear from you. Whatever crime James Phillips has committed he has paid for it over and over again, both in conscience and in his present terrible position."

"But where is he, sir? Have you any idea?"

"I think we will find him," said Blake. "We are gradually narrowing down the circle now, and Salcoth Island will prove the final phase. To my mind there is no doubt whatever but what Phillips set off to try to get to Salcoth Island and possess himself of the incriminating papers before those two scoundrels could do so."

"It's a curious position," he went on, with one of his grave smiles; "we are all in the same race, we have all started at different time and all with the same common goal—a little hut on the south beach of an island that is a mere pin-point on the map of the world!"

CHAPTER 12.

At Salcoth Island.

On a great lichen-covered rock a man was seated, his elbows resting on his knees, his chin on his hands. On his left there ran a long line of beach on which a grey sea was breaking monotonously, the voice of the surf rising and falling to the lift of the tide.

It was a grey desolate spot, and a thin sea mist moving in great swathes, circled now and again around the lonely figure.

From afar came a curious medley of sound. now and again a sharp clear bark, then a rumbling noise, following by a chorused called. Once, as the figure sat there, there came sliding up out of the mist, a wet glistening object. It moved cumbrously, heavily, and the man's dreamy eyes lighted on it.

It was a great seal, wet from the sea. It raised itself on its awkward flappers and stood for a moment, its whiskered snout tilted upwards. The man could see the lift and fall of the grey whiskers as the beast watched him.

He made a motion with his hand, and the huge, ungainly animal, turning round with a swing, went flopping back along the beach to plunge into the surf.

James Phillips, for it was he, watched the trail of the seal until it had vanished, then once again his brooding fit descended in him. His long voyage to Salcoth Island had been performed without mishap. He had touched at Vancouver and had succeeded in persuading one of the sealing vessels to land him on the island.

It was really too early in the season for Salcoth, and the sealer had gone on, leaving James Phillips on the beach with his kit around him.

He had felt very desolate and alone as he stood there, but presently, arousing himself, he had lifted his kit and had struggled up the rocky beach on to the higher land beyond.

He had found a hut out of which a trail of smoke was rising, and presently he had introduced himself to a squat fur-clad figure, whose snub nose and pock-marked face was unmistakable.

The Eskimo had a smattering of English, and in the phlegmatic manner of his type had displayed no surprise at seeing this solitary Englishman on the island.

James Phillips had made arrangements with the man to live in the hut, and a space had been provided in one corner for him to sleep.

But it soon revealed itself to Phillips that his search was not going to be easy. This hut was on the east beach, and, presently, the owner of the hut explained the reason of that.

It appeared that eight or nine years before, the seals had, for some unknown reason, completely deserted the south beach and had made new breeding quarters on the east side of the island.

This is by no means a strange happening, for these wonderful animals of the sea have little laws and tennets of their own, and their life study is a fascinating one.

James Phillips plied the Eskimo with questions, but the man was just as dense as possible. The Grangepool banker had discovered that there had been another hut on the south beach, but it had been demolished years before.

The owner of the hut held up nine fingers to give Phillips an idea of the length of time. It was a heart-breaking discovery to make, and Phillips began to search.

The south beach was a great stretch of boulder-clad ground behind two spurs of land. It was the best part of two miles from point to point, and day after day Phillips searched up and down the long beach, trying to discover the site of the old hut.

But as day followed day, despair gradually began to eat into the man's soul. The place was a wilderness of rocks and boulders, and it seemed to him as though he would never find what he was in search of.

Yet he continued his task with the dull determination of despair. As soon as the grey dawn broke he would rouse himself from his uncomfortable bed, snatch a hasty meal of such foor as the Eskimo's slender store could afford him, then with a piece of dried meat and a handful of hard biscuits, together with a bottle full of water, the weary man would step out of the hut into the mists of the island towards the south beach.

All day long he would keep up his search, halting only for a few moments to make a midday meal. The coming of night would find him spent and exhausted, trudging back over the trackless island to the hut.

It was only after a week of this aimless prowling that he began to continue the search with something like a system. He marked off on the rocks the various portions of his search so that he could start again on the following morning, and thus, square by square, cover the entire stretch of beach.

He realised now that his search might take him months, for there was very little chance of any indication of the site remaining after the long lapse of time.

Even if part of the building had been left there was little doubt but what the swift growing moss, that covered the rocks on the island, would have effectively concealed it.

Phillips's only hope lay in his being able to discover what had once been the fireplace, for ashes and burnt wood are the only things that resist the steady march of lichen.

As he sat on the boulder, chin in hand, the man's ceaseless brain went back over the long years of the past. He straightened up and stretched his arms above him.

"By Heavens, I have paid," he murmured in a hoarse voice. "From the very first moments that I used Marle's ill-gotten gains, my peace deserted me."

He drew a deep breath.

"Twenty years!" he went on. "Twenty years of utter agony. Oh, Heavens! I wonder if it is worth while?"

He stood up and looked about him. Below, on the edge of the beach, the surf was foaming. Phillips, with the weary movements of a man dog-tired, began to pace towards the edge of the beach, slipping from rock to rock.

He gained a great ledge of black rock at last, around which the sea was foaming. It was an ugly sea, snarling and hungry. The man folded his arms and looked down into the swirling waters.

"Just a plunge," he said, "a moment's agony, and then—peace!"

He was weary and hungry, and his long fruitless search had gradually sapped him of his courage. His body swayed forward, then, suddenly a new thought came to him and he drew back.

"No," he said, "not yet. For my little girl's sake I—I must struggle."

The mists cleared slightly and gave him a view of the sea. From the shore, as far as the eye could reach, lay the grey waters, and Phillips could see little black dots moving along the surface.

He had a few words with the Eskimo on the previous night, and the man had told him that the seals were coming, coming in their thousands now, to the east beach.

Phillips watched the little wet heads as they moved on through the water, now vanishing with a momentary flick of their flat tails, then emerging again, always moving on and on round the headland towards the east beach.

And the chorus from beyond the range of boulders was rising higher and higher, and, at last, urged by a curiosity that he could not resist, the gaunt man made his way along the shore and round a bend where he could see the east beach.

It was alive with black ungainly forms. They were roaring and champing, and now and again there would come up to his ears the battle-cry of two great seals as, their long white teeth gleaming, they would charge at each other in a fierce fight that would decide which was to rule.

Around the two fighters there would gather eight or nine female seals watching the battle quietly. There was something very human about it all; and, fascinated, Phillips forgot, for a moment, his troubles.

So absorbed was he in watching the stirring scene that he did not notice a cloud of mist gathering. It came eastwards, and, presently, he found himself enveloped in its folds. It was a real sea fog, heavy damp, and it wiped out his entire vista.

He roused himself to his position then, and as he did so, darkness came on.

"I'll have to get back," he said as he turned.

A faint misgiving stirred him as he realised that it was next to impossible for him to find his way, and it was only then that it dawned on him that this particular portion of the beach was utterly strange to him, he had not been there before.

Salcoth Island was not a very big place, only some four miles broad by five miles wide, but James Phillips realised that it was quite big enough for him to lose himself.

He knew that the nights were bitterly cold and he was rather thinly clad.

"I'll have to get back to the hut at once," he thought, leaping down from the boulder.

He stumbled forward for a hundred yards or so, and it was only when he went sprawling across the wet body of a seal that he realised he was going in the wrong direction, heading for the beach.

As a matter of fact, he was now in the midst of the seals, and a second or so later he realised his danger; for, as he took another pace forward, there came a snuffling grunt, followed by the swift champ of teeth, and a huge shape flashed out from the midst and two white tusks snapped as they passed him.

Now the fangs of a full-grown male seal can give a nasty wound, and although Phillips, with a quick movement evaded the swift rush, the fang cut a strip clean out of his sleeve.

The great brute sprawled on; and Phillips leapt over its thick body. He had a stout stick in his hand, and, as the seal wheeled round again, Phillips poised himself and swung the stick above his head.

He knew that his antagonist was only fighting for its home. Phillips had unconsciously stumbled right into the little circle that the male seal is lord and master of, and the animal was quite entitled to resent the intrusion.

The seal came on again, and the bank manager brought the stick down with a whack, landing full on the animal's skull. The stick broke, but the blow was effective for the seal dropped and Phillips, whipping round, went off at a rush, stumbled over another smaller seal, then finally gained the higher ground above.

He came to a halt, gasping for breath, unnerved slightly at the nearness of his escape.

"By Jove, I must be careful," he thought, "if I got in amongst them they would tear me to pieces."

He knew enough about the animals to appreciate that this was the only time when there was any real danger. It was the breeding season and both male and female seal were ready to fight for their young.

He began to move forward cautiously now and found himself stumbling through the boulders. The cries of the seals behind him gave him an index to their whereabouts, and he kept on and on until, at last, the cries died away into an occasional reverberation of sound.

"What the dickens am I to do," the man thought, coming to a halt. "I'll never find the hut in this mist."

He realised then his folly, for he had omitted to put a compass in his pocket, but he had been so accustomed to making his way back in the daylight that he had not troubled to take any notice as to the exact position of the little shelter.

From the south beach it had always been plainly visible, for it had been built on a higher point above the east side. Now, however, the mist and the gathering dusk, concealed its position.

Gradually the mist grew colder and colder, and presently Phillips found it necessary to swing his arm across his chest to keep himself warm.

The Alaska nights are chill; and out there the cold is as keen as a knife. He had long ago eaten the humble ration of dried meat and biscuit, and he began to feel the pangs of hunger keenly.

He stumbled on for the best part of two hours and, at last, sheer exhaustion brought him to a halt. It was pitch dark now and the mist was still hanging over the island, so that he could not even see a solitary star.

"It's no good," he told himself. "I'll have to find some place to sleep to-night."

He moved on for a little while longer, then presently tripped over a boulder and clutched at it to save himself. The boulder was a big one and, struggling to the other side of it, Phillips discovered a little hollow, covered with moss, below. He felt around it and decided that the place would serve as a slight shelter.

"Never again!" he told himself as he dropped wearily into the hollow. "In future I must get back to the hut before the dusk comes on."

He made himself as comfortable as possible and tried to sleep, but it was a fitful slumber at the best. The cold was so acute that he found himself waking up time after time, his teeth chattering; and his limbs aquiver.

He had to rise up and stamp to and fro now and again, beating on his chest to restore the circulation. It was just after one of these painful experiences that a new sound came to him.

From out of the fog there came a low hoot, the note of a steamer's siren. It sounded for all the world like a bull-calf bellowing in the dusk.

He listened. The sound was repeated again and again, but the whirling mist made it impossible for him to locate the quarter from whence it came.

The siren was sounded three or four times, then there was silence, and although he strained his ears, Phillips could not hear any further sound.

The morning came wet and chill, with the fog still brooding over the island. Stiff and sore the bank manager arose to his feet and, ravenous now, began to move onward again.

The fog baffled him, and he had another encounter with the seals on the east beach before he realised that it would be better for him to keep along the shore, as a guide.

The result was that, after three hours steady search, he saw the black hulk of a hut looming up in front of him. A gasp of relief broke from the man's lips, and he staggered forward, turning round the corner of the little shelter and pushing the door aside, tottering into the interior.

It was empty, and Phillips, crossing to the range of shelves beside the fireplace, drew down a tin of biscuits, and, grabbing a handful, began to eat hungrily, voraciously.

There was a fire burning in the open space, and beside it stood a smoke-blackened tin, containing about half a pint of coffee. He poured the liquid out into a shallow pannikin and sipped at it, crouching over the fire to warm himself.

When he had taken the edge off his appetite, and had dried his clothes slightly, Phillips began to wonder what had happened to the owner of the hut.

As a rule the squad fellow hardly ever left the place except for a few moments at a time.

Suddenly, Phillips glanced at the corner in which his bed was placed, then he rose to his feet with a muttered exclamation. For, beside the cot was lying a pair of small leather shoes. The manager of the Grangepool bank crossed to the rude cot, and picked up the shoes.

They were obviously of European manufacture, and so small that Phillips's hand could easily span their length.

"What does this mean?" the man thought.

He had never seen the shoes there before, and he knew that the Eskimo did not possess such things. The discovery of the shoes made him glance around the hut, and presently he found something else of interest.

It was an oilskin coat, and, on one of the wooden pegs behind the door, he saw a sou'wester hat hanging. Then, most curious of all, close to the fire were one or two ends of cigarettes.

They were the oval Egyptian type, gold tipped.

"There must have been visitors here," Phillips murmured, "no doubt they have gone out with the Eskimo. By Jove, that explains the siren last night!"

He went out of the hut, and stood for a moment gazing moodily at the thick bank of fog. He knew that the hut was only about one hundred yards from the beach, and beyond it lay the bay in which, no doubt, the mysterious ship was at anchor.

But the fog effectively hid it from view, and, at last, James Phillips began to move down towards the shore, a strange misgiving at his heart.

He reached the surf at last, and turning to his left, moved along it. He had covered about a hundred yards when presently he caught sight of a boat rising and falling on the water. There was a figure in the bow, and Phillips peered at it, then gave a low shout. The man in the boat stirred, looked round, then leapt into the surf and waded ashore.

"That you, Skipper?"

It was a Yankee drawl, and as Phillips drew nearer, the man stopped and peered at him.

"Hallo, who on earth are you?" the sailor asked.

"I've just come from the hut," said Phillips.

He glanced at the boat, and noted that the space where the name of a vessel is usually marked, had been newly painted over.

"Came from the hut, did you?"

There was suspicion in the man's face, and he drew back, eyeing Phillips closely.

"Well, what do you want?"

"Oh, nothing," the Grangepool bank manager returned, "only I was lost on the island last night and I couldn't get back to the hut. I heard the siren going and that guided me here."

"What are you doin' on Salcoth Island anyhow?" the sailor went on, "it ain't exactly what you'd call a holiday resort."

"Oh, I'm here just for a—a purpose of my own," Phillips returned.

"Does anybody else know you're here?"

"I don't think so," said the banker slowly.

He saw that the man was obviously ill at ease, and presently he slipped his hand into his pocket and drew out a little wad of American notes. The sailor's eyes glinted as Phillips undid the rubber band.

The Grangepool banker counted out five ten-dollar bills, and folded them together.

"I want some information." he said. "I'm not going to do any harm but I'd like to know what has happened. Why you have

130

Rare Sexton Blake Bust created by Eric Parker (1926).

The cover of Sexton Blake Library No. 1. September 1915.

The cover of Sexton Blake Library No. 2. October 1915.

The cover of Sexton Blake Library No. 3. November 1915.

The cover of Sexton Blake Library No. 4. December 1915.

Two of the many early magazines which featured Sexton Blake. The issue of 'Boy's Herald' from 1909 contains a Blake serial entitled 'Sexton Blake at Oxford' and the 1920 copy of 'Nugget Weekly' contains another serialised adventure, 'The Fakir's Secret'.

A selection of covers from 'Union Jack' the magazine that carried Blake stories every week for the best part of its long life.

SPECIAL CHRISTMAS NUMBER

A Love Story Every Week

The Crime of the
Christmas Tree

The Mystery of the
SIPING VAMPIRE

A tale of the weird

AWESOME EERIE UNCANNY! Was the tomb of the Hentys haunted by the un-dead? This is the finest yarn combining the supernatural with detective work you have ever discovered! Featuring SEXTON BLAKE, Tinker, and Pedro the BLOODHOUND. Complete Inside.

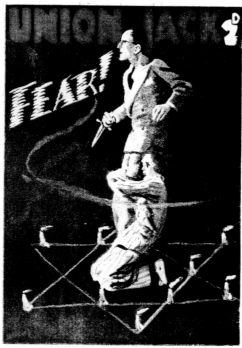

FEAR!

Fear of the *Unknown*; fear of the awesome and uncanny!
A THRILLER WITHOUT A GUN — a real creepy thriller,
yet a genuine Sexton Blake detective story
just the same. Complete inside.

SEXTON BLAKE — PEDIGREE BLOODHOUND

The Mystery of
BLIND LUKE

'The Ghost of Rupert Forbes', one of the 'Boys Friend Library' series. This Sexton Blake story was reprinted from 'Union Jack'.

This page:
Two of the cards from the 'Sexton Blake Card Game' produced by Waddy Productions.
Opposite page:
The second Sexton Blake Annual (1940) with a cover illustration by Eric Parker.

SEXTON BLAKE
ANNUAL

SOUVENIR BOOK OF THE
WORLD'S GREATEST DETECTIVE
WITH A RECORD OF HIS MOST
FAMOUS CASES, INCLUDING:
HIS FIRST CRIMINAL INVESTIGATION, HIS
MEETING WITH YVONNE, HIS LONG FEUD
WITH GEORGE MARSDEN PLUMMER AND
HIS ADVENTURES IN THE WAR

The only Blake strip to appear in 'Super Detective Library'.

Sexton Blake meets Raffles in this hardback novel published by Dean & Son.

The first four issues of Sexton Blake's own magazine, 'Detective Weekly'.

More 'Detective Weekly' covers.

Another selection of Sexton Blake library covers including bottom right, the final issue in magazine format.

come here, and who you are waiting for now."

"Hand 'em over," said the sailor, extending a brown paw.

Phillips shook his head.

"Not until you've given me the information," he said.

The lean jowl of the American widened into a grin.

"Right," he returned, "that's fair. Now, fire away, what do you want?"

"Who are you waiting for?"

"For my skipper, Captain Baydoe, and two friends of his," said the sailor.

"Do you know the names of his friends?"

"Nope."

"What are they like?"

"One of them is a huge feller, big as a house, an ugly customer I should guess, while his pal is a little wizened monkey, with a face that'd frighten a nipper into a nightmare."

Phillips drew back, his face bloodless. He had never forgotten the appearance of the man he had thought was Marle, and the wizened, shrivelled figure that had accompanied him.

"They—they are here!" Phillips broke out, half to himself, "here, on this island!"

He took a pace towards the sailor, and thrust the folded notes into the man's hands.

"Where did you come from?" he asked, "and what is the name of your vessel!"

"Her name is the Paul S. Modie," the sailor returned, "we're from 'Frisco."

"What are you here for?"

"Well, we thought we were after seals, but the old man is a bit previous. It'll be another week or two before we can get in among 'em."

"Then why did you come ashore?"

"Oh, that's our passengers' business," the sailor returned. "They have gone to the south beach for some reason or other. There ain't no seals there now, but that's where they were bound."

Phillips reeled backwards, and the sailor, with a quick leap, caught him by the arm.

" 'Ere, steady on, mate," he said, "what's happened to you?"

With an effort the hounded man regained control of himself. He passed a hand across his forehead, and found that it was wet and clammy to the touch.

"Nothing—nothing," he said.

James Phillips looked at the sailor.

"I won't question you any further," he went on, "but if you feel under any obligation to me, keep quiet on what has transpired between us."

The sailor spat on the beach.

"You bet your life on that," he said. "I ain't ever goin' to say that I've seen you. Captain Baydoe is a rough horse when he's roused. I'll be as dumb an an oyster, an' I hope you'll be the same."

He touched his cap to Phillips, and the bank manager turned and staggered back up the beach again. He realised now what had happened. Marle and his vulture-faced companion had followed him to Salcoth Island, and were even now, at that very moment, searching south beach for the old hut.

He, Phillips, had so far failed to find the hut, but Marle was bound to know where it had stood. The man would be able to go to the spot at once, and the Seafoam's papers and deposit-note would be in his possession.

A groan broke from Phillips's lips, and he wrung his hands together.

"It's just my fate," he said, "all my efforts have been in vain. That brute will gain possession of the papers, and I shall be a ruined man. He will be able to go back to Grangepool and produce the deposit-note, and the bank will pay him the money. They will discover then what I did, and my daughter will find herself the child of a—thief."

All his pent-up agony flooded him, and his tall, thin figure seemed to shrivel. He groaned aloud.

"Marle here—here!" he muttered.

The scrape of a foot on the boulders ahead roused him. He glanced forward, and there came through the folds of mist a little squat figure, which he recognised at once as being the owner of the hut. Phillips rushed towards the man and caught him by the arm.

"Hallo, you!" the Eskimo said, "you no get back. Dashed cold last night."

"I was lost," Phillips said, "but, tell me, what about the men who came to your hut. Where are they? What are they doing?"

The Eskimo jerked his thumb over his shoulder.

"They over there," he said. "I got fed up. They look for something, same as you."

"At south beach do you mean?"

"Yes."

Another question came to Phillips's lips.

"Did you tell them that I—I was here?"

The man's broad face turned towards him.

"No," he returned, "they no ask me."

Here again was an example of the phlegmatic nature of this curious race. Captain Baydoe and his two companions had not asked the man if there was anyone else on the island, and the Eskimo had not troubled to enlighten them.

Phillips drew a breath of relief.

"Good," he said, "if they don't know I am here, there is still a chance for me."

He turned to the little man with whom he had lived for so long.

"Why did you come back?" he asked.

"I hungry," said the man, a state, by the way, in which he always seemed to be. "They no want me, and I no want them. I come back for food."

"Well, look here," said Phillips, "I am going on to the south beach. But if they come back to the hut, don't you mention that I am here. You understand. Not a word about me."

"I no mention you to anyone," said the Eskimo, making a promise which, although Phillips was little aware of it, was to have a curious result.

"Right."

The banker released his hold on the man's arm, and swung off into the grey mists, while the Eskimo, without even turning his head, trudged on to the hut.

James Phillips was assured of his way now, for, by keeping a sharp watch on the boulders as he passed, he could recognise the marks he had made. At the end of an hour's steady trudging, he found himself within earshot of the surf breaking on the south beach.

His pace broke to a slow walk, then he began to pick his way carefully over the moss-covered ground, stopping every now and again to listen. His cautious advance was continued for some time, then suddenly he came to a halt, every nerve on the alert.

A voice had come to him through the fog, a deep, penetrating voice. He was not able to make out what it said, but it guided him, and, dropping on his hands and knees, Phillips crept forward from boulder to boulder until, at last, he was close to where the murmuring voices arose.

He found himself behind a huge rock, and worming his way up this, he raised his head over the top.

Instantly, the shape of the ground in front of the boulder told him that here was the site of the old hut that he had been in search for so long. It was flat and smooth, covered with a soft green carpet of moss.

The fog was not so dense now, and he could see the place quite clearly. About ten yards away, seated on a low boulder, was the figure of a man in oilskins. He was puffing contentedly at a briar pipe, and the scent of the tobacco came to Phillips's nostrils.

About five yards away were two figures. The taller of the two had a short-handled tool in his hand, with which he was scraping the moss from the ground. The other figure, a wizened creature, was leaning over the cleared space, examining it intently.

Phillips saw now that already a great portion of the space had been removed, and the surface was broken.

"I guess you've gone far enough that way, come a little more to ye're right."

The man seated on the rock had moved the pipe from his lips, and his drawling voice sounded.

Carlac straightened his broad shoulders and dashed the sweat from his face. It was tough work removing the year's growth from the ground, and the giant criminal was bathed in sweat.

They turned, obedient to Baydoe's suggestion, and started work again, Carlac scraping the moss aside while Kew hovered over the cleared space with a sharp implement in his hand which he drove into the surface, loosening it.

Motionless James Phillips knelt, watching; then at last there came a quick cry from Kew's lips.

"All right!"

Carlac dropped the tool and bent forward. Kew was digging feverishly at a certain spot in the cleared ground. Gradually the hard surface was removed, and Carlac, pushing Kew aside, caught at the embedded object and tugged.

The box came up out of its twenty-year-old hiding-place, and a moment later the rusted hinges had been broken off and Kew's lean hand closed round the papers.

He stood up and glanced at them, Carlac's head thrust over his shoulder.

The log-book, one or two certificates, and an envelope bearing the crest of the Grangepool bank.

Yes, they are all here—ship's papers and the deposit note."

What happened then Phillips was never able to explain. It seemed to him as though a sudden mad impulse drove all caution from him.

Kew and Carlac, intent on their discovery, did not hear the quick scrape on the boulder. Captain Baydoe looked up and saw the long, gaunt figure poise itself. He whipped the pipe from his lips and opened them to shout. But before he could make a sound the figure had launched itself straight out from the rock in one mighty leap, hands thrust forward, fingers open.

It was a mad effort, and came near to success. Phillips' lean body landed straight between the two men, and Kew, taking the full force of the impact, was sent rolling over and over on the lichen-covered ground.

A snarling yell broke from Phillips' lips and his hands closed over the precious papers, snatching them out of Carlac's grip. The giant criminal, taken aback, was sent staggering a pace or two.

The shrill shriek broke from Phillips's lips, and he whipped round, pressing the papers to his breast. In another moment he would have escaped, and neither Carlac nor Kew could have stopped him.

But as he leapt away the Yankee skipper thrust a hand into his pocket. When it appeared again the arm was extended, and a whiplike crack sounded.

There was a scream and, half-way in his leap for safety, Phillips reeled and collapsed, the papers escaping from his clutch and scattering on the damp moss around.

There was a rush, and Carlac was on top of the bank manager. Phillips, with a groan, made an effort to rise.

"I only winged him," came the calm voice of Baydoe.

The bullet had torn a path through Phillips' thigh, and although he was half fainting with pain, the man put up a grim fight. But Carlac was too much for him, and at last the gigantic criminal, seizing Phillips by the beard, dashed his head down on a projecting rock.

The lean bank manager went limp his hands falling by his side. For a moment Carlac bent forward, peering into the face

132

of the man beneath him, then an oath broke from his lips and he leapt to his feet.

"It's Phillips!" he said, turning to Kew.

The professor had paid no attention to this struggle; he had been busily engaged in collecting the scattered papers. This task was completed now, however, and he, too, came forward to peer into the upturned countenance lying on the wet moss.

"So it is," Kew returned. "But how did he get there? If He——"

"Ho-o-o!"

Suddenly from the mists there came a long, warning note from a siren. Captain Baydoe, who had been engaged in taking the discharged cartridge from his revolver, gave vent to a quick cry of alarm. He darted across to where Carlac and Kew were bending over Phillips' body.

"You heard that?" he said. "That's the signal! Quick! We've got to get out o' here sharp!"

"What do you mean?"

"I told my mate to sound as soon as there was any sign of the Russian patrol-boat anywhere about," said Baydoe. "and that's the signal. If you fellers want to get out o' here safe, you'd better scoot at once! Come on, there's no time to waste!"

It was obvious that Captain Baydoe was alarmed, and he was not the type of man to be in that state without good cause. Carlac looked at his rascally confederate.

"What about this man?" he asked.

Baydoe dropped to his knee and put his hand on Phillips' heart; then they saw him start, and lean forward close to the bearded face.

"You needn't trouble him gentlemen," he said; "he—he's gone!"

"Dead?"

"Yes."

The skipper of the Paul S. Modie was moving now, and he beckoned to Kew and Carlac.

"If you are coming with me you must come now," he said.

And with a last glance at the prone figure of Phillips, the two master-criminals slid away into the fog at the heels of the captain, while on the wet moss the long figure of James Phillips lay stretched, mute and still, his fingers clutching at the soft growth.

CHAPTER 13.

Closing In.

"Do you see yon bank o' fog?"

Captain MacPhail of the Mary Barton, Vancouver, stretched his finger out, and Blake, standing beside him on the little bridge, nodded his head.

"Weel," said the Scotch skipper, "that's hangin' over Salcoth Island."

He cocked his eye at Blake.

"I'll gang in if ye like," he went on, "for I could find ma way blindfolded in there, but it's a bit risky."

The Mary Barton was a snug little steamer, used principally for coasting purposes along the bleak Alaska coast. Blake and his party had chartered it mainly because the skipper, Andy MacPhail, knew the island.

As a matter of fact, old Ben Wade had found in Andy an ancient acquaintance, and so the bargain was made and the little Mary Barton chartered.

She proved herself to be absolutely seaworthy, and the voyage to the bleak island had been covered without mishap of any kind.

"Time is rather precious, you see," said Blake, "and I think, if you don't mind, you had better try to get ashore."

"Ye want to see the seals, I suppose?"

"Yes, that's it."

Whatever Andy MacPhail might have thought about the little party he had never put any questions. He was quite content to accept his money and leave the voyage entirely in the hands of his passengers.

The Mary Barton gave a preliminary hoot, then, its engines turning at a slow rate, began to nose its way into the fog.

Blake left the bridge and went into the bow where Tinker, MacLeod, and Ruth were seated. The slender figure of the girl was wrapped in a comfortable oilskin-coat, and her face, peering out from beneath a sou'wester, was aglow with happiness and health.

"Salcoth Island is just ahead," said the detective, coming forward.

"Yes, Ben has told us already," said Ruth, getting up and leaning over the bow. "But I do wish this fog would clear away."

"So does our skipper," said Blake, with a smile. "Anyway, he's going to risk it and get us in."

There was a a few moment's silence, while the broad bow of the Mary Barton moved forward, then suddenly there came a cry of delight from the girl.

"Oh, look—look!" she cried.

Tinker and Hector leapt to her side and followed her pointing finger. On the crest of a wave there appeared the sleek head of a seal. The creature swam for a moment, then dived, revealing a circle of black sleek body. Another and another followed, and soon the Mary Barton was moving in a swirl of seals that dived and swam and played a hundred tricks around her slow-moving bow.

Ruth and her companions watched with fascinated interest, and presently Tinker felt a hand on his shoulder, and turned to see the healthy, ruddy countenance of old Ben by his side.

The old chap's eyes were gleaming, and he was peering into the water.

"There they are, the beauties!" he said. "It's years and years since I saw 'em last, but I can feel the touch o' their sleek bodies

133

even now."

"There are so many of them," said Ruth. "Where are they going?"

"They're all heading for the beach, miss," said Ben. "If ye wait a minute you'll hear the calls of the others. They are all making their little homes there, and it'll be a great to do, I promise you."

The Mary Barton came nearer and nearer to the shore, and at last the ceaseless cries and calls of the inhabitants of the beach came to their ears.

Suddenly Ben straightened up, peered ahead for a moment, then wheeled on Blake.

"We're goin' wrong," he said. "This isn't south beach."

He pointed to a huge headland that was standing out from the island, towards which the Mary Barton was being steered.

"Are you quite sure?" Blake asked.

The old tar laughed.

"Am I sure, sir?" he returned. "I know every foot of Salcoth Island. We are heading away from the south beach now."

He and the detective went across the deck, and Ben climbed the little bridge to the skipper's side. As soon as the old tar mentioned the coast, the skipper nodded.

"Yes, you're richt," he said, "it's the east beach I'm headin' for. Ye told me ye wanted to see the seals."

"Ah yes, that's my mistake!" said Blake. "I understood that it was the south beach that the seals were on."

"Naw, naw, ye're wrang there!" said old MacPhail. "They changed their quarters ten years ago. It's the east beach they are on noo."

"Oh, well, that's after my time!" said Ben. "I know the seals have little ways all o' their own. Last time I was here they were on the south beach."

The skipper's hand dropped on the signal bell; then he turned to Blake.

"I'm at your service, sir," he said. "Is it the south beach ye want?"

"Yes."

Another clang sounded, and now the Mary Barton took a long sweep seaward, finally heading towards the shore again. But now it moved away from the cries and calls, and presently they died down into the distance.

It was only a bit of sheer bad luck that had brought about that manoeuvre, but it was fraught with great results. For as the Mary Barton moved onward, from the fog there came a long hoot of a siren.

"Hallo, there's someone else up at the east beach!" said MacPhail. "That's rather strange, for it's too early for the seals yet."

The listened, but the sound was not repeated, and the Mary Barton continued her way round the dangerous coast of the little island.

Yet that hoot was the same signal as had drawn Captain Baydoe and the two nefarious scoundrels away from the south beach. Carlac and Kew, stumbling along behind the American skipper, finally reached the east sisde, to find that the boat had already been launched and the sailor was waiting for them to clamber into it.

The quickly pulled themselves on board the boat, then the sailor, pushing off, took to his oars and rowed swiftly out towards the Paul S. Modie.

Captain Baydoe was the first to climb on board, and as soon as he did so he was met by the mate.

"What's the matter?" the skipper asked.

The mate pointed towards the huge headland.

"I just caught sight of another vessel coming in here," he explained. "It turned tail just before it reached the headland and vanished again; but you told me to let you know as soon as any other vessel did appear, so I sounded the signal."

"Couldn't you make out what it was?"

"No, the fog was too bad. But I know it was under steam."

Captain Baydoe drew back and turned to Carlac and Kew.

"Might be all right," he said; "but it might not. It ain't worth while taking any chances though. You see, we are not allowed here. It's Russian property."

"What do you advise?" Kew asked.

"Well, if you gentlemen have done what you wanted to do, I say sheer off as soon as we can."

There was no reason why the two should wait any longer, and they agreed with the skipper's suggestion. Baydoe was obviously anxious to get away from the prohibited bay, and, in quick time, the Paul S. Modie was turned seaward and moved out from the little beach.

"You see, just around that headland is the east beach," said the captain. "And that's where the seals are gathering now. No doubt, if that was a Russian cruiser, it was first of all making for east beach to see if any of our crew were there. As soon as they find out there's no one there, they'll come round here and have a look at us. It strikes me we are just in the nick of time."

In that opinion, of course, Captain Baydoe was mistaken, but he was not to know that. Anyhow, his abrupt departure saved his two rascally passengers.

It was three hours later before the Mary Barton came to anchor at south beach, and one of its squat boats went flashing down into the water.

Ben—and one of the sailors tumbled in and held it steady while Ruth, Tinker, and Hector MacLeod went down the ladder into the boat. Sexton Blake was the last to leave, and MacPhail thrust his bearded face over the side just before the boat pushed off.

"I'd ha' come wi' ye," he said; "but ye are all right with old Ben there. He knows his way aboot here as well as I do."

The little boat was rowed off into the fog, and presently it ran ashore. the mist had begun to move uneasily now, and Ben, raising his head, sniffed.

"It's all right," he said. "there's a wind coming up now, and the fog'll be gone in a little while."

He and his companions trudged ashore, leaving the sailor behind to guard the boat. Ben was striding ahead with Blake by his side, and the old salt was silent for a long moment.

"I've seen this beach alive with 'em," he said at last. "It's very strange how they should leave it all now. It don't seem right somehow."

The fog was rapidly moving, and presently they were able to see the boulder-strewn beach with the black, rugged ground beyond.

"I don't see any sign of the hut," said Blake.

Ben came to a halt on a flat-topped boulder and looked around.

"No, it's gone as well. But it's all right, sir; I know just exactly where it used to stand."

The old sailor stood for a moment studying the ground, then his memory guided him aright, and he turned on his heel and began to move off over the rocky ground.

The old fellow seemed to be wonderfully agile, for, despite his years, he soon put a gap of twenty or thirty yards between him and the rest of the party. Hector and Tinker had dropped behind to help Ruth over the rough places.

"By jiminy, that old fellow can shin it all right," said Hector, panting and struggling up the rocky slopes.

Ben had now reached the top of the beach, and had turned to his left, making his way between the boulders.

"I—I am very sorry," said Ruth, glancing at Tinker. "I know you could get on better without me."

Her slender Ankles and thin shoes were hardly adpatable for the hard ground they had to cover. Tinker smiled down as he held her arm.

"That's all right, Miss Phillips," he said. "We will get there soon enough."

They went on for the best part of a quarter of an hour; then suddenly they saw Blake hurrying back towards them. Tinker gave one look at the stern countenance of his master, then came to a halt.

"What is it guv'nor?" he asked.

"Oh, it's—it's all right," Blake returned, with a swift glance at Ruth. "Only I don't think you need come any further. Ben has—has found the place where the hut was, and I am afraid that we-—we are too late."

Ruth had been studying Blake's face, and suddenly her quick intuition brought dread into her heart. She came forward, catching the detective by the arm.

"You are hiding something from me, Mr. Blake," she said. "Quick! Let me know. What is it!"

There was a gentle expression in Blake's eyes, and he looked down at her.

"Well, Miss Phillips, I am afraid that we have—have found you———"

"You mean you have found my father!"

With a quick cry the girl broke away from Blake, and, hardly stopping to see where she placed her feet, she darted off over the rough ground.

"Is that right, sir!" Hector asked.

Blake nodded.

"Yes," he said. "Ben discovered him lying close to the site."

"Is he—is he dead?"

"I'm afraid so."

Blake had not paused to examined the body, his first kindly thought being to save the girl from this unneeded agony. Ben was still kneeling over the figure when there was a rush of feet, and, with a groan, Ruth dropped on her knees beside the ragged, bearded man.

"Dad—dad!" she wailed.

She leaned forward, raising the head and straining it to her breast. As she did so, Ben, who had drawn aside slightly, saw the fingers twitch.

With a shout, the old fellow leapt to his feet.

"By Heavens, he is still alive! Mr. Blake—Tinker! Quick!"

The came up with a run, scrambling over the rough ground. Ruth, with her father's head still clasped to her breast, glanced up at them.

"I saw his fingers move." said Ben. "He's not dead; I'm sure of it."

The detective went up to Ruth and drew her aside; then a brief examination told him that Ben's words were true. The life had not quite left James Phillips's body.

There was a great bruise at the back of the head, and the bullet had made an ugly wound in the thigh. But the man still breathed.

Instantly Ben whipped off his heavy coat, and Tinker did the same: then the garments were knotted together, and the unconscious body of Mr Phillips was placed on them. Tinker and Hector acted as stretcher-bearers, and they carried their burden back along the beach followed by Ruth.

Blake had stepped aside, and was examining the moss-covered space. He saw the place where the moss had been scraped from the earth that had once been the foundations of the hut, and the black gap out of which the box had been drawn. Then, under the boulder, he discovered the iron box with the lid forced open.

"There's been a bit of a fight here, sir." said Ben.

"Yes," the detective returned, "and it only occurred recently, within the last two or three hours I should think. You can see the earth is quite freshly dug, and from the condition of the man's wound I shouldn't think it could have happened more than an hour or two ago."

Ben looked round him.

"Can't think what men want to fight for in a rotten place like this," he murmured.

Blake turned to his companion with a smile on his face.

"Look at this," he said.

The detective held the box in his hand.

"This is the cause of the fight," he went on. "We have come across half the world for the same cause; only, unfortunately, we have arrived just a little too late."

"But if it only happened two or three hours ago they may not have gone yet," said Ben. "There ought to be a chance of collarin' the rogues."

A swift memory returned to Blake, and he looked at the tanned face by his side.

"You remember that siren we heard——" he began.

"By jiminy—yes!"

"I'm afraid that meant the signal for departure for these brutes," Blake went on. "In all probability they caught sight of our boat, and I'm afraid they have given us the slip."

He and Ben turned and followed the melancholy group ahead. James Phillips was lifted into the boat and rowed back to the Mary Barton. As soon as the injured man was made comfortable below Blake sought out the skipper.

"You need not waste any more time on this side," he said. "You can take us round now to where the seals are. I suppose there's a hut or something there?"

"Oh, yes," said Captain MacPhail. "the Russians leave someone to look after the seals. They're mostly Eskimo."

The Mary Barton was under way again, and this time MacPhail cracked on all speed, with the result that within two hours he had made anchor in the little bay oposite the Eskimo's hut.

Blake and Ben went up to the hut and had a word with the Eskimo. the detective's quick eye caught sight of the small shoes which, in his haste, Kew had not been able to recover.

The Eskimo, in his broken English, gave an account of what had happened, so far as he knew, and Blake was able to reconstruct the grim scene that had taken place on the south beach.

"They've got the best of us, Tinker, and that's the long and short of it," Blake said afterward, when he and his young assistant were alone in the cabin together. "But there's one point in our favour now. It is evident that they believe that James Phillips is dead, and although they have the Seafoam's papers and the deposit note they may find it difficult to turn that deposit note into money."

"And what are we going to do now, guv'nor?" Tinker asked.

Blake smiled. One item of news that the Eskimo had given the detective was worth much to him. He had told Blake the name of the vessel on which Kew and Carlac had arrived, and also its port. The native of the island had recognised Captain Baydoe again, for it was not the first time that the Yankee skipper and his little vessel had visited the island.

The Eskimo's statement, coupled with what Blake had already discovered in 'Frisco, assured him on one point.

Captain Baydoe had left 'Frisco on one of his usual sealing expeditions, and it was not likely that he would leave these seas until he had accomplished his mission.

This meant that Kew and Carlac might be kept practically prisoners on board the Paul S. Modie until the sealing operations were completed.

"They might be kept on board for a month or more," said Blake. "Anyhow, they are sure to be delayed some time. Of course, should they sight any vessel making for port they will no doubt get on board; but we have got to take that risk."

He glanced at Tinker quietly.

"We are going to head straight for England," he said, "and there's just a possibility of us getting there ahead of these two scoundrels. If we do—well, we can prepare a very grim reception for them."

But Sexton Blake was not aware of the curious game of hide-and-seek that was being played around the island. Captain Baydoe, of the Paul S. Modie, had no intention of deserting the sealing-ground. It had only been the fact that the mate had imagined the Mary Barton to be a Russian cruiser that had caused the Yankee skipper to leave the east beach.

He had borne away northward, describing a wide sweep, and dusk had found the Paul S. Modie heading for the east beach of Salcoth Island again.

"I'm going to take the risk," the skipper said. "It would be better if I waited a week or two; there would be more seals then. But it doesn't matter. There must be quite a heap of bachelors on the beach, as it is, and, as you gentlemen seem in a durned hurry to get back again, I'm going to take the risk now. I ain't goin' back empty-handed.

Kew and Carlac had pleaded in vain with the skipper. But on his own boat Baydoe was absolute monarch, and they had to fall in with his wishes.

And so, in the darkness, every boat of the Paul S. Modie was launched, and the crew tumbled into them, ready for their attack on the creatures on the east beach.

It was a highly unlawful proceeding, for not only was it Russian territory, but it was also too early in the season. That attack on the beach would probably mean the desertion of it by the seals, and would practically ruin the island.

But none of these thoughts troubled Baydoe, and as the skipper took his place in the last boat, he glanced up at Kew and Carlac.

"We shall be busy all night," he said, "an' if you like you can come ashore with us."

"We might as well take the opportunity," Kew said; and the two men dropped down the swaying ladder into the boat.

By the time they reached the beach the crew were already at work. The two criminals could hear the slaughter, the thud of heavy clubs, and the whimpering moans of the dying animals. The crew of the Paul S. Modie seemed to have gone mad, and the east beach fairly ran with blood.

Kew and Carlac took no part in the one-sided battle, they drew away at last, and Kew scrambled up the beach, heading for the little hut.

A faint light was streaming through a crack in the wall, and the wizened man pushed open the door and entered, followed by Carlac. The eskimo sat up and stared at the intruders.

"Hallo—you back again!"

"Yes."

The man grinned.

"Plenty visitors to-day," he said.

"What do you mean?" Kew broke out, striding forward.

The Eskimo held up two stumpy fingers.

"Two men come here," he said; "one man took your shoes."

His small eyes twinkled.

"They found other man on south beach. You no finish him."

The phlegmatic way in which the Eskimo referred to the crime made Carlac scowl. He strode up to the squat figure and stood over the cot.

"What are you driving at?" he said.

The native of the island seemed quite unconcerned, and gave a brief report of Blake's visit and what had transpired. When Kew heard that Phillips had been taken on board the Mary Barton and was still alive, his vulture face hardened. He questioned the Eskimo closely, and at last the great truth dawned on him.

"There can be no mistake about it," the wizened criminal said, wheeling on his confederate—"it is Blake—Blake turned up again!"

Carlac glanced at his companion.

"What's to be done?" he muttered.

"Baydoe must take us back to the coast at once," Kew snapped. "He can land us anywhere he likes, but we must get away. It's only a blind piece of luck that has brought us back here to find out what we have done, and we must make the best use of it."

He turned and hurried out of the hut, with Carlac at his heels. When they had gone the Eskimo arose from his cot and closed the door behind his unwelcome visitors.

Kew and Carlac regained the beach, and the wizened professor went in search of Baydoe, while Carlac waited by the boats. Just what argument Kew used to persuade the obstinate Yankee, Carlac was not able to discover, but half an hour later a shrill whistle sounded, and in a few moments Baydoe and Kew appeared on the beach.

Again the whistle sounded, and from every quarter of the beach men came hurrying, bearing with them their dripping burdens.

Baydoe had chosen his men skilfully, and the boats were filled to the gunwales with the reeking cargo.

It took the best part of an hour to get the boats alongside the Paul S. Modie and swing them aloft, but the task was accomplished at last, and an hour before dawn the 'Frisco sealer was steaming out of the bay once more, heading coastwards.

"We've a tough job ahead," said Kew, "but we have one pull over Blake. That is, he doesn't know that we know he has been on the island and that he has taken off James Phillips alive. We must use that against him."

CHAPTER 14.

In An Old Disguise.

"Oh, look at that poor old man, daddy! Let me give him a penny!"

A little dot of a child, trotting along by her father's side, came to a halt and pointed a chubby finger.

Seated on the edge of the kerb, on a low camp-stool, was a grotesque figure. It was that of a bent, silver-haired man. A tattered hat was drawn over the brow, and over one eye was a black patch. On the pavement stood one of those dingy organs, and the beggar was turning a handle slowly to the accompaniment of a torrent of wheezy notes that had no sort of melody in them.

Opposite where he sat was the entrance to Grangepool Station. It was a bright day, and there were a good number of people about the streets.

The little girl took the copper from their father's hand and, running across the pavement, dropped it into the tin pannikin.

"Thank 'ee kindly, missy!" said a hoarse voice, and the child, running back to her father's side, went into the station.

At the entrance a couple of porters were standing chatting to a policeman. One of the indicated the man.

"He doesn't do so badly, that old fellow," one said. "That's the sixth copper I've seen him get within the last half-hour."

"And he ain' been here so long, either," the other porter put in.

"No, that's true," said the policeman; "only a couple o' weeks at the most."

One of the porters grinned.

"He's a queer-looking chap," he said; "but, by jiminy, I think his missus is funnier than him! Have you ever seen her?"

"No, can't say I have."

"Oh, she comes along about six o'clock and keeps him company. They're about the rummiest pair I've ever seen."

All through the long day the ragged, grotesque figure sat with his organ. At about two o'clock he drew out a red handkerchief from beneath the stool, and, opening it, produced a chunk of bread and cheese, which he munched at contentedly.

He seemd a pathetic, lonely figure, and the little tin pannikin attached to the crazy organ was a mute appeal that few passers-by could resist.

At five o'clock the London express steamed into the platform, and its passengers emerged from the wide entrance to the station. The beggar-man at the corner of the pavement began to turn his organ anew, the sibilant feeble notes rising above the clatter and noise.

There was a big number travelling by the evening train, and the bearded face of the mendicant was lifted, watching the stream as they came out.

Presently there emerged from the entrance a couple of youthful figures—a tanned, good-looking lad, and by his side a sweet-faced girl, whose cheeks had also been tanned by sun and wind.

They came to the edge of the kerb and halted, while a porter signalled for a cab. The vehicle drew up a few inches away from the man with the organ. The young man passenger helped the girl into the cab, then turned to the driver.

Just for an instant the music of the organ ceased.

"Fourteen Fairview Avenue, New Town."

The wheezy notes of the organ started anew, and the cab rattled off, while the porter, pocketing the tip, returned to the station. Ten minutes later, when the man emerged and looked down the pavement again, he noted that the organ-grinder had vanished.

"Gone—eh?" he muttered. "Ain't goin' to wait for his missus to-night. Must have had an extra good day to-day."

Meanwhile, the organ-grinder, with his flimsy organ suspended over his back and carrying the folded camp-stool under one arm, was hobbling along through the main streets of the busy town.

It seemed to be as much as he could do to move; his legs were bent under him, and he hobbled painfully, slowly, along the edge of the kerb.

He turned at last into a quieter street, made his way along it, then found himself at last in a lane which led into a long range of allotment gardens. At the far end of the gardens a feather of smoke was rising into the air, and towards this spot the organ-grinder headed.

He turned by a clump of trees and went towards a shabby-looking caravan. From the little tin smokestack of the caravan the smoke was rising lazily, and as the mendicant reached the short flight of steps that led to the door of the vehicle, it opened, and a figure appeared in the narrow doorway.

It seemed a very fair match for the grotesque figure on the steps. It was a wizened woman, dressed in drab garments that hung loosely round her shrivelled frame. Over the head was drawn a shawl, beneath which a fringe of grey appeared. The eyes were covered with a pair of smoked glasses, and her lean, gaunt face was almost concealed beneath the folds of the shawl.

The shuffling figure at the front of the steps swung the small organ from its shoulder and slipped it under the caravan, then climbed the steps, while the woman at the head held the door open with a wrinkled, claw-like hand.

The door closed behind the tottering figure, and as soon as it had done so a great change came over the bent form. The legs seemed to straighten, the whole figure grew tense, and the crouching body stood up until its bulk almost filled the caravan.

"They have arrived."

It was the deep voice of Count Ivor Carlac that sounded, and the wizened figure at the door whipped round towards him.

"You are sure?"

The hoarse voice came from between the thin lips, and with a quick movement Kew drew the smoked glasses from his eyes. Carlac strode across the caravan and dropped on to one of the bunks.

Hector MacLeod and Miss Phillips are here. They came by the five o'clock train, and have gone up to the house in Fairview Avenue."

"Then that means that the girl has come to prepare for her father's return," said Kew, an evil smile crossing his vulture face. "I knew that sooner or later the man would return again. All his interests lie here, and we had only to wait."

Carlac leaned back in the bunk.

"It's been a cursed long wait!" he put in. "It's been all very well for you, you could get a rest here, but I had to squat on the pavement there, day after day, until I felt as though I'd never be able to straighten my body again."

Kew's cackling laugh came across the caravan.

"You played the part to perfection, Carlac," he said. "No one would have suspected that you were anything but what you appeared to be."

Carlac shot a glance at the grotesque, wizened figure on the chair.

"You also looked the part," he returned grimly. "I have seen just such villainous old hags as you look in caravans before."

He arose to his feet and crossed to a locker, opening the door and taking out a black bottle. He measured out a generous portion of the contents and drank it.

"That's better!" he said, tossing the dregs on to the floor. "And thank heavens there is no more of that organ business! I got sick of the sound of it!"

"And so did everybody else, I should think." Kew put in. "But you are quite right, that side of our task is completed."

The scoundrels were biding their time. They had not ventured to make any appearance at the bank to claim the money in the name of the dead man. Kew was too clever to risk that.

But his discovery on Salcoth Island, the proof that James Phillips was still alive had given him all the information he required. He had built on the fact that sooner or later James Phillips would return to his native town, and it was then that the scheme of blackmail would be renewed.

And now, after many days of waiting, the appearance of Ruth Phillips at the station was the signal for a new move.

At half-past six that evening the workers in the allotment gardens heard the creaking of rusty wheels and the caravan that had stood for the past two or three weeks in the vacant ground beyond, came rumbling down the lane.

The huddled figure of Carlac was seated in the shafts holding the rope reins, and a word or two of chaff were passed up to him as he drove on.

The caravan turned and continued its way up the rising ground that led to New Town. It was a heavy pull for the animal between the shafts, and the best part of an hour elapsed before the caravan reached Fairview Avenue.

It went along the road, then turned to the left where a space of green turf, beside a high wall, gave it room to turn. The van was backed on to the turf and the horse loosened from the shafts, while Kew, still in his disguise, emerged from the vehicle and began to build a fire, erecting a tripod over it. In a few moments the fire was burning and a kettle full of water was hung on the tripod above the flames.

Presently a policeman came along, and after a doubtful glance at the fire, came towards it. Kew's replies to the man, delivered in the cackling voice, seemed to satisfy him, for, after a nod of his head, the representative of the law went down the road again.

As soon as the policeman had vanished, Carlac appeared from the caravan. He had changed his disguise now, having removed the grey beard, and being dressed in the blue sailor suit in which he had first appeared in front of James Phillips.

"I am going to have a look at No. 14," he said. "There is another train from London arriving about nine and our man may have come by that."

Kew smiled.

"I think you are only wasting time," he said, "but still you can have a look if you like. In my opinion our man will not arrive at Grangepool Station at all."

He pointed down the wide road.

"This is the main road from London," he went on, "and I think it will be along there that he will come."

"Perhaps you are right," said Carlac. "but there is no harm in my seeing."

He slid off into the darkness, and, finding the lane that ran along the back of the houses in Fairview Avenue, the huge criminal followed it until he came to the wall of No. 14.

It was about nine feet high, but it proved a very slight obstacle to Carlac. He leapt up and caught at the parapet, and with an effortless pull of his arms he was across the top of the wall, and the next moment had dropped into the garden at the other side.

There was a light burning in one of the lower rooms, and the yellow gleams struck a shaft of light along the path. Carlac, guided by the beam, made his way along the path and finally reached the window. He saw that it was the kitchen, and presently a figure moving from an inner doorway revealed itself to be that of Ruth Phillips.

The girl had slipped into a blue overall, and she was carrying a small tray containing tea-things.

She seemed smiling and content, and as she moved across the kitchen, Carlac's eyes rested on the tray for a moment. Then a glint came into the eyes, for he noted that there were three cups and saucers on the tray.

Drawing back from the window, Carlac moved to the angle of the house and reached the broad balcony that ran around the front part. He climbed on to the balcony, slipping over the rails, and, keeping close to the wall, found himself at last beside a window, the blind of which had been drawn.

He noted, however, that the lower part of the window was slightly open, and, dropping on one knee, reached forward, catching at the bottom of the blind, and lifting it.

It was the interior of the study that he was peering into, and, seated on a chair, with his back to the window, was the sturdy figure of Hector MacLeod. Ruth, standing beside the small table, was just in the act of depositing the tray on it.

There was a little spirit kettle with the blue flame burning briskly, and the girl's eyes were alight with excitement.

A murmur of voices came to Carlac's ears, but he could not catch the drift of the conversation. Now and again Ruth would glance impatiently at a little watch on her wrist, and every moment saw her turn her head towards the door.

For the better part of twenty minutes Carlac knelt there, watching the scene, then suddenly, there came to his ears the hum of a motor. It was coming down Fairview Avenue from the direction of the high road, and as he stood there, Carlac saw the white lights from the head lamps glimmer. The lights described an arc, then he saw them glaring on the white gate, sending a criss-cross pattern on the drive.

A figure in chauffeur's uniform came out into the glare, then the gate was opened, and a moment later the car, which proved to be a big touring one, came up the drive, it's rubber wheels grating on the gravel path.

Carlac leapt to his feet, for he realised that as soon as the white lights shone on the balcony, his presence there would be revealed. He had only just time to slip into a dark corner of the balcony, then the car emerged from a bend in the avenue and came to a halt outside the front door.

The door was opened and a little shaft of light issued. The slender figure of Ruth Phillips appeared, poised for a moment, then, with a quick cry, the girl ran down the steps and flung herself into the arms of a man in a heavy travelling cloak who had just alighted from the car.

Father and daughter exchanged a fond embrace, then, holding on to her father's hand, Ruth led him up the wide steps. Carlac leaned forward, trying to catch what it was that the excited girl said, but the whirring of the motor drowned her words, and he heard the front door close.

Then the car, after turning and backing in the narrow drive, went back towards the gate again.

With a stealthy rush Carlac was across the balcony and had taken up his position at the open window again. He was just in time to see the tall figure remove the heavy cloak.

It was James Phillips right enough, and the gaunt, hollow cheeks were mute testimony of the fight the man had had to make for his life.

Ruth assisted her father into the chair, and Hector MacLeod poured out a cup of tea. The man seemed to have little life in him. He accepted the ministrations in a dull fashion and mumbled his thanks.

Presently Hector Macleod seemed to ask a question to which Phillips replied, for a moment later the youngster, with Ruth by his side, hurried from the room. Carlac heard them go to the front door and was just in time to throw himself face downwards on the balcony when Ruth and Hector appeared on the steps.

They ran down together into the drive, and Carlac listened to the patter of their feet until they died away.

It seemed to the master criminal as though this was the exact moment he had been waiting for. Raising himself, Carlac strode across the balcony, reaching the door. It had not been closed, and a push was enough to send it back on its hinges.

Carlac stepped into the wide hall, closing the door behind him. He made no sound as he crossed the hall and opened the door of the study. He stepped into the room, his eyes seeking the figure in the arm-chair.

James Phillips had drawn the chair up towards the fire, and the cup of tea, untasted, stood on the little table by his side. The bank manager's face was thrust forward and the eyes were fixed and staring.

Carlac crossed the room slowly and was close to the table before Phillips sensed his presence.

"That you, Hector?"

The question was spoken without the man raising his head. The deep, curt laugh that Carlac gave made Phillips swing round.

There was a cry and a swift leap. The little table and the cup of tea were dashed to the floor, and, white and tense, James Phillips faced the huge figure in blue.

"No, it's not Hector, James Phillips," said Carlac; "it's someone more important."

"You—you!"

Carlac's broad criminal face was set and grim. He strode up to the nerveless man, fixing him with his eyes. Beneath that fierce gaze Phillips was like wax.

"I have waited a long time for this, James Phillips," Carlac went on. "I knew that sooner or later you would come back to Grangepool, and now I want a settlement."

Phillips was staring at the face, the broad nose and iron-grey hair.

"You—you want a settlement!"

"Yes," said Carlac. "I hold the deposit note that you gave twenty years ago in return for twenty thousand pounds. That money you misappropriated; you must now deliver it up."

His eyes were as cold as steel.

"Before I leave this room you must give me satisfaction. You have had the money and you will have to refund it."

"I—I can't refund it. I do not possess anything like that sum."

"Then what you do possess I shall have," the relentless scoundrel went on. "Every penny you have belongs to me. I am going to give you a chance, Phillips. You will either refund the last farthing or the story of your crime will be published abroad."

There was a wailing cry from the thin figure of James Phillips, and the man dropped on his knees in front of Carlac, gripping at the master criminal's broad palm.

"No, no; don't do that, for Heaven's sake don't do that," the bank manager broke out. "I have only just recovered from a—a terrible illness. It was you and your friend who brought me near to death's door. I am weak and—and incapable of doing anything just now. Give me a chance, man; give me a chance."

"What money have you in your possession?"

Still in his kneeling position, Phillips fumbled with his coat and presently drew out a bulky pocket-book.

"There's six hundred," he said. "It is all I have with me. It's yours—take it—take it!"

He pressed the book into Carlac's hand. The criminal's fingers closed over it, but his laugh was short and curt.

"Six hundred is nothing," he said; "you are worth more than that."

"But I have no more in my possession at this moment, I—I swear it. Give me time—let me find out just how I do stand, and I promise you that to the best of my ability I will—will repay you."

There was no mistaking the dread and terror that hung on the man's life. Carlac felt that James Phillips was going to be an easy victim.

"Listen to me," he said; "I will give you twenty-four hours. By this time to-morrow night, eight o'clock, you must meet me at the corner of this avenue and you will have in your possession at least ten thousand pounds in gold and notes. Understand—ten thousand pounds. That is only half of what you owe me. Get up!"

He caught at the thin shoulders and drew the man to his feet. James Phillips tottered a pace and dropped into the chair.

"I will—will do my best," he said, "only you must—must promise that you will not reveal my secret?"

"That all depends on yourself," the master criminal replied. "Remember you have twenty-four hours."

As the words left Carlac's lips he heard a thud on the outer door, followed by the sound of a key in the lock. With a swift rush the criminal was across the room and had lifted the lower half of the window. He swung the blind aside and slipped his great bulk through the gap, then, turning round, he fixed his eagle eye on James Phillips's face.

"Until to-morrow night," he said.

Then, dropping the blind, he vanished, just as Ruth and Hector MacLeod darted into the room, to find Phillips lying stretched in the chair with bloodless lips and eyes staring vacantly at the ceiling.

Dad—dad! What has happened? Oh, in heaven's name speak!"

Ruth flung herself on her knees beside her father, clutching at his cold hands.

James Phillips turned his head towards the girl, his lips moving, but no words coming from them. It seemed as though the ordeal he had gone through had bereft him of speech, and, at last, assisted by Hector, Ruth half led, half carried her father up the stairs and into his bed-room.

Hector MacLeod assisted the nerveless man to undress, and it was not until he was safely in bed that Hector left the room. He found Ruth dry-eyed and tearless, waiting in the hall. The girl was white to the lip.

"What can have happened?" she asked, turning towards Hector.

"I don't know," the youngster returned, "he seemed quite all right when we left him,"

The girl caught his arm.

"Oh, I am so afraid," she broke out. "I was so happy before he came, I thought that everything would be just all right now. But he seems worse than ever."

Hector MacLeod was silent. Indeed, he could find no words to use to help the girl in her fears. A sudden wish leapt into his heart.

"If only Mr. Blake was here," he said. "I cannot understand why he went off as he did."

The little party had arrived together at Liverpool, and Ruth and Hector had been taken with James Phillips to one of the private nursing homes there. When they returned to the hotel, at which Blake and Tinker and Ben had put up, it was to discover that the trio had gone.

There was only a short note from Blake addressed to Hector, stating that he had arranged to look after James Phillips until he was well, then he was to arrange to get him back to Grangepool.

These orders, although Hector did not quite understand them, were carried out to the letter. He and Ruth had waited in Liverpool until the time came when Phillips was able to travel.

In his note, Blake had suggested the best way to get the bank manager back to his home, and Hector had carried this out. He and Ruth had travelled with Phillips to the nearest junction, then, after chartering a car to take the bank manager the last portion of his journey, Ruth and Hector had gone on by train.

They had arrived in Grangepool as already explained, and had hurried at once to the house to prepare for the coming of the broken man.

"If only Mr. Blake would turn up," Ruth sighed. "I cannot understand why he deserted us. It seems so—so strange of him."

"He must have had some reason," said Hector, "Mr. Blake is not the sort of man to desert anyone. Sooner or later he will turn up, and we shall find it will all be right."

But, even as he spoke the words, Hector MacLeod felt a dull misgiving, and it was with a heavy heart that he left the house in Fairview Avenue that night, and made his way down to the station hotel.

"I don't like it," the youngster thought, "it was all right while Blake was with us, but the job is too big for me, and I wish to goodness he would turn up again."

His wish was to be fulfilled sooner than he expected.

CHAPTER 15.

Conclusion.

I ain't goin' to argue with you. You agreed to put in a month's work for me, and you've only put in a fortnight. If you don't stick to it, I don't pay yer."

Mr. Tobb, greengrocer, stuck his fat legs apart, and, placing his hands on his hips, scowled at the two figures opposite him. He was standing in the little shanty that looked out over the allotment gardens, and it was evident that he was in a roaring temper.

The figures in front of him were dressed in shabby clothes, and were as unkempt and untidy a couple as one could meet in a day's march.

The younger of the two had been carrying a hoe over his shoulder, and this he had now deposited at the worthy greengrocer's feet.

"Ye understand," Mr. Tobb went on, "no work, no pay!"

"Well, we ain't goin' to work no longer for you, and that's flat," said the older of the two, "an' if you don't pay up we'll summons you, you see if we don't."

"Summons away," Tobb bawled out, "an' don't you give me any of yer sauce either. Clear out o' my garden, quick!"

There were other workers dotted her and there on the allotments, and the greengrocer's irascible voice carried to various quarters.

The two unkempt figures wheeled round, and stalked away down the narrow path between the rows.

"Lazy tramps that ye are, serves me right for givin' ye work," the exasperated greengrocer bawled behind them. "It's a good riddance to bad rubbish, that's what I says."

The two figures slouched along, shoulders up, hands thrust in the pockets of their trousers. As they passed through the allotments, they had to undergo a running fire of chaff. Now and again, the slimmer figure would turn and throw back an apt reply, but at last the ordeal was over, and they found themselves in the little lane.

As a rule they turned to the left, heading for the old town, but this evening it was to the right that they moved, trudging on along the lane until they had left the gardens behind, and were passing through the quiet streets.

"I am afraid we have left it a bit late, guv'nor."

"No, it's quite all right, Tinker. I have a shrewd idea where these two rascals are hiding."

It was Sexton Blake's voice that issued from the ragged figure of the allotment worker. The disguise was perfect. A five or six day's old beard on the chin; the greasy cap, and the unkempt hair was typical of the vagrant.

From the dilapidated boots to the dirty red handkerchief, Sexton Blake looked the part.

It was almost dusk before they had left the allotment gardens, and Blake and his companion wended their way through the streets, heading for New Town. Presently they emerged on the broad high road. that ran out of Grangepool, and a messenger boy wheeling past on a bicycle was hailed and stopped.

"Caravan? Yes, there's one just up the road a bit," the boy said, "it's next to Mr. Porter's field."

The youngster went on his way again, and the two vagrants continued their trudging along the grass border of the road. They climbed the slope, and presently caught sight of the battered van standing in the little stretch of grass.

Blake came to a halt, and dropped on to the greensward, while Tinker followed his example.

"I'm pretty sure that's the van, guv'nor," he said.

"Yes, that's it, right enough, Tinker," Blake returned, "we have been watching it too long to be mistaken."

Little had Kew and Carlac dreamed that as they passed to and fro each day to the caravan, that in the allotment gardens a couple of pairs of eyes had watched their going.

Clever though the criminals were, they had not realised that their every move was being observed, and although they had slipped away in the night times, the following day had found Blake on their track.

"Where abouts are they now, guv'nor?" Tinker asked as, leaning back on his shoulders, he nibbled at a blade of grass.

The darkness had increased, and there was only a few stars gleaming in the sky. Ahead of them they could see the caravan, and, by its side, a dull glow revealed the presence of a small fire.

Blake was watching the glow, and suddenly he saw it leap into flame, as a thin figure stood over it, feeding it with a few scraps of brushwood.

"They are quite close to Fairview Avenue," said Blake; "the top of the avenue is only a few yards down the road. I have no doubt but what Hector and Ruth and Mr. Phillips have arrived home by now. In fact, I expect Carlac saw Hector and Ruth come by train yesterday. That would be the signal for their departure from the allotment."

"I wish we had followed them last night, guv'nor?" Tinker said.

"Perhaps it's just as well that we didn't," Blake returned, "for they are still here, and it is evident that they haven't been very successful."

He was silent for a moment, then he turned to his young assistant.

"We will have to divide forces now, my son," said Blake, "I think the best thing you can do is to go down to Fairview Avenue, and find out what is going on there. Be careful how you go, and don't let anyone see you. When you have found out how things are, you can come back and wait for me here."

"And what are you going to do, guv'nor?"

Blake nodded towards the caravan.

"I am going to tackle Kew," he said, and his voice was stern and severe.

Tinker rising to his feet, slipped across the road and vanished into the dusk. Blake waited four or five minutes before he, also, arose. He kept well in the shadows of the high wall as he approached the caravan, until, at last, he found himself within twenty yards of it.

Close to where he was the horse was browsing. Blake could hear the crisp crunch of the animal's teeth as it cropped at the short grass.

Flat on his face, the detective began to move through the grass until, at last, he was under the side of the caravan, close to the steps. About five yards away from him there was the fire, and, seated on an upturned box, was the grotesque figure in female clothing.

Once the figure turned its head, and Blake saw the hawk-like features of Kew standing out against the faint glow from the fire.

The wizened man seemed impatient. He moved restlessly in his seat, sometimes rising, and listening, then resuming his box again, with a low-voiced murmur of impatience.

Somewhere in the distance a clock chimed the hour of nine, and Kew rising again, thrust the box aside with a sweep of his foot, and began to pace up and down in front of the fire.

Ten minutes passed, then a sudden thought seemed to strike the criminal. He came to a halt in the middle of his pacing, wheeled towards the van, and, striding forward, climbed the short flight of steps.

Blake heard the boards creaking beneath his weight, as the criminal crossed the vehicle, then, later the sound of a key being turned in a lock came to Blake's ears.

Noiselessly, the detective wriggled out from his cramped hiding place, and, kneeling beside the flight of steps, raised himself until, at last, he was level with the glass-panelled door.

The door was slightly ajar, and through the gap Blake saw the shapeless figure of Kew. The criminal was kneeling in the centre of the van, and in front of him lay the reed organ. Even as Blake watched he saw the top part of the organ wrenched upwards, and Kew, thrusting his claw-like hand into the interior, began to draw out paper after paper.

An expression of grim satisfaction crossed Blake's face. For he realised what these papers were: They were the contents of the box that Kew and Carlac had found on the lonely site on Salcoth Island.

It was just those very papers that had made Blake adopt such a strange way of finishing his case. He knew that while Kew and Carlac were in possession of them, James Phillips would always be under fear of blackmail.

Blake's first duty was to get possession of the papers, and here was his opportunity.

The thought that has sent Kew hurrying into the caravan had been a quick suspicion of his companion. Carlac had told Kew of the interview he had had with James Phillips, and of the appointment that had been made for that night.

It had been fixed for eight o'clock, and when nine had struck, Kew, his impatience gradually rising, had suddenly suspected that Carlac might have played him false.

If the big criminal had possessed himself of the papers, and had sold them to James Phillips, it was more than likely that he would play a double game.

But now, as the long fingers of the professor turned the various papers over, he realised that his suspicion was unfounded.

"No," he said aloud, "they were all right, and while they are in my hands I am safe enough."

He arose to his feet, folding the papers into a bundle, which he thrust into the loose, shapeless garment he wore.

He then replaced the top of the organ, and crossing to the locker, thrust the instrument back into its hiding place, closing the lid.

As he did so he heard a board creak. There was a mirror above the locker, and Kew threw his head up and glanced into it. Just for a moment he had a fleeting vision of a grim, rugged-face staring at him.

Quick as a flash Kew leapt aside, thrusting his hand below the pillow of his bunk. But even as he withdrew his hand, an iron grip fell on his wrist, and, flinging himself round, Kew struck at the unknown intruder.

His hand now free from beneath the pillow, and in it was a long, gleaming tube. Blake had pinned Kew's wrist against the side of the bunk, but the talon fingers were still gripping at the tube, and twice Kew tried to level it.

But Blake, putting up all his strength, succeeded in keeping the hand rigid.

It was fierce battle, all the more deadly because it was carried on almost in silence. Kew had dropped his shawl, and the false grey wig had fallen away from the head, revealing a hairless cranium.

In the loose folds of his robe the man looked more like a vulture than ever, and his eyes, glaring and white, peered from the red-rimmed lids like those of the bird of prey.

Slowly and remorselessly Blake tightened his grip until the bones of the wrist creaked to his pressure. He had flung his other arm under Kew's shoulder, and the side of his hand was pressing against the lean throat.

The men hardly moved their positions as the deadly pressure continued. Kew battling for his life, tugged and writhed and swayed. There was a wondrous strength in the lean, wizened shape, and it was all Blake could do to hold the hand down.

Suddenly, Kew made another desperate effort, and, just for a moment his hand moved from the hard side of the bunk. The tube dropped, but even as its hollow end swept towards Blake, the detective drove his arm forward and up.

Kew's knuckles rapped against the side of the bunk, there was an oath and a scream, then the tube fell, and a faint click sounded. There was muffled report, such as an air rifle gives. Something flashed out of the tube and burst against the wall above Kew's head. A greenish smoke hung for a moment over the two men, enlarging rapidly, descended on them both.

Blake felt a burning sensation in his eyes and nostrils, and, quick as a flash, he dropped to the floor, dragging Kew with him. He knew that it was a poison gas that the skilled criminal had tried to use on him, and there was only one way to escape from it.

With Kew's lean body clasped in one arm, Blake wormed his way to the door. One swing of his disengaged hand saw the door open, the Blake and Kew went sprawling down the steps, rolling over on to the green grass.

Blake had never released his hold on his enemy, and, when they fell together, the detective, with a quick swing, was uppermost. Kew's body was rigid, and his arms hanging motionless by the side. The vulture head was back, the eyes closed.

Blake, peering at the face, drew back with a quick breath, for he saw that there was a faint greenish hue on Kew's lips.

It was evident that the poison had reached Kew first, and its deadly effect was apparent.

Raising himself to his knees, Blake felt in the folds of the garment, and presently his fingers touched the little packet of papers. He drew them out and slipped them into his pocket.

He stooped again and glanced at the figure at his feet. There was no sign of motion, for it seemed to Blake as though the gas had done its work swiftly and well.

As he bent over the figure, there came to his ears a crash, followed by a shot. Blake straightened up, and, leaping over Kew's prostrate body, darted into the road. There was another flash and a report, and he saw the blue flame flick out in the darkness.

Dropping into a run, Blake sprinted along the road, and found himself beside the lane that ran down at the back of the houses in Fairview Avenue. It was from that quarter that the sounds had come, and he made off up the lane as hard as he could pelt.

The darkness deceived him, and, as he darted on, someone came tumbling over the top of a wall right on his shoulders. Blake, taken by surprise, was carried off his balance, and, a moment later, a pair of powerful arms were around him, and he was pinned to the ground.

The detective made a quick effort which saw him release one of his arms, then he swung round with his opponent, reeling up against the wall on the right.

Blake drew back his fist, and was about to dash it into the face of the man he was struggling with, when the unknown raised his voice.

"Quick, Tinker—quick! The beggar's getting away!"

Blake fist dropped, and he peered into the face.

"Why, it's MacLeod, isn't it?"

There was a gasp, and the arms around his body were released. Blake moved aside, and Hector scrambled to his feet. Another rush and a scramble sounded, and Tinker came shinning over the wall.

"It's Marle," Hector broke out. "He—he got away into the lane. I followed him, and he fired at me twice."

Instantly Blake realised his mistake. There were a number of dark doorways set in the wall higher up, and he had not paused to examine them.

He whipped round, and, followed by Tinker and MacLeod, went sprinting off up the lane. They emerged on to the high road, and, turning to the left, headed at once for the caravan. Blake was ten yards ahead of his companions, and, as he reached the fire, Tinker heard his master give vent to a word of dismay.

He had left Kew prone and helpless beside the little heap of cinders, but there was no trace of the ungainly figure now.

"They have got away, I'm afraid," said Blake. "come on, Tinker, we must search."

"Listen, guv'nor!"

Tinker gripped at his master's sleeve, and held up his hand. The trio strained their ears, and there came back to them, faintly, the rapid beating of horse's feet."

"It's the van horse," said Blake, leaping towards the vehicle.

His surmise was correct, for the animal, that had been browsing peacefully on the sward behind the caravan, was gone, and, although they listened again, the hoof-falls were not repeated.

"It—it was all my fault, guv'nor," Tinker broke out. "I ought to have known that the beggar would make a dash for it."

Hector turned to Blake's assistant.

"It was as much mine as yours, Tinker," he said. "I ought to have kept a better watch."

"What happened?" Blake asked.

They had turned now, and were retracing their steps towards Fairview Avenue. Tinker's report was a very brief one. He had made his way to the house, and, gaining admission by the back wall, had stumbled across Hector in the kitchen. Hector had told Tinker that James Phillips had insisted on going out an hour before, and had not yet returned.

Ruth was beside herself with fear, and Hector had been trying to prevent the girl from going out in search of her father. Tinker and Hector had made a hurried plan, and, while Hector waited in the house, Tinker had gone off in search of Phillips.

He found the wretched bank manager locked in a fierce struggled with the burly figure which Tinker had recognised at once as being that of Carlac.

James Phillips, rather than allow himself to be blackmailed, had made a desperate attempt to kill Carlac, and it was only the master criminal's swiftness that had saved his life.

Tinker had only been in the nick of time, for Phillips was pinned to the fence of his own garden, with Carlac at his throat.

The young detective had not stopped to consider his actions, but had leapt at the ruffian. Carlac had struck out at Tinker, sending the lad reeling; then, the huge criminal had darted through the white gate, while tinker, gathering himself together, had made after him.

Carlac had flashed across the garden and down beside the house with the young detective at his heels. The youngster had called out to Hector, and the plucky bank clerk had leapt out of the kitchen just as the huge criminal came down the path.

It was well for Carlac that he had been in that garden before and knew his way, for the two youngsters were close on his heels by the time he had gained the barrier.

He had leapt on to a wooden barrier, which had given way, and that was the crash that Blake had heard. Then, from the top of the wall, Carlac had fired a shot which had grazed Hector's temple.

The criminal had dropped into the lane, and Hector, drawing himself up on the wall, had run along the parapet like a cat, following the man below.

Near the head of the lane, Carlac had fired **again**, and this time the bullet had caused Hector to lose his balance as he ducked, sending him toppling into the garden below.

The youngster had clambered on to the wall again, and seeing a dark figure beneath, had flung himself bodily on to it, with the result that the reader already knows.

"It's rotten luck!" MacLeod broke out. "I don't know what we shall do. It seems to me as though Mr. Phillips is going to be hounded by these men for the rest of his life."

They turned into Fairview Avenue now, and were approaching No. 14. Blake caught sight of a lean figure resting against the gatepost, and darted forward. He was only just in the nick of time, for Phillips had already raised his hands to his temple, and the dull muzzle of a revolver gleamed between his fingers.

A quick snatch saw the weapon dragged from his grasp, and James Phillips turned a white face round towards the trio.

"That's a cowardly way, Mr. Phillips," Blake said; "only a coward would think of doing that."

A low cry broke from the bank manager's lip's, and he reeled against the gatepost.

"Let me die—let me die!" he said. "It's no good! Those brutes will hound me all my life, and the crime of years ago can only be wiped out by my death."

"You are wrong there," said Blake. "Those men will hound you no more. Come, and I will explain."

He took the man's arm, and they walked up the broad drive together. Two minutes later a silent party was gathered in the study, James Phillips in the deep armchair, while Blake stood at the table, with the little pile of papers in front of him.

"Here are the records of the Seafoam's last voyage to Salcoth Island, and also the deposit note which Marle received from you. Nat Marle died in Laidstone Prison quite recently, and his testimony can never be given against you."

It was the first time that James Phillips had heard the truth, and he listened to Blake's words with breathless interest.

"Marle dead—Marle dead!" the man repeated over and over again.

"Yes," said Blake. "So far as Marle is concerned he can never claim his ill-gotten gains."

Then, with a quick pace forward, Blake stepped up to James Phillips and put the papers into the trembling hands.

"But you will remember, Mr. Phillips, that that twenty thousand pounds did not belong to Marle. He had swindled his employer, Malcolm MacLeod, and the rightful owner stands—there!"

He pointed towards the bronzed youngster. Phillips raised his sunken eyes and looked at the lad.

"Yes, yes; I know that," the bank manager said brokenly. "But you will admit that I—I did my best for you, boy. It was only when that first letter came from the prison and I knew that the past was rising up against me, that I—I got rid of you. Can you forgive me for that, Hector?"

MacLeod felt a small hand steal into his, and he closed his own round it.

"There is nothing to forgive, sir," he said, "and if you feel you are under any debt to me—well, I know an easy way of repaying it."

"You mean that? Can I repay it in any way?" Phillips said quickly.

Hector stepped aside, and drew Ruth forward.

"Give me your daughter, sir. I have loved her for years, and she is more to me than any more in the world."

James Phillips arose to his feet, and, coming forward, placed the Seafoam's papers and deposit note in Hector's hand.

"They belong to you," he said; "but if you are in earnest about what you said just now, I am only too ready to agree."

There was a little fire burning in the grate. Hector, releasing his hold of Ruth for a moment, stepped forward, and, with a quick swing of his hand, tossed the precious deposit note and ship's papers into the heart of the flame.

A cry came from Phillips's lips, and he held out his hands. Ruth caught at one, while Hector gripped the other.

"Father!" they cried in unity.

For a moment they stood together in a warm embrace, then Hector lifted his head and looked round him, while a cry broke from his lips.

"They—they have gone! Why, hang it, they've gone!"

Blake and Tinker had indeed disappeared.

It was some five or six days later before Hector received any communication from the great man that had helped him so much, and then the message was laconic enough:

"Kew and Carlac still at large, and while they are Tinker and I will be busy. You, however, need have no further fear, and we both wish you the best of happiness and luck, and all good wishes to your charming bride."

But how Blake and Tinker finally ran Professor Kew and Count Carlac to earth, is another story.

THE END

THE SHADOW OF HIS CRIME

OR, HOUNDED DOWN

THE PROLOGUE
I.
Clench and Cavendish, Financiers

The clerks in the spacious general offices of Messrs. Clench and Cavendish, Financiers and Company Promoters, of Throgmorton Avenue, were preparing to leave for the night, but in the private sanctum of the partners, there were many signs suggesting that work was not yet at an end.

Jasper Clench, a tall, lean man, with a pale, shrewd face, lit by keen grey eyes, was poring over a private ledger, whilst his partner, Richard Cavendish, was seated at the opposite side of the table, counting the immense pile of bank-notes before him, and making them up into batches of £5,000.

Richard Cavendish presented in appearance a striking contrast to his stern-visaged partner. Cavendish was a trifle short and stout, and possessed a merry, fresh-complexioned countenance, and a pair of twinkling black eyes. He at all times looked sleek and prosperous, from the top of his well-oiled head to the toes of his immaculate patent boots, and it was for this reason that when a client was doubtful about some investment he or she had made with the firm, it was Mr. Cavendish who attended to the reassuring interview.

Cavendish was the owner of a glib tongue, and a manner as sleek and oily as his looks. He could talk the most doubtful would-be invester over to his side, and convince one who had lost heavily by the collapse of one of the firm's companies, that he was taking a pessimistic view of matters, and ought to try again.

Despite Richard Cavendish's powers of oration, however, both partners realised that the time had arrived when London was decidedly too hot for them.

During the last six months the number of dissatisfied clients calling at the offices had umpleasantly increased. The Easy Investment Syndicate, the Cape Diamond Concessions, and the Greshamly Rubber Company—all three concerns, which Clench and Cavendish had floated upon public money—had somehow gone smash, and now clients were becoming far too inquisitive over their "Great Eagle" shares.

Two days ago, an aggressive American client, handling a dog-whip suggestively, had tried by force to gain an entry into the private sanctum; and only yesterday there had been the widow who had openly wept before the clerks and declared that she had been swindled.

The Great Eagle Gold Mining Co. was the last "little affair" with which Messrs. Clench and Cavendish had amused themselves.

A well-known mining engineer—who, by the way, was now very much missing from Britain, and enjoying some of the firm's money upon the Continent—had journeyed to Brazil, where the site of the Great Eagle properties was situated, and he had sent home a glowing report that the ground was positively teeming with the precious metal.

Upon the strength of this, Messrs. Clench and Cavendish had sent out thousands of alluring prospectuses, and filled the pages of the Press with hosts of gripping advertisements, and their energies had not been in vain.

There are always plenty of people in this curious world of ours who are stupid enought to think that by expanding a little capital, they can become millionaires without the slightest trouble to themselves, and the abundance of "fish" Clench and Cavendish's "nets" had caught pleased the swindlers mightily.

They did not trouble that when the crash came many thousands of hard-working men and women would lose their lives' saving—their all! Like all men of their class, they were selfish to the last degree, and they were out for every pound they could rake in.

But now, as we have already said, investors wanted news as to how the Great Eagle Properties were progressing, and the company promoters knew that it was time they discreetly withdrew from the scene of their scoundrelly operations.

Jasper Clench closed the ledger and locked it carefully, and, lighting a cigar, he sat watching his partner until the latter had completed his count of the notes, and had stowed them away in a portmanteau, which stood by his side upon a chair.

"Well?" Clench asked, in the hard voice that was characteristic of him. "You found my calculation was correct?"

Richard Cavendish rubbed his fat hands together, and smiled his sauve smile.

"Precisely," he murmured. "The notes total just over two hundred and fifty thousand pounds, and there's a like sum in easily-negotiable securities—altogether half a million, my friend. Half a million to bolt with! It's not so bad!"

Clench nodded; but he did not return the other's smile. Indeed, it was seldom that he troubled to evince any sign of pleasure. He was always the hard, calculating man, whose one thought was the making of money. Mammon was the god he worshiped, and nothing else mattered.

"There will be another ten thousand to add to our haul by the first post to-morrow morning," he said thoughtfully, as he examined the end of his weed to make quite certain it was burning evenly. "That foolish old women at Merton promised to send me a cheque for the shares she wishes to take up, immediately she arrives home to-night. I convinced her that the cheque must be left open, and advised her to send it by registered post. As soon as it comes to hand in the

145

morning, we can cash it, and get along to your yacht."

Cavendish drummed his fingers upon the table and looked doubtful.

"Wouldn't it be almost as well to leave to-night?" he asked slowly. "The yacht could sail by this evening's tide."

Clench made a deprecating gesture with his hands.

"And leave old Mrs. Burton's ten thousand behind?" he asked, with something like a sneer in his voice. "Bah, man, where is your nerve?"

"I don't know about nerve!" his partner retorted. "To be too daring is to be foolhardy. The police are paying us far too much attention of late. The big man, whom I spoke of the day before yesterday, was hanging about again to-day, when I went out to lunch."

Clench sat a little more upright in his chair.

"You are sure of that?" he asked sharply.

"Yes," Cavendish agreed. "There may be no harm in him, but to my way of thinking, he looks very like Scotland Yard." He shuddered perceptibly. "I'm not anxious to see the inside of one of her Majesty's prisons. With all our other coups we have left a loophole through which we could wriggle and clear ourselves; but with this Great Eagle business we could do nothing but return the bulk of the money we have netted, leaving but a most inadequate profit for ourselves, if we wanted to escape doing time for fraud. We planned to make this our last great coup—to leave England with every penny of the public's money—and there's no sense in hanging back to add a paltry ten thousand to the half-million we've already cleared."

"Oh, we shall escape safely enough," the other protested, "and we shall take every sovereign with us. Let me see you lock that bag away in the safe, then we'll leave until the morning. Hark! That is our cab drawing up, now."

Cavendish hesitated, fidgiting with his podgy fingers.

"Then you are going to stick to your original plan?" he asked.

Clench's cold, grey eyes looked back into those of his partner, and his thin lips curled into a sneer of contempt.

"Of Course!" he snapped. "You ought to have been a woman. You haven't the pluck to be a man—and a rogue. Put the stuff away, and let us get out into the open air. The atmosphere of this stuffy place makes my head ache."

He watched his partner whilst he took up the portmanteau and placed it within the massive safe, which stood behind the door. When Cavendish had locked the safe, Clench turned to the door leading to the general offices, unlocked it and passed through.

"I'm going next door to buy some cigars," he said, over his shoulder. "I'll see you in the cab.

Richard Cavendish nodded, then stood looking after him with clenched hands. The merry light had died from his eyes, and his face was not at the moment a pleasant spectacle to behold. The flabbiness seemed to leave his cheeks, his jaw was harshly set, and his whole aspect was sinister in the extreme.

"You sneering, pig-headed brute!" he snarled, when his partner had passed out of hearing. "You can stay and be nabbed if you're so minded, but you won't have me with you when you are arrested. I've tried to talk sense to you, but you won't listen, so I've got to look after myself. I'm going to take my share to-night, and by morning my yacht will be miles out to sea."

• • • • • •

Over the City hung that curious stillness that is always noticeable after about ten o'clock at night and Throgmorton Street was deserted save for the solitary constable, who was steadily pacing along upon his beat, his footsteps scarcely audible by reason of the thick goloshes covering his boots.

The man glanced into Throgmorton Avenue as he drew abreast of it, but the courtway was apparently as empty as the thoroughfare in which he stood, and he passed on indifferently, inwardly counting the hours before he would be off duty and able to seek his bed.

The pad, pad of the constable's footsteps died away into silence, and they had scarcely done so, ere a dark figure emerged from the shadows cast by the buildings in the court. It was a short, stout form, and as the moonlight fell upon the man's face the features of Richard Cavendish were revealed.

Cavendish, who was carrying a gladstone bag, boldly stepped across the court and paused before the door of the building wherein lay the offices rented by his partner and himself. He tried the door, and to his satisfaction he found that it was unlocked, a fact that showed that one of the porters or cleaners was still within the building.

Cautiously, for he had no special desire to be observed, the stout swindler pushed open the door, and glided into the hall, then upon tip-toe he made his way to the door, upon which, even in the semi-gloom, could be read the legend "Clench and Cavendish—Private."

Cavendish took a bunch of keys from his pocket, inserted one in the lock and turned it noiselessly. A moment later he stood within the office, breathing hard in his excitement, the door once again securely fastened behind.

He lost no time now in carrying out his object. he whipped out a pocket electric torch, and, keeping the white beam of light low, so that it should not be seen by anyone who might chance to pass the glass door, he guided his footsteps to the safe, wherein lay the gigantic sum with which he had arranged with his scoundrelly partner to decamp upon the morrow.

Yet again, the swindler's bunch of keys was produced, and he placed one in the lock of the safe. There was a soft click, then Canvendish had tugged open the massive door and the contents of the safe lay at his mercy.

He took a grip upon the handles of the portmanteau, and, lifting it out, he placed it upon a chair. Then he picked up his gladstone and stood it upon the table.

At that moment Richard Cavendish had no intention of defrauding his co-swindler. He merely meant to possess himself of his share of their ill-gotten gains, and to sail away with all speed in his yacht, which was lying at anchor off London Bridge. But when he opened the portmanteau, and once again feasted his gaze upon its valuable contents, a sudden gleam of avarice leapt into his eyes, and he was assailed by an overmastering statue carved in stone, although his brain was working quickly. In the darkness his eyes were still glinting greedily, and his lips were compressed temptation.

"Why not take all?" he whispered to himself, staring down in fascination at the rolls of notes and securities. "After all, it is not Clench's money." It did not occur to him that neither was it his. "He has swindled honest men and women to obtain it, and it would only be a case of the biter bit."

Richard Cavendish put out his electric torch and stood as motionless as a in a thin straight line.

What should he do? he asked himself. He had never liked Clench—indeed, during the last few weeks of their partnership, he had began to feel that he hated him. Time after time he had been stung to the quick by some sneering remark of his partner's, and——

Richard Cavendish closed the portmanteau with a snap and locked it, and now his mind was made up.

"I'll do it!" he muttered. "I'll take the whole half-million. With a sum like this I need never return to Britain. I can change my name, and live a life of luxury and ease. And when my son grows up, he will never know that his father was once dishonest—a swindler! Somehow I'm glad that——" He shrugged his shoulders impatiently. "At times, I am a sentimental fool!" he rasped. "I mustn't waste time! The farther away from British shores my yacht can be by the morning the better! If Clench overtook me, he would kill me!"

He took up the portmanteau and, staggering beneath its weight, he crossed to the door. He turned the key, passed out, and relocked the door behind him; then without being seen by a living soul, he quitted the building and made his way into Throgmorton Street, where he hailed a passing hansom.

Richard Cavendish had taken the whole coup. Jasper Clench, swindler, had been swindled!

II.
A Dramatic Arrest and a Vow of Bitter Vengeance

There was a deep frown upon the brow of Jasper Clench as his cab slowly conveyed him through the dense fog that, with the coming of dawn, had descended upon London like an all-enveloping blanket. That morning he had called at his partner's private house in order that they might journey to the City together as was their custom, but to his surprise he had discovered that Cavendish had left home with his baby son and the child's nurse late upon the preceding night, and had not since returned.

Clench had made endless inquiries of the servants as to the reason for his partner's sudden departure from home, but none of them appeared to know what reason their master could have for his somewhat peculiar action.

It never occurred to Clench for a moment that his fellow-conspirator might have stolen a march upon him, yet he felt curiously worried by what he had ascertained, and a hundred times he had cursed the fog during his journey from suburban Wimbledon to town.

The swindler sighed with relief as the Jehu at last guided his horse into Throgmorton Street, and he lost no time in alighting and paying off the man when the court in which his offices were situated was reached.

As he groped his way through the choking mist into Throgmorton Avenue the company promotor collided violently with a bulky form, and he trust it unceremoniously out of his path.

"Where the deuce are you coming to?" the man queried pugnaciously. "Do yer want all the blessed path?"

Jasper Clench paid no heed, but kept straight on until he disappeared through the doorway of his office-buildings, and the burly man, who might have been a well-to-do tradesman, if one might judge by his general aspect and attire, indulged in a grim smile.

"You seem in a hurry, Mr. Clench," he muttered beneath his breath. "I wonder what has become of your precious partner? I don't think he's passed in yet; still, he may have arrived early."

He turned and whistled softly, and almost instantly the figures of three more men loomed out of the fog. They were all of a similar stamp to the fellow with whom the swindler, Clench, had collided—big, burley, and strong. They, too, might have been men of a hard-working, tradesman class, yet when one looked the second time one was struck by something strangely official in their bearing.

"How long have you been waiting about here, Hemmings?" the first man asked, addressing one of the newcomers.

"Since eight o'clock, sir."

"Ah! Clench has just gone to his office. Have you seen anything of the man Cavendish?"

"No sir, I've kept my eyes skinned, but he hasn't passed me to the best of my knowledge."

The questioner nodded.

"Right!" he answered gruffly. "Keep within hailing distance. If the other beauty don't turn up soon, we will make sure of getting Clench first. Cut away with you. We mustn't be seen together."

The three large men disappeared into the fog once more, and the first man entered the courtyard and took up his stand at a spot whence it was just possible through the mist to observe any person leaving or entering the building wherein Clench and Cavendish carried on their questionable business.

Jasper Clench had stopped to speak to his head clerk. He had made enquiries as to whether his partner had put in an appearance, but it was only be answered in the negative. he still wore a puzzled frown as he unlocked the door of his private room and passed within.

His first action was to examine the contents of the letter-box, and a cynical twitching of his thin lips proclaimed that he was experiencing a feeling as near to pleasure as he was capable of, as he selected a registered envelope, addressed in a feminine hand. The missive, had, of course, been signed for by one of his clerks and afterwards slipped into his private box.

He ripped the letter free from its covering and saw, as he had expected, that it contained the promised cheque for ten thousand pounds, promised him by his client of Merton. he stowed it carefully away in his pocket and hummed a tune as he turned to his table.

The air, however, ceased with startling abruptness, and the swindler stood staring at the gladstone bag which was in evidence before him. That it was his partner's property he realised at once, for it bore the initials "R.C." upon its side, but what bewildered Clench was that he was sure the bag had not been in the office upon the previous evening.

"Now what the dickens can this mean?" Clench said in a puzzled tone. "The clerks say he has not been in, yet the first thing I find——"

He stopped short, uttered a gasping cry, and fairly lept over to the safe, the door of which was standing a few inches ajar. With shaking hands he wrenched open the massive steel door, then he went reeling backwards, his always pale face the colour of chalk, every drop of blood gone from his lips.

"Gone!" he screamed hoarsely. "Gone!"

Like a drunken man he swayed to his knees before the safe, groping blindly within as though he could not put faith in the evidence of his eyes.

"Gone!" he raved again. "The cur! The dirty, thieving hound! The treacherous scoundrel! He has robbed me—robbed me! I——"

The door opened sharply and the bulky form of the man who had been waiting in the court without stepped quickly into the office. He was followed by his three companions, who stood in the background.

Clench gained his feet, clutching at his temples, and his wild eyes fixed themselves vacantly upon the stern faces of the intruders.

"What—what does this mean?" he asked shakily. "I can see no one this morning. I——"

"You will have to see me, I think, Mr. Jasper Clench," the foremost man snapped grimly. "I am Detective-Inspector Rayner, of Scotland Yard, and I hold a warrent for your arrest upon a charge of fraud!"

Jasper Clench clutched at the edge of the table for support, his knees shaking beneath him, his mouth agape with surprise and horror.

"It's a lie!" he stammered, his voice almost hysterical. "It's a foul lie! I am an honest business man and——"

"You will have every opportunity of proving it!" Inspector Rayner answered gruffly, as he took a sharp step forward and snapped the handcuffs upon the swindler's trembling wrists. "I don't mind telling you, however, that I wouldn't give a brass farthing for your chance! James Teddington, the engineer sent out to prospect the Great Eagle Mining Properties, has died as a result of an accident in Paris. Before he breathed his last he confessed how you and your partner had bribed him, how he had found not an atom of mineral on your land, but had sent home a false report that the place was a modern Tom Tiddler's ground. Now, I'm telling you no more. I must warn you that anything you say may be taken down in writing and used at your trial in evidence against you!"

"Great heavens, this is terrible—terrible!" Clench moaned. "And to think that my partner has escaped—escaped with every penny of the money we have made together! Curse him, I say! I'll serve my time! I'll——"

"What's that?" Rayner asked sharply, startled out of his official manner. "You said your partner, Cavendish, has gone with the money?"

"Every penny of it!" Jasper Clench laughed horridly, mirthlessly. "Every penny of it!" he raved. "We were to have sailed with our haul in his yacht this morning, but you'll find it weighed anchor last night! Oh, yes, you'll find it gone, right enough! Oh, I pray and hope that you may find the viper—I would serve a double sentence to know that he will suffer as I shall suffer!"

His eyes blazed like living coals with the awful hatred that consumed him.

"Whether he be caught or not!" he cried hoarsely, 'I'll be even with him! If I have to serve ten—fifteen years I will not forget! When I come out, I'll hound him down! I'll hound him down, you hear me! And when I find him, I will deal out to him the most bitter vengeance ever devised by the brain of mortal man!"

———

THE STORY: TWENTY YEARS HAVE ELAPSED

CHAPTER 1
The Reception at Sir Digby Cranston's

Outside the residence of Sir Digby Cranston, in Berkely Square, an awning had been erected from the gate to the imposing entrance and a strip of carpet ran beneath, reaching to the edge of the pavement. The windows were ablaze with lights, and all through the evening a host of carriages and motor broughams had rolled up to discharge elegantly-cloaked ladies and immaculate debonnair men, at whom the loungers who hung about the spot gaped with something very like awe.

Sir Digby Cranston, who was a very wealthy gentleman and a keen and well-known collector of precious stones, was holding a reception to celebrate the return of his only child, Elice, from France, where she had been nobly acting as a Red Cross nurse, and although the evening was as yet young, a vast and distinguished gathering had put in an appearance.

A myriad festooned lights illuminated the spacious reception-room, playing upon the khaki uniforms of the officers, the conventional black coats of the civilians, and the pearly white shoulders of the women. An orchestra, concealed in an alcove behind a cluster of ferns and palms, was playing a dreamy air.

A gentle breeze, scented with the sweet, refreshing odour of roses, was wafted from the direction of the archway forming the entrance to the conservatory, fanning the faces of the guests as they chatted vivaciously together.

Sir Digby, a distinguished-looking man of sixty, attired in faultless evening dress, stood by his daughter's side as she received the fresh arrivals. Elice was a charming girl of twenty-one, simply yet daintily gowned, and it was noticeable that her right arm rested in a sling. Venturing too near the firing line to tend the wounded and dying, she had been wounded by a splinter of shell, and she was a girl to be admired, for she had bled for her country.

Sir Digby Cranston's eyes were continuously straying across the room to where a women sat alone, slowly using her fan, the lights lending additional charm and lustre to her fair golden hair.

The nobleman was a widower, and perhaps this was the reason for his obvious fascination where this woman was concerned. To merely say that she was beautiful would be to most inadequately describe her. She was dazzling, there was something about her—personality perhaps—that irresistibly invited attention and held the gaze.

She might have been twenty-five—perhaps a little less, and her complexion was pale and creamy. Her eyes were dark and melting, her lips full and alluringly red, and she made a picture such as surely no artist could faithfully portray. She was attired in some glistening stuff that fell sheerly away from her rounded shoulders; and Sir Digby told himself that he had never seen this women look so charming.

And yet she was not of high birth. She was simply his private secretary, and he knew her as Miss Hammond, from Chicago. Upon many occasions since the girl had come to him with testimonials from an American millionaire, Sir Digby had seriously thought of asking her to be his wife, yet it was possible that he would have suffered with a stroke of apoplexy could he have known her true identity, or have guessed that her glorious masses of hair were merely a skilfully-made wig.

Broadway Kate, the wife of Ezra Q. Maitland, the man who surely could be termed the greatest criminal at large, found it convenient at times to assume male attire, and for this reason she was wont to keep her hair cropped to her well-shaped head, merely adjusting a wig, such as she was now wearing, when appearing as a member of the fair sex.

For many years Kathleen Maitland had been a criminal. When she had first married her husband, Ezra, he had been a successful and straight-forward business man in New York, and they had been supremely happy. Their happiness, too, had increased a hundredfold when they had been blessed with a child—a baby girl.

Olive, their little daughter, had reached the age of four, then misery—misery in a hideous form—had descended upon them like a thunderbolt. Little Olive had fallen ill and died, and this had turned Kate's husband, for the bad.

It had been small swindles and robberies that he had indulged in at first; but soon, confident with success, Maitland had engaged in colossal crimes that had startled the world. Where the man led, the woman had followed, and thus Kate became her husband's partner in crime.

Maitland was possessed of a cool, reasoning brain, and time after time he had outwitted the astute American detective, Fenlock Fawn, who continuously failed to obtain any definite evidence against the master criminal.

New York, Petrograd, Paris, and London had been visited by Maitland in turn, and in each city he had succeeded in hoodwinking the police and detectives until, in the last-named, he crossed the path of Sexton Blake, the famous logician and criminologist of Baker Street.

The alert, clever brain of the master detective had been pitted against that of the master criminal, and upon each occasion, although Maitland's supreme conceit had not allowed him to admit it at first, Sexton Blake had proved that he was the better man, and the criminal had only escaped the clutches of the law by, metaphorically speaking, the skin of his teeth.

Broadway Kate sat abstractedly fanning herself until she heard Sir Digby announce that some private theatricals were about to take place in an adjoining room, then she rose to her feet and carelessly strolled to the archway leading into the conservatory.

Through this she passed and made her way between the long lines of ferns, palms, and rare blossoms until she gained the small garden at the rear of the premises.

She crossed a corner of the miniature lawn, and approached a clump of evergreens. As she reached them a dark form of a man emerged from the shadows.

"It that you, Ezra?" she asked, in a low tone.

"Bet on it!" the man who had met her agreed. "Waal, how are things shaping?"

"Real fine, I guess," Kate replied quickly. "As I thought, the jewels have been on view during the evening."

Ezra Q. Maitland—the man was he—chuckled softly and pressed his wife's hand in the darkness.

"Good girl!" he said appreciatively. "And they will be in the house all night?"

"Yes," Kate informed him. "Old Sir Digby will lock them in his safe, which he considers to be as secure as the Bank of England. You have had made the key of which I gave you the wax impression?"

Maitland grinned.

"You bet I have," he drawled. "I wasn't likely to let the grass grow under my feet. Kate, we are in luck! If there's any truth in the rumours I've heard, Sir Digby's collection of sparklers are worth something like two hundred thousand pounds, and even in dealing with that thief, Israel Samuels, we ought to clear seventy or eighty thou.!"

The woman lit one of her daintily scented cigarettes.

"Have you written to Sammuels?" she asked.

"Yes, I've replied to his note," Maitland answered, "and he's open to to the deal whenever I bring the stuff along. But I mustn't stay. If you were found talking to me out here, it would be difficult to explain my presence. By the way, where is the safe situated?"

"In Sir Digby's study."

"And the position of that?"

"Over there to the right. You can see the French windows quite plainly from here."

"Good! I shall be right along just before dawn. I suppose they'll keep this poppy show up to well into the early hours of to-morrow morning?"

Kate nodded.

"I reckon they are bound to," said she. "I shouldn't come here until well after three."

"Make it half-past," Maitland said, after a moment's thought. "That will give me time to do the job and make myself scarce before daylight. You will be able to open the windows for me, of course?"

"Yes."

"Good!" Maitland said again, as he turned to depart. "I'll get right along and lie low until the right time! Say"—he suddenly swung round upon his heel—"give me a kiss, girl! I've not seen you for four whole days!"

Kate held up her lips to his, and just for a moment the master-criminal held her in his arms, then he released her and vanished silently into the gloom. The woman stood staring in the direction he had gone for nearly a quarter of a minute before she moved to retrace her steps to the house.

"How I wish we could start afresh!" she muttered, a catch in her voice. "How happy we could be, just he and I together and——"

She tilted her shoulders and sighed wearily.

"That can never be," she said, "until we have made the tremendous coup we have been planning for so many months—a haul that would keep us in luxury in some distant land for the rest of our lives!"

CHAPTER 2
Maitland at Work

One by one the lights in the windows of Sir Digby Cranston's mansion had been extinguished until the house was enshrouded in darkness, and the strip of garden at the rear was only illuminated by the waning light of the moon.

From a distance came the voice of a clock chiming the half-hour after three, and the sound had scarcely died away ere Ezra Q. Maitland, his coat collar turned up to hide any vestige of white, a mask concealing the upper portion of his sinister features, stole along the alleyway which was connected with a garage, and which ran along at the rear of the wall enclosing Sir Digby's garden.

When Maitland reached the nobleman's premises, he paused and listened intently, smiling grimly as, after a second or two, he assured himself that all was silent as the grave.

With a quick, neat spring, he gripped the top of the garden wall with his muscular hands and drew himself up, to afterwards drop noiselessly to the other side. Stealthily he stole over the tiny lawn and darted behind a clump of bushes at the spot where he had previously met his wife.

Crouching down, but out of sight, Maitland lay peering through the bushes. He knew that it was past the time at which he told Kate he would arrive, and he wondered how long she would keep him waiting. He cursed softly as the dew from the grass found its way through his clothes and damped his flesh with its icy touch. The morning was cold for the time of year, and the criminal's wait was to be anything but a pleasant one.

Ten minutes, a quarter of an hour dragged by, and he wished he could smoke a cigar. He took one from his case, but hesitated for the present to light it, fearing its glowing end might be observed by someone from one of the windows.

Maitland lay watching the French windows of Sir Digby's study for another five minutes; then, with an impatient gesture, he placed the cigar between his teeth and felt for a match.

He swore under his breath as he discovered that he had omitted to bring with him his vesta case, and he began rummaging in his pockets in the hopes of finding a stray lucifer.

At last he found one in his vest-pocket, struck it upon his trousers, and applied it to his weed; then he lay puffing at the smoke until a light suddenly sprang up within the study.

The master-criminal gave something like a sigh of relief, and, tossing away the cigar, he rose to his feet, for the windows had opened, and the slender form of his wife emerged on to the lawn. She was attired in a neat travelling costume, and carried a small bag, and it was noticeable that her hair was now of raven black, also her complexion was more ruddy and the curve of her brows had changed.

"Is all quiet?" Maitland asked, as he reached her side.

"Yes," Kate replied. "You can get right along with the job; but you'd better be quick."

"Why are you late?" her husband asked. "I've been fooling around for the last five-and-twenty minutes."

"I am sorry," Kate replied, "but I fell asleep. I had had a tiring day. You'll have to look slick, because the butler is an early riser. He's often about a little before five."

"I reckon I shall be miles away by the time the old fool rubs the sleep from his eyes," the master-criminal grinned reassuringly. "Is it safe to leave these lights going?"

'Yes, I imagine so. No one can see them from the lane at the back."

"Right! Come along. Guess I'll give you a helping hand over the wall before I start work."

Broadway Kate hesitated, her eyes wistful.

"I'll stay with you until you've got the jewels," she said. "We——"

"Say you'll do nothing of the kind, my girl," her husband returned sharply. "There's always a chance of having to make a sudden bolt over jobs like this, and if you were with me you'd be in the way. Besides, I've no wish to let you sample prison life, and you're not taking the risk. Come along, and don't waste any more time."

Kate sighed resignedly, then allowed him to take her arm and gently propel her towards the wall.

Cunning and unscrupulous criminal though he was, Maitland had one redeeming feature—his great love for his wife. He worshipped the ground upon which she walked, and Kate, knowing this, was always ready to obey him without question.

By the wall they paused, and the master rogue spoke quickly to his fair companion.

"I reckon we'll give America a turn again after this Kate," he remarked "I've been planning that for some time past, and I've arranged with Wang"—he was referring to his Chinese servant and confederate—" to meet at Euston. You will both catch the first possible train to Liverpool and meet me at the Great Central Hotel. Good-bye for the present.

"Good-bye, Ezra!" the women returned, her lip quivering. "Be careful, and, mind, no violence if——"

"Don't worry," he interrupted. "I'll be successful, and the 'sparklers' will be in Samuels's hands before old Sir Digby finds out they are gone!"

He stooped and kissed her, then he assisted her over the wall and cautiously retraced his steps towards the house.

Maitland entered the study, the windows of which Kate had, of course, left ajar.

Almost at once he espied the safe, which was built into the wall upon the opposite side of the apartment.

He lost no time in getting to work. He took from his vest pocket a glittering key, and, with deft fingers, inserted it in the keyhole of the safe.

He pressed it gently, then more firmly, only to finally curse beneath his breath, for the key would not turn.

Maitland drew the key from the lock and took from his pocket a tracing of the original one, which Kate had handed to him together with the wax impression she had managed to secure.

The criminal's eyes keenly studied the formation of wards, then he produced a tiny file and a miniature bottle of oil, for he had detected a slight difference at one point.

He set to work patiently, despite the tiresome task that lay before him. He had to proceed by guesswork, and he knew that if he filed the ward a little too much, there would be no chance of his gaining the haul he was seeking.

Four times he inserted the key in the lock to find that it would not turn, but at the fifth attempt there came a soft clicking sound as the lock of the safe shot backwards, and, with a chuckle of exultation, Ezra Q. Maitland pulled open the heavy door.

To discover the prize for which he was seeking was the work of a moment. No less than seven leathern cases lay within the safe, and, upon making a swift inspection, the American crook found, as he had expected, that they contained Sir Digby's famous collection of precious stones.

He removed the cases, and placed them upon the table, opening the lids in turn. Diamonds, rubies, sapphires, emeralds, and host of other gems were in evidence, and as the rays of the electric lights fell upon them, they glittered and scintillated until Maitland's eyes were dazzled.

He stood for a moment gazing exaultantly at his coup, mentally resolving to ask from the "fence," Samuels, five thousand over the price he had originally intended to let it go at. His piercing eyes were glinting like stars through the holes in his mask, and their brilliance vied with that of the heap of stones lying before him.

He roused himself from the spell the magnificence of the jewels had cast over him, and whipped two wash-leather bags from his pocket. He filled them to the brim with the sparkling gems, and concealed them about his person, but even now there was still quite a quarter of the collection left upon the table.

Maitland grabbed up a handful of the stones, meaning to place them in his breast-pocket, but before he could do so, he received one of the greatest and most alarming surprises of his life. The door of the study suddenly opened, to reveal Sir Digby Cranston, attired in a dressing-gown and slippers, carrying a candle in his left hand, a businesslike-looking revolver in his right.

The old nobleman came very near to worshipping his collection of jewels, and he was always nervous and restless, when they were in the house during the night, although he had always believed that his safe—the safe that Maitland had succeeded in opening in less than twenty minutes—was more or less burglar-proof. Upon the present occasion, he had lain awake for just over two hours after he had seen his last guest off, and retired to rest, and he had been obsessed with a strange feeling that his collection of gems was in danger.

He had tried to think that he was allowing himself to be over-imaginative, and stupidly nervous, but at last, unable to court repose, he had decided to journey down to his study to satisfy himself that all was well.

Despite his fears, Sir Digby had scarcely expected to find a burglar at work in the room when he pushed open the study door, and he was almost as surprised at seeing Maitland as was the master-criminal at suddenly being confronted by him.

Sir Digby took a startled step backwards, a cry of alarm bursting from his lips, then, in a glance, realising how matters stood—that he was in danger of losing the greater part of his treasures—he levelled his revolver and pulled upon the trigger.

There were two deafening reports, one following sharply upon the other but it was Ezra Q. Maitland who had shown the most promptitude. Long experience had taught the master-criminal that at such times as these, it was the man who fired first who lived to tell the tale, and he had not hesitated when Sir Digby had flung up his right arm.

Like lightning, Maitland's hand had dropped to his hip, his fingers had gripped upon his weapon, which he had fired almost the instant it was out of his pocket without appearing to take the slightest aim, and Sir Digby's bullet tore its way harmlessly through one of the drawers of a roll-top desk, as the nobleman fell heavily upon his face.

Maitland did not stop to see how badly the old man was injured, not did he trouble about the remainder of the jewels. He spun round upon his heel and rushed madly through the windows, raced across the lawn with the speed of a hare, and gained the garden wall. With an agile spring he was sitting astride it, and as he dropped to the opposite side, he could hear the sounds of excited voices from the house, whilst lights were springing up in the windows.

The criminal cursed at what he considered his ill-luck, then pressing his elbows to his sides, he positively flew up the alleyway, and vanished into the gloom.

And back in the study, Sir Digby Cranston lay inert and still, the blood from and ugly wound upon his temple dyeing the expensive carpet, a dull, ominous red, whilst his daughter Elice, who had just rushed into the room, was upon her knees by his side.

"Help, help help!" the girl cried wildly, her eyes dilated and filled with horror. "Help, help, murder! My father has been murdered!"

CHAPTER 3
At Baker Street

Tinker, assistant to Mr. Sexton Blake, the famous detective of Baker Street, yawned and rubbed his eyes, as the clock upon the mantelpiece of the consulting-room chimed the half hour after four, and he rose from the great easy chair in which he had

151

been reclining, and stretched his arms wearily above his head.

"Well, I'm jiggered!" the young detective muttered, still sleepy and dazed. "I must have dozed off in that chair last night whilst I was sitting up for the guv'nor. Great Scott! Half-past four! Then this means that the guv'nor hasn't been home all night! Pedro, you red-eyed old scoundrel why didn't you wake me?"

Sexton Blake's clever and sagacious bloodhound rose and stretched himself, much as his young master had done, and afterwards squatted upon the hearthrug, and blinked sleepily at the lad. Then he stalked forward and affectionately fawned upon Tinker, who patted his massive head.

"I suppose you're not to blame, Pedro," the lad went on. "I'll bet you were playing at shut-eye before me. What do you want? Some coffee?"

He indicated the coffee pot and Pedro bayed softly. It was seldom he refused anything either of his masters took to eat or drink. Tinker picked up a pair of Indian clubs, removed his coat, and indulged in a little invigorating exercise, whilst the hound watched him with superior indifference.

After a few minutes of this the young detective picked up the pot and vanished to make the promised coffee. When a quarter of an hour had elapsed he returned, poured himself out a cup of the steaming beverage, and gave Pedro his share, with much milk added, in a saucer.

"Now, where the dickens is the guv'nor?" Tinker mused, when both he and Pedro had quenched their thirst. "It's too bad of him to leave me in the lurch like this. Ugh! I feel cramped and sore sitting in that beastly chair all night, and I've got a kink in my giddy neck. It feels as though it's going to walk round the corner. It's no use turning in, now, so I'll wait till Mr. Blake turns up. Now, let me see. What did his note say?"

He drew a slip of paper from his pocket, and perused the hastily pencilled words upon it.

"Just discovered whereabouts of Fenson," (they ran), I am going with Inspector Martin to arrest. You can sit up for me if you like, as I expect to be home just before midnight.—S.B.

Tinked frowned, and his young face momentarily took on a grave expression.

"Humph!" he grunted. "I'm hanged if I like this. Fenson is a dangerous beast, and wouldn't be taken without a struggle. I hope nothing happened to the guv'nor. Still, nothing can have happened! I should have heard from Scotland Yard before now if he had been injured. I wonder what's kept him."

He replaced the message in his pocket, and sat for a few seconds gazing thoughtfully at Pedro.

"My lad," he said, at length, "you might as well go through that latest trick I've taught you. I don't want you to forget it, and we haven't practised it for several days."

He groped beneath the couch, and brought forth a soldier's helmet and a toy gun, with a result that Pedro put his tail between his legs, and hastily vanished under the table.

"Come here, sir!" Tinker ordered, with mock severity in his tones. "Laziness is a vice——"

He made a quick grab, and, securing the hound's collar, dragged him from his cover.

"Good Pedro, stand up!" he commanded.

With a bored expression upon his doggy countenance, the hound rose upon his hind legs, and his young master clapped the helmet upon his head, and tucked the gun in the crook of his right forepaw.

"Shoulder arms!" Tinker cried. "Quick march!" Then beating time to the refrain he commenced to sing, whilst Pedro, looking utterly foolish and disgusted, solemnly marched across the room.

> "When we're wound up the 'Watch on the Rhine'!
> How we'll sing, how we'll sing 'Auld Lang Syne'!
> You and I, Hurray! we'll cry!
> Everything will——"

The door opened sharply, and Sexton Blake and Detective Inspector Martin, of the C.I.D., stood upon the threshold of the room, regarding the bizarre spectacle in amused surprise.

"Well, I always thought so," Inspector Martin remarked, "although I didn't like to air my opinion until I was sure. When a young man gets up at a little before five in the morning to qualify for the proprietor of an educated animal show, he needs to interview a brain specialist."

"Oh I'm not potty, sir," Tinker retorted, winking at his master. "I'm merely looking ahead."

"What do you mean?" Martin asked.

"Why, you see, sir," Tinker explained, as he took the helmet and gun from Pedro, and tossed them out of sight beneath the couch, "if the detective's business failed we could go in for a penny gaff. Pedro knows lots of tricks, Mr. Blake would make an excellent wizard and fortune-teller, with a little make-up and the togs, whilst you needn't be idle."

"And what could I do?" Martin suggested, with an air of condescending amusement.

"Why, if you let your hair and whiskers grow, you'd make a jolly fine Wild Man from Borneo," Tinker answered coolly, "We'd shove you in a cage, and all you'd have to do would be to dance and howl a little and——"

"Be quiet, Tinker!" Sexton Blake ordered sternly, for he had seen that the cheeks of his official colleague had flushed wrathfully. "Suppose you give us some of that coffee I see you have made. We are both tired and worn out."

The famous detective removed his hat and light dust coat, and tossed them aside, then he sank wearily into an easy-chair, and signed to Martin to do the same. Sexton Blake had spoken the truth when he stated they were both fatigued. His always pale face looked drawn and haggard, and there were dark marks about his eyes, whilst even Inspector Martin had lost some of his ruddiness of complexion, and looked heavy-eyed and worn.

Tinker poured out the required beverage, and handed a cup to both the inspector and his master. As Sexton Blake stretched forth his long, slender hand to take his cup, Tinker saw that his wrist was bandaged.

"You are injured, sir!" he said anxiously.

"Only a graze, lad," the detective replied, with a shrug. "How is it you are up so early?"

"I haven't been to bed, guv'nor," Tinker explained. "I was waiting for you to come in, and fell asleep in the chair. I didn't wake till about half an hour ago."

"Fenson led us a dance," Sexton Blake said. "We found him in an opium den down East, but he fought like a madman when we attempted to arrest him, managed to break free, and eventually gained the roofs. He had a revolver, and we couldn't get near him for some time. He gave us the slip altogether once, but, quite be chance, we got upon his track again, and he is now safely under lock and key. Hallo"—as the telephone bell rang sharply and insistently—" who ever can be ringing up at this hour?"

Tinker crossed to the instrument, and took down the receiver.

"Hallo!" he said. That is Sir Digby Cranston's house at Berkeley Square? Yes; these are Mr. Blake's room. He's in, but he's been upon a case all night, and——

"What is the trouble, lad?" Sexton Blake asked, rising from his chair, his weariness leaving him as if by magic. "Sir Digby Cranston is a friend of mine. What has happened?"

Tinker swung round from the telephone, his face evincing the keenest excitement.

"It's Sir Digby's collection of jewels, guv'nor!" he announced quickly. "Nearly all the stones have been stolen, and Sir Digby, who surprised the burglar, has been badly wounded!"

Sexton Blake elevated his eyebrows and whistled softly.

"Let me speak," he said, taking the receiver. "Ah, that is Miss Elice, is it not? Yes, I am Sexton Blake. When did the robbery occur?"

For several minutes the detective conversed with Sir Digby Cranston's daughter, who was at the other end of the wire, and ere he had finished, Inspector Martin was standing listening eagerly by his colleague's side. Curiously enough, like his friend, the Scotland Yard man seemed to have forgotten his fatigue, now that there was work to do.

"What has really happened, Blake!" Martin asked, as the detective hung up the receiver. "The man has got clear away?"

"Yes," Sexton Blake replied. "Sir Digby held a reception last night to celebrate the homecoming of his daughter, who has been acting as a Red Cross nurse at the front, and his renowned collection of precious stones were on view during the evening. He couldn't sleep when he went to bed, and had a presentiment that his jewels were in danger. He went downstairs just to satisfy himself that all was well, and upon entering the room in which his safe is situated, he found a masked man bending over the cases which had contained the gems, and which were standing upon the table.

"Sir Digby tried to fire, but the burglar managed to shoot first, and bolted with the best part of the collection."

"Are you going to take up the case?" the official asked eagerly.

Sexton Blake nodded as he lit a cigar.

"Yes," he agreed. "As you may have heard me tell Tinker, Sir Digby is a personal friend of mine, so, tired though I admit I am, I cannot well refuse. Besides, this is no ordinary robbery. The Digby collection must be worth something like a couple of hundred thousand pounds! I have inspected it, so I know."

"Phew!" Martin ejaculated. "Do they know of the robbery at the Yard!"

"Yes; Detective-sergeant Jones is already upon the scene of the crime."

"Oh, is he!" Martin snorted. "That's the man who, quite by a fluke, got ahead of me in the Mortlake forgery business. Got ahead of me, mind you, his chief, and coolly took all the credit! I haven't liked the beggar since!"

"Naturally not," Sexton Blake responded drily, and we wondered just what sort of "fluke" had enabled his friend's subordinate to score. "Are you coming along to Berkeley Square?"

"Of course I am!" Martin answered. "I'm longing to dress Mr. High-and mighty Jones down!" he added aggressively. He grinned viciously. "Won't he be pleased when I turn up!"

"Suppose we leave off discussing this person with whom you seem to be riled," Sexton Blake suggested mildly as he slipped into his dust-coat and donned his hat. "Minutes may count if we are to run the thief to earth and regain the jewels."

"Do I come with you, sir?" Tinker asked eagerly, as his master and the Scotland Yard man moved towards the door.

"No, my lad, not at present," Sexton Blake returned. "But later there is a chance we may require both you and Pedro. If we do, I shall telephone, so don't go out upon any account."

———

CHAPTER 4
Sir Digby's Story

Elice Cranston bent over her father as he stirred uneasily and awoke from the troubled sleep in which he had lain since the departure of his medical man.

The baronet was lying in his bed, and the ugly wound in his shoulder had been dressed after the bullet fired by Ezra Q. Maitland had been extracted. The old man's face was ghastly, his lips were bloodless, and his eyes unnaturally bright with the agitation that was obsessing him. The doctor had looked grave when he had made his examination, but he had given it as his opinion that with careful nursing Sir Digby would recover in due time.

The nobleman had refused to be warned as to allowing himself to become excited, and he had insisted upon telling his daughter what had happened in the study, requesting her to at once communicate with his friend, the great private investigator of Baker Street.

"I wonder how much longer Sexton Blake will be?" the baronet asked petulantly. "You—you said that he was up when you 'phoned, Elice?"

"Yes dad," the girl replied, laying her cool white hand upon his feverish brow. "He promised to come here at once and he cannot be a great while. Ah, hark! There is someone upon the stairs now."

There came a tap on the door, and in response to the girl's order to "come in," the butler appeared.

"Mr. Sexton Blake and Detective-Inspector Martin have arrived. Miss Elice," the servant announced. "Shall I show them up?"

"Yes, yes!" Sir Digby exclaimed eagerly, before the girl could reply. "Let them come to me at once!"

"Dad, you must really keep calm," Elice insisted, with the gentle tone of authority in her sweet voice that her training as a nurse had gifted her with. "All the jewels in the world are not worth your life, and you know what Doctor Tilling said."

"Hang Tilling!" the baronet snapped, raising himself painfully upon his pillows, despite the restraining hand his daughter put out. "I want to sit up, Elice, so that I may tell Blake what has occurred! Confound you, sir!"—this to the butler—"Haven't I told you to show 'em up immediately!"

The man, who was a very old retainer, looked troubled, and glanced towards his young mistress. Elice inclined her head to show he was to obey, for she kew that the longer her father was kept waiting to see the famous criminologist to whom he wished to pin his faith, the worse his condition would become.

The butler disappeared, and presently returned to announce:

"Mr. Sexton Blake and Detective-Inspector Martin!"

Sir Digby turned so quickly that he jarred his wounded shoulder, and his face twitched with pain. He forgot his agony the next moment, however, as Sexton Blake and the burly red-faced official from the Yard entered the room and approached the bedside.

"I am glad that you have come, Mr. Blake," Elice said, as she gave the detective her hand. "Father is most anxious that you should take up his case!"

Sexton Blake smiled into the girlish face.

"I don't think there will be any difficulty in that, Miss Elice," said he. "Fortunately, I am enabled to commence my investigations very soon after the crime has taken place, which often simplifies matters. With luck, I may pick up a clue that will enable my colleagues and myself to quickly get upon the track of the burglar. But let me introduce you to Detective-Inspector Martin, of Scotland Yard."

Formal greetings having been exchanged, Sexton Blake and Martin drew chairs near the bed.

"Do you feel able to give me the details of the case that are available, Sir Digby?" the private detective asked.

"Yes, yes, Blake!" Sir Digby returned quickly. "I've been badly injured, but, by James, if I were dying, I think I would use my last breath in doing all possible to help you get on the scoundrel's track! Three-quarters of my beautiful collection gone—stolen by this villain, who——"

"Do not distress yourself, Sir Digby," Blake interrupted soothingly, for a flush of colour had sprung into the old man's ashen cheeks, and he was shaking with intense agitation. "You may rely upon the best efforts of both Martin and I, and there can be no good purpose gained in your upsetting yourself. At what time did you come downstairs and find the burglar in your study?"

"Let me see! At about half-past four, I suppose it would be. I had a strange feeling that all was not well, and, just to satisfy myself, I rose and secured a revolver and candle, making my way downstairs. You can judge of the shock I received when I saw the masked man in the room. I threw up my weapon to fire at him, but he was took quick for me. He fired first, and I remembered no more until I found my daughter and Tilling—my doctor—stooping over me. I was in bed, and Tilling had dressed my wound. Mr. Blake, at all costs, whatever else you have to shelve, I implore you to leave no stone unturned to get my treasures back! I will compensate you for any loss you may sustain, pay any fee that——"

Sexton Blake held up his hand sharply.

"We are personal friends, Sir Digby," he reminded the nobleman quietly. "The question of fees need not be entered into—at least until the case is brought to a conclusion. What is the value of the stones that are missing?"

"I cannot accurately say, for I have not been well enough to check the part of the collection the scoundrel left behind him. Quite three-quarters of the collection have been taken, however, and I should imagine the thief's haul is a little less than one hundred and fifty thousand pounds in value."

"I see. Would it be possible for you to obtain me a detailed list of the stones that are missing?"

"Inspector Jones has already requested that," Sir Digby answered, "and I have promised to let him have it, although I had quite forgotten until now. Do you think you could compile the necessary particulars, Elice?"

The girl looked doubtful.

"I doubt whether I could, dad," she replied. "You see, Mr. Blake"—turning to the detective—"I have been away from home practically since the outbreak of the war. Doubtlessly you have added to the collection during my absence, father."

"Yes," Sir Digby admitted, frowning. "And I have also exchanged and disposed of a certain number of stones. However, Miss Hammond could lay her hands upon the necessary lists and would be able to assist you, Elice."

"I wonder where Miss Hammond is?" Elice said thoughtfully. "It has just truck me that I have not seen her since the alarm was given."

"Humph! She must be a heavy sleeper then," the wounded nobleman grunted. "The shots that were fired roused the whole household, did they not?"

Elice inclined her head.

"Yes," she agreed. "It is indeed strange that Miss Hammond was not awakened."

"May I inquire who this Miss Hammond may be?" Sexton Blake queried.

"My secretary—an American girl of remarkable beauty and intelligence, Blake," Sir Digby answered. "You had better awaken her, Elice. She will not mind being disturbed under the circumstances."

The girl rose to her feet and moved towards the door.

"I think," Sexton Blake suggested, "that, with your permission, Sir Digby, we will take a look at the study. I presume the jewels

154

were locked in your safe before you retired?"

"Yes. The safe was opened with a duplicate key. It was left in the lock."

"Indeed! It would almost seem, then, that some person in the house was in league with the thief."

"Yes; although for the life of me. I can't think whom it could be. All my servants have been with me for years, and I have every confidence in their honesty."

"Have you the key to hand?"

"No; but Mr. Jones, of Scotland Yard, has it. He is downstairs still, I expect. Oh, how I wish I had hidden my collection in this room! But, there, it is of no use repining now!"

The baronet sank back feebly upon his pillows, and Sexton Blake and Martin followed Elice from the room, as she beckoned them.

"I will take you to the study, gentlemen," she said.

The two detectives followed the girl down the imposing, thickly-carpeted staircase, and she quickly led them to the room in which Sir Digby Cranston had so dramatically surprised Maitland some two hours ago.

An alert-eyed young man, with a drooping moustache of a sandy hue, a fresh complexion, and square, determined chin, turned from the safe which he had been examining. He was quietly dressed in a dark grey suit, and there was little of the detective about him, although Martin, had he been inclined to admit the truth, could have told you that Detective-sergeant Jones was one of the ablest young officials at the Yard.

A constable stood respectfully in the background, watching his superior, and he drew himself up and saluted smartly as Martin swaggered in behind Sexton Blake. Elice whispered a word of excuse to the latter and left them.

"Hullo, Jones!" the worthy official growled. "So you've been put on this case."

Jones nodded coolly.

"Yes, sir," he answered. "The assistant commissioner sent for me as soon as we received the news of the robbery, and I came straight away here."

"Humph! Have you discovered anything of value?"

Not a great deal, at present. The robbery was well planned. The burglar came prepared with a duplicate key."

"May I see it?" Sexton Blake requested.

Jones produced the article in question, and Sexton Blake took it between his long, white fingers. He scrutinised it closely, noting that one of the wards had been recently oiled and filed.

"Depend upon it, he had an accomplice in the house," Martin said. "It's a rotten old safe, anyway. If the fellow had not secured a duplicate of the key, he wouldn't have had much trouble with it. Fancy keeping jewels to the value of two hundred thousand pounds in a thing like this, Blake?"

"It is certainly unwise, my friend," Sexton Blake admitted, as he sank to his knees before the safe and examined it closely.

"Unwise! I call it sheer idiocy!" Martin growled. "Some people fairly ask to be robbed, and we chaps at the Yard get all the trouble. Why, in the hands of a cracksman who knows his work, that safe would be as easily opened as would an ordinary sardine tin! What're you looking for? Finger-prints?"

Behind his chief's back. Mr. Jones smiled. It struck him that what Sexton Blake was doing was rather obvious. The Baker Street detective had produced his lens and was going over every inch of the polished steel door and its brass fittings.

"I am afraid you'll be disappointed in that direction, Mr. Blake," Jones said. "I've already searched for impressions, and there's not a ghost of one!"

Sexton Blake paid no heed to him until he had made a thorough inspection of the door through his lens. Then he rose, smoothed the creases from his knees, and shook his head.

"Not a sign of an impression," he said. "The man escaped through these windows, I take it?"

"Yes," Jones replied. "They were open when I arrived. Save for removing the jewels that were left behind, Miss Cranston had thoughtfully left the room just as it appeared when she rushed in to find here father upon the floor. She thought he was dead at first, for the front of his dressing gown was stained with blood, as also was the carpet."

Sexton Blake glanced keenly round him.

"And you have touched nothing since?" he queried.

"I have disturbed nothing, although I have, of course, made a thorough examination," the Scotland Yard man returned.

Sexton Blake backed towards the door, and, as was his custom, he made a survey of his surroundings, nothing escaping his keen grey eyes. He saw the dark, wet stain upon the carpet, which told him the spot at which Sir Digby Cranston had fallen when he had been wounded, and in his mind's-eye he imagined how the room had appeared when Elice had first entered.

He pictured the inert form of the nobleman lying stretched at full length upon the floor, the jewels scatted about the table, the safe yawning open, and the windows ajar. He stepped over to the gas-heating stove and stood before the massive fireplace, but there was nothing in or behind it—not even a scrap of paper—that would serve as a clue.

"Have you been in the garden as yet?" he asked, addressing Jones.

"I have taken a look round," the sergeant replied, "and I have found little save that I know the exact spot where our man scaled the wall. A brick had been dislodged and lay on the mould of the flower-bed beneath."

"A flower-bed is directly beneath the wall, then? There are surely some traces of footprints there?"

"Yes. I have the measurements here," Jones answered, as he drew a notebook from his pocket. "There was a women in the business, I imagine."

"How do you know?" Martin asked eagerly.

"There are two sets of impressions at the foot of the wall," the dectective-sergeant explained. "One set were made by a women. You can tell by the shape of the heel."

Martin sniffed.

"Of coure you can!" he snapped. "I don't need to be instructed as to how to distinguish the footprints made by a man from those of a woman."

"I was not suggesting such a thing, sir," Jones retorted calmly. "I merely explained how I was fairly certain a women was in the case. I say fairly certain, because even the elongated heel isn't always a proof that the marks were made by a member of the fair sex. I was once taken in very successfully by a crook who purposely wore ladies' shoes when at work."

"That's nothing to do with the matter in hand," Martin returned. "We've got to catch the man who stole Sir Digby Cranston's jewels, and whilst we are listening to your experiences as a detective, he's gaining a longer start of us. When you are as old as I and——"

"Let us get into the garden and investigate," Sexton Blake cut in, and his manner was impatient, for he had no wish to listen to a passage of arms between the rival officials. "We shall learn more there than is possible here, I think."

He stepped to the windows, released the catch, and a moment later stood on the strip of path that divided the house from the miniature lawn.

Sexton Blake moved slowly over the grass, his eyes scanning the ground, but he saw nothing to interest him until he stepped behind the bushes, in the cover of which Ezra Q. Maitland had lain in wait for his wife.

At once the detective saw that the grass was crushed and flattened, and he knew that someone had crouched at the spot for a considerable time. He sank to his knees, and beneath his lowered lids his eyes were steely and bright as he picked up the stump of a match which had been partly burnt.

"Our man believed in living in style, my friend," Sexton Blake said, looking up at Martin, who was standing over him, with Detective Jones by his side.

"How do you know?" the official asked, with a frown of puzzlement.

"Because this match enables me to deduce that he was recently frequented one of the most expensive and select hotels in the West End of London," Sexton Blake answered quietly.

'Oh, draw it mild!" the worthy official grinned. "How the deuce can you tell that from the stump of a match?"

"In this particular instance, quite easily," the Baker Street detective replied. "Take a look at it. It is not an ordinary match by any means."

The Scotland Yard man took the charred fragment of wood from his colleague's hand and glanced at it in his best official manner. Sexton Blake had been correct in stating that it was not an ordinary lucifer. It was broad and flat in shape, and stamped in the centre were the letter "R.H."

"I don't see that it affords us much information," Jones who was looking over his superior's shoulder, said indifferently.

"On the contrary," Sexton Blake objected, "it tells me that it was once in one of the matchstands in the American or buffet bar of the Royal Hotel in the Strand. These matches are peculiar to the institution in question, they being specially made for the proprietor, who has a mania for the initials signifying his hotel to appear on practically every article in use there. The glasses, the crockery-ware, the table-linen and cutlery all bear the initials 'R.H.' in some form or another.

"It is a habit of mine to notice facts that would escape, or only momentarily impress the average person. It is fairly safe to assume that our man, when taking a drink at one of the bars, discovered he was without matches, and took several from one of the stands before passing through to his rooms or making for the street. He must have been a resident at the hotel, otherwise he could not purchase refreshment at either of the bars."

"The reasoning is sound enough," Martin admitted, "But, after all, it does not identify the man who stole the jewels. Indeed, there is every reason for it to be possible that it was not he who dropped this fragment of match."

"On the contrary, I do not think that there is much doubt about the lucifer having once been in the possession of the cracksman," Sexton Blake returned, with quiet conviction, as he took the scrap of wood from Martin's hand and carefully stowed it away in his wallet. "Look at the grass and note how it has been pressed down behind these bushes. The fact seems to indicate that the man lay here for some good while, possibly watching for the house to be wrapped in darkness before he made his attempt to steal Sir Digby's treasures."

"Or he may have been waiting for his accomplice," Detective Jones put in.

Blake nodded.

"You are, of course, referring to the woman whom you have deduced went over the wall with the man?" he said.

"Yes!"

"We will take a look at the footprints later," Sexton Blake answered. "For the present, there may be more to be found here. Phew!"

"What have you dropped on?" Martin asked, stooping eagerly forward, for Sexton Blake had given a long, low whistle.

"This," Blake answered, holding up a partly-smoked cigar, which he had just unearthed from beneath the bushes.

"It's an Indian brand!" Martin said, as he took the find between his finger and thumb and sniffed at it.

"Precisely! It is a Trincomalee!"

"What!" Martin started. "The kind smoked by Ezra Q. Maitland?" he ejaculated involuntarily. "Jove, Blake do you think——"

"We must not jump to conclusions," the Baker Street detective protested, with a deprecatory gesture of his hands. "Trincomalees are certainly the brand of cigars smoked by Maitland and are very rare in England, but the finding of this butt here does not necessarily proclaim that the American was the burglar."

"As with the match," Jones said, "the cigar may not have been smoked by the criminal, although there's indication that it was."

"I fancy I follow the direction in which your thoughts are running," Sexton Blake said. "The cigar was thrown away almost immediately after it was ignited, which might mean that our man, supposing he was the smoker, saw that the time for him to act had arrived, necessitating his tossing the weed away."

"That's just what I was deducing, Mr. Blake. Do you think that Maitland has cropped up again in his affair? By James! It's more than likely when one comes to think of it! He's been quiet for a long while now, and Sir Digby Cranston's jewels would mean a haul that even Maitland would consider worth going for! The woman might have been his wife, eh?"

156

"It is more than likely," Blake agreed. "But let us prove the theory to be an actual fact before we rely upon it. Perhaps you'll lead us to the spot where the man and women scaled the wall?"

Jones nodded.

"This way, gentlemen!" said he.

He started off across the lawn, and presently paused before the wall that cut off the garden from the lane at the rear. He indicated with his foot a brick that lay in the soft mould of the flower-bed beneath, and pointed to the cavity it had recently filled.

Sexton Blake sank to his knees, quite heedless that the gound was damp with the dew that had fallen during the night. His brows were drawn together, his lips compressed, as he studied the footprints that were in evidence in the soft earth. As Jones had said, they appeared to have been made by a man and a woman, for one set was very small and dainty, whilst the heels of the person responsible for them had sunk deeply into the ground.

Blake rose and drew himself to the top of the wall with a quick, neat spring. He glanced from side to side, then once again dropped to earth and stood by his companions.

"Hallo!" Martin said at that moment. "What's wrong with Miss Cranston? She seems upset about something!"

Sexton Blake and Jones swung round in the direction in which he was looking. Elice had just emerged from the study windows and was hastening towards them in a manner that suggested something out of the common had occured.

Her breath was coming a little sharply, and her cheeks were flushed with excitement, as she reached the three men.

"It's Miss Hammond, gentlemen," the girl answered quickly. "She has completely disappeared, and her bed has not been slept in!"

Sexton Blake's eyes glinted as instinctively he darted another glance at the impressions in the mould of the flower-bed.

'I would suggest that you allow us to see her room," he said. Then, meaningly, "We have ascertained that a women was mixed up in the robbery, Miss Cranston."

Elice, caught her breath and her eyes opened wide with astonishment.

"But, Mr. Blake," she protested, "you cannot think that my father's secretary had any connection with the man who committed the theft of the jewels?"

The detective tilted his shoulders.

"We know that a woman, for some reason, climbed over the wall into the lane at the rear of the garden," the detective said, non-commitally. "Also, the duplicate key could not have been obtained by the burglar, without assistance from an accomplice in the house."

"But Sadie Hammond could have had no hand in the crime, Mr Blake!" Elice cried. "She came to my father with references from an American millionaire, and was one of the nicest of girls. We were very great friends, and I cannot for a moment believe her to be dishonest."

"Yet her sudden disappearance is peculiar, to say the least of it, Miss Cranston," Sexton Blake persisted. "With your permission, we shall take a survey of her apartment without delay."

"Of course, if you think it necessary, I will take you to her room."

"I believe it to be most necessary. Were the references from this—er—millionaire ever confirmed?"

"You mean did my father correspond with him to ascertain whether the testimonials were genuine?"

"Yes."

"I am almost sure that he did not, Mr. Blake. Dad was always a trifle lax in business matters."

"Exactly. I should not be surprised if these references proved to be forged, but we will cast no futher doubts upon Miss Sadie Hammond's honesty until we have had an opportunity of searching her room. You said she was, as her name implies, an American, if I recollect rightly?"

"That is so. She hailed from Chicago."

Sexton Blake seemed thoughtful as he and his companions followed the girl back to the house and up to the first floor.

Elice led them along a corridor, and paused before a door at the far end. Throwing this open, she displayed to view a tastefully-furnished bedroom.

One glance at the bed sufficed to tell the detectives that Elice had been right in stating that it had not been slept in. Sexton Blake ran his eyes over various pieces of furniture the room contained, and moved over to the dressing-table.

His eyes narrowed as he stood for a moment regarding the array of articles dear to the feminine heart which stood there. Bottles of perfume, a tiny jar of face cream, a box of rice powder, a tube of lip salve, and an expensive box of assorted chocolates lay about in disorder.

Sexton Blake took up the stump of a tiny cigarette, but upon examination it proved to be a "My Darling" State Express, a brand that is specially sold for ladies and which could be purchased at any good-class tobacconists. Blake was about to turn away when he caught sight of a quantity of hairpins lying in an ornamental glass tray, and at once he was struck by the fact that they were of two distinct kinds.

Quite a dozen were composed of tortoise-shell, and were of an amber colour, whilst there were three of the ordinary black wire description. Blake turned to Elice.

"Your father's secretary was a blonde," he said.

It was a statement rather than a question.

"Yes, Mr. Blake. Her hair was very beautiful, and of a fair golden hue."

"Can you remember ever seeing here with her hair undressed? I mean, with it falling about her shoulders?"

"No," Elice replied slowly, after a pause. "Never to the best of my recollection."

"I rather thought not, Miss Elice," Sexton Blake said, a trifle drily. "Had you done so, you might have detected that what you believed to be tresses of natural and exceptional beauty were nothing more than a skilfully-made wig."

"A—a wig!" Elice gasped. "Why do you think that?"

"Because," Sexton Blake returned quietly, although there was suppressed excitement in his keen, grey eyes, "there is, in my mind, but little doubt that Sadie Hammond was merely an alias for Kathleen Maitland, or 'Broadway Kate', as she is known by the police of nearly every civilised country in the world, one of the cleverest and cunning female criminals of the twentieth century."

"Broadway Kate!" Elice seemed astounded, bewildered. "The wife of the man who attempted to steal the Great Belgian Relief Fund!" she said tensely.

"The same," Sexton Blake admitted.

"But what makes you so sure, Blake?" Martin asked eagerly. "You said just now, when you found the end of a Trincomalee cigar in the garden, that we could not be sure that it had belonged to Ezra Q. Maitland, although——"

"And since then," Blake replied, "I have secured a clue that has made me practically certain of the identities of the thieves. Let us put two and two together. We know that the secretary, who is known as Sadie Hammond, is of American origin. So is Broadway Kate. Secondly, the secretary came to Sir Digby, who, by the way, is a renowned collector of precious stones, with references that might quite easily have been forged.

"We must note that Miss Hammond would know that the jewels would be kept in the house all last night, for they were to be on view at the reception, and naturally could not be sent to the bank until this morning. Miss Hammond, in her position as private secretary to Sir Digby, would doubtless have frequent opportunities of taking a wax impression of the key of her employer's safe.

"Now, although Miss Hammond would be tired and would need rest after the whirl of a reception last night, her bed has not been slept in, and she has mysteriously disappeared. A burglary occurs, and we discover footprints at the foot of the garden-wall which show that a man and a woman have stood there. A brick is dislodged, which practically proves that they scaled the wall, and thus escaped from the premises.

"Behind a clump of bushes, where some person has obviously lain in wait for some time, we find the stump of a cigar, which, upon examination, proves to be a Trincomalee, a brand that is always smoked by Ezra Q. Maitland, but otherwise seldom found in Britain.

"The cigar had scarcely been lighted before it was tossed aside, seeming to suggest that the smoker had only just commenced it when he found that the time for him to be active had arrived. Therefore, it would appear that it was the cracksman to whom the cigar belonged. What is more likely than that Miss Hammond, who was his accomplice, appeared from the study windows before he had an opportunity of taking more than a few whiffs at the weed? She possibly would open the windows for him to enter and commit the burglary. I noticed that they showed no signs of having been forced.

"Now the Trincomalee cigar suggests Maitland, but it is hardly sufficient proof to lay the crime at his door without some further definite indication to that effect. We have the clue we need here. I refer to these hairpins.

"Miss Cranston tells us that Sadie Hammond was a blonde, which these amber-coloured hairpins at once suggested to my mind. If she were a fair woman, why on earth should she need black hairpins? Do you begin to see what I am aiming at?"

Martin rubbed at his chin and looked puzzled.

"I'm afraid I don't quite understand what——" he began. "By Jove! Yes, I do! We know that Broadway Kate keeps her own hair, which is dark, cropped short to her head, so that she may easily assume the character of a man, and when she appears as a member of her true sex, she wear a wig! She was known as a blonde as Sadie Hammond, but before she left here——"

"Precisely—she changed her wig for a dark one, by way of disguise, so that she should not be easily traced," Sexton Blake concluded.

"She took the light-coloured pins from her fair wig," Jones put in, his manner evincing the keenest interest in the private detective's methods, "and used ordinary dark ones to pin the hair of a black wig into place, leaving two behind her."

"Exactly!" Sexton Blake agreed. "It is Ezra Q. Maitland and his beautiful yet criminal wife whom we have to seek. When we find them, we shall regain your father's jewels, Miss Elice. I think it would be as well for you to go to him and set his mind at rest by imparting to him that we are hot upon the track."

"And now we are off to the Royal Hotel in the Strand, Mr. Blake," Sergeant Jones suggested.

Sexton Blake inclined his head as he took out his cigar-case.

"Yes," he said. "We shall inquire for a guest who knocked up the night-porter just after dawn, presuming that Maitland returned there immediately after he had fled from here. With luck, we shall clap the darbies on his wrists before an hour has passed."

And Inspector Martin grinned in his beard as he jingled the handcuffs that always reposed in his tail-pocket.

———

CHAPTER 5
At the Royal Hotel

It was just after six-thirty that a taxi-cab, in which were seated Sexton Blake, Detective-inspector Martin, and his subordinate, Jones, dashed up to the imposing entrance of the Royal Hotel, which is near Charing Cross Station, and one of the most exclusive and expensive institutions of its kind to be found in the great world of London.

Almost before the cab had drawn up Sexton Blake had alighted, and he was quickly followed by his companions. The Baker Street detective paid the chauffeur, tipping him liberally; then the detectives mounted the steps leading to the hotel's entrance-hall.

A sleepy-looking porter was languidly cleaning the brass plate upon the doors. He paused in his work, and stared heavily at the early visitors.

"We wish to see the manager, my man," Inspector Martin said pompously. "Is he about?"

The porter scratched his head, and slowly a grin appeared upon his usually expressionless countenance.

"Lor' no sire!" he answered. "'E ain't in the 'abit if staying hup all night!'"

"Don't try to be funny, my good fellow!" Martin snapped. "It doesn't suit you! You will have to rouse him, if he is not yet up!"

The porter grinned again, in a manner that irritated the short-tempered Scotland Yard official to no little degree.

"You may be right sir," he said; "But, then again, you might be wrong, an' if you was to arsk me, I should say you was wrong, by long chalks! Why, bless me, he'd sack me on the spot if I disturbed him at this 'ere h-hour in the mornin'!"

Sexton Blake pushed his way forward. He drew half-a-crown from his pocket and slipped it into the man's ready palm.

"We wish to see the manager upon a very important matter," said the detective. "But, firstly, you may be able to give us some information. For how long have you been upon duty?"

"I ain't long come, sir."

"Can you tell me if any of your guests have entered here since you arrived?"

"No sir. They ain't astir so early as this."

"We have reason to believe otherwise, at least, where one of your patrons is concerned. Has the night-porter left?"

"I don't think so, sir. I haven't noticed him go out."

"Can you get into touch with him should he be still upon the premises?"

Yes sir. If you'll wait half a minute I'll see if 'e's still about."

Sexton Blake nodded.

"Please do so at once," he ordered, in that quiet tone of authority that was at times characteristic of him, and which seldom the highest or lowest found possible to dispute. "The matter is urgent."

The porter touched his cap and disappeared. He quickly returned with a sturdy man of middle-age at his heels.

"This 'ere's the night-porter, sir," the former announced. "This is the gen'lman who give me half a dollar an' wants ter know things, Bill."

Sexton Blake took the obvious hint, and a similar tip found its way into the night-porter's pocket.

"I want to know if one of your gentlemen knocked you up, soon after daylight, my man?" the detective said.

"There was one—yes, sir," the man informed him. "But how you should know that, beats me, there being no one about when I lets him in!"

"It doesn't matter how I know of the arrival," Sexton Blake returned. "Who was this man?"

"A Mr. Charles Blenkarn, sir."

"An American gentleman?"

The porter looked still more surprised.

"Yus," he agreed. "He came in all of a fluster like, and guessed and reckoned at me like one o'clock. He gave me a couple of bob, sir, an' said as how he was sorry he had troubled me. I didn't know him, but I looked up his name in the visitors' book, found everything was all right, an' let him through."

"Thank you! Was his wife with him?"

"No, sir. He ain't got one, to my knowledge. Anyway, there was only his name entered in the book against the number of his room."

"You did not see a lady waiting outside, for instance?"

"No, sir. If you remember, I said as how there was no one about when I lets him in. Howsomever, his wife might have been waiting outside out of sight somewhere, for he didn't stay in his room long."

"He went out again, then!" Sexton Blake exclaimed sharply.

"Yes, sir. Arter about ten minutes, just as I was 'aving a do—I mean shovin' me legs up and restin' 'em, down comes his nibs again. 'Hi'm, sorry, porter, I guess,' he says, 'but I reckon I've got to trouble you again,' he says, 'I've an appointment that I must keep at half-past six,' 'You're an early bird, sir,' I says, as I opens the doors for him. 'You bet, porter,' he says, grinnin' all over his face. 'An', say, I've caught the worm! Good-mornin,' an' I guess I'm much obliged to yer,' he says. An' with that he hops down the steps and fairly scoots down the Strand."

"We must see the manager immediately, my man," Blake said, turning to the other porter.

"But what'll he say, sir?" the fellow asked, hesitating.

"I expect he'll say a good deal when he knows the truth," Sexton Blake answered a little grimly. "Take this card up to him. He will understand when he sees it."

The porter took the slip of pastecard, and started as he read the name engraved upon it.

"You're the great detective, sir!" he exclaimed, in an awed voice.

"I am a detective—yes; and these gentlemen are representatives of Scotland Yard. Please hurry! We have little time to spare."

Without more ado the fellow took his departure, and a few minutes later he reapeared, and requested the three detectives to step into the entrance-hall. He showed them into a small but comfortably furnished office, situated near the cloak-room, informing them that Mr. Raymond, the manager, would be with them in a few moments.

It was, however, quite a quarter of an hour before that gentleman put in an appearance, and Martin and Jones had been fidgeting with impatience although Sexton Blake had seemed careless of the time that was passing. He had been sitting languidly in an easy-chair, the lids drawn low over his eyes, drumming the tips of his long, nervous fingers together as was his custom when deep in thought.

Mr. Raymond proved to be a dapper little man, with a monocle and neatly waxed moustache. It was a habit of his never to appear in public unless he was well-groomed and sprucely attired, and although he had been agitated and exceedingly ill-at-ease when he had been informed that detectives were seeking information as to one of his guests, he had stopped to shave and fully dress before leaving his bedroom.

"You are Mr. Sexton Blake?" he asked, as the famous detective rose and formally bowed.

"That is my name," the latter agreed. "These gentlemen are Detectives Martin and Jones, of the C.I.D.. We have been inquiring about the doings of one of your residents—a Mr. Charles Blenkarn."

"So I have been informed," Raymond answered, tugging at his moustache, and looking worried. "I—er—trust, gentlemen, that there is no serious reason for your seeking him?"

Sexton Blake lifted his shoulders expressively.

"I wish I could answer in the negative, Mr. Raymond," said he. "But I cannot; for the simple reason the man you know as Blenkarn is in reality one of the most badly 'wanted' men in London at this moment."

"Good heavens!" The little manager let out the exclamation explosively, and he seemed to grow limp as he lowered himself into a chair. "Who—who is he?" he queried weakly.

"He is Ezra Q. Maitland," Sexton Blake replied quietly. "A man who, you will possibly be aware, is being sought by the police of well-nigh every civilised country, save, of course Germany and Austria, for whom he has in the past worked as a spy."

Raymond gasped, and mopped his brow with a daintily scented handkerchief.

"The villain!" he cried, recovering himself. "To—to think that he has had the audacity to come to the Royal! Mr. Blake, I beg—I beseech that you will not make this matter public— It will ruin our reputation for all time!"

"You may rest assured that we shall hush the matter up, as we have done when he has been discovered at other select hotels," Blake answered reassuringly. "I take it that you will assist us in all your power to enable us to get upon his track?"

"With pleasure I will!" the little man exclaimed jumping up like a Jack-in-the-box. "I trust that you may catch him, gentlemen! I hope he may get a life-sentence!" he added feelingly. "What can I do for you?"

"Allow us to search his room."

The manager started towards the door, but paused as he reached the threshold.

"There could not possibly be any mistake?" he queried doubtfully.

"None whatever," Sexton Blake assured him. "You have heard that he knocked up the night porter just after dawn, stayed in his room for a short time, and then hastened out again?"

"Yes."

"He had just returned from committing a robbery involving something like one hundred and fifty thousand pounds. He has probably taken his departure for good, meaning, perhaps, to leave the country before, as he believed, the crime could be traced to him. Indeed, I believe it to be most likely."

"Phew! He's made a haul this time!" Raymond breathed excitedly. "Follow me, gentlemen. I'll—I really beg your pardon, Mr. Melson. Did I hurt you?"

The last portion of his remarks had been caused by reason of his stumbling over a stooping figure, as he had hurried from the office. The man whom he had addressed as Mr. Melson had been bending to tie up his shoe-lace, and had been just a little to the left of the door, so that he had not been visible to the four men until they had stepped from the office.

"It's quite all right, Raymond," Mr. Melson said; and Sexton Blake darted a keen glance at him as he noticed that his voice contained the slightest trace of a nasal twang. "I guess it was my fault for stopping just by your office. I had no idea you were in there, though. You are about early."

"Yes; and you, too, sir," Raymond replied. "An early stroll, perhaps?"

"Yes; I haven't been able to sleep very well. Touch of neuralgia, I reckon. Good-morning, Raymond!"

"Good-morning, sir!"

Sexton Blake paused for the fraction of a moment to stare after the tall, gaunt figure of the man whom the manager had addressed as Melson, for the detective knew that he had lied when he had said that he had not been aware that the manager was in his office.

The excitable little gentleman had been speaking in a high-pitched, almost shrill voice, by reason of the disturbing news Blake and his companions had brought him, and unless Mr. Melson was stone deaf he must have known that the office was occupied.

When he had first emerged from the room and seen the manager stumble over the stooping figure, Sexton Blake had asked himself if Melson had been playing the eavesdropper, and as the latter's unmistakable twang had fallen upon his ears, the detective had momentarily asked himself if this man were Maitland—if, after all, Charles Blenkarn was not their man?

But a glance at Melson's lined careworn face removed all doubt from Sexton Blake's mind. Melson's eyes were grey, whilst Maitland's were of a jet, piercing black in hue. As he followed the manager up the long, wide staircase leading to the first floor, Sexton Blake put Melson from his thoughts, thinking that perhaps he had merely sought to overhear what was being said in the manager's office out of mere inquisitiveness, but the detective would have been surprised could he have seen Mr. Melson's expression as he gained the street, and heard the words he uttered.

"By heavens!" he had muttered, rubbing calculatingly at his chin. "Then I was not mistaken! The man is Maitland without a doubt, and these people are seeking to arrest him. If I could only save him, it would be the opening with him that I have planned. With his fine brain to work the scheme I have in mind——"

"I'll do it, I reckon!" he murmured. "I'll order my car and follow them. If there's the ghost of a chance——"

Meanwhile, Sexton Blake, Martin and Jones had followed the debonair little manager to the room that "Mr. Charles Blenkarn" had occupied. As Sexton Blake had half-expected, the apartment was in the wildest disorder, showing every sign of its recent occupant having made a hurried departure.

Drawers were pulled open to their fullest extent, articles of clothing lay in confusion upon the floor, whilst in the grate was a heap of ashes, suggesting that a quantity of letters, or other documents, had been hastily burnt.

"A Trincomalee," he said meaningly.

He began poking about amid the heap of ashes in the grate, then a sharp exclamation left his lips, and he gained his feet, a charred scrap of paper held between his finger and thumb.

Inspector Martin and Jones stepped eagerly to his side as he moved over to the table and smoothed the scrap of paper out upon it. Two corners of the paper, which was of the cheapest variety of note, were burnt away; but, in spite of this, it was at once plain to the detectives that it had once been a letter, for a number of ill-formed, misspelt words were still discernible upon its surface.

This was how Sexton Blake's find appeared as he laid it upon the table and perused it:

Sextons Blake's eyes were very bright and hard as he turned quickly to his colleagues.

"This is the most valuable clue we have discovered!" he said, with unwonted enthusasm in his voice.

"But why?" Martin asked, his brows going up in surprise. 'It only tells us that somebody was sorry because he was not in when Maitland called upon him—or that is how I take it. Then it goes on to say that the writer got something—a note, by the look of it—and that he can do the deal if the stuff is brought to him."

"Yes; and the stuff referred to means, of course, the jewels."

"Of course; but there's no address or signature showing, and possibly neither ever appeared on the letter, so we don't know who wrote it, or from whence it came," Martin objected. "We are no better off than we were before we found it."

Sexton Blake laughed silently, and moved towards the door.

"Where are you off to?" Martin asked, glaring at his friend, for he detested anything that mystified him, and he could not understand Blake's obvious exultation.

"I am going to the shop in Cleever's Rents, a slum just off the Minories, where a gentleman named Israel Samuels ostensibly sells second-hand clothes," the private detective returned calmly. "But I must first make a call in Villiers Street."

"Samuels, the 'fence'!"* Martin and Jones cried together.

"Samuels, the man we have always thought to be a 'fence'," Sexton Blake corrected. "We have never proved it, you know, although I fancy his race is nearly run."

"You think that Maitland has gone to him to dispose of the jewels?" Martin jerked. "But how do you know? There's nothing on the letter to show that it comes from him, and—'"

"There I must differ from you," Sexton Blake interrupted. "There are a dozen indications to definitely prove that Israel Samuels

---

*Receiver of stolen goods.

161

was the writer of this message to Maitland. Only a few days ago I secured a specimen of his handwriting from a reformed crook, and you may rely that I took the trouble to carefully study it. The shaky writing, the twist of the 'e's', the formation of the 'l's' and the 'r's' are unmistakable—even the spelling of the words is characteristic of the man! We may arrive too late to arrest Maitland, but at all events we shall regain the Digby collection, or the part of it that has been stolen. I must go to Villiers Street whilst you get off post-haste to the Yard for a search warrant."

"Why are you going to Villiers Street?" Martin asked

"Because," Sexton Blake said, with the ghost of a smile playing about his lips as he drew a handsome diamond ring from his finger, "I require a disguise, and I am going to call on a friend of mine there who always keeps a variety in readiness for me. Impersonating a crook who I am almost certain has done business with Samuels, I shall go to his shop on the pretence of selling this ring, which, of course, he will think I have come by, by dishonest means. You will be waiting near at hand, and should I find that Samuels has someone in his shop-parlour, I shall take it to be Maitland and immediately arrest him. I shall telephone Tinker, and, in a good disguise, he will be hanging around by the shop door. As soon as he sees me clap the handcuffs on old Samuels, he will signal to you. You will then enter the shop at once to assist me with Maitland. It may not be an easy matter to secure him, for he will be desperate, and will possibly fire free unless I am too quick for him. You had better bring two or three plainclothes men with you, in case the inhabitants of Cleever's Rents attempt to effect a rescue of our prisoners. I happen to know that they are not in love with law and order."

Martin nodded, and his chin went forward aggressively as he felt his biceps.

"Won't pay 'em to interfere with us!" he grinned. "I haven't been in a scrap for a long time, and I believe a shindy would do me good! We'll have friend Samuels this time if we have to ransack the old blackguard's shop from cellar to attic! He's worried me for years, and now that we've got something tangible to go on, I'll lay him by the heels or resign my position—go into the country and grow cabbages!"

———

CHAPTER 6
Escape

Cleever's rents is not one of the nicest localities in the metropolis. Far from it, many would say, when they took in its cracked and broken windows, stuffed with rags or paper, its garbage-littered gutters, its poverty-stricken aspect, and its narrow dimensions.

Upon either side, tall, gaunt-looking houses tower up towards the strip of sky that is visible between them, many of them sheltering a family in every room. Pinched-faced, ill-clad children of all ages seem to play continuously on the steps, in the puddles and gutters, save when a Council school officer takes it into his head to risk that part of his person getting broken by paying a visit to the slum.

There is a gin-palace standing upon the corner, which always seems to be doing a brisk trade, and at night the sickly light from its windows is the only illumination Cleever's Rents receives or requires, for the inhabitants detest too much light for many reasons, and the two lampposts that are in evidence have been rendered hors de combat long since.

It was to this part of the globe that Ezra Q. Maitland had wended his way after he made his hurried exit from the Royal Hotel, and now, with his soft hat pulled well over his eyes, and his coat collar turned up, he was pausing before a dingy shop which stood exactly opposite the public-house.

Over this establishment, which was outwardly a wardrobe dealer's, known to the Cleever's Rents residents as an "ole clo" shop, was the faded and weather-beaten inscription—"I. Samuels."

Save for the ancient articles of wearing appeal in the dirty window, there was nothing to indicate the nature of Mr. Samuels's calling; but he was known by half the criminals in London—also by Scotland Yard, although its members had never been able to secure any definite charge against him—to be one of the most adroit "fences" and benevolent old crooks who ever drew breath.

The shop was open, despite the fact that the hour was not quite seven o'clock, for long experience had taught Mr. Samuels that it was often at an exceedingly early hour that his numerous "friends" desired to do a deal with him.

After a quick, furtive glance about him, Ezra Q. Maitland tried the door, found it unlocked, and pushed it open, He stepped into the close, fusty atmosphere beyond conscious as he did so that an electric bell was buzzing somewhere in the rear of the premises.

The master-criminal had not long to wait for the appearance of the man with whom he had come to do business. A tattered curtain concealing the entrance to the shop-parlour was thrust aside, and the wizened countenance of old Israel Samuels peered out.

He was very old, ugly and unclean. He possessed a parchment-like skin, a hooked nose, and evil, beady eyes. A skull-cap was upon his head, concealing to an extent its baldness, whilst he was attired in a disreputable red dressing-gown, over the front of which streamed his matted grey beard.

"And what can I do for you, my tear?" the old reprobate queried, regarding Maitland with a half suspicious look as he tottered forward and stood behind the counter, rubbing his bony hands. "It'th a pleathant mornin', to be sure, ain't it?"

Maitland's reply was to take a step forward, pushing back his hat and turning down his coat collar; then, in a trice, the neat black beard and moustache that had concealed his features were whipped away, and his sinister eyes were looking into those of the Jew.

"Holy smoke! If it ain't tear Mithter Maitland!" the old man exclaimed, throwing up his dirty hands. "Vell, vell, vell, thith ith a pleathure, to be sure! Come you in, my tear, and ve vill do bith'nith with ourselves together!"

"Get right along, and don't talk so much," Maitland advised shortly. "My time is limited, I guess."

The old man chuckled cacklingly, seeming in no way offended by his client's manner.

"Come in—come in, my tear," he muttered, lifting the flap of the counter and standing aside for Maitland to pass through.

The master-criminal followed him through into the shop-parlour, where there was an overpowering odour of kippers, which caused the refined soul of the Yankee crook to positively revolt within him.

His hands had dropped carelessly into his jacket-pocket as he had followed the old "fence" into the room, for none knew better than Maitland how handy it was at times to be lighting on the draw when visiting such a place as this.

Not that he was by any means afraid of the decrepit Samuels; but the old man knew the nature of the business upon which he had come, knew that he probably carried a vast quantity of jewels upon his person, and Maitland did not trust him.

Samuels had been expecting his visit, and he was quite capable, if it suited his purpose, to employ one or more of the ruffians of his acquaintance to be at hand to treacherously attack and rob him—Maitland—of his ill-gotten gains.

However, a sharp survey of the stuffy little parlour, with its worn and broken furniture and array of unhealthy-looking wax flowers, convinced Maitland that he and the Jew were quite alone, so he dropped his long frame into an easy-chair standing near the table and watched Samuels from the corners of his eyes as he, too, seated himself.

"Vell, my tear?" the "fence" asked eagerly. "You've got them?"

Maitland nodded leisurely as he carefully lit one of his strong Indian cigars.

"Bet on it," the master-crook answered, in a drawling tone. "Say. I told you I was after jewels to a value well over a hundred thou., and I ain't a man to boast without cause as a rule."

"You haf them vith you?"

"Of course. Think I've come here for the pleasure of just sittin' and looking at a crooked-beaked old scoundrel like you?" the Yankee queried. "Say, I guess you'll open your eyes when you know what the stuff really is. Now that the job's over, I guess I've no objection to letting you into the know. It's the Digby collection that I've lifted; or, rather, three-quarters of it!"

"The Digby collection!" The old Hebrew's jaw dropped in blank surprise. "My vord!" he gasped. "How in the name of all that'th vonderful did you do it, my tear?"

"I reckon that's got nothing to do with you, my friend," Maitland retorted. "Suffice it for you that I've got the 'shiners' here, and the sooner I've exchanged 'em for banknotes the better I shall be pleased. Take a look at 'em!"

He had taken the two wash-leather bags from his pocket, and now, with a quick twist of his hands, he had emptied their contents upon the newspaper that lay upon the table to serve as a cloth.

The unset jewels went rolling over the table, Maitland scooping them together so that they did not fall upon the floor. Even in the dim light of the little parlour they shone and blazed with a myriad lights, and old Samuels caught in his breath with admiration, while his wizened face depicted innate greed.

Without a word, he screwed a powerful magnifying-glass into one of his evil old eyes, and for the next ten minutes he was poring over the master-criminal's haul, picking up stone after stone in his fingers and submitting it to an exhaustive scrutiny.

"Say," Maitland drawled at length. "Suppose you hustle some. I reckon I don't feel too secure here."

"Vhy?" Israel Samuels queried sharply. "You haf not been followed?"

"No; I reckon not. But I've a good reason for wishing to get to the other side of the Herring Pond without much delay. I've had an uneasy feeling yesterday. A man who is staying at the hotel I have been using opened the door of my room when I was taking off my disguise for a snooze. It ain't like me to be careless, but I guess I'd omitted to lock the door. He apologised, and said he had made a mistake; but whether that was gospel or no, I can't say. He may have looked into my room on purpose, although I don't think so, for I made inquiries and found that his name was Melson, that he hailed from America, and was reported to be a millionaire and a well-known Wall Street man, which seems harmless enough. However, let's get going!"

Old Israel Samuels slowly removed the glass from his eye, drew up his sloping shoulders until they well-nigh touched his ears, and he rubbed his skinny hands until the joints cracked.

"Of course, my tear," he lisped. "I can give you something for the stuff as a speculation; but I fear it vill not be a great deal."

"Why not?" Maitland asked sharply, his eyes snapping.

"Vell, you see the jewels are tho well known and so eathily trathable, my tear," old Samuels answered. "I should haf to keep them monthth yearth, before I dare dispoth of them; elth haf to cut them about, vitch vould lessen them in value."

"Well, what do you say to eighty-five thousand pounds?" the criminal asked.

"Vat?"

"Eighty-five thousand pounds."

"Eighty-five thouthand grandmother!" the 'fence' repeated scornfully. "My tear Mithter Maitland, you ought to know better, indeed you ought. I can only gif you thirty-thouthand, and then I consider I am being moth generous!"

"See here!" Maitland hissed fiercely, his piercing eyes glinting dangerously. "Don't you try any tea-garden tricks with me, you avaricious old skeleton! I'll make it eighty thou., not a penny less!"

Old Samuels shook his head vigorously.

"I tell you it can't be done, my tear," he protested. "Look at the risk I run!"

Maitland rose to his feet and began slowly putting the jewels back into the bags.

"Vhat'th the game?" the Jew asked, a trifle anxiously.

Maitland made a deprecating gesture.

"I reckon I'm takin' 'em elsewhere," he said determinedly.

"Stay a minute, my tear. Suppoth ve thay thirty-five—look here, forty thouthand pounds paid on the nail!"

"Go to the dickens!" Maitland said politely. "You have heard my price!"

"Vell, as you're an old friend of mine, ve'll stretch a point and thay thixty thouthand, half to be paid now and half next veek."

Maitland pointed to one of his eyes.

"I calc'late there's not a sign there," he drawled.

"A sign of vhat?"

"Green! Do you get me? You might move sudden, like!"

The Jew threw up his hands in horror.

"My tear Mither Maitland," he gasped, "I vouldn't do thuth a thing! Now, if you'll take my termth—Hark! Vhat's that! There is somevon in the thop!"

For a moment the two men stood rigid. Maitland had laid the bags upon the table, and his fingers were gripping upon the serviceable automatic that reposed in his jacket-pocket.

"Who can it be?" he asked tensely.

"Anybody at 'ome?" a hoarse voice asked from the other side of the faded curtain.

"Comin', comin'," the Jew cackled. "It'th alright, I think," he said to Maitland. "Stop here a moment and I'll thee who it ith."

He tottered towards the door, pushed aside the curtain, and emerged into the shop to peer from beneath his shaggy brows at the rough-looking man who stood before the counter.

The latter was attired in a pair of patched corduroys, a ragged coat, and a cap of a loud, check pattern, drawn forward over his eyes. A scarf was about his neck, knotted beneath his right ear; he was unshaven and flushed of countenance. He was clutching hold of the counter as though for support, and it seemed that, although the day was so young, he had been inbibing more than was good for him.

"'Allo, me ole cock-spadger!" the man said with a leer. "'Ow're yer—hic!—fluffing it? Why, it must be four year since I saw yer dirty face larst!"

He lurched forward over the counter and tried to shake the "fence" by the hand. Old Samuels peered at him keenly, then he gave a sharp exclamation.

"Toby Grimes!" he ejaculated quickly. "I thought you were still in——"

"'Ush!" Mr. Grimes protested with a shudder. "Don't mention me 'otel at Portland, Sammy, cos I got fed hup wi' it! I 'ad ter complain to the manager, I did! Cos why? Cos the place was so expensive! Did they play billyards? No!—hic—but they used ter play shove 'apenny on the tables, an' I lorst me pore old dad's forshun like wildfire! Nah, I'm agoin' ter tell yer this——"

"Vhat d'you vant?" Samuels asked impatiently. "Haf you come here to do buthnith, or only to vaste my time, ain't it?"

"I've come ter do a deal, me lad!" Grimes said, suddenly losing his balance, sprawling forward over the counter, and embracing old Samuels lovingly about the neck. "'Ere'—he drew himself up with drunken dignity—"don't you get a-talkin ter me like thet 'ere, cos I won't 'ave it. Many'as the deal we've done together, an' now, arter me first day on ticket-o-leave, I've brought yer something thet'll make yer eyes hopen!"

He dived his fingers into his vest-pocket and drew forth a valuable diamond ring.

"Vhere did yer get it!" Samuels asked sharply.

"Wot's that got ter do wi' you?" the other asked aggressively. "'Ere, gimme a fiver for it?"

"Put it avay, you fool!" the "fence" urged. "Don't flash it about in the thop! There's somevon outside now, and——"

"Hoh, it's halright. It's only me son, 'Arry. Nice feller—hic!—is 'Arry! Ever met him?"

"No, and don't vant! I'll gif you two pounds for that ring, Grimes, my tear."

"Let's come inter the parler an' talk it hover mate. We——"

"No, no! Come back! There is an acquaintance of mine in there already!" the "fence" protested quickly, as he grabbed at the other's sleeve.

"Then in that case, my friend," the man whom Israel Samuels had taken for an old associate snapped in a low tone, I am going to chance arresting you, for I imagine I know who your friend is! Quick, Tinker! Get a hold on him!"

The old Hebrew uttered a gasping cry and went tottering back, staring dully at the handcuffs which Sexton Blake—the reader has guessed at Grimes's true identity—had snapped upon his wrists.

Simultaneously with the clinking of the steel, the door had been dashed open, and Tinker, well disguised and attired in a suit of rags, had entered and sprung over the counter. He gripped the "fence" by his fettered wrists, bent him backwards, and clapped his hands over his mouth so that he could not cry out to alarm the man in the shop-parlour.

With the speed of an arrow released from a bow, Sexton Blake was round the counter. He thrust the curtain aside and entered just as Maitland was re-adjusting his disguise.

A sharp cry of surprise and dismay burst from Maitland's lips. With his left hand he made a grab at the two bags of jewels, which lay upon the table, whilst he whipped his rovolver out of his pocket with his right.

"Who the deuce are you?" he snarled, swinging up his weapon. "Stand back! or, by heaven, I'll let daylight into you! Ah! a plague upon you!"

Sexton Blake had known that the position was desperate, and not for the fraction of a second had he hesitated. He had drawn his automatic as he darted from the shop to the parlour, and as he had seen Maitland's arm go up, he had sent his weapon whizzing through the air.

His aim had proved remarkably true. The heavy butt of the revolver had struck the master-criminals knuckles, and, with a snarl of pain and rage, he had involuntarily released his hold upon his shooting iron. It went clattering to the table, and Maitland let fall the jewels as Blake hurled himself at his throat.

Locked in each other's arms, the two men went swaying across the room, stumbled over a chair, and crashed to the floor. They rolled over and over, Maitland cursing savagely, Sexton Blake preserving a grim silence.

The master-criminal fought like a madman, every evil passion in him roused, for he believed that he was the victim of some traitorous trick of the "fence," Samuels. He never for a moment thought that this rough-looking man, with the apparently drink-blotched face, was his arch-foe Sexton Blake.

Crash! Blake's bunched fist thudded into Maitland's face, landing fully between his eyes with a force that caused the American's senses to reel. In a flash his arms were pinned to the ground, and his opponent was kneeling upon his chest.

"Who the tarnation thunder are you?" the criminal rasped, glaring up vindictively into the face of the man above him. "What's your game?"

"My game is to arrest you, Ezra Q. Maitland," Sexton Blake said grimly, "and to regain Sir Digby Cranston's jewels!"

A great cry escaped the master-criminal, and he seemed scarcely to believe the evidence of his senses as the well-known voice fell upon his ears.

"Sexton Blake!" he breathed hoarsely. "Sexton Blake!"

"Very much at your service!" the detective snapped. "Your hands please! Thank you!"

Click! Maitland suddenly found his wrists drawn upwards and jerked together; then next instant, one of the fetters was snapped home. He struggled fiercely, desperately, managing to drag one hand away, and at that moment there was a loud commotion from the shop.

Old Samuels had suddenly fastened his yellow teeth into Tinker's palm, and the lad had let out a yell and released his hold of the Jew. With surprising agility and strength, considering his age, the "fence" had flung the surprised lad from him and made a rush for the shop-parlour.

In old Samuel's brain was but one idea. If only he could assist Maitland to escape with the jewels he would be safe, for no evidence of any value could be brought against him. He was far too artful to allow of any stolen property to remain on his premises once he had bought it. He was in the habit of having it removed at once to a private house in Streatham, where he was known by another name and very seldom allowed himself to be seen.

As the old man disappeared through the doorway, Inspector Martin, Jones, and a couple of plain-clothes C.I.D. men dashed into the shop, but they only found Tinker, who was hurriedly picking himself up, in view.

Old Samuels raised his arms above his head as he saw Blake and the Yankee crook struggling upon the floor; then, putting forth all his strength, the "fence" brought his manacled hands crashing down upon the back of Sexton Blake's unprotected head.

The steel fetters added to the effect of the blow, and for a moment red lights danced before the famous detective's eyes. He went reeling sideways, and Maitland, swift to take his opportunity, flung off the enemy and leapt to his feet.

"The jewels! Take the jewels!" old Samuels screeched. But Maitland was not such a fool as to delay for even an unnecessary second now that he had a chance to make a bid for freedom.

He knew that were he captured the police would hand him over to the military authorities, when he would be court-martialled and, without doubt, sentence of death as a spy would be passed upon him. He went across the room like a flash of lightning, to collide, as he reached the threshold, with Detective-sergeant Jones.

Thud! Maitland's fists crashed fairly and squarely into the unfortunate Scotland Yard man's mouth, and he collapsed in a huddled heap. Inspector Martin, who was close upon his heels, pitched over his inert form before he could pull up, and fell sprawling to his hands and knees.

Sexton Blake jumped to his feet, although his head was singing dizzily. He made a mad leap for Maitland, but quick as thought the criminal seized one of the plain-clothes men, swung him around, and sent him staggering into the private detective.

Partly owing to his dizziness, partly because of the impact which which the Scotland Yard man's body collided with his own, Sexton Blake lost his balance and fell heavily.

All was confusion and pandemonium! Martin caught sight of old Samuels and clutched at his legs, bringing him down with a run. Maitland had only one man to contend with before he was able to quit the parlour, and he aimed a swinging blow straight for the point of his jaw.

The plain-clothes man, however, ducked neatly and attempted to wind his arms about the crook's body, but Maitland was just the fraction of a second too quick for him. He took a step backwards, sprang forward again, and seized the detective in a vice-like hold.

At that moment Tinker appeared in the doorway, and Maitland's piercing eyes blazed like living coals with hatred and excitement. With the strength of a Hercules, he swung the Scotland Yard man above his head and sent him hurtling through the air straight for Sexton Blake's assistant's chest.

Nimbly, Tinker dodged aside, but it was impossible for him to entirely escape the flying body of the detective. The latter's heavy boots came into violent contact with the lad's head, and Tinker staggered backwards.

By an effort he kept his balance, but the Scotland Yard man was dashed heavily against the counter. It was a crazy structure, and it could not stand such rough usage and keep it equilibrium. It heeled over and fell with a cloud of dust that set Tinker, the official, and the criminal coughing.

Tinker flung himself at Maitland just as Sexton Blake, who had picked himself up, came rushing from the parlour, but, with a speed born of desperation, Maitland raised his foot and savagely kicked Tinker below the belt.

The lad collapsed like a stone, all the breath knocked out of him, and before he could save himself, Sexton Blake had stumbled over him and fallen again.

Maitland did not wait to see what the result of his treacherous attack upon the young detective had been. he fairly jumped across the shop, flung open the door, and dashed into the street, slamming it to behind him.

He pressed his elbows to his sides, and flew round the corner by the gin-palace, to find himself in the Minories. He heard the shouts of his pursuers in the rear as he came abreast of a handsome car, and realised that the man who was sitting in the driver's seat was calling to him.

"Quick! in with you!"

So surprised was Maitland that he momentarily stopped as he heard the words. They had come from the individual seated in the car, the engine of which was throbbing as though in readiness for the motor to be sent pulsing forward at the shortest notice.

In a flash the criminal recognised the person at the wheel as Mr. Melson, the reported millionaire, the man who had looked into his room at the Royal Hotel, and seen him undisguised.

"Hurry, you fool!" the man from America cried, leaning forward from his seat. "I know you are Maitland, but I want to save you from arrest!"

For the space of a couple of seconds the criminal hesitated, scarcely realising that he heard aright. Then he had sprung into the tonneau of the car, and Melson had sent it humming forward.

Maitland hardly knew why he had obeyed this man. For all he knew he might be a detective, and was now determined to drive him to the nearest police-station. The master crook was half inclined to spring out again, despite the speed the car was gathering, but something told him to lie low and trust to luck that his unexpected ally was genuinely anxious to help him elude his pursuers.

Inspector Martin, Tinker, Jones and Sexton Blake swung round the corner into the Minories as the car dashed onwards towards Tower Hill.

"Where is he!" Martin gasped, pulling up so suddenly that Tinker trod upon his heels. "He—he's vanished!"

"He's hiding in a doorway!" Sexton Blake panted; and. although he saw the car as it throbbed onwards, rapidly disappearing round a bend in the road, he little dreamed of the strange rescuer who had come to his arch-foe's aid. "Come along, Martin! We'll have him yet! He cannot have got far away!"

But, despite the little party of detectives searching exhaustively for upwards of an hour, no trace of Maitland could they find, and at length they were forced to give up the task, admitting themselves for the time being baffled, mystified, nonplussed!

It was not to be long, however, before Sexton Blake and the man who had sworn to sooner or later take his life, were again to come to grips!

———

CHAPTER 7
The ex-Swindler

The sun was blazing down from a perfectly cloudless sky, and it was nearly noon as Mr. Melson's long, grey touring car pulled up before the Magnificent Hotel, upon the front at that ever gay and vivacious seaside resort of the Kentish coast—Margate.

The sea was as calm as a mill-pond, hosts of happy, laughing children played upon the sands and paddled their sun-tanned little feet in the foam, whilst farther out bathing was in full swing.

It was hard to believe that not very far away thousands of men were fighting and dying, suffering and bleeding in a stupendous and deadly conflict, such as history had never known in the past, and, please God, will never know again.

At the popular pleasure haunt things seemed to be progressing much the same as usual, save that there was a curious and significant absence of young civilians of the male sex. Every young fellow between the ages of nineteen and twenty-five or so was in khaki, with but very few exceptions. Soldiers were everywhere, looking cheerful enough, for they were proud of wearing the King's uniform, and if, in a few weeks or months, they were to be crushed and slain by the great German war machine, they didn't let the thought trouble them now. With the true British spirit, they lived only for the present, entertaining and making happy their sweethearts or amusing their wives and children as the case might be.

Mr. Melson alighted from his car and turned to Maitland, who was now seated carelessly in one of back seats. Only a moustache now disguised the astute Yankee's features, for his false beard had been torn away in the great struggle he had made for freedom in the stuffy little shop in the East End of London, but he seemed to feel fairly secure as he slowly puffed at one of his favourite smokes and gazed idly about him.

"Why the tarnation thunder have you come to this mad-headed place?" the criminal asked, looking upon the animated scene about him with a sneer curling his lips.

"It's as safe as anywhere else, I guess," Mr. Melson answered, with a lifting of his shoulders. "You'd better come into the hotel. I am going to engage rooms for us. I've already told you that I want to speak to you in strict privacy, and the sooner I've got what I want to tell you off my chest the better I shall feel. I calc'late we are going to do business together, my friend."

"Really?" Maitland raised his brows, and his manner displayed no particular gratitude for the service his companion had rendered him. "Waal I guess I'm on if there's enough money in the stunt! Say, do you think we shall be traced? Blake is a 'cute card, and if he tumbled that I was in this car he'd move heaven and earth but what he'd find it!"

Melson laughed softly, and shook his head.

"Sexton Blake may be fiendishly clever, but I don't think he'll find this car very easily," he said, with conviction. "I changed the number plate before we were more than eight miles out of London. It was a false number that was on the car when I picked you up in the Minories!"

"You are real smart for an amateur!" Maitland said, nodding approvingly.

"Perhaps I am not such an amateur as you appear to imagine," Melson answered in a curious tone.

Ezra Q. Maitland studied his companion's features from beneath his lowered lids. The criminal took in the extreme pallor of the reputed millionair's clean-shaven face, saw the deep lines that so strongly marked it, noted the deep-set, cold grey eyes. And the crook wondered. Somehow, he could not help thinking that Melson was a man who had suffered—suffered deeply and bitterly, and Maitland asked himself what could be the man's object in wishing to gain his co-operation. Was it some great crime he was planning? Some stupendous robbery or swindle that——"

"Say, I guess you'll know me in the future Maitland," Mr. Melson drawled cynically.

The Yankee started, and roused himself.

"I beg your pardon!" he said. "But you interest me. And, by the way, suppose you drop using my real name? It's not too healthy for me, I guess, to have it shouted about. Call me Kerney—Luke O. Kerney; that will meet the case, I think."

"Suppose we get into the hotel and see about a meal?" Melson suggested. "We can give orders for it to be served in a private room, and can talk after we've disposed of it."

"Right-oh!" Maitland answered. "But, say, what of this stunt you want me to participate in? Is it likely to keep me in England long—for more than a few days?"

"Yes," Mr. Melson returned, with conviction. "Possibly you will be working for me for several weeks."

"That's if it's worth my while, I reckon," Maitland reminded him coolly.

"It will be worth your while, my calculating friend," the other stated reassuringly. "I don't care what the job costs me, for I reckon I've got the dollars. Ten, fifteen, twenty thousand pounds, it's all he same to me, as long as I gain my ends."

Maitland licked the ashes from his cigar, and nodded.

"Very well, then," he said. "I guess I'll get one of the hotel attendants to sent a wire to my wife and servant. They are at Liverpool now, awaiting me, but I'll instruct them to meet me at a rendezvous in London."

"All right; but you'd better be careful how you word the message."

"You bet. We always arrange the next name we are to pass under long before we move from one place to another. It is more convenient. My better half is known at the Great Central Hotel—the place where she is staying—as Mrs. Kerney, and it will be in that name that I shall send the message. Let's get right along."

It was some half an hour later that Maitland and the mysterious Mr. Melson, from the States, having despatched an excellent luncheon, were sipping their liqueurs and smoking their cigars in the private sitting-room thay had engaged at the Magnificent.

Maitland turned from the window, whence he had been lazily surveying the shimmering sea, and his keen eyes met those of his companion.

"Suppose," he drawled, as he toyed with the little glass of Creme de Menthe before him, "you tell me just how the wind blows?"

Mr. Melson leant forward, regarding Maitland through the blue smoke of his cigar.

"Do you recollect the Great Eagle Gold Mining Swindle that startled the whole of the United Kingdon some twenty years ago?" he asked slowly.

Maitland puckered his brow.

"I can't say that I do," he answered. "Why, I couldn't have been more than about fifteen then, I guess, and such things didn't trouble me."

"No, I suppose not," Melson returned. "Then it will be necessary for me to give you a rough outline of the manner in which a partner and I engineered that and other coups of a questionable character and planned to bolt with a sum of half a million pounds sterling!"

The master-criminal's eyebrows elevated, and he grinned.

"Say," he exclaimed enthusiastically, "you're some genius, I guess!"

Melson shrugged wearily, and displayed no enthusiasm.

"I have often regretted since that I did not keep honest," he replied quietly. "By heavens, I have been repaid for going wrong—repaid a hundredfold! Listen! I am going to tell you a story of the past—a story that will explain to you why I am a man with an obsession—one who lives for but one object—to be bitterly revenged upon a fiend who betrayed me!

"Twenty years ago a man named Richard Cavendish and I—I was known than as Jasper Clench—were in business together as financiers and company promoters, in Throgmorton Avenue, London.

"We never played the game honestly. From the commencement of things we swindled, but we both were clever, and for years the police could not succeed in gaining any evidence against us condemning enough to warrant our arrest. We saw to that, and always we managed to keep clear of the law ourselves, although more than once our agents made slips and paid the penalty.

"There were scandals—black scandals—in connection with our names; but—well, you are a man of the world, and you will know how easily the British public forgets and how simple is the inexperienced person with money to invest.

"Well, matters went real strong for many years until the affair of the Great Eagle Mining Swindle. Both Cavendish and I felt that we had gone a little too far, so we realised on every available asset, to find that we were jointly worth £500,000, with which we meant to bolt.

"It was arranged that we should quietly get away in my partner's yacht, taking with us the whole of our resources in notes and easily negotiable securities. The whole of our wealth was hoarded together and placed in a portmanteau upon the day previous to that which we were to set sail.

"Cavendish wanted to get away that night, I remember, but my accursed greed urged me to wait for a large amount that was to arrive from a silly old woman upon the following morning. We came to words over this particular bit of business, but in the end, as was always the case, my will predominated over that of my partner, and, after locking the portmanteau in the office safe, we left for the day, agreeing to meet upon the next morning.

"I recollect that it was terribly foggy on the morning fixed for our hurried departure, and I was half frantic with impatience, as my cab crawled towards the office. When I arrived there, however, I found that the payment I had been expecting from my client had arrived by registered post, and my good humour was restored.

"I wondered what was detaining my partner Cavendish, for he was not in evidence, and my clerk told me that he had not as yet been to the office. I was about to settle down to wait for him, when I caught sight of a gladstone bag bearing his initials. I stared at it, for I knew that it had not been in the office when we had parted upon the previous evening. "A moment later, I saw that the safe door was standing ajar, and upon darting over to it, and flinging it open, I found that the portmantea—the bag containing our hoard of half a million—had vanished!

"Cavendish had stolen a march upon you?" Maitland suggested; and he could not suppress a smile, for the cunning piece of treachery appealed to him.

"Yes!" Melson rasped, his grey eyes suddenly flashing with badly suppressed fury. "The cur had come to the office during the night, opened the safe with his key, and made off with my share of the plunder as well as his own!

"I think for the moment I went mad! The next thing I realised, was that plain-clothes men had burst into the office, and that a pair of handcuffs had been clapped upon my wrists.

"I wildly demanded an explanation, for I could not see how any real proof that the Great Eagle business was a swindle could have been obtained! But, my heart sank like lead, when I heard that the engineer whom we had sent out to survey, and report upon the property had died in Paris, making, prior to breathing his last, a full confession that he had been bribed by us to say that the worthless Great Eagle mines were an Eldorado!"

"And Cavendish?" Maitland asked.

"He got clear away, the hound!" Mr. Melson—it will be easier to call him by his assumed name—cried, his hands clenching, his lips snarling down uglily. "He showed the authorities a clean pair of heels, and doubless lived the life of luxury and indulgence, whilst I—I ate out my heart in prison—worked in the quarries until my hands were scarred and bleeding! Oh, yes, there's not much question about the viper having enjoyed himself! I can picture him spending money like water in some distant land, where he would pose as a self-made millionaire!

"During those long, sleepless nights in Portland, I was wont to lay, and picture him eating of the choicest foods, drinking of the most expensive wines that his treacherously gained money could purchase! By perdition! How I've suffered! But I'll be revenged! I'll be revenged!

"I got ten years, but gained a remission of my sentence owing to good conduct. I have submitted to the insults of the warder—men who were not fit to lace my shoes—without a murmur, because I knew that each day I was spared in that awful place meant that I was nearer to getting even with Richard Cavendish!"

"When I was released, I sought my wife and child. I had a little money hidden away. I had kept it as a reserve fund, foreseeing the possibility of our plans going wrong! It was just over a thousand pounds, so that I engineered my search without much difficulty!

"You can judge of my feelings when I, at last, found that my poor wife had died. She had never dreamed that I was anything but an honest business man, and, from what I gathered, she had never been well since she received the shock occasioned her by the news of my arrest!

"But, it was not that that really killed her, Maitland! She had died of slow starvation, for the luck had gone against her! Indirectly, it was Richard Cavendish who was responsible for my darling's death! She did not suspect that either Cavendish or I were crooked, although it had been arranged that she, and my daughter, together with my partner's wife, were to meet us to accompany us upon the yacht. The two women thought that it was merely a long pleasure trip that we had promised ourselves, after a period of strenuous work!"

"Am I wandering? Perhaps, I am. I know that my troubles are of little interest to you. Let it suffice that, at last, I found the hovel in the slums where my poor wife had breathed her last. She had obtained work as a seamtress, and day and night she had worked to provide food and a home—such as it was—for our baby girl. She had at length fallen ill, but had still attempted to slave to protect the little one from the agonies of starvation, although she had, I realise, cared little for herself.

"She had got behind with her work, and fine after fine had been imposed upon her by the avaricious grab-all for whom she had worked. Since my return from America, I have made a point of searching for him, and bringing him to ruin. With my wealth it was quite easy, and I paid him back in his own coin, grinding him down as he had ground my wife, for I am not a man to easily forget or forgive!

"He is now a drink-sodden wreck of humanity, begging for coppers in the gutter, holding horses heads for the price of a drink!" He laughed harshly, and tossed his cigar into the grate; he had ruined it, for in his intense emotion he had crumpled it in his hand. "But that has really nothing to do with my story. Let me return to the time—it would be from eleven to twenty years ago—when I stepped from prison to again enter the free world.

"I have told you that I found my wife had died. I began to search for my little daughter. At last, I discovered that she had been taken in and cared for by a woman who had lived in the same house as my wife. It was some considerable time before I traced her, for she had been forced to change her quarters, owing to difficulty in paying rent. Out of pure good-heartedness, this woman had, for the time being, adopted my child. I gave her fifty pounds when I took little Violet away, and since then I have seen that she has been free from want.

"I went to America, taking my little daughter with me. She was then ten years of age, and has since blossomed into a very beautiful woman. I made money, Maitland! I always had a good headpiece on me, and I found it almost as easy to pile up the dollars by fair means as by foul! I started on very little capital, but by sheer hard work, and honest, though sharp dealing, I soon began to amass a fortune!"

"My luck never deserted me! Everything I touched seemed to turn to gold. I toiled every day and night to increase my wealth, ruthlessly crushing all my weaker opponents. Always there was my goal in the eye of my brain. My revenge upon the man who had betrayed me—the black-hearted hound to whom indirectly the death of my wife was due!

"In seven years I found that I was a millionaire several times over, but even then I did not stop in my rush for fortune! I continued to slave for money; it was my god, and nothing else—save my one great determination, to get even with Richard Cavendish—entered my mind!"

"And, now that you have come to England?" Maitland asked. "You have found this man?"

"Yes," Melson answered, in a hard tone. "My agents found him at Newmarket a month ago. From what I can gather, he has repented of his old life, and has been returning anonymously the amounts out of which we swindled out clients twenty years ago. He has had a phenomenal run of luck on the Turf. He races straight enough, it is pure good fortune when he wins, and very seldom that he comes a cropper.

"He owns a number of thoroughbreds, and time after time, his stable had brought off tremendous coups. By the way, you may have heard of him. He has changed his name to Riverton!"

Maitland whistled.

"Gee!" he ejaculated. "Do you mean he is John Riveton, the owner of the winner of the Two Thousand Guineas?"

"Yes."

"Then he is a rich man, from all accounts."

"No; on the contrary. I believe he is comparatively poor, for every available pound has been used to pay back our former dupes."

Maitland's lips curled into a sneer.

168

"The fool!" he muttered. "Say, what are your plans for vengence. After all, I reckon it ought to be easy for you to give him a dose of what you have been through. A few words to the police, and he would be arrested, would he not?"

"Of course, but that, my friend, is to come later. Bah! Do you think it would satisfy me only to know that he was in prison, and undergoing misery and humiliation such as I have endured? No! The viper shall be repaid a hundred fold. I intend to strike at him through his son!"

"He has a son, then?"

"Yes, and it is where he is concerned that I require the help of a man like you. I believe you are rather a clever forger?"

Maitland laughed softly.

"You pay me a compliment," he drawled. "But what has my skill in penmanship to do with your proposed revenge?"

"I will tell you," Melson replied. He had grown more calm now, and was lighting a fresh cigar. "Laurence Riverton, the son, is employed as a cashier in Fisher's Banking Syndicate, in Fleet Street. He has, by some means, discovered the truth about his father's past life, and has refused to touch a penny of his money, until every amount due to the people who were once our clients has been paid.

"My agents report that father and son are, in every other way, the best of friends. Laurence takes a deal of interest in horses, and is at his father's stables pretty well every week-end. He is said to be a good horseman, and has, I believe, ridden several of his father's candidates in over-the-sticks events."

"I think I'm beginning to see daylight," Maitland said. "You want me to work some hanky-panky business that will get Master Laurence into the deuce of a shindy at the bank?"

"Precisely," Melson agreed. "Look here!"

He drew from his pocket a cheque, and handed it to the master-criminal.

Maitland laid it upon the table before him, and studied it with narrowed eyes. He pursed his lips, then very grimly he smiled. The cheque was for seven thousand pounds, and had apparently been made out by someone who was inexperienced in penning such documents.

"By Colombus!" Maitland ejaculated, as he handed it back across the table. "I calc'late there's possibilities in that slip of paper. It would be the easiest thing in the world to add a 'ty' to the word seven, and slip in an extra nought over the dot signifying to seventy thousand pounds!"

"Exactly. That was my idea," Henry Melson said, with a hard little smile playing about the corners of his thin-lipped mouth. "You know whom the drawer is, of course?"

"I reckon so. He is a big bookmaker in Bond Street, and rumoured to be the straightest man of his kind in the United Kingdom. Say, what was the matter with him, I wonder, when he signed and passed that cheque?"

Melson smiled coldly.

"He had dined rather well with me," he said. "He has had a splendid time over the recent Irish racing, and was in high spirits. This cheque he paid to me was practically the only amount he had to pay over Long Lady, the outsider that won at forty to one the other day. He told me he had done remarkably well since the racing in England had been cut down, and the Irish meetings have become so popular. We went back to his office after our lunch, and he gave orders to a girl in his employ to draw me a cheque in settlement of my winnings.

"She, I imagine, was a new addition to his staff, and seems a bit slow and dull. Perhaps she had been rather hurriedly taken on to replace some young fellow who has enlisted. Anyway, she was an amateur at cheque writing. Charles McDonald is reported to be a careless individual in business matters; but I reckon he would have spotted the opportunity this cheque held out to a crook if it had not been for the mood he was in, and the fumes of the champagne that were in his brain.

"He handed it me with a flourish, not ever troubling to cross it, and after a few minutes conversation I left him.

"It was not until I arrived at my hotel that I noticed the lax manner in which the cheque had been made out, and simultaneously realised that it was drawn upon the bank in which the son of my enemy is employed.

"In a flash, the germ of a plot entered my brain, and I have been trying to puzzle out some way of altering this cheque, so that the swindle should appear to have been committed by young Riverton. There are many chences of getting at him, for to watch the man I so deeply hate, I have set up a neighbouring establishment at Newmarket, where I have a string of racehourses, although there I am not known as Melson. I race in the name of O'Mega—Cyrus O'Mega. I have frequently changed my name, in order that my old partner, should he encounter me and suspect my identity, would find it impossible to prove whom I really was.

"I have altered greatly, and I do not think Cavendish would know me, should he run into me unexpectedly I have managed to scrape up an acquantance with his son, and the young man generally pays me a visit when he is at Newmarket to see his father. I think now you have the full details of the position, and undertstand at what I am aiming. Can you devise some scheme by which my great end can be attained?"

"I guess so," the criminal answered. "But before we talk of that, I reckon there's one thing—or, rather, two—that I'd like to know. The first is how did you cotton that I was whom I am? Secondly, how much do I make out of this business, providing I am successful in bringing about what you desire?"

"I will reply to the second question first," Melson returned. "I don't care what my vengeance costs me! I will guarantee you ten thousand pounds if Laurence Riverton is disgraced and arrested. Will that be satisfactory?"

Maitland hesitated.

"Waal, you are a rich man," he said insinuatingly. "Another five thousand wouldn't break you."

"We clinch it at that!" Henry Melson agreed, with such readiness , that the American crook inwardly reproached himself for not asking more. "Fifteen thousand pounds shall be yours upon the day young Riverton is in the hands of the police, and I will pay all expenses in connection with the matter. Now, as to how I discovered your identity; it was really by chance."

"I had seen you upon several occasions at the American bar at the Royal, and from the first your figure seemed familiar to me. It was, however, quite by a fluke that I entered your room and saw you undisguised. I knew you in a moment then, for I had

169

seen you in Wall Street at the time when you startled New York by the coup you made over cornering wheat. You sailed very near the wind, then, my friend."

Maitland nodded.

"Correct," said he. "It was mighty near to swindling, and Fenlock Fawn's fingers itched to get busy with his handcuffs; but I was just within the law, and I could afford to chuckle up my sleeve. I am going to my room to think. Of course, I will accept the commission you wish to entrust to me."

"There is one last word," Melson said. "I am determined to take no risks in this matter. You must carry out whatever plot you conceive entirely alone and upon your own responsibility. I have had just over eight years' experience of prison life, and"—he shuddered—"I would sooner blow out my brains than pass beyond those bleak, grey walls a second time."

CHAPTER 8
The Experiments of Ezra Q. Maitland

Mr. and Mrs. Luke O. Verney had been for two days at De Feyer's Private Hotel and Boarding House in Bayswater, and it is fairly safe to say that since their arrival they had formed the topic of most of the conversation during meal-times at that cheaply, yet excellently managed institution.

They were looked upon as something of a mystery, and accused of possessing customs and manners that stout and garrulous Mrs. De Feyer, the worthy lady who acted as their hostess, described as "'aughty."

It did not suit the good woman's ideas and tastes when the very American Luke O. Kerney had calculated he and his wife would partake of their meals in the privacy of their sitting-room. Unless her guests were willing to sit at the long table in the harshly furnished dining-room, over which she was wont to preside, Mrs. De Feyer usually got it into her head that they had something to hide.

In the present instance, the landlady was perfectly correct, and could she have seen what was taking place in the quarters of her newly-arrived guests, her suspicions would have been increased a hundred-fold.

Ezra Q. Maitland had decided that it was as well to shift his quarters several times after his narrow escape from Sexton Blake. He had therefore, after wiring his wife at Liverpool, altering their arrangements, gone from the Magnificent Hotel at Margate to another at Broadstairs, where, under the name of Robson, he had spent the night.

Thence he had taken train to London and met his wife at a restaurant in Charing Cross Road, and from there they had journeyed to Bayswater, and engaged rooms at Mrs. De Feyer's third-rate hotel.

The master-criminal and his wife had just finished lunch, but they were not resting and chatting over their coffee, as Mrs. De Feyer was picturing as she discussed them at length with her other paying guests.

The dishes and cutlery had been pushed to one side of the table, and the cloth had been rolled back. The door was securely locked, and Maitland, who had removed his coat and rolled up his sleeves, seemed to be deeply interested in a curious experiment he was making.

Before him upon the table was an array of bottles, all neatly labelled, and containing liquids of various colours. He had just poured ten drops of a green fluid into a cup that was quarter-filled with water.

Broadway Kate who was now disguised by a wig of a rich, bronze-brown hue, was holding a second bottle in readiness for Maitland to use, and she seemed as deeply engrossed in the experiment as was her husband.

The Yankee carefully recorked the bottle he was holding, and placed it beside the others, then he took the bottle from his wife and slowly and carefully measured out ten drops from that, his thin lips moving as he counted.

The liquid in the cup had taken on a pale green colour, but now a remarkable change took place, as the criminal added the chemical from the vessel he was handling. The latter liquid was colourless, but it had the effect of turning the contents of the cup to a bluish-black shade, similar to that of ordinary writing ink.

"Now for the acid," Maitland ordered; and Kate took up a small paper packet and tipped its contents—a greyish powder—into the cup.

Maitland patiently stirred the liquid with a glass rod until the powder had dissolved. Then he seated himself, lit a cigar, and, taking out his watch, sat smoking for precisely ten minutes.

At the end of that time, he rose, and shifted the smoke to the extreme corner of his mouth.

"It ought to be O.K. now, girl," he said. "We'll test it."

Kate handed him a pen, provided with a new steel nib. Maitland carefully wiped it with his pocket-handkerchief, as though to make certain that it was perfectly clean, and that no covering of grease was upon its surface. He dipped the nib into the ink-like concoction in the cup, and, drawing a sheet of notepaper towards him, he scrawled upon it a few meaningless lines.

'He waited for them to dry, then produced from his pocket-book the cheque which the bookmaker, Charles McDonald, had given a few days previously to Mr. Henry Melson. The criminal carried it, together with the sheet of note, over to the window and scrutinised both long and earnestly.

"Too dark," he said at length. "Just a dash of blue, and the shade will be identical."

It was to a bottle holding a liquid of a bright blue colour that he went. He drew the cork and let fall five drops into the cup. He stirred it well, and, after cleansing the nib with scrupulous care, again made a test of the liquid.

When it had dried, and he had once more compared it with the ink upon the cheque, he chuckled with satisfaction.

"Exact!" he commented. "Now let us see if the vanishing trick works all right."

He blew out a wreath of smoke, and lay the cheque upon one side. He held the sheet of notepaper between his fingers and thumb, and, seating himself, sat with his eyes fixed upon it. It was noticeable that the first impressions that Maitland had made had become very, very faint. From a blackish-blue they had changed to a light brown hue; in a few minutes they were yellow, and a little latter they had faded away altogether.

A similar thing happened with the scrawling lines that the astute crook had more recently penned upon the paper. When, after roughly about twenty minutes, they had completely vanished from the surface of the paper, the criminal began to puff hard at his cigar, until its end was glowing fiercely.

He took the weed from between his teeth, and for the space of ten to fifteen seconds he held it directly beneath the spot upon the sheet of notepaper at which had recently appeared the ink lines.

When he finally replaced his cigar in his mouth and turned the paper in his hand, Broadway Kate, who had been intently watching his procedure, gave an exclamation of approval, for the impressions were again in evidence, outlined as plainly as they had first appeared.

"I thought I hadn't forgotten how to make the stuff, Kate," her husband drawled. "Do you remember the fraud we worked in Petrograd with it? We netted a cool five thousand dollars then, and the secret is going to bring us many times that amount on this occasion. It was a good speculation when I bought the secret of this particular invisible ink from that chap in the Bowery, and I reckon its infallible."

"It will will resist all tests to discover it once it has faded?" Kate said.

"Yes, except, of course, the test of heating. But let me get to work on the cheque. Humph!" He picked it up and examined it. "The writing's not hard to copy."

The criminal drew up his chair to the table, and using an ordinary pen and ink, he covered a sheet of paper with repetitions of the letters "ty," and the nought sign. From time to time his keen glance darted towards the cheque, and thence back to his efforts upon the paper.

Finally, he seemed to be satisfied, and changing the pen and ink in favour of his new nib and the concoction in the tea-cup, he placed the cheque directly before him, and slowly set to work.

He deftly added the letters "ty" after the word seven, and joined the "y" up with the word thousand. A moment later an additional nought had found its way amid the figures and Ezra Q. Maitland grinned down in evil exultation at his handiwork

The master-criminal did not stir until the additions he had made in the specially prepared ink had entirely faded away, leaving the cheque as it had originally appeared—for seven thousand pounds; then with great precision he folded it and replaced it in his wallet.

"It's a cinch!" he declared with conviction.

CHAPTER 9
The Big Cheque

Fleet Street at twelve-thirty on a Saturday morning!

True, not quite such a busy Fleet Street as it is to be seen on any other week-day, for many of the publishing offices are closed until Monday morning. Your editors, subs, artists, authors, and even certain classes of printers are prone to take somewhat long week-ends. But all the same, signs of busy life meet the eye upon every side.

Newspaper-boys on cycles dash hither and thither, others on foot rush to and fro, their glaring placards fluttering before them. Men and girls hurry this way and that along the wide pavements, all eager to complete their business for the day and seek their respective pleasures. Pleasures? Well, not in every case, strictly speaking, for many of them are going to put in an afternoon's war work, making munitions or packing them, striving to get recruits for Lord Kitchener's ever-increasing army, or brightening the lot of some crushed and mangled hero from the battlefield.

In the true sense of the word the first two tasks cannot be termed pleasures, yet, if such a contradictory statement can be excused, they are little else, for to engage in the slightest effort towards crushing the German barbarians must fill the breast of any true patriotic man or woman with a feeling of pride and satisfaction.

In half an hour the doors of Messrs. Fisher's Bank would close for the day. Laurence Riverton, cashier, sighed with relief as he glanced up at the clock and realised the fact.

In many ways office life did not suit him, yet for reasons that have previously been explained, he had refused to lead a life of idleness and independance, and energetically stuck to his post in Messrs. Fishers' Banking Syndicate, Limited, where he had been engaged for several years.

Immediately upon the outbreak of war, Laurence had offered himself for a soldier, fired with enthusiasm, and eager to fight for his country and king. But the luck had not been with him. A slight tendancy to eye-trouble had stood in his way.

It was nothing really serious, and did not necessitate his wearing glasses, save when he was engaged with his ledgers, yet it would have barred him from accurate shooting, and the medical man who had examined him had regretfully shook his head as he looked upon the young fellow's stalwart lithe-limbed form.

Laurence Riverton was a picture of British manhood. He must have stood six feet in his socks, and was proportionately broad. He was fair-haired and handsome, possessed of regular, clear-cut features that spoke of distinction, and a pair of large, frank blue eyes.

He was a man made for an open-air life, and inwardly he heartily detested the stuffy banking premises, where from nine-thirty in the morning till four in the afternoon he received and paid out every description of money—notes, gold, silver and copper, until he became cynical and indifferent where even the most colossal sums were concerned.

The young cashier's thoughts were far away as he sat upon his stool, momentarily idle. Without knowing that he did so, he stared unseeingly at the bald patch upon the crown of a fellow-cashier's head; then unconsciously his eyes wandered up the row of black-coated men who stood or sat in their places before the long counter, busily taking or paying-out money as the case might be.

Right at the rear of the long room, Mr. Septimus Fisher, the managing-director of the bank, was fussily dressing-down a long-suffering office youth for surreptitiously reading a periodical with a highly-coloured cover, upon which some Buffalo-Bill-like person was cooling shooting a Redskin whilst he flourished a bowie-knife in the snarling visage of another.

Mr. Fisher did not believe in boys reading literature of the thrilling order. He had strange ideas, and was wont to dub all boys' books as penny dreadfuls. Certainly, he had just cause in the present instance, for that illustration was truly a 'shocker"; but Septimus Fisher tarred all youths' periodicals with the same brush, and this was not the only direction in which he was narrow-minded.

He was a "kill-joy" nothing more or less. If he had had his way, picture-palaces, music-halls and theatres would have ceased to exist, whilst clubs and taverns would have been burnt to the ground. He believed that to even read the racing news meant that one was upon the direct road to ruin, and he termed football a dangerous and uncivilised game.

War he held as horribly sinful and barbarous, and he was always the prime mover in a "peace-at-any-price" campaign. He was the author of many letters to the Press, giving reasons why we should love the enemy, forgetting that the ruthless shelling of Scarborough, the air raids upon undefended towns, the atrocities in France and Belgium, and a hundred-and, one other dastardly actions had for ever made the bullying Power across the North Sea a nation to be looked upon with contempt and loathing.

To look at Mr. Septimus Fisher was to realise the true character of the man. He was thin to emaciation; his face was sallow and sour in expression, the eyes narrow and mean, the mouth drawn down at the corners in a look of perpetual misery, possibly occasioned because all men were not as he. His iron-grey, mutton-chop whiskers were the emblem of fussiness, as was his old-fashioned polo collar, with the austere black bow tucked precisely beneath the wings. He was short of stature, wizened of frame, cheaply dressed, and innocent of any kind of jewellery.

Laurence Riverton turned to hide a smile of contemptuous amusement, as the shrill of his employed rating the unfortunate boy brought the cashier back to his surroundings.

With a start, he realised that a customer was standing before the counter directly in front of him, and almost simultaneously became aware that the man was smoking a very strong cigar.

"I'll take it short," the latter said coolly, as he pushed a cheque across the counter to the young man.

Laurence took up the cheque; then his brows went up, used though he was to paying out large amounts, for the cheque was for no less a sum than seventy thousand pounds.

Just for a moment the young cashier stared at the pink slip of paper; then, as he saw the signature—"Charles McDonald," in bold round-hand characters—he pulled open his drawer and took out a sheaf of rustling notes.

He had never cashed a cheque for so large an amount before upon the signature of this particular client, yet he had frequently dealt with far larger ones which had been paid through another bank, and he knew that Charles McDonald, the well-known, self-advertised bookmaker of Bond Street, frequently paid out colossul sums in winnings to his numerous clients.

"Guess I've touched lucky," the man upon the other side of the counter drawled, and Laurence did not notice the anxious look that for an instant was in his piercing eyes.

The cashier nodded and smiled.

"You have indeed, sir," he agreed; then he turned and whispered to the man next to him. "There's a very big cheque here from Charles McDonald," he said. "I suppose it is all right to cash it, or would you see the guv'nor first, just as a matter of form?"

"I shouldn't trouble old Fisher this morning," the other cashier grinned. "He's in the most ratty mood you could possibly imagine. He nearly bit my head off when I went into his private room just now. Anything's all right from McDonald. He's eccentric, you know."

"All right," Laurence said. "I shall have to get you to lend me some notes to make up the amount, if you don't mind, Smithson."

"How much will you require?"

"Ten for a thousand, if you've got them," Laurence answered, making a quick calculation. "Thanks!" as he took the notes and pushed an I.O.U. towards his colleague. "I'm much obliged!"

He quickly took the numbers and pushed roll after roll over the counter towards the man who had presented the cheque.

"I think you will find that correct, sir," he said.

The American—such Laurence had taken him to be, by reason of his speech and twang—nodded, and leisurely began counting the notes.

The cashier had an opportunity of studying him whilst he was thus engaged, and realised that he looked just the sort of individual to have dealings with the Bond Street commission agent.

He was attired in a suit of quietly sporting design, and a handsome gold tiepin was just visible beneath his brown beard. His moustache was elaborately curled at the ends, and in every way he was debonair and well-groomed. His cheeks were ruddy, as though he were accustomed to spend much of his time in the open air, and there was just that touch of "horse" about him that must essentially cling to the habitual race-goer.

"That's O K , I guess," he drawled, as he stowed the notes away in his breast pockets. Gee! But it's the first time I've ever hit Charlie up like this! He's generally had all the luck. Say, do you know him?"

"A little," Laurence answered. "He is always a good sportsman, and doesn't seem to mind paying out any amount."

"That's because he's always on the right side in the end, sonny," the American chuckled, one of his lids drooping. "It's the bookie who always comes out on top, never you fear! Waal, good-day to you! I guess I'll go and make a hole in this boodle! I can afford to!"

He nodded affably, turned upon his heel and strolled from the bank, whilst Laurence Riverton, after cancelling the cheque without again glancing at it, placed it in his drawer with the others he had that morning taken and cashed, afterwards entering the amount in his ledger.

He little dreamed of the manner in which the Yankee's pulses had raced whilst he had apparently chatted so calmly. He was

172

not aware that already three characters upon this cheque had shown a face-value of seventy thousand pounds were slowly fading from sight, not could he foresee the dark clouds that were swiftly gathering and hanging over him, or guess that he had ever been confronted by one of the most unscrupulous criminals the world had ever known—Ezra Q. Maitland, blackguard, gentleman, thief, swindler, and scoundrel in general by instinct.

It was three o'clock. The City was beginning to grow deserted, and the majority of the business houses had disgorged their streams of workers, who had wended their way towards tram, tube, or 'bus.

Fleet Street had grown strangely quiet, although in certain newspaper offices, where work hardly ever ceases, the machines were still thudding busily away.

An hour and a half ago, Laurence Riverton and the other clerks employed at Fisher's Bank had taken their departure, and the door had been securely closed by the night watchman, whose duty it was to make his appearance on Saturdays at a little before closing-time, to remain upon the premises over the week-end.

Yet the managing-director of the firm was still in his private room, poring over a private ledger.

"Well, well!" Septimus Fisher muttered, as he closed the book with a snap, rose, and locked it in his safe. "The war doesn't seem to affect us so much as one might imagine! Our profits are good and have appreciably increased this month. Humph! Now what about this holiday question? It's scandalous that they should expect holidays at such times as these! Yet"—he smiled a thin smile, and rubbed his bony hands—"it's just as well that my clerks do have vacations, for it gives someone else a chance of constantly going through their books, which is often a check upon their honesty. Now, let me see!"

He re-adjusted his spectacles, and drew a memorandum book towards him.

"Humph, humph!" he sniffed. "Castle goes away this week, and will not return for a fortnight. Then Edwards takes three weeks. Bah! It's awful to think what dead money all these stupid customs—this ridiculous laziness—costs the bank! Edwards draws six pounds per week, which means that every year we pay him eighteen pounds for lazing about at some seaside resort for a matter of twenty-one days! Ah, Lane resumes his duties on Monday morning! I trust that he will return to work full of new vigour and conscientiousness; but I doubt if he will—I very much doubt if he will! Then there is Riverton; he goes after Edwards. Now, that reminds me!"

He closed the book, and took a letter from one of the pigeon-holes in his desk. It was addresses from the Riverton Training Stables, Newmarket, to Laurence Riverton, Esq., 45, Park Road, Forest Hill, and ran:

"Dear Mr. Laurence,—If you can get away from town this Saturday afternoon and can come to the stables, it will, I venture to think, be to your advantage. We are trying Serious Symons with his stable companions, Octopus, Wuffy, and The Luck, and it will be a trial that will do your eyes a bit of good! Of course, you already know the certainty both your dad and I consider Serious Symons to be for the Gold Cup race, which the Ascot authorities have agreed to be run at Newmarket this year, on account of the war. Barring accidents, I cannot see anything to beat him, and if you will allow me to take the liberty of advising you, I would urge you to chance a substantial bet on him. Trusting you will turn up I remain, yours very sincerely,

JACK HAYNES, (Trainer)."

The letter was a fortnight old, and it must have been a curious idea of right and wrong that had prompted the head of Fisher's Banking Syndicate to keep it in his desk, it not being his property, and having come into his possession quite by accident upon the morning it had been received by his cashier.

Laurence Riverton had been suffering from a bad cold and whilst in the presence of his employer on the morning that the letter had been delivered at his home, he had suddenly and violently sneezed.

Quite naturally, he had whipped out his handkerchief, and, unnoticed by him, the letter had fallen from his pocket to the ground. The mean, little eyes of Septimus Fisher had seen it instantly; but he was always anxious to take opportunities of spying upon his clerks, so he had held his peace, and when Laurence had quitted his room, he had picked up the epistle and perused it.

As he had realised that it was from a trainer of racehorses, Septimus Fisher's face had gone black with astonishment, for he had heard, despite his abhorrence of sport, of the famous racehorse owner, John Riverton, but until now had had no inkling that the latter was the father of his cashier, Laurence Riverton.

The old hypocrite had tried to tell himself that he was pained and shocked to learn that Laurence was even interested in the running of thoroughbreds, but, in reality, it was a feeling of suspicion—a mean, unreasoning suspicion as to the honesty of his cashier—that had been predominant in his narrow mind.

If a man put so much as a modest "shilling each way" upon the chance of a racer, Septimus Fisher at once determined that he was going to the bad or that he was already a confirmed rogue. Like most persons of his class, Fisher had never taken the trouble to go to a racecourse to study the many phases of life that are always to be seen there.

Had he done so he would have known that the rogues and crooks of the Turf are very much in the minority. True, there are a class of men—ay, and women, too—who make their living by tricking and "rooking" others in racing matters, yet to one of this order there are a thousand others who follow racing because they love horses, perhaps betting a little for the mere fun of the thing, or, on the other hand, never risking so much as a soverign, even when it is their own candidate who is running.

Fisher only looked upon the black side of things. He was for ever picturing honest men becoming thieves because they betted madly and ruthlessly, and he saw a ruined home, a starving wife and children, in every harmless navvy reading a sporting edition of a newspaper.

Therefore, it was only natural that he should look upon Laurence Riverton with the gravest and blackest suspicion now that he had discovered that he took pleasure in things connected with thoroughbreds.

Even as he folded the letter and stowed it carefully away in his desk, he told himself that it would be evidence against his clerk should Riverton at some future time fall to temptation and rob the bank.

The day was Saturday, and, as usual, the cashiers and other clerks left at about one-thirty. Mr. Septimus Fisher went to the strong-room immediately the last man was off the premises and the porter had closed the doors upon him.

Fisher had opened the door of the strong-room with his private key, then he had gone through Laurence Riverton's cash, checking it by his books. It was not out by so much as a penny-piece, and for the time being the old kill-joy's suspicions were proved groundless, although it must not be thought for one moment that they were entirely removed or lulled.

He made up his mind there and then that he would keep a constant watch upon his sportively inclined employee. And to-day he meant to repeat the examination he had made a fortnight previously.

He rose from his desk, took his keys from his pocket, and left his private room, locking the door behind him.

He passed along a corridor, and paused before a heavy iron door at the far end. This he unlocked, displaying a flight of stone steps leading down to the vaults below the bank.

He switched on the electric lights, for the place was dark and gloomy, then he descended the steps until he reached the flagged floor below. He turned to the left and reached the door of the strong-room, which was fitted with a combination lock in addition to one of ordinary make.

He placed a huge key in the latter, and turned it, next manipulating the combination and tugging open the massive door. He stepped within the strong-room. Again his fingers touched a switch and the place was flooded with light.

Upon a long shelf that ran along one side of the wall, were twelve articles that looked like shallow boxes. The were in reality the drawers which fitted into the counter before the cashiers as they sat in the long room above attending to the requirements of Messrs. Fisher's clients.

At the close of the day the drawers were removed from the counter, and a lid specially made to fit over them adjusted and locked. They were then carried to the strong-room, and the keys were given into the charge of Mr. Fisher.

The old banker went straight to the drawer marked with a figure eight, unlocked and removed the lid from it. Then, drawing a stool up to the shelf, he began going through Laurence Riverton's cash and notes, checking the amounts of each batch or bag with the entries in a small ledger that was also in the drawer.

They proved perfectly correct, and Fisher took up a bundle of cheques secured by an elastic band. He released them, and laid them upon the shelf, and one by one he checked them with Laurence Riverton's booking.

Presently Mr. Fisher's eyebrows contracted sharply, and spidery lines appeared upon his dome-shaped brow. He drew a long breath, and for a second or two sat staring from the entry book to a cheque drawn upon the account of Charles McDonald for the sum of seven thousand pounds.

Of a sudden he jumped to his feet with a husky cry, his thin face twitching, his eyes bolting from his head.

"What!" he almost screamed. "No, no! I must have made a mistake!"

He began to feverishly recount the gold and notes, losing his reckoning more than once, and beginning his check again.

At length, as the last batch of five-pound notes fell from his hand, he clutched at his temples wildly, and seemed for a moment incoherent.

"Sixty-three thousand pounds!" he spluttered, as he at length recovered himself. "Sixty-three thousand pound short in his money! Taken to back this horse that his father's trainer recommends to him! Oh, I know! I am a fool! I am familiar with human nature! The scoundrel! The thief! But I'll make an example of him! I'll, I'll——"

He snatched up the ledger and Charles McDonald's cheque, and went rushing towards the door, forgetting that he had left the lid of the cash drawer standing by the wall. He quitted the strong-room and locked the door with trembling fingers, then he went pelting up to the ground floor. At the top of the stairs he met the watchman, who looked at him in askance.

"Is anything wrong, sir!" the man asked respectfully.

"Wrong! Wrong!" Septimus Fisher waved his hands helplessly in the air. "It's more than wrong!" he groaned. "The bank has been robbed—robbed of sixty-three thousand pounds!"

"Good gracious, sir! You—you can't mean it, sir!" the watchman gasped. "When? How? Who could have done it, sir?"

"I know the identity of the culprit, my good fellow!" Septimus Fisher said, with almost a trace of grim satisfaction in his high-pitched, querulous voice. "The thief is one of my own cashiers. It was Mr. Riverton! There can be nothing gained by keeping the matter secret, for it will all come out in the papers after his arrest! Get on to the police at once. Try Snow Hill! I should think that would be the nearest station. Make sure you are in communication with the officer in charge, and put him through to my private room!"

"Very good, sir," said the excited watchman; and he hastened to the nearest instrument, whilst old Fisher disappeared into his sanctum.

Once alone, Septimus Fisher sank limply down in the chair before his desk and clasped his head in his hands. He was not used to experiencing excitement, and his head was aching madly. His brain was in a whirl, and as yet he could scarcely credit the evidence of his senses.

He sat with nervously twitching hands and blanched, scared face. He kept looking from the cheque for seven thousand pounds to the entry in the book for ten times that amount, with the air of a man who was trying to convince himself that he was not the victim of a hallucination—that his imagination was not playing him a sinister trick.

"Ah!" Septimus Fisher grabbed at the receiver of the telephone which stood upon his desk by his side as the bell whirred noisily. He clapped it to his ear, and found himself in touch with the official in charge of Snow Hill Station.

"Is that Mr. Fisher!" came the query.

"Yes, yes!" Fisher returned. "You are Snow Hill police-station?"

"Yes; your watchman has just rang us up and says that your bank has been robbed of a large amount. We——"

"Quite right! Quite right!" the banker agreed, in his petulant tones. "One of my cashiers has falsified his books to the extent of sixty-three thousand pounds!"

"Ah! Then it is really a case of embezzlement?"

"Yes, on a gigantic scale. The scoundrel has evidently fallen to sudden temptation. He required the money to bet with to—

to—er—back a certain horse! I happen to know it!"

"I see. When did you discover this deficiency in his accounts?"

"To-day, sir. To-day that ever is! He is now doubtless at—er—Tattersalls place at Newmarket or Epsom or somewhere"—Septimus Fisher's knowledge of racing matters was somewhat hazy—"ruthlessly betting with the money he has stolen. He has entered against a cheque for seven thousand the figures seventy thousand. He received and paid out the cheque to-day."

"You have, of course, made certain that the difference between the amount of the cheque and the entry is not a slip of the pen?"

"Of course I have!" Fisher snapped irritably. "I have been through his cash in hand twice!"

"And the name of this cashier, Mr. Fisher?"

"Laurence Riverton. He is the son of a Mr. John Riverton, of Newmarket, sir. A man who helps to blacken the world by running racehorses, sir! If I had my way——"

"I have made full notes of your information, sir," the official at the other end of he wire cut in, somewhat hastily. "It is a matter for Scotland Yard, with whom I will at once get into communication. You should hear from them within half an hour of my informing them of the facts of the case. You will be at the bank, sir, for some time?"

"Yes."

"Then very good, Mr. Fisher. I expect one of our men from the C.I.D. will join you in an hour, at the outside. I do not anticipate that we shall have much difficulty in running this man Riverton to earth."

"I hope not, sir—I hope not!" Septimus Fisher grated. 'He deserves ten years, and I hope that he gets it!"

And, with this charitable wish, he rang off, and again fell to glaring at the cheque drawn by M. Charles McDonald in favour of Henry Melson for the sum of seven thousand pounds.

———

CHAPTER 10
Sexton Blake Incredulous

"My dear Martin, almost from the first you ought to have known that the man was innocent."

Sexton Blake settled himself more comfortably in the roomy easy chair in the recess by the fireplace, tossed away the end of a cigarette and placed the tips of his long, nervous fingers together. He was regarding his colleague, Detective-Inspector Martin, from beneath drooping lids, and his attitude was languid, almost listless.

Three days had elapsed since the raid upon the shop of the "fence" Israel Samuels, and that benevolent old villain was now cooling his heels in a police-cell, with the prospect of a long spell of enforced confinement before him, during which he could think over his many sins.

Sir Digby Cranston had been overjoyed to recover his jewels, and according to a telephone message from his daughter that Tinker had taken that morning, the baronet was already beginning to show signs of making a wonderful recovery. If the truth be told, the old nobleman loved his jewels almost to the extent of worship, and their recovery had acted upon him as a tonic, doing him far more good than the skill and labours of half the specialists in Harley Street.

Sexton Blake and Martin had but one regret where the case was concerned—the complete escape of the master criminal from the States. Ezra Q. Maitland had vanished as though the earth had opened and swallowed him up, and although half the detectives of the C.I.D. were seeking him, not the vestige of a clue could any of them find as to his whereabouts.

Sexton Blake and Tinker had also been busily engaged in attempting to pick up their old enemy's trail, but they, like the Scotland Yard men, had for the time being failed. The detective had thought of the car he had seen vanishing in the distance when he had entered the Minories with Martin and the others, and upon consideration it had struck him that Maitland might have been able to escape in it, although he had been certain that it was not the crook who had sat at the steering wheel.

But, unfortunately, the car had been too far away for any of Maitland's pursuers to be able to make out the number, even if at the moment they had taken the trouble to try to note it, so Blake had no means of tracing the vehicle.

Inspector Martin lit his pipe and stared through the smoke at his friend. The latter had that morning put him upon the right track in a murder case that had been troubling the worthy official for the past three weeks, and he had called to inform Sexton Blake that a successful arrest had been duly carried out.

"Don't see how you knew Garner wasn't the man, Blake," the Scotland Yard man growled. "We found the piece of blue serge upon the nail in the dentist's gate, and there was a spot of blood upon it. Garner was the last man to be seen leaving the murdered man's house, and upon searching his rooms, we found the coat with the piece of material missing. We know now that he was the victim of circumstances, but even you must admit that the evidence was mighty black against him, at any rate, from the first appearance of things."

Sexton Blake nodded slowly and drummed his fingers together.

"Of course," he admitted, "unless one was very observant. Now, to be candid, Martin, you are really not quite observant enough." The official sniffed and shrugged his broad shoulders slightly.

"I'm as observant as most men," he protested. "I don't go about with my eyes shut."

Sexton Blake indulged in one of his rare smiles.

"I never insinuated such a thing," he objected. "You look, you see, yet you do not observe. As a test, shut your eyes and tell me how many pictures there are upon the walls of this room."

"No looking!" Tinker grinned, glancing up from some work he was doing at his desk by the window.

"Well, I'll be hanged if I'm going to fool about over this matter!" Martin growled, with a good-humoured grin. "I don't know, for I've never counted 'em."

"Precisely. You don't know because you have never taken the trouble to observe," Sexton Blake answered. "You have been in this consulting room some hundreds of times, and you must have seen the pictures, yet you cannot say how many there are, because you have not been observant enough to count them. Now, that is where we differ, my friend. There are nine. I know, because I have observed. There are twenty stairs leading from the hall and five from the hall down to Mrs. Bardell's sacred domains. I know these details for a similar reason. Now, with the Streatham murder case there was quite a lot that would have escaped the eye of the ordinary individual.

"The dentist was stabbed by a left-handed man. The position and nature of the wound proved that. Then again the piece of serge cloth that was adhering to the nail in the gate was soaked with rain. Upon the night in question we had in London a short, sharp shower, but the rain had entirely ceased by eleven o'clock, and there was no further downfall until several days later. Yet, the hands of the clock upon the mantel in the murdered man's consulting-room, which had been damaged in the struggle that ensued and stopped, pointed to a quarter before two.

"I took particular care to ascertain from the policeman, who had been upon the beat running past the house, at what time the rain had stopped in Streatham upon the night in question. After a little thought, he told me that it must have ceased well before midnight, as it did in the neighbourhood of Baker Street.

"Obviously, then, the man Garner had passed out of the house and left a portion of his coat behind long before the dentist had been stabbed, otherwise the piece of material would not have been saturated with rain. A little investigation proved, too, that Garner was not accustomed to using his left hand in preference to his right. The trace of blood upon the piece of serge looked ugly at first, then, in a flash, the explanation came to me, proving ridiculously simple. Garner had had a tooth drawn, and, of course, the blood had come from his lacerated gums. You followed how I traced the real culprit, and—Hullo, the 'phone again. See what it is, my lad."

Tinker obediently rose from his seat and crossed to the instrument.

"Hullo!" he said, as he clapped the receiver to his ear. "Yes, this is Mr. Blake's rooms. Scotland Yard? Right. Yes, old—I mean Mr. Martin is here, Sir Henry."

The Inspector jumped up like a parched pea from a shovel.

"The Chief Commissioner?" he asked quickly.

"Yes, Sir Henry Fairfax, sir. He's excited about something, the silly old josser!"

"S-s-sh!" Martin hissed warningly. "He'll hear you! Gimme the receiver! Hullo, Sir Henry. Yes. Martin speaking. I beg your pardon. No, I can't hear very well!"

"Tell the dear old thing to shout, sir," Tinker advised; and Martin turned a crimson, threatening face towards his tormentor as he hastily clapped his hand over the mouthpiece of the instrument. "His dulcet tones—"

"If you don't shut up, I'll break your silly head!" Martin snarled darkly. "Mr. Blake, throw him downstairs or something. He's—"

"Keep quiet, Tinker," Sexton Blake ordered. "Don't interrupt. The matter may be urgent."

Martin removed his hand from the mouthpiece. Then for the next few moments he was carrying on a conversation with his superior. Finally, he rang off and turned excitedly to Sexton Blake.

"There's been a big embezzlement at Fisher's banking house, in Fleet Street," he said. "Sir Henry knew that I was likely to be here, so rang up in the hopes of catching me. He wants me to go along to the bank at once. He seemed glad I was here."

"Of course," Tinker murmured, with a glance of awed admiration towards the official.

Martin did not deign to to reply verbally. He attempted to quell Tinker with a look of contempt that ought to have made him collapse then and there. It only made him grin, however.

"Do they know who is responsible for the theft?" Sexton Blake asked, as he reached for his cigar-case and took out a weed. Martin nodded.

"Yes," he returned. "A cashier in the bank's employ has entered a cheque in his ledger as seventy thousand pounds, and it is really only for seven thousand."

"And he is sixty-three thousand short in his cash in hand?" Sexton Blake queried, making a swift mental calculation.

"Yes," Martin agreed. "Not a small amount, is it?"

"Hardley," Blake said a little grimly. "What is the culprit's name?"

"Riverton!"

"What!" Sexton Blake sat upright in his chair, and the newly-lighted cigar fell from his hand. "Did you say his name was Riverton?"

"Yes," Martin said again, and he regarded his friend curiously, for it was seldom that Sexton Blake was wont to show much animation.

"Do you know his Christian name?" the private detective asked sharply.

"It is Laurence. He is the son of John Riverton, a racing man, of Newmarket. From what I can hear, the son has got into a mess over horses."

"Fiddlesticks!" Sexton Blake snapped, with an impatient gesture of his hands. "It's impossible!"

"I only know what I've heard," Martin protested, with a careless raising of his brows.

"Of course," Sexton Blake admitted, as he picked up his cigar. "But, you see, I happen to know young Riverton personally, and I should be ready to stake my reputation that he is not the kind of man to turn thief! He is a member of one of my clubs, and is as straight as a die! He is far too sensible to back a horse for more than he could afford!"

"Well, he's the money short, anyway," Martin answered. "He's an amateur criminal, and ought to be fairly easily found. I suppose I'd better say good-bye and get along to the bank at once. Hullo, what's on?" as Blake rose and flung off his dressing-gown.

"I am coming with you, with your permission," the Baker Street detective answered quietly.

"Surely there's no need. The matter is simple enough, although there's a good deal at stake. I'll guarantee I'll have him clapped in a cell within twenty-four hours, Blake."

"That," Sexton Blake answered, "is just what I wish to avoid, if it is at all possible."

"You mean——"

"That I don't believe Riverton stole the money," the private detective returned, with conviction.

"To me, it seems rather obvious that he did," Inspctor Martin objected. "You will think so, too, when you know the full facts of the case, as I have heard them from Sir Henry Fairfax. Each cashier at the bank removes at the end of the day his drawer containing the money he has received. He is provided with a special lid, which fits upon the top of the drawer and is locked. The key is then handed over to Mr. Septimus Fisher, the head of the bank, and he returns it when the cashier comes the next morning—or rather Monday morning in this case—so that the man may make up his accounts before the bank is opened some half hour later.

"Mr. Fisher was for some reason suspicious of Laurence Riverton, and went through his books and money in hand. He discovered the deficiency and at once communicated with Snow Hill Police Station, whence the Yard learnt the news."

Sexton Blake was thoughful for a moment, a deep line between his eyes.

"What made Mr. Septimus Fisher suspicious of his employee?" he asked.

"I don't know," Martin replied. "You still intend to come?"

"Yes," Sexton Blake replied. "I shall not believe that young Riverton has turned crook until I definitely prove it for myself. If I find that I have been mistaken in him, I will never consider that I am a judge of human character again. Tinker, my jacket and hat. You had better come along too. You have been indoors a good deal of late and a blow in the car will do you no harm."

A few minutes later Sexton Blake's great, grey car was standing before the house in readiness to start, and at a sign from his master Tinker climbed into the driver's seat.

Martin and Blake took their places and the lad threw in the clutch, sending the car humming forward.

When they reached Fleet Street they were not long in espying the palatial building in which the firm of Fisher carried on their business, and Tinker brought the car smartly to a standstill in the kerb.

"Wait here, lad," Sexton Blake ordered, as he alighted followed by the Scotland Yard official. "Should I want you, I will let you know."

He mounted the steps with the Inspector, and the latter tugged with official vigour at the bell, the doors being tightly closed. It was not long before the detective's summons was answered by a constable, and he saluted respectfully and stood upon one side as he recognised Inspector Martin.

"Anyone about?" Martin asked gruffly.

"Yes, sir. Detective-sergeant Hemmings is with Mr. Fisher in his private room."

"Lead the way," Martin commanded, with a curt nod. "Mustn't lose any time."

The man saluted again and swung round upon his heels. He led his superior and Sexton Blake to Septimus Fisher's sanctum, where that gentleman was closeted with a broad-shouldered individual, whose appearance at once suggested the official detective force.

"Detective-Inspector Martin and Mr. Sexton Blake," the constable announced, for the famous private investigator was well-known to him.

Septimus Fisher looked a trifle surprised as he heard the name of the latter detective.

"This is entirely a matter for the police, Mr. Blake," he said fussily. "I cannot see my way to incur the directors unnecessary expense in this unfortunate matter."

Sexton Blake looked at the little, shrivelled-up banker much in the manner of one who is studying a newly-discovered curiosity. At first glance, the detective knew the kind of man he had to deal with, taking in the mean, squinting eyes, the sour, jaundiced face, and the general appearances that betokened a suspicious nature.

"I beg your pardon," he murmured, with a raising of his brows.

"I said that I could not allow of there being any unnecessary expenditure over this audacious theft," the little banker repeated irritably. "However cheaply you worked, my fellow-directors would consider your fees superfluous and unwarranted."

"Exactly," Sexton Blake agreed, and there was a suggestion of sarcasm in his voice, "I quite realise what you mean, Mr. Fisher. I shall, however, neither charge nor expect any remuneration for what I do here. Your director's pockets will be no lighter by reason of my taking an interest in this case. I am working upon behalf of Mr. Laurence Riverton."

"What! You have seen him!" the banker shouted excitedly.

Sexton Blake shook his head.

"Why, no," he returned, "yet all the same it will be upon his behalf that I shall work. He is a friend of mine and I am anxious to prove his innocence of the crime that has been laid at his door."

Septimus Fisher laughed spitefully.

"You will indeed be a clever man to do that!" he sneered.

Sexton Blake tilted his shoulders and the lids drooped almost sleepily over his eyes.

"I have been called clever in the past," he said indifferently, "and perhaps I shall live up to my reputation in the present instance. However, I will leave that for others to judge after I have cleared up the case. Why did you deem it necessary to check your cashier's accounts?"

The banker flushed confusedly, for the question had been fired at him with a suddenness that had taken him off his guard.

"I had—er—grown suspicious that his habits were scarcely those that a young man in his position should cultivate," he answered.

"My chief gave me to understand that Riverton had got into a mess through betting," Martin put in. "Is that correct, Mr. Fisher?"

"I—er—believe so."

"You do not know for certain?"

"Well—er——"

"We must be in possession of the plain facts of the matter," Martin said gruffly, and his eyes were fixed keenly on the banker's face. "If you will answer our questions straightforwardly——"

"I—er—will, of course, do so," Septimus Fisher interrupted. "I will admit that I do not know definitely that Riverton is in any trouble over his indiscretions in the direction of horse racing, yet—"

"Yet you know that he has been indiscreet?" Sexton Blake put in, in a hard voice.

Septimus Fisher turned upon him almost fiercely.

"Any man who goes racing is indiscreet, sir!" he snapped, with feeling.

"I do not agree with you," Sexton Blake objected bluntly. "The running of thoroughbreds is the finest sport a Britisher could follow, and it is only the betting when it is carried to extremes that is harmful. There are blackguards upon the Turf as there are in every other walk of life, but, there are also thousands of straight, honest men who make a legitimate living out of breeding and racing."

"We shall never agree, sir!" Fisher retorted sharply.

"Possibly not," the detective answered carelessly. "We are both allowed to have our own opinions. I do not wish to argue the matter, and merely wanted to point out to you that because a man is a judge of a horse and is interested in Turf matters it does not necessarily signify that he is a villain. We may assume, I suppose, that you know Mr. Riverton's father to be an owner of racehorses?"

"I am aware of that fact now, but the younger Riverton was never honest enought to inform me of his father's Turf connection. I only discovered that my cashier was interested in racing by reading this letter a fortnight ago. You will see that it suggests he should make a bet upon some horse that is shortly running, or has already run, at Newmarket."

"It is to run next week," Sexton Blake said, as he perused the epistle the banker had handed him.

"What is it?" Martin asked, with ill-suppressed eagerness, for he knew that Riverton's stable was always bringing off "good things," and wondered whether the letter contained a tip.

"It is Serious Symons for the Gold Cup."

"Do Riverton's say it'll get there?" Martin suggested, craning his neck and trying to read the letter over his friend's shoulder. "Of course"—he had caught the indignant glance that Septimus Fisher was levelling at him—"if it wins and young Riverton has backed it, he might want to refund the money he is short of now."

"How did this letter come into your possession, Mr. Fisher?" Blake asked casually, as he handed it over to his colleague.

"It fell by accident from his pocket whilst he was conversing with me in this room."

The detective made no comment, but his eyes had grown cold as he turned away.

"With your permission, we'll take a glance at the cash in Riverton's till and his books, Mr. Fisher," Martin suggested.

"I have the cheque and the ledger in which his cash is entered here."

"You have verified the amount of money all told in the till of the accused, Hemmings?" Martin asked, turning to his subordinate.

"Yes, sir."

"I think we'll just check the amount, as a matter of form," Sexton Blake said. "It would be just as well, you know."

"All right," Martin answered. "We'd like to do as Mr. Blake suggests, sir"—turning to the banker.

The detectives were conducted by the guide to the strong room and shown the till, which still stood open upon the shelf with its fellows.

Sexton Blake and Martin went through the contents and agreed upon the amount, then the former picked up a slip of paper.

"I see that it was necessary for Mr. Riverton to borrow ten thousand pound notes from someone named Smithson," he commented. "What exactly does that mean?"

"Oh, merely a matter of one cashier obliging the other," the banker explained. "Riverton, I suppose, ran short of a thousand pound notes, and gave Smithson—the cashier who sits next him—an I.O.U. until they made up their accounts on Monday morning—or rather, when they ought to have made up their accounts. It is my firm believe that Riverton never will return to the bank!"

"Can we verify this I.O.U. business?" Martin queried.

Fisher nodded.

"I can unlock Smithson's till, and doubtless we shall find the I.O.U.," he said.

This was done, and the slip of paper Laurence Riverton had handed his fellow-clerk was brought to light and examined.

"It would be utterly impossible for anyone to tamper with Riverton's money whilst he was absent for a few moment from the counter?" Blake asked.

"Practically so. It is a strict rule of the bank that a cashier must lock his till should he leave his place for the shortest period. Besides, Riverton would check the amount of money he had in hand with the entries in his ledger before he placed the lid upon the till and locked it. Had he have been such a serious amount short and had had no hand in the deficiency himself, he would naturally have reported the affair to me immediately."

"I follow you, Mr. Fisher. No one could gave got at the money after the till was locked?"

"No one! All the keys and locks of these tills are of a different pattern and there are no duplicates. Only one key exists to each lock and these are given into my charge at the close of each day."

Sexton Blake was silent for a moment. He began to sort the various articles in Laurence Riverton's till, and presently came to an A.B.C.

"Mr. Riverton has gone to Newmarket," he said suddenly.

"How do you know?" Martin jerked.

Sexton Blake pointed to the figures "2.13" that appeared on the cover of the railway guide.

"There is a train from Liverpool Street for Newmarket at that time," said he. "He has evidently gone down to see his father."

"He may not have written that memorandum to-day," Septimus Fisher objected.

"He did," Sexton Blake assured him. "Look at the ink. It is quite bright, which proves that the figures have been recently penned. Had the note been made yesterday or before the ink would have had time to become dull and faded slightly. We shall now examine his book and the cheque about which there is the question, if you will permit us, Mr. Fisher."

The banker inclined his head in agreement.

"Come up to my office," he said.

The little party quitted the strong room—after Fisher had relocked the tills. He also secured the strong-room door and set the combination; then, in company with the detectives, he made his way to his private room.

He stepped over to his desk, indicated an open book which lay there and produced the cheque for seven thousand pounds. Sexton Blake's eyes narrowed as he saw the name of the drawer.

"Charles Macdonald," he murmured. "Of course, the big commission agent of Bond Street."

"The same, Mr. Blake," the banker admitted.

The detective ran his fingers down the entries in laurence Riverton's ledger until he came to the name McDonald. He saw that the figures "£70,000:0:0" had been boldly entered against it in the cash columns.

"Strange," he muttered. "I must admit that at first sight matters look black for young Riverton. However, there are several points that are against his being the thief. For instance, if he had robbed the bank of this amount, does it not strike you that it would be little short of madness for him to go to his father's place in Newmarket?"

"He may have relied upon the deficiency in his cash not being discovered until Monday, Blake," Martin suggested.

"Yes, that is so. Now, I wonder why it was necessary for him to borrow from his fellow cashier, Smithson."

"It was a bit cool if he actually borrowed the money to increase his haul," Inspector Martin remarked.

"Decidedly cool," Sexton Blake returned a little drily. "Do you know Mr. Henry Melson, the man to whom the cheque is made out, Mr. Fisher?"

"No; I have never heard of him before. But that is not at all extraordinary. Mr. McDonald deals with all classes of people, and is always putting on new clients."

"Exactly. I suppose he would take a bet from anyone, provided no money was sent before the race?"

"If he knew they were good for the amount they were staking."

Precisely. I wonder if it would be possible to get into touch with the man Smithson?"

Fisher thought for a moment.

"It so happens that it would," he answered. "He is a hardworking man and has a large family, so he is not averse to adding to his income. He sometimes takes work home, and he has an arrangement with a call-office near at hand, in case I wish to ring him up."

"Ah, that is indeed fortunate—that is, if he will be in to-day!"

"I imagine he will," Fisher stated. "He took home a good deal of work, I know. If you will excuse me, gentlemen, I will endeavour to get into communication with him."

He sat before his desk and drew the telephone towards him. He gave a number, and after some little delay, whilst the cashier was fetched from his house, he was put into touch with him.

"May I speak?" Sexton Blake queried, after Septimus Fisher had explained what had occurred at the bank. "Thank you! I am a detective, Mr. Smithson. Can you tell me why it was necessary for Mr. Riverton to borrow ten thousand-pound notes from you this morning?"

"Yes," came the reply. "He required them to make up the amount of a large cheque he was cashing."

"Do you know who drew the cheque?"

"Yes. It was one of our largest customers, a Mr. Charles McDonald."

"Do you know the amount of the cheque?"

"No; but it was a large one. Mr. Riverton mentioned that it was a big amount, and asked my advice as to whether he should speak to Mr. Fisher before dealing with it. I said I thought there was no need, as Mr. McDonald deals in large sums and is a trifle eccentric."

"Thank you! That is all I wish to know. Good-bye!"

Sexton Blake replaced the reciver and turned to the others.

"We shall search for Mr. Riverton at Newmarket," he said. "Will there be any objection to our taking charge of this cheque, Mr. Fisher?"

"No; so long as you take care of it, and return it in due course."

"I will be personally responsible for it," Sexton Blake answered. "Have you noticed, by the way, anything peculiar about it?"

"Yes; it is very carelessly made out. These blanks that appear between the words and figures show the utmost inexperience."

"Just so. Indeed, a moderately clever forger could easily alter this cheque so that it read as though it had been made out for seventy thousand instead of seven thousand pounds."

"Why, yes, it would be quite easy! But that has not been done, so there seems little to be gained in putting the point forward." Sexton Blake scrutinised the cheque for along moment, holding it close to his eyes at several different angles.

"It does not appear to have been 'faked', certainly," he answered, as he folded it and put it away in pocket-book.

"You wish, I take it, to charge Riverton with his embezzlement?" Inspector Martin queried, when they stood upon the steps of the bank.

"Yes!" old Fisher snapped, his thin face setting harshly. "I shall show the villain no mercy! The law must take its course. Good-day, gentlemen! I sincerely hope that you will find him and place him under arrest before many hours have passed."

"I, too, hope that we find him without delay," Sexton Blake returned. "We shall then possibly learn that what precise mode of trickery has been employed to swindle both him and you."

"I fear I don't understand, Mr. Blake," Septimus Fisher returned cynically. "The man is a thief! The case is most clear. All men in his position who follow the pernicious so-called sport known as horse-racing must sooner or later overstep the mark!"

Sexton Blake shook his head at him reprovingly

"We must not get upon that subject again, Mr. Fisher," he said quietly, "or we shall not get to Newmarket to-day. I would like to say a word in your ear before we part. If you are so fully convinced that our finest sport is sinful, why do you increase the profits of your bank by accepting and using the money of one of the largest bookmakers in the United Kingdom? It is scarcely practicing what you preach, you know. There is one other thing. When another person's property comes by accident into your hands, the most honourable course would be to return it to him. I am referring to the letter Laurence Riverton dropped in your office. It was not over honest to read it, you must admit. I wish you good-day, sir!"

And with that the detective strolled down the steps and gained the car, leaving the little wizened banker positively speechless with indignation.

"My word, Blake, but you riled him!" Martin chuckled, as Tinker started the car.

"He deserves to hear a little broad-minded speaking, my friend," Sexton Blake answered calmly, as he lit a cigar. "The man is a hypocrite—an out-an-out hypocrite! There is no other description to fit him!"

CHAPTER 11
Laurence Riverton's Love

No one at Newmarket dreamed of questioning whether Mr. Cyrus O'Mega, the gentleman who had recently bought up a well-appointed racing stable and a palatial mansion attached, was an American, and precisely what he seemed—a wealthy man whose sole object was to follow the sport he loved.

His manner and little eccentricities of speech seemed to proclaim his nationality without a shadow of a doubt; and had any of the "lads" employed by him been told that he was in reality a Britisher, that in London he was known under the alias of Henry Melson, that Cyrus O'Mega was merely another alias, and that his true identity was Jasper Clench, ex-convict and swindler, they would not have believed their informant.

Indeed, they might have questioned his veracity in a manner that was far more forcible than polite, for Mr. O'Mega had always proved, despite a tendency to sternness, that he was fair and just to the last degree.

There was not a lad in the stables, too, who would not have risked his very life for his employer's charming daughter. Violet O'Mega—as they knew her here at Newmarket—was as gentle and kind as she was dainty and beautiful, always ready to listen to the troubles of others, or to lend a helping hand to those in need. In addition to this, she was a born horsewoman, and could sit the most troublesome steed as though it were part of herself, a fact that speedily earned her the admiration of all the stable hands.

The O'Mega stables were situated in a valley upon the heath, at no great distance from the famous race-course. Usually there were from ten to a dozen thoroughbreds in training here, and, though he was practically a new-comer to the Turf, Mr. Cyrus O'Mega's candidates had already won for him several good races. At the moment, Cyanin, a smart three-year old, which the reputed millionaire had recently purchased, was considered something of a "good thing" for the Gold Cup, to be decided upon the following Tuesday, although "the heads" admitted that it would find Serious Symons, a racer trained at Riverton's stables, very hard to beat.

There had already been quite a lot of betting at the London clubs upon the forthcoming event, for now that racing had been so curtailed owing to the war, an occasional meeting at headquarters was thought quite a lot of. Cyanin and Serious Symons were to-day quoted as co-favourites at four to one, and considered by many keen judges to be wonderfully evenly matched.

The weather, if the present conditions lasted, promised to be excellent for the meeting, which commenced upon the following Tuesday.

All day long the sun had been shining radiantly, and the heath looked gloriously fresh and green. It was drawing towards late afternoon and a gentle breeze had sprung up—a breeze that was deliciously scented with the smell of the rolling turf, and was at once refreshing and invigorating.

The lads had completed their work for the day, and the stable-yard was deserted as Henry Melson sauntered down the steps of his house, crossed to the great gates and entered. He was accompanied by Ezra Q. Maitland, although now the master-criminal appeared strikingly different to the brown-bearded, sportively-dressed man who had visited Fisher's Bank that morning.

He had gone back to his character of Luke O. Kerney, from America, and appeared as he had done in the De Fayer Boarding House at Bayswater.

His guise was a truly marvellous piece of work, and Maitland was soon to thank his lucky stars that he had taken so much trouble with it. But more of this anon.

He looked to be about sixty years of age. A grey wig covered his own dark hair, and was secured in place so skilfully with spirit gum that the keenest pair of eyes could not detected that it was not natural. A beard and moustache of the same hue adorned his pale face, and even his eyebrows now possessed a whitish tinge, whilst their slant had completely altered. To complete the metamorphosis, a pair of tinted spectacles concealed Maitland's eyes. This was an old trick of his, and one that he had found very, very useful in the past.

"Thank goodness, we can talk here!" Henry Melson said, as he lit a cigar and proffered his case to Maitland. "It was impossible to say anything before my daughter, and I have been burning to know how the business went off."

"It worked like a charm, I reckon," Maitland grinned. "I walked into the bank and held my cigar beneath the spots of the cheque that I had treated with the invisible ink. The additions making it read as seventy thousand came up all right, and young Riverton paid out the amount in notes with hardly a murmur."

"He did make some demur, then?"

"Yes, but nothing to speak of. He had to borrow from the cashier next him and asked if he should go and see the manager, the cheque being for so large an amount to cash forthwith. The other advised him not to, however, and he paid me out."

"He didn't mention the amount to the other clerk?"

"No, fortunately. I kept cool and counted the notes before I left the bank, but once I was outside I hailed a taxi and told him to drive like the dickens to Charing Cross. I got another taxi there, and went to Westminster Bridge, then in a third cab went back to my hotel at Bayswater. You see, I meant covering my tracks all Sir Garnet!"

"You are a clever villain, my friend," Henry Melson said. "You have the notes with you?"

"Yes. I guess I understood that young Riverton would be paying you a visit this evening?"

"He is almost bound to do so. He never visits his father's stable without looking us up. I reckon"—he smiled in a very sinister manner—"my daughter attracts him."

"Gee!" Maitland chuckled. "Quite melodramatic! The son who is to be ruined to pay off an old score against the father in love with the daughter of the man who has betrayed him! Really, I guess it's real extra!"

"The position is assuredely a trifle complicated," Henry Melson agreed. "But I do not think Violet cares a rap for him. Riverton will possibly be in time for tea. If such is the case, you should get your opportunity easily enough. I will suggest that you and he go to the bath-room to wash your hands. He is almost sure to remove his coat, and you know when to do then. Hush! Here comes my daughter!"

Maitland turned to see a slim, girlish form entering the stable-yard.

Violet Melson was not unlike her father, yet her face lacked the pallor and stern expression that was always apparent upon his.

Her hair was auburn chestnut, which Joshua Reynolds loved to paint, with eyebrows to match; mouth just a little trifle large, yet as sweet and expressive as her dark hazel eyes.

Her complexion and figure were eloquent of youth and health, and when she spoke her voice was full of that music that womanly refinement and delicacy combine to give, albeit it held a trace—the very slightest trace—of a twang that long years spent in America had irresistibly gifted it with.

"Poppa, do you remember your promise?" the girl said, as she reached the side of the two men. "You said you would take me right along to see Cyanin. I haven't had a chance of looking him over since he was cured of that touch of coughing."

Henry Melson's expression softened as he smiled into the beautiful, eager face.

"Of course I remember, little girl," he said tenderly. "You would like to see him now?"

Violet nodded.

"I should so much," she answered. "I do hope that he will win."

"I guess he'll be somewhere there at the finish, Vi," the millionaire said, with conviction. "The cough was nothing. In fact, I believe it only existed in my trainer's imagination. Joe Sparks is a good fellow, but just a wee bit pessimistic. Care to take a peep at the colt, Kerney?"

"Bet on it, Mr. Melson," Maitland drawled. "If——"

"Hush!" the American warned. "Not that name here. Kerney. Try to remember the other."

A troubled look sprang into his daughter's beautiful eyes.

"Why is it necessary to pass under a false name here, dad?" she asked impulsively. "You have always put me off when I have asked you to explain and——"

"My dear child," the ex-swindler protested, "heaps of people race under a nom-de-plume. I"—he hesitated momentarily whilst his brain worked quickly for an excuse—"I do a great deal of business with people who are not in agreement with horseracing, and I am anxious that they should not know that I have anything to do with it. You must be careful not to disclose my secret to anyone. Mr. Kerney knew me in America, and, as he met me here some days ago quite be chance, I had to let him into the know, I guess."

"Oh, I reckon you can rely upon my discretion," Maitland remarked, with a light laugh. "Is this the stable he's in?"

"Yes," Melson said as he took a key from his pocket and unlocked the door. "This way. Isn't he a beauty?"

"He's more than that!" Maitland exclaimed, genuine admiration in his tones. "It's got to be a real good horse that'll beat him. I guess I'll chance a pony on him, anyway."

"Back him each way and you are on a dead certainty, Kerney," Harry Melson said, with quiet assurance. "He's bound to get in the first three barring a serious spill, or some such unforeseen accident. Ah, Cyanin, you cute old card, I believe you know you could beat everything in the race if it suited you!"

He was stroking the thoroughbred's velvety nose, and the beautiful creature seemed to greatly appreciate the caress.

He was indeed a splendid colt, bright-eyed and alert in appearance. Every curve of his glossy body spoke of enormous speed and breeding, whilst his temper seemed to be good, and there was nothing of the "rogue" about him.

Violet moved forward and laid her hand upon his long, slimly-made neck.

"You dear," she said softly. "I am sure you are going to win for us."

"I'll spend my winnings on a new gown for you if he does, Vi," Henry Melson said. "I wonder who that is in the yard?" he said, his head raised sharply in a listening attitude.

"My I come in?" said a voice from without, and Violet exclaimed with a curious eagerness:

"I believe it is Mr. Riverton!"

She proved to be right, for a moment later the figure of the young cashier from Fisher's Banking Syndicate was framed in the doorway. His eyes lighted up, just for an instant, as he saw that Violet was present.

"Come in, Riverton, my boy!" Henry Melson bade cordially, although he had averted his head to hide the hatred in his eyes. "It'll give you a chance of seeing Cyanin. You can hedge, so that you don't lose over the money you've put of your father's horse for the Gold Cup next Tuesday."

Laurence Riverton laughed good-naturedly as he came forward and shook hands with Violet and her father.

"As a matter of fact," said he, "I haven't so far put a penny on Serious Symons, my dad's candidate, although I think he'll win."

"You think he'll beat Cyanin?" Maitland asked carelessly.

"It will be a close thing between them, sir," Laurence answered, with a non-committal shrug of his shoulders.

"You must let me introduce you to my friend, Laurence," Henry Melson said. "I had forgotten you had not met before. This is Mr. Luke O. Kerney, from the States. Mr. Kerney—Mr. Riverton, the son of a neighbouring owner."

"I am very pleased to meet you, Mr. Kerney," Laurence responded formally, as he extended his hand, although for some strange reason he at once took an instinctive dislike to the American. "Will you be here for the meeting next week?"

"I guess so, unless I get some urgent cable that will make it necessary to sail by Monday's boat to New York," Maitland replied. "So your dad owns Serious Symons, the co-favourite with Cyanin?"

"Yes. Apart from the other horses' chances, the race will be a rattling good one to watch," Laurence said. "My father is as keen on the chance of his horse as Mr. O'Mega is about his, and he has just cause. To my way of thinking, there's not a pin to choose between the two. They will fight it out to an exciting finish."

"We must get back to the house," Melson said at that moment. "It is long past tea-time. Of course, you will stop, Riverton?"

"Well, really, I feel almost ashamed to," the young man laughed. "I declare I am for ever walking in at tea-time."

"Oh, nonsense!" the millionaire protested. "Why, we only see you on Saturdays. Take Violet along, will you? But what about your horse? Did you ride over?"

"Yes. May I leave him in the stable?"

"Certainly. Bring him in and put him in that empty stall there. There are some oats going begging, and he can amuse himself."

"I won't detain you for more than a few seconds," Riverton exlaimed, as he hastened from the stable.

He returned almost at once, leading a superb black gelding. He made the animal comfortable in the stall Henry Melson had indicated, then the little party walked towards the house, Laurence and Violet some little distance ahead of the two elder men.

If the truth be told, Laurence Riverton looked forward to the few hours he was able to spend in the society of the slender girl by his side. From their first meeting he and Violet had been irresistably drawn to each other, and Laurence found himself desiring wealth as he had never wanted it before.

Although he tried to hide his feelings, he was passionately in love with the girl. Her pure, sweet face, with its great, dark eyes and wistful mouth maddened him until he found tender words—eloquent, earnest words that would have told her of his love—upon the very tip of his tongue, and it was only by exercising all the will-power at his command that he had prevented himself opening his heart to her and clasping her in his arms.

Laurence had heard rumous that the man he knew as Cyrus O'Mega was a millionaire, or something very like one, and he told himself that for the time being at least Violet was not for him—a poorly-paid cashier in a city bank.

True, had he been so disposed, he could have altered his sphere of life almost immediately by accepting the allowance his father, John Riverton, had offered him. But Laurence had made a solemn vow—a vow that he meant to keep at all costs.

When he had returned from Harrow after a few months at the renowned college, he had quite by accident discovered that his real name was Cavendish. He had been idly searching through the drawers of an old writing-desk, had touched a spring that disclosed a secret cavity beyond one of the pigeon-holes, and brought to light documents that had proved without the least doubt that his father was the swindler Richard Cavendish, the man who had fled from London twenty years ago with half a million pounds out of which he had defrauded the misguided persons who had entrusted to him their investments.

A strong code of honour had always been one of Laurence's most cherished possessions, and immediately he had confronted his father with his knowledge. Then the old man had broken down, and, little by little, the lad heard the black story of the past.

He had learnt how his father, when he had been a partner in the firm of Clench & Cavendish, had treacherously betrayed his co-swindler and decamped with the whole of the haul they had made. He heard of the two long years that his father had spent in Buenos Aires in reckless extravagance and self-indulgence, then how, with a little capital, he had returned to the land of his birth, and, by pure luck, made money upon the turf.

He heard of the death of his mother, and how her decease had changed his father—made of him a saddened, chastened man. He was told of the great resolve Richard Cavendish had made to refund every penny to his former dupes, or, in the event of their having died, to their nearest relatives.

Fortune had seemed to be with Richard Cavendish in the desire to make reparation that obsessed him. In whatever direction in turf matters he speculated, he came out on top with but very few exceptions, and year after year the men and women who had been swindled by Clench & Cavendish received anonymously a portion of the money they had lost.

"I had hoped you would never know, lad," the ex-swindler had said. "But now that you've discovered my secret I have told you the whole truth. Heaven knows I am repentant, and I am doing my utmost to right the many wrongs I have done my fellow-beings!"

Laurence had felt sorry for his father, for he had known that he was sincere in every word he uttered. Yet from that day the young man had refused to touch a penny of his father's money, and had given out his intention of working for himself until the last portion of the amount out of which his father had defrauded his clients had been returned. He had steadfastly kept his word. He had not gone back to Harrow, but by the influence of the headmaster he had secured a position as junior clerk in Fisher's Bank. He had worked energetically until he gained his present position as cashier.

It was probable that he would soon be handing in his resignation to his employers, he thought, as he walked by the side of the girl he worshipped. He knew nothing of the sinister plot against him, and had no presentiment of what was shortly to transpire. If his father's horse, Serious Symons, won the Gold Cup, Richard Cavendish—or John Riverton, as he was now known—would be in a position to make his last repayment and would also be in pocket by a very large amount.

The prodigal swindler had pinned his faith to his candidate for the important event at Newmarket upon the following Tuesday, and had backed Serious Symons for many thousands of pounds several days ago, securing a long price about him. Laurence and his father had that day engaged in a long conversation, and the young man had agreed to throw up his position in the bank and once again live with his father in the event of the "certainty" coming off.

If Serious Symons did win, the young man intended to go straight to Violet and lay his heart at her feet, for then he would be in a position to offer her a home and luxuries such as she had been accustomed to. None but herself knew what the result of the big race would mean to him. Often he had dared to believe that he had seen the light of love shining in Violet's eyes when she had been conversing with him; he believed that she cared, and——

"How preoccupied you are, Mr. Riverton!" the girl said, suddenly breaking the silence that had fallen between them, and smiling up at him archly. "One might be forgiven for thinking you were shouldering the troubles of the world, or——"

"Or?" he prompted, recovering himself with a start.

"That you were in love," she said innocently. "I have heard that when a man is in that condition he is as silent as an owl."

"Do I look like an owl?" Laurence queried, smiling.

"No; but—"

"But, after all, perhaps, I am very much in love," he finished, and his voice in spite of the stern hand he was keeping upon himself. A flush of pink sprang into the girl's cheeks, and she veiled her eyes with her long lashes as she turned her head aside.

"Here we are at the house!" she said, with the air of one who wishes to change an embarrassing subject. "Will you unlatch the gate? The catch is stiff!"

"Guess I could do with a wash, O'Mega," Ezra Q. Maitland said, when they had entered an expensively furnished room, in which tea was laid. "Don't trouble to call a servant! I reckon the bathroom will suit me, and I know where to find it."

Henry Melson nodded.

"Sure you would not like some warm water? There will be none there," he answered.

"No; don't trouble," Maitland drawled. "What do you say, Mr. Riverton, to keeping me company? A rinse will do us real good, I reckon."

"Yes, I'll come with you," Laurence answered. "It is hot to-day, and a wash will refresh us, if we may be excused."

He glanced at Violet, and she inclined her head. Then the two men wended their way to the first floor, where Maitland pushed open a door.

He waved his hand towards the washhand-basin.

"After you!" he said politely. "Guess I'll get a cigarette going for a moment. I'm partial to a smoke before a meal."

Laurence Riverton unsuspectingly removed his coat, and hung it upon a hook behind the door. He turned on the tap, and partly filled the basin, and a second later he had buried his face in the cool, refreshing water.

Like lightning Maitland acted. He wipped from his pocket a roll of crisp bank-notes, and deftly thrust them into the breast-pocket of his victim's jacket. When Laurence removed his face from the basin, it was to find Maitland seated upon the edge of the bath, carelessly making smoke-rings and watching them slowly travel towards the ceiling.

When some few minutes had elapsed, and the master criminal and the cashier were taking their places at the tea-table, Henry Melson darted a questioning look at his cunning and unscrupulous ally. It was to see Maitland incline his head, and just for a fleeting moment Henry Melson's face wore an expression of fiendish triumph, and his eyes blazed like living coals.

The last step towards ruining the son of the man who had betrayed him twenty-years ago had been successfully taken.

———

CHAPTER 12
A Dramatic Arrest and a Condemning Find

The big, grey horse reared, then pawed the ground impatiently, as his mistress pulled him up and, shading her eyes, gazed towards the sinking sun. Like a blazing fireball, it was slowly disappearing behind a belt of trees, casting a dull red glow over the distant hills. It was a glorious sight, and when seen on the silent, lonely heath was enthralling—almost awe-inspiring.

Laurence Riverton turned in his saddle and looked back to where the girl sat upright upon her horse. She caught his glance, roused herself from her reverie, and galloped to his side.

"Isn't the sunset splendid?" she said in admiration.

Laurence nodded, although inwardly he was longing to tell her that there was that before his eyes infinitely more beautiful than the glare of the dying sun.

"You like England, Miss O'Mega?" he asked.

"It is wonderful!" Violet Melson returned. "So peaceful, so quiet—especially here upon the green heath. I don't think I ever wish to go back to America."

Again Laurence inclined his head. Then for a moment silence fell between them as they rode onwards.

After tea had been taken at Henry Melson's house, Violet had expressed her intention to ride to a distant cottage to take a parcel of delicacies to an old dame who was ill, and Laurence had jumped at the chance to accompanying her, pointing out that the girl would have to pass his father's stable upon her journey. Violet had seemed pleased that she was to have Laurence's company, and the young man's heart had pumped madly as he had helped her into her saddle and they had ridden from the stable-yard.

He was experiencing a feeling of regret now because they were rapidly nearing the Riverton stables. He was racking his brains for an excuse to accompany her to her destination, and afterwards ride back with her, but so far he had failed to find words in which to put the suggestion forward.

As it was to happen, Violet Melson was never to complete her intended journey.

A bird fluttered noisily from a clump of bushes as the thud of the horses' hoofs alarmed it, and Violet's steed swerved badly and reared. The girl kept her seat with the ease of an experienced equestrian, and brought her whip down smartly upon the animal's flank.

The chastisement only seemed to madden him, and he went careering forward, to pull up suddenly, with his hoofs planted hard to the ground. Then the brute appeared to do his utmost to unseat his rider. He flung up his head, trying to strike the girl in the face, but Violet drew back sharply, tightening her rein. Next the horse arched his back, then flung up his hind-legs, and lastly reverted to his rearing tactics.

It was all to no avail. Violet sat in her saddle as though she was strapped there, moving her supple body to suit the ever-changing attituides of the horse. She did not use her whip again until the animal's temper had exhausted itself; then she flicked him several times, and sent him prancing forward.

Laurence Riverton galloped after her, a great anxiety in his heart; but he could do nothing save watch, and as he saw the horse begin to quieten down he heaved a sigh of relief.

"He is a high-spirited brute, Miss O'Mega," the young bank clerk said, as he rode to her side. "I don't know whether it is quite safe for you to ride him."

"Oh, Satan is harmless enough!" Violet returned, stroking the horse's neck. "He gets out of hands at times, but—"

She broke off, listening intently

"What is that?" she asked.

Laurence Riverton raised his head, and he, too, listened for a moment.

"An aeroplane, I think," he said. "Yes; look! There it is—right over those trees! You can just see it—a speck in the clouds."

They both reined in their horses, and the girl sat gazing upwards, her hand raised to shade her eyes.

"It is coming this way," she said. "It's not a German machine, I suppose?" she added, with a laugh.

"I don't expect so," Laurence answered. "We should have heard some distant firing, if such were the case. Jove, but it is travelling! Look! It is getting quite distinct now!"

He was right, the aircraft was speedily approaching them, and now the roar of her engine could be plainly heard.

Louder and louder the noise grew, and soon they were able to make out the shape of her.

"A British biplane," Laurence said. "She must be making sixty to seventy miles an hour!"

They sat motionless, their eyes upon the oncoming aircraft. It was making a bee-line for them, and would pass, unless the pilot altered the course, directly over their heads. It was flying quite low, and could not have been more than seven or eight hundred feet above the ground.

The roar of the engine became a reverberating din as the aeroplane sailed above them. It was a fine sight to see, and Riverton sat fascinated until——

A startled cry came from Violet, and the young man swung round. The girl's horse had been frightened, for the second time within the last quarter of an hour. The crackling hum of the engine of the biplane had struck terror into the sensitive animal's breast, and it had suddenly swung round and dashed away across the heath.

Laurence brought round his horse like lightning, and went speeding away after the girl, for he had realised that a terrible danger menaced her, in spite of her skill as a horsewoman.

The aeroplane was rapidly disappearing, the sound of its engine growing fainter and fainter in the distance, but the mischief had been done. Satan had got the bit between his teeth, and was well nigh wrenching the girl's slim arms out of their sockets as he tore madly onwards, and all her efforts to slacken his pace were worse than useless.

The horse was making striaght for a stone wall dividing two fields, and upon the opposite side was a quarry, open, and from forty to fifty feet deep. It lay just behind, in the centre of the wall, and, as the stone was valuable, the owners kept it open, and work went on there now and again. The wall, which was all loose, rough stones, was there to warn people who did not know the country of the danger, and to remind those who did of the quarry's existance.

The maddened horse was heading straight for the very worst part of the wall, just as the spot where the quarry lay upon the opposite side. It would at the pace it was making, take the wall at a leap, and it was resisting all efforts of the girl to turn it in its wild career.

Laurence Riverton's head began to swim, and his mouth grew parched. He drove his spurs into his horse until the unfortunate animal whinnied and fairly bounded into the air.

"To your left!" he yelled hoarsely. "To your left, for Heaven's sake!"

He might have shouted to the dead for all the good his warning did. The girl was powerless to stay the foam-flecked animal beneath her or to swerve him, and, with white, set face and starting eyes, she realised that unless a miracle happened she was doomed.

Nearer and nearer to the wall Satan drew, and Laurance Riverton rode as he had never ridden before. His horse was almost as frenzied as the girl's but he was still well under Riverton's control. At all costs he must reach her and drag her from the saddle, even at the cost of a broken limb. If she went over the wall, and hurtled into the depths of the quarry——

Laurence shuddered, and, if it were possible, his face grew even more ghastly than it had been before he had pictured what was likely to happen.

Again and again he spurred his horse, and to his joy he found that he was gaining upon Satan and his terrified rider.

Crack! crack! crack! His whip went up, and descended three times with the rapidity of lightning, and his horse reared with the pain, but somehow it found itself urged forward, and now it was almost at the heels of the uncontrollable Satan.

The wall was but a dozen feet away! Laurence Riverton set his teeth, and again his spurs were driven home. With a last burst of speed, his horse shot forward, and now the two animals were travelling neck and neck.

Laurence's lips moved in a silent prayer to Providence to watch over them as he leant sideways in his saddle.

"Take your feet from the stirrups!" he shouted; and almost at once the girl understood and obeyed.

Just what happened then, Violet hardly knew. She felt herself gripped about the waist; then she was positively hauled from the saddle.

Laurence had taken a hold upon her slim form with both arms, and jerked her from her seat in the very nick of time. He saw the wall before them, and flung himself from the back of his own steed, endeavouring to hold the girl so that she should fall upon him. He had no thought for himself and was ready to sacrifice his life so long as she was not injured.

There was a terrific thud as the bodies of the girl and the man came to earth, rolled over, and violently struck the stonework.

Almost simultaneously the air was rent by a shrill whinny of terror as Satan went soaring over the wall and saw the yawning quarry beneath him. He went crashing downwards, whilst Laurence's horse, unable to stop in its wild pace, collided with the crumbling stonework of the wall, sending a portion of it rattling down into the quarry.

The poor creature collapsed in a heap, but staggered to three legs, as Laurence Riverton, blood upon his ashen face, reeled up. One of the horse's forelegs was badly broken, and Laurence shuddered at the sight, dazed, sick, and giddy though he was.

Fortunately he was able to put the animal out of its misery with very little delay, for he was carrying a revolver—a habit he had attained since being attacked by a party of Apaches when upon a tour in Paris.

There was a sharp report and a dull thud, and Laurence Riverton's horse was mercifully disposed of. The young man tried to return the weapon to his hip-pocket, but his strength gave out, he swayed, swung round upon his heels, and pitched to the ground by the still form of the girl he secretly loved.

. . . . . .

"Laurence! Laurence, lad! What has happened?"

Riverton looked up feebly to find his father bending over him.

John Riverton, alias Richard Cavendish, had altered greatly in the twenty years that had passed since he had fled from England with his ill-gotten gains. He was bearded now, and his hair was quite white; whilst, like his ex-partner, his face was deeply lined with care and suffering. Just now he was grey, to the lips, his eyes burning with anxiety.

"Laurence, speak to us!" he said. And now the young man became aware that Jack Haynes, his father's trainer, was also kneeling by his side.

The bank clerk raised himself weakly upon his elbow, becoming conscious as he did so that he was terribly stiff and sore. His eyes fell upon the form of his horse, then travelled to the spot where Violet Melson lay upon the grass, the trainer's coat propped beneath her head.

In a flash memory returned to him, and, stifling a groan, he gained his legs.

"Violet—Miss O'Mega!" he said. "She—she is not badly injured?"

"She don't appear to be, Mister Laurence," the trainer said reassuringly. "She got a nasty knock on the head and is stunned, but there are no bones broken."

"Thank Heaven!" Laurence breathed, as he knelt beside the girl and gently stroked her hair from her damp forehead. "How did you find me?"

"Haynes had been for a walk and passed this way, Laurence," John Riverton explained. "He examined you both to see if he could do anything for you, and, finding he couldn't, he came and informed me of what had taken place. You've had a nasty spill, by the look of things."

"Yes," Laurence said grimly. "It was only by inches that I managed to snatch Miss O'Mega from certain death. Her horse was frightened by the noise of an aeroplane that passed overhead; he got the bit between his teeth and went like a rocket straight for the quarry wall. I only snatched Miss O'Mega from her saddle in the nick of time!"

"The horse went over the quarry?" John Riverton asked, in a hushed voice.

"Yes!" Laurence shuddered. "Thank Heaven, he went over riderless!" he said earnestly. "We had better see if he is quite head, or lying maimed and injured. We must climb down and put a bullet through his head, poor beast, if he has not given up the ghost. You poor old Dick!" he said, stooping for a moment as he passed his dead horse; and a lump had risen in his throat. "I had to shoot him, father. He collided with the wall and broke his leg!"

He jumped, and clutching the edge of the quarry wall, drew himself up. For a moment he sat astride it, then carefully he lowered himself to the narrow strip of ground that divided it from the frowning quarry upon the other side.

A glance downwards speedily convinced him that Satan was no more. He was lying with his head doubled up in a gruesome manner beneath him, and there was not an iota of doubt that his neck was broken.

Laurence rejoined the others, and told then what he had seen. He crossed again to the side of the unconscious girl, stooped, and tenderly lifted her in his arms.

"We must take her home and let Mrs. Lee attend to her, dad," he said, referring to his father's housekeeper. "I can carry her, dad. She is no weight to speak of, and we are not far from home."

The little party started away over the heath, Laurence Riverton tenderly bearing the girl. A wisp of her luxurient hair was brushing against his face as her head lay upon his shoulder, and Laurence longed to press his lips to hers. He refrained from doing so, however, not wishing to cause comment upon the part of his father and the trainer.

When the Riverton stables were reached and Violet had been carried into the drawing-room of the house, which, like that of Henry Melson, was attached to the stables, Laurence gently deposited her upon the couch and arranged a cushion beneath her head, whilst he rang the bell and summoned the housekeeper.

Mrs. Lee proved to be a motherly sort of person, and she was quickly endeavouring to bring the girl to her senses. John Riverton stood over the couch, regarding Violet's pale face intently for a while, and presently he drew his son aside.

"You said she was Miss O'Mega," said he. "Is she a relation to the American Cyrus O'Mega, our neighbour whom you visit?"

"Yes. His daughter," Laurence replied.

John Riverton frowned and passed his hand across his wrinkled brow.

"Somewhere I seem to have seen her before," he said slowly, with the air of a man who was trying to recall some long-forgotten incident in his past life.

"Perhaps you have encountered her upon the heath, dad?" Laurence suggested. "She rides a good deal, and is fond of the open air."

The elder man shook his head.

"I don't imagine so," he said, after a moment's pause. "Perhaps, after all, I am mistaken, or it is merely a chance resemblance to—— By Heavens, I know now! She is like Clench—Jasper Clench, my old partner!"

Laurence Riverton started.

'Impossible!" he cried, almost indignantly.

"It is not impossible! It is true!" the elder Riverton persisted, moving quickly towards the coach and gazing down long and earnestly at the unconscious girl. "And yet—and yet—— Perhaps it is merely a trick of my imagination!"

The housekeeper was looking at him curiously, for the one-time swindler was trembling with agitation. He turned away and moved towards the door. Laurence followed him, and, once in the hall, his father said:

"I am going to smoke a cigar in the open air, lad. Whether or no I am imagining that yonder girl features are like those of the man I betrayed, the shock has unnerved me. Laurence, you love her?"

The young man caught his breath and started with surprise.

"Yes," he said, his voice full of emotion.

"I knew it," John Riverton answered quickly, laying his hand upon his son's broad shoulder. "I knew it from the manner in which you looked at her when she was lying unconscious upon the heath. Why do you persist in leading your humdrum existance—you cannot call it life—boxed up in that bank? Why not throw it up at once and live with me here?"

"You know the decision I have made, dad," Laurence answered firmly. "Until every penny is paid back——"

"I know lad," the old man interrupted. "But within a few days I shall be able to refund the last instalment to them all and be a rich man into the bargain."

"If Serious Symons wins," his son reminded him.

"If he wins!" John Riverton laughed enthusiastically. "Can he lose?" he asked. "He is trained to the minute, and there is nothing to beat him. With your help here at the stables, we can be even more prosperous. You will be in a position to make the girl you love your wife, if she'll accept you, and——"

"I shall not speak until Serious Symons has won, dad, and my future is assured," Laurence protested, although at the moment he did not really comprehend the strength of his love, nor foresee how forthcoming events were to loosen his tongue. "I do not wish to dishearten you, but there are other horses in the race, one of them practically on a level with your candidate in form and class."

"You mean Cyanin?" John Riverton asked; then, eagerly: "You have seen him?"

"Yes, to-day. He is a 'gentleman', there can be no doubt of that, and whatever beats him will go close."

"It will be Serious Symons," the elder Riverton said, with conviction. "He beat Cyanin when he was a two-year old, and will beat him again."

"I am not so certain," Laurence objected. "I wish, dad, you had not risked quite so much on his chance. But let us hope for the best. The dye is cast now, for better or worse."

"For better or worse," John Riverton repeated. "Let us hope it is for the former. It means much to both you and me."

He passed along the hall, opened the front door, and strolled down the steps, taking out his cigar-case. Laurence turned back to the room, but a glance showed him that Violet was still in an unconscious condition, and the young man followed his father out of doors.

As he joined him, and the two men moved leisurely down the drive, the gate at the far end was opened sharply to admit of a burly individual, who walked with a noticeable swagger, and a tall, lean gentleman, very quietly dressed and pale of face.

"I wonder who they can be?" John Riverton said, removing his cigar from between his teeth and stepping to gaze at the intruders. "I do not know them."

"Can they have heard of the accident by the quarry and have come to inquire after Miss O'Mega and myself?" Laurence suggested. "They may be the owners, or——"

He did not finish his sentence, but stood waiting until to the men drew nearer. Suddenly he gave an amazed exclamation.

"Why, it is Sexton Blake!" he said.

"The great detective!" John Riverton cried. "Good heavens!" His hands clenched, and beads of perspiration started to his brow. "Can it mean that after all these years—— No, no! It is absurd! I covered my movements too thoroughly for that! What can they want?"

'Sexton Blake and his companion—Detective-Inspector Martin—pulled up as they reached the two men.

"Mr. Laurence Riverton?" Inspector Martin asked officially, although he knew well enough that the younger of the two men was he, for Sexton Blake had had no option but to admit the identity of his friend.

"That is my name," Laurence said, his eyes widening. "But you have the advantage of me. Mr. Blake, I am glad to see you." He held out his hand, and without hesitation the detective gripped it. "Allow me to introduce you to my father."

Sexton Blake bowed formally, whilst Inspector Martin looked awkward and ill-at-ease.

"What has brought you to this part of the globe. Blake?" Laurence Riverton asked.

The detective, for once in his life, seemed momentarily at a loss for words.

"We are here upon very unpleasant business, Mr. Riverton," he answered at length. "This is an official friend of mine. Detective-Inspector Martin, of Scotland Yard." He was watching the cashier's face closely as he spoke, but saw there only an expression of growing bewilderment. "There has been either a gigantic swindle or an embezzlement at your bank."

"Good heavens!" the young fellow gasped. "It—it is not in connection with anything I have dealt with?"

"Unfortunately for you, sir, it is," Inspector Martin said gruffly. "We require to know why you entered a cheque, drawn in favour of a Mr. Henry Melson by the commission agent Charles McDonald, for seven thousand pounds as seventy thousand—just ten times as much?"

"What!" Laurence Riverton reeled back as though he had received a blow in the face. "I—I don't understand!" he gasped, passing his tongue across his dry lips. "The—the cheque was for seventy thousand pounds!"

Martin turned to Sexton Blake.

"Perhaps you will show it him, Blake?" he suggested.

The detective produced his wallet, and took from it the slip of paper in question, holding it so that the young Riverton could see it.

The cashier seemed paralysed for a few seconds, and he stood with dilated eyes, staring stupidly at the cheque. He tried to snatch at it; but Martin struck up his hand.

"What, in the name of Heaven, does this mean?" Laurence asked hoarsely. "It—it cannot be the same cheque."

"It is the same," Martin said coldly. "You must know, sir, what this means."

Laurence uttered a great cry, and the blood rushed into his cheeks.

"Do you dare to insinuate," he blazed indignantly, "that I—I have robbed the bank?"

"You are certainly sixty-three thousand pounds short in your cash," Martin retorted grimly. "We have checked it with Mr. Fisher and know."

"Oh, this is preposterous!" Laurence cried. "Mr. Blake, you do not believe that I am a thief? I——"

"I do not as yet know what to believe, or think, Riverton," the Baker Street detective answered, with a helpless gesture. "I have known you for some years, and always found you to be a man of honour. Yet there are many matters you must clear up before you can remove the charge that has been laid upon your shoulders. Personally, I believe that a fraud has been skilfully planned and engineered, and you are the victim of it. Are you willing to swear on oath that when you cashed this cheque it was for seventy thousand pounds?"

"I do swear it, Blake!" Laurence cried, in ringing tones.

"You could not have made a mistake. For instance, your mind was not preoccupied with other matters at the time this cheque was presented?"

"No; not to any extent, anyway. But, I am sure—I am positive—that it was for seventy thousand pounds! Why, I made a remark to one of my fellow cashiers because it was for such a large amount. It is most unusual for a cheque running into five figures to be left open."

"Of course. That was what at once struck me. Mr. Fisher, however, seemed to think little of the matter, declaring that Charles McDonald was a most eccentric man."

"That is so, and it was for that reason that I did not speak to Mr. Fisher before dealing with the matter. Good Providence! I can hardly believe my eyes! The cheque I cashed was for seventy thousand. I would say so if I were upon my deathbed, and it is utterly rediculous to entertain the idea of a mistake. I have never over or under paid a cheque that has been presented in the past. I am more than certain that I should not make such a blunder as to multiply thousands of pounds by ten!"

"Laurence, there must have been some hideous error made by Mr. Fisher," John Riverton said, in a voice that was unsteady. "My boy, surely if you exercise your mind you can think of something that will explain——"

"I can't, dad!" the cashier protested, almost wildly. "Now that I look at it, and study it, it is the identical cheque that I cashed this morning for seventy thousand! I know, because I noticed then the splash of red ink on the back. You see it is there."

He clutched at his temples.

"Am I going mad?" he panted. "Did I really make this awful blunder?"

He lowered his hands, allowing them to slowly sink down his chest until they fell limply by his sides. As his right hand was passing over the spot in his jacket where there was fitted an inside pocket, there came a peculiar rustling sound, and Inspector Martin's eyes suddenly glinted.

Just for a second or two the Scotland Yard man stood tense, then his body swayed forward, he sprang at Laurence, and secured his arms in a vice-like hold.

The young man struggled frantically to break free, but strong though he was, he found himself at a disadvantage.

"What is the meaning of this outrage?" he gasped, ceasing to struggle. "Let me go!"

Martin did no such thing. It it were possible, his grip tightened for a moment, then Laurence found himself swung backwards over the burly official's crooked knee, and Martin's hand was groping in his inside breast-pocket.

With a quick jerk, the official had wrenched out a handful of crackling banknotes, and he let Laurence go so suddenly that the young man stumbled and all but fell to the ground.

Next moment Martin had let out a shout of triumph, and was flourishing his find before Sexton Blake's eyes.

"A portion of the stolen notes!" he jerked excitedly.

———

CHAPTER 13
Blake's Questioning

Laurence Riverton came reeling forward, his eyes blazing dangerously, his fists clenched.

"You fool!" he hissed between his teeth. "You blundering fool, you are mad!"

"I think not, my young friend," the Scotland Yard man retorted gruffly. "We took a note of the numbers of the notes that had been paid out on the cheque you have falsely entered, and these are a portion of them."

"You lie!" Laurence blazed. "But—but——" He caught in his breath with a sobbing sound, and his jaw dropped blankly. "Those notes are not mine," he cried wildly. "I have not possessed such an amount in my life. They are for thousands of pounds."

"I quite believe they are not yours," Martin said, with an attempt at grim humour. "I expect Mr. Fisher will endorse your opinion. You must consider yourself under arrest upon a charge of embezzling sixty-three thousand pounds from your employers. I would warn you that anything you say may be taken and used at your trial in evidence against you."

"But I have no knowledge of how the notes came in my pocket!" Laurence said thickly. "I vow I am telling you the truth. Someone must have put them there."

Sexton Blake was lighting a cigar, and his eyes were very bright and keen. He was searchingly studying the young man's face through the smoke of his weed, and the detective somehow felt that Laurence's dazed, almost frantic astonishment was genuine.

What did it mean? the detective asked himself. Was it possible that Laurence Riverton was the victim of a deep-laid, subtle plot? He had experienced such cases in the past, And——

There are five thousand pounds here,' Inspector Martin said. "What have you done with the balance?"

"I tell you that I have never had it in my possession!" Laurence cried. "When I cashed this cheque, it presented a face value ten times more than now. In some remarkable manner it has changed—the figures and lettering have altered. I have no way of telling how these notes came upon my person, and I have no knowledge of the whereabouts of the missing fifty-eight thousand pounds. I solemnly pledge you my word, as a man of honour, that I am telling you the truth! I am mystified, baffled! My head is swimming, and I can hardly believe the evidence of my eyes!"

"Let me see the notes, Martin," Sexton Blake requested.

The Scotland Yard man handed them over. There were five of them, each for a thousand pounds face value.

The Baker Street detective slowly inspected each note in turn, turning them, and also examining their backs. When he came to the last note, he suddenly raised it close to his eyes, and pursed his lips.

"An oily thumb mark," he said. "It appears to have been made quite recently. Mr. Riverton, you will have no objection to showing me your thumbs?"

Laurence obeyed instantly, and the detective minutely examined the under portions.

"The mark was certainly not made by you," he said, with assurance. "Tell me, what was the man like who presented the cheque, and in whose name the cheque was made out?"

The cashier described him as accurately as his memory would allow.

"He was an American, I think," he said, in conclusion.

"An American!" Sexton Blake looked thoughtful. "I have heard his name somewhere just recently," he murmured. 'Melson—Melson! I wonder where it could have been? I may keep this marked note, Martin and the cheque, for the time being?"

'Certainly, Blake!" the inspector agreed.

"Good!" Sexton Blake answered. "I have a theory that I want to test with the cheque, and there is just a chance that this thumb mark may be repeated in my collection at Baker Street. Like the name of Melson, the impression seems strangely familiar to me, yet for the moment I cannot recall where I have experienced it in the past."

"This is a terrible affair, gentleman!" John Riverton said, his face drawn and anxious. "Will it be necessary for my son to accompany you, inspector?"

'Yes," Martin said, with a lifting of his shoulders. "The evidence against him is too damning to allow of anything else."

"By Jove! But I'll not be put to this indignity!" Laurence Riverton rasped, losing his head a little. "If you dare to lay a finger upon me, it will not go well with you."

"Laurence, my boy, I beseech you to be calm!" the elder Riverton pleaded. "It is useless to resist the law."

"I am innocent, and I won't be treated like a felon!" Laurence blazed "Stand back, you cur, or——"

Martin hurled his huge body forward, and his handcuffs were swinging in his hands. There was a sharp smacking sound, and with something very like an oath, the burly official went reeling backwards, blood streaming from his mouth.

"Don't be a fool, Riverton!" Sexton Blake advised sharply. "You are——"

His voice was drowned by an angry roar from Martin, as he again sprang at his intended prisoner. There was a short, quick scuffle as the two men closed. Next moment they had thudded to the ground, and were rolling over and over upon the gravel of the drive.

Laurence Riverton fought like a madman. The amazing charge that had so suddenly been brought against him had for the time being made him very near a madman, and he was not responsible for his actions. He struck blow after blow at his adversary until Martin suddenly got a hold upon his wrists and clicked on the fetters.

Roughly, Martin jerked the young man to his feet, and turned an anything but friendly look at Sexton Blake, who had not troubled to take any part in the arrest. Martin's expression plainly meant, "Why did you not come to my assistance?" but Sexton Blake purposely ignored it.

In spite of the apparently indesputable proof that young Riverton had committed a theft on a gigantic scale, Sexton Blake still adhered to the opinion he had voiced when he had first heard of the embezzlement over the telephone at Baker Street.

"You'll get it hot for this, my young spitfire!" Martin snarled to his prisoner, as he wiped the blood from his face. "It would have paid your to come quietly in the first place."

"I am sorry, officer!" Laurence Riverton answered, with almost a tone of weariness in his voice. "The shock of this fearful accusation had turned my brain. I again tell you that—— Ah, don't let her see these handcuffs!"

He had tried to turn away, and pull Martin after him; but he was too late.

Violet Melson had emerged from the house, upon the arm of old Mrs Lee. She was tremulous and weak from the recent accident, and had only just regained her senses; but when she saw the man who had saved her from death, she seemed to obtain new strength, and hurried down the steps.

"Laurence," the girl said, unconsciously using his Christian name for the first time. "I want to thank you for saving my life. Mrs Lee has told me all that happened, and——"

She stopped dead, and her eyes grew startled as she saw the shining wristlets the young man wore.

"Oh, what does this mean?" she asked, catching her breath. "Laurence—Mr. Riverton, why are you handcuffed?"

Laurence was silent for a moment, his eyes lowered, his cheeks flushed with shame. Then he raised his head sharply and his gaze was frank and fearless as he looked into the face of the girl he loved.

"I am the victim of a foul conspiracy, Miss O'Mega," he said, in a low voice. "I am accused of an enormous embezzlement, and circumstantial evidence is black against me, but I want you to believe that I am innocent!"

He held out his manacled hands supplicatingly, and after a moment's hesitation the girl impulsively took them in hers. Her hazel eyes were suddenly filled with tears, and even at that critical moment Laurence was capable of feeling a thrill of joy, for

188

he knew that she cared.

"Laurence, I do believe you guiltless of this charge!" she breathed, her fingers tightening upon his.

"Heaven bless you for those words, darling!" the young man said huskily. "Oh, you cannot realise how much this assurance means to me. Violet, it is wrong of me to speak now, but I cannot longer keep silent. I love you, dear, love you better than life itself! May I come to you when I have been proved innocent and released?"

Just for a few seconds—seconds that seemed like an eternity to the wrongfully accused man—the girl was silent, a flush of pink stealing into her cheeks, her long lashes drooping over her eyes, then she somehow found herself quietly sobbing upon his breast, her arms wound about his neck.

"I love you, too, Laurence!" The words were spoken so low that the young man was forced to bend his head to hear. "You have saved my life, and I am ready to place it in your keeping!"

With a choking lump in his throat, Laurence pressed his lips to hers. He tried to speak, but his heart was too full to allow of words. He was supremely happy, yet the black shadow of suspicion—the shadow of a false and terrible charge—was hanging over him, marring the bright future that would otherwise have been his.

"Come along, sir," Inspector Martin urged officially. "I can allow you no longer!"

"You shall not go, Laurence!" Violet cried passionately, as she released her arms from about his neck and swung round, facing the Scotland Yard official, give them your word that you will not attempt to leave the country! My father is rich and will make himself responsible for any amount, if——"

"It is useless, dearest!" Laurence protested gently. "The law must take its cause! I am sure that right must conquer wrong in the end, and in due course I shall be freed! Mr. Blake, your are silent. You do not believe that I have turned dishonest?"

"No!" Sexton Blake answered readily. "I have thought you innocent from the first, and I am going to leave no stone unturned to prove you so!"

Laurence gave a cry of mingled joy and gratitude.

"You will work for me—use your skill on my behalf?"

The detective inclined his head, and he did not appear to see the little smile of contemptuous amusement that was playing about his official colleague's lips.

"I have given you my word," Sexton Blake said simply.

And Laurence Riverton felt that a great weight had been lifted from his mind. He again turned to Violet.

"Good-bye, dear heart!" he said, in a subdued, shaking voice.

. . . . . .

It was some three-quarters of an hour later that the door of Henry Melson's study was burst open and his daughter, looking ill and haggard, entered and flung herself at his knees, to burst into a paroxysm of grief.

"Gracious, child, child, what is wrong?" the millionaire asked, in surprise, as he caressingly stroked the bowed head.

"It is Laurence, dad—Mr. Riverton—he has been arrested!" Violet sobbed. "He saved my life! Satan took fright near Wellstread Quarry, and was going straight for the wall. Laurence snatched me from my saddle in the very nick of time—risked his life to save me!"

"Heavens!" the old man whispered tensely. "And—and then?"

"I was unconscious from a blow on the head I sustained in the fall from my horse, and Laurence carried me to his house! When I recovered, I found him in charge of a detective, accused of embezzlement! They have taken him to prison, and—and I think my heart is broken! I love him so!"

A hoarse exclamation burst from the lips of Henry Melson, and he stared down dully at the grief-wracked girl.

"You—you love him!" he choked aghast. "Oh, my heavens! What have I done?"

———

CHAPTER 14
Identifying the Thumb Impression

Sexton Blake was once again at Baker Street.

An hour had elapsed since his return from Newmarket, and Inspector Martin had departed with his prisoner. Laurence Riverton was now in a cell at Bow Street, charged with the gigantic embezzlement of sixty-three thousand pounds from his employers; but during the journey up to Liverpool Street, Sexton Blake had further questioned the accused young man, and it had been with the light of new hope in his eyes that Laurence had taken leave of the famous detective.

Like many others before him, he had been impressed by the quiet assurance of the great criminologist, and Sexton Blake had undertaken to do all in his power to prove that the young cashier was the victim of a carefully thought out conspiracy—a mean yet cunning plot to ruin him and for ever blight his life.

Sexton Blake had removed his jacket, and now he was attired in his well-worn dressing-gown. He had drawn a chair up to the table, and the wallet containing the thumbed banknote and the fatal cheque was before him.

Tinker was standing by his master's side, his young face bright and eager, for he was never happier than when watching Sexton Blake at work.

"You really think Laurence Riverton is innocent, guv'nor?" Tinker asked, as he laid a reference-book upon the table near the hand of his friend and employer.

"My dear lad," Sexton Blake answered protestingly, "you surely heard what I said to the elder Mr. Riverton when he got through on a trunk call just now?"

"Of course, sir, but——"

"By this time, lad, you ought to know me well enough to realise that I never raise false hopes."

"I know, sir, but—— Well, this case beats me up till now," the assistant said frankly. "There's no getting away from the figures and words on the cheque, and the notes that were found in his pocket——"

"I am aware of all that," Sexton Blake cut in, a little drily. "Yet I am also aware that Laurence Riverton spoke the truth when he said he had no knowledge of how the notes came into his possession. It was also true that when the cheque was presented this morning it read as being made out for seventy thousand pounds."

"But, how, sir?"

"The letters and the extra nought needed were added."

Tinker scratched his head and looked badly puzzled.

"Then where are they now?" he asked.

"They have disappeared. They were meant to disappear."

"They have disappeared? They were meant to—— My aunt! I get you, guv'nor!" the lad cried. "Invisible ink!"

"Yes," Sexton Blake agreed. Something like that, I fancy. We will put to the test in a few moments. Ah, you have brought the book of thumb impressions. Let us see if——"

His voice trailed off into thoughtful silence as he took the marked bank-note from his wallet.

He spread it upon the table.

"The powder, Tinker," he ordered.

The lad seemed to know what was required, for he immediately went to a shelf and took from it a small tin box, placing it in the hand the detective stretched out for it.

Sexton Blake removed the lid, displaying a powder within, not unlike black pepper. He shook a little of this over the spot upon the note where the impression of the oily thumb was faintly visible, making quite certain that it was entirely covered.

For the space of a minute Sexton Blake sat patiently waiting. Then he shook the powder back into the box and pushed it aside.

The result of his experiment was the desired one. The mark had now turned to an intense black, and was clearly outlined upon the surface of the paper. Blake sat for a few moments intently studying it. Afterwards he began to turn the pages of the reference book.

Upon every page was a series of thumb and finger impressions, most of them made by notorious criminals whom the detective at some time in the past had been instrumental in clamping in gaol.

They were numbered, and from an index at the foot of each page it was possible for Blake to ascertain the identity of the man to whom a certain mark belonged. Time after time it has been definitely proved that a thumb-mark cannot lie, and this harmless-looking book was, metaphorically speaking, worth its weight in gold to such a man as its present owner.

At first the lad had been eager and expectant, but as he saw his master turn page after page until he had almost reached the end of the book Tinker began to think that after all the mark upon the banknote, which had promised to be a valuable clue, was to prove no help to them.

The last page! Even Blake was beginning to lose hope. Then, as he came almost to the last impression in his collection, he started and caught his breath sharply.

"You got it, sir?" Tinker asked excitedly.

Sexton Blake did not at once reply. He sat with his eyes fixed upon the book, unconsciously showing the excitement that was inwardly gripping him by biting his underlip until the blood was drawn. Then he leapt to his feet, and his fingers sought a switch that would supply him with extra light.

Sexton Blake sank into his chair again, bending eagerly forward over his desk. He was holding the banknote near his eyes, and again and again he compared it with the impression in the reference-book. Finally, he very deliberately placed the note back in the wallet and took out the cheque. He resorted to the box of black, powder once again, and slowly and carefully covered its face with the chemical.

He made sure that not a fraction of an inch of the slip of paper was left uncovered, and took out his watch. It seemed as though he might be afraid that his eagerness might prompt him to dust the powder from the cheque before sufficient time for it to take effect had lapsed. When a minute had ticked away, Blake emptied the powder back into the box anbd discovered that quite a number of finger and thumb impressions were in evidence.

At once he recognised the mark of Laurence Riverton's thumb, repeated three times. The cashier had, of course, handled the cheque when he had cashed it.

There were five more marks, not counting those made by fingers, and for the next two minutes the detective was carefully comparing them with the mark that interested him in his book.

The result was—nil! Sexton Blake, however, was quite patient and undaunted by his lack of success.

Once more the powder came into use and upon this occasion it was the back of the cheque that was treated.

Again the jerking out of the timepiece; again the long minute's wait, in which the only sound that broke the stillness of the consulting-room was the ticking of the watch and the breathing of the man and the lad.

After what seemed an enternity to Tinker, who was always keenly interested in his master's methods, Sexton Blake returned the powder to the tin again, replacing the lid, and signalled to the lad to return it to its place upon the shelf.

It was characteristic of the ever-methodical Blake that he made no attempt, in spite of the tremendous excitement that was obsessing him, to look at whatever marks might have been brought to light upon the cheque, until he had seen his assistant remove the article which he had used and now wished to dispence with.

The detective's lids were raised sharply, and his eyes were very keen as he at length looked to see the result of his labours.

As upon the face of the cheque, there were a number of marks, and almost immediately Sexton Blake gave a little exclamation of satisfaction.

The impression he had found upon the bank-note was repeated on the back of the cheque, although in the latter case it was very, very faint.

190

And he had an identical mark in his book of reference, made by the thumb of one of the most notorious criminals of the twentieth century.

Sexton Blake looked up at his assistant, and smiled slightly as he saw the tense, expectant look on the young detective's face.

"We are up against Maitland again, my lad," he said, very quietly.

"What!" Tinker fairly shouted the word. "You're not joking, guv'nor!"

"I have never been more in earnest, Tinker." Sexton Blake returned. "Ezra Q. Maitland is in this plot against young Riverton, although, why"—he made a helpless gesture with his hands—"it is, at present, absolutely impossible to imagine! Yet, be that as it may, it was Maitrland who was responsible for the great swindle that was worked at the expense of Fisher's Bank this morning, for the impression of his thumb appears both upon the thousand-pound note that was found in young Riverton's pocket and upon the cheque.

"Maitland has handled both, yet whether it was actually he who cashed the cheque, whether Henry Melson is a new alias of his, and whether he personally put the five notes in his victim's jacket-pocket, we have yet to find out. By the way, look up the name of Melson, will you?"

Tinker crossed to a bookshelf, and took down a thick, red-bound volume bearing the letter "M." He swiftly turned the pages and read aloud:

"Melson, the Right Hon. Sinclair. Member of——"

Sexton Blake held up his hand.

"I know the desription by heart, lad," he said. "Said to be upon the verge of bankruptcy, in the hands of moneylenders, etc., etc. It would not be that young man, the Melson we want, should Henry Melson not merely be an assumed name of our old enemy. There is only one entry?"

"Yes, sir."

"Humph! Put the book away. Tinker. It can tell us nothing. By the way, does the name strike you as familiar?"

"I can't say it does, guv'nor," he answered at last.

Sexton Blake frowned and looked puzzled. He sat for a few moments slowly stroking his clean-shaven chin.

"It is most annoying," he muttered presently. "It is unlike me to forget, yet I feel, that I have heard this name within the last few days, and cannot recall when and where. However, it will come to me sooner or later. We shall now go to the laboratory."

"You are going to test the cheque, sir?"

"Yes; for signs of invisible ink having been used upon it. There seems to be no other deduction to arrive at. We know that Maitland is in this, which makes me doubly convinced upon the point of young Riverton's blamlessness in the matter. What else, then, could be the explanation? He is an experienced bank clerk, who can boast that he has never made a mistake even in a few pence in cashing cheques for his employer's customers. It is, therefore, a million to one against his first error being for many thousands of pounds. Besides, he specially noted the cheque, because it was for such a large amount, and made mention of it to the man seated next him at the bank counter.

"There is no doubt that the cheque really did bear a face value of seventy thousand pounds when it was handed to Riverton to be cashed this morning. Therefore, additions which have since faded away were then in evidence upon its surface. Let us try what we can do in the laboratory."

A few minutes later Sexton Blake and Tinker were standing before the long, marble shelf that ran down one side of the detective's well-appointed experimenting-room.

The cheque was upon the slab before them, Blake was bending over it, applying some colourless fluid from a tiny bottle, and Tinker was at hand to give him any assistance he might require.

Chemical after chemical the detective used, pausing from time to time to examine the cheque through a powerful microscope. It was all to no purpose, however, and at the end of three-quarters of an hour Sexton Blake had to admit failure.

Abstractedly he helped Tinker put the various bottles away, and returned to the consulting-room. Here he dropped into his favourite chair, slowly drew out his cigar case and lit up.

For several minutes Sexton Blake sat haunched up in his chair, the tips of his fingers pressed together, the lids drooping over his eyes, until a person who he did not know him might have been forgiven for thinking he was dozing.

Tinker, who knew that his master was thinking deeply, quietly seated himself, and took up a book to read. He had hardly settled down, however, before his master roused himself, and sharply gained his legs.

"It has come to me, Tinker," he said quickly. "I know now where I have encountered the name of Melson. It was in the Royal Hotel, in the Strand, when we were upon the track of Maitland. When we came out of the manager's office, he stumbled over one of his guests, who was apparently adjusting his shoelace just outside the door. It struck me then that the man was listening. Somehow, I now feel more certain of it."

"Do you think he's in with Maitland, sir?"

"I will not go so far as that," Blake answered. "However, I think it might be worth our while to look Mr. Melson up."

"You will go to the Royal Hotel?"

"Yes; I shall question the manager, Mr Raymond." A smile played about the corners of his lips. "When he learns that I am seeking information about another of his guests, he will begin to think that his beloved hotel is being turned into a high-class thieves' kitchen. Come along, my lad. We'll not trouble about the car. We can get a taxi at the end of Baker Street, I expect."

. . . .

Sexton Blake sat in the private office of Mr. Raymond, manager of the Royal Hotel, Strand. An attendant had shown him in, and gone in search of his spruce little master.

The detective had not long to wait. The manager presently hurried in, an anxious look upon his pink and white face.

"Good evening, Mr. Blake," he jerked. "If you have come about the man Blenkarn, or Maitland, we——"

"No; it is not about him that I wish to see you, Mr. Raymond," the detective said. "Do you remember that when we were here before—I mean the Scotland Yard men and I—you spoke to one of your guests who had stopped to tie up his shoelace outside this office door?"

"Er-Yes. I remember the incident faintly. Yes, it was Mr. Melson. But——"

"A Mr. Henry Melson?"

"Yes. He has left the hotel now. Surely, you cannot want him, though, Mr. Blake?"

"I may want him very urgently, although whether or no it will be quite in the way that you mean, I cannot at present say," the detective rejoined. "What do you know of him?"

"He is an American millionaire, if all the reports I have heard are true. A man well known on Wall Street, and well connected in the States."

"Do you know anything else regarding him?"

"No; except that I hope for more guests like him. There's no doubt about his being possessed of pots of money. He may or may not be the millionaire the rumour says he is, but he must be fabulously wealthy. He has drank of the very best wine we have in our cellars, and never ordered cigars less than two shillings apiece."

"And he has paid for these expensive items?" Sexton Blake suggested, smiling.

"Of a certainty. He left here somewhat suddenly, but sent a cheque in settlement of his bill, requesting that his luggage should be sent on. That, by the way, reminds me. We have omitted to enclose a photograph belonging to him."

"Of himself?"

"No; of his daughter. A very charming girl, Mr. Blake—a very charming girl."

"From where did he write for his luggage?"

"From Newmarket. Doubtless he has gone there for the racing next week. We were instructed to send his luggage to the cloak-room at Newmarket Station, to be called for."

"Just so. He gave you no address there?"

"No."

"Could you tell me if you have ever seen this Mr. Melson and the man you now know to have been Maitland in conversation?"

"Never. I do not think they knew each other."

"Thank you, Mr. Raymond," Blake said. "I am much obliged for your kindness in so readily giving me this information. By the way, could I see the photo of Mr. Melson's daughter? I do not know that it will be of any advantage to me, but I have a fancy to see it."

"I have it in my desk," Raymond said. "Excuse me for one moment."

He turned to his roll-top desk and opened it, it having been closed for the night. He took a photo of the cabinet order from one of the drawers, turned, and handed it to the detective.

Sexton Blake took the picture in his hands, then ever so slightly he started, and a deep frown appeared upon his brow—a frown of mingled surprise and puzzlement.

Mystery or mysteries! The girlish face depicted in the photograph was that of Violet O'Mega, the girl for whom Laurence Riverton had that day declared his love!

———

CHAPTER 15
The Interview with Laurence Riverton

Sir Henry Fairfax, Chief Commissioner of Police, looked more than usually serious as he faced Sexton Blake, who had just been shown in to him.

At all times Sir Henry's position was no sinecure, and of late there had been a great number of involved cases, with a public outcry when certain of them had not been cleared up satisfactorily. This was apart from the extra worry and work caused by the great war; and now there was this latest crime at Fisher's Bank. Although circumstantial evidence was so black against Laurence Riverton, the case was enshrouded in mystery, and Sir Henry was in grave doubt as to whether the balance of the sixty-three thousand pounds that were missing would ever be recovered.

If Laurence Riverton was indeed the victim of a plot against him, Sir Henry realised that someone had made a tremendous haul with every possibility in favour of keeping it. If, on the other hand, Riverton had embezzled the money, an obstinate nature would urge him to keep silent as to its whereabouts. And the chief commissioner dreaded the tongue of Septimus Fisher, the bank's managing-director, if the money were not regained. Sir Henry had heard of Mr. Fisher in the past.

"You are working upon the bank case, Mr. Blake?" Sir Henry suggested, as he indicated a chair.

"Exactly," Sexton Blake agreed. "Has any further statement been made by Laurence Riverton?"

"No," Sir Henry replied. "All the indignation he showed when he was formally charged has vanished. He seems dazed, almost in a state of collapse."

"An innocent man would be."

"You still think he is innocent—that he is the scapegoat of some clever swindler."

"I think he is the dupe of Ezra Q. Maitland," Sexton Blake replied calmly.

"What!" Sir Henry leapt from his chair. "Good heavens, you don't say that man is in this?" he cried excitedly.

"He has certainly handled both the cheque and one of the banknotes that were found in young Riverton's pocket," the Baker Street detective answered.

Sir Henry sat back in his chair, his lips parted, his eyes fixed half incredulously upon his companion's pale face.

"Just why have you called here?" he queried at length.

"I want an order to interview Laurence Riverton alone."

"Quite alone?" he asked.

"Yes; without even a gaoler present."

"Really, that would be a trifle unusual, Mr. Blake," the commissioner objected hesitatingly.

"Yet I think it might be most necessary in clearing up the case," Sexton Blake answered. "I want Riverton to place his whole confidence in me. There may be some black page in his past—some indescretion, shall we call it?—that he has atoned for and tried to forget—which is at the bottom of the conspiracy against him."

"You mean that he may have done someone a bad turn and they have sought to be revenged upon him by making him appear a thief?"

"Something like that—yes. You will give me the necessary letter?"

The commissioner frowned, hesitated for a second or two, then pulled a sheet of official-looking notepaper towards him. For the next few moments the silence was only broken by the scratching of his pen as he wrote and signed the order the private detective had requested.

"You will let me know as soon as you discover anything definite about Maitland?" he asked, as he pushed the letter across the table.

"Yes, Sir Henry," Blake agreed. "I will wish you good-night—and many thanks!"

"Good-night, Blake!"

The detective was very thoughtful as he left Scotland Yard. As he emerged on to the embankment he espied a disengaged taxi, and raised his hand sharply. The vehicle pulled into the kerb, and the detective instructed the chauffeur to take him to Bow Street.

When he arrived there and presented the commissioner's letter to the superintendent in charge, that official looked astonished. He read the letter through twice, but made no comment upon it. He called a constable, and whispered a few words to him, showing him the order from Scotland Yard.

Almost at once the man beckoned Sexton Blake to follow him, and it was only a few seconds later that the detective found himself being ushered into the cell in which Laurence Riverton was imprisoned.

He sat there on a wooden bench, his face between his hands, and he did not attempt to look up until the clang of the door roused him.

"Mr. Blake!" he gasped, as he recognised his visitor. "You—you have discovered that I——"

"I have not definitely cleared you," Sexton Blake interrupted kindly, for he anticipated what the young man had been about to say. "But I have proof that a clever and unscrupulous criminal is mixed up in the affair. Now I want you to answer a few questions, placing your whole confidence in me."

"You may rely that I will do so, Mr. Blake."

"Good? We are quite alone; you will see that the door has been closed, and there is not even a gaoler within hearing, for I came armed with a special permit from the Chief Commissioner of Police. Tell me, who is the girl who was present at your arrest?"

A flush of pink sprang into the cashier's ashen cheeks.

"A Miss Violet O'Mega. Blake, I was a cur to speak as I did to her, but the words were out of my mouth before I could suppress them. She is the daughter of Mr. Cyrus, a neighbour of my father's. He is the owner of Cyanin, the co-favourite with my father's candidate for the big race at Newmarket next Tuesday."

"Have you ever had reason to doubt that O'Mega was really her name?"

"Great heavens, no!" Laurence cried, almost indignantly. "Why do you ask such an extraordinary question?"

"Because," Sexton Blake said quietly, "she and her father passed under another name when they stayed at the Royal Hotel in London."

"But—— Oh, you must be mistaken! Why should Mr. O'Mega wish to change his name?"

"That is just what I am anxious to find out. It will surprise you, perhaps, when I tell you that Mr. Cyrus O'Mega was known as Henry Melson at the Royal."

"As Henry Melson!" Laurence Riverton rose unsteadily from his bench, to regard Sexton Blake almost stupidly, like one who doubts the accuracy of his hearing. "As Henry Melson," he repeated—"the name of the man to whom the cheque was made out!"

"The same. What do you make of that?"

"I—I do not understand! There must be some grave error somewhere!"

"There is no mistake. A photo of the Miss Melson who stayed at the Royal was inadvertently left behind when their luggage was sent on to Newmarket Station—to Newmarket, mark you. The picture was that of the girl whose life you saved this afternoon—Miss Violet O'Mega!"

Laurence Riverton sank back to his seat, his hands shaking as he let them drop between his knees.

"What can it mean?" he muttered dully. "What can it mean?"

"What kind of man is the person you know as Cyrus O'Mega?" was Sexton Blake's next question.

"An elderly gentleman—about sixty, I should think."

"He was nothing like the man who cashed the cheque?"

"No, certainly not! The person to whom I paid out seventy thousand pounds this morning was apparently quite a young man, with a neat brown beard and moustache. Mr. O'Mega is grey, and his face is lined—lined deeply, as though from the stress of a hard business life. Mr. Blake, there is some deep mystery here, which I am beginning to fear will never be explained away."

"Perhaps the mystery is even deeper than you can as yet understand," Sexton Blake answered. "I told you that a notorious criminal was mixed up in the case. He is a master of crime—an expert evil-doer—an arch-fiend, of whom the world would be well rid. I refer to Ezra Q. Maitland, the man who has thrice attempted to betray Great Britain to Germany, the scoundrel who all but got clear away with an enormous sum raised for the relief of the suffering Belgians."

"Maitland!" Laurence cried. "How do you know?"

"It was he who was responsible for the thumb impression on the note found upon you," Sexton Blake explained, "and upon closer investigation, I discovered that the impression was repeated upon the cheque."

"This—this ought to be enough to clear me!" Laurence exclaimed eagerly.

"It will go a long way towards doing so, but we must have more substantial proof," Sexton Blake said. "Have you ever come into contact with Maitland in the past? I mean in such a manner that he would wish to do you a bad turn?"

"Never to my knowledge, unless he was passing under an alias!" the cashier declared. "But, there, so far as I know I haven't an enemy in the world."

"Are you positive of that?"

"Why yes. I have always led a straight, decent life, and treated my fellow men honestly, as I would have had them treat me."

"There is no incident connected with your past that would cause some person or persons a desire for vengeance against you? Remember, we are quite alone, and you promised to give me your whole confidence."

Laurence slowly shook his head.

"There is nothing I can call to mind," he began. "I wonder"—he had started—"I wonder—— No, no; it cannot be!"

"Of what were you thinking?" the detective asked quickly.

"Of—of my father; but I cannot tell you of that. It is a secret—a secret he has kept closely guarded for years."

"Do you mean that in the past he has committed some act that he wishes to keep from the knowledge of the world?"

Laurence hesitated.

"Yes," he answered, in a low tone, after a while.

"Why not be perfectly frank with me?" Sexton Blake asked. "Remember, I am not an official detective, and anything that passes between us here will go no further without your permission."

"You mean that? You mean that you will give your word of honour that whatever I tell you—even if I confess that my father had once committed a great crime—it will remain a secret for all time in your breast?"

Sexton Blake inclined his head.

"My lips would be sealed," he said. "You have my word of honour as a gentleman."

"Then you shall know all," Laurence Riverton said, with a swift making up of his mind. "My name is not really Riverton. It is Cavendish. My father was the Richard Cavendish, of the firm of Clench and Cavendish, who absconded twenty years ago with a sum of half a million pounds. He had swindled thousands of hard-working men and women out of their life's savings—their all. But I swear that he has repented of his sin! Mr. Blake, have I done wrong in telling you this? Will you feel it your duty to communicate with the police, and——"

Sexton Blake drew himself up, with an indignant look in his eyes.

"I have given you my word," he said coldly.

"I am sorry," Laurence pleaded flushing. "But, you see, my father was never arrested, and although he has atoned for the past and paid back nearly every penny of the money out of which he has defrauded those who once trusted him, a word to the police and he would pay the penalty for his dishonesty."

"He has repented then, and is making good?"

"Yes. To give him his due, he stints himself to make reparation every day of his life. As you doubtless are aware, he has had wonderful luck upon the Turf, and has won large sums of money by backing his own candidates. Believe me, Mr. Blake, every possible penny of his winnings has been spent to right the great wrong he done years ago. After each big win he has anonymously despatched an instalment of money he owes his old clients, until now only a comparatively small sum remains to be sent. If Serious Symons wins the Gold Cup on Tuesday, my father will be in a position to send the last payment to his former dupes."

I faintly remember the case," Sexton Blake said, after a little thought. "Can you give me any further particulars of it?"

"Yes. You will doubtless recollect, when I recall the fact to your mind, that Jasper Clench, my father's partner, was arrested and sentenced to ten years' penal servitude."

"Yes; it all comes back to me," Sexton Blake agreed. "I was a mere lad then, but even in my schooldays I studied crime and the ways of criminals. Did not your father escape with the whole of the money and leave Jasper Clench to bear the brunt of matters? I seem to remember that Clench made a dramatic outburst at his trial."

"You are right. Clench swore that he would be revenged upon my father, if he had to wait a lifetime. But, after his release from Portland, he completely disappeared, and has never been heard of since. Has he suddenly become active, and is my present predicament the outcome of his vengence?"

"Your father did not know where he went?"

"No; he simply vanished. The earth might have opened and swallowed him up."

Sexton Blake lapsed into silence, and he did not rouse himself until a gaoler knocked upon the door, to intimate that the time Sir Henry Fairfax had allowed for the interview had elapsed.

The detective rose to his feet.

"There are two more questions," said he. "Can you remember any time during to-day—that is, since you left the bank—when anyone could have placed those five-thousand-pound notes in your pocket?"

"I cannot say that I do," Laurence answered helplessly.

"For instance, you did not remove your coat for any purpose, and leave it out of your sight. Perhaps whilst you were doing something to one of your father's horses?"

Laurence Riverton puckered his brow and thought for a long moment. Presently he brought his hand sharply down upon his knee.

"By Jove! I've got it!" he cried. Yet"—his face fell—"it could not have happened then."

"When?"

"When I went to the bathroom to rinse my hands with a friend of Mr. O'Mega's—a Mr. Luke O. Kerney."

"An American!" Sexton Blake exclaimed, with a trace of suppressed excitement in his usually level accents.

"Yes; I should take him to be one from his drawl and way of expressing himself."

"You removed you coat to wash?"

"Yes; I hung it behind the door, and turned my back whilst I filled the basin and rinsed my hands."

"And this man Kerney was behind you? He would have had an opportunity of slipping the notes into your pocket?"

"He would certainly have had a chance of doing so., but what good would it have done him? He could have no grudge against me. I will vow I have never met him in the past!"

"Be that as it may," Blake said. "It will be necessary to ascertain more definite information about Mr. Luke O. Kerney, I think. Now cast your thoughts back. Did you here this man Kerney speak of a motor?"

"Yes. But why do you ask?"

"Because the impression upon the bank-note was caused by an oily thumb. That at once suggested a car or motor-cycle to my mind."

"By heavens!" Laurence exclaimed, and now he was trembling with excitement. "Mr. Blake, I believe you are on the right track! Luke O. Kerney arrived at Mr. O'Mega's stables at Newmarket in a car, and he mentioned that upon the road he had had a slight breakdown. It was nothing serious, and he was able to put it right himself."

"We have hit upon the correct solution of the oily thumb-mark, I imagine, Riverton," Sexton Blake said. "He would be almost sure to get his hands smeared with oil whilst repairing the part of the mechanism of the car that had gone wrong. He evidently did not properly cleanse his thumb, thus we get the impression of it when he hurriedly placed the notes in your pocket."

"Then you think that Kerney did it?"

"I do," Sexton Blake answered grimly. "I also think that he is Ezra Q. Maitland. A thumb impression never lies! The rule has been proved over and over again, and there has never been an exception. Do you recollect——"

"Time's up, sir!" the gaoler said, drumming again upon the door.

"Do you recollect any peculiarity that was marked in both the man who presented the cheque and this Mr. Luke O. Kerney?" the detective queried taking no notice of the interruption.

"No; I cannot bring myself to think they were one and the same man, if that is what you mean, Mr. Blake, although they were both Americans."

"You did not observe any striking mannerism about the man who brought the cheque to your bank?"

"No; save that he appeared to be a vigorous smoker."

"In what way?"

"I doubt if the fact is worth recording," Laurence said. "He was smoking a very strong cigar, and I noticed that he had puffed at it until the end was glowing redly—fiercely. But there, there can be nothing in that!"

"On the contrary," Blake returned, his eyes gleaming and hard in expression. "I believe you have supplied me with the most important clue towards proving your innocence!"

"But how——"Laurence began.

"I will not further raise your hopes until I am sure," Sexton Blake said, with a gesture of his hand. "I am going home to make a further experiment with the cheque you cashed. If the theory I have arrived at proves correct, I will lose no time in letting you know!"

And with that Laurence Riverton had to be content.

———

CHAPTER 16
Violet Melson Calls

"Miss O'Mega is awaiting you in the consulting-room, sir."

Sexton Blake was met by Tinker with this information as he entered his house at Baker Street with his latchkey.

The detective elevated his brows, produced his watch, and glanced at it.

"Then Miss O'Mega looks like spending the night in London, Tinker," he said. "There is no train back to Newmarket to-night."

"She must have been waiting quite an hour guv'nor. I think she has booked up to stay at the Royal, in the Strand. She asked to be allowed to use our 'phone, and go on to the manager. She said she must see you before she went away."

Sexton Blake mounted the stairs and entered his consulting-room. As he appeared, the slightly built girl who had been seated by the window rose, and took a timid step forward.

Voilet Melson looked very different to the girl who had defiantly disputed Inspector Martin's authority that afternoon. Her distinctly pretty face was white and drawn, and there were dark marks about her eyes, suggestive of bitter tears.

"You may get to bed, Tinker," Sexton Blake said.

The girl did not seat herself when Sexton Blake drew forward his most comfortable chair, in preference to the one she had been occupying upon his entry. She stood fidgeting with her gloves, seemingly nervous and ill at ease, although Sexton Blake was smiling reassuringly.

"Mr. Blake," she said quickly, with much the suddenness of a nervous person taking a plunge into cold water, "forgive me for staying until such a late hour, but I could not go away until I had interviewed you."

"You had much better sit down, Miss O'Mega," Sexton Blake insisted; and this time the girl obeyed him unhesitatingly. "You have called upon behalf of Mr. Laurence Riverton?"

"Yes," Violet answered, a proud little smile upon her lips. "I love him. I will declare it to all the world in defiance of the hideous charge that has been made against him. I have come to you because—because"—her voice broke pathetically—"you said to-day that you thought him innocent, and because I believe I can trust you with a secret."

Sexton Blake bowed.

"You may rest assured of my discretion, Miss O'Mega," he said.

Violet Melson hesitated, her little hands clasping and unclasping nervously as they lay in her lap.

Mr. Blake," she said suddenly, "I do not trust my father's friend!"

"You are referring to Mr. Luke O. Kerney," the detective murmured, with the air of one who is not asking a question, but stating a fact.

"Why, yes," Violet admitted, in surprise. "But I—I don't understand how you read my thoughts, for that is what you must have done. I had no idea that you knew, or had ever heard of Mr. Kerney."

"I am not quite sure whether I know him or not," Sexton Blake returned enigmatically. "I have, however, heard of him within the last hour. Why do you mistrust him?"

Violet bit her lip, and seemed momentarily at a loss for words.

"I really hardly know," she said at length, "save that I witnessed a strange scene between him and my father soon after I had returned, and—and——"

"Soon after you returned home and told your father of Mr. Riverton's arrest?" Sexton Blake prompted.

"Yes, yes," Violet exclaimed eagerly, clutching at the words. "It was soon after I returned home. Mr. Kerney was handling a great number of banknotes. Under the circumstances, I thought the fact of his being in possession of so many was significant."

"How many notes would you consider he had?"

"I could not say with any certainty," the girl answered, "but there were three to four thick rolls."

"Is that all you came here to tell me, Miss O'Mega," the detective asked, his lids drooping over his eyes, although he was in reality keenly studying his fair visitor's expression.

"Yes, Mr. Blake," Violet answered, after a distinct pause. "I—I thought that what I had seen might put you upon the right track. I have no reason for suspecting Mr. Kerney other than his having so many notes upon his person. Yet—yet——"

She lapsed into silence, and her eyes fell as she plucked at the lace upon her sleeve.

"You are sure that this is all you intended to communicate to me?" Sexton Blake queried quietly.

"I—I—— Of course I am sure, Mr. Blake."

"Miss O'Mega, you are not," Sexton Blake said gently, but very firmly. He had leant forward in his chair, and now his eyes were fully open and looking into those of the girl in a manner that seemed to penetrate to her very soul.

"Really," she protested feebly, "I guess you must let me know my own mind best."

"Like many other women who have been in trouble, you do not know your own mind, Miss O'Mega," the detective persisted. "Please hear me out, and forgive the liberty I take in differing with you. You came here fully intending to place confidence in me—to unburden your soul to all that was worrying you. You have altered your mind at the last moment. Why?"

Voilet stared back into the handsome, clever face of the man opposite her. Her lips were quivering, and she looked very effeminate and miserable at the moment.

"Why not tell me everything?" the detective murmured, a curiously tender note in his voice. "It would be for the best in the end."

A sob shook the girl's fail form. She seemed to shrink, and her shoulders shook convulsively, as she was overcome by a fit of heart-broken weeping.

Sexton Blake remained silent, knowing that the outburst would do much to steady her nerves and leave her quiet and confident.

"Mr. Blake," she said suddenly, looking up, and drying her eyes, "I hesitated to tell you all I had seen, because I think that my father is involved in this terrible business. I impulsively made up my mind that I would come to you and tell you all, but at the last moment my courage failed me. You—you will promise that my father shall come to no harm by reason of the information I am about to impart to you, either directly or indirectly?"

"I have already given you my word that my discretion may be counted upon," Sexton Blake said simply.

"I hate to think such a thing," she said, "but, somehow, I cannot help believing that my father knows a great deal about what has happened to-day. I have told you that I saw Mr. Kerney with a great number of banknotes in his hand. I entered the room unheard by either him or my father, for I was wearing a pair of light shoes, and the carpet of the drawing-room, in which they were seated, is very thick, rendering one's footsteps almost noiseless.

"I paused upon entering, for my father and his friend seemed to be engaged in a quarrel. Their voices were raised, and upon the face of Mr. Kerney was an expression that I can hardly describe. It was fiendish, should I say?" She shuddered. "It was the face of a criminal—a would-be murderer! He had removed the coloured spectacles he is in the habit of wearing, and his eyes were blazing with passion.

"I heard my father say 'I forbid you to use the fifty-eight thousand pounds you have over. You ought to have used more of them, and let them be secured by the police.'

"Then Mr. Kerney said something about it being quite safe to change them in France, as French notes bear no numbers."

"You are sure that he said that?" Sexton Blake asked sharply, his lids, which had been drooping again as he leant back in his chair, fingers tip to tip, going up quickly.

"Yes, those were his words. I am sure. My father began to reply, and I caught the words: 'We must arrange for the police to find them.' Then Mr. Kerney turned in his chair, saw that I was present, and kicked my father upon the shin so violently that he gave a cry of pain.

"Mr. Blake, what can it all mean? Upon no account must my father suffer, even if he is connected with this foul plot against the man I love! Yet I would have you get to the bottom of the mystery and clear Laurence Riverton."

"You have noticed nothing strange in your father's manner of late?" Sexton Blake suggested.

"Well, no—that is, nothing stranger than usual. He was always a strange man, and I believe there was a time when he had to work hard for a very meagre living. I have very little recollection of my father in my childhood. He was away from home for many years, and was not by my poor mother's bedside when she passed away in poverty, in the East End of London. My father is not an American, as is generally supposed. He is a Britisher; but long years in New York have caused him to cultivate many Americanisms which are misleading in the direction of his nationality.

"I seem to dimly remember him when I was quite a baby—a little atom that could just toddle about. Then he vanished out of my life, and as I grew older and asked my mother about him, she used to cry and say that he was abroad, working hard to provide a home for us later on.

"My mother seemed to grow poorer, and we nearly starved. In fact, we should have done so had it not been for the kindness of a neighbour little better off than we. One morning I crept to my mother's squalid bed, to find her hand was cold and curiously stiff.

"I was but a child, and at first I did not know that Death had laid his grisly finger upon our little home. I tried to rouse my mother; then, growing frightened, I called for the women who lived in the room beneath the garret we occupied. They told me my mother was dead.

"I was taken away by the neighbour who had been my mother's friend, and the years dragged by. Then my father found me, and shortly afterwards we sailed for America. At first we lived cheaply, but soon we moved into a much larger house, and my father began to heap expensive luxuries upon me."

"I know now and understand that he made money by working hard upon a little capital he had brought out from England. He was called 'The Gloved Millionaire' before very long, and——"

"Why was he given that nickname?" Sexton Blake asked.

"Because it was a habit of his always to wear gloves, even when he dined."

"Do you know why?"

"Yes. He had been doing very rough work before his return to England, and his hands were scarred and the nails broken."

Ah! Sexton Blake allowed the exclamation to softly escape his lips, and sank back in his chair. "Please proceed," said he.

"There is little more to tell, Mr. Blake," Violet said. "My father grew tremendously rich, until he practically retired from active business, leaving his affairs in the hands of a competent manager.

"We came to England, and a few months ago my father suddenly bought up a racing stable and house at Newmarket, expressing his intention of breeding and training thoroughbreds."

"Do you know your father's reason for calling himself O'Mega at Newmarket and Melson in London?" Sexton Blake asked.

"You—you know of that?" Violet had started. "I—I had no inkling that——"

"It is my business to know things, my dear young lady," Sexton Blake murmured. He smiled. "If you are anxious to keep your identity secret you should be careful not to leave photographs behind when you move from one place to another."

"Did I leave my photo somewhere?"

"Yes; at the Royal, where your father was known as Henry Melson."

"Melson is our name—or so I have always understood. My father took the stables in the name of Cyrus O'Mega for business reasons, I believe."

"Did he explain the change of name away by hinting at business reasons to you?"

"Yes."

Sexton Blake was silent for several minutes. His brows were drawn together, his lips compressed into a thin straight line. It was evident that he was thinking deeply. He seemed oblivious of the presence of the girl.

"Mr. Blake"—Violet had leant forward, and her hand was resting timidly upon his sleeve—"you will prove Laurence Riverton innocent?" she pleaded.

Sexton Blake looked up with something very like a start.

"I promise you I will," he said simply. "You woulf perhaps like to stay and see an experiment?"

"I do not understand."

"If you will kindly turn the tap connected with the gas-heating stove, I will show you what I mean. It is just by your hand there."

The girl manipulated the tap, and, stooping, Blake struck a match and ignited the fire. He then turned to his safe, unlocked it, and took from one of the drawers the cheque signed by Charles McDonald for seven thousand pounds.

He waited until the asbestos balls had began to glow redly, then he knelt by the stove and held the cheque before the bars.

After a few seconds had elapsed, Sexton Blake removed the cheque from before the fire and examined it. Cool and unemotional man though he was, he gave a shout of triumph then, for the letters "ty" had appeared at the end of the word seven, and an extra nought was now apparent amidst the figures, making the cheque read "seventy thousand pounds."

Sexton Blake was never given to being theatrical, but it was with something of a flourish that he handed the pink slip of paper to the watching girl.

"You see," he exclaimed—"You see!"

Violet drew a quick breath as her eyes took in the metamorposis that was apparent in the cheque.

"It has changed—it has altered!" she cried. "It is now for the amount that Laurence declared it was for when he cashed it this morning. Mr. Blake, what does this mean? My brain is whirling with the stress of all this mystery!"

"The explanation is simple enough, Miss Melson," Sexton Blake returned, a little grimly. "The cheque was forged to represent it as being an order to pay out just ten times as much as it was originally made out for. It was treated with invisible ink, which would only appear upon heat being applied! Your fiancee gave me the clue quite by chance to-night when he mentioned that the man who cashed the cheque was a very vigorous smoker, and that he had puffed his cigar until its end was glowing fiercely.

"Of course, he stood holding the cigar beneath the spots upon the cheque where the invisible additions had been made. Thus, when he handed the cheque over the counter, the added 'ty' and the nought sign had been brought out, and Laurence Riverton naturally cashed it for seventy thousand, instead of seven thousand pounds. When he put the cheque in his drawer, after having entered it, the 'faked' lettering and nought sign slowly faded away."

"But what is this?" Violet cried, and her voice was hoarse and tremulous with emotion. "This cheque is made payable to—

to my father."

"Yes," Sexton Blake answered slowly. "I fear he is very deeply implicated in the plot against your lover. I am sorry to give you this shock, Miss Melson, but I think it better that you should know the truth at once. You, however, have an assurance that no word of mine shall bring your father harm?"

CHAPTER 17
Sexton Blake's All-night Sitting

It was two o'clock in the morning as Sexton Blake, carrying a lamp, ascended the stairs and entered his consulting-room.

The detective's clothes were covered with dust, and his face was smeared with it. But then he had been engaged in a very unclean job in a very unclean place—the cellars beneath the house.

It was there that Sexton Blake kept file upon file of old newspapers, dating back for the matter of some twenty to twenty-one years. He had been searching for a record of the trial of Jasper Clench, which had taken place so many years ago, and the newspaper page protruding from his jacket-pocket proclaimed that he had been successful in securing what he sought.

Sexton Blake turned out the lamp and placed it upon the sideboard. He then brushed his clothes, passed into his dressing-room, and indulged in a refreshing wash.

When he returned to his consulting-room, he had removed his coat and vest, and he donned his dressing-gown and sank into his favourite chair.

Very slowly and methodically the detective filled and lit his oldest and blackest pipe, then he settled down to think out the complicated case in connection with Fisher's Banking House.

An almost startling theory had come to Sexton Blake after his interviews that evening. Mr. Raymond, the manager of the Royal Hotel, had convinced him—even before his conversation with the girl whom two hours ago he had seen safely to her hotel—that Henry Melson and Cyrus O'Mega were one and the same man. The photo of Henry Melson's daughter was the picture of Miss O'Mega. There had been no doubt about that, and later Violet herself had admitted that her father raced under the non-de-plume of O'Mega, and that Henry Melson was the name she believed to be really his.

Henry Melson was the man to whom the cheque was made payable. Then how, if Melson was not implicated in the plot against Laurence Riverton, had the cheque got into the hands of Maitland, and been cashed for ten times its real value? It appeared to Sexton Blake that Henry Melson must have known Maitland when they had both been staying at the Royal Hotel, and had later coerced him into committing the swindle upon the bank in such a manner that it would look as though Laurence Riverton was guilty of a tremendous embezzlement.

That this had been Maitland's intention, there was no shadow of a doubt. Otherwise the master-criminal would hardly have parted with five thousand pounds and taken the trouble to place the notes in his dupe's pocket.

Mr. Melson, Sexton Blake was certain, had been listening outside the door of Raymond's office when he—Blake—and the Scotland Yard men had been discussing Maitland. Was it possible that Melson had helped Maitland to escape them, in order that he might participate in the plot that was being hatched against the young cashier at Fisher's Bank?

Sexton Blake remembered the car that he had seen humming away up the Minories when Maitland had given them the slip after the raid upon the shop of the "fence," Israel Samuels; and he wondered if, after all, the criminal had been concealed in the vehicle—if it had been Henry Melson who sat at the wheel?

Presuming that Henry Melson and Maitland had conspired together to ruin young Riverton, what was the object of the millionaire? Obviously he wished to pay off some grudge of the past—to be bitterly revenged. Yet it could not be against the younger Riverton personally that Melson was seeking vengeance. Who, then? Why, the elder Riverton,. It was logic, based upon Sexton Blake's principle that two and two always made four; not sometimes, but all the time.

Voilet Melson had said that her father had been known in America as "The Gloved Millionaire," because he had worn gloves, even at meals, to hide the disfiguring scars that were in evidence upon his hands. When she had asked her mother for her father, she had been told that he was abroad. "Abroad," the detective shrewdly suspected, meant "prison." That would account for Henry Melson's scarred hand and broken nails when he had suddenly returned to claim his child. Then what other deduction could be arrived at than that Henry Melson was in reality Jasper Clench, the ex-partner of Laurence Riverton's father?

Every deduction pointed to this being the case. In the twenty-year-old newspaper report, Sexton Blake had read of the wild outburst of Clench when he had been sentenced, how he had sworn that before he died he would seek out the man who had betrayed him and make him suffer as he was to suffer.

The attempted ruination of Laurence Riverton's life was the form that vengeance had taken. Jasper Clench had sought out his old partner, and had tried to strike at him through his son.

Sexton Blake had thought over the story Violet Melson had told him, and the fact of Melson's friend—Kerney—being in possession of so many banknotes, together with the conversation the girl had overheard, seemed to almost prove that he was Maitland. The detective had warned the girl upon leaving her to say nothing of what she had told him to her father, and had reiterated his promise that no hurt should come to him.

There was but one course open now—to go down to Newmarket in a disguise and keep an eye upon this Mr. Luke O. Kerney until he gave some indication that he was indeed the master-criminal.

Sexton Blake placed his pipe upon the mantel, and lit a cigar carelessly, so that it burnt all down one side. The hours dragged by, and at length the grey light of dawn streamed through the Venetian blinds, displaying Sexton Blake haunched up in his chair, the front of his dressing-gown snowed with ash. His face was expressionless as that of a Sphinx, his eyes half-closed, an observer might have thought that he was asleep.

Eight o'clock struck upon the marble clock on the mantel, and the door opened sharply.

Pedro bounded in, and fawned upon his master, but he suddenly desisted, sneezed badly, and bolted from the room again, his tail between his legs. The smoke-laden atmosphere of that room was too much for him.

Tinker, who had followed the hound in, stood gazing at the huddled figure of his master.

"You've not been to bed guv'nor," he said reproachfully. "You'll be knocking yourself up if you go on like this."

"I have been thinking, lad," Sexton Blake said, rising and placing his hand affectionately upon his assistant's shoulder. "But don't you worry about me. I will sleep later on to make up for any all-night sitting. Pull up the blinds."

Tinker obeyed, and Sexton Blake waved his hand towards a chair. He gave the lad a full account of his deductions, much to Tinker's interest and surprise.

"Then you think this chap Kerney is Maitland, sir?" the assistant asked excitedly.

"Yes. Fate appears to have once again willed that he shall cross my path," Sexton Blake answered.

"And you'll arrest him at once, sir?" Tinker asked. "We must get a warrant and——"

"We must make certain of his identity first, Tinker," his master interrupted. "We shall go down to Newmarket by the first train this morning, and Pedro will accompany us."

"You and I will take it in turns to hand about the O'Mega, or Melson stables, in a suitable disguise, until we have proved that Kerney is our man. Hurry up, my lad, and order breakfast. We have no time to lose. Now that Maitland—if the man is he—has carried out his plot and has a sum of fifty-eight thousand pounds in his hands, he might clear out of Newmarket, and England, without a moment's notice to his co-conspirator!"

CHAPTER 18
The Capture of Blake

"My heavens, Maitland, I have got to steel my heart to go with this business!"

Henry Melson passed his hand wearily across his brows as he utterd the words.

He was seated in his study, in company with Ezra Q. Maitland, who was smoking a cigar and slowly sipping at a brandy and soda he had just mixed himself from the tantalus and syphon upon the sideboard.

The crook stared curiously at his companion. Henry Melson looked ill and haggard, his cheeks seemed to have grown sunken, and he appeared strangely old and careworn.

"What the tarnation thunder is the matter with you?" the master criminal queried, as he flicked the ashes from his cigar.

"What you suggested has happened," Melson said huskily.

"You mean?" Maitland asked, with a raising of his brows.

"That my girl has given her heart to the son of the man who betrayed me," Henry Melson answered. "I have said nothing to you before. I knew on Saturday, and this is Monday, but I've been trying to forget—trying to put my little girl's tear-stained face from the eye of my brain—trying to forget the agonised tone of her voice when she told me of his arrest!"

Maitland grinned.

"Don't be a bigger fool than you can help," he said callously. "I reckon the gal will soon forget him when he's breaking stones in chokee!"

"Silence!" Henry Melson cried, his eyes blazing. "How can you speak so lightly under the circumstances! Violet is an impressionable girl. She will never put him out of her mind!"

"Waal, let her keep him in it!" the Yankee drawled. "Do you mean to say you will go back now? Think of how you have suffered! Think of the sneers and gibes of the warders who used to bring you your skilly! Think of the coarse work that tore your hands! Think——"

"Enough!" Henry Melson rasped, drawing a long, quivering breath. "I am never likely to forget the past. You are right, perhaps. I will go on with my great venegence! You have wired for your servent?"

"Yes. What's the time now? My watch has stopped."

"Just six o'clock," Henry Melson answered, looking at his timepiece.

"Then the yellow villain will be here before long, I guess," Maitland answered. "I instructed him to catch the first train after receipt of my wire."

"And you think he will manage to get into the stable and leave no trace of foul play having been employed?"

"I reckon I'm sure of it. Wang is as cunning as a wagon-load of monkeys, and as agile as any one of them. I put a code word in my wire that he will understand, and he'll bring with him some deadly poison that leaves no trace."

Henry Melson nodded slowly, his eyes narrowing. At the moment his pale face was transformed into that of a fiend. His eyes were gleaming with hatred, his lips snarling from his teeth.

"Good!" he muttered. "It will be the last blow for Richard Cavendish before his finds himself in the hands of the police. If Serious Symons won the Gold Cup, his great aim would be accomplished, for he would be able to send the last of the money to those we defrauded. I have got into touch with one of our former victims, and I have learnt from him that only one further payment remains to be made to refund all that he invested in our companies. But the horse shall not win, and Richard Cavendish shall eat out his heart in prison, knowing that he is still in the debt of the fools who trusted him. Hark! There is someone outside now, I guess!"

He was right. Footsteps were heard in the corridor, and there came a tap upon the door. In response to Henry Melson's command to "come in," a footman entered.

"A person to see Mr. Kerney," he said, with a haughty sniff.

The next moment he was gasping with indignation, for the caller—a thin evil-looking Chinaman, attired in European clothes—had unceremoniously pushed him aside and shuffled into the room.

He was Wang, Ezra Q. Maitland's Oriental servant and accomplice, a scoundrel to his skinny finger-tips, perhaps even a little more callus and unscrupulous than his notorious master.

"You may go, Giles," Henry Melson said, making a gesture to the servant, who was favouring the Chinaman with a supercilious stare.

The door closed behind the man, and Wang shuffled forward to bow low before his master.

"What orldels?" he piped, in his thin voice.

"You have brought the stuff? You understood the wire?"

"Yes, most illustrious one," the Chinaman agreed. "Wang quite allee lightee undelstand. Bling lots of poisons—all vely, vely deadly."

"You slit-eyed scoundrel!" Maitland grinned. "I believe you like messing with those beastly drugs of yours. Say, it's a horse—a racehorse—we want put out of the way."

Wang smiled in a curiously sinister manner.

"The vely thingee!" he piped, displaying a tiny phial. "A little of this on a needle, a scratch, and gee-gee tulnee upee his toes qulite allee lightee!"

"Then listen here," Maitland ordered, plucking at his sleeve and drawing him near. "I guess I'll give you your instructions. The job's got to be worked to-night!"

· · · · · ·

Eleven o'clock had struck, and not a light showed in the Riverton Training Stables, with the exception of the faint glimmer of the lamps placed above the stalls of the horses, whilst, so far as could be seen through the trees, the ex-swindler's house was also in darkness.

Yet towards the wall surrounding the extensive stable-yard crept the figure of a man. It was a lean, diminutive figure, almost apish in shape and movement as it glided through the gloom.

Something trailed down the man's back. It was a greasy pigtail, which had somehow escaped from the large cap that was drawn over its owner's head, previously securing it in a coil.

Wang—the maurauder was he—glanced about him furtively as he crouched in the shadow of the wall; but alert-eyed though he was, he did not perceive the dark shape that suddenly darted out of sight behind a clump of bushes.

The night was not an ideal one for the purpose, for although the sky was cloudy and threatening from time to time the clouds would pass from the face of the moon and the countryside was flooded with its sickly, yellow light.

The Chinaman remained where he had crouched for fully half a minute. Then, as he heard no sound from the opposite side of the wall, he straightened his skinny body, made a quick leap, and clutched at the top of the brickwork.

The next moment he was scaling the wall, and had dropped upon the other side to again wait for a few seconds in silence, listening.

There was a faint rustling from the direction of the adjacent bushes, and the form that had been concealed behind them again appeared.

The man had evidently been shadowing the Chinaman, for he now went slowly towards the spot at which the former had climbed the wall.

The shadower was a typical specimen of the tout and hanger-on, so frequently to be met with in the neighbourhood of racing stables. He was attired in a very shabby suit of loud checks, with a dilapidated cap to match, pulled low over his eyes. A gaudily-tinted scarf was wound about his neck and knotted under his left ear, whilst cracked and patched leggings adorned his lower limbs.

His face was unshaven and tanned, and even the keenest observer would have failed to recognise him for whom he really was.

Sexton Blake never did things by halves, and this latest disguise of his was one of the most skilful pieces of work in the direction of the art of make-up that he had accomplished for some time past.

The detective, with Tinker and Pedro, had journeyed to Newmarket upon the preceeding day and put up at a small inn there, where he was well known to the proprietor—a fact that enabled him to enter and leave in various disguises, if he found it necessary.

Most of the day he had been watching the Melson—or O'Mega—stables, but he had not, as yet, caught a glimpse of the man who was known as Luke O. Kerney. Sexton Blake had been about to turn his steps towards his inn as dusk commenced to fall, when a thing had happened that had caused him to change his plans.

He had seen a Chinaman enter the house, and in a flash he had realised the man's identity, although he had been some hundred yards away and unable to see his features. Instinct had told Sexton Blake that the caller was Wang, Maitland's accomplice and servant, and he knew that he was without question, upon the right track.

He had lain hidden behind a rise in the ground, his eyes glued upon the house. For two hours he must have waited, then his vigil had been rewarded by his seeing the lean, shuffling figure of the Chinaman slip from the gates opening into the drive.

Sexton Blake had decided to follow the Oriental, although he counted him as very small fry as compared with his villainous master. Blake was, however, pleased now that he had taken the course he had adopted for, he reasoned that some very sinister motive was in Wang's mind now that he knew his quarry's destination.

Sexton Blake stood with his ear pressed against the wall, and he heard the faint sound of the Chinaman's dragging footsteps as he moved across the yard towards the stables.

The detective waited until the sound ceased, then made his way round to the gates. There was a flash of light as Sexton Blake whipped out his pocket-torch and examined the massive padlock with which they were secured. Next moment the torch was back in his pocket, and he was holding a bunch of skeleton keys between his fingers.

Quickly the detective set to work. He meant to enter silently by the gates, for he dared not scale the wall for fear of alarming the wily Chinee and giving him a chance to slip away in the gloom. Had he mounted to the top of the wall, his figure would have been silhouetted against the sky, and it was a hundred to one on the marauder seeing him and taking fright.

Besides, Sexton Blake had a whim for catching Maitland's servant red-handed, and——"

Click! Blake had found the key to fit the lock, and one of the gates swung slowly inwards as he gently pressed upon it. With the stealth of a cat, the detective entered the stable-yard and darted to the wall, to press himself flat against it.

He heard a slight sound from the direction of the stable-door, and saw Wang's form darkly outlined against it. Only his arms seemed to be moving, and Sexton Blake immediately knew what he was doing. He was attempting to pick the lock.

Tensely, the detective waited until he saw the door move inwards and the Chinaman glide through. Then Sexton Blake ran noiselessly across the yard, crouched down by the door, and peered cautiously into the stable.

He heard the horses stirring uneasily, although they were not making sufficient noise to arouse the stable lads, who slept in the rooms provided for them in the upper portion of the building. It was the light from a dark lantern held by Wang that was causing them to be restless, for the Chinaman was going from stall to stall, examining the occupants.

Wang stopped before a handsome-looking thoroughbred, and the watching detective knew that it was Serious Symons, John Riverton's candidate for the Newmarket Gold Cup, he having recently seen a photo of the horse in one of the illustrated papers, and noted the splash of white upon its forehead.

He saw Wang take something from his pocket. Had he been nearer, he would have been able to discern that it was a tiny phial, and a packet of ordinary needles. The Chinaman uncorked the phial, drew out one of the tiny steel instruments, and dipped the point in the greenish liquid in the miniature bottle. Then he passed the dark shade over his lantern.

Sexton Blake knew that the time had come to act. He leapt up and steeled himself for a spring that would land him at the back of the doper; and at the moment he had no inkling of the danger he himself was in.

A few seconds before, a man had come tearing towards the stables, his elbows pressed to his sides, his breath coming pantingly between his teeth. He had seen the gates standing ajar and had cautiously entered the yard to almost at once observe the crouching form of the detective by the stable door.

Ezra Q. Maitland—the newcomer was he—had pulled up quickly and watched, knowing by the stature of the bent form that it did not belong to his accomplice, Wang.

The master-criminal began to creep forward, his fingers gripping hard upon a life-preserver that lay in his jacket pocket. Nearer and nearer Maitland drew; and now the heavy weapon was swung above his head.

At the very moment when Blake rose and poised his body to hurl himself forward, Maitland's foot foot kicked against a stone, and Sexton Blake swung round on his heels.

He flung up his arms to protect himself, but he—was the fraction of a second too late. The life-preserver descended with a sickening thud upon his temple, and he collapsed like a log at the master-criminal's feet.

A startled gasp came from inside the stable; and Wang, dropping the bottle of poison and the needle, darted towards the door, whipping out an ugly-looking knife.

A word from Maitland, however, reassured him, although his slit-like eyes were full of surprise at seeing his master. He put the knife away and shuffled into the yard.

"Whoee thlis?" he asked, in a whisper, as he caught sight of the detective's still form upon the cobblestones.

"I reckon I don't know, yet;" Maitland returned quickly, in the same low tone. "You haven't killed the horse?"

"Noee!" Wang answered. "Me goo back and doee it now!"

"You'll be doing nothing of the kind!" Maitland hissed sharply.

"But youl orldels, mastel, were to——"

"Don't argue!" Maitland snapped. "I came here to stop you injuring the brute. I am playing a game of my own and I guess I want him to win! I was only in the nick of time, for I couldn't give old Melson the slip before. Here! come right along! Let's get away before someone hears us and gives the alarm!"

He turned to dart from the yard, then paused, and stopped over the unconscious detective.

"I wonder whom he can be?" he muttered, removing Sexton Blake's cap. "By Columbus! A wig! Here, cast your glim this way for a moment!"

The yellow beam from the Chinaman's lantern shot out as he slipped back the slide and played upon the drawn face of the detective, from whose head Maitland had snatched a sandy wig.

The master criminal peered down at his victim, then a low cry burst from his lips, and, snatching out his handkerchief, he rubbed vigorously at Sexton Blake's face, removing some of the grease paint from the skin.

"Perdition!" Maitland muttered, his hands shaking as he drew back. "It's Sexton Blake!"

"Sexton Blake!" Wang recoiled, as though he had been shot, and so startled was he was he all but dropped his lantern.

"S-s-s-h! You fool!" Maitland snarled, recovering himself by a great effort. Let us get away from here slick. Catch hold of his legs!"

But Wang's formidable knife was out, glinting wickedly in the gloom.

"Why not killee him right nowee?" he asked callously. "Dead men tellee no tales, and——"

"Do as I order you, you yellow scum!" Maitland blazed. "By heavens he shan'n't die quickly. Besides, if his death were reported in the papers, your mistress would know that you or I killed him. I reckon Kate's against murder, and perhaps that's a good thing for me. Hustle, some, will ye?"

The Chinaman replaced his knife and seized Blake's legs, whilst the master criminal got hold upon him beneath the armpits. They stealthily carried their burden from the stable yard and quickly made away from the Riverton buildings.

"Whele takee him?" Wang asked, pausing after they had covered some distance and were out of sight of the stables.

"To the quarry over there!" Maitland said, pointing across the heath to where could be seen the wall that surrounded the dangerous cavity. "We will leave him there! It's odds against his being found before he starves to death, but that's his look-out. Sometimes the quarry isn't worked for weeks. On the other hand, some of the stone might be required and workmen go there to-morrow."

"You notee think that?" Wang said, with an evil smile.

"I don't," Maitland answered callously, "otherwise I should find some other means of disposing of the spying hound, for if he were at liberty I should stand a poor chance of keeping away from the Tower of London's shooting range."

They were silent until they arrived at the quarry wall; then Maitland ordered:

"Over with you!"

Wang let fall the detecive's feet and nimbly scaled the wall. Maitland was soon astride it; and, dragging Sexton Blake's limp body over, he handed it down to the Chinaman, who stood upon the quarry's edge.

Some five minutes later they had succeeded in scrambling down the treacherous side, and Maitland shuddered as his eyes fell upon the dead Satan—the horse that had so nearly carried Violet Melson to a swift and terrible doom.

"Look!" he said, pointing to the quarry's side. "There is a working there. Bring him to it."

They carried Sexton Blake over the yawning cavity in the rocky earth to find that it went back into the side of the quarry to extent of some six feet.

"Put him right inside and go and find some rope," the master-criminal ordered. "There ought to be some over by those trucks and things."

Wang dropped the detective roughly into the cavern-like hole; and, turning upon his heels, made his way in the direction indicated. Maitland glanced after him a trifle anxiously, for Sexton Blake had stirred uneasily, and it seemed that he was about to regain his sesnses.

Long before the detective opened his eyes, however, the Chinaman had found a length of stout cord and the detective had been bound hand and foot.

"So, my friend," the criminal hissed, as Sexton Blake's lids flickered and he looked up feebly and blinked in the glare of Wang's lantern, "you're conscious again. Say, look at me, and I guess you'll cotton on to what's happened!"

The detective stared up dazedly, his mind for the time being a blank. His head was aching horribly, and he was experiencing a sensation for all the world as though two keen-bladed knives were being driven through his temples.

Maitland knelt beside him and stuck his hate-distorted face near that of his enemy. He was not wearing his spectacles now, and his true features seemed to peer out nakedly from behind his disguise.

"Maitland!" Sexton Blake said, memory returning to him with almost overwhelming suddenness. "So we meet again!"

"Yes, you cur!" the criminal snarled, striking his arch-foe a brutal blow between the eyes that caused his brain to reel again. "We meet again, but under very pleasant circumstances—for me! Do you know what is going to happen to you?"

Sexton Blake shugged as well as he was able, and his air was almost that of weariness.

"I suppose that is rather obvious," he said. "You have brought me here to murder me. It is what I should expect from you."

"You happen to be wrong!" Maitland sneered. "We could have put your light out in Riverton's stable yard if we had been so minded. But I've a fancy to give you a sporting chance, Sexton Blake."

"Indeed!" the detective murmured, with a raising of his brows and his manner as cool as though he had been discussing the chances of a fine day upon the morrow in some society lady's drawing-room. "You appear to have developed a sudden vein of kindness. Why?"

"Because it's long odds against your chance coming off, you clever, cunning fiend!" Maitland snarled, his passion suddenly returning to him. "We are going to leave you here on the chance of your being found! Do you get me?"

"I think so," the detective answered simply. "If no one comes to the quarry I shall die of starvation."

"Yes!"

"I thought there was some good reason on your part for not putting me out of the way expeditiously," Sexton Blake retorted. "That explains the sudden trait of humanity," he added, with a sneer curling his finely chiselled lips. "But why not leave me to take my sporting chance? You can do no good by stopping here to talk of my possible end."

"You're a cool card, Sexton Blake," Maitland said. "By James, I can always admire you, in many ways. What a pile of money we should have squeezed from this gullible world of ours if we had worked together, instead of against each other."

"That would have been out of the question," Sexton Blake answered. "Even if I were dishonest, I should hardly care to associate with a contemptible spy and would-be murderer!"

"Bah! Don't goad me too far!" Maitland rasped, his hands clenching. "I guess I'd better leave you, or I might take a fancy into my head to kill you outright. But listen to my plans before I go! It will be pleasant when you are slowly starving, to think that I have netted a fortune."

"There was no need for you to trouble about Serious Symons to-night. I never intended him to be injured, although I agreed with Melson——"

"With Clench," Sexton Blake corrected coolly.

Maitland started violently.

"You—you know whom he really is?" he gasped. "But, after all, I am not surprised. I'll admit you are clever, I guess."

"As I was saying, I never meant Serious Symons to be 'got at,' because I calc'late it's to my advantage for him to win. When he has done so he'll bring John Riverton many thousands of pounds, and I mean to lay my hands on some of them. I've already got a haul——"

"Fifty-eight thousand from Fisher's bank, to be precise," Sexton Blake said, with the air of a man stating a known fact; and he smiled slightly as he saw Maitland start again. "But go on; I am really interested."

"I reckoned you would be!" the criminal grinned. "To know that you are beaten and your man's getting away with fortune ought to please you! Waal, I guess John Riverton's got to part up when Serious Symons gets home! As you know whom Melson is, you have possible been clever enough to find out the identity of John Riverton. But I guess I'll tell you, if you haven't. He is Richard Cavendish, a swindler who escaped from England twenty years ago with half a million sterling, and he's never been arrested."

"I calc'late I'm going to touch him for something like twenty-thousand; and, with that added to the other, I sha'n't have to trouble society again by preying on it. If he don't pay up and smile, you can guess what'll happen. He'll do about ten years, unless the judge happens to be in a sympathetic frame of mind, which ain't likely. He signed to Wang, who roughly forced a knotted handkerchief into the detectives mouth, to serve as a gag. With a mocking smile, Maitland turned away.

"Good-night, Sexton Blake!" he sneered. "Good-night; and pleasant dreams to you!"

CHAPTER 19
At Newmarket

Racing again, and Newmarket woke into life!

In the "ring" all was bustle and excitement, the race for the Gold Cup being the next upon the card to be decided.

Well-dressed men were seeking to know the odds, brazen voiced book-makers were shouting them. Money was swiftly changing hands, and the tick-tack men were experiencing one of the busiest moments of their day.

In the cheaper enclosures the noise was even more deafening. The smaller punters were betting rapidly, favouring little else save Cyanin, Serious Symons, and a member of the "dark" order called Claudian, about whom there were mysterious whispers. He was a four-year old, and was said to have run well in Ireland, when he had finished fourth to a famous crack in a big event.

The war seemed to make but little difference to the attendance, save that upon every side it was possible to see a khaki uniform.

Line upon line of spectators pressed forward to the rails as the horses to contest the Gold Cup were paraded. There were a dozen in all, and the race promised to be an interesting event. Although, upon public form, Serious Symons and Cyanin seemed to hold the rest of the field safe, the rest were good horses, one and all, who had run well in the past; and more than one seasoned backer chanced a bit on an outsider.

The horses looked a handsome lot as they passed the stand, the gorgeous silks of the jockeys and the glossy coats of their mounts shimmering in the soft warm sunshine. It was a glorious day for racing, bright and sunny, yet cool, owing to the gentle breeze that was blowing across the heath.

Three to one was obtained about both Cyanin and Serious Symons, and every bookmaker had been mentioning the latter, although since the morning there had been conflicting rumours afloat concerning him.

Some had said that he was too ill to run, others that he was dead. There had been a whisper going round that he had been "got at"; but no one had seemed to know the real facts of the case. Even the "heads" in the "ring" had appeared ignorant concerning the truth.

"When Jack Haynes, Riverton's trainer, had been approached regarding the colt, he had been very reticent. He had smiled enigmatically and vouchsafed no definite information. In his heart, however, was a fierce anger, for that morning he had found the lock of the stable door picked and the fragments of the bottle of poison that had fallen from Wang's hands upon the ground.

"A favourite collie had sniffed at the green fluid in a portion of the broken glass and died with a proptitude that was almost uncanny. Still, Jack Haynes was a man who believed in letting the public go hang when they wanted information about horses in his care, although he never misled anyone. He had, therefore, kept his own counsel as to what had precisely happened.

The bookmakers had been careful, and kept Serious Symons co-favourite with Cyanin. Their caution, as they had now discovered, was warranted; for at the last moment Serious Symons had been brought into the paddock and he was now the foremost in the parade.

Up in the stand, Henry Melson had smiled grimly as he had listened to the gossip concerning his one-time partner's horse, and he did not happen to be looking when the animal passed the stand. Someone shouted:

"There he is, as fit and well as can be! There's Serious Symons. Who said——"

Melson turned swiftly, and his glasses went up to his eyes.

"By heavens!" he cried, swinging round on Maitland, who was by his side, in company with Violet. "What does this mean? Wang has——"

"Hush!" Maitland hissed warningly. "What are you talking about?"

"The—the horse!" Henry Melson faltered pointing to the colt as it broke into a canter and left its fellows behind. "Look! It's with the others!"

"Great pip! Yes!" Maitland ejaculated, turning his head aside to hide the little grin that would come to his lips. "The yellow scoundrel! He—— But, don't say any more now! People are looking this way! By James, Mel—O'Mega, Wang shall suffer for this!"

Henry Melson stood staring after the horse, his glasses held in shaking hands. He was dumbfounded; for that morning the master-criminal's oriental servant had sworn that Serious Symons had fallen dead in his stall, when scratched with a needle which had been dipped into the deadly poison he had brought with him from London.

"The careless idiot must have killed the wrong horse!" Maitland whispered in the elder man's ear; and there was splendidly feigned anger in his voice. "The fool! I'll make him smart when I get at him. I'll tan his yellow hide, I guess!"

Henry Melson lowered his glasses, his face very harsh, his eyes unnaturally bright.

"May it fall and break its neck a yard in front of the post!" he breathed. "But"—he shrugged—"even if it beats Cyanin, I still have another weapon to use against the cur who——"

He broke off and lapsed into silence, eagerly waiting for the cry that would tell him that the race had started.

Things began to get busy now and the bookmakers in the cheaper enclosures were doing an even more rapid business, although the betting had been brisk for the last twenty minutes.

In this noisy and more animated crowd a young man, with a baby moustache, of which he seemed excessively proud, was strolling aimlessly about. He was immaculately attired, and his stockings were of a delicate pale blue, whilst he cultivated a really spendid creation in neckwear.

More than once his "knut-like" appearance had caused a disgusted Tommy to intimate aloud that he would look better in khaki, but Tinker, assistant to Mr. Sexton Blake—the "knut-like" look was a very good disguise—paid little heed, for he knew well enough that he hand his master has worked ceaselessly in the interests of Great Britain since the outbreak of the war.

If the truth be told, Tinker was a trifle preoccupied. He was wondering why his master had not returned to the inn upon the preceding night, and feared some harm had befallen him. The lad knew how dangerous was the work of his master and himself, when pitted against the master-criminal from America, the man who had sworn to one day take their lives?

"'Ere y'are, me young sportsman!" a bookie yelled, as Tinker paused to study the prices scrawled upon the slate. "What's yer fancy?"

"Serious Symons," Tinker answered, rousing himself and fishing out two half-crowns.

"Fifteen bob to a dollar the Solemn Bloke!" the penciller said to his clerk. "An' as good as fifteen silver shillin's in yer pocket, mate!"

"Glad you think so," Tinker murmured; and passed on, after taking his ticket.

"Three ter one Cyanin! Three ter one Serious Symons! Eights Claudian! Ten the Rook! 'Ere, walk up, ladies an' gents! Ten ter one bar two!"

The bookmakers were shouting against each other now, all eager to lay the odds.

One unfortunate penciller was suffering from a cold, and had almost lost his voice. He believed, however, in the motto "Business as Usual," and was doing his best to attract attention to himself, much to the amusement of his competitors, who were chaffing him unmercifully.

"Say, George!" a loud-voiced bookmaker jeered. "If yer stands there wheezing much longer, you'll take root!"

"Well, if I does take root," the afflicted one squeaked, "I 'opes I don't grow into a thing like you!"

"'Ere, watcher mean, yer red-nosed welsher!" the other snarled.

"If yer calls me a welsher ag'in, yer worm, I'll put me fist against yer heye!" the man with the cold retorted angrily. "Can't a cove shout if he likes wi'out——"

But the little exchange of compliments was stopped by the magic roar that went up from a thousand throats.

"They're off!"

A dead silence after the thunderous outburst—a silence that was impressive and could almost be felt. Those who carried glasses had them glued to their eyes, watching to see how the horses had got away.

Up in the stand John Riverton was anxiously watching for his colours. It meant so much to him if Serious Symons won. He would be able to repay the last of the money to his swindled clients of years ago and know that his one great object in life was accomplished to the full.

The first mile covered at a hard pace and the field beginning to tail off. There were soon only five horses seriously contesting the race, the others having dropped hopelessly behind, one by one.

Serious Symons was near the rails and coming along swiftly, yet steadily. Cyanin was a little in the rear, but he was moving well and his jockey seemed to be nursing him.

The other three who were near consisted of the "dark" horse, Claudian, a big, slashing five-year-old called Tressady, and a smart chestnut colt named the Hope.

Ah! Claudian had had enough of it and was swiftly falling behind. A green jacket grew more and more in the rear and the Hope was accounted for. Tressady's jockey was using his whip, but it was useless. As many a keen judge had predicted, the race was really to rest between Serious Symons and Cyanin, the favourites.

Only a furlong to go. Cyanin was running well, and so far his jockey had found no cause to force his pace. Serious Symons was still hugging the rails, and a howl went up as, for a moment, it looked as though Cyanin was attempting to "bore" him.

On, on flew the two thoroughbreds, their long necks stretched out as though they could scent the winning post. Fred Brown, on the Serious One, had his whip out now and was using it, causing his mount to fairly jump forward.

Cyanin was badly in the rear for the space of a second or two, but his rider followed the other jockey's tactics and Cyanin, too, bounded forward until the two horses were racing neck and neck.

All was wild confusion. Their names were both being yelled with equal persistency upon every side, until suddenly Fred Brown again urged his horse to a last supreme effort.

Serious Symons was a length ahead, two, three, and——

"Serious Symons! Serious Symons w-i-n-s!"

The shout developed into a din, echoing and re-echoing over the heath, then Serious Symons shot past the post, a winner by four lengths, and cheer upon cheer went up from those who had entrusted him with their money.

And up in the stand Henry Melson was muttering a savage curse, whilst his ex-partner was almost delirious with joy, forgetting for the time being the black shadow that was hanging over his son, the one being in the world for whom he cared.

"Thank Heaven!" was John Riverton's muttered comment. "At last I can fully repay and look the world in the face again!"

. . . .

Tinker ceased his restless pacing, and pausing before the window, stared out into the quaint, hedge-bordered lane in which his inn was situated.

The lad looked anxious and worried. Upon his return from the races, which he had visited purely to kill time, it was to find that Sexton Blake had not returned; and Tinker was beginning to have grave fears as to his master's safety.

The lad turned from the window with an impatient gesture, and sank down in a chair. Pedro, who realised by instinct that something was troubling his young master, solemnly stalked over to him and pushed his cold muzzle into his hand.

"I wonder where your master is, old chap?" Tinker muttered, caressing one of the faithful hound's enormous ears. "It's unlike him to go off like this without leaving some word for me. I'm beginning to fear the worst! My aunt! But if that brute's killed my guv'nor, I'll never rest until I've put the rope about his neck!"

Tinker's hands clenched savagely, and his young face took on a hard, determined expression. He tried to put the thought from his mind, but somehow it refused to go.

Time after time Ezra Q. Maitland and his scoundrelly servant, Wang, had come within an ace of sending Sexton Blake to his last account, employing the most fiendish means to attain their end. Tinker remembered how Maitland had all but succeeded in suffocating his arch-enemy after the clearing up of the case of the Belgian Relief Fund, he remembered how Wang's devilish pet had stabbed Sexton Blake in Rome, and——

"We'll try to find him, Pedro!" Tinker exclaimed, suddenly rising to his feet. "I can stand this suspense no longer. If I spoil some plan of the guv'nor's by appearing on the scene at the wrong moment, I'll chance the wigging he'll give me. Come, lad. Find your master."

Pedro bayed softly and capered joyously towards the door, as Tinker snatched up one of the detective's caps and moved across the room.

When they had passed down the lane and stood outside the inn, Tinker stooped and pressed the cap to his four-footed friend's muzzle.

"Good Pedro! Find!" he ordered. "Seek your master!"

The hound whined wistfully; then, after quickly sniffing round in a circle he raised his head and gave tongue. The next moment he was tugging upon the leash Tinker had affixed to his collar, anxious to be off upon the scent of the man he loved so dearly.

Down the lane went the hound, Tinker breaking into a trot to keep pace with him. The scent was many hours old, but, it being that of Sexton Blake, and so well known to the dog, he had little difficulty in following it.

Now and again he hesitated, but it was never for long, and always he picked up the scent again and pushed onwards until Tinker found himself traversing the heath.

Soon he knew that Pedro was making for the O'Mega stables, but when he arrived there he abruptly turned and made off in another direction.

Straight for the neighbouring establishment, owned by John Riverton, Pedro made, and passed through the gates into the stable-yard.

He passed a couple of lads who were standing talking together, and for a moment they were too surprised to resent the intrusion.

"Here, old sport, what's the game?" one of the stable lads asked, seizing Tinker by the arm and earning a warning growl from the dog that made him jump back a pace with undignified haste. "Taking the dog for an airing in our stable, or merely come ter look at the gee-gees?"

Tinker turned a serious face towards the speaker, so serious, in fact, that the stable hand almost immediately changed his tone, for he was a decent enough young fellow at heart.

"What's the trouble, mate?" he asked.

In a few sentences Tinker explained whom he was, and the reason for Pedro having led him into the yard.

"By jingo! So your're Sexton Blake's assistant, eh?" the stable lad exclaimed. "Well, then you can bet it was your guv'nor who stopped Serious Symons being killed last night. You heard that some cur tried to 'get at' him?"

Tinker nodded.

"It was true, right enough," the stable hand said. "We found a bottle of poison smashed on the stable floor, and when one of the trainer's dogs sniffed at it, he pegged out quicker than greased lightning."

"I am afraid something has happened to my guv'nor," Tinker said, gulping at the lump that would rise in his throat. "Will you let me have a free hand and allow the dog to go where he likes!"

"Betcher life, mate, if it'll 'elp you," the other replied.

Tinker thanked him and allowed Pedro to move forward. The hound had been tugging vigorously upon the leash, and as soon as he was given his head he moved to the stable door; but there, after sniffing round for a while, he came to a dead stop.

Again and again Tinker tried to make him pick up the scent, but always with the same result. Pedro would nose the ground for a second or two, then squat upon his haunches and look up wistfully into his young master's face.

'I think I can reason out what it means," the lad said huskily at last. "The guv'nor was drugged or knocked over the head and carried from here. That is why the scent ends."

Dejectedly he left the stable and wandered aimlessly over the heath. There was a great, gnawing terror at his heart—an agony of dread. Who had attacked Sexton Blake and carried him away? If it were Maitland, Tinker felt that there was little hope of his ever seeing his master again alive.

Unconsciously he wandered on, until he almost collided with the wall shutting in the Wellstread quarry. He pulled up sharply, rousing himself from his reverie, and lent upon the wall, not noticing that Pedro was excitedly sniffing at the grass at the spot where Sexton Blake's legs had dragged when Wang had dropped them to scale the wall on the previous night.

Then suddenly Tinker missed his companion. He called to the hound, but received no response. He whistled shrilly, but still Pedro did not come.

For fully a minuite the lad stood waiting, wondering where the dog had gone. Then Pedro came tearing madly round the wall, fawned upon him, and turned, and disappeared the way he had come.

Tinker followed him, to find that he had paused, and was looking back as though intimating that he wished his young master to follow. A sudden hope flashed into Tinker's brain, for the hound was evidently wild with excitement and wanted him to descend the quarry.

Pedro had squeezed his way through a broken part of the stonework, and was baying incessantly from the opposite side of the wall.

Like one possessed, Tinker scaled the wall, and Pedro bayed again as he appeared. The hound began scrambling down the precipitous side of the quarry, and Tinker, beginning to feel certain of what his show of eagerness signified, speedily, yet more cautiously, followed him.

When they reached the bottom of the pit, Pedro bounded away to the opposite side and disappeared into a cavity which workmen had made in the stone. The lad sprinted after him and whipped out his electric-torch. He flashed its rays into the dark-hole, and a whoop of joy left his lips.

"Guv'nor!" he cried. "Dear old guv'nor! So weve found you, after all!"

The lad's eyes were moist as he tugged at the knots of his master's bonds. He was well-nigh frantic with relief, for Sexton Blake was conscious, and, save for the ugly bruise upon his temple, he seemed little the worse for his adventure.

The last knot was loosened and Sexton Blake struggled free of his bonds. He tried to rise, but it was only to fall back helplessly, for his limbs were numbed and useless.

"Thanks, lad!" Sexton Blake murmured, as he snatched the gag from his mouth. "That's right, rub my legs! I'll be all right in a moment, but the circulation stopped for awhile. I have been here all night!"

"What has happened, sir?" the lad asked quickly. "It—it was Maitland?"

"Yes, Tinker," the famous detective answered, a trifle ruefully. "It was Maitland again. He took me unawares and stunned me. But I'll tell you all about it later. Our first step must be to arrest him."

"You know where he is, then, guv'nor?"

"I imagine I shall find him," Sexton Blake replied, his eyes glinting grimly. "He rather foolishly informed me of his plans, which he intended carrying out whilst I slowly starved to death—a thing that you have prevented. You have saved my life again!"

He laid his hand upon his assistant's shoulder.

"You're a good lad, Tinker," he said simply.

And that was all the praise that the young detective needed. He understood.

CHAPTER 20
A Surprise for Maitland

John Riverton's brows contracted as he read the name upon the slip of pasteboard his butler had just handed him.

"Luke O'Kerney!" he muttered. "I have never met him in the past, so far as I can recollect.

"He says his business is most important, sir," that servant said. "He said it was imperative that he saw you to-night, and at once." John Riverton's frown deepened.

"I suppose you'd better show him in," he said. "He possibly represents some charity, and after my big win to-day——" He waved his hand.

"Show him in here, James," he said. "I may as well see him and get it over, I suppose."

The servent bowed and departed. He returned a moment later to usher Ezra Q. Maitland into the room.

The master criminal bowed as the door closed behind the servant, and there was a confident little smile on his lips.

"Good-evening, Mr. Riverton," he drawled, coolly helping himself to a cigar from a box standing upon the table. "I am glad that you decided to see me."

"Please state your business, Mr.—er—Kerney," John Riverton answered coldly. "My time is limited."

"So is mine, I guess," Maitland returned, nodding. "Still, I don't anticipate that I shall keep you long Mr.—er—Richard Cavendish!"

A strangled cry broke from the prodigal swindler, and he reeled to his feet. His jaw was dropping badly, and he was trembling like a delicate leaf in a breeze.

"You—you have made some mistake!" he faltered, licking his parched lips. "My—name—is—not Cavendish, but——"

"No; somehow it don't look like it, does it!" Maitland grinned sarcastically, as he allowed his long body to sink into a luxurious chair. "Bah! Quit on it! I know you well enough! You are Richard Cavendish, ex-swindler, ex-thief—a man who ought to have done penal servitude, but hasn't!"

"You fiend! You cur! I'll kill you!" the one-time swindler raved wildly, suddenly clutching at the poker and darting across the room towards his visitor. "I'll——"

"Stand back!" Maitland was steadily covering him with a revolver. "Say, I'm reckoned a mighty good shot," he drawled, "so I advise you to keep calm. Put that poker down. You hear me!"

"Who are you?" Cavendish asked hoarsely, allowing the heavy implement to drop from his nerveless fingers. "How do you know me? Why have you come here, and what do you want with me?"

"As to who I am," Maitland answered. "you have my card. I guess Kerney ain't my real name, but that doesn't matter. It need not concern you how I've tumbled to your identity. Suffice it for you that I know it, and am ready to give you away to the police unless you fall in with my demands."

"Then it's blackmail you're after?" the racehorse owner asked with a sneer.

"Precisely," Maitland answered coolly. "You might have known it from the first. To-day you have won many thousands of pounds. I am going to relieve you of exactly twenty-five of them."

"And that," said a deadly level voice, as the door was suddenly flung open, "is just where you are wrong, Ezra Q. Maitland!"

The master-criminal leapt to his feet with a dismayed oath, and his hand holding the revolver went up sharply.

There was a deafening report from the doorway, and Sexton Blake, who had entered with Tinker, cast aside his smoking weapon and leapt forward. Maitland gave a scream of pain, and his revolver clattered to the floor.

Sexton Blake had known that it was no time to hestitate when dealing with Maitland, especially when that astute crook held a shooting-iron. He had fired rapidly as soon as he had seen the weapon in the master-criminal's hand, and his bullet had grazed his fingers.

There was a short, sharp scuffle as the two men closed, then Sexton Blake treated his arch-foe to a neat back-heel and they thudded to the floor. Tinker, who had sprung to his master's aid, did the rest. There was a click, and the lad had snapped a pair of handcuffs upon Ezra Q. Maitland's wrists.

"Better search him, my lad," Sexton Blake ordered coolly.

"There are notes here for thousands, sir!" Tinker cried excitedly, as he snatched roll after roll from the snarling criminal's pockets. "And a cheque for fifteen thousand pounds signed by Henry Melson!"

"Ah, the little haul from Fisher's bank, and the price of his black treachery," Sexton Blake said quietly, as he took the note and the cheque from his assistant's hand. "This, I think, we will destroy at once. You'd better 'phone for the police, Tinker."

The detective deliberately tore the cheque in halves, then taking a vestacase from his pocket, he took out a match, struck it, and applied it to the two portions of the cheque which he had placed together.

Whilst Tinker stepped over to the instrument, which was fitted up in one corner of the room, Sexton Blake watched the cheque slowly burn, finally crumpling the ashes in his hand.

"This is the end of me, Mr. Blake," John Riverton—or Richard Cavendish, as it may now be better to call him—said brokenly. "You were listening outside the door. You heard whom I really am?"

"Yes," Sexton Blake answered; "but your secret is safe with me."

"But not with me!" Ezra Q. Maitland laughed harshly, as he struggled up upon his elbow. "Give me my freedom , and I'll keep my mouth shut. Otherwise, Sexton Blake, your precious swindling friend shall see the inside of a prison. Do you get me?"

Sexton Blake turned his back upon him without reply, and drew Richard Cavendish aside.

"You will have to leave England at the earliest possible moment," he said. "I cannot agree to his terms, but I have given my word that it shall be through no action of mine should you eventually suffer for your past misdeeds. You understand?"

"Yes, Heaven bless you!" John Riverton muttered. "And—and my boy?"

"I can prove him innocent immediately," Sexton Blake returned, with quiet assurance.

Twenty minutes later an inspector and a constable had driven from Newmarket Police Station, and Maitland was led away. He turned as he reached the door.

"I guess I'll keep mum till the morning, Sexton Blake," he drawled. "You might find you've made a mistake and get me released by them."

"I might; but I very much doubt it," Sexton Blake retorted coldly.

The telephone-bell rang sharply, and John Riverton moved over to it and took down the receiver. He listened for a moment to what was being said at the other end of the wire then the receiver fell from his hand, and he staggered back, with working face and twitching hands.

"I see it all!" he cried. "O'Mega, my neighbour, is Jasper Clench! Oh, I have been blind not to realise it before! Mr. Blake, I have just been speaking to him. He is dying—lying upon his deathbed."

"His deathbed!" Sexton Blake exclaimed sharply. "I don't understand!"

"He has fallen from his horse, and his spine is injured," Richard Cavendish explained breathlessly. "The 'phone is fitted up by his bedside, and he is quite conscious, he has been speaking to me. He has told me that he was responsible for the false accusation against my son. He asks me to forgive; but I—I can't! He——"

"You must!" Sexton Blake interrupted firmly. "Come, if he is indeed dying, we must not lose a moment. Don't let him go to his last account without your assurance that you will forgive him fully. Remember the past—the treacherous action you took against him."

Just for a moment Richard Cavendish hesitated, then he made for the door.

"You are right!" he said. "You are coming, too?"

"Yes," Sexton Blake answered simply.

. . . . . .

Henry Melson, otherwise Jasper Clench, looked up feebly as there came a tap upon the door of his bedroom. He was lying upon his back in his bed, his body wracked with pain. He had been riding into the town when his horse, taking fright at a recklessly driven car, had thrown him awkwardly. The doctor, who was with Voilet by the bedside, looked grave. He had given it as his opinion that Jasper Clench had but a few hours to live, unless something akin to a miracle happened.

Voilet, who had been sobbing quietly and holding her father's hand, rose and opened the door.

She found a servant without, who had brought Richard Cavendish, Sexton Blake, and Tinker up to the sick-room.

The girl beckoned them, and they entered.

The eyes of the two men who had been partners in crime twenty years ago met in a long gaze, then Jasper Clench lowered his, with a dry, repentant sob. Richard Cavendish crossed to the bed, sank down besides it, and took the hand of his one-time partner.

"I tried to ruin your boy, Richard," Jasper Clench said huskily, "but I want to make reparation. I employed the criminal, Maitland, to——"

"I know, Jasper," Cavendish interrupted gently. "Mr. Blake has told me everything as we drove over. You must try to forget—and live."

"Can you forgive me, Richard?" Jasper Clench asked, in a broken voice.

"If you can forgive me, Jasper," Cavendish replied, as he pressed the supposedly dying man's fingers.

For a few moments Cavendish remained kneeling by the bedside. Then a thing happened that put a dramatic end to the touching scene.

A servant came rushing up the stairs, and burst into his room without the ceremony of knocking.

"Which of you gentlemen is Mr. Sexton Blake?" he asked excitedly, looking from one to another.

"I am he," the detective answered, stepping forward. "What is wrong?"

"It's a message from the police-station, sir!" the man panted. "One of the policemen who had your prisoner—what's his name?—Maitland, has just arrived at the station with a broken arm."

207

"And Maitland?" Sexton Blake asked, grasping the man by he sleeve. "He——"

"Has bolted with the car, sir!" the man finished. "He snapped the chain of his handcuffs, flung the policeman into the road, and knocked the inspector senseless with a blow from a heavy spanner that must have been lying in the bottom of the car.

"Tell the police I will be at the station as soon as I can get over," Sexton Blake answered; and the man took his departure.

"You'll come at once, sir, won't you?" Tinker asked, for his master seemed in no way inclined to hurry himself.

"There is plenty of time, Tinker," Sexton Blake answered, with a significant glance at Richard Cavendish. "Perhaps, if he gets away, it will be for the best, after all. Now that he's got a start, there's not much likelihood of catching him. He'll abandon the car a few miles away and change his disguise in some way. But we shall meet again ere long."

"It seems a shame to let the beast go, sir!" Tinker protested. "And yet"—in his turn he looked towards the swindler, who had made every reparation in his power, but had never paid the penalty of the law—"I think I understand."

———

EPILOGUE

Two months had elapsed, and the summer was drawing to its close. Yet the sun was shining brightly, and the roses in Jasper Clench's garden at Newmarket were still in bloom.

The millionaire had not died. A specialist had advised an operation and it had been successfully performed, dragging the ex-company promotor from the very jaws of death.

On this bright, warm day in September, Clench was seated in an invalid-chair upon the verandah of the magnificent house attached to his racing stables.

Richard Cavendish, who had been reading to him from a sporting paper, was seated by his side. The two men were watching the figues of a man and a girl as they wended their way, hand in hand, amid the rose-bushes.

They were Laurence Cavendish and Violet Clench, and they were whispering together as they walked—whispering of the love that was in their hearts.

The release of Laurence Riverton had taken place within twenty-four hourse of Ezra Q. Maitland's daring escape from the police, for the evidence that Sexton Blake had laid before Sir Henry Fairfax, of Scotland Yard, had conclusively proved the young man's innocence.

The detective had demonstrated to the Commissioner how the invisible ink upon the cheque was brought to light by heating, and there had been the fifty-eight thousand pounds in notes—notes bearing numbers coinciding with those missing from Fisher's Bank—which Blake had taken from Maitland to substantiate his plea upon Laurence Riverton's behalf, to say nothing of the tell-tale thumb marks upon the banknote and the cheque.

"What do you say, Cavendish, to allowing your horses to be trained with mine here?" Jasper Clench asked, suddenly looking round at his companion. "Don't you think it would be a good idea?"

Cavendish nodded.

"I think it should work well," he answered. Then with a smile: "We should be partners again, Jasper."

Jasper Clench allowed his eyes to wander to the stalwart form of the young man whom he had once tried to bring to ruin, and from him to the slim, girlish figure by his side.

"Yes, partners again," he murmured. "Partners like our children, Cavendish. They are partners in a great and wonderful love."

"Heaven bless them!" Richard Cavendish said earnestly.

And he, too, sat watching the lovers until they disappeared amongst the roses.

THE END

THE RAJAH'S REVENGE

CHAPTER 1

In Far Kashopore

Kashopore, the capital of Puljara, lies in the angle of a sluggish river. It is one of the chief cities in the North-West of India, and the caravan road that skirts the high walls of the town is always alive with life and movement.

A benign British Government may supply trains, but the native of India, true to his immemorial custom, prefers to travel by road, slowly, easily, with many halts and hindrances. All day long the red dust rises from the wide roadway, all day long the sun blazes through the iridescent haze; and from dawn until dusk, man, woman, child; horse, camel, sheep, and goat, trudge to and fro.

At the great gateway of the town an armed guard is posted. They are quartered in a red stone building inside the gate, and the sentinel on duty is dressed in khaki, with scarlet cuffs and collar. On the great turban is placed the mark of his Highness, the Rajah of Puljara, Mahommed Ali Kahn.

His Highness is an enlightened prince. He stands in favour with Britain, and his city is a model of cleanliness and prosperity. He cannot make his people clean—no power on earth could do that; but he has seen to it that the streets are cleared and that the lazy folk no longer deposit their garbage in that most convenient of places—the next-door neighbour's door!

The palace is a massive structure, standing isolate on the banks of the stream. A white wall divides it from the city, and along this wall are innumerable stalls, littered with commodities of all kinds. It is really the market-place of the town, and the voices of the hucksters and dealers arguing heatedly over the value of their wares, resound all day.

About two o'clock on a blazing afternoon, two men emerged from a house close to the palace, and, turning to the left, made their way leisurely along the line of booths, beside the palace wall. They were a badly-assorted couple. Dressed in white drill, and wearing wide pith helmets, their faces, tanned though they were by the sun, were unmistakably European.

A sherbet-seller, from Mirzapore, jerked his thumb at them as they passed.

"The hawk and the bull are out again!" he cried, in his high-pitched vernacular, a cackle of laughter greeting his remark. And, indeed, his simile was well chosen.

One of the men in white, was a huge, broad-shouldered fellow, whose every movement hinted at the giant strength of his limbs. His face beneath the pith helmet might have been carved out of solid granite, so hard and fierce were the jaw and lips. His eyes were set deep in his head, and looked out at the swarming life seething around him, with the grim contempt of a man accustomed to be obeyed.

The other was the exact opposite. Small-limbed, almost dwarfish, with a great head and narrow, sloping shoulders, he tripped along vainly trying to keep in stride with the long, swinging movements of his companion.

But if the thin body was that of a weakling, there was no suggestion of that infirmity in the face. It was like a hawk. Keen, remorseless, thin of lip, long of nose, with small, beady eyes that were ever turning to right and left, restless, never still. The pith helmet did not hide the high-domed forehead, and one could see that the cranium was quite bald, a fact which added to the vulture-like appearance of the thin, cruel face.

A strangely assorted couple, truly, and yet well-matched.

Count Ivor Carlac and Professor Kew!

What had brought them to India? There was no one there to ask that question. India is one of the safest hiding-places in the world, and the unscrupulous European flourishes there, like a bay-tree.

They seemed to be prosperous, too. A diamond flashed on one of Carlac's fingers, for the huge criminal had always a weakness for gems; their clothes were of the finest, and the shopkeepers in the town knew that they had money to spend. They were living with a carpet-merchant, and had engaged a suite of rooms and servants, paying in advance. They had been in Kashopore over a week now, and seemed to be just ordinary sightseers, interested in the wonderful old city, with its long history of siege and battle, rapine and loot.

At the great iron gate that stood in the palace wall, Carlac halted for a moment. Through the magnificent scroll-work of the gate he could see the interior of the outer courtyard, with its tall cypress-trees, and mosaic paths. A trooper of the rajah's bodyguard came clanking to the gateway, a long, curved blade swinging at his supple thigh.

As the man emerged through the gate, Count Carlac hailed him.

"His Excellency, Colonel Bryce," he said, nodding to the palace.

The upright trooper clicked his heels together, and gave a real military salute. He had served his time with the Bengal Lancers, and had not forgotten his English training.

"His Excellency has gone out, to Briuth, on the Cashmere Road, sahib," came the reply, in perfect English. "He does not return until dusk."

A gleam of satisfaction came into Carlac's eyes as he thanked the trooper, and the man passed on.

"You are satisfied now, Kew?"

The little, wizened professor nodded.

"I was never so impetuous as you, my dear Carlac," he returned, in his thin, sibilant tones. "You always take things for granted; I always make sure."

The big man laughed.

"Quite right," he returned; "and perhaps it is that which makes us such a suitable couple to run in harness together. Anyhow I vote that we start for the Cashmere Road. We have plenty of time. I know that Bryce and his daughter will not be returning until dusk, but we might as well see that everything is ready for them."

His lips lifted in a hard smile, that found a reflection in his companion's face.

"It is the first step in a big move," said Kew, as he turned away. "We have tackled many things in our time, but this is biggest of them all."

"All the more reason why we should succeed." came the reply. "It is only your small criminal—the area thief and clothes-snatcher—that fills our prisons. The big men keep outside."

A shadow crossed Kew's face.

"Not always, Carlac," he returned, with a quick shiver. "We have both known what it is to serve under the broad arrow."

They were striding along through the narrow, thronged streets, and presently they reached a portion where a great, black building thrust its forbidding walls up over the barrier of the palace.

Kew pointed to the structure.

"And heaven help the man who was put in there," he went on. "English prisons are bad enough, but that one—ugh!"

It was the prison in which the rajah's evildoers were confined. Count Carlac glanced at it, and shrugged his shoulders.

"There is no chance of us finding quarters there," he returned, little dreaming how the future was to make him remember this remark, and to prove its falsity.

It took them the best part of half an hour to elbow their way through the good-natured crowds and emerge through one of the east gateways. The gate opened out on to a broad road, which ran on through a double row of tall trees, past paddy-fields and dykes, rising always until, with one long great sweep, it vanished into the hills beyond, tilting and winding until it struck the cart-road down to the Juman, thence on to Sringar.

They continued along the road, and finally Carlac came to a halt, at the end of the trees.

"What did Chandra Lal say?" he asked, turning to his companion. "Something about the old temple and the rajah's shooting-box, wasn't it?"

"Yes. That was the safest place for us to wait. The attack will be made from a paddy-field close to the temple. We can hear Chandra's signal from the temple."

They had a three-mile walk in front of them, but this was a by-road, and the only living thing they met was a dusty fakir, shuffling along in his rags, with his begging-bowl hanging from his lean waist.

Carlac, inspired by some feeling that he could not quite define, dropped a few pice in the bowl, and the fakir muttered his thanks.

"A gift to fortune—eh?" Kew said, with his dry smile. "It isn't often that you give anything away."

"I want to pull this particular business off," said the bigger rogue. "Don't forget that there are ten lakhs of rupees at the end of it, if we play our parts well."

The small eyes of Professor Kew glinted avariciously.

"Yes. One hundred thousand pounds," he said slowly, "and in gold!"

His thin hands clenched, and he laughed, a thin, cackling sound.

"No awkward notes to be traced from place to place, no bonds or jewels to sell. Just gold. Good, clean, yellow gold. That is the stuff, Carlac."

Dusk saw them moving along the edge of a high growth of canes, and Carlac caught sight of a dark, round dome, showing up the waving heads of the thick plantation.

"The temple," he said.

Five minutes later they found themselves entering the dark interior of the ruined place of worship. It was just a little wayside shrine erected to some forgotten god, and as Kew went deeper into it, there came from its depths a sibilant hiss!

The master criminal drew back, smiling, into the shadows. Kew's nerves had always been like steel.

"All right, my friend," he murmured. "We won't disturb you or your brood. You keep inside, and we'll be content with the entrance."

One of the big blocks of masonry that formed the shrine had fallen, and Carlac and Kew seated themselves on the hewn stone. The hush of an Indian summer was brooding over the scene. Now and again there came to their ears the soft rustling of some fugitive breath of wind, running along the tops of the waving cane. Once a night-bird, at least a yard wide from tip to tip, came dipping towards the doorway, only to poise and flutter back as it caught sight of the two motionless men at the entrance.

"A-r-r-r!"

A long call, such as the camel man voices to his team, sounded. Ivor Carlac leaped to his feet.

"That's Chandra. They are coming!"

Kew also arose.

"Plenty of time yet, my friend," he returned. "We have got to wait until the attack is made. Our noble rescuer part must be done well if we are to make the proper impression."

They plunged into the thick growth on the left, and found a path which led them through the field. There was a feint light from the stars, and Carlac, moving ahead, was able to pick his way.

At last they reached the dry ditch that divided the field from the road, and, dropping into this, Carlac began to follow its tortuous course.

"Help! Help!"

A sweet English voice, lifted in terror, broke the silence.

The wizened professor, staggering along behind his giant companion, chuckled aloud.

"There it goes! All right, my dear Miss Bryce. Be scared to death if you like. All the better for us. We are coming!"

A hundred yards was covered at a run, then Carlac leaped out into the road. Ahead of him he saw a mass of indistinct shapes gathering around a couple of plunging horses.

"Halt! Halt, there!" he cried, in his deep, commanding voice.

Kew leaped to his side, and together the precious pair darted headlong into the welter of struggling figures. Carlac caught sight of a tall, thin man in khaki, struggling desperately with three white-robed forms.

Like a bull Carlac charged straight into the melee. His powerful hand gripped one of the attackers by the neck, and a jerk saw the native go sprawling on his face into the ditch.

Thud!

Carlac's fist shot out, catching the second man on the jaw. With a howl of pain the man released his hold on Colonel Bryce, and went reeling back to measure his length on the dusty road.

"Bravo! Well hit sir!" the colonel gasped, as he found himself free.

Kew had gone on towards the horses, where the flutter of a white dress told him who the other victim was. A brawny ruffian had wrapped his arms around Muriel Bryce's slender body, and had dragged her clean out of the saddle. Kew with a monkeylike quickness, darted round and leaped full on the fellow's back.

His thin hands, with their hard knuckles, dug into the neck, just where it joined the spine. It is an old trick of the ju-jitsu expert, and by it a man can be rendered senseless. Muriel's captor shrieked aloud at the numbing pressure, then his hold gave, and, with a swing of his body, he released himself from Kew. Kew plunged forward again, but the man, leaping aside, flung himself across the road and vanished, with a rustle, into the field.

It had all happened so swiftly that when Colonel Bryce looked round he found that the swarming band of rascals had vanished, leaving his daughter and the two figures in white drill on the road.

Kew had stepped forward and caught at the horses' bridles, soothing the frightened animals.

"By James, gentlemen, that was what I call a neat little rescue!"

The quiet, cultured voice of the British officer sounded, and Bryce crossed towards his daughter, who caught at him quickly.

"Oh, dad!" she cried, clinging to him for a moment.

All traces of excitement had died away from Bryce. He patted his daughter on the cheek, then turned and smiled through the dusk at the huge figure of Carlac.

"It's all over, my dear," he said, "thanks to the quick intervention of these gentlemen. But, by James, I must admit that the rascals fairly had us!"

Kew came forward leading the horses, and Bryce held out his hand.

"I am extremely obliged to you, sir," the courtly gentleman said. "I had been warned about this attack, but I paid no attention to it. As matters have turned out, the warning was more serious than I thought."

Carlac smiled inwardly. It had been part of his plan to warn Bryce of the impending attack.

"These hounds were evidently determined to have you, sir," Carlac said.

"Not much doubt about that," Colonel Bryce returned. "But the way you polished them off was a perfect eye-opener. You must be tremendously strong."

He looked admiringly at the great, massive frame of the master-criminal. Carlac had always been proud of his strength, which was far above the ordinary.

"I am glad that I was able to help you, sir," he returned. "And now, as it is all over, perhaps you had better mount. It is getting late."

Bryce started forward, and caught Carlac by the arm.

"My dear fellow, you don't think that I am going to let you go like this," he broke out.

Again Carlac was playing a part. He wanted to make it appear as though reward was far from his thoughts.

"But it is all over, sir," he said, "and you and your daughter have a long ride in front of you."

"I don't care twopence about that!" the colonel returned. "I insist on knowing your names. Hang it, man, even if you do not think much of what you have done, we have a different opinion! Eh, Muriel?"

The slender girl nodded her shapely head.

"I was frightened to death," she admitted. "That brute dragged me clean out of the saddle."

A shudder ran through her frame at the memory of the tenacious arms and the hot breath of the ruffian so close to her face.

"I am glad that we arrived in time, Miss Bryce," Kew put in, in his suave tones. "It was your scream that we heard."

The girl turned round at the mention of her name.

"Then you know my father and I?"

It was a slip, but Kew covered it at once.

"We saw you ride out from the palace this afternoon," he explained. "We are living quite close to the palace, at the house of Saljar Ral, a carpet-importer.

"Ah, I've heard about you!" said Bryce. "You have been living in Kashopore for about a week, I believe? You are Count Kaldross and Doctor Kay?"

There were the names that Kew and his companion had chosen. They were near enough to the real ones to save their owners from making mistakes.

"My name is Kay," the wizened man returned, bowing to Muriel.

"Well, look here, doctor!" the colonel went on. "I don't know how long you are going to be in Kashopore, but I insist on you both being my guests until you leave!"

211

"We are going to England on the twenty-third," said Carlac, with a swift glance through the dusk at his companion.

Colonel Bryce, little dreaming of the trick that was being played on him, rubbed his hands together.

"Nothing could be better," he returned; "for I, too, am going to England on that date! In fact, we're all going—Muriel as well. It is quite a big——" He stopped, as though he had been about to reveal more than he ought to. "Anyhow, I insist on you both coming to see me to-morrow morning!" the colonel went on. "I will leave orders at the main gate of the palace, and you will be brought at once to my quarters. You promise me that?"

He held out his hand to Carlac, and the count shook it.

"If you really insist, colonel," he returned. "But, at the same time, I think that you are making much of nothing. Anything that my friend and I did, we were only too glad to do. There is no need of going any further in the matter."

But before the colonel and his daughter cantered off, they had been assured that the two men would call on the following day, Kew stood in the centre of the roadway watching the horses until the darkness had swallowed them up. Then, turning his head, he glanced into the canes.

"Chandra!"

A rustle, and a stout, squat figure came waddling over the ditch.

"Is the sahib pleased with his servant?" the fat Bengali asked, with a grim chuckle.

"Yes; it was well done. Here!"

There was a chink of gold, and the stout palm closed tightly.

"And there's an extra rupee for the man I attacked," said Kew, in his thin tone. "Tell him to rub oil on his neck to-night, and by the morning the pain of it will have gone."

Chandra laughed aloud.

"The sahib has fingers like steel," he said. "The man swears that he felt the life being drawn out from behind his ears, as one draws water from a bag."

"'Twas only a Japanese wrestling trick," said Kew, "It was taught me by the emperor's own wrestler, in Tokyo."

Chandra vanished into the dark field; then Kew joined Carlac.

"Was Chandra satisfied?"

"Yes. I gave him twenty pounds. He and his gang never had so much money in their lives before.

They moved along the road at a slow pace, Carlac's brow drawn, his lips set.

"The first move to get at his Highness's war-chest has panned out well enough," he began at last; "but we've a long way to go yet."

"We have prepared our ground," said Kew, "here in Kashopore, and in London, at Downe Square—everything possible has been arranged. It all depends on the rajah now. If he still sticks to his plan—still decides to hand over his war-chest to Colonel Bryce for safe transit from Puljara to London—then we have little to trouble over. The ten lakh of rupees are as good as ours."

"We've got to get Colonel Bryce to ask us to join his party when he starts," said Carlac.

"I'll bet you that he does that to-morrow! Why shouldn't he?" Kew smiled to himself in the dusk. "We've proved ourselves very useful, even as a bodyguard. No, you need have no fear on that point, Carlac. When his excellency Colonel Bryce, military adviser and British representative at the court of his Highness the Rajah of Puljara, leaves for England on a very important mission, he will have two additional members of his suite—you and I.'"

The lights of the city presently loomed in front of them, and they entered the gateway, a sentinel moving out to open the wide gates. For in Kashopore, in common with many other cities in India, the main gates of the city were still closed from sunset to sunrise.

Under ordinary circumstances Carlac and Kew might have been forced to spend the night in one of the dak-bungalows that are always to be found close to a big city for the use of belated travellers, but this time they were allowed in at once.

"His excellency the colonel-sahib's orders," was the reply which the tall sentinel gave when questioned by Kew.

The wizened man turned and grinned at his companion as they passed on into the narrow thoroughfare.

"There you are!" he said mockingly. "Already you have proofs that our worthy friend the colonel thinks a great deal of us. By to-morrow morning you may rest assured that we will belong to his personal suite."

Carlac smiled at the cold, mocking voice.

"I think you're right, Kew," he returned. "And, by Jove, we must take full advantage of it. We have a clear field, and if we fail it will be our own fault. Within a couple of months from now we ought to be sharing a hundred thousand pounds."

The magnificent gift which the Rajah of Puljara had promised to England, ten lakh of rupees, had caused no little stir when it was first announced. The rajah himself had arranged that he should hand over the treasure to His Majesty King George, and the Indian potentate was travelling to London to perform that ceremony. It was this news that had first stirred the cupidity of Kew and his companion.

They studied up every detail concerning the gift. They read every report, and discovered the following facts:

The money, in solid gold, was kept in an iron-bound chest in the palace at Kashopore.

The chest itself was a historical one, for it had been presented to his Highness by his people on ascending the throne. Kew, setting to work in his grim way, soon found a photograph of the chest in a local museum, together with an exact description of its measurements. The curator of the museum little dreamed to what use his information concerning the treasure-chest was going to be put. That same night Kew sent off a long letter to a certain address in London, where an antique dealer, a perfect master at the art of faking old furniture lived.

The two scoundrels also discovered that Colonel Bryce, the British representative at Puljara, was a prime favourite with the old rajah, and that the colonel had been commissioned to take charge of all the details concerning the great gift. He had to travel to England with the precious chest, and await the arrival of the rajah, who was due to follow by a later steamer that sailed a week after.

Here then was the best opportunity to steal the chest. A project that fascinated the master intellects of the two criminals. It wanted courage and daring and skill, attributes which both men had to a high degree.

It was Carlac who discovered that Colonel Bryce owned a house in London, in Downe Square. He got the address of the house, and, to add another link to their long chain, another letter was sent off, this time to a certain Flash Harry, one of Carlac's old gang.

The rest of the plot consisted in the two men worming their way into the confidence of the genial colonel, and this, thanks to a very old but useful trick, had now been accomplished.

"We have absolutely nothing to fear," said Kew that evening, as he and Carlac sat in the quietly-furnished room that they had rented in the carpet-dealers's house. "Chandra Lal would never betray us; he would be clapped in the rajah's jail as an accomplice as quick as possible. To-morrow, at the very urgent entreaties of our friend the colonel, we will take up quarters in the palace, and remain there until the party starts for England.

He rubbed his lean hand over his bald skull, grinning the while. Perched on the heap of high cushions, with his thin legs tucked under him and the light from the lamp shining full on his yellow face, he looked more of the bird of prey than ever.

"This is the sort of affair that I delight in," he said. "There are risks attached to it. "You and I, Carlac, have to face the powers of two Governments, the British and the Puljara. There is not the slightest doubt but what the treasure will be guarded day and night. He, he! We have our work cut out for us!"

Carlac had flung his huge frame on a low divan and was pulling at a long pipe. He blew a fragrant cloud from his lips before making a reply.

"You seem pleased to find it difficult,"—he put in, at last. "And I suppose you're right. There is only one thing I hope, and that is that a certain man, whom we both know, is kept out of it."

Across Kew's face the shadow of a scowl spread. He leaned forward.

"Why do you talk of that individual?" he asked hoarsely. "We have had quite enough of him in the past!"

"Oh, I don't know," Carlac returned, "the thought just came into my head!"

"Then banish it!" snapped his companion. "That man has been a thing of evil omen to me, and to you. Without his interference we would both have been rich men now. Able to move about the world and enjoy everything that came our way."

He started to his feet suddenly, and raised his clenched fists in the air. The lamp threw his grotesque shape on the dull wall behind him. He looked like some demon from an old-world picture, in his long, loose robes.

"I swear that if Sexton Blake crosses my path this time, I will not rest until one of us goes under," he muttered, his voice thin with suppressed feeling. "Too long he has been like a Nemesis in my path. There must be an end to one of us, and if he intervenes now, let him look out for himself!"

Then, just as suddenly as it had risen, his rage died away, and he was his old, cool, inscrutable self again, smiling out of his lashless eyes at Carlac.

"Sounded frightfully dramatic and all that, I suppose," Kew said; "but I mean it. And now, let's get ready for our visit to-morrow."

He seemed to be assured of his welcome at the palace, for he packed everything in readiness for the move.

And neither he nor Carlac were disappointed. Colonel Bryce met them on the marble steps that led into his private suite, and the colonel's handshake was of the warmest.

"I was afraid that you would not come," he admitted, leading the way down a tapestry-hung corridor and into a spacious, well-lighted room, where at a table a sturdy youngster, in neat-fitting khaki, was seated, hard at work on a heap of documents. "Vernon, here is Count Kaldross and Dr. Kay. They have turned up you see."

Lieutenant Vernon, attache to the colonel, drew his long legs beneath him, and arose to shake hands. He had a keen, bronzed, good-looking face, a typical young officer such as one meets anywhere in clubland.

"Pleased to meet you, gentlemen," he said, revealing a set of white, even teeth; "and I'm jolly glad you've turned up. Miss Bryce was doubtful about it, and it was quite on the cards that I should have to go and hunt for you, although I hadn't the remotest idea where the dickens I could find you."

Carlac was studying the bronzed face, and a slow smile crossed his heavy jowl. Vernon was a member of Colonel Bryce's suite, and was, therefore, a potential enemy.

"I don't think that we have much to fear from you," he decided. "A brainless cub. And all the better for that!"

It is not always advisable to judge a man by his first impressions. Lieutenant Vernon was young and rather dandy in the matter of dress; but he was not altogether without brains, as the future was to prove.

Nothing could exceed the warmth of the welcome that the two arch-scoundrels received. Muriel Bryce was particularly kind to them both, and Vernon, head over heels in love with the beautiful girl, was inclined to scowl a little when he found himself so very much in the background.

It was arranged that Kew and Carlac should take up their residence at the palace, and they did so. And it was also arranged by the colonel that they should travel to England together.

"My dear chap, it is my convenience that I am studying," the colonel admitted. "I might tell you that this journey of mine is going to be a most anxious one."

They were seated at the dinner-table, with cigars and liqueurs. Carlac had cunningly suggested that the presence of his companion and himself might embarrass the travellers.

"In what way, colonel?" Kew's voice was quite steady.

"Well, I'm taking with me a chest with a king's ransom in gold, inside it," the colonel returned. "And, 'pon my word, I

213

don't like the job one little bit."

"Colonel Bryce is referring to the rajah's gift to our King," Vernon put in. "I suppose you've heard about that?"

His grey eyes were fixed on Carlac, but that individual was a master of the art of self-control.

"I'm afraid I haven't," he returned. "Kay and I have been in the hills—Thibet and Darjiling—for the past two months. We were quite out of touch with civilisation."

The colonel arose to his feet.

"Well, if you care to come along with me, I'll show you the thing we've got to travel with. It might interest you."

Muriel who was seated next to Vernon, noted a frown cross the handsome face, as the two strangers arose and followed their host.

"What are you frowning at?" the girl asked, with a quick, roguish laugh.

Vernon turned to her.

"The colonel is much too trusting," he said. "Of course, I know that the treasure-chest is safe enough here in Kashopore. No man could get it outside the palace and live to tell the tale. But, later on, it might be different."

Muriel laughed.

"Stuff and nonsense!" she said. "I think that you are in a very suspicious mood this evening, Mr. Vernon. You surely don't think that these two men are likely to steal the chest?"

"Well, I—I——"

Muriel arose to her feet, her nose in the air.

"I'm surprised at you!" she went on. "After all, these gentlemen saved dad and I, and if that doesn't make them worth cultivating in your eyes, then you don't think very much of—of me!"

She was about to hurry away, when Vernon, leaping forward, caught her by the arm.

"You know that I think all the world of you, Muriel," he said, in a deep, passionate voice. "Why do you tease me like this?"

The girl looked up into his love-filled eyes, then her own melted. With a quick movement she leaned forward and gave him a butterfly-like kiss.

"I'm not teasing, dear," she said. "Only, I do think you are much too suspicious. I really think that it's this stupid war-chest. I shall be glad when it has been safely handed over to the rajah."

Vernon released her, and stepped back a pace.

"Perhaps it is the beastly chest," he returned. "And you are certainly quite right. I, too, will be jolly pleased when it has gone. It's far too heavy a responsibility for my liking."

Colonel Bryce had lead the way down a narrow flight of stairs and into a small, vaulted room. He lighted a lamp, and held it aloft.

"There is the war-chest," he said.

It was a massive, solidly made receptacle. The carving was deep, and toned with age. Iron bands, riveted through the solid wood, gave it an appearance of strength.

Kew and Carlac stepped forward to examine the chest. Despite the fact that they had nerves like steel, neither could control the swift thrill that ran through their veins.

Here was the very treasure that they had set out to obtain, by foul means or by fair. Locked beneath that heavy lid were piles upon piles of golden coins. A king's ransom!

"You do not seem to take much trouble to guard it, colonel," Carlac said. "I did not notice any sentries."

Colonel Bryce laughed.

"No man in the world could shift that chest from here," he said. "Try and move it."

Carlac caught at the stout handle, and put out all his vast strength. The chest did not budge an inch.

"Gold is heavy, you see," their host went on. "It takes four men to shift it. Besides, there is not a soul in Puljara would dare even to lay his finger on that chest. It is the rajah's property, and sacred. It means death to anyone who touches it without his permission."

The two rogues followed him back into the dining-room. Kew was quiet and thoughtful, leaving the conversation to his companion.

For as they stood over the chest there had come to the wizened professor a foreboding that he could not define. The breath of some far-off danger, chilling his soul.

"Death to anyone who touches it!"

That black prison that they had passed in the morning. Would it one day open its gates to swallow——"

With an effort he drew his thoughts back, and into his beady eyes there came the old look of greed and avariciousness. These two passions that had turned him from a skilled, clever physician, one of the greatest surgeons that the world had ever known, into a hunted criminal, with every man's hand against him.

I'll risk it," he thought, his vulture face hard and set. "It is a far cry from London to Kashopore, and the rajah cannot reach me in England."

Was he right or wrong?

CHAPTER 2
Tinker and Muriel

That's the worst of a great, hulking dog like you, Pedro. You cannot be taken out in the daytime, like an ordinary pup! You're too big and hefty, and people want to make a fuss of you."

Tinker, his hand tight on the strong leather leash that was attached to the collar of the great bloodhound, Pedro, voiced his grumble in what was rather a kindly tone.

As a matter of fact, the young detective was only too glad to snatch every opportunity he could get to take the big hound out for a stroll. Pedro, under ordinary circumstances, usually lived in the East End, for there was no convenience for him at Baker Street. But Tinker was constantly bringing the dog to the chambers, and there it remained until the old landlady fired up and insisted on it being taken back to its quarters.

"She hasn't grumbled yet, old man," the youngster went on; "but that's because you're getting jolly artful. Who taught you to stow yourself away below my bed every time the old dear comes upstairs—eh?"

He laughed as he spoke, and Pedro, turning his huge head, gave a wave of his tail that was as eloquent as speech.

They had turned westward, through the maze of streets that lie between Baker Street and Edgware Road. Crossing that busy thoroughfare, Tinker went on down a broad, quiet street, and presently turned into a small square. He was heading for Hyde Park, but was shaping a rather erratic course. He had nothing much to do, and London, in the half-gloom that the fear of Zeppelins had necessitated, had its fascination.

"Well, if that isn't most annoying!"

Tinker was almost within touching distance of the stooping figure before he realised that it really was a human being. The voice was a charming silvery one, and Tinker came to a halt. As he did so the girl looked up, and gave vent to a little gasp as she saw the slender youngster with the huge hound by his side.

"Goodness, how you frightened me!" she gasped, rising to her feet.

It was quite thirty yards to the nearest lamp post, but there was just sufficient light to allow Tinker to see that the face turned towards him was a charming one, and that the girl was in evening dress, without a hat. A soft cloak had slipped from one smooth, white shoulder, and she drew it into its place again, at the same time running a small hand through her hair.

"I'm very sorry, miss," Tinker began, raising his hat.

"Oh, that's quite all right!" came the laughing reply. "But—well, it was really that great dog with its big eyes that made me jump!"

"Have you—have you lost anything?"

"Yes; and I'll never be able to find it, either. It is a jewelled comb."

"Where did you lose it?"

The girl waved her hand vaguely.

"Somewhere about here," she returned. "I just came out for a breath of fresh air, and walked across to the gardens. I did not notice that I had dropped the comb until I came back here."

She looked down at the pavement.

"It is one of a set, and very valuable. An Indian rajah made me a present of them on my last birthday. I believe they are worth about sixty pounds each!"

"Phew! You don't want to lose a thing worth that amount, miss!"

She seemed a sweet, friendly woman. She chatted away in a bright manner, and Tinker decided that she was worth helping. He knew that there would be very small chance of her getting her ornament back again if she waited until the morning. Your London milkman, dustman, and newspaper boy are as honest as the day, but there are others less honest who haunt the better-class thoroughfares in the small hours—vagrant prowlers, like the carrion dogs of the Oriental cities, seeking whatsoever chance may throw in their way, from gutter and drain.

"I suppose it isn't really worth while searching," she went on, with a little sorrowful shrug of her shoulders. "I'm sure that no human being could find my comb on a dark night like this."

Tinker smiled, and his hand slipped down the leash, loosening it.

"You're quite right, miss," he returned, "no human being could find your comb, but there's an old fellow here who has something better to guide him than eyes."

The girl looked round as though expecting to see a third person. Tinker smothered a laugh.

"I mean the dog, miss," he said. "he is a bloodhound, the wisest and best in the world."

His companion turned towards him with a quick swing.

"That dear old doggie?" she said. "Do you really mean to say that he can find———"

"Give me one of your combs," said Tinker.

The girl handed him the jewelled ornament out of her hair without a moment's hesitation. It was a little proof of instinctive trust, which made Tinker all the more eager to help.

"Here, Pedro!" he said.

The hound snuffled at the comb.

"Oh, poor thing! How can you expect him to find it?"

"Seek!"

It was certainly a hard task. As a rule Pedro's work was the tracing of human beings. Tinker stepped back, watching the hound. It was a real test, and his pride in the wonderful sagacity of his beloved companion would not dare him to think of defeat.

"Seek, old man—seek!"

There came from the hound a half impatient snuffle. Pedro glanced first at Tinker, then at the intent, eager girl by his side. Then the big hound stepped out on the roadway, and his muzzle nosed at something on the ground.

With a quick laugh and a cry of delight, the girl darted towards the dog, stooped, and lifted the object.

"He—he thinks we were both such fools!" she cried, tucking one slender arm round Pedro's massive throat. "And so we were, you dear thing!"

"Did he find it?" Tinker asked.

The girl held up her hand; the comb was sending a red, dull glow from between her fingers.

"Of course he did! Don't you see what it was? These great big eyes of his had found it long ago, and he was just thinking to himself how foolish we both were."

She made a pretty picture, stooping there in the shadows, one arm round the hound's neck, her small mouth open, her white teeth gleaming.

"Good old Pedro!" said Tinker.

He was genuinely delighted with the hound, and as the girl arose, he reached out and replaced the leash.

"But you mustn't go like that!" his companion said. "I—I am really very much obliged, and—and———"

She was just about to offer some sort of reward, but the movement that Tinker made brought her to a halt. She flushed in the darkness, then, with a laugh, held out her hand.

"My name is Muriel Bryce," she said; "I live at number five. Won't you please give me your name? I should love to come and see this dear, clever dog some time."

Tinker hesitated for a moment, then gave his name and address.

"I'm afraid that you won't have much chance of seeing Pedro there, however," he added; "it is only now and again that we have him with us."

"Well, I'll risk it, and—and thank you so much again. Good-night!"

Muriel and Tinker shook hands; then, after a pat on the hound's head, the slender figure tripped off down the pavement and turned into the porch of a small house. She waved to Tinker as she vanished, and the lad raised his cap.

"No that is what I call a real English lady, Pedro," Tinker murmured, as he resumed his walk—"no side, no swank—just real good breeding!"

At the corner of the square he glanced up and read the name.

"Downe Square—never heard of it before."

He saw now that it was a very tiny oasis of a place, with not more than half-a-dozen houses on each side. Bayswater and Mayfair are dotted with just such similar havens of quiet.

Tinker went on down the street that led from the square, and presently there turned the corner a slow-moving taxi. The driver was keeping close to the kerb, and was looking up at the houses as he moved along.

Catching sight of Tinker and the dog, the driver slipped his clutch for a moment.

"Where's Downe Square, mister?" he asked.

Before Tinker could reply an extraordinary thing happened. The door furthest away from the pavement opened, and a figure in a dark cloak leaped out, swinging towards the driver.

"Keep your mouth shut, you fool!" a harsh voice rasped. "If you don't know the way, keep quiet!"

Tinker saw the cloaked figure lean forward and knock the driver's foot aside, so that the spinning clutch was re-engaged and the taxi shot forward.

"Here, what the blazes———"

There was a jar and a crash, and the driver took control of his vehicle again. The cab stopped and the driver, infuriated at this high-handed proceeding, leaped from his seat.

"Yer might have bust the blinkin' keb up!" he bellowed. "Wot do yer mean by it, hey?"

Tinker and Pedro stood on the edge of the kerb to watch the scene. The driver, obviously enraged, danced up to his passenger, his fists clenched.

"Come on, yer monkey-faced skunk!" he bawled. "I'll giver yer, interferin' with my———"

He never completed his remark. As he rushed at the cloaked form an arm was extended, and Tinker heard a faint coughing sound.

Chough!

There was no flash, no report, but the driver, as though struck by some deadly missile, threw up his hands and fell flat on his back in the middle of the road. The cloaked figure, wheeling round, without as much as another glance at the heap at his feet, sped off up the street and vanished.

It was only then that Tinker really moved in the matter. Pedro, for some unaccountable reason, had commence to strain and whimper at his leash.

"All right, old man" Tinker murmured. "I don't suppose that the driver's very much hurt. Probably a punch in the jaw, although neither you nor I saw the blow."

He stepped out towards the man lying in the road.

"Come along, old chap!" said Tinker, stooping forward. "You can't be so badly hurt as———"

He touched the driver, and at the pressure of his fingers the shoulder moved round and the head fell back. Tinker peered for a moment into the upturned face, with its fixed, dull eyes and drawn back lips. A cry of utter amazement broke from the young assistant.

"Good heavens, he is dead!"

There was no mistake about it. The unfortunate man had been terribly punished for his brief and natural anger. The discovery shocked Tinker. and for a moment he stood irresolute; then, realising that there was only one course to pursue, he drew a police-whistle from his pocket and sent a shrill summons through the deserted streets.

Pheep! Pheep!

An answering call came, and two minutes later a stalwart constable came upon the scene. A half-a-dozen words from Tinker gave the man the bare details of the affair, and also the identity of the speaker.

"I've seen you often, Mr. Tinker," the constable said; "and, anyhow, I recognise your dog."

He pointed to Pedro. The hound was still betraying a curious impatience, and his head was turned always in the direction of the square—the direction that the mysterious fare had taken.

"Not much good of you trying to follow him," Tinker said; "you haven't even got his scent."

Yet Pedro still strained and whimpered, and it was only when Tinker, at the suggestion of the constable, took the dead man's place at the wheel of the cab, that the hound gave up his importunities. The driver had been lifted into the vehicle, and, with the constable inside with his gruesome charge and Pedro on the step beside him, Tinker drove the taxi to St. Hugon's Hospital.

"I should say that he died of suffocation." The house-surgeon gave his verdict in the uncertain voice of a man in doubt. "Yet, on your story, it does not seem possible."

Tinker and the constable, with an inspector who had come from the nearest police-station, were standing in the surgeon's room. The brief examination of the body had just concluded.

"It beats me!" the young detective returned. "As far as I could see, there wasn't a blow struck. The other man simply stretched out his hand and there was a soft sort of cough, and the driver went down like a nine-pin!"

There was nothing further for him to do at the hospital, and he and the inspector went out together. The officer was obviously ill at ease.

"A nice sort of case to have to tackle," he grumbled. "No blow struck, the surgeon not really sure how the poor beggar came by his end, and—and not so much as a clue to go on to find the man that did it."

"Except that he had asked the driver to take him to Downe Square," Tinker put in.

The inspector shook his head.

"We're not even sure of that," he returned. "The driver asked you for Downe Square, but how are we to know that his fare was actually going there? It might have been one of the streets off it, or the driver might even have been looking for a short cut."

There was certainly a possibility that the inspector's gloomy diagnosis of the case was correct.

"And to-morrow the papers will be full of it. 'Another Crime of the Darkness. Waht are our police doing?' That's the sort of headline they'll put up, I'll bet!"

Despite the tragedy that he had witnessed, Tinker could not help smiling at the tone of voice.

"Anyhow, it is not your fault," he said, consolingly. "No man could have foreseen what happened."

Yet when he parted with the inspector Tinker felt that in someway or other he had been the indirect cause of the crime. He had no reason to apply to justify this assumption, yet deep in his heart the feeling arose and grew that it was the fact of the driver stopping to ask him the way that had resulted in his death.

Then a sudden thought flashed into his mind, and he came to a halt.

"By Jove! It is possible that the murderer recognised me?"

He remembered that he had been standing under a lamp-post when the taxi drew up. Anyone inside the vehicle could easily have seen his face.

Then Pedro's strange behaviour formed another link. Had the hound, with its deeper sagacity, recognised some old enemy?

Tinker looked down at the big hound with a half-rueful expression on his face.

"By jiminy, my son, I'm beginning to think that you and I play the wrong roles. It ought to be you that had charge of the leash, and I ought to be wearing that collar. You've proved to-night once that your eyes were keener than mine—and I shouldn't be surprised if you were right the second time."

It was too late to do anything now, however. The criminal, stranger or ancient enemy, had made good his escape. It would have been worse than useless to attempt to trace him, even with the aid of the hound. Pedro might have been able to follow the man had they started at once, but now it would be necessary to get some article of clothing belonging to the unknown—and that was an impossibility.

"No; you've got clear away, whoever you are," Tinker muttered. "And the only question that concerns me now is: why did you want to keep the address that you were going to away from me?"

He could find no answer to that problem then, and indeed, clever though the youngster was, he was not to be blamed for that.

Tinker could not know that it was the sight of his keen, well-remembered face, and more particularly the sinewy shape of the great bloodhound, that had aroused a sudden panic of fear in the heart of a rogue.

Professor Kew's iron nerve had deserted him for the moment—for it was he who was seated in the vehicle.

He had come back from a momentous visit. Earlier that afternoon he had gone to the address of the antique-dealer, and had been shown the result of his letter.

A great chest, the exact counterpart—carrying, iron bands, everything—of that which stood in the strong room in No. 5, Downe Square!

A taxicab, had been chartered, and Kew had seen the chest safely handed over to a lynx-eyed individual, who had been introduced to him by Carlac as "Flash" Harry.

It was the initial move of their great scheme in London, and the professor had been weighing over the various details on his return journey to Downe Square. Then, as though by sheer chance, he had caught sight of the lad and dog—the loyal servants of the only man in the world that Kew hated and feared.

And what followed had been the result of that panic. His death-tube that he always carried had not failed him, and he had escaped.

But he was in a welter of fear as he entered the quiet home of the man he intended to victimise, and he made for his bedroom at once, to pace up and down, hands behind back, his vulture head on his breast.

He had killed a man, but that thought did not trouble him. It was the appearance of Tinker so close to Downe Square that kept the brooding man, pacing up and down long into the night.

CHAPTER 3
At the Antique Dealer's

"He was such a hard-workin' chap, sir"—the tearful voice had a subdued pathos in it—"and he didn't have an enemy in the world. Heaven knows what me and the kiddies are going to do now."

Sexton Blake glanced compassionately at the drab figure seated on the edge of one of the comfortable chairs in his consulting-room. Tinker, always nervous in front of a grief-stricken woman, cast a quick, appealing look at his master.

When "Mrs. Todd" had been announced by the landlady, neither Blake nor his assistant had any idea who she was. But her opening remarks soon told Tinker that it was his adventure of the previous evening that had brought her here. She was the wife of the dead taxi-driver, and it appeared that the police-inspector had sent her on to Baker Street.

"Why was he killed?" the woman asked again, turning a tear-stained face to Blake. "He never 'armed anyone in his life. I know that my Joe was a bit hasty-tempered-like, but he never did no harm to anyone."

Sexton Blake was a busy man, and the case of the murdered taxi-driver was hardly one of the type that he cared to tackle. It was one of those street crimes that the police make their province, and under ordinary circumstances Blake would have taken no part in the investigations.

But the appeal of the poor and destitute class always made a big impression on the great detective's charity. And this forlorn creature, in her tears and misery, had found the best way of appealing to him for help.

Half an hour later, when he dismissed her, there was a shadow of hope in her faded eyes. Tinker saw his master slip something into the work-worn hand, and heard the woman's murmur of thanks. When Blake came back into the consulting-room, he eyed Tinker with the ghost of a smile on his finely-chiselled lips.

"So your little stroll last night had a sequel to it—eh?"

Tinker flushed.

"I didn't want to trouble you, guv'nor," he explained. "I knew that you were busy enough as it was. Besides, there was really nothing to be done."

"That was quite right, old chap," said Blake; "but this poor woman puts a different complexion on the affair. By a foul deed she has been robbed of the bread-winner of her little home. That is a far greater tragedy in the lives of the poor than of the well-to-do. We must try and help her, Tinker."

He glanced at the notes he had taken. The woman lived in Whitechapel, and the cab was garaged close by. It was her husband's own private property, having been bought by instalments.

Blake had taken the number of the vehicle, and also the place that it usually stood when out for hire.

"It's not going to be an easy task," he said; "but there is just a remote chance of us tracing the taxi's movements yesterday, Anyhow, we will have a try."

It was a hard task.

They found out that Todd had not been seen on his usual stand on the previous day. Inquiries at the garage, however, gave Blake the information that Todd had been hired for a wedding, that had kept him busy for the whole of the afternoon. The wedding-party had gone to an hotel, and finally Todd and two other drivers had taken their guests to their respective homes.

"The job must have kept him on the go until about eight o'clock, sir," the garage-owner said; "then, I suppose he went on to try and pick up a casual or two. But, maybe, Steve Jones could help you to find out what happened afterwards. He was with Todd at the wedding-party. "

Blake got the address of Steve, and finally ran his man to earth, in a little flat in a high tenement building. Steve had evidently not yet turned out for his usual day's work. He was a short, thick-set man, and seemed inclined to talk.

Blake's news concerning Todd's death seemed to shock his listener. After giving Jones a brief account of the tragedy, the detective began to question him.

"Yes, that's right," said Steve; "me and Todd was both at the wedding. And, by jiminy, I thought that they was never going to finish. It was arter six o'clock before they left the hotel—and some of 'em wasn't half lively, either."

"Where did you go?"

"Oh, Todd and me drove off together," the driver explained. "We got our money, and then, as we was both jolly hungry, we went down to the shelter in Shapper Street, and had a bite. While we was there a 'phone message came for a taxi, and I went off first. Todd thought there might be a chance of picking up something and he followed me."

"Did you see him again?"

Steve was silent for a moment.

"I couldn't swear to it, you see, mister," he said at last; "and, as this might mean a police court job, I likes to be sure." The great detective smiled at the man's caution.

"You are quite right," he said; "it is always best to be careful. Still you are not giving evidence on oath now, and if there is any little point that you think might help, let me have it."

"Well, sir, it's like this. I stopped at the address where the 'phone message came from, and picked up my fares. They were a long time about it, and they'd got some heavy luggage with them. But when I turned to leave, I did think that I saw Todd's cab. It was crawling down the pavement towards me, and I gave him a wave of the hand. But there was a gent, signalling at the same time, and, if it really were Todd, he didn't see me. You know, it's pretty dark in London at night-time."

"Where did you pick up your fares?"

"Anton's, 30a, Luer Road. It's an antique furniture shop."

Blake nodded his head.

"I know Anton," he said.

"He's a queer chap, that," Jones put in; "but it weren't him that I took in my cab. They was customer's of his, I reckon. They'd bought an old box, or something, from him. Blimey! It was heavy! I'd to get down and give them a hand to fix it on the luggage-step."

Small, almost trivial, details, these. Yet Blake's vast brain treasured them all. It is only by a system of this kind that, bit by bit, scrap by scrap, the great mysteries of the world are solved.

"And how far away was the cab which you thought might have been Todd's?"

"Just underneath the next lamp-post," said Jones. "Of course, mister, I ain't swearing that it was his—only at the back o' my mind I do think that it was."

"You would make a very good witness, Jones," Blake said quietly, "and one that could be relied upon."

The taxi-driver stood up.

"I'd like to do something to 'elp, sir," he said. "Todd was one of the best, he was. It's a blinkin' shame that he should be murdered. He never did anyone any harm. Maybe a bit hot-tempered, but that's nothing."

Tinker had waited at the entrance to the building, and when Blake appeared, the young assistant glanced keenly at his master.

"Any luck, guv'nor."

"I shouldn't like to venture an opinion just yet, Tinker," Blake returned, "but we have a little line to work on now."

This time it was to Anton's place that Blake journeyed, by taxi. As he entered the frowsy, dingy shop, the thin, lean-faced proprietor came forward. Anton recognised Blake at once, and held out his hand, the usual inscrutable smile on his lips.

"And how is Mr. Blake?"

Blake returned the greeting, and looked around him. No one had ever been able to point an accusing finger at Lew Anton. His business was at least genuine. He was a maker of false antiques. His little workshop at the back of the premises had seen more spurious Chippendale and Jacobean furniture turned out to deceive even the connoisseur than any other maker in London.

"Nothing in the almost antique line for you this morning, I suppose?" Anton went on, rubbing his long, clever fingers together. They were stained and hacked by much handling of tools and polishes, for Anton did most of his better-class work himself.

"No, Anton, I'm not on the buy. I want a little information."

The antique dealer pursed his lips.

"You know my unvarying rule, Mr. Blake. A customer's business with me is a sacred trust."

"That's all right, old chap!" laughed Blake, who understood the man perfectly. "I'm not going to find out whether somebody's cherished treasures are really genuine, or samples of your work."

Anton looked relieved, and half apologised.

"It wouldn't be fair to them, you know," he explained.

"What I want to find out is the movements of a certain taxi-driver," said Blake. "He was observed to pick up a fare close to your shop, and I was hoping that you might have noted it."

"That's a difficult question," the dealer murmured. "When is it supposed to have happened?"

"Last night. Just about the same time as a customer of yours 'phoned for a taxi to take away a box from here."

"Ah, yes! That was between eight and nine, I should think. I couldn't swear to the time, of course."

"That would be about the time."

Blake briefly repeated the details what he had had from Jones. Anton listened quietly, then shook his head.

"I'd like to help you, but I'm afraid I cannot," he said at last, "for, as a matter of fact, I did not go out of my shop. The—the article that was being taken away was very weighty, and I had to send my assistant along with the customer to help carry it to the taxi."

"I suppose your customer could not help me?"

The antique-faker smiled—a wintry smile.

"Now, of course, you are stepping on forbidden ground," he put in. "I dare not give you my customer's address!"

Blake was well aware of the old fellow's prejudices, and the detective had to confess that Anton's attitude was the correct one.

No individual cares to have it known that his cherished antiques are really only clever fakes, and the mere fact of Anton supplying one with articles was quite sufficient to label them as fake.

"That makes it rather awkward, Anton," said Blake, "for I am very anxious to trace this taxi."

The lean proprietor shrugged his shoulders.

"I don't think that my customer could help you, in any case," he went on. "If you inquire, you will find that the chest"—he mentioned the article almost before he was aware of what he said—"has been taken to Paddington Station—left-luggage office. I believe it is intended to travel to the East."

That information certainly settled matters so far as that particular channel of information was concerned. Blake, clever though he was, could hardly be expected to trace an unknown proprietor of a left-luggage article through London!

"That has settled it!" the detective agreed, revealing no trace of disappointment on his face. "And now, have you anything to show me? I have five or six minutes to spare."

Anton's intellectual face lighted up; then a quick shadow of disappointment crossed it.

Blake had often visited the little shop, and his keen knowledge of antiques had made Anton relish his opinion.

"If you had only come along here yesterday, Mr. Blake," he said, "I would have shown you something worth while?"

He drew himself up, all the pride of the artist shimmering in his faded eyes.

"A masterpiece!" he said. "It is the best thing I have ever done! I would have defied even the great Hindu artist himself, who designed the original, to have made a more perfect duplicate!"

"But if it's gone, what's the use of arousing my desire to see it?" Blake laughed.

And then the pride of the artist conquered for a brief moment the caution of the man of business.

"After all, I don't suppose that there can be much harm!" Anton muttered, half to himself. "The chest is going back to India—probably on its way there now!"

He had no reason to think otherwise. Professor Kew, who was just a mere customer so far as Anton was concerned, had been cunning enough to tell the dealer that his work was to be sent out to India for comparison with the original. Kew had taken this course in order to arouse the professional pride of his dupe. He had been successful, for Anton's work on the chest was a masterpiece of elaborate and careful copying; but by the false statement, Kew was to lay himself open to future discovery.

"Yes, I'll show you the photographs."

He slid behind the counter, and returned presently with a sheaf of faded photographs. They were of the chest, and gave views of each carved side and top. Dim though the were, Blake could pick out the exquisite carvings and tracery.

"And you really made a copy of this?"

The face of the dealer flushed with pride.

"I was at it, day and night, for the best part of three months," he said, "and I give you my professional word that in every detail—line for line, grain, and finish—my duplicate equals the original!"

"Then, by Jove, I should have liked to see it!" said Blake. "It looks like one of those old Indian chests that one rajah sent to another in the old fighting days either as a war indemnity or as a peace offering."

"I don't know its history," said Anton, truthfully enough. "I was only interersted in the work."

Blake and Tinker spent half-an-hour in the old fellow's shop, and Anton came to the door to see them off.

"It's been very interesting, guv'nor," Tinker said, in his dry way, "but we haven't got much forra'der!"

"That's true!" the great detective returned. "And yet, I don't know! I am inclined to trust to the word of Jones. He is a cautious sort, and is not likely to make a mistake."

He glanced at his assistant.

"Anton is as close as an oyster, but both you and I know that some of his customers are very queer fish. I am half-inclined to think that the unknown fare who was picked up by Todd in Luer Road was the same man that murdered him.

"But it was much later than that when I saw the taxi at Downe Square, guv'nor.

"Yes, that's so. But we won't theorise any longer. I'm going to make another effort, and if this is unsuccessful I will confess myself at fault."

Tinker placed his hand over his waistcoat.

"I could make an effort on a decent steak, guv'nor!" he said, and his lugubrious tone told Blake that he meant it.

It was now well on in the afternoon, and they had breakfasted early.

They turned into a restaurant, and had a meal; then Blake chartered another taxi.

"Paddington!" he said to the driver.

Tinker's eyes brightened as he caught the word.

"You think that——"

"I'm not going to think anything!" came the quiet reply. "I'm just experimenting."

An hour later, however, Tinker had proofs that the unerring instinct of his master had not been at fault. They traced the chest, to find that it had been left in the luggage department only a very short time, the owner returning an hour or so later and removing it. The porter, who assisted in the task, gave Blake a description of the two individuals who had claimed the weighty object.

"One of them was a big, burly gent,—looked like a Colonial—and the other was a tall and rather flashily dressed."

A very meagre description, and neither of them tallying with Tinker's brief memory of the under-sized man in the long cloak.

The chest had been placed into a hooded cart, and the porter had not noted any name on the vehicle. And that was all they could discover about the chest.

But outside the station Blake found an intelligent railway policeman, who filled in a great gap.

He had seen Todd and his taxi, and had observed the cloaked man alight. He noted this particularly, because the cloaked man had ordered the driver to wait for him. The stranger had gone into the station, and had remained there for about half an hour. He had reappeared at last in company with a burly man, who had evidently entered the station by the Underground. The two men waited until a hooded cart had entered the covered portion of the station; then the cloaked figure had gone back into his taxi alone.

From the policeman's description, there was no doubt but that the man who had spoken to the unknown murderer was the same as had gone off with the spurious chest.

"And that is as far as we can go just now, Tinker," Blake explained, as they left the station. "You see, one of my theories was correct. The man who waited at the lamp-post outside Anton's shop was interested in the removal of the chest. We have proved that conclusively."

Tinker nodded.

"It's been a hot job, guv'nor," the lad said admiringly. "And it looks so blinkin' simple now it's been done!"

Blake laughed.

The whole art of following up clues depends on one's ability to eliminate the unnecessary, old chap," he explained. "I'm not going to theorise, and we must just accept what we have actually found. Todd, driving his cab, left Paddington at an hour that would just give him time to reach Downe Square about the moment that you were there. We have filled in all his day for him, and by doing so we have established one great fact—that is, that the man who engaged him in Luer Road was the actual murderer."

"That was the point, guv'nor," the quick-witted assistant agreed, "for, of course, Todd might have picked up half a dozen fares from the time Jones saw him last until I witnessed the crime."

They had both spent a thoroughly fatiguing day, and were glad to make their way back to Baker Street. A telephone message was waiting for Tinker, asking him to ring up the police-station. He did so, and heard the inspector's report.

"Nothing doing, guv'nor," the lad said, as he replaced the receiver. "They've been all round Downe Square and the neighbourhood, but no one seems to be able to help them. The inspector is inclined to think that it wasn't Downe Square that the taxi was making for, but some street beyond it. Perhaps he is right, you know, for the driver didn't ask for a number—only for the square itself."

"That's a rock that we might very likely split on," said Blake. "However we'll see! The inspector is entitled to his own opinion, and certainly he ought to know the type of people who live in that neighbourhood."

A high tea was waiting for them, with fresh buttered toast and the scones that, on special occasions, the landlady condescended to bake for them. Tinker had a wolfish appetite, and made a great meal. Half-way through it, the door of the dining-room was pushed aside, and Pedro, yawing, came into the room, to lay his great head on Blake's knee and wave his strong tail.

"Hallo, you rascal!" Blake said, patting the sage head. "So you haven't been banished yet? Better lie low, then!"

The entry of Pedro aroused an almost forgotten memory in Tinker's mind.

"I can find a good home for him, guv'nor," he announced with a grin, for he knew that Blake would not part with Pedro for all the gold in the world.

"Indeed?"

"Yes, and, by jiminy, it's at Downe Square, too!"

Blake looked up.

"It seems to me as though that square is bulking very large in your life, old chap."

"I'd forgotten all about Pedro," Tinker admitted. "The other affair wiped it clean away."

He gave his master an account of the little adventure in the gloomy square and the clever way in which Pedro had found the jewelled ornament.

"And the young lady said that she was coming round here to see old Pedro again!" Tinker grinned. "I'd like to see our old dame's face when she does come to the door and asks about 'that dratted dog'!"

"I'm afraid Miss Bryce will be doomed to disappointment unless she hurries up!" was Blake's remark. "And, by the way, her name sounds rather familiar. Do you know anything about her?"

"Not a word except that she's every inch a lady!" said Tinker gallantly. "And she wears wonderful combs—worth fifty pounds each, and were given to her as a birthday present from a rajah."

He heard his master give a quick breath, and looked. Blake's face had changed completely—the lines of deep thought about the eyes were plainly visible, the lips were set, and the whole countenance was set and grim.

"A birthday present from a rajah! And she lives in Downe Square!"

He rose abruptly from his chair and went out of the dining-room. Tinker heard the door of the study close, then quiet footfalls sounded.

The lad reached out and patted Pedro.

"That's done it, old man," he said; "somehow or other the guv'nor's got his thinking cap on, and that means you and I will have to amuse ourselves for the rest of the evening."

He knew that it was his remark that had roused some quick idea in the master brain of the man he admired.

Tinker, shrewd and keen-witted, tried to discover what it was, but he failed.

"Can't be done," he muttered, pushing his chair back. "I am a jolly clever young man, but when the guv'nor get busy, you can push me back in among the 'also tried's,' Pedro. But I'll bet that whatever it is, there's nothing against the little lady you and I met last night. She was just a peach and a picture, and if I weren't a pal of yours, Pedro, I'd be jealous. For she certainly didn't put her arm round my neck, nor—nor kiss me under the ear!"

CHAPTER 4
The Theft of the War Chest

In one of the rooms on the second floor of No. 4, Downe Square, there had gathered three men—Professor Kew, Count Ivor Carlac, and the third, an overdressed, sleek rascal, known to his associates as Flash Harry.

The house, situated next to No. 5, had long stood vacant, and the agents had only been too glad to let it on a short lease. Flash Harry, representing himself as the confidential secretary to a wealthy man who desired to keep his name out of the affair, had told the agents a very plausible story. He had made out that the house was to be used as a nursing home for wounded and convalescent colonials, hinting that his employer was a rich Canadian.

The first three months rent had been paid in advance, and a number of workemn had been engaged on the place. Carpenters and plasterers were constantly in and out of the house, lending colour to Flash Harry's story.

He himself furnished a couple of rooms and gave out that he would take up residence there as soon as the alterations were completed.

The local firm of builders who had undertaken the work of altering the house little dreamed that their legitimate business was serving to cover an elaborate fraud.

None of the neighbours thought that there was anything wrong when they heard the sound of hammer and chisel going long into the night. It was known that the work was being pushed forward at express speed so that the place might be ready for its future inmates as soon as possible.

Kew's active brain had organised the whole affair, and now he was there to make his final arrangements.

"I don't see what you've got to worry about, gents," Flash Harry commented: "everything has gone just like clockwork. I've had the grate and wall pierced, and there's a gap big enough for four men to walk through into the room next door. And the job has been done by my own pals—who daren't give me away."

He crossed to the black marble mantelpiece that looked solid enough, in all conscience, and tapped it.

"A fine piece of work," he grinned, "although I say it who shouldn't."

Carlac glanced across at him, then looked at Kew.

"I agree with you, Harry," the burly criminal returned; "you have done extraordinarily well. Our friend, however, seems to have developed nerves—and it's the first time I've ever known him to do the like."

Kew was seated on the edge of a chair, his shrivelled figure curled up in its usual bird-like pose. The hawk face lifted, and the beady eyes turned on Carlac.

"I have developed nerves—but that does not mean that I am afraid." he returned, in his clear thin tones. "It only means that we have to be little more cautious."

"But we've been cautious enough, haven't we?" Flash Harry commented. "Take that old chest, for instance; it came in here in full view of the workmen this morning—disguised as a sideboard. The trick of fitting false legs and a false back to it was a masterpiece, I reckon!"

He grinned towards the object he named. Already the legs and back had been moved from the great chest and a covering of tapestry had been flung across it as it stood in the corner of the room.

"I give you all that," the grim-visaged professor said. "It is not the chest nor the work that you have performed here that I am troubled over. It was the fact of meeting that young cub, Tinker."

He had made a confidant of Carlac in the matter, but the broad-shouldered criminal shook his head.

"I think that you were mistaken this time, Kew," he returned; "there is no conceivable reasons to connect Tinker's appearance with our presence here. It was just an unfortunate coincidence; and the only thing I find to regret in the business is what happened after you set eyes on him."

Kew's cruel lips lifted in a passionate smile.

"Meaning the death of the taxi man," he said. "Oh, I am not concerned about him! He was a blundering fool, and would have caused trouble. I had to get away at once and without being recognised. The man would have detained me—he had to be removed."

He dismissed the matter with a wave of his lean hand.

"But, still, I am prepared to give in to you in this case, Carlac," he said. "If you are of the opinion that Blake knows nothing about us, then let us carry the final move out."

"Now?"

Kew arose to his feet.

"Why not. It is just five o'clock. The faithful Abdul will be squatting outside the door of the treasure-room, tulwar over his knees, his keen ears on the alert. We could not choose a better occasion."

Now that the cool voice proposed the actual deed, Flash Harry, a craven at heart, began to have qualms.

"Couldn't we wait for a bit," he muttered; "it's early yet. Perhaps later on there wouldn't be so much chance of us being heard. We—we might trip over something, then——"

"There are a hundred 'mights' that could happen," Kew's cutting voice returned; "what we have to do is to guard against all of them, and be very careful."

He turned his back on Harry, addressing Carlac.

"Now is the best time," he explained; "you and I are out of the house. We know that, this afternoon, Colonel Bryce and Lord Eagley, of the Foreign Office, both inspected the chest and its contents, assuring themselves that everything was correct. You hear the colonel say that that was going to be done. If the chest vanishes and the duplicate is put in its place now, who can blame us?"

The strong face of the tall criminal lighted up in a quick sarcastic smile.

"We don't want anyone to blame us," he returned grimly; "but, all the same, I think you're right. Now is the time."

He slipped out of his jacket and rolled up his sleeves, revealing the great bulging muscles of the forearm. Flash Harry eyed the powerful limb admiringly.

"I always said that the count ought to have been a wrestler," he said; "there's a muscle for you. Lord, he could tackle the pick of them, he could."

He had also removed his coat as he spoke, but Kew did not follow the example set by the other two.

A sudden tense silence descended on the man. Carlac, with a quick, light tread, reached the chest and nodded to Flash Harry.

"We'll get it as near to the fireplace as we can," he whispered, in a low tone.

The chest had been weighted with heavy blocks of lead, and it was all that Flash Harry could do to carry his end across the room.

Kew had already removed the rugs and fire implements from the hearth. He looked up at Carlac, who nodded his head.

"Right," the powerful man muttered.

Kew, stooping down, caught at the bars of the grate and pulled. Noiselessly the whole back portion of the fireplace swung upward and outward, leaving a gap four feet high and about four feet wide. Through the gap it was pitch dark, but the light from the room they were in shed a faint gleam into the interior beyond, revealing the edge of a carpet and an ornamental hearth.

"The glim—quick—out with it," Harry breathed. And Kew, leaping back to the gas-jet turned out the flame.

Carlac lowered the corner of the chest, and stepping into the open gap, listened for a moment. There was no sound and at last he turned his head.

"Pocket-torch!" he breathed. And a long slender tube was thrust into his hand.

A little bulb of light leaped from between his fingers and raced for a moment over the carpet, to settle at last on the square outlines of the rajah's war-chest.

"Right, come on. Careful now!"

Anton's masterpiece was lifted, and with noiseless steps Carlac and Flash Harry entered the other room, dipping low to avoid the uplifted grate. They tip-toed across the chamber, and resting their own burden for a moment, tackled the heavy treasure-chest. It was almost more than they could manage; Carlac, strong as a bull, was capable of swinging his end, but Flash Harry, tug though he did until the sweat stood out in beads on his forehead, could not make it stir. Suddenly the man felt a breath at his side, and the voice of Kew sounded.

"Now lift!"

The great chest came up in answer to their combined efforts, and the slow painful journey towards the gap began. It was well for them that the chest had been deposited quite close to the grate of the room. They had only to carry it some ten or fifteen feet, and yet, by the time that it had been set down in the other room, Carlac was panting for breath. Flash harry collapsed over the top of the chest with a stifled groan.

"I—I'm—beat!" he muttered hoarsely.

There was a movement by his side. Kew darted to the table and opened a small case, returning a moment later with a small phial.

"Drink that—quick!"

Flash Harry never knew what it was that trickled down his throat, stinging and potent. But it seemed to drive the fatigue from his limps like a charm. His swimming brain cleared and he straightened up.

"Gee! That's better—what have we to do next?"

"Put the other chest into its proper place," Carlac whispered; "come along."

This time Kew took no part in the business beyond holding the torch so that his two confederates could put the false treasure-chest exactly over the place occupied by the real one. They had worked with feverish energy and the moments had seemed as long as hours, yet no more than ten minutes could have passed from the moment that Kew raised the grate until, after a careful inspection on his hands and knees by Carlac of the carpet in the other room, it was lowered into its place.

"We haven't left a mark behind us," he said, brushing the dust from his knees as he straightened up. "I think that that has been very neatly carried out."

Flash Harry was leaning against the wall wiping the sweat from his streaming face. Kew had lighted the gas again by now, and the trio of rogues eyed each other in silence.

"That must have weighed half a ton," Flash Harry breathed. "It's the heaviest thing I've ever tackled."

Kew bent over the wonderfully carved box. His beady eyes were flaming with the old avaricious glare.

"It was gold, my friend," his thin tones piped; "solid gold! If the burden had been twice as heavy we would have managed it."

The man leaning against the wall laughed.

"I didn't think you were so strong, professor," he admitted; "you certainly helped me. I couldn't have managed my end alone."

Kew chuckled.

"That was not strength—simply will-power," he returned. "I willed that we should lift the chest. And we did."

There was something uncanny about him, and Harry turned away with a half-shiver. He had always been afraid of Kew. Carlac was more of his type of leader.

"Well, now we've got it, what's to happen?"

He put that question in a bantering tone, and Carlac smiled.

"We have a safe place for it," he said; "but we cannot remove it just now. To-night we will call for it, and you must keep your eye on it until then. And don't forget about this," Kew went on, indicating the grate that he had now closed. "Your workmen will have to get busy at once, bricking in."

The chest was removed to the corner, and the piece of tapestry arranged over it once more so that it looked like a couch.

Not a word was said to Harry concerning his honesty, nor was it needed. For Flash Harry knew his men, and the world would not have been wide enough for him to find a hiding-place in, had he attempted to play the double game with them. He had been promised his reward—and it was a generous one. With that he had to be content.

Kew and Carlac left No. 4 by way of the narrow garden in rear of the house. It let them out into a narrow lane once used by tradespeople of a bygone generation, but now given over to a few stray cats.

It ended in a range of stables down one of the side streets that led into the square. The two rogues had tidied themselves before leaving No. 4, and there was no trace of the mighty effort he had made on Carlac's face as he rang the bell and entered the home of his genial host, Colonel Bryce.

The colonel himself was just descending the stairs as the two criminals entered. He came forward with outstretched hand, a picture of kindly welcome.

"I am hoping that your search for berths has been unsuccessful, Count Kaldross," he cried.

Carlac shook his head.

"Then I'm afraid I must disappoint you, colonel," he returned. "Dr. Kay and I have fixed up to sail in a White Star from Liverpool to-morrow morning."

"But how unfortunate," Bryce went on. "I do wish that you could wait over the week-end. I believe his Highness will be in England by Tuesday at the very latest. I am sure that he would be glad to see you, for I have mentioned your valuable services to him."

"We did very little, colonel," said Kew, in his bland, smooth tones.

"Well, I don't know so much about that," the officer returned. "You took your turn at watching the chest on board ship, and would have done the same here if I would have allowed you. That's a jolly sight more than most people would care to do."

Carlac bowed.

"It was a very small return for your many kindnesses, colonel," he replied. "And now I'm afraid that the doctor and I must get to work on our packing. We really ought to catch the midnight express for Liverpool to-night."

They went on up the stairs and along the corridor. Beneath a shaded electric-bulb was seated the great, turbanned figure of a trooper of the rajah's bodyguard. The man sat motionless, as though carved out of bronze, his curved sword across his massive knees, the keen blade shining beneath the reflected light from the bulb above him.

Kew gave Abul a word as he passed.

"It is all well with thy master's treasure, Abul?"

The white teeth of the Indian shone beneath the black beard. Abul nodded his head.

"I am here to guard it, sahib," he said simply, "and all is well."

The face of the doctor twisted into a mocking grimace as he went down the passage and into his own room. He found one of the colonel's valets at work, laying out his evening dress.

"I'm packing up to-night, Carter," said Kew. "The count and I start for America in the morning. You might get my clothes together."

"Very good, sir," the servant returned.

To Kew there was a grim comedy about his presence in the house that evening. He had tricked his host and the grim-jawed sentinel so cleverly, that neither suspected him. He was going to eat Colonel Bryce's food, drink Colonel Bryce's wine, and at the end of it, he would leave Downe Square with Colonel Bryce's treasure-chest.

"A rogue can never be a gentleman," the grinning schemer decided, as he descended the stairs. "It is just Colonel Bryce's bad fortune that he should be in charge of something I covet. And what I covet I get."

Carlac was already in the drawing-room talking to Muriel Bryce. Over the girl's white shoulders the eyes of the criminals met and lingered for a moment.

Muriel turned to the professor and began to chat to him, echoing her father's regrets at the departure.

"We shall quite miss you," she said, in her bright, friendly tones. "After travelling so far together, it does seem a shame."

Later on Lieutenant Vernon and the colonel appeared, with a silver-haired aristocratic-looking man, whose name Kew did not catch. They all went into the dining-room, and Kew and his companion enjoyed what they knew was to be their last meal in the well-conducted house.

Colonel Bryce was in excellent spirits that evening, laughing and chatting with his guests in turn. Only seasoned rogues such as Kew and Carlac could have sat through that meal and enjoyed it as they did.

Just at the end of the meal the colonel raised his glass and nodded to the men he trusted so implicitly.

"Your health, count—and yours, doctor. My only regret is that you have to leave us."

Behind his hand Vernon sent a quick whisper across to Muriel.

"Thank goodness! It's about time the did go!"

He received a very indignant glance for his pains, but it did not seem to upset him very much. He leaned back in his chair, smiling to himself.

From the very first this young officer had had his doubts about the two adventurers who had come so unexpectedly into the little circle. He had watched them as a cat watches mice, yet—and he was honest enough to admit it—Vernon could not find a single suspicious incident to hinge his doubts upon.

In every way they had proved themselves genial companions—ready to share anything that might come along.

Still, despite all this, the doubt had never been killed, and now that they had announced their departure, the young officer was candid enough to admit his satisfaction.

"I can't help it, Muriel," he said later on in the drawing-room, when his charming young hostess took him to task over his whispered speech. "I suppose I am a suspicious fool; but it's all due to that confounded war-chest! Only let the rajah come and take the thing away and I'll be as different as possible. But while the colonel is responsible, I feel on guard, and I cannot trust anyone. Count or no count, friend or foe!"

It was a long speech for the usual monosyllabic Vernon to make, and the girl smiled up at him.

"We'll try and be nice to them for to-night. They leave at eleven."

And, true to their statement, Kew and Carlac did leave No. 5 at a few minutes before the hour named. Their baggage, a very light load—for they had given it out that most of their heavier traps were returning to America direct—was stacked up in the taxi that had been sent for, and the farewells took place in the lighted hall.

In the darkness of the cab Kew leaned back in his seat, and Carlac heard him chuckling softly.

"Of course we'll write to you when we get to America, my dear Miss Muriel," the thin voice muttered: "but we may never set foot there."

Carlac turned his head and looked out into the darkened streets.

"You needn't make fun of the girl," he said slowly. "After all, she was kindness itself to us; and I, for one, shall always remember her as a sweet, good-hearted child."

Kew's chuckle lifted in a cackling laugh.

"So that's it, eh?" he sniggered. "We grow sentimental on the eve of departure. My dear Carlac, that is perhaps the funniest thing you have ever said. You rob a girl's father of his treasure, then wax sentimental over the girl."

"I am, perhaps, just a little human," the broad-shouldered criminal returned. "You, apparently, have no claim to that feeling."

"None whatever!" snapped Kew in his usual remorseless tones. "I was out for gold, and had no time for stupid sentiment. I have got what I sought, and am quite content."

They reached the station, and Kew called to a porter directing him to take the baggage to the night express. This was done so that the taxi-driver might be able to prove that his fares had really gone to the station and taken train there. But on the platform the two rogues claimed their luggage again and had it removed to the cloak-room, then left by another exit.

"It would have been better for us to travel to Liverpool," Carlac mentioned: "but we cannot risk that. Flash Harry is straight enough, but the responsibility is too great for him. We can't expect him to guard that chest himself."

"We don't want him to," the wizened man by his side returned grimly. "We have to get that chest away from Downe Square to-night."

He was pacing along the dark pavement, his head bent forward, his hands clasped behind his back. Carlac could almost feel the vast contentment that was radiating from his evil companion.

"This is our last big effort, Carlac," Kew said. "Gold is untraceable, and we can retire to any part of the world we like, and be always sure of a welcome."

"Always excepting India," Carlac put in, in a half-thoughtful tone.

"What do you mean?"

The tall criminal shrugged his shoulders.

"I was thinking of the Rajah of Puljara," he said. "You remember what was said about the chest. It was sacred, and anyone touching it with sacrilegious hands———"

"Nonsense! An old woman's tale that!" snapped the little figure by his side. "I have no room for superstitions."

He threw back his great head and laughed.

"The Rajah of Puljara may be all-important in his native state, but he has little authority in London. We are safe enough from him, my friend."

Yet Carlac's words had left their impression on the quick intellect of the professor, and before his eyes there came a sombre vision. The outlines of the gloomy prison at the Palace of Kashopore.

Almost unconsciously Kew shivered.

"Why on earth did you mention that fool's story," he snapped. "It would have been better had we forgotten its existence."

It was the dim forebodings of what fate held in store for them that had stirred his evil heart. For Puljara was to see them again, and the prison in the bustling town was to open its gloomy doors to them, as the beginning of an existence that was worse than death.

But all this was veiled in the mists of the future, and for the moment, the success that they had achieved blinded them to everything else. They were on the threshold of a new and splendid life, with a treasure awaiting their disposal.

The height of their dreams had been attained.

"Good-morning, Abul!"

Lieutenant Vernon came to a halt in the corridor and nodded to the great shrewd Indian trooper. Bright-eyed and sleepless, Abul, faithful servant of his master, the Rajah of Puljara, acknowledged the greeting with the stately dignity of his race.

"Good-morning, sahib!"

The young British officer glanced admiringly at the big, bearded figure. Abul's ceaseless guard of the room in which the great treasure-chest stood, had become a thing of wonder and astonishment to the inmates of No. 5. The staff of English servants that ran the household were all openly afraid of this bronze god with his naked sword. Abul had arranged a bed at the door of the room, and there, when fatigue overcame him, he was supposed to sleep. But no one in the house could ever swear that they had seen him at rest, and his endurance was the subject of much chatter below stairs.

"You have not tired of your watch yet?"

"No, sahib."

The young officer smiled.

"Well, you won't have long to wait now. His Highness is due in London on Tuesday."

"That is good news, sahib."

The trooper had risen to his feet, and he stretched his superb limbs, resting the point of his sword on the ground.

"I, Abul, will be glad." he admitted. "This London is no place for a man used to the hills. Ah! but the nights are long and dismal. I would rather spend a month on the hills with the stars as companions, than a day here in this gloomy city."

"You're quite right there, Abul," Vernon returned. "London is pretty rotten just now—worse than it usually is."

It was about nine o'clock in the morning, but most of the household were up and about. Colonel Bryce, an early riser himself, saw to it that the others followed his example. The breakfast gong began to rumble, and Vernon, with a nod to the trooper, hurried along the corridor and descended the stairs.

"Good morning, Lieutenant Vernon," said a demure voice, and Muriel, looking as pretty as a picture, stepped out of the morning-room, a laughing greeting on her lips and in her eyes.

Vernon cast a quick glance to right and left. There was no one about. With a deft movement he slipped his arm around the slender waist and kissed the fresh young lips.

"Oh!"

"I couldn't help it, darling," the ardent young officer whispered, "you looked so perfectly sweet and charming."

"But if dad——"

"I wouldn't care," came the reply. "I mean to tell him at the very first opportunity. I am to get my captaincy next week—and after all, the colonel married your mother when he was only a subaltern, with very little prospects."

He looked down at her, the love shining in his eyes.

"I'm no end of a patient lover," he announced. "but I really must have a kiss now and again."

Muriel smiled and gave his arm a little affectionate pressure. She knew that this clean-living lad was hers, heart and soul. And she returned his love with interest. But, girl-like, she revelled in the power she had over him, keeping him at her beck and call from daylight to dusk.

They entered the breakfast-room together, and a moment later Bryce joined them. He was dressed in riding-clothes, for he made it a custom to have an hour's canter in the park after breakfast.

"Thank goodness we'll soon have the great load taken off our minds," he said. "I've had a cable from his Highness. He arrives in London at ten o'clock on Tuesday morning."

"Have you engaged his suite of rooms, sir?"

"I'm going to see about them to-day," said Bryce: "As a matter of fact, there were hopes that he might have found suitable quarters at York House, but they cannot be spared. However, the Ritz has promised to keep their best apartments for him, and I think they will suit."

He cast a half-laughing glance at the fresh young faces in front of him.

"A rajah isn't an easy person to handle, Vernon," Bryce said slily. "In fact, he's almost as bad as a—a wife!"

He saw the red tide in the charming countenance of his daughter. The colonel bent his head and laughed quietly over his plate.

He was not so blind as he pretended to be, and the little love-match between his secretary and his daughter had his entire approval.

As soon as the breakfast was over the colonel arose to his feet.

"Come along, Vernon," he said. "We've got to make the usual visiting rounds."

Every morning and evening the senior officer and his subordinate had made it their duty to enter the room in which the chest was stored and see that everything was correct. Very often Muriel accompanied them, and she, too, arose.

"I always feel as though I ought to be carrying a rifle at the slope," she whispered to Vernon as he stood aside to allow her to pass out into the hall.

The colonel led the way upstairs, Muriel and Vernon behind him. As the grizzled head of the veteran appeared above stairs, Abul, the sleepless, leaped to his feet and stood to attention.

The morning ceremony was gone through.

"Halt! Who goes there?"

"Visiting Rounds!"

"Advance, Visiting Rounds! All's well!"

The colonel stepped forward, and Abul, taking a key from his belt, held it out. The lock on the door clicked, and Abul, pushing the door aside, entered.

The room was a small, square one. It was empty, save for a strip of wonderful carpet in the centre of the floor, and the big iron-bound chest. There was a curtain at the window, and Vernon, stepping up to it, drew it aside so that the faint light might fall full on the chest.

"All is well, Abul," said the colonel, nodding towards the heavy box, "and soon I will be able to meet thy royal master and tell him how well thou hast kept thy bond."

Abul's eyes glinted.

"I am my master's slave," he said, with a proud humility that sat well on his powerful face. "I have but done my duty."

Muriel had crossed the room and was now close to the window where she stood talking to Vernon in a low tone. Her eyes were wandering aimlessly, and presently they concentrated on something that seemed to be jutting out from beneath the great war-chest.

"What is that?" she asked in a low tone, extending a dainty finger.

"Vernon stared for a moment, then, crossing to the chest, he stooped.

"By Jove!"

The colonel and the dusky trooper wheeled round.

"What is it, Vernon?" the colonel's voice rang out sharply.

The young officer was looking at something in his hand, and there was a puzzled frown on his face. At the colonel's question he straightened up, then came forward, his hand outstretched.

"Did you—did you move the chest yesterday, sir?"

"Move it! Certainly not! How could I?"

"I—I thought that you might have done, for—for I have just found this sticking to one corner."

It was a fragment of tapestry of a cheap quality, and small though the scrap was, there was sufficient of it to show that it was new and unsoiled.

For a moment the colonel looked at the innocent scrap of material, then his eye travelled to the chest and riveted itself there.

Lew Anton had done his work remarkably well. Grain and texture, outline and measurement had been exact and minutely accurate. Ninety-nine men out of a hundred would have been taken in, but Colonel Bryce happened to be the hundreth person.

He had been haunted by that treasure chest and what it contained. He had dreamed of it at night, and had worried over it by day. Every detail of its carved panels were known to him, he could have closed his eyes and described every single line of it.

And now he was looking at the stout iron handle. Anton had done his best even in that detail, but the skilled faker knew that there was his only weakness. Newly-wrought iron can never be made to resemble old. The Hindu who had fashioned the original had done so using only hammer and chisel, fashioning it laboriously, slowly.

"By heavens! That is not the rajah's chest!"

Colonel Bryce almost screamed the words as he darted forward and dropped on his knees in front of the faked receptacle. His hands were clutching at the iron handle, and, as his fingers passed over it, doubt became certainty. The handle was smooth to the touch of the fingers, whereas the old handle had been pitted by the taps of the maker's hammer.

"Oh, Colonel! You—you must be mistaken!"

Vernon's face was bloodless as he darted to his chief's side.

"No, no—I'm right! This handle—I can tell by the very touch of it! And look at the very panels—they are fakes—fakes, I tell you!"

With an effort the grizzled-haired man arose to his feet. His face was grey as it turned first to Vernon then to his daughter.

"Get me my keys, Muriel, please," Colonel Bryce said in a voice that was strained and hoarse. "Quick, dear, you know where I keep them!"

Muriel fairly flew along the corridor and into her father's bedroom. There was a secret drawer in the little bureau which only her father and Muriel knew. The bunch of keys was found, and the pale-faced girl hurried back to the room.

When she entered, Abul had just been trying to lift the chest, and had succeeded.

Horror was visible on the face of the two Englishmen as they looked at the huge trooper.

Abul had never been able to move the treasure-chest singlehanded before. There again was proof that something was wrong.

Muriel never forgot that moment of breathless doubt that followed. Her father's hand trembled slightly as he found the heavy gold key that fitted the lock of the treasure-chest. Slowly the various locks were tried, and the key did not fit. Anton had only been able to produce the outer appearance of the locks. He had nothing to guide him so far as the hidden mechanism was concerned.

"It will not open!"

"Oh, dad! Try again! Perhaps——"

"Your sword, Abul!"

The trooper held out the great carved blade and, stepping back, the colonel swung the tempered steel aloft.

Crash!

A fury seemed to descend on Colonel Bryce as he smote at the faked masterpiece. Great swathes of wood flew out at each powerful stroke, and at last, the lid was cut away from its fastening and slipped down on to the carpet.

"We have been betrayed," the colonel said in a thin voice. "Look! The rajah's treasure has vanished."

The dull bars of lead on the heap of rags at the bottom of the chest could not be mistaken. Vernon reeled against the wall of the room, sick and dazed.

"Gone! Gone!" he muttered, scarcely able to realise the truth.

It was Abul's voice that sounded at last. The trooper reached out a powerful hand and placed it on the colonel's sleeve.

"We have been tricked by cunning thieves, sahib," he said. "But the fault is not thine. It is I, Abul, who must bear the burden of shame."

His bearded face twitched, and into the eyes there came a look of deadly menace.

"I have been false to the trust that my master placed upon me," the man went on, in deep, vibrating tones. "I am in the dust. Allah help me!"

He made a sudden move forward, and his hand caught at the sword in Colonel Bryce's grasp. Instantly Muriel realised what was going to happen, and with a stifled scream she leaped forward, gripping at Abul's arm.

"No, don't do that, Abul," she breathed. "It is not your fault. No one could have been more faithful than you."

She drew him away, and looked into the bronzed face.

"I will tell his Highness," she vowed. "He will not blame you, and your life is too precious to be taken as you mean to do."

She had averted a tragedy. Abul lifted her small hand and placed it against his forehead.

"My life is in the mem-sahib's hands," he said slowly.

It was Muriel who brought the tension of the situation to an easier pitch.

"After all, none of us are to blame," she went on. "We have done everything in our power. You, dad, and you also, Mr. Vernon, have never neglected anything possible. If some evil wretch has stolen the treasure, how can we be blamed?"

She had the woman's instinct to bring solace to her troubled menfolk, and she succeeded. Colonel Bryce passed his hand across his forehead and sighed.

"What is to be done?" he asked wearily. "The treasure has vanished—spirited away! What can we do?"

"The police——"

Muriel turned to him with a quick shake of her head.

"We have to try and keep it out of the papers; if we can," she said, in her wise way. "Don't let us give up hope so soon.

There may just be a remote chance of getting the chest back before the rajah returns."

Her brave words had a very slender foundation, yet they brought a certain amount of comfort with them. Bryce went up to his daughter and placed his hand on her shoulder.

"You are the pluckiest of us all, Muriel," he said. "I must admit that this discovery has absolutely shocked me out of all power of thought. What can we do?"

His haggard face and tired voice fairly wrung Muriel's heart. Her lips quivered for a moment, and then suddenly there came into her mind a great inspiration. Vernon had crossed to the chest, and was leaning over it. Muriel cried out to him.

"Come away, Mr. Vernon! Please don't touch it. I—I have thought of someone who—who might be able to help."

She drew her father towards the door, and beckoned to Vernon to follow. Abul, his head hanging, his sword, which the colonel had now handed him, swinging aimlessly in his strong hand.

"Close the door and lock it," Muriel said, in a low voice. "Let Abul mount guard again, just as though nothing had happened. We must keep it away from the servants as long as we can."

Abul was listening to her eagerly, and he took up his post again beside the door, while the colonel turned the key.

"You are in charge, dear," the old officer said, with a faint smile. "But I confess that I do not see what good it will do."

"You must have patience," his plucky daughter returned. "I am going out, and—I thought that Mr. Vernon might come with me. I am going to bring someone here who is just the cleverest thing in the world."

Her intense eagerness carried everything in front of it. She hurried into her own room and slipped into a cloak and hat. In five minutes she was ready, and had joined Vernon in the hall. Outside the door a taxi was waiting, and also the groom in charge of the colonel's hack.

"I couldn't ride to-day, dear," Bryce said. "Send the man away. And don't be long; I cannot wait."

The charger was sent back to the stables; then Muriel and Vernon entered the taxi.

"Baker Street!" Vernon repeated. "And who lives there, Muriel? It isn't a visiting neighbourhood."

"And this isn't a visiting expedition," said Muriel, a grave light in her eyes. "Oh, I hope and pray that this move may result in something!"

She turned towards her companion, her eyes shining.

"I am putting all my faith in the sagacity of a dog," she announced.

Vernon leaned back and stared incredulously.

"A dog? But, I say, Muriel——"

"Yes, just a dog. But one of the most wonderful creatures in the world. Listen!"

She gave him a brief account of the little incident in which Pedro had played such a quaint part. Then went on:

"The boy who was with him—Tinker was his name—said that Pedro was more used to tracing men. It must have been human beings who removed the real treasure-chest, and if that wonderful dog can only find out how they did it, we may be able to trace them."

Her intent manner gradually inspired Vernon. By the time they reached Baker Street, the young officer was almost as eager as his companion.

But when the landlady opened the door they had their first disappointment.

"He ain't in, miss," the old dame said. "Gone out, as usual. There ain't no trusting to that Tinker, I can tell you. Of course, you 'ad an appointment with him and he's gone and forgotten——"

Muriel checked the ready flow.

"No, I didn't have any appointment," she returned; "but it is most important that I should see him."

"Mr. Blake's at home, miss. Maybe he'll see you."

Muriel slipped a card into the old dame's hand. When the found themselves alone in the waiting-room, Vernon turned to Muriel.

What name was it that the old lady mentioned?" he asked.

"Blake," said Muriel.

Into the young officer's face a light leaped, and he smiled.

"By Jove, Muriel, I believe that you have done the best thing, after all!" he said. "I don't know Tinker or Pedro, but I have heard of the name of Blake. He is one of the greatest private detectives in the world! I've never met him, but he has a great reputation in India."

The return of the landlady saw them ushered upstairs and into the consulting-room, where, a few moments later, Sexton Blake entered.

The keen, clean-cut face, the deep-set, steel-blue eyes, and the general air of alert, steadfast confidence, impressed Muriel at once. She arose with a half-blush, and held out her hand.

"I'm afraid that we are disturbing you, Mr. Blake," the beautiful girl began.

"That's quite all right, Miss Bryce," Blake returned. "I know that it must be something important that brought you from Downe Square so early."

"Then you—you know me?"

Blake smiled.

"Tinker told me of a little adventure he had," he explained.

The girl nodded her shapely head.

"Yes, yes. And it is really through that adventure that I am here now. I want Pedro. Is he here?"

By way of reply Blake stepped to the door and gave a low whistle. Pedro came slipping round the edge of the door, to be pounced upon by Muriel at once.

"You dear!" she said, wrapping her arm round the massive neck.

"Pedro is not very popular with our landlady," Blake explained, turning to Vernon, "and so we have to keep him in the background when he is here."

Muriel arose to her feet.

"I want him to come with me this morning," she said. "There—there is a big task in front of him, but I think he can manage it. Will you lend him to me?"

Or, better still, perhaps Mr. Blake would come with Pedro," Vernon put in. "Perhaps it is asking rather a lot from you, Mr. Blake, but I can assure you that the matter is a most important one, and would probably interest you."

He glanced at Muriel, who gave an encouraging nod. Both of them felt that they could not trust their secret into better hands than those of this quiet-voiced, clever man.

"A thief, or thieves, I should say, for it is the work of more than one person, have removed a certain valuable article from number five, and it is absolutely vital that it should be traced at once."

"What is it that has been stolen?" asked Blake.

Vernon lowered his voice.

"I take it that you will treat what I say as strictly confidential," he went on; "for, as a matter of fact, there are very grave issues hanging on it."

"You have my promise," said Blake.

"Good! Then you must know that it is a treasure-chest, with over ten lakhs of rupees in gold, that has been stolen. It is the property of the Rajah of Puljara, and was in the keeping of my chief, Colonel Bryce."

It seemed to Vernon as though Blake was paying very little attention to his statement. The detective was leaning back in his chair, and there was a curious light, half-smiling, half-thoughtful, in the steel-blue eyes.

"The matter is most urgent, Mr. Blake," Vernon said, a trifle annoyed.

Blake hurriedly arose.

"Quite so, and I will come with you now."

Pedro's leash was produced and adjusted on the wide collar, then a start was made for Downe Square. It seemed to Muriel that Blake hesitated for a moment as he passed the house on the left of No. 5.

"It is the next house, Mr. Blake," she said; and the detective turned his head and smiled.

"Yes, I know. That is number four."

Colonel Bryce eyed the strange man and the bloodhound rather dubiously when the entered his study, where he had been pacing to and from. But as soon as Muriel introduced Blake, the colonel's manner altered.

"Delighted to meet you, Blake!" the old Indian veteran said, giving the detective a warm grip. "Your reputation has reached all India, and you are something of a tradition there."

"We are in luck, sir," Vernon put in, "for Mr. Blake has promised to help us in this terrible affair."

They climbed the stairs, and Abul arose at their coming. Blake's eyes rested for a moment on the bronzed face of the trooper; then a kindly light came into the steel-blue eyes. He saw that the man was suffering agonies of mental torment, and, in his kindly way, Blake had to speak a few words of comfort.

"Have no fear," he murmured, using the clipped speech of the hillmen; "thou art not yet disgraced. Thy treasure is safe."

Into Abul's dark eyes came a flame. Who was this man who spoke to him, not in the usual Hindustani of the British, but in the exact vernacular of his own people?

"Thou sayest, O Protector?"

"I bid thee have courage. Thy hour of dismay has passed."

The door of the room was opened now, and Blake entered.

He gave one glance at the damaged chest, then, to the astonishment of the little group behind him, Blake flung back his head and laughed.

"So much for Anton's masterpiece!" he said aloud.

Bryce looked indignant.

"I hardly see anything to laugh at here, sir!" the distracted old fellow began.

Blake turned quickly, a quick apology on his lips.

"I'm sorry, colonel! It was rather thoughtless of me. I forgot that you do not know as much as I do concerning this chest and its owners."

"Do you mean to say that you know——"

A faint sound came to their ears, and brought the colonel's protest to a halt.

Blake flung a quick glance around him; then, crossing the room, picked up a fragment of the broken chest and struck the wall—three quick taps.

To the utter amazement of Bryce and his companions, there came an answer to the signal. Two taps, and after a pause a third.

Using the piece of wood deftly, Blake began to tap out a message. Vernon a skilled signaller, clutched at Muriel's arm.

"It's Morse," the young officer whispered breathlessly. "By Jove, this is a thriller, if you like."

"O.K. This is Blake here," the officer read, following each long and short pause between the beats.

Again a silence, then a rumbling sound, as though someone had loosened a handful of bricks in the chimney. Then at last the whole grate itself began to move, and a cry broke from Muriel's lips.

"Look—look!" she gasped.

Back swung the massive grate, revealing the adajcent room, and a slender figure standing in the gap, supporting the hinged portion.

"All right, guv'nor," came the voice of Tinker.

Blake turned to his watchers.

"I think we might as well go through, colonel," he said, in a laconic tone. Like a man in a dream, Bryce moved forward, stooping to avoid the edge of the gap. As he passed out of sight, Muriel heard him give vent to a great cry. Darting after him, the girl saw her father kneeling in front of a square, black object in the corner. The colonel's arms were stretched over the top of the chest, and he was drawing great sobbing breaths of joy.

"The rajah's chest! It is here—here! Thank Heaven!" his thin, trembling voice cried.

Muriel was by his side in a moment, and her hand slipped around his shoulders, holding him tight.

"Oh, dad—dad!" the girl breathed, tears of relief streaming down her cheeks. "It—it is a miracle—a miracle!"

Yet there was little of the miraculous in what happened. Fortune, the fickle jade, had simply swung its wheel in the usual elusive way, and a great opportunity had been taken advantage of. But that incident demands another chapter.

CHAPTER 5

In Which a Small Mystery is Given Quite a Simple Solution

Tinker had been quite right in his remark concerning Blake. The chance word that the young assistant had dropped awoke a quick memory in the brain of his master. On leaving Tinker, Blake had gone into his study and turned up the files of his newspapers.

It was a long search, but at last he discovered what he sought. It was full descriptive article, dealing with the splendid present that his Highness the Rajah of Puljara was about to make to his Emperor, King George of Great Britain.

Ten lahk of rupees, in gold, to be handed over by the rajah in person. The reporter who wrote up the story had made as much of it as possible, and Blake read the account from beginning to end. A paragraph near to the finish caught his eye.

"His Highness's military adviser, and trusted friend, Colonel Bryce, the British representative at Kashopore, has been commissioned to bring the treasure to England."

Blake replaced the file of newspapers in their accustomed place on his shelves, and began to pace up and down his room.

"There is not the slightest doubt but what Tinker's acquaintance of last night is Colonel Bryce's daughter. The jewelled comb from the rajah settles that identity."

The active brain worked at the various threads, selecting the useful from the superfluous.

"Circumstances sometimes combine to bring about strong coincidences," Blake muttered; "but I'm inclined to think that there is very little coincidence about this affair. The man who murdered the taxi-driver was going to Downe Square. He was interested in the fate of the faked Indian chest, and what I have to do now is to try and connect the one with the other. That ought to be easy."

He stepped to the telephone, and gave a number. It was the editorial offices of one of the great newspapers, and a few moments later Blake recognised the voice that sounded over the wire.

"This is Sexton Blake, Mr. Walterley."

"Oh, all right! What do you want, old chap? Anything exciting?"

"Oh, no! I only want a little information."

"Right—fire away!"

"When does his Highness the Rajah of Puljara arrive in England?"

"Next Tuesday, I believe."

"Do you know if this treasure of his is already in London?"

"Yes; Colonel Bryce is in charge of it. He lives in Downe Square."

Blake mentally thanked the powers of the fourth estate then; there was little happening in London that these keen news-gatherers did not know.

"One more question. How does he propose to hand over the money? Ten lakh of rupees is rather bulky, isn't it?"

"Oh, there's going to be quite a ceremony at Buckingham Palace! There will be all sorts of big bugs there, and his Highness is to be presented to his Majesty. The treasure is in an old Hindu chest, a unique speciment of ancient workmanship, I believe."

"Ah!"

The editor caught the faint breath of satisfaction.

"What about it, Blake?"

"Oh, there's no news for you!"

"But look here, you artful beggar, don't forget the 'Independent' if there is any story attached. Fair exchange, you know."

"Right you are! If there is anything to be made out of it you'll have the first scoop."

Blake replaced the receiver, and turned away, well content. In his mind now there was no doubt left; the chest which Anton had laboured on, the original photographs of which Blake had inspected, was a duplicate of the rajah's treasure-chest.

That meant that there was some great crime hinging. A startling robbery had either been perpetrated, or was within an ace of it.

Blake slipped into his bedroom, and made a hurried change of attire. It was in the rough garb of a working-man that he finally slipped out of the house in Baker Street. A glance at his watch told him that it was close on ten o'clock. Downe Square was not very far away, and presently Blake found himself turning into the quiet oasis. He crossed to the garden side of the square and moved along. In his hand was a small wicker-basket, such as the average artizan invariably carries. In appearance and manner he looked the typical British workman, making his way home from some belated job.

Opposite No. 5 he came to a halt for a moment, pretending to light his pipe. He saw that the windows of the colonel's home were all lighted, with heavy curtain drawn over them, in accordance with the new lighting regulations. Once a figure paused in front of the window on the left of the porch, a thin man, with stooping shoulders. Blake little dreamed that it was the shadow of his ancient enemy, Kew; but he was to make that discovery later. As the reader is already aware, this was the night that Kew and Carlac were to make their pretended departure; and already the real treasure-chest, with its store of hoarded gold, had been removed from the house.

Blake examined the house quietly. He saw that it stood at the end of the square, and there was only a blank wall on the right, beside which the pavement of the side street ran. The most daring thief in the world would not venture to carry off such heavy booty as the treasure-chest in that direction.

Moving along the gardens, Blake halted in front of No. 4. He saw now that the front of the house was partly concealed by a structure of poles and platforms—the usual builders' scaffolding. The lower part of the house was in darkness, but, as he watched, Blake saw the glimmer of a light appear for a moment in one of the windows of the first floor. It was only a passing glint, such as might come from a lamp being carried past an open doorway, but it was quite sufficient for the quick eyes of the great detective.

"I must have a closer inspection," he muttered, glancing to his right and left. There was not a soul moving, and the hooded lamps scarcely did more than intensify the darkness. Blake walked boldly across the street, reached the scaffolding, and finding a convenient ladder, climbed to the first platform, which ran along below the window-sills of the rooms on the first floor.

He chose the window through which the glint of light had appeared. It was closed and fastened down, but it was a feeble barrier against Blake. From the little basket he withdrew a long, slender screwdriver. It was inserted between the two halves of the window—a faint scrape followed, and the catch slid back.

A moment later the intrepid man had opened the lower half and had slid into the room. He closed the window behind him and stood still for a moment, listening.

Faint and far off there came to his ears a sharp tapping sound. For a moment Blake was puzzled, then he located it. It was the sound that a mason's trowel makes on brick!

"Humph! Perhaps I've had all this trouble for nothing!" he muttered. "It sounds as though the workmen were still busy here."

He realised that if he were caught there might be some awkward questions to answer. But Blake knew that his identity would be quite sufficient to satisfy any doubts.

"I'll risk it," he decided. "If they are genuine workmen, I can easily make up some yarn about looking for a job."

He had grown accustomed to the darkness now, and was able to pick out the dim outlines of an opened doorway. He crossed towards it, and found himself in a wide corridor, that seemed to run back the whole length of the house. The corridor was pitch dark, but, near the far end, a pencil of light revealed the presence of a closed door. The door was on his right as he faced it—on the same side as No. 5.

He moved along the corridor with noiseless feet. Close to where the pencil of light was shining, Blake almost fell over a board lying in the centre of the passage. He stooped and felt it, and his fingers came in contact with a cold, wet heap in the centre of the board. The unmistakable tang of wet cement!

"Mortar!" the detective muttered, coming to a halt. "By Jove, I believe that I have made a——"

He had moved on a pace or two, and was opposite the door. He heard the lock click, and with a quick bound was past the doorway, and had flattened himself out against the wall behind.

The door opened towards him, and through the gap Blake saw the dark outlines of a man's figure.

The head moved to and fro, then it was turned towards the interior of the room.

"Must 'ave been a rat, or summat," a hoarse voice muttered. "Anyhow, there ain't anythin' here, Harry."

"All right, Joe! Maybe it was my imagination. But I'm all a bundle of nerves to-night."

That voice—where had he heard it before? There was something familiar in the tones?

The door was closed, and a few moments later the dull tap, tap commenced anew. Blake, dropping on one knee, slid along to the keyhole and peered through. There was a light standing on a small table immediately facing him, and behind it he saw two shadowy figures at work. They were kneeling in front of the grate, and beside the one on the right stood a small heap of bricks—bricks of the clear, glazed type that are usually used for a certain kind of ornamental grate.

There was still no indication that the presence of these men had any sinister meaning. Then suddenly the taller figure turned to reach for something on the table. He was in shirt-sleeves, with his white cuffs rolled back. Blake caught sight of the sleek face, with its trim black moustache and small, criminal eyes, and the man's identity leaped out of the great storehouse of his brain.

"Flash Harry!"

Immediately the whole aspect of the case was changed. The man was a known, habitual criminal—one of the type that are bound to go crooked. It was for no good purpose that he was there hard at work in that room.

The cool detective, kneeling in the darkness, realised now that all his calculations were working out remarkably well.

"A room in No. 5 is immediately behind that grate and wall," the detective muttered. "There is no doubt that. And you are bricking in the fireplace, or, at least, have started to do so. That means that your other job is done!"

There was every indication of an elaborate, far-sighted plan, and Blake was well aware that it was not the brain of Flash Harry that had worked it out. The criminal was never of the leading type. There was some other brain behind it all.

"Yes, you've done what you had to do, and the question is—what has become of the swag?"

The fact of there being a duplicate chest was sufficient to give Blake a reliable guide. The rascals had removed the chest and its treasure intact, replacing it with the faked one. What had they done with the real, the valuable chest?

231

He tried to get a wider range of vision, but the narrowness of his spyhole prevented him from doing so. He saw, however, that the room had a deep bay on the left, with a window that evidently opened out on the back of the premises.

As he knelt there, turning over these questions, a new sound came to his ears—the sharp hoot of a taxi. The men in the room also heard it, and Flash Harry moved out of Blake's vision, heading for the concealed window. The flame of the lamp on the table flickered suddenly—a mute proof that the man had flung open the window.

A soft laugh came to Blake's ears.

"That's them!" he heard the voice of Flash Harry drawl. "They're just leaving next door. Lor,' they're cool 'uns, they are! Carlac is bad enough, but that monkey-faced Kew——"

The listener behind the door drew one deep breath.

Kew and Carlac.

Instantly the puzzle fitted itself. There was no doubting now who the murderer was! Mentally Blake blamed himself for not realising the truth before. There was only one man in the world who could deal out death suddenly, noiselessly, as had happened to the driver.

Professor Kew!

"We'll have to get on with it!" The voice from the room sounded again. "It's got to be finished, and we've got to clear out before they come back!"

Carlac and Kew were to return! That could only have one explanation—the treasure-chest must be there in that very room!

A bold man is always open to take risks, but Blake was clever enough to realise that against four desperadoes he had little chance. Whatever he was going to do would have to be done quickly.

And, first of all, the treasure-chest had to be saved. Under no circumstances should he risk its removal from that house! He made up his mind at once and arose to his feet.

His fingers sought for and found the knob of the door. He tried, and found that it turned at his pressure. With a quick push, Sexton Blake thrust the door aside and stepped into the room.

A shout of dismay came from the window, and Flash Harry's long body leaped across the intervening space towards the detective.

"Here! Who the blazes——"

Crack!

There was no time for ceremony. As Flash Harry closed with Blake, the detective swung his bunched fist up in a fierce hook, which landed plump on its mark. It caught the rushing man full on the point of the jaw, and sent his head back with a jerk that threatened to crack the neck. Flash Harry spun round, smote the air wildly with the hands for a second, then went down, on his back, on the floor.

Before Blake could turn round, the other rogue was on him. The steel trowel in the man's hand flashed in the light of the lamp, and Blake had to duck swiftly to avoid the murderous cut. His fingers closed on the sinewy wrist, and, with his other arm wrapped around his antagonist Blake, swayed across the room. He tripped over a piece of loose tapestry, and the length of material came away.

Blake had a brief vision of the black panels and iron bands of the treasure-chest; then a violent plunge from his antagonist saw them roll over on the floor, half-enveloped in the smothering folds of the tapestry.

The detective's antagonist was a burly rogue, and was putting up a grim struggle, knowing that prison awaited him.

A groan sounded from the huddled heap beside the table, and Flash Harry arose dizzily to his feet. Blake was now on top of his man, and the trowel fell with a clatter on to the floor. The detective's cap had dropped off in the struggle, and Harry, tottering forward, glared down at the clean-cut face. Blake looked up for a moment, and their eyes met; then the criminal, with a hoarse shout of fear, leaped back.

"Blake!" he gasped. "That's done it! We're nabbed!"

The very name of the detective seemed to take all the courage out of the cowardly man's heart.

His confederate, putting up a grim struggle with Blake, turned a red, streaming face toward the man beside the lamp.

"Quick—curse you! Out him! The lamp!"

The shout seemed to rouse Flash Harry from his stupor of fear. His hand, trembling violently, caught at the lamp, and he raised it. But in doing so it tilted over to the left, and, with a last flicker, the light went out.

There was a crash, and the lamp was splintered on the wall only a few inches above Blake's head. Then Flash Harry, rushing across the room, leaped out of the doorway, and Blake heard his feet echoing along the dark corridor.

"You cur! You cur!" the man on the floor snarled, writhing desperately to escape from the iron hold of his captive.

There was a last furious struggle, then something cold settled over his wrists, and there was a metallic click.

"You did your best, my friend," Blake's level tones murmured, "but I was one too many for you."

A savage snarl came from his feet.

"If that skunk hadn't bolted, you wouldn't be able to crow!" came the grim reply.

Blake was on his feet now, and presently he found the gasjet and lighted it. the man who had been working at the bricks had raised himself to a sitting position, and was glaring with sullen fury at the detective.

Blake looked at the fellow closely. He was distinctly of the lower order of criminal—low forehead, scowling brows, and drooping chin.

"How much of this job were you responsible for?" he asked.

The man jerked his head at the fireplace.

"I'd to brick that up," he said. "That's all I knows about it—and that the truth, guv'nor!"

He watched the detective cross the room, and bend over the great chest. Blake tried to lift the massive box, but it resisted

232

his most powerful effort. It had evidently not even been tampered with.

"I'm inclined to believe you," he went on, turning towards his prisoner, "otherwise you must have been a fool to work away there when over a hundred thousand pounds in gold was close to your elbow!"

The brute face of his captive was tilted up.

"You—you're kiddin', mister!"

Blake smiled grimly.

"I'm not," he said, pacing his hand on the chest. "In this box is enough gold to make you or anyone else a rich man."

"And I never knew anything about it!" the pinioned man muttered. "Flash Harry told me that the swag had gone! Blow me, if I'd ha' known——"

His covetous eyes glared at the chest, and Blake smiled grimly; then, at a signal from him, the fellow arose to his feet. Blake made up his mind on a certain move.

"Hold out your hands!"

The thick wrists were extended, and Blake unlocked the handcuffs.

"Clear out!"

"Wot's that?"

The man leaned forward, with bewilderment writ large on his face.

"You can go!" said Blake. "Don't think it worth while to charge you! I am after bigger game than you. But I shouldn't trust Flash Harry in future, if you take my advice!"

The man whipped round, and fairly bolted for the door. Blake followed him along the corridor, down the wide staircase, and saw his thick figure slip out into the dark square.

"It was the best thing I could do," Blake muttered to himself. "You were hardly worth keeping, and there is just a chance that you might want revenge on Flash Harry. In that event, you may prove yourself useful."

He stood for a long moment in the dark doorway, musing to himself.

He knew that, so far as the treasure-chest was concerned, it was safe now. There could be little doubt but what Flash Harry would seek out Kew and Carlac, and warn them of what had happened. It was useless for Blake to wait there any longer.

A slow footfall came to his ears, and presently the bulky figure of a constable loomed into view. Blake stepped out of the doorway of No. 4 and approached the man in blue.

It was the same constable as had come in reply to Tinker's call, and when Blake gave his name the constable was all attention.

"Give your inspector my compliments, and ask him to put a man on special watch here to-night," said Blake. "I will send round my assistant in the morning to explain matters. If anyone does attempt to enter the house, they have to be arrested at once."

It was obvious from the policeman's face that he would have given up his pension to have questioned Blake, but his discipline held him in check, and he saluted.

"All right, Mr. Blake!" he returned. "I'll wait here myself until the inspector comes round. I'll see that everything is all right."

Blake went off, a quiet smile on his lips.

"I'm very much afraid that you will find it an easy job." was his inward comment.

And he was quite right, for, when Tinker went round to No. 4 early in the morning, it was to find that no one had been near the house. The youngster had received instructions from Blake to clear away the half-completed brickwork. It was Blake's intention to make a report of the case to Scotland Yard, and allow them to deal with the matter, but the visit from Muriel had altered all that, and so it came about that Blake played the quiet drama in the previous chapter.

CHAPTER 6
The Arrival of the Rajah

"It seems incredible!" Colonel Bryce said, a pained look on his fine face. "These men were my guests, and I was under a debt of gratitude to them."

They had removed the war-chest into the colonel's house, and Sexton Blake had told them of the manner of men they had entertained. Lieutenant Vernon had not been able to conceal his satisfaction at finding that his suspicions were justified, but the young officer kept silent, for he noted how badly his senior took the news.

"They are absolutely unprincipled scoundrels," said Blake slowly. "There is no deed too vile, no artifice too low for them to use, provided that they can attain their object."

He glanced at the colonel quietly.

"Apart from this robbery, the man that you knew as Doctor Kay committed a murder only two days ago."

He gave an account of the incident of the taxi-driver.

Muriel shuddered and drew closer to her father.

"Oh dad, how terrible!" the girl murmured in a shocked tone.

The evidence that Blake placed in front of them was much too strong to be refuted in any way, and so the ugly truth was forced on Colonel Bryce. He had been duped and deceived.

"I suppose you blame me, Mr. Blake," the clean-minded old officer said with a swift glance at the detective; "and, on the face of it, it certainly looks as though I were not the proper person to be in charge of a great treasure."

Blake shook his head.

"I cannot see that any blame can be attached to you, sir," he returned. "These men wormed their way into your confidence, and from what I know of them they would act in such a manner as to remove any possible shadow of doubt being attached to them."

"That is quite true, Mr. Blake," Vernon chimed in; "for I must confess that I had my suspicions that all was not fair and above board with them, but, although I watched them at every possible opportunity, I never once caught them napping. They must be men of iron nerve."

"They are," said Blake, "and it is only by the merest of chances that I succeeded in thwarting them. Had I been an hour or two later the chest would have disappeared and I doubt very much if it could have been traced."

The colonel made a quick gesture with his hand.

"Don't speak of it," he said, "it is too terrible. What could I have said to his Highness? He has trusted me and I had failed. The rajah is a very just and upright man, but he never forgives a mistake."

"He need never know," said Blake. "There is no reason why he should."

"But that will mean that these blackguards will get off scot-free," Muriel put in indignantly. Woman-like, she had changed her opinions immediately and thoroughly, and was now the bitter enemy of Carlac and Kew.

"That cannot be helped, Muriel," her father put in slowly. "If Mr. Blake was to make a case of it, the whole affair would have to come out. Apart from my own part in the matter, I don't suppose the Foreign Office would allow Blake to proceed."

"I am sure they would not," said Blake. "These sort of cases are better kept in the background. We do not want the world to know that we have men in England so vile as to rob a generous ally."

"How I wish I could meet them just once," the high-spirited girl breathed, her eyes flashing.

"You may yet have that opportunity, Miss Bryce," Blake assured her, little dreaming of how true his words were.

They left the treasure-chamber at last, and Blake noted that Abul had taken post inside the room this time. A sudden misgiving ran through the detective's mind.

"By Jove, I'd forgotten that Abul understands English," he muttered to himself. "He has heard the whole story. That might prove deucedly awkward."

He kept his misgivings to himself, however, and, after arranging a few minor details with the colonel and the inspector of police, Blake left No. 5.

In order to keep the real crime a secret, Blake had told the inspector that a gang of thieves had tried to break into the colonel's house by way of No. 4 but that he, Blake, had got wind of the affair and had spoiled the game before the ruffians could accomplish their object. The half-bricked grate lent colour to this story, and as the colonel backed him up, the detective felt that there would be no further inquiries made concerning the affair.

Nor was he mistaken in that.

The Tuesday afternoon papers recorded the arrival of his highness the Rajah of Puljara and suite at the Ritz. A paragraph followed dealing with the presentation at Buckingham Palace, and on the Thursday Blake and Tinker received two cards, which, signed by the King's chamberlain, was sufficient to allow them to enter the courtyard of the palace.

It was a gorgeous spectacle. The Rajah, in his glittering robes, appeared from a royal carriage, followed by two of his sons, slim, dusky-faced princes, aglow with jewels. From another carriage there poured out half a dozen attendants among whom, towering head and shoulders above the others, Blake picked out the giant figure of Abul. The huge chest was drawn forth, and the six men, moving together in a steady rhythm, carried it into the palace.

Colonel Bryce, Vernon, and Muriel were also visible, and the girl, catching sight of the quietly-dressed detective, flashed him a quick smile and bow as she went past.

Of the ceremony inside the palace, the newspapers made a great story. The rajah had been received by the King, and, after receiving the chest and the rajah's oath of fealty, King George bestowed a glittering order on the rich princeling. The whole affair created no small stir, coming as it did in the middle of the grim and world-racking struggle, for it proved to Britain's enemies that Britain's rule in India was a wise and kindly one, ensuring loyalty and devotion from that swarming country.

"If Kew and Carlac had succeeded in their job, it might have meant a split between the rajah and the Government," said Blake to Tinker later on, in his study. "For that reason alone I am glad that we are able to get the better of the heartless ruffians."

Tinker sighed.

"And they're getting away with it, guv'nor," the lad muttered gloomily. "It does seem a blinking shame. They deserve to be punished."

"I'm afraid that our hands are tied, Tinker," his master responded. "I had a word with the Foreign Office about it, and they are absolutely against making any sort of fresh move in the matter. Their chief anxiety is to keep the affair away from the rajah, and so long as they do that they are quite content."

Yet, despite all the precautions taken, the Rajah of Puljara heard the news.

On the evening after his splendid reception, the great man was alone in the magnificent chamber of his suite in the hotel when one of his personal attendants entered.

"Abul, of the guard, desires a word with thee, Protector of the Faith,."

"Admit him."

The long-limbered trooper swung into the room, halting on the threshold with a low salaam.

"Well, Abul, what is it?" The rajah spoke in quiet English, with scarcely an accent. It was the tongue he favoured when addressing his soldiers, most of whom had served their time with the British Indian troops.

"Thy servant's heart is heavy," said the trooper, advancing across the chamber. "A secret weighs upon it."

"Let me hear it, Abul."

And so, in the quiet tones of his trooper, the rajah heard the truth, How near his treasure had been to being stolen, of the miraculous way that the great English detective had intervened, almost at the eleventh hour.

Yet as he listened, it was not the fact of his gold being removed that seemed to rouse the great man's ire.

"They laid hands on the sacred chest," he muttered through his crisp black beard. "By Allah, but that demands a punishment."

"They took the chest away, Commander of the Faithful," Abul went on, "under the guise of friendship they played their thief's tricks."

"Who were the dogs?"

Briefly and concisely Abul told all he knew concerning Carlac and Kew.

"They came to Kashopore, did they?" his Highness repeated. "We will inquire into that. Whoever befriended them there was no friend of ours."

He leaned back in the armchair, resting his bearded chin in one strong palm. Abul, standing stiffly to attention, waited for his master to speak.

"They have set their evil hands on a sacred thing, and have soiled it with their touch," said the rajah slowly. "Had I known I would not have offered it, soiled as it was, to the great King. They have made me a mock and a jest, and I dare not tell the Emperor of this meanness that has befallen me."

His lips lifted suddenly, transforming the whole face. There was something tigerish and remorseless in the slow, cold smile.

"But all that they have done they shall pay for," said the Rajah of Puljara quietly. "and I take the oath now. Allah, aiding me, these miscreants shall taste my vengeance, I swear it."

He raised his bejewelled hand aloft and Abul made a quick salaam. He knew that his master never took an oath idly.

"Anything that thy servant can do will be done," the trooper said.

"Thou wilt play thy part, Abul, but for the moment I will have to trust to one, cleverer than art thou."

He arose to his feet and crossed to a small bureau from which he drew a small plain-bound note-book. Turning over the leaves for a moment, his Highness found what he sought—an address.

"Nazra Ali Ben Dhur, Cheapside, Oriental agent," he read aloud.

Abul's eyes quickened. He had heard that name before. It was well known in Kashopore. Ben Dhur was his Highness's secret agent in London, as well as the trade representative for Puljara.

"Thou wilt wait until I call thee, Abul," said his master. "I have a letter that thou hast to deliver for me."

The trooper's eyes were flames of keen contentment as he bowed himself out of the chamber. He knew that his master was planning revenge—a revenge such as only the Oriental mind can plan.

Ten minutes later an envelope was handed to him, addressed to Ben Dhur. Late thought it was, Abul started off on his errand at once. It was 8 o'clock before the trooper reached Cheapside, and he had some difficulty in finding the number. It was up a dim courtyard, and Ben Dhur's offices were on the second floor. A charwoman, cleaning the stairs gave vent to a half-shriek of alarm as the huge turbanned figure came striding up the stairs.

"Mr. Dhur! Oh, yes, he's in the office all right. But you oughtn't to go about like that, mister. You'd frighten a woman to death with that great sword of yours. Ain't decent, that's what I calls it."

Abul grinned as he went on up the stairs, and presently he found himself in a room filled with the odours of the East. Sweet smelling spices, dried fruits and spices. The trooper's nostrils dilated as he breathed the familiar air.

"I might be back in the bazaars of Kashopore," the home-hungry man said, as a figure in European clothes came shuffling out of a small inner office. "Thou art Ben Dhur?"

"That is my name."

Abul thrust out the note.

"A message from his Highness, the rajah," he explained.

Ben Dhur adjusted a pair of spectacles on his hooked nose and peered at the envelope with his small, weak eyes.

"Come into my room," he said. "It will be safer there."

Abul followed him and stood like a statue, while Nazra broke the seal of the envelope.

The letter seemed to cause him a great deal of dismay. He read it twice, then his thin fingers went up and caressed his beardless chin.

"Hast thou any knowledge of this?" he asked.

"All I know is that my master is in haste," came the non-commital reply.

The bent figure shrugged its shoulders.

"Aye, that may be," he replied; "but this is no easy task that has been set me. Were we in Kashopore it might be otherwise, but here in England the authorities do not care for such matters."

The trooper grinned.

"I may tell thee that the authorities will trouble themselves but little over this matter," he said, and Nazra chuckled.

"Ah, I have caught thee, close of mouth. Thou dost know all about it, then. Then who are these two men?"

"Dogs!" returned Abul. "They tried to steal the rajah's treasure. They have to be punished."

He came a pace nearer. In his eyes a grim light was shining.

"I will help thee to the end of my strength, Ben Dhur," he said; "for these men played a double part with me and his Excellency, Colonel Bryce. Under the guise of friendship they stole into his house and cloaked their designs with soft words. Revenge awaits me if I can but get them into the hands of my master."

"And where art thou to be found should I require thee in haste, oh revengeful one?" the wizened dealer asked, a smile on his twisted lips.

"No. 5, Downe Square; the home of Colonel Bryce," came the reply.

"Good, friend! Await a message from me there."

Abul left the dingy office with a feeling that the weird proprietor would not fail. There had been something in Ben Dhur's quiet manner that had made a big impression on Abul.

"He was known to be as sly as a fox at Kashopore," the big trooper muttered to himself, "and I see that repute did not lie in his case."

Nor was he mistaken, although just how Ben Dhur came to get on to the tracks of Carlac and Kew is a mystery that remains unsolved.

. . . . . .

There is a quiet courtyard, not very far from Finsbury Square, which the average Londoner has no knowledge of. Tucked away as it is behind tall buildings, offices chiefly. Mardal Court consists of a dozen houses, most of them dilapidated, shabby places, where a curious type of tenant lives. No doubt there are one or two respectable families in the court, but they, in common with the others keep themselves very much to themselves.

Flash Harry, when in funds, lived at No. 6. It was generally understood that the hard-faced woman who tenanted the house was an aunt of his. Anyhow, he seemed to be the only human being who received any sort of favours from her. As she paid her rent regularly and did not break the law openly, she was allowed to remain, although the police were well aware of the type of character who formed the lodge element of her establishment.

It was into this quiet house that Carlac and Kew vanished on the night of their great failure. As Sexton Blake had anticipated, Flash Harry, fleeing from capture, was just sufficiently brave to go and seek out Kew and the master-criminal and tell him what had happened. He found them at the stables where the van in which the treasure-chest had to be removed was waiting, the horse ready between the shafts. They had only just arrived from the station, and as Flash Harry's breathless report fell on their ears, a cold fury descended on Kew.

He turned to his broad-shouldered companion, his eyes glinting like coals of fire.

"Well, my friend what have you to say to it now?" he rapped out. "After all my suspicions were not so far from the truth. That sleuth-hound, Sexton Blake, has turned up, just as I dreaded he would!"

Carlac was silent. He was leaning against the side of the stables, his great arms folded over his chest, a look of sullen rage in his eyes.

"He has beaten us," the thin voice of the professor went on bitterly; "we have been tricked out of our plan just as though we were a couple of foolish schoolboys. By Jove, how he must enjoy this triumph of his."

It seemed as though Kew was much more upset over the fact that Blake had beaten him, than the actual loss of a vast fortune.

"What could have put him on to the affair?" Carlac asked at last. "There was no possible chance of his knowing the exact moment when we shifted the chest. We had not made any definite plans. How did he know that we had completed our job at No.5."

The reader is aware that all these question had a very simple answer. It had been sheer luck, coupled with a gift of close deduction that had made Blake's coup so wonderfully successful. But this was, of course, unknown to the two criminals.

"Someone gave us away," croaked Kew; "that is very certain."

His hawk eye had lingered on Flash Harry for a moment, and that worthy rogue had stormed out a violent protest.

Their game was up, and it was obvious to them both that they would have to get into secret quarters for a while. Flash Harry's suggestion that they would find safe lodgings with his aunt was accepted, and Kew and his confederate took rooms there.

They had ventured out only once during the days that had followed, and that was on the afternoon that the rajah visited the palace. Kew's face was a study as he saw the carriage with the precious chest swing past, and he went back to Finsbury in a gloomy silence that Carlac made no attempt to break.

"There is not sufficient room in this world for Blake and I," was his only remark. "One of us will have to give way."

At about ten o'clock on the evening of Abul's visit to Ben Dhur, the last-named gentleman turned into Mardal Court, followed by another dusk-skinned man who seemed very loathe to do more than enter the quiet back street.

"The house is No. 6, Ben Dhur, and it will not be good for me to be seen with thee."

Ben Dhur's hook nose twitched, and he glanced at his companion.

"Meaning thou art afraid, Gilga Lal?"

The slim man bowed. Your oriental never denies a really obvious truth.

"It is the little man that I fear," he observed; "he is cunning, and is a wizard. He kills a man with a breath—I have seen and I know, Ben Dhur."

"Very well, I will go on alone. But listen."

He whispered for a few moments in the other man's ears, who received his instructions with a nod.

"And if you fail, Ben Dhur, what shall I——"

"Away with thee, lackbrain! I will not fail!" came the quiet reply.

It was the hard-faced aunt of Flash Harry who answered Ben Dhur's soft knock on the door. She glanced doubtfully at the stooping figure of her visitor.

"Who told you that a gentleman named Kew lived here?" she asked.

Ben Dhur spread his hands.

"A friend," he returned; "a friend who has his interests at heart. Tell him that I only desire a few moment's speech—and I am quite alone."

She closed the door in his face, leaving him to cool his heels on the step while she went up the stairs with the message. Kew and Carlac were together in the sitting-room, and Kew's hairless brows drew together in a quick frown as the woman made her report.

A Hindu, you say?" the professor muttered. "What can he want with me? How does he know I am here?"

An evil life makes its own burden. Kew hesitated for a long moment before finally making up his mind.

"All right, send him up."

As soon as the woman had vanished he turned to Carlac, and thrusting his hand into his breast pocket he drew out the deadly nickel-plated tube of death.

"Turn the light out in your bedroom and stand just inside the door," said Kew. "At the first suspicious sign, level that tube and touch the button. Be careful of your aim, for it is instant death."

Carlac took the terrible weapon with the air of a man accepting a snake.

"I'd rather trust to a revolver——" he began.

"And waken the whole neighbourhood," came the grim retort. "If this man is a spy, we've got to silence him and get away from here at once. He must not have the opportunity of giving the alarm, nor must anyone hear the slightest sound."

There was the sound of a footfall on the stairs, and Carlac, with noiseless strides crossed the sitting-room and vanished into the room on the left. The light in the bedroom vanished, and Carlac, turning round, took up position in the half-opened door, standing well back in the shadows, the tube positioned between his powerful fingers.

"Come in!"

Kew's thin voice sounded in reply to the knock and Ben Dhur entered. He stopped for a moment, his rheumy eyes blinking in the bright glare. Kew had taken up a position that made it possible for him to watch his man closely.

"What do you want with me?"

Ben Dhur cringed.

"Do I address the great sahib-doctor, Kew?" he asked.

His voice was the true whine of the servile native, his whole attitude that of a vast abasement.

"That is my name," said Kew.

Ben Dhur came further into the room.

"If I give the doctor-sahib some good news, will he pay for it?"

Instinct had made Ben Dhur strike the right note. Kew knew his East like an open book, and was aware of the fact that every native of India has his price.

"It depends on the news—and the price," came the non-committal reply.

"My news is worth fifty English sovereigns—and not a penny less. It concerns someone whom the doctor-sahib has cause to hate beyond all other men?"

"His name?"

"Sexton Blake."

Kew leaned forward, staring into the grey-bearded face.

"How do you know that I hate this man?" he rasped.

Ben Dhur cringed a little lower.

"We have ways of finding out things, sahib. You know that even here, in this cold country, news travels among we wanderers."

It was quite true, and Kew knew it.

"What is your news?"

"His Highness, the Rajah of Puljara—may Allah protect him—has heard that a gang of thieves came near to stealing his treasure."

A half-smothered sound came from Kew's lips, to be checked almost as soon as it came.

"Go on," he muttered.

"His Highness the Rajah does not know how near he came to losing it, but he has heard that this Sexton Blake played a big part in the thwarting of the thieves and so he has decided to honour him. To-night, when his Highness returns from the theatre, he desires that Blake and his companion, the youth named Tinker, should have audience with him. And he is presenting this man Blake with a diamond necklace worth a mint of money, ten thousand pounds has it been valued at!"

Kew gave vent to an oath. He had no reason to doubt this man's story. He knew that the ruler of Puljara was vastly rich and given to mad, generous impulses. If it was true that Blake's deed was known, there was every possibility that the rajah, out of sheer gratitude, might lavish some valuable gift on the fortunate man.

Blake had saved the rajah from a great loss of prestige. Had he arrived in London to find his treasure-chest stolen it would have been a disgrace that history would have made notorious.

"Worth ten thousand pounds," Kew muttered aloud, twitching at his thin lips. "By Jove, what a reward?"

Ben Dhur came a little nearer.

"Does the doctor-sahib relish the thought of his enemy receiving this vast present?"

"I'd rather see him dead at my feet," the arch-scoundrel broke out in sudden passion. "He gains that very reward through——" He stopped in the nick of time, and the hard look came into his eyes again.

"But why should this story interest me?" he went on.

"Because in it there is a chance of the sahib finding sweet vengeance," Ben Dhur muttered, in a low tone. "I can help the sahib to trick this detective out of his jewels."

"How?"

Ben Dhur had never glanced at the dark doorway on his left, but now he jerked a thumb towards it.

"Thy friend, who standeth in the shadows there, will have to play a part," he began.

There was a creak, and Carlac strode out of the doorway, eyeing the stooping figure of the visitor from beneath ruffled brows. Ben Dhur gave him a low, cringing salute.

"Thou hast heard all, so I need not repeat my story, sahib," he went on imperturbably, although there was a glint in his eyes that revealed how he had enjoyed the quick surprise he had sprang upon the two nonplussed criminals.

"If you have a plan, out with it," Carlac snapped, throwing himself into a chair.

"My brother is the messenger that his Highness has chosen to go and bring the detective Blake and his assistant, the youth, Tinker, to his suite of rooms," Ben Dhur went on; "and my brother likes not his task, for the jewels are of value, and there will be no reward for him out of the giving of them."

He nodded towards Carlac.

"His Highness the rajah starts for Puljara early to-morrow morning, and there is no chance of his knowing that a deceit has been practised upon this man Blake, nor the youth, and——"

The alert brain of Kew read the riddle that lay behind the guarded words. He leaned forward, tense and eager.

"You want my friend and I to impersonate Blake and his companion?" he said.

Ben Dhur's smile was a treat to behold. It spread all over his wrinkled face.

"The doctor-sahib is right," he said; "but, and he does this, my brother and I will want our due rewards. Fifty English sovereigns for me, and hundred for my brother."

"By Jove, and you'll have them!" Carlac roared, leaping to his feet, carried away by the sheer recklessness of the enterprise.

And, as a matter of fact, it was certainly a risky undertaking. To accept the jewels from the hand of the man they had already tried to rob, was adventure enough, but when it was coupled with the knowledge that they were impersonating the two beings in the world that had foiled them, the whole became doubly enticing.

Kew indicated a chair.

"Sit there," he said to Ben Dhur. "My friend and I will have to consider this thing."

He stepped into the bedroom, followed by Carlac. Kew lighted the gas, then turned round.

"Well, what do you think of it?" he asked slowly.

"There's enough risk in it to frighten anyone," he admitted; "and yet, after all, we have a fighting chance of carrying it off."

He laughed aloud.

"His Highness never met us while we were at Kashopore, and he has never met Blake or Tinker. You are a master of disguise, Kew, and I don't think that this is beyond you. Blake is about my height, and you are slim enough to make a good Tinker. If we could pull it off, we'd have turned the tables on that sleuth-hound to some purpose."

It was really that part of the scheme that appealed to them both. The thought of impersonating Blake, of receiving the reward that he was entitled to, was tempting beyond words.

But in his cautious way, Kew put in a word.

"It might be a plant."

"In what way?"

The question baffled the wizened professor. It is was one of Blake's schemes, why should he go to all this trouble? He knew where they were—the fact of the Hindu visiting them would prove that, if he were in Blake's pay. Why not arrest them at once?

"If Blake or the police were behind this, we'd have been under lock and key by now," Carlac went on; "and Blake is the only one who knows our connection with the affair—if he does really know that?"

It was the old question rising again. For while Kew was convinced in his own mind that Blake had knowledge of their complicity in the affair from the very outset, and he based this belief on the purely chance meeting with Tinker, Carlac, who was really nearer the truth, did not agree with him.

Another question came into Kew's mind, and he slipped into the sitting-room for a moment. Ben Dhur was seated exactly as he had left him, on the extreme edge of the chair.

"Will Colonel Bryce be accompanying his Highness?"

Beneath his heavy brows the eyes of Ben Dhur blazed for a moment. From that question he drew a favourable response to his schemes.

"No. His Excellency the colonel is no longer in favour in the sight of his Highness the rajah."

It was a cunning response, for it was just what would have happened under ordinary circumstances, when the rajah heard of the incident of the treasure-chest.

Kew withdrew his vulture-shaped head.

"We'll risk it," he said to Carlac. "If that man is a liar, then he's the greatest in the world."

CHAPTER 7

The Rajah's Ruse

"Going out again, Abul? I'm afraid that his Highness runs you almost off your feet."

Pretty Muriel Bryce cast a glance of sympathy at the tall figure of the trooper. Abul, wrapped in his long cloak, was just crossing the hall of No. 5, Downe Square, when Muriel, coming out of the drawing-room caught sight of him.

The brawny trooper turned, with a low salaam. Muriel was a great favourite with all the servants in the house, and in

Abul she had a most devoted worshipper.

"I am always ready to answer my master's call," the trooper returned.

There was a light shining in his eyes, and he seemed to be labouring under an unusual excitement. The clock in the hall chimed the hour of eleven.

"I expect you won't be back until after midnight," said Muriel. "But I will tell one of the servants to leave some supper for you."

Abul smiled.

"The mem-sahib is always kind and thoughtful," he returned; "but she troubles too much over her slave. I may not be able to come back to-night. If his Highness needs me, I will stay by his side."

He salaamed again, and Muriel went back into the drawing-room, a little puckered line of thought on her smooth brows. Lieutenant Vernon was seated close to the piano, and he looked up as the girl entered.

"Hallo, darling, you've got you thinking-cap on? What's troubling you now?"

He caught at her hand as she passed and drew her on to the arm of the chair. Muriel laughed.

"There is not anything really to worry about," she admitted at last, "and yet, I'm just a trifle worried. Why should Abul have to go to the rajah so late as this?"

"Dunno," Vernon returned; "and I'm not sure that I care very much. What has Abul's movements to do with us, anyhow?"

"Nothing, I suppose; and yet it seems strange that the rajah should send for him, without telling dad. After all, Abul is dad's servant."

Vernon was well aware of the strict etiquette of the rajah's court, and now that Muriel drew his attention to the apparent slight on Colonel Bryce, the young subaltern looked grave.

"By Jove, I never looked at it in that light, Muriel; but you are quite right!"

"There is something wrong," said Muriel. "His Highness kept dad waiting for a long time to-night, and then sent word that he didn't want to see him."

She looked at Vernon.

"Do you think it is possible that he has found out something about the treasure-chest?"

"Great Scott, no—at least, I hope not! Whatever put that idea into your dear little head?"

"I couldn't say, but I feel somehow that there is a cloud over dad—and I'd give anything to find out the truth. You know what sort of man his Highness is. He would never really forgive dad if he found out about the affair."

"Of course he wouldn't; but he isn't going to find out. We are all as mute as oysters where that is concerned."

The lovely girl nodded her head towards the hall.

"Oh, I know that we wouldn't give it away; but what about Abul?"

"Nonsense, Muriel! Abul is as faithful as the day."

Yet even as he he voiced his protest, Vernon felt that this clever girl was not very far out.

"Abul is faithful; and he is in the service of the rajah," Muriel pointed out. "Perhaps his loyalty made it impossible for him to keep silent."

Vernon tugged at the little moustache on his lip. There was a rueful expression in his eyes.

"By Jove, Muriel, you are making me think!" he said at last. "You are quite right about the rajah's changed attitude towards the colonel. I was at the hotel this evening, and there was hardly a soul would speak to me. And, as a rule, the attendants are only too glad to have a jaw."

His sweet-face companion heaved a sigh.

"It's an awful nuisance," said Muriel, "for it will make it so awkward for us all when we go back to Kashopore. Dad has to go there as British representative, even although the rajah might not like to have him. I do wish that we could do something, dear."

Vernon shrugged his shoulders.

"I don't see what we can do," he admitted candidly. "We daren't ask the rajah if he has discovered anything, for that would put the fat in the fire at once."

It was certainly an awkward situation if Muriel's surmises were correct; but it was one that could not very well be altered.

"We'll just have to wait and see," her lover said at last. "His Highness will probably be going back to Puljara some day this week, and we will be following him. If he still gives us the cold shoulder at Kashopore, we will know then that your idea is right. After all, if we hang on long enough, the affair will blow over. His Highness thinks no end of your dad, and he will gradually forget."

Muriel made a slight movement.

"And meanwhile, we've got to go about like naughty children, who have been found out!" she cried indignantly. "Well I, for one, won't do that!"

She looked so deliciously tempting with her air of indignation, that Vernon drew her to him and kissed her soft, red lips.

"I'll bet his Highness does not hold out very long against you, you beautiful dear," he murmured. "Besides, we may be worrying ourselves without cause."

But had he been able to follow Abul that night, Vernon would have had ample proof given him that the rajah was not only aware of what had happened, but had already taken steps to assure revenge—and a revenge of his own particular type.

Abul, swinging through the dark streets at a swift pace, found himself close to the big hotel at last. He turned down the quiet side-street from Piccadilly, reached the corner, and halted. A shadow detached itself from the dark doorway of a house opposite, and came forward.

"Thou art Abul?"

"That is my name."

"Here is a message for thy master, his Highness the rajah," said Gilga Lal.

"From Ben Dhur?"

"Yes."

Abul took the message and looked at the brown face in front of him.

"Why did not Ben Dhur deliver this himself?"

White teeth glimmered in the dusk.

"Because it was arranged that I should do so. I waited for a sign, and when it came I followed out the orders I had received. I telephoned——"

"So it was you who spoke to me on the telephone?" said Abul. "I thought that it was not the voice of Ben Dhur."

"Ben Dhur is busy, and cannot leave the side of the men he has found," came the reply. "My orders were to tell you to come here and take this note. I was also warned to make haste, for there is little time to lose. My advice to thee, O Abul, is to go to they master with this letter. Delay kills the best of plans."

He slid away into the darkness, and Abul made his way back into the hotel, seeking out the suite of rooms in which the rajah lived. There were signs that a move was about to be made. The attendants were busy packing great cases and boxes. Abul, with the privilege of a trusted retainer, went at once into the small room that the rajah reserved for his study. He found the ruler of Puljara seated at a desk, smoking.

As soon as Abul entered, the rajah turned and held out his hand.

"The message from Ben Dhur?"

Abul's eyes widened.

"Your Highness knows then?"

The ruler of Puljara chuckled.

"That old fox Ben Dhur spoke to me this afternoon, about an hour after he had seen you," came the quiet response. "He has done as I expected, and has arranged a trick, the guile of which will surely ensure its success."

He had opened the letter as he spoke, and he read its contents.

"Well done, Ben Dhur!" said the rajah, leaning back in his chair with a smile of deadly meaning on his heavy lips. "The delivery of this letter means that he has succeeded in his design. And now we have to prepare for his coming—you and I, Abul."

"I am at my prince's commands," said Abul.

The rajah rose to his feet.

"Listen, and I will give thee an account of Ben Dhur's plan."

He stepped across to the door and saw that it was shut. Then in a low tone he gave Abul a brief account of the wily way in which Ben Dhur was to place Kew and Carlac into his hands.

"Avarice brings them here," the rajah ended, in a dry tone, "and avarice will hold them. Thou wilt play the part of Ben Dhur's brother, the man who for one hundred English sovereigns would betray his ruler."

"Not all the gold in the world would make me do that, protector!" said Abul.

The rajah clapped him on the shoulder.

"But this is only a game, Abul, and I can trust thee to play it. These rogues would recognise thee, for they must have met thee often enough in the house of Colonel Bryce, whom I have not yet forgiven for his silence on this matter."

Abul ventured a word for his chief.

"It was only the desire to keep trouble from thee that made the colonel-sahib hold his peace," the staunch trooper put in.

The rajah shrugged his shoulders.

"Well, that may be, but I will consider it later. If I am successful to-night, I may find it in my heart to forgive."

And inwardly Abul vowed that the scheme would succeed, as much for the sake of Colonel Bryce as for his own personal desire for revenge on the two wily rogues who had played such a despicable part.

"Thou wilt disguise thyself in the robes of one of my attendants," said the rajah. "Ben Dhur has promised to bring his men here to the hotel. Thou wilt go and wait for them, demanding their names and bringing them into my presence."

"And after, your Highness?"

Over the heavy features of the ruler there stole a grim smile.

"After, two men will leave the hotel in thy company. They will be dressed as the two visitors, and thou wilt see them safely away. See to it that their departure is observed."

He rubbed his hands together.

"And to-morrow morning we travel by motor-car to Southampton, where a special suite of cabins have been taken for us on a liner that starts at noon. I have already told the Foreign Office that my visit comes to an end now; urgent State matters makes it necessary that I should return to Puljara at once."

Abul's eyes were glinting as he listened, and he knew what lay behind his master's words.

"Go now and prepare thyself," the rajah ended; "and remember much depends on thee."

Ten minutes later a gorgeously-robed figure appeared in the wide foyer of the hotel and seated itself in one of the deep chairs. The staff of the Ritz is well accustomed to the gorgeous apparel of Eastern grandees, and no one paid any particular attention to the seated man.

About midnight a taxi drew up at the door of the hotel, and the porter saw a couple of men alight. One a huge, broad-shouldered individual, the other a slim, youthful figure, muffled in a heavy overcoat.'

A third individual, leaning back in the dark interior of the taxi, bent forward for a moment and whispered into the ear of the shorter individual.

240

"My brother is waiting—I see him yonder in the hall, doctor-sahib. All is well."

Kew had often given proofs that he was a master of the art of disguises, but his skill surely reached its greatest height that evening.

It had been a fairly easy matter to disguise Carlac, and the big criminal was a striking double of Sexton Blake. But it was on his own individuality that Kew had made the greatest transformation. Wig and grease paint, false eyebrows and paraffin wax, used with the deft touch of a master, had worked a miracle on the wizened face. The glow of youth was on it now. It had been filled out, made young, and his step was as light as that of a lad's as he followed the taller rascal across the pavement into the lounge.

Abul, his beard dyed grey, blue-tinted spectacles over his eyes, had to stare for a long moment before he realised that the men crossing the hall were indeed the two rascals he had lived with so long.

It was a case of diamond cut diamond, but neither Carlac nor Kew did more than cast a perfunctory glance at the gorgeous-robed figure who arose and came towards them.

"Thou art Mr. Blake and his assistant, Mr. Tinker?"

Abul put the high pitch of age into his voice. He spoke loud enough for the porter to hear him.

"Yes, that is correct," Carlac returned.

"His Highness the Rajah of Puljara is awaiting thy coming."

Abul wheeled with another low bow, and the two men followed him in silence.

The last lingering suspicion that Kew had died then. They were in one of the finest hotels in the world. They were met as honoured guests.

"A steady nerve now, old chap, and we've won," he whispered in a low aside to Carlac, an unusual cheeriness in his thin voice.

They found themselves in narrow corridor at last, and presently their guide halted and knocked on a door.

A strong voice sounded, and the door was opened by the robed guide, who stood aside to allow them to enter, following them through the doorway.

Standing beside his desk was the regal figure of the rajah. He was dressed in a plain frock-coat of European cut, and his breast was a blaze of Orders. He looked every inch a prince.

"The English detectives, your Highness," announced Abul.

The rajah waited for the two men to approach, then he bowed.

"I am pleased to make your acquaintance, Mr. Blake," he said, in perfect English. "I have heard of you, even in far India, but have never had the pleasure of meeting you before."

Carlac could play the game of bluff as well as most men, and he slipped into the part he was playing easily enough.

"I trust that your Highness has enjoyed your visit to our country," he said.

Across the heavy lips of the rajah a fleeting smile passed. These men were certainly cool blackguards, and the rajah always appreciated courage, even in the evil.

"My visit would not have been so pleasant were it not for you, although others tried to keep that story away from me."

"It was very little I did," the mock-detective went on—"hardly worth mentioning, in fact."

Kew was quite content to allow Carlac to do all the necessary speaking. The professor had disguised himself wonderfully, but he doubted his ability to change his voice to the quick, youthful speech of the irrepressible Tinker.

The rajah turned, and lifted a wide morocco-covered case. Opening it, he allowed the case to tilt forward. The rays of light from the shaded electric-bulb behind him sent a dazzling light over the shimmering gems. They seemed to sparkle, to take fire, and against the velvet lining of the case their radiance found a perfect setting.

An expert in gems Count Carlac had no need to be told that the necklace was worth every penny of the price that the mysterious stranger had mentioned. Diamonds have their market value the world over.

The rajah lifted the necklace from the case and turned round.

"I desire to reward you," his strong voice continued; "your deed must not go unrecognised."

There was a double meaning in his words, although both Kew and Carlac failed to see it at the moment.

"Would you accept these jewels from me as a fair return for what you and your companion did?"

Again there was a mocking note in the voice. The stern-jowled man was deliberately playing with words, and was enjoying the grim comedy to its utmost.

"If you consider what we did as worthy of a reward, your Highness, of course, we will accept anything you might choose to bestow upon us."

"Anything, Mr. Blake?"

The rajah stepped aside a little, and made an almost imperceptible gesture.

Carlac bowed.

"We will accept anything at your hands."

"Good! By Allah, you have sealed your own doom out of your own mouths."

As the words left the rajah's lips, Carlac heard a footfall behind him. Before he could move there descended over his head a thick muffling cloth. At the same moment, Kew, standing a little to the left, was served in the same way. Instantly the catlike cunning of the professor asserted itself. Instead of trying to struggle with his assailant he dropped straight down on to the floor. The result was that Abul, who had cast the cloth over the professor's head, stumbled forward, tripping over the wizened form and dragging the cloth way with him.

"Help! Hel——"

Knowing what lay before him, Kew, in sheer desperation, raised his voice in a shrill appeal; but, before the second cry was completed, Abul had recovered himself, and his brown hands closed the folds of the cloth, pressing against Kew's lean

241

throat.

A heavy thud beside him told the professor that Carlac had been thrown on to the thick carpet of the room.

"Strangle that old hound!"

It was the rajah's voice, commanding, arrogant, and it came to Kew through the thick folds of the heavy cloth. The powerful fingers of Abul were tightening their grip, and, with one mighty effort, Kew twisted himself round so that he was able to thrust his hand into his breast-pocket. An icy-cold shiver ran through him as he realised that he was unarmed. The death-tube had been left behind in the house at Finsbury!

A quick spasm of rage made the vulture-man snarl in the muffling folds. What a fool he had been! He had given the tube to Carlac, and had forgotten to get it back again! For the first time for many a day he was without that potent weapon which made him stronger than any other man. Little dreaming of the escape he had had, Abdul clung to the writhing, quivering form. He was seated straddle-legged across Kew's hunched-up body, and the look in the eyes of the trooper was that of man enjoying a long-delayed triumph.

His remorseless fingers closed tighter and tighter; he could feel the convulsive movements of the wiry rogue beneath him. And then, at last, there came the last violent effort, and Professor Kew gave up the fight. His clawing hands fell back on the carpet, and his twitching limbs were still.

Abul drew the cloak aside, revealing the ugly face, with its smeared make-up. Quickly a gag was placed between the swollen lips, and Kew's hands were tied tightly behind his back. Then, and not until then, did Abul glance around him.

Close to the desk was a heap of struggling forms. The rajah had drawn aside, and was watching the fight with glittering eyes. There were two of his finest troopers pitted again Carlac, and, although the huge criminal had been taken by surprise, he was giving the sinewy men all they could do to hold him. His head, muffled in a baglike cloth, swayed to and fro, and his powerful arms had gripped at the bodies of his two assailants. The man who had first cast the muffling bag had drawn the cords tight, and it was just as well for them that he had done so, for Carlac, unable to see, could only rely on the grip of his powerful fingers.

As Abul glanced across towards the struggling heap, he saw the huge criminal make a mighty effort that carried him almost on to his feet. The rajah's troopers, tough though they were, were dragged up at the same time, each drawn forward by one of Carlac's great arms.

Into the centre of the chamber the master criminal staggered blindly, his assailants with him. One of the troopers gave vent to a groan of agony, and the cracking of a bone sounded. A muffled roar came from the hooded giant, and, with a mighty swing of his arm, Count Carlac flung the injured trooper aside. The Hindu, his hand pressed against his ribs, fell heavily on his face, and through his clenched teeth another half-strangled groan came. It was only sheer courage that prevented the plucky man from crying aloud in his pain.

The other trooper was now tackling Carlac single-handed, and they fell into a wrestler's grip, swaying across the room, twisting and feeling for a master-hold.

The rajah turned towards Abul, and made a movement with his hand.

"That dog is too strong, and the noise may be heard outside. End it, Abul!"

As he spoke, he indicated a heavy steel weight that stood on the desk. Abul obediently picked up the weight, and darted towards the two men, locked in the fierce grip. He was only just in the nick of time, for, as he drew near, Carlac twisted sharply, and in another moment the Hindu trooper was lifted clean into the air in a Cumberland fall. He circled right over Carlac's muffled head, and came down on the carpet with a thud that fairly shook the room. Abul, swinging the weight aloft, closed with the panting giant.

Crack!

The weighty weapon came down on Carlac's hard head with terrible force. The huge criminal tottered, clutched at the air, then, like a pole-axed ox, he dropped first on his knees, then swayed slowly forward until he was lying face-downwards at the feet of the rajah.

Tough though the fight had been, it had only lasted for a few moments. The rajah, stepping quickly to the door of his room, opened it, and looked up and down the narrow corridor. There was no one to be seen, and he turned towards Abul again.

"Go to the top of the corridor and wait there," he said. "In a few moments, Mr. Blake and his companion will leave here. See to it that they are safely escorted out of the hotel."

Abul salaamed and went out into the corridor, walking up to the head of it and waiting patiently. Ten minutes later the door of the rajah's study opened, and two figures appeared. The taller one was carrying a morocco-covered case, and in the dim light of the corridor Abul saw that the face was that of a white man.

In silence he led the two through the hotel and out into the darkened street. A taxi that was waiting close to the portico crawled up, and someone thrust his head out of the window.

"Come along, Mr. Blake!" a sleek voice said.

The porter of the hotel opened the door, and the two men in european clothes entered. Abul, stepping back, allowed a swift smile to cross his lips, for the voice that sounded from the depths of the taxi had been the voice of a certain cunning man known as Ben Dhur!

"A fox indeed!" muttered the trooper, as he turned away. "And his Highness was not mistaken when he trusted this matter into his hands."

The porter watched the taxi vanish into the dimly lighted thoroughfare, and resumed his position at the door. It was just one of the ordinary incidents of his employment. There was nothing mysterious in it, and yet he had been a witness of the final act of a crime that is now very seldom heard of in England. The kidnapping of two men had been safely accomplished, without the slightest sign of the crime leaking out.

Early on the following morning there was a rare bustle in the little side-street beside the hotel. A fleet of motor-cars and a huge motor-lorry was waiting his Highness the rajah and his retinue. Into the lorry was stored the heavier luggage, amongst it being two huge, bulky wicker baskets. The rajah's servants, personally loaded the lorry, and travelled with it down to Southampton, also carrying the luggage on board. Much of the baggage was stored in the hold, but the wicker baskets seemed to be particularly valuable, for they were placed in a large, empty cabin that his Highness had specially reserved for his valuables.

The liner sailed at noon, and the long voyage began. The rajah seemed to be in a very gracious humour, for he laughed and chatted with his men, one of whom seemed an invalid, for he had been helped on board.

None of the ordinary stewards were allowed to go near the deck cabins set apart for the rajah. As is with Indian princes, the rajah had his own cook and his own special food, and an armed sentry stood day and night on the cabin occupied by his master.

There were very few other passengers on board, and not the slightest suspicion of what was really happening ever appeared.

Bound hand and foot and gagged, lying in the half-light of the store cabin, Carlac and Kew were being carried away to a captivity worse than death itself. Twice a day they were fed by an armed man, who watched them, dagger in hand, in turn as they ate.

They knew that the first sound from them the dagger would strike—once, and once only!

In their crime-stained lives, these two hawks on society had often found themselves in grim corners, but both of them knew that this was in a niche by itself.

Once, the guard who brought their food chanced to be Abul, and Kew, cunning always, ventured to speak to his guard.

"It is forbidden that I should speak to thee, thief and dog!" muttered Abul. "But this I will tell thee!"

He leaned forward.

"You laid evil hands on the sacred chest," he said, "and for that, death is the punishment. But the manner of thy death lies in the hands of my master, the rajah."

The under-current of cruelty that is always to be found in the Indian nature, no matter how educated he may be, asserted itself for a moment.

"But it will be a death worthy of thee," the trooper went on—"a death that will come slowly, and with many halts, but it will come!"

He lapsed into silence again, and Kew did not dare question him further.

It was not possible for a man like Kew to repent; he was too deeply stained in villainy for that. But he found a grim and rather curious consolation in the fact that Carlac was to share in any horrors that might follow.

Kew had always been the doubtful one of the two. He had hesitated to trust the oily-tongued Ben Dhur. Kew's eyes grew red with rage as he thought of that cunning rogue, who had proved cleverer than he. But Carlac had appeared to accept the story so readily, that Kew's more cautious nature had been lulled into a false security.

And now they were going to pay for that folly.

He knew that there would be no hope of mercy from the rajah. The man's face was sufficient indication of the pitiless nature that lay behind it!

No; they had made a mistake, and they would have to pay! All the grim stories that the natives of Kashopore had to tell about the dark prison returned to Kew, and he remembered his own and Carlac's forebodings concerning the place.

The long days passed, and as the voyage drew to its close Kew began to count the hours.

He saw his fate looming in front of him, misty, yet always threatening.

Then once a strange, almost grotesque idea came into the wizened criminal's head, an idea so curious that he laughed—a smothered sound behind his gag. Carlac glanced across the narrow cabin, and saw Kew's vulture face looming in the dim light. It was distorted in a grin, and the huge criminal wondered what manner of thought could have brought that expression there.

For into Kew's mind had flashed the question: "Could Sexton Blake save us?"

Small wonder that the professor found humour in the idea. Sexton Blake was their sworn enemy, had thwarted them time and again in their evil plans against the world. Surely he would be the last man in the world to stretch out a saving hand!

Yet the future was to prove that that thought was based on solid foundations. Kew was clever, but he had never been able to fathom the true greatness of the man who was his chief opponent. Blake was against all crime! He stood for law and order, the right of civilisation against desperadoes and rogues.

Kew dismissed the thought as being a mad, hopeless one. But he was wrong there, for events were to turn into the very course he derided.

And how that came about will now be explained.

CHAPTER 8
Flash Harry's Plea

"Thank goodness you've arrived at last, Mr. Blake. The chief has been 'phoning all over the place for you."

Lord Witherly, assistant secretary to Sir Milder Dane, Secretary for Foreign Affairs, tucked one arm under Blake's, and led him along a carpeted corridor.

"I'm very sorry," said Blake, "but I only received the message ten minutes ago. I was out of town yesterday."

"Lucky dog," sighed his lordship, who contrived to do as little work as any healthy young civil servant, but thought he had the world's cares on his youthful shoulders! "Fancy getting a holiday at this time."

He stopped at a well-polished mahogany door, and knocked twice.

"Come in," came a clear, penetrating voice.

Lord Witherly drew back with a swift wink to Blake.

"Not likely," he muttered, below his breath. "That's the lion's den this morning, and I'm no Daniel."

Sir Milder certainly looked a trifle annoyed, very different to his usual urbane self. He and Blake were old acquaintances, and Blake was rather surprised at the cold formal bow that the Foreign Minister gave him.

"Morning, Blake. I'm glad you've turned up at last. I've been waiting in for you all morning."

There was a movement close to one of the big windows, and a tall figure came forward towards the desk. Blake recognised the aristocratic features of Colonel Bryce, and gave him a bow.

The colonel's nod was frigid in its severity. A slight shade passed across Blake's face. One of the most even-tempered men in the world, he was yet quite independent and not used to greetings of this type.

"I only arrived at my chambers to-day," he said; "I did not leave any address, so my assistant could not forward your message."

"You were not in Paris by any chance?" Sir Milder asked.

Blake looked into the keen face.

"Why did you ask that question, Sir Milder," he queried.

Sir Milder toyed with his pen for a moment.

"I know that you have some diamonds to dispose of and I thought that Paris would be the readier market at this time of the year."

Blake's clear eyes widened, and his lips lifted in a smile.

"Diamonds to dispose of," he repeated; "is this a joke on your part."

The Foreign Minister shook his head.

"I never joke during office hours," he said; "and I am quite serious on this matter, Mr. Blake."

There was a cold note in his voice that made Blake stare.

"I see that there is some sort of story attached to your question. Perhaps you will be good enough to explain," he said.

"Need I tell you? I am simply hinting at the fact that his Highness the Rajah of Puljara made you a present of a very handsome diamond necklace previous to his somewhat sudden departure for Kashopore, last Tuesday."

The explanation was so astounding that Blake threw back his head and laughed. But a moment later he checked himself, as he noted the grave looks of the other men.

"I beg your pardon, Sir Milder," the detective said hurriedly; "but, really, your story is so absolutely amazing that I had to laugh."

Sir Milder's eyes widened.

"You—you deny it then?"

"It seems hardly worth denying," Blake returned easily; "I have never met the Rajah of Puljara in my life, and I certainly see no reason why he should give me a necklace—or anything else for that matter of it."

Colonel Bryce who had been a silent listener until that moment, suddenly chimed in.

"But we have proofs that you called on his Highness on the night before his departure and that you were with him for some time, and when you and your assistant——"

"What? Tinker in this as well?"

"Our witnesses state that he accompanied you," came the curt retort; and when you left the hotel you were carrying a morocco-covered case, the description of which I recognised at once. It was ordered by me at his Highness's request, two years ago, and contained a diamond necklace that his Highness deeply prized.

Blake was looking just a trifle bewildered now, and sir Milder, leaning back in his chair, studied the keen, clever face intently.

"All this sounds to me like the veriest rubbish, Colonel Bryce," the detective said; "I can assure you that I was never near the hotel, nor was my assistant. I did not know that his Higness had gone until I read it in the afternoon papers on the following day."

"Can you let me have proofs of this?"

Blake's face changed, and he arose to his feet.

"I am not in the habit of giving proofs to any statements I might make." he said stiffly; "and I do not think that you have any right to demand them."

He looked steadily into the eyes of Colonel Bryce.

"You seemed glad enough to accept my statements on another affair that happened not so very long ago," Blake went on; "I would not remind you of it, but it seems to me that your attitude has changed a great deal since then."

A flush crossed Bryce's face, and he made an impulsive move forward.

"I—I hate to—to put these things to you, Blake, and that's the honest truth," the harassed old soldier broke out; "but things have happened that have upset me and everybody else here."

The Foreign Minister leaned forward.

"Perhaps I might explain," he said; "his Highness the Rajah of Puljara, is a prince with whom the British Government desire to keep in friendly terms. We had arranged a programme of entertainments for him, and suddenly, without a word of warning, he announces his intention of going home. His message was not received until the morning, and when I sent up to the Ritz it was to discover that he had already started for Southampton.

"What made him go away so swiftly?" Blake asked.

The colonel was about to speak, but Sir Milder silenced him with a gesture.

"I'm coming to that presently," he explained. "Of course, there was a big to-do here, and I had to try and find out what had happened."

He reached out and drew a small sheaf of folded blue papers towards him.

"Here are the various reports from the men I sent off," he went on. "In the first place, it was discovered that his Highness only booked his berths late on the same evening, somewhere between eight and ten o'clock. It was done by 'phone to the steamship offices at Southampton."

He withdrew another slip.

"I sent a man to the hotel, and his inquiries proved that orders to pack were not given to the rajah's suite until quite late on the same night. Indeed, there was some difficulty in chartering the requisite number of motor-cars."

"He went to Southampton by road. Why?"

Blake was leaning back in his chair, now listening intently.

"We do not know. But he certainly did travel by car, and so did all his suite."

"Finally, this report was handed to me," the Foreign Minister added; "and I must say that when I read it first it seemed scarcely credible. It stated that you and your assistant, Tinker, were received by his Highness somewhere about midnight; that the story which the hotel servants heard from the rajah's staff, was to the effect that you had rendered him a great and valuable service, in return for which he had made you a handsome present. You were seen to both enter and leave the hotel, on the latter occasion carrying the case that Colonel Bryce identifies by its description."

"Then all I can say is that the man who gave you that report was either mad or very much deceived," the detective returned, in a grave tone.

He turned towards Colonel Bryce.

"I am beginning to read a little of this riddle," Blake went on; "I take it that you heard this report, and promptly came to the conclusion that I had told the rajah about the treasure-chest."

His voice was rather cold, and Bryce moved uncomfortably.

"If I have been mistaken I can only apologise," the polished old gentleman said quietly; "but I think that you will admit it has been a most trying time for me."

"Colonel Bryce is, perhaps, the worst off of us all," Sir Milder explained; he waited on the rajah that evening, and was refused admittance. That in itself was a severe blow to anyone like the colonel here, who had been on such friendly terms with his Highness. Then again, the fact of the rajah leaving England without even telling Colonel Bryce that he was doing so, hints pretty clearly that the old feeling of friendship between them has vanished."

He dropped his official manner for a moment, and looked at Blake.

"It is beastly serious, Blake," he said, "we cannot afford to quarrel with the rajah, and Bryce was the only man we could really trust at Kashopore. You can understand how awkward it will be now. We do not know whether it is advisable to send Bryce out again to Puljara."

The colonel drew a deep breath.

"But I mean to go," he said. "If the Government does not send me as their representative; then, by Jove, I'll go as a mere ordinary visitor. I'm going to get at the bottom of this matter if it takes me the rest of my life."

Blake looked at the old fellow with a sudden pang of sympathy. He could appreciate the feelings of the colonel now. For years Bryce had been in a high position, the favourite of a ruling prince, and the trusted agent of his Government. It was only human that he should feel his position keenly now, and resent it to the uttermost.

"I quite understand," said Blake. "But I can assure you of my innocence in this matter. I have never met his Highness, and if he has heard about the treasure-chest, it is certainly not from my lips."

He spoke the words slowly, with a ring of sincerity in his tones that could not be mistaken. Sir Milder gave vent to what was little else than a grunt of relief.

"Thank Heaven for that, Blake," he broke out; "I was really dreading to hear you say something else. For, you see, any ordinary man might have been quite justified in telling the rajah, and claiming a fair reward. We know that it was only your skill that prevented that daring robbery from being successful."

He looked at Bryce, and his whole aspect had changed.

"Blake's explanation only makes the mystery more profound," he went on "but I do not mind that. As he is implicated in it—well, he will jolly well have to take the matter up and find out the truth."

He spun round on Blake, smiling slightly.

"They state here that you saw the rajah, and that you walked off with a pocketful of diamonds, Blake," the Foreign Minister ended. "Well, now what I want from you is another report—and the true one, this time."

"And you shall have it, Sir Milder," the detective returned in a grim tone.

It was seldom that Blake allowed his feelings to interfere with his usual routine, but he certainly felt that in this matter he had been served rather badly. The mysterious report concerning his supposititious visit to the rajah must have had some sort of foundation. There was no reason why the foreign secret agent should have pitched specially upon him. Obviously some cunning brain had been at work to foist this foolish charge on to his shoulders.

"I hope you have forgiven me, Blake," said Colonel Bryce later, when he and Blake found themselves in the street together. "Sir Milder told me about the report yesterday, and I even went to the trouble to call at the hotel myself. It is certainly the fact that the general impression there is that you did call and did receive a present from the rajah."

He looked half-apologetically into the steely eyes by his side.

"But I think I ought to tell you that there was one member of my household who ridiculed the idea from the very first," the old officer went on; "my daughter and I had quite a storm over it. She refused to listen that both you and Tinker were incapable of doing such a thing—and, at the bottom of my heart, I agreed with her.

Blake's keen face softened. It was just what a girl like Muriel Bryce would do. No matter what official reports were there as proof, she trusted more to the dictates of her own honest heart.

"I am very grateful to Miss Bryce," said Blake, "and I do not blame you. After these reports I could blame no one for assuming that they were true."

They were heading towards Piccadilly, and Bryce turned to Blake.

"Why not go to the hotel now?" he suggested; "that is where the trouble really exists."

"That is just where I am going," said Blake.

He soon had cause to forgive any doubts that might have arisen in the mind of the colonel. For the big porter on duty at the door came to a halt as Blake and the colonel approached. He was the same man as had been on duty when Carlac and Kew entered the hotel. Proof of the wonderful skill that the professor had diplayed in his disguising of his ally were speedily evidenced.

The porter touched his cap, saluting.

"So you've met Mr. Blake, colonel?"

Sorely troubled though he was, Colonel Bryce could not repress a smile.

"You recognise this gentleman then, porter?"

The porter grinned.

"Ra-ther," he said, "and I only wish I was in his shoes. It ain't everybody as can walk out with a pocketful of jooels!"

It was not worth while for Blake to attempt to put the man right, but he realised now that a subtle and deep trick had been played on the hotel and its staff.

They found the manager in his office, and Blake introduced himself, then gave the manager the true side of the story.

"Of course, it has nothing to do with us, Mr. Blake," the manager went on, "but it seems as though his Highness has been tricked by someone."

That was a side of the case that had not appealed to Bryce or Sir Milder. But the colonel saw its point at once.

"You are quite right there," the old officer put in, "for if some masquerading rascal impersonated Blake, his Highness was certainly defrauded."

Blake was silent for a moment.

"Is the suite that the rajah occupied still vacant?" he asked.

"Yes. Would you like to see it?"

Blake nodded, and he and Bryce went along the splendid corridor. Bryce indicated a side corridor at the end.

"His Highness's private study was down there," he said; "I know that, for he kept me waiting for two hours and then sent word into the corridor that he did not want to see me."

The manager unlocked the door of the small room and Blake entered it.

"I'm sorry to say that it hasn't been tidied up yet," he explained. "We are working the hotel with a very small staff just now and the most I could do was to have the floors swept."

Blake crossed to the desk and halting there glanced around him. That curious sense that could not be named and yet asserted itself so often, that feeling that some people called psychic and others auto-suggestion, came to him as he stood there.

Something had happened in that room that had a big bearing on the curious mystery he had been called upon to unravel. Bryce and the manager, standing in the doorway, saw the face of the detective change slowly. The eyes, always unfathomable, became luminous, and the clean-cut features drew together in a strained intent expression.

Blake's eyes travelled to the floor, along the walls, and suddenly he stepped forward and tilted a chair back. There was a fragment of something attached to the leg of the chair—attached so firmly that Blake had to take out his knife and scrape it off.

Bryce saw him peer at the little object in his hand, then a quiet laugh sounded.

"Would you mind looking at this, colonel," said Blake, "it might amuse you."

Bryce came forward and glanced down at Blake's palm. It seemed to the colonel as though it was a scrap of hair that lay in the hollowed hand.

"What is it?"

"A false eyebrow," came the reply; "just goldbeater's skin and cleverly placed hair. A little spirit gum is still attached to it—and I had to removed it forcibly from the chair."

He glanced across at the manager.

"The leg of a chair isn't the usual place for an eyebrow, is it?" said Blake, and his companion smiled.

"But how on earth did it get there?"

"If you look closely at it you will note that there is a little human skin attached to one portion, colonel," the detective went on, indicating a smaller white patch against the transparent goldbeater's skin background; "and that can only mean it was violently wrenched from the person who was wearing it at the time!"

He folded the scrap and placed in in his pocket-book.

"And there is one other point about it, that I don't suppose you could have noticed," he added; "that eyebrow is exactly the same shade and shape of my assistant's, Tinker."

"Then it means that the manager is right, and someone else did impersonate you here? By Heavens, the rajah ought to be warned!"

It was proof of the old officer's loyalty that he should still think of his old chief—even although that chief had left him without a word of farewell.

"I should not be in a hurry to do that, colonel," Blake put in quietly; "for the rajah might not be pleased to learn that he had been tricked. Our first duty is to trace the tricksters and try to recover the jewels. Then, perhaps, it might be worth your while to travel to Kashopore and hand them back to his Highness."

The colonel struck his hands together.

"If that were only possible," he broke out, "it would put everything right."

But that was an event that had never to happen, as Blake was soon to realise. He went carefully through the remainder of the suite of rooms but found no other traces of the mysterious visitors.

A tradesman's account, lying on a littered table caught Bryce's eye, and he picked it up and glanced at it.

"I see that his Highness has gone off and forgotten to pay this bill," he said; "I'll settle it for him."

Blake glanced idly at the bill. It was from a local stores.

"Two 7ft. by 4ft. wicker baskets, lined and padded, with double hasps and extra locks, to be delivered immediately."

The date on the bill proved that the baskets had been delivered on the last day of the rajah's visit to England.

"I think I remember about them," the manager said, after a short pause; "they were brought very late. In fact it was rather a special favour on the part of the stores as they were closed when the rajah gave the order."

"About what time was the order given, do you know?"

"I'm not sure, but I could easily find out. I'll 'phone through now."

The manager was not quite sure what association could exist between the two big wicker baskets and the case that Blake was dealing with, but he was anxious to be of help. He came back to the rooms after a few minutes' interval.

"The order was given about nine o'clock," he announced.

Blake turned to the colonel.

"It seems as though his Highness only made up his mind to leave England somewhere between eight o'clock and midnight," he observed.

"It certainly appears so," the officer agreed. "and it's very curious, for his Highness is not the sort of man to change his plans quickly. The average eastern prince likes to move entirely by a set programme."

"But perhaps something very important happened," said Blake, in his quiet voice; "something so important and interesting to his Highness that all other ideas gave way before it."

The colonel looked at him, earnestly. He saw that Blake was hinting at some definite point, but he could not follow the suggestion.

There was nothing further to be gained by staying at the hotel, and at Bryce's invitation, Blake and he went on to 5, Downe Square, together. Muriel came out of the drawing-room as soon as she heard her father's step. The girl's eyes brightened with delight when they rested on Sexton Blake, and she hurried forward with outstretched hand, a warm greeting on her lips.

"I'm so glad to see you, dear Mr. Blake," Muriel cried. "I've had to listen to such a lot of nonsense about you that I have been quite worried to death."

Her father smiled.

"All right, Muriel, I take back everything I said," he put in; "but Mr. Blake himself will assure you that even he is puzzled over the whole sorry business."

They went into the drawing-room for a moment, and Muriel fired off a torrent of quick inquiries, to which Blake gave accurate replies. He saw that Muriel was just as swift-witted as a girl of her education and class could be, and the complications of the case made it useful for him to have as many opinions as possible. Whether he acted on these views or not was quite a different matter.

"I knew that you had never been anywhere near the rajah," Muriel affirmed stoutly; "and for my part, I'm glad that he has been swindled."

"Hush, Muriel——" her father began.

The girl gave a little petulant stamp of her tiny foot.

"Yes, I am glad," she repeated, "and I don't care who hears me say so. He's an ungrateful creature, and there is only one person worse than him—and that's Abdul!"

Blake looked at her.

"What has the faithful Abul done?"

"Faithful, indeed!" Muriel cried. "We were all mistaken in him, Mr. Blake. He cleared out on the night before his Highness vanished, and we never saw him again! Isn't that true, dad?"

Bryce nodded.

"Abul has gone," he said, "but I don't blame him exactly. I suppose he heard that his Highness was going, or his Highness may even have ordered him to accompany him. After all, Abul was only my orderly, and was really the servant of the rajah."

"I don't care, he ought to have told us," said the girl; "and it's very suspicious. I do believe now, that, if his Highness did know about the attempted robbery, it was Abul who told him!"

Across the slender shoulders of the girl the eyes of the men met. Blake nodded his head.

"That is the first surmise that strikes me as being near to the truth that I have heard concerning this matter, Miss Bryce," he agreed quietly. "I have always had a lingering doubt in my mind concerning Abul. He was loyalty itself, but he was the rajah's man."

He turned to the colonel.

"You know the East as well as I do, colonel," the detective went on, "and don't you think it more than likely that Abul would not be able to keep his secret from his master. You know what sort of fellows the native troopers are. They regard their rulers as small deities, and to keep a secret from his prince must have been a terrible burden to Abul."

Colonel Bryce drew a deep breath.

"I have been trying to convince myself that Abul had nothing to with it, Blake," he said, at last; "but I'm really afraid that it is as you and Muriel suspect. The poor fellow simply could not keep his peace, I suppose. That would explain his Highness's anger with me, and I do admit that it was perhaps justified. But you have yet to fit in the other part of the story—the visit of the two individuals who passed themselves off as you and Tinker."

Blake shrugged his shoulders.

"I am less concerned about that now than I was," he admitted. "After all, I can prove that neither Tinker nor I was near the Ritz that evening, and it occurs to me that it is hardly worth while pursuing the investigation further. The only one who has lost anything by it is his Highness the rajah. He is the poorer for a diamond necklace, but as he does not complain, why should we?"

"Bravo, Mr. Blake!" Muriel cried, clapping her hands. "that is just exactly my feelings in the case. The rajah has treated dad most shamefully, and if he has been cheated out of his beastly old diamonds—well, it only serves him right!"

But her impetuous speech brought no answering smile on the face of her parent. There was a certain quiet dignity in the old colonel's manner as he looked at his daughter.

"That's not my opinion, Muriel," he said. "After all, I am still his Highness's military adviser and English attache. I am also still the British representative in Puljara. If his Highness has been defrauded, it is my duty to see that matters are put right."

Muriel stepped back and made a little pout with her lips, at the same time casting a rather loving glance at the old gentleman.

"So Mr. Blake, for my sake, if not for own, I hope you will continue your investigations."

It was then that Blake asked a question over which Muriel puzzled her head for the rest of the evening.

"I will do so on one condition."

"As many as you choose."

"One will do. And it is this: If I start on the case you will not attempt to withdraw from it at any future time. I mean that whatever developments take place, I may rely on your aid, no matter who may be implicated."

Colonel Bryce was silent for a moment; then held out his hand.

"I do not follow your meaning, sir," he said, "but there is my hand and my promise. No matter who may be drawn into this matter, you will have my active aid and support."

They exchanged grips; then a few moments later Blake left the quiet house, refusing the colonel's invitation to stay to dinner. Half-way down the square the detective heard the quick tap, tap! of small feet and the swish of a silken skirt. Muriel Bryce, her lips parted, her cheeks red with the run, caught his arm.

"You do walk so quickly," she panted. "I had ever such a run!"

Blake stopped.

"I did not know that you were following me," was his obvious response.

"I simply had to," the girl went on. "What ever do you mean by what you said to my dad? Who do you suspect?"

Her large lustrous eyes were fixed on Blake's face with an anxious light in them. Quick as a flash Blake divined the fear in her heart. He pressed her hand gently.

"I do not suspect Lieutenant Vernon—nor yourself."

Muriel blushed and laughed; but there was obvious relief in her eyes.

"Of course, it was absurd," she admitted. "But you were so strange over the matter that just for a moment——"

She came to a halt, and laughed again.

"And you won't tell anyone that I came after you to—to inquire?"

Blake raised his hat.

"Not for the world!" he assured her; and she turned away, to hurry back through the dusk to her own home.

Blake went on, a grim smile on his lips.

"Certainly not Vernon nor you, Miss Bryce," he repeated. "But to me it seems as though someone is going to be drawn into the web whom the colonel will be rather anxious to shield rather than expose."

He had made one or two simple deductions, and his own observations had filled in the blanks.

The fact that he had found the false eyebrow wedged on the bottom of the chair-leg was proof enough to him that the story of the bogus detectives' visit to the rajah was right enough, and they had actually been in the same room as his Highness.

But how came it that one of the false brows, with a piece of the wearer's skin attached to it, was found in the room? It meant that the disguise had been torn off during the visit!

No other explanation was possible. By design or accident, the individual disguised as Tinker had lost part of his disguise, and lost it in what had obviously been a painful way, for it had been torn from its place.

Yet the hotel staff testified that the two detectives had walked out of the hotel apparently unharmed, bearing their treasure with them.

This was a pretty problem to solve, and Blake strolled along turning it over and over in his mind.

The rajah must have seen these two men, otherwise they could not have gone off with the jewels. He must have handed the case to them, and yet must have known that he was being tricked!

That was not possible. The false eyebrow, with its mute testimony of violent removal, debarred that theory. The man who had impersonated Tinker had been unmasked in the very presence of the man he had tried to deceive. It was unbelievable that after such an occurrence that the rajah should hand over the princely reward.

Then his mind turned to another channel. How did the rajah come to associate his name and that of Tinker's with the stolen treasure-chest? Here a simple reply was forthcoming. Abul had told his Highness.

Abul had told his Highness everything, for Abul knew the whole story from start to finish; knew the cunning parts that Kew and Carlac—that Kew and Carlac——"

As the names came into his head, Blake came to a pause, and quick thrill ran through him.

Kew and Carlac—Tinker and Blake!

"By Jove! Can it be possible?"

As a man moving through a fog, Blake began to see a light dimly in front of him. He remembered how Abul vowed vengeance on the two rogues. The chest was a sacred thing in the eyes of the rajah himself. Was it possible that all that masquerade that had taken place was nothing more or less than a drama of revenge?

It was seldom that Sexton Blake ventured into the doubtful paths of theory. As a rule he preferred to follow the evidence, but it was beginning to dawn on him now that ordinary methods would not avail him.

He was up against one of these intricate, subtle schemes so dear to the Oriental mind. There was something of the Arabian Nights in this vague drama.

Had Abul tricked Kew and Carlac into delivering themselves into the very arms of the man they had tried to rob?

For over two hours Blake trudged along street after street in a brown study, his clear mind tussling with the intricate puzzle.

And gradually, by eliminating all other possible solutions, building the whole fabric up on the slender evidence of the false eyebrow and its strip of human skin, Blake came as near to the true solution of the matter as it was possible for mortal to do.

"The rajah knew these men were trying to swindle him for the second time. Abul, no doubt, was at the bottom of it. Kew is a master of the art of disguise, and under his hands Carlac could easily pass himself off to a stranger as me," thus his thoughts decided. "They went into the Ritz, but they never left it. These baskets," his retentive memory picked up that point suddenly and clearly—"these baskets, ordered at such a late hour, were intended for human freightage. That was why they were padded. Yes, I am willing to stake all I possess on it. Carlac and Kew are in the hands of their enemy, the Rajah of Puljara."

He came to a halt and looked about him, to discover that his wandering footsteps had taken him into Regent's Park. He turned, and headed back for Baker Street.

"I will make sure first," thought Blake. "Kew and Carlac were always difficult rogues to trace, but Flash Harry is a different proposition. I will have a word with him, and see if he knows where they are. If they are still in England, then all my fine theories are dreams. If not, then I will be satisfied that there is something in the deductions method after all."

. . . . . .

Three days later a certain over-dressed man, mingling in the crowd outside a music-hall, felt someone touch him on the arm. He turned with that quick animal-like movement of head which betrays the criminal type.

"All right, my friend," Sexton Blake said, in his quiet voice, "don't get alarmed. I'm not out after you to-night, only I want a few words with you."

Flash Harry recovered his nerve quickly enough, and he grinned.

"That's good, Mr. Blake!" he said. "I ain't the sort to bear malice, although you did give me a thick ear the last time we met."

He led the way through the throng, Blake close to his side. They reached a quieter thoroughfare at last, and Flash Harry shortened his pace.

"Now then, what's the trouble? Mind you, if it's any pal of mine you're after, I'm mum!"

"I'm after no one," said Blake gravely; "and when I do go after anyone, I never accept help from your kind—a fact that you know well enough."

"I give in there," said the known crook. "You don't usually need a lot of help—worse luck for them as you're after."

"Have you seen anything of Kew and Carlac lately?"

"No."

"Are you sure?"

"Ain't seen 'em for years and years."

Blake looked into the shifty eyes.

"That's a lie," he returned slowly. "I know that they were working with you on the treasure-chest affair. But that's all over and done with. What I want to know is if you've seen them since last Monday night?"

Flash Harry drew a quick breath, and Blake saw that his shot had told.

"Look here, Mr. Blake," the crook began, "if you're kidding me, say so! What has happened to 'em? Have you landed them both?"

"Then you have not seen them since that day?"

Flash Harry was silent for a moment.

"Give me your word that you ain't trying to down them for something, and I'll tell you the whole truth!"

"I give you my word that neither Kew or Carlac will come to any harm out of what you tell me," said Blake, finding it easy enough to make that promise—which, even although made to one devoid of all traces of honesty, the detective meant to keep.

"Right! Well, it's like this. I knew where they were staying—I stay there myself now and again. Last Monday I had a talk with Carlac, and left the house about eight o'clock. I didn't get back until after theatre-time, maybe about half-past eleven, and my—and the landlady who keeps the house, told me that Kew and the chief had gone out."

To Flash Harry, Count Carlac was always the chief.

"I waited up for them until past two, but they didn't turn up; and they ain't showed their faces there since."

"And you have no idea what has happened to them?"

Again the rogue hesitated.

All I knows is, that the landlady of the house told me, that shortly after I left someone came along to see Kew. He was in the house for the best part of three hours, and they left together."

"Who was the visitor?"

"Dunno. Only my—the landlady said he was a little, dried-up monkey of a man—not English. The sort of men what come round to sell you carpets and bits of tinselled shawls."

"A Hindu, perhaps?"

"Yes."

Flash Harry saw Blake's eyes light up suddenly.

"What is it, Mr. Blake? I don't worry much about Kew—he can look after himself. But the chief—oh, he was something of a man, he was!"

And so did criminal honour criminal. Blake's smile was grim as he looked into the pleading face.

"If what I think is true, neither you nor anyone else will ever set eyes on Kew or Carlac again," he said. "They are both in the hands of an enemy who is just as cunning and ruthless as they are."

He was about to turn away, when Flash Harry caught his sleeve.

"Look here, Mr. Blake, I'll tell you summ'at else," he said, in a hoarse voice. "I had a look in their bedrooms afterwards, and found a lot of grease-paint and spirit gum on the dressing-tables. And they had togged themselves up in different clothes, 'cost the landlady saw them both as they went out. She hardly recognised the professor. She—she swore he was just like a young lad."

"Then that settles it," came the deep-voiced reply; "and only a miracle can save the man you are fool enough to admire and call chief. He is in the hands of someone who is a law unto himself, far away from England—someone who has every cause to seek vengeance."

Flash Harry was by no means a fool. He read the daily papers diligently, and now, at Blake's words, he was able to make a shrewd guess at the truth."

"I've got it—I've got it!" he cried. "The Rajah of Puljara has gone back to India, and he's taken the chief and Kew with him. That's it—that's it! He is out for revenge over that treasure-chest affair."

Again his fingers caught at Blake's sleeve.

"Don't let him torture them, guv'nor," the man whined. "that's what his game will be. It's bad enough to swing, or to serve a long stretch in quod, but torture—ough!" He covered his face with his hands for a moment, then looked up again.

"You could save 'em, Mr. Blake, if you tried," he went on. "There ain't a crook in the world as would hide long from you. You've beat the best of us always in the long run. But you've always been fair. You've stood up before to-day and stopped a mob from lynching someone as richly deserved it. Don't let this human tiger torture two white men, even although they are just like me, bad 'uns and crooks."

He gave a gulping sob, and turned to hurry down the street. Blake stood motionless on the pavement, a prey to many curious emotions. There had been something of the grotesque in the scene; the thought that Flash Harry should plead to him, Sexton Blake, to save these two human birds of prey from their fate, had been humorous enough—and yet there was a touch of pathos in it, that made its presence felt.

The man had pleaded for his chief, the only being in the world that he admired, in his warped, criminal way. He had even wept as he pleaded.

A sentence came into Blake's mind.

"Torture two white men!" Flash Harry had said. That was true. There was no doubt but what the rajah's revenge would turn to some terrible torment.

Then his duty, strange though it appeared, came into the detective's mind. He was always on the side of justice. The Rajah of Puljara had broken the old ancient laws of Britain, that law of habeas corpus, which had formed the basis of Magna Charta, the beginning of Britain's freedom.

This Indian prince had broken the law, and white men, even although they were criminals, had a right to the protection of their race, in a case like this.

A quizzical smile broke over Blake's lips as he walked along the pavement.

"This is distinctly a new role for me to play," he thought. "In the past I have always been against Kew and Carlac, now it would seem that force of circumstances—and the rough, but very eloquent, pleading of another blackguard, only a shade less evil than themselves—makes it necessary for me to be on their side. I wonder if it will be as thankless a job as it seems."

Only the future could answer that; but Blake had made up his mind, and having done so, nothing could change it.

CHAPTER 9
The Learned Fakir of Kashopore

Kashopore, the changeless, was simmering beneath the heat of an ardent sun. In bazaar and narrow streets the natives lolled in the shade, or walked along close to the low-roofed houses. Now and again a pack of scavenger dogs would raise a din of snarls and yelps, as someone of their group settled a quarrel; but they were the only creatures that seemed to have any sort of energy. It was noon, when the sun was at its fiercest, and most of the wealthier natives were safely sheltered in their homes, in rooms shaded with long, heavy sunblinds.

In a white-painted house, which, by its cleanliness and general air of care, stood out in marked contrast to those around it, under a striped awning on the roof, a girl in a cool, white summer dress was seated in a comfortable chair, swinging a fan to and fro.

By her side stood a little table, with a syphon and a glass, and stretched out on a strip of carpet at her feet was a lithe young officer, in white drill.

"What's interesting you, Muriel?" asked Vernon, looking up lazily. He saw that the girl's eyes were fixed on some distant object. Muriel came back to earth with a little start.

"Interesting me?" she cried. "Oh, the usual place. His Highness's palace—that we are no longer allowed to enter."

From the roof of the white-painted house, Muriel could see the towers and minaretes of the great palace, a quarter of a mile away. In the blazing sun they stood out clear, alabaster-like against the cloudless sky.

"Oh, hang the palace!" Vernon returned. "Between ourselves, Muriel, I would much rather be here. There was a bit too much of the ceremony business when we lived in the palace."

The British residency was certainly a comfortable place, occupying a little niche of rising ground close to the river. A garden of about a couple of acres kept it slightly aloof from the neighbouring houses, and, as Vernon said, the life there was much more simple.

Muriel shrugged her shoulders.

"That's because you are so lazy," she cried. "You hated having to dress up in your official uniform, and attend the court. But, for my part, I must say I regret the quarters we used to occupy. For instance, we had more servants than we knew what to do with—and didn't have to pay them, either. It is very different now. I've got to manage on dad's official pay, and it's not quite so easy as it sounds."

The young lieutenant smiled. The only son of a wealthy manufacturer, Vernon did not trouble himself where money was concerned.

"I've already suggested how that can be altered, Miss Obstinate," he murmured.

Muriel tossed her head.

"As if dad would hear of you standing your share of the expenses! It is too absurd!"

"As a mere aide-de-camp, it might sound rather asbsurd," the youngster went on; "but as a son-in-law—well why not?"

Their love-affair had progressed slowly. The colonel had been told of Vernon's affection, and had made no very great objection. He pointed out, however, that his daughter was very young—just turned eighteen—and at least two years ought to pass before the wedding took place.

"By that time we shall see if you are both of the same mind," the old officer explained. "I don't believe in marrying in haste."

Vernon fumed a little, but he was forced to submit. But he never lost an opportunity of pointing out how much better it would be if the embargo were removed, and he could marry the girl he loved at once.

Muriel laughed.

"I don't suppose dad would hear of it, even under those circumstances," she returned. "and, anyhow, we have two whole years to wait."

She rested her firm, white chin in her cupped hand, and stared again at the palace.

"I can't make it out," she cried. "The rajah seems friendly enough. Yet we have been here for over a fortnight now, and he has only sent for dad once."

"But we've had heaps of game, and other very useful presents from him," Vernon remarked; "that shows he isn't quite antagonistic."

"But there is something missing," said Muriel, "I'm sure of that. If there weren't, we would have been back in our old quarters."

Colonel Bryce and his small staff had not been long in following the rajah back to India. The Foreign Office had decided that it was best that Bryce should return at once, and the old soldier, well-accustomed to constant moves and changes, had started off on the long journey, ten days after the rajah had sailed. The rejoicings over the return of their ruler had only just teminated in Kashopore, when the Bryces arrived to take up their quarters at the residency. The rajah had promptly sent a welcoming message, and daily there arrived from the palace many little luxuries for the colonel's table. But Muriel was quite right in her statement that the rajah had only granted one audience to the British representative, and then it had been a very short one, for his Highness had been dressed ready for a boar-hunting expedition.

Secretly Colonel Bryce felt his new position keenly, but he allowed no indication of his feelings to reveal itself in public. He knew that the inhabitants of the town were watching every move, and that the enemies to British rule, who are to be found everywhere in India, were rejoicing in the fall of this favourite of their ruler's.

"I don't understand it," said Muriel. "The rajah seems friendly, and yet he won't have us near him. Why should that be?"

"Give it up," said Vernon lazily. "I never was very good at conundrums, and, besides, it's too beastly hot to think."

Muriel's eyes flashed.

"You are too lazy for words," she said; "I don't think you care a bit really."

Vernon raised himself on his arm for a moment, and looked at the slender, graceful figure of the girl he loved.

"You are quite right there, Muriel," he said. I don't care very much what happens so long as I can spend most of my day with you. Palace or residency—or mud hut for that matter—would be quite good enough with you to share it."

His quiet speech brought a flush into the girl's cheeks. She leaned forward and put her hand on his head.

"It is a very sweet speech, sir," she said. "and I forgive you."

She leaned back in her chair again and looked across the shimmering roofs of the city spread out like an intricately-patterned carpet. The residency stood high, and the whole of the city could be viewed from the wall of the roof. Across the

251

gap stood the rambling structure of the palace. Suddenly a bright flash from one of the high towers caught the girl's eye. She shaded her eyes, staring at the tower, and once again the flash came.

The sun was striking on some bright object and its rays were being reflected across the city.

"Have you got your binoculars, dear?"

Vernon stretched out a lazy hand and picked up the little leather case from beneath the low wall.

"Here you are!"

Muriel took the glasses out and adjusted them. there was a long silence, then the girl drew a quick breath.

"It is his Highness," she said. "He seems to be very interested in something that is going on in the palace. He is watching from the tower and is using a pair of glasses. I caught the flash from one of the lenses a few moments ago. Do look, Vernon, there's a dear."

With a sigh of protest, Vernon drew himself up from his comfortable position and took the glasses that were held toward him. He leaned on the low wall and levelled the binoculars.

The powerful glasses picked up the top of the tower. The tall figure of a man in dark, close-fitting robe was leaning over the edge of the tower, glasses raised to his eyes, watching something that was happening below.

There was no mistaking the burly figure.

"Yes, it is the rajah right enough," said Vernon, "but what the dickens does he find to amuse himself up there?"

He was still watching the figure. It seemed to be keenly interested, for it did not move a muscle, nor did the head and arm supporting the glasses shift.

"What is he looking at?"

"Vernon changed his glasses round, trying to pick up the other man's view. The high wall of the palace made an unbroken line, and the object that held the rajah's attention, whatever it was, was hidden behind the guarding walls.

"The prison lies in the direction that he is staring at," the young officer commented at last, "but I'm hanged if I can see anything."

He returned the glasses to Muriel, who levelled them again at the tower. She watched for a minute or two, then suddenly the attitude of the man on the tower changed. He lowered his glasses from his eyes and straightened up. Quite clearly Muriel Bryce saw the rajah fling back his head in an unmistakable laugh. He beat his hands together as a man might do who had seen some act worthy of applause.

"This is really too much," the girl cried. "I shall simply die of curiosity in a minute. What is it that's going on in the palace?"

Two minutes later the rajah had vanished from the tower, and although Muriel waited, hoping that he would reappear, he did not do so.

But on the following day at exactly the same hour and in exactly the same place the rajah appeared again. His actions were almost similar to the previous day. First the long watch, then the applause, and retirement.

This time Muriel was the sole witness, for the colonel and Vernon had gone off early in the morning together, and were not expected back until sunset.

"If I could only get a word with Abul," the girl thought, "I might be able to get something out of him. I'll really have to find out what it is that interests his Highness so much, and always at the same hour of the day. It's a mystery, and I hate mysteries, they fag the brain so."

But Abul, the huge trooper, had been careful to keep within the confines of the palace ever since the colonel and his staff had arrived at Kashopore. This in itself was quite sufficient to satisfy Muriel that her surmise concerning Abul had been correct.

"He's afraid to face us," she decided, "and yet, I don't think I would have said much to him. He couldn't keep that secret away from his prince."

She arose from her chair and leaned over the low wall for a moment, glancing down into the little courtyard beneath. Beyond the courtyard stood a beautifully wrought-iron gate which opened into the roadway.

Whizz!

Muriel caught sight of a dirty, ragged figure beyond the gate. The man raised his arm and suddenly jerked it forward. Something shot past Muriel's head and fell on the carpet beneath the chair.

"Oh! You—you brute!" the girl cried, dropping back from the wall, her cheeks white.

The fellow had deliberately aimed at her, or at least had seemed to do so. The brief vision she had had of the man told her he was of the wandering fakir type, a pest that neither time nor change of customs seems to be able to remove.

"If I were a man I'd—I'd run down and give you a good hiding, you wicked wretch," the girl thought, her breath coming and going in little indignant gulps. "I'm sure that I never done anything to harm you or anyone else."

She glanced round and her eye caught a white object lying beneath the chair.

It was a sheet of common notepaper, tied around a small stick! The missile that had whizzed past her head.

"Why, what on earth——"

Muriel dropped on her knees and fished out the stick from below the chair. The note was tied to it with a piece of soft rag. With eager fingers the girl untied the knot and opened the note.

"If Miss Bryce would like to meet her old friends, Sexton Blake, Tinker, and also Pedro, she can do so by coming to the East Gate at sunset this evening."

Muriel had to read the note twice before the meaning of it dawned on her. Then with a quick run she was leaning over the wall again.

"Fakir! Holy One!" she called, her eyes fixed on the gateway.

There was no reply, but later on, glancing to the left at a spot where she could command a view of the roadway running between the houses, Muriel saw the figure of the fakir pass, and after him, at the respectful distance that disciples must move, strode another slender form, at whose heels there plodded a great sturdy hound.

Muriel almost cried aloud with vexation.

"Oh, why didn't he stop," she cried. "Why are people so annoying just now?"

Sexton Blake in India?

It seemed incredible; and yet Muriel remembered that they had lost touch with the detective in a most abrupt manner. From the afternoon that he had called and she had run after him to ask him a certain question, Sexton Blake seemed to have vanished into thin air. Even the Foreign Office, where Colonel Bryce made inquiries, did not seem to be able to give any news; and although Muriel did manage to call once at Baker Street previous to her departure to the East, it was only to learn that Blake and his assistant had gone off somewhere for what was evidently a long visit, as they had taken a lot of clothes with them.

And now, in Kashopore, of all places, they had turned up, detective, and assistant, and bloodhound.

"I feel as though I was moving in a sort of dream," Muriel finally admitted. "There is no mistaking Pedro, even if the others were only disguised. I must go to the East Gate."

It was not such a risky proceeding as it might have been. Muriel Bryce was known to everyone in Kashopore, and they also knew that she stood high in the favour of their ruler. Apart from that there was always the shadow of the British power over her. It would be a brave man who would venture to attack the girl in that city, a brave and a mad one, for his act would bring a summary punishment on all Kashopore.

But it is doubtful whether any thought of danger ever entered the eager girl's head. She dressed herself in her riding-habit and ordered the syce to bring round the polo pony that her father had given her. Sunset found her riding through the narrow streets, and every now and again one of the crowd would send a salaam to her, which Muriel always returned with a sweet smile and bow.

The English rose had plenty of admirers in teeming Kashopore, and she was safer in the crowded streets than anywhere else.

Half an hour saw her reach the East Gate, and she cantered beneath the wide arch, taking the red roadway on the left.

The lighted guard-room, occupied by the gate sentinels, made a yellow background against which her slender figure stood out clearly. Something came snuffling out from the dusk, making the pony shy.

"Steady, Ron, you silly old thing; it's Pedro, the darling."

Muriel rode astride, and in a moment she had swung herself out of the saddle and was kneeling in the red dust, patting the flanks of the great hound who gasped and panted his delight at this meeting.

"Good evening, Miss Bryce," a quiet voice said.

Muriel looked up at the ragged figure in front of her. The begging bowl, attached by a cord to the sunburnt throat, the long staff, and naked, dust-covered feet, were all in keeping with the dusky face and straggling beard. But the voice and accents were those of an Englishman, and one that she recognised at once.

"Mr. Blake," she said, rising to her feet and holding out her hand.

Blake extended the bowl as though it was a present that the girl offered him.

"I am the Wandering One for the time being, Miss Bryce," he said, "and I am always to be found outside the little Temple of the Vines."

Muriel drew a swift breath.

"But how extraordinary," she exclaimed eagerly. "I heard the servants talking about a very wise beggar-priest, who had taken up his quarters at that very temple."

Blake bowed, and the shadow of a smile crossed his bearded lips for a moment.

"It is wonderful how a good knowledge of the native tongue and a certain amount of commonsense helps a man to build up a reputation," he returned. "But I'm glad to hear that my advice has been found to have the real stuff in it."

The slender girl in her neat riding-habit was walking along the roadway, Blake by her side, while the slender figure whom Muriel recognised as Tinker, and Pedro, followed them at the respectful distance that a disciple should keep from his master.

"But you are perfectly splendid," Muriel went on, glancing with critical admiration at Blake. "I never saw anything like it. You would deceive the eyes of the sharpest native."

"It is more than likely that I will have to do that sooner or later." said Blake in a dry tone. "Always assuming that the one you refer to is the head of his people."

"You mean the rajah?"

"Yes."

"But what—why——"

She halted and looked at her companion.

"Is it because of something that the rajah has done that you are out here in this disguise?"

Blake bowed.

"Because of something which I think the rajah has done would be perhaps the better way of putting it, Miss Bryce," he corrected.

"But this is really interesting," the vivacious girl went on. "You know, I suppose, that dad and all of us are in disgrace. That is to say, his Highness refuses to give us our old quarters in the palace, and has never invited us to see him yet?"

"But his Highness sends you very many presents for your table," said the disguised detective. "For instance, there was a fine buck brought over yesterday."

"Goodness! You know as much about our business as we do," Muriel went on. "I hope that we are not added to the suspicious list!"

Blake laughed.

"I wouldn't have sent that message to you, if you were," he pointed out.

"Well, that's consoling, anyhow. And now, tell me, how long have you been in Kashopore?"

"Tinker and I arrived just exactly three days behind his Highness."

"You must have travelled very fast."

The keen jaw of the detective twitched for a moment.

"I meant to get here before him, if I could, but I was held up in America. I went round the other way, you see, Miss Bryce. One travels faster on land than by sea."

"But what was all the hurry about?"

The man by her side came to a halt. The roadway was in darkness now, and there was no sign of other pedestrians.

"I cannot take you into my confidence yet, Miss Bryce," Blake said, in a quiet tone; "but I promise I will do so as soon as I clear up one or two points. Meanwhile, I want you to help me."

"I'm sure I'll do anything I can."

"I want you to find out what his Highness did with a very splendid specimen of a Bengal tiger which arrived in Kashopore on the same day as I did. As a matter of fact, it travelled by the same train, and had a much better compartment than Tinker and I. It was taken to the palace in a gorgeous gold car; and I hear that the rajah is highly delighted with his purchase."

"I never heard anything about that," said Muriel; "but I shouldn't be surprised if he did buy a tiger. He has quite a small zoo, in the palace."

"This particular tiger had quite a history," said Blake. "during the journey I had a word or two with the man in charge of it. It is a man-eater, and has never been in captivity. It was caught in a pit, and was kept there for over a week, as it was much too strong to be handled by the villagers. They were very pleased when his Higness sent down for it. He paid quite a big sum of money for his latest pet."

"Well, it is all news to me, Mr. Blake," said Muriel, "but I'll try my best to find out. Unfortunately, our changed conditions make it rather harder than it might have been."

Blake was silent for a moment.

"Don't you think that his Highness might desire to keep you away from the palace, for reasons apart from the ones you think?"

He put the question in a quiet tone, as one might do who was mentally puzzling out the reply himself.

"Oh, I'm sure it is all through that unfortunate robbery!" Muriel cried.

"Yes, Miss Bryce, I agree that the robbery is at the bottom of it; but the point I want to decide is, if the rajah is still nursing a grievance against Colonel Bryce. In this case, I don't think that he would trouble to send so many presents. I should imagine that the rajah is the sort of man who makes an enemy and allows him to remain one."

"I see your point, Mr. Blake," said Muriel thoughtfully. "And it certainly does seem rather strange. If the rajah feels friendly enough to send us gifts, he ought to feel friendly enough to give us back our old quarters."

"Where were your quarters?"

"Right in the centre of the inner courtyard," said Muriel, with a half-regretful sigh. "They were lovely! Just a little tower quite by itself. It was reached by a passage from the main buildings, of course, but we could close an iron door in the passage, and were completely shut off from the others."

"Perhaps you would describe the tower to me?"

"It was eight-sided, and three stories high. The ground floor was divided into two rooms, one we used as the dining-room, and the other the kitchen. Upstairs were the study and one bedroom, and there were two other bedrooms on the next floor. Above that was a flat roof, and in the centre of the roof was a building, that we used as a store. In summer time I've often slept up on top of the little store. It was a delightful place. It had a wall about four feet high all round it, and it was fairly well sheltered by the other towers of the palace."

Then Blake asked a question which made Muriel draw back a pace.

"It would be possible for anyone in one of the higher towers to see the whole of the roof and the little store, of the quarters you once occupied."

"Why, of course! Good gracious, how foolish of me! I have only just thought of something most extraordinary."

Before she could go on, Blake had taken the very words she was about to utter, from her lips.

"You mean that you have found out where the rajah keeps such a steady watch on, during the two hot hours of the afternoon?"

"You have seen him, then?"

"No. But you forget that I am a very wise fakir, Miss Bryce. And even the palace servants come to have a word with the wise."

His quiet laugh brought an answering smile on the girl's lips.

"I have been puzzling my brains all day," Muriel admitted. "I saw the rajah and his glasses. What is it that keeps him so very intent?"

Blake shook his head.

"That is more than I can find out," he said, and his low voice now had taken a sterner note; "but I mean to do so. You, perhaps, might aid me?"

"How?"

Blake leaned forward.

254

"When his Highness sends another gift, try and have a word with his messenger," he said, "and say to the messenger that you think it a shame that the rajah should have turned a man-eating tiger out into your old quarters, to roam about the rooms just as it pleases?"

"But—but has he really done that?"

"The messenger's manner will soon prove whether he has or not," the detective returned grimly; "and that is the other item of information that I want you to gather for me."

He drew back from her, with a low salaam.

"I am always to be found at the temple of the Vine," he went on, and now his voice had changed into the sing-song whine of the mendicant priest; "the mem-sahib can always see me there."

A shadow had loomed up out of the dusk. It was a tall native, white-robed, and turbaned, striding out through the dust. Muriel, with a final nod to Blake, climbed into her saddle and turned Ron's head homeward.

Her brain was a whirl of thought and doubts. Blake had not asked her to keep his presence in Kashopore a secret, but instinct told the girl to do so, until he gave her permission to speak.

What was his object?

The question arose in her mind, and she puzzled over it, while Ron cantered on through the east gateway and turned into the narrow, winding streets of the old city.

One thing was sure, he was there to watch the rajah, and by doing so he was taking his life in his hands. Only a man with vast courage would dare to stay in Puljara, with such a mission to perform. It was like going into the lion's den, for the rajah's word was law in his own little kingdom.

Muriel almost shivered as she thought of the long odds that Blake would have to face.

"It would be an act of madness on the part of any other person," she murmured. "Two men and a dog against his Highness and all his bodyguard and people. It is enough to make one laugh, if it didn't make one feel more inclined to cry!"

And she did shed just one tear, then her little head went back, and she straightened her supple form.

"But I will help him!" she vowed. "I know that there is nothing mean or underhand in his task. Whatever he has to do is bound to be on the side of justice and truth. I'll help him to the bitter end."

A splendid resolution, and one that Muriel Bryce was to carry out. And yet, had she known the whole truth, she might have hesitated to give that promise. For the mission that Sexton Blake had taken up was the rescuing of two rascals who, to many people, had richly deserved their fate. Somewhere in that vast palace Count Carlac and Professor Kew were held in bondage. That fact Blake had now proved beyond the shadow of doubt. A word picked up here and there, a half-frightened confidence made darkly, all went to prove that two white men had travelled with his Highness as captives, that they had been seen to enter the palace and from that moment no sign or word had been heard of them.

Blake had made his way to the little temple in the midst of the paddy-field when he left Muriel, and on reaching the shelter, Tinker and Pedro came up to their master.

"I suppose you heard most of the chat, Tinker?" Blake asked.

The youngster—Tinker—might have been one of the thousands of slim native boys who are to be found swarming in the East. A ragged robe, half opened at the breast, revealed the clear amber skin, which could stand the light of the sun and the test of water successfully, the white teeth and black, sleek hair were typical of the race. His feet, naked in the dust, had the real hard sole now of one who goes barefooted in all seasons.

"Yes, guv'nor; and I was sorry that I couldn't have a word with Miss Muriel. She's a real trump, right through."

'She will help me, Tinker," the detective went on; "and she has a keen brain, while her nerves are of the best. Yes, I think that she will be of great use to us."

Tinker had entered the temple and had lighted a small native lamp, the smoky flames dispelled a little of the darkness, and Tinker began to prepare the supper. A simple meal, but quite sufficient to the seasoned campaigners. Rice and dates, with a cup of coffee, and a plentiful supply of small, appetising rice-cakes.

Tinker had adjusted a scrap of ragged cloth over the narrow door of the temple, so that they might be concealed from any chance wayfarer. Not that there was a big likelihood of anyone coming that way. The temple was rather remote, and the path to it through the paddy-fields was a haunt for snakes, and, by the word of the natives, ghosts. Blake had filled his briar, and, leaning back against the wall of the temple, he was puffing away contentedly. Tinker had flung himself upon a heap of rugs, with Pedro's head on his knees.

Wo-o-ouf!

Pedro seldom growled. The nearest thing he could do was a sort of subterranean bark which came apparently from some deep recess in the thick throat. A moment later Blake heard the crackling of reeds, and, with a quick movement, arose to his feet. His pipe was thrust into a safe crevice in the wall, and he stepped up to the doorway.

The quick panting of a man was heard, and a hand reached out and tugged the flimsy cloth aside. Blake saw a white-robed figure standing in the dusk, then the new-comer leaped forward through the doorway and closed the cloth over it again.

Blake watched the sweat-covered face, and noted the quick, laboured breathing. The stranger was covered from head to foot with dust, and there were thorn scratches on his face and hands.

"Thou art pursued, perhaps?" Blake asked, in the vernacular.

The man turned towards him, and shook his head.

"I do not know. I heard no sound. But they saw me as I climbed the gate, and fired. Look!"

He held out his left hand. Blood was caked on the wrist.

"Only a scratch, but my heart was within an inch from where the bullet struck," the fugitive continued, "yet I have beaten the dogs!"

His face, seamed and lined with care, turned to Blake.

"They were watching for me night and day," he went on; "I have had to hide like a rat. But I beat them in the end. His Highness will not have the joy of watching Chandra Lal in terror."

"He who breaks the law must pay." said Blake in the whine of the class he was representing.

The fugitive threw back his head.

"Well spoken and well played!" he cried. "I was warned that thy disguise was beyond praise, and by Allah, they were right."

Tinker had started to his feet at a bound, and the dust-covered man backed away against a wall, stretching his hand, palm forward, out towards them.

"I am a friend," he whispered; "it is true that I know you are white men—but that makes it better for me."

Blake had not moved, but his eyes were as hard as granite as he watched the face of the intruder.

"Who are you?" he asked.

"My name is Chandra Lal, but that will convey nothing to thee. But when I tell you that I was a friend of two men, Carlac and Kew, here in Kashopore, and that I know of your mission here——"

Blake made a signal to Tinker, who stepped back to the heap of rugs. The detective nodded to Chandra Lal.

"You either know too much or too little, my friend," said Blake, in a grim voice and speaking in English. "Sit down, and if you are a friend, prove it."

Chandra Lal's eyes brightened, and he drew a breath of relief.

"I was not sure, even when I spoke," he muttered, sending a quick glance at Blake; "verily, you are the image of all fakirs. I had heard of your powers, Mr. Blake——"

"What, even the name?"

Despite his self-possession, Blake could not avoid the slight sigh of surprise. Chandra Lal smiled.

"There is but little mystery in it, sahib," he went on. "I have a brother in London, Gulga Lal, who writes to me. He sometimes does services for a certain Ben Dhur—whom may Allah destroy, for a cunning fox!"

"I do not know either of these two men," said Blake.

"That is so, and yet you know of them," said Chandra Lal quickly. "Ben Dhur is the man who tricked Carlac and Kew into going to his Highness. My brother helped him in the task—but my brother did not know that I had once served Carlac and Kew.

Little by little the story came out. Chandra Lal's brother, little dreaming that Chandra was in any way implicated in the matter, had written a long account of the trick. And he had added the information that, by some means or other, known only to himself, Ben Dhur had picked up, that Sexton Blake, Tinker, and Pedro had left for Kashopore, in a mad attempt to save the guilty men.

This last item of information must have leaked out through Flash Harry. Ben Dhur had, no doubt, set someone to talk to the fellow, and Flash Harry was a known talker

"And when did you receive this letter?"

"Only yesterday, protector," said Chandra Lal; "but some of the information was but stale news to me. I knew that the sahibs, Carlac and Kew, were prisoners at the palace, before it came. By Allah, I had plenty of proof of that."

He explained what had happened to Blake. Two days after his Highness's arrival, one of the ruffians who had been hired by Chandra Lal to carry out the mock attack on Colonel Bryce, had been brought before the rajah charged with another offence. In order to try and save his own skin the man had told the story of the trick that Kew and Carlac had played upon the British representative.

"I was warned just in the nick of time," said Chandra Lal; "a friend in the palace sent word to me that an order for my arrest had been made out. I hid from them until yesterday, when that letter was carried to me by one I could trust."

He looked at Blake.

"Twice I have caught sight of you and your companion, sahib," said Chandra Lal, "and when my brother menioned that there was also a dog with thee, and that thy powers of disguise were so world-famous, I guessed that the ragged fakir was no other than the great English detective. To-night, hearing that you lived at the Temple of the Vine—My friend passed thee on the roadway but two short hours ago. Thou wert talking to the daughter of the colonel-sahib.

Tinker emitted a grunt from his corner. Not even on the broad high road were they safe from listening ears.

"And so I determined to seek thee out," Chandra Lal ended; "for as thou art here as an enemy of the rajah's, it might be that thou wouldst help me to get away from his accursed State."

"And is that so difficult?"

"They say no man can get away from Puljara, if its ruler desires otherwise," he said. "I know that many have tried, but I have yet to hear of a success. So long as you remain here, all is well, but it is when the frontiers have to be passed that you find how strong is the arm of the prince."

"Which certainly sounds dashed cheerful so far as you and I are concerned, Pedro, old chap," Tinker whispered into the dog's ear. "It looks as though we're going to do this beggar-boy act for the rest of our natural lives."

But he smiled as he spoke, and his eyes travelled across to the strong, bearded face of the man whom he loved to look up to as master as well as friend.

"But if his Highness can hold the guv'nor—then he's a greater man than I think he is," the lad added, "and, meanwhile, no matter what this wily man says, my money's going on Baker Street every time."

CHAPTER 10
A Terrible Vengeance

The grey fingers of the dawn came out from the east, touching with delicate grace the dark shadowy towers of the palace. As the light increased a man lying on a heap of unsavoury rugs below the four foot wall of the round-shaped building on the roof of the tower that had once been occupied by Colonel Bryce, stirred uneasily, then sat up, casting the rugs to one side. The morning light was striking full on his face—and it revealed with pitiless accuracy the lines around the eyes, the sunken cheeks, the straggling, unkempt beard.

Slowly the huge man arose to his feet, stretching his arms as one who was still weary. In the centre of the narrow circle was an iron trapdoor, and beside it stood an earthenware jug and a platter filled with a heap of rice.

"Our usual supply," said Count Carlac aloud, as he stepped towards the jar.

He was hardly recognisable. His clothes hung about him in a limp manner, hinting of a gaunt frame beneath. His beard covered the broad, powerful jaw from ear to ear, and his eyes, hollow globes of light, were fixed, and had that rigid stare that comes to one who has spent long hours beneath a burning sun.

He lifted the jar to his lips and took a careful drink. He knew that it had to last all day. Then, holding the jar in one hand, he turned and crossed the narrow roof, to stoop over another bundle of rugs.

"Might as well waken up," said Carlac, "it is the only hours of the day, that are worth while."

The bundle of rugs moved, and out of their folds came the hawk-face of Kew. The change in him was not so apparent as on his heavier companion. The sallow cheeks were, perhaps, a trifle hollower, the eyes burned more brightly, but the hairless face and the hawk nose, the thin cruel lips and the lashless eyes, had not changed in their expression.

"I am not sure that I wanted you to waken me up," the thin, birdlike voice said; "I was dreaming—pleasant dreams." Carlac held out the jar.

"Dreams are not much use to us," he said, in his harsh voice; "we have to prepare for—for our day's task. And remember that that jar has to last us until to-morrow. They dare not supply us with more, even if they desired to do so."

Kew sipped at the fluid, then placed the jar carefully into a niche in the wall by his side, then, with a smothered groan he arose stiffly to his feet. Stepping to the low wall he peered down on to the roof of the tower. From the top of the wall to the flat tiles of the roof, was a drop of about eighteen feet. The wall of the roof of the tower was about five feet high, just high enough to prevent anyone in the courtyard below seeing what was going on on the other roof. Kew looked down into the moatlike gap that ran round their prison, and, keeping close to the wall, walked round the little circle of the roof.

"No, it is not there yet," he said.

"Of course not," Carlac returned; "it only appears when his Highness is there to watch the fun!"

He spoke words in a hard tone, but there was a touch of fear in his voice. He had seated himself on the iron trapdoor and was eating the rice from the platter, scooping it up with his fingers for want of a better utensil.

Kew dropped into a squatting position by his side and began to eat. A silence fell on the two men, and the sun, rising in its golden splendour, found them just finishing their meal. The fragments that remained were placed in the niche with the jar of precious water, then Carlac, drawing his rugs into the only part of the wall that afforded a slight shade, stretched himself out on them, his head resting on his arms.

Kew, restless spirit ever, began to walk up and down the stone flags, halting every now and then to cast a glance on to the other roof. Carlac watched him for a long while, then his impatience found vent to speech.

"You are only tiring yourself out, quite needlessly," he muttered. "If you will be advised by me you will save all your strength—you will need it soon enough."

Kew halted and shot a glance at his companion from beneath his hairless eyelids.

"I cannot sit down," he snapped; "leave me to do as I please. You will find me ready enough when the hour comes." He drew a quick breath.

"How are we going to get out of this?" he went on, his eyes glinting. "There must be some way of doing so. There never was a prison yet that could not be made to open."

Carlac nodded towards the trapdoor.

"There is the only means of escape," he pointed out, "it is not closed. A child can raise it—but neither you nor I dare to do so."

The hawk nose of Kew twitched as he looked at the trapdoor. He knew that it was unfastened—and knew that it had been left in that condition deliberately. Through it they could drop into the stores, and the doors were open that led from the stores on to the roof. On the roof of the tower was another black gap which hid the staircase that led down into the interior. Yes, it seemed easy enough for them to make a descent from their uncomfortable eerie.

But it was the guardian of the tower, the custodian lurking in one of the hidden rooms, that held them in a bondage light but remorseless.

Noon came and went. The sun grew hotter and hotter, Kew, wearied at last of his ceaseless pacing to and fro, had dropped into a sitting position, leaning against the wall. Suddenly a word from Carlac roused him.

The huge criminal had risen to his feet.

"Get ready, Kew," Carlac's deep voice said; "his Highness has just taken his seat for the show. Look, there he is!"

To the right there arose a tall tower. The tallest in the palace. A man's figure in dark robes came forward and leaned over the wall. The sun caught and reflected its light on a pair of glasses that the newcomer held in one jewelled hand.

A feeling of reckless—bravado came to Carlac, and hollowing his hand around his lips, he sent a loud hail across the stirless space.

"Salaam, you brown devil! We are still here, and ready!"

Kew, watching the figure of the rajah, saw the heavy lips go back in a swift smile, and the rajah made an answering gesture, a mocking return to the defiant salute.

Then from below the tower there came a chorus of noises, the shouting of men, and the beating of drums—a perfect demon's tattoo.

"Look out for it!" Carlac whispered. "they are driving it up from below."

He crossed the low parapet, and watched the black gap in the roof below. A long minute passed, then to the ears of the two men there came a low, savage snarl, which, starting on a deep note, rose to a grating, angry cry; up through the black gap there came the sleek, evil head of a huge tiger!

"Here it is!"

With an effortless bound the tiger came out of the gap, to turn and send a full-throated snarl back into the cool chamber below. A spear, with a bright steel point, flashed out at it, and its curved paw struck twice at the weapon, then, driven back, it sank snarling on to its haunches, and the iron trapdoor arose, blocking the gap. The tiger was a prisoner on the lower roof.

Carlac had drawn back, and he looked at Kew. The wizened professor had torn a strip of material from the rug, and was binding it round his thin fist.

"To-day it will be hungrier than it was yesterday," the professor's thin voice sounded; "and it will try all the harder. Better get ready."

Carlac had slipped out of his coat, and had rolled up his sleeves. Swiftly he bound up his right fist, from knuckles to elbow, using an old wrapping that he found beneath his own pile of rugs.

Sc-cr-cr!

The stroke of steel-like claws against the side of the circular store sent a swift thrill through the listeners.

"Already?" Carlac breathed, trying to force a smile. But his lips were bloodless, and the eyes had narrowed into mere pin-points. Instinctively they both moved towards the wall, and peered over—into the very jaws of the brute below. The man-eating tiger had stretched itself full length up the wall, its jaws gaping, its snake-shaped head back. For a long moment Kew stared down into the cold, unwavering eyes beneath. Animal hate glared up into the human hate, then the sinewy beast dropped lightly on the hot roof, and began to pad slowly round and round. And now began that terrible sentry-go, which the solitary witness on the high tower opposite had watched so intently for days.

Round and round went the sleek, striped shape, and round and round above it moved the two ragged, weary men. Not for one instant dared they withdraw their eyes from the brute. They knew what was going to happen, and as they crept round they had to be ever on the alert.

There was something terrible in the silence, broken only by the soft, shuffling sound of the two pairs of feet, as they moved round and round on the sun-scorched flags, and the softer pad, pad, of the great paws below.

"Ah!"

It was a half-strangled cry, almost of relief, that broke from Carlac's parched lips. For the tiger, maddened by the steady watch above, had crouched suddenly, and made his spring. Eighteen feet is a tremendous height even for such an agile brute as a tiger. The paws, with the great talons, curved against the top of the wall for a moment, slipping, clutching, seeking a hold. Carlac, leaping forward looked down into the great yellow jaws, then, with a courage that might have made him a worthy man had it not been for the criminal streak in him, the giant criminal sent his fist crashing between the brute's eyes.

The tiger seemed to know what was going to happen. There came up a thin, angry snarl, and one great paw flashed at the arm that had dealt it such a blow.

It was well for Carlac that his bandages were thick and tight. For as the tiger fell backwards on to the floor beneath, a great shred of cloth fluttered down with it, and Carlac staggered back against Kew, white to the lips.

"It—it nearly had me that time," the big man breathed. "It's as cunning as possible. It has tumbled to our game, and waits for the blow. Sooner or later it will get its hold, and you or I will follow it head first."

"That has yet to happen, my friend," Kew breathed. "And, meanwhile, the rajah seems to have enjoyed it."

He pointed towards the tower opposite. The rajah had dropped his glasses, and was clapping his hands together. The cold brutality of the action seemed to madden Carlac, for he shook his fists in the air, and raved out a torrent of words.

Kew caught his arm.

"Save your breath, Carlac," the professor said, in his grim way, "and save your strength for the other tiger, who, at the moment, is much the more dangerous of the two."

He had been watching from the wall all the time, and Carlac came to him, peering over. The great brute, snarling softly to itself, was running its red tongue, catlike, over its sleek skin. It had evidently been bruised a little by its backward fall. It halted in its operations, as Carlac's shadow fell across it. Carlac looked down into the small eyes, and noted the hate that blazed into them.

"There will be very little quarter for us when you do win," the huge criminal muttered to himself.

They watched the brute in silence. The tiger arose at last, and stretched itself, then started to cross the roof, heading for the higher wall. Instantly both men started into life.

Kew, snatching up a handful of rubble, cast it at the sleek back, while Carlac, leaning down as far as he dared, sent a mocking shout at the animal.

A wild snarl broke from the great cat's lips, and, wheeling round, it charged at the wall.

Its leap was a badly-judged effort, and it landed two feet below Carlac, who had swiftly drawn himself up again. The hot, fetid breath from the open jaws fanned his white cheek, and then, spitting and clawing desperately, the striped brute went down on the lower roof again.

Kew leaned against the wall, and wiped the sweat from his forehead. He was plainly suffering from a sudden rush of fear. "We must keep it away from that other wall," he broke out. "And, by Jove, that was a near shave!"

It was the other wall that they feared. For if once the tiger climbed on to its broad top, there would only be a narrow gap between it and the roof of the shed. Both Carlac and Kew realised that from the other wall it would be an easy matter for the powerful brute to launch itself clear across the gap, and up over their low wall, on to the circular roof. And when it did that, their fight came to an end. Unarmed, cut off from retreat, what chance would they have?

It was far better for them to goad the tiger into his furious attempts to leap from the roof below, than to let him find out the weak spot in their defence.

Slowly the sun moved on over the brazen sky. The sweat was pouring from Carlac's lean cheeks, and the long ordeal was beginning to tell on him. Three times within the same number of minutes did the tiger attempt to reach his goal, and once; for a terrible moment, his head was level with the wall, while one vicious paw struck out to right and left, with that swift, deft aim that marks the attack of all animals of the cat tribe.

It was Kew who saved them then. Carlac had been sent reeling by one of the vicious swings, and in another moment the tiger would have scrambled on to the wall, when Kew, stooping suddenly, picked up the platter containing the remains of the rice heap, and with a shrill scream cast the plate into the brute's eyes.

The rice had been highly spiced and peppered—in itself a cunning attempt at torture, for the seasoning engendered a terrible thirst. But now it served another purpose, for the pepper stung the brute's eyes, and, half-blinded, it reeled from its hold. Kew, rushing in then, sent it down once more by a blow from his wrapped-up fist.

A tornado of cries and snarls followed, and the tiger, rolling over and over on the roof, clawed and scraped at itself in a wild fury.

It was only then that the rajah, bending forward slightly, gave any signs of anger. His hand was raised, and his voice sounded. A moment later and the hard grate of a bolt being removed came to the ears of the panting, exhausted men on the sun-baked roof. Carlac, tottering to the wall, glanced downward. The iron trap-door shot out of sight, revealing the black gap.

The tiger seemed to hear the sound almost as soon as his still triumphant foe, for he arose, and with a couple of bounds had reached the trap-door.

His sinewy limbs folded beneath him, and a moment later he had vanished into his lair.

"All—all over for this afternoon!" Carlac croaked, through parched lips.

His face was drawn and bloodless, and has he leaned against the wall, Kew realised that there was yet another danger to be met. Sooner or later this eternal fight against such terrible odds would have its effect on the brain of the giant criminal. Carlac's strength of arm made him the chief guard of the little tower, and the greater part of the struggle was carried out by him. But Kew knew now that the ordeal was sapping away more than the mere strength of his companion. Carlac's eyes were fixed and staring, and his lips were moving, although no sound came from them.

"Show's over—show's over," he said, finding his voice again. "The next performance will take place at the same time to-morrow."

He reeled forward, and with a quick bound Kew was at his side. The professor's hand was stained with blood, when he looked at it. Carlac managed to reach his heap of rugs, then collapsed, and Kew, after a hasty examination, saw that there was a great wound running down the whole length of the big forearm. The tiger's claws had left its mark.

The wizened criminal went to work to bind and clean the wound. Perhaps it was as much self-preservation as anything else that made Kew put out all his skill in the little act. He arranged a rug over one part of the wall, so that Carlac might have some shade, sprinkling water on the rug, to make it cooler beneath.

If Carlac became feverish all was lost. Kew knew that he himself, alone and unaided, could not hope to beat back the incessant attacks of the fury-filled, hungry animal. That afternoon the attacks had followed each other in quick succession, proving that the animal was getting mad with hunger. Soon it would reach the ravenous stage, and not even the opening of the trap would make it vanish into the cooler rooms beneath. Unless he had Carlac to help him then, the game was up.

Right through the rest of the long, hot hours, Kew sat beside the little shelter, tending the man who lay breathing heavily beneath it. Now and again the wizened professor would raise the edge of the rug and glance at the flushed face, with its black, tangled beard. Occasionally he would reach for the jar of water, and, moistening a rag, would place it over Carlac's broad forehead.

It was a fight with everything against Kew, and yet, when the day came to a close, his touch on Carlac's wrist found it cool and the pulse normal. Carlac came back from his heavy sleep to see the soft stars shining above, and the birdlike figure of Kew silhouetted against the sky, like some fantastic picture.

"Feeling better?"

The voice was hard enough, and Carlac sat up.

"Yes, I'm all right." He stretched out his hand, and Kew held the jar forward. Carlac emptied it with one long pull.

"It strikes me that I was pretty near to collapse," the tall criminal went on. "The pace was a little too hot for me, I suppose."

He arose to his feet, and went across to the wall. All around him arose the high buildings of the palace, shutting out all hope of a glimpse at the outer world. The faint lights from the city shone into the sky, and Carlac stretched his arms out in a gesture of impotent rage.

"It hardly seems worth while," he said, turning to Kew. "Why not put an end to it."

He pointed into the darkness below. They could easily find a way out of their torture, if they chose.

Kew's cackling laughter jarred on the still summer air.

"Not while I retain my senses!" he put in. "While there is life there is always hope! The tiger can be faced. But your way is a poor one, and gives us no earthly chance."

He came to Carlac's side, and rested his chin on his cupped hands, his elbows on the low parapet. Far away in the distance arose the low hills, over which the high-road ran. Along the shadow of the hills there came gliding into view a little snake of light, winding to and fro, and presently they heard, far off, the shrill, clear whistle of a train.

"That is our road to freedom," said Kew. "If we could only reach the railway——"

The snake of light crawled on and vanished. Carlac, who had been watching it closely, suddenly reached out his hand and caught Kew in a fierce grip.

"Look!" he said. "Over there—just beneath the hills! I thought I saw a light! Yes, there it is again!"

In the blue dusk a light appeared, vanished—appeared, vanished. Long flashes and short flashes.

"It has nothing to do with us," said Kew.

But Carlac was able to read Morse Signalling, and he began to count the flashes.

"Long, short, long, short—C. Short long—A. Short, long, short—R."

A deep breath came from him.

"Keep quiet!" he whispered, in a hoarse voice. "They are spelling out my name!"

Kew stiffened into attention at once, and watched the light as it flashed and faded, now with a long interval of light, then with a short of one.

"Remember the words!" whispered Carlac. "I will spell them out:

"'Carlac. Chandra Lal sends greetings. Have courage. Send reply if possible.'"

Kew darted across to his heap of rugs, and returned with a little metal box. It was one of those petrol self-lighting patents, and had escaped the careful search of his custodians owing to the fact that it had slipped into the torn lining of his coat.

One of the rugs, almost tinder-alike, thanks to the heat of the sun, was torn into strips, and Kew released the spring of the box. A little flame leaped out, and was held to the strip. Leaping on the parapet, Kew waved the flaming rag round and round above his head until it had burned itself out.

There was a long moment of waiting; then, away in the distance, came an answering flash, proving that the flaming signal had been seen.

Kew dropped on to the circular floor of his prison, and peered up into the face of his companion.

"Well, what about the easy way out now?" he asked, in his quiet, sardonic tones.

Carlac folded his hands and laughed silently.

"That is all over and done with," he returned. "But I am puzzled! Chandra Lal may have dictated that message, but I'll swear he never sent it!"

"Why not?"

"He knows nothing of telegraphy," said Carlac. "'I know him well enough! The hand that signalled that message was an expert's."

"But what does it matter?" the professor put in drily. "We have received the message, and that is quite enough for me!'

"They must have been nine or ten miles away," Carlac went on. "the country round Kashopore is as flat as a billiard-table, and they would have to travel to the foothills before they could reach a place where their light could be seen and read."

"They have taken a risk," the professor returned. "for if we could read it, so could others!"

"Unless they knew the exact position of this tower, and trained the light on it," Carlac went on. "In that case, only the people in the palace and around its immediate vicinity could have seen the light."

He wheeled on his companion.

"And by Jove, they have chosen the very best hour to escape detection!" he went on. "they change the guard just now, and the night watch relieves the day one. His Highness and his staff are at their evening meal. Yes, it is the very best moment they could have chosen!"

There was another long silence; then Kew shrugged his shoulders.

"It is all very well," he said slowly; "but, even now, I fail to see how Chandra Lal can help us. He was clever enough in organising a mock attack, but I don't think him quite capable of tackling the rajah and his bodyguard!"

Carlac's bearded face was wearing a grim, intent expression.

"There is someone else behind Chandra Lal!" he said. "I'll swear to that!"

"But who can it be? Not a soul in the world knows what has happened to us! At least, I mean, not a soul from our part of the world. Chandra Lal may have found out about us, but England is the only place we could expect real help from, and I doubt very much if they would even trouble to come to our rescue if they knew our plight. You forget that we are what is termed law-breakers—beyond hope of redemption. If we die to please the whim of a rajah, no one will trouble themselves very much."

His hard, cynical tones grated on Carlac. The latter pointed out to where the point of light had shone like a star of hope in the darkness.

"Someone out there has other views concerning us, Kew." the huge criminal returned, "and there are white men who would not hear of others being tortured in this diabolical way, even although they were as we are, outside the pale of the law."

Kew turned away on his heel, with a shrug of his shoulders.

"Have it your way!" he snapped. "But, candidly, I do not build up hope on Chandra Lal's signals. We are only sure of one thing, and that is that to-morrow will bring his Highness and the tiger, each of them as hungry for blood as they possibly can be. That is what we have to face, and the rest is in the regions of wild dreams and fancies."

He walked across to his heap of rugs, and stretched out on them. Carlac remained standing beside the wall, his eyes turning now and again towards the darker mass in the distance which marked the bulk of the hills. But there was no further signalling, although he waited for over an hour, and at last he was forced to turn away and seek his pile of rugs.

In its way, the torture which the rajah was inflicting on these men, was a masterpiece. The anticipation, the certain knowledge that as each afternoon came so would the gaunt, hungry brute appear, to prowl round and round the little store, seeking for a chance to leap, the long-drawn agony of the spell of waiting, was as cruel as was the actual fight that took place. And day by day the tiger would grow fiercer and fiercer, as its hunger increased, while day by day the two wretched men on the roof above would grow weaker and weaker, until the end came when, too powerless to check the climbing brute, they fell victims to his powerful paws.

That was the culminating feast that his Highness the Rajah of Puljara, stripped now of the veneer of civilisation that cloaked him when abroad, looked forward to.

We cannot judge him, for the East has laws of its own. Kew and his confederate had broken what was almost a Divine law so far as the rajah was concerned. They had set thieving and sacrilegious hands upon a treasured relic. Their deaths would have to be examples to others, grim warnings of what might happen to rogues who plotted against the might of their prince.

But this time his Highness was to be baulked of his anticipated revenge. Kew and Carlac, after all, had been punished enough in the dread days that they had already spent. The crowning horror was fated not to happen.

And the being who was to bring that miracle about was a ragged fakir who at that moment was striding along a narrow cart-track that ran from the railway station beside the foothills down to the plains around Kashopore. Beside him stepped a lighter figure, and in the grasses in front there appeared now and again the sinewy shadow of a great hound.

It was Sexton Blake and Tinker returning to the Temple of the Vine, and any doubt that Blake might have had concerning the fate of the two men had vanished now, for it was he who had sent the signal, naming Carlac, and had received the waved reply. Chandra Lal had picked out the exact spot from whence the light would be seen on the little tower, but the Hindu had not stayed behind to mark the result of the signals.

Capture meant death so far as Chandra Lal was concerned, and he was taking no chances.

"The English sahibs are always brave," was his explanation; "but a coward lives the longer, and life is sweet."

CHAPTER 11

How Blake Entered the Palace

"You seem jolly pleased to get rid of us, Muriel!" Lieutenant Vernon said, with a light laugh. "I feel the green-eyed monster, Jealousy, rising in me!"

He looked down at the lovely face of his sweetheart, and Muriel returned his smile.

"Now, that's just like a man!" she said quickly. "You come to me and say that dad and you decided to have a day's sport with some friend, and that you may not return to-night. Although I ought to feel hurt and pained at your neglect, I hide all that, and even help you get ready, and because I do that, you promptly accuse me of some dark motive!"

Her lover put his arm round her.

"But there is something, Muriel!" he urged. "I can see it in your eyes! They are shining like stars with something that looks to me like suppressed excitement. And why do you spend most of your time on the roof, watching the palace?"

A tell-tale colour arose to Muriel's cheeks for a moment, but she laughed the shrewd question aside. Vernon was right, however, and Muriel was really glad when, an hour later, the tall, erect figure of her father, mounted on a fine white Arab, cantered throught the gateway of the quiet Residency, followed by Vernon. The young officer turned in his saddle, and waved his hand to Muriel, who was watching their departure from the roof. The girl fluttered her handkerchief in reply; then the two riders vanished, and Muriel dropped back into the soft cushions in the deep easy-chair.

"Thank goodness they have gone!" she decided. "That sounds frightfully wicked and all that, but I don't mean any harm. Only I must have the place to myself if I am to help Mr. Blake!"

A message had come across to the British representative that the rajah was about to send over a basket of fruit. Muriel received that message, and, knowing that Colonel Bryce was going to start at once on his hunting expedition, the girl kept the message to herself. Her father, punctilious always in matters of these kinds, might have postponed his departure in order to receive the rajah's gift in person, and this was just exactly what Muriel desired to avoid.

It was about noon when the messenger from the palace arrived. Muriel saw the tall, uniformed figure, with two black servants following behind, bearing the great basket, come through the doorway. She leaned forward, stared for a moment, then arose to her feet with a quick gesture of satisfaction. Her eyes were bright, and there was a mischievous smile on her lovely lips.

"Abul—at last."

For it was the stalwart trooper that the rajah had chosen as messenger this time.

Muriel crossed the room, and went down into the cool reception-chamber, seating herself in the big chair usually occupied by her father.

"When the king is away, the king's daughter takes his place, I suppose," the girl thought.

There was always a certain ceremony attached to the giving and receiving of the gifts.

A knock sounded on the door, and the fat major-domo of the house entered, his chubby face full of a tremendous dignity. As head-servant to the British representative, he was no small personage in his own estimation.

"A messenger from his Highness, the maharajah, desires speech with her excellency, the mem-sahib," he droned, in a nasal tone.

Muriel always preserved a very straight countenance during these little ceremonial affairs.

261

"Tell the messenger of his Highness to enter."

Round spun the fat butler, to draw aside the heavy folds of the curtain.

"Enter, O messenger from his Highness, et cetera, et cetera."

The stalwart figure of Abul, looking every inch a soldier in the neat uniform of blue and gold, strode over the threshold. Already the rajah's servant had heard the clear voice of Muriel, and the tan on his cheek was slightly pale as he bowed low before her.

"Greetings and salutations, your excellency!" said Abul, in a voice that had an undercurrent of apology in it." "The Prince of Puljara desires thee to accept this unworthy gift from his hands."

The two black slaves had placed the basket on the floor. Muriel, rising to her feet, went up to the basket. Exquisite grapes, melons and exotic fruits came out of the basket, each in a beautiful dish of silver filigree-work.

Murmuring her thanks, Muriel accepted the gift in the name of her father, and the two black slaves followed the butler out of the reception-room. Abul was about to do the dame when Muriel, with a quick movement, touched him on the arm.

"There is no hurry for a moment, Abul," she said, a smile on her lips. "I want to have a word with you."

She went back to the big chair and seated herself in a graceful, easy pose. One slender arm was resting on the high arm of the carved chair, and her chin was on her rosy palm. Against the carved black wood of the chair she made a wonderfully beautiful picture of gracious, womanly beauty.

Abul, standing ill at ease in the centre of the room, had only ventured to give one glance in her direction; then his eyes were fixed on the carpet, and remained so.

"Why have you deserted us, Abul?"

The sweet voice had just a little thread of regret in it, and there was something plaintive in the question. Abul stirred uneasily.

"I have been busy, mem-sahib," he began. "I—I——"

"When I was a small child you used to say that you were my slave and bondsman, Abul," Muriel went on; "you used to swear that there was no service in the world that you would not do for me. Have you changed since then?"

The big trooper drew a deep breath.

"I have not changed," he returned; "but I——"

"You have changed, Abul," the girl went on relentlessly. "You have played the part of a false friend. Oh, Abul, I never thought that you would be capable of such a thing!"

The brown fists of the trooper were clenched, and his face was twitching with emotion. Abul had realised that this interview had to happen sooner or later. The man had realised that this interview had to happen sooner or later. The man had a great, fervent admiration for this sweet, kindly English girl, and had dreaded the moment when he would have to stand in front of her clear eyes. He had tried his best to get out of the duty which had been imposed upon him, but the head of the household had insisted on his taking the duty, and as the rajah himself was not to be seen that morning, Abul could do nothing else but obey.

"The mem-sahib uses harsh words to her servant," the tall trooper said.

"Yet are they not justified, Abul?"

The turbanned head was nodded.

"Yes, they are justified," he returned, disdaining to shield himself behind a lie. "Yet the mem-sahib must know that Abul also had to be loyal to his prince."

Muriel smiled.

"Yes, I know, Abul, and for that reason I have forgiven you. You told the rajah of what had befallen the treasure-chest; but I forgive you."

The trooper leaped forward and dropped on one knee, raising the girl's hand to his lips.

"The mem-sahib understands," he said, in thick tones. "Abul would die for her, but he could not face his master with a secret in his heart and a lie on his lips."

"True, Abul," said Muriel, who secretly sympathised now with the man, "and you are forgiven."

He arose to his feet, his brown, handsome face alight, as though a great weight had been lifted from his sterling, honest soul."

"Thy slave had been troubled sore over this matter," he admitted, and thy forgiveness has healed him."

Muriel leaned forward.

"But I have not yet forgiven his Highness," she said, with girlish candour. "Why does he keep us away from the palace? I think it is mean of him!"

She spoke in English now, and Abul smiled.

"Thy old quarters have been changed," he explained; "all the furnishing and fittings have been removed. His Highness found it so on his return, and has made another use of the tower."

"Yes, and I know the use he has made of it," the girl went on. He has turned a great, savage tiger out into our rooms. Oh, I do think that that is very unkind of him!"

She had been watching Abul's face, and she saw the quick, startled look that flashed for a moment in the man's eyes.

"A tiger, mem-sahib?"

"Yes, Abul—a tiger!"

A little line of annoyance appeared between her smooth brows.

"Are you going to deny that?" she went on. "Are you still ready to speak to with a tongue that lies?"

It was almost pitiful to watch the expression on the trooper's strong face. Loyalty to his ruler tugged him one way, while the old affection that he had in his heart for this winsome young girl tugged in the opposite direction.

"Mem-sahib," he broke out, "I—I would not lie to thee."

"Then there is a tiger in our old quarters?"

The trooper nodded his head.

"Some other person has told thee, so that cannot be laid at my door," he returned, half to himself.

Until that moment Muriel had not been sure that Blake's extraordinary story was correct. But Abul, by his admission, had proved it, and the look of wonder that came into the girl's eyes made him lower his own.

"But—but it is so strange," Muriel went on. "Why should his Highness allow a great hungry beast to roam at will through those lovely rooms? Surely there was room enough for it in his tiger-house?"

Abul shrugged his shoulders.

"I am not in the confidence of my prince," he said; a blank look coming over his face. "The mem-sahib must ask his Highness for the reason of all this."

"I will when I get a chance," the high-spirited girl returned. "But his Highness is just the same as you are, Abul—he will not see me."

Abul's eyes smiled.

"The prince perhaps fears that he may say too much—even as I fear," was his reply.

Muriel leaned forward.

"I know that there is something being hid away from me and from my father, the colonel," she said, in a quiet, low tone. "And it must be something evil, or there would be no reason to hide it from our knowledge. If you should see your master, Abul, you can tell him that I wonder at the change that has come to him. I always looked on him as a prince whose every action was worthy—who would not stoop to lie and deceive. He has dropped from that high position in my mind, and I feel that it is better that we should live outside the palace while this black mood is upon him."

"I—I will try to deliver thy message."

The girl bowed.

"And were it not for the fact that Kashopore would wonder at it, I would send back to him all his gifts," she went on, her fine eyes kindling. "If we are not to be admitted to his friendship, we do not want the gifts from his table. We are not beggars at his gateway!"

Abul flushed beneath the scorn in her tongue.

"It is not in that light that his Higness send the gifts," he broke out. "I know that he still regrets the change that has taken place, and looks forward to the hour when the colonel-sahib can return again to the palace."

"The colonel-sahib could return to-day," Muriel put in quickly. "It is his Highness who makes the delays."

And then Abul was tempted to say more than he ought to have done.

"Let the mem-sahib have just a little more patience," he urged. "I know that within the next day or so all will be put right, By to-morrow, his Highness expects——"

He came to a halt swiftly, and his face flushed. Muriel caught at the meaning of his words, but cleverly enough, did not continue to question him on that line.

"And when shall I see thee again, ungrateful?" she asked, her mood changing swiftly into a kindly, bantering one.

"As soon as I can get away from my duties," Abul returned eagerly. "I have heard that the ruins of an old city have been found in the hills, full of wonders from the past. Perhaps in the near future the mem-sahib would like her slave to show her these ruins?"

These two had been on many similar expeditions together, for Colonel Bryce knew that in Abul, Muriel had a guardian who would gladly give his life in her defence.

"That will be splendid!" the girl cried, clasping her hands together. "I will let you know when I can go."

Abul drew up and salaamed again.

"I must return to the palace now, mem-sahib," he said, "and I have been told to state that his Highness will send a further gift of some silken stuffs that have been brought to him from Kashmir to the mem-sahib herself this evening. The messenger will arrive an hour after sunset.

He went out through the doorway, and Muriel sat for along time thinking deeply. When she did move at last it was to go across to the little bureau in the corner where she wrote a long note. A silver-toned bell brought the stout major-domo into the room.

"I want thee to do me a service," said the girl. "I want to consult a fakir, a most wise man, who lives in the Temple of the Vine. Take this letter to him, and hear his reply. I want him to come hither this afternoon, if he is at leisure."

"It will be as the mem-sahib commands," the head servant returned; "and I will deliver the message with my own hands."

The old fellow was as good as his word, and late in the afternoon the ragged figure of the fakir came through the gateway of the Residency, to be led across the courtyard by one of the servants and up to the roof, where Muriel awaited his coming.

Blake murmured a greeting, and dropped into the easy squatting position which the native of India always uses.

"What did the white girl want with him?" he asked, so that the servant who was retiring might hear.

"I have heard your wisdom and piety," Muriel returned, "and would hear some advice to profit me."

The servant had vanished by now, and her mood changed. She leaned forward, her lips apart, excitement shining in her eyes.

"Oh, I do wish that you had come a little sooner," she breathed, "the rajah has been on his tower again, and I know that something has happened. He seemed more excited to-day, and he was clapping his hands together as though the spectacle pleased him. What it is, Mr. Blake?"

Blake's eyes glinted through the heavy brows.

"I think I can enlighten you on that point, Miss Bryce," he said. "But, first of all, have you found out what I asked?"

"Oh, about the tiger. Yes, you were quite right. Abul came to-day, and I made him practically admit it."

"Abul—eh?" said Blake with a smile. "I don't suppose that he enjoyed the interview exactly."

Muriel Bryce answered his smile with a quick, mischievous pout.

"I gave him a good talking to, if that's what you mean," she returned; but I didn't really get a lot of information out of him. He did say, though, that by to-morrow there would be some sort of change. I couldn't quite fathom what he meant——"

"By to-morrow," the disguised detective repeated. "That is worth knowing. It means that whatever has to be done must be done at once."

He looked at Muriel Bryce for a moment, then he leaned forward.

"I said I would take you into my confidence as soon as I found it possible, Miss Bryce," said Blake; "well I am now going to keep that promise. I came here to Kashopore because I was practically assured in my own mind that his Highness had carried out a most daring abduction. When he left England so hurriedly, it was to prevent any inquiries being made concerning his movements. At this present moment there are two white men prisoners in his hands, and they are being tortured."

"Oh, Mr. Blake!"

"They are men who deserved punishment of some sort, but not of the kind that his Highness is inflicting on them," the stern voice went on.

"They are criminals, and you have had experience of them both."

Muriel's eyes lighted up suddenly.

"You—you don't mean those two scoundrels who tried to steal the rajah's treasure-chest?"

"Carlac and Kew are at present prisoners in the palace, and their quarters are in the tower that you used to occupy."

For a moment Muriel sat back, breathless with bewilderment; then a sudden thought came to her making her start with horror.

"But you said the—the tiger was there?"

So it is, Miss Bryce," the calm reply came. "Abul himself could not deny that."

"I don't understand," Muriel went on. "If Carlac and Kew are prisoners, and the tiger is there with them, how can they live?"

"That is the only point that I have not yet cleared up," said Blake; "but I have proof that the two criminals are held prisoners in the tower, for I signalled to them and received a reply. To me it seems as though the rajah has evolved some terrible form of torture, and——"

"Oh, of course, I think I see now," the girl broke out. "He watches something that takes place every afternoon. To-day I saw him, and he seemed more excited than usual. He clapped his hands as though applauding some act or other—and it was in the direction of the smaller tower that he was looking."

Blake nodded his head.

"I have no doubt but what you are correct, Miss Bryce," the detective returned. "Carlac and Kew are giving his Highness some form of savage entertainment, and the scene of that entertainment is the top of the tower. But what it is is more than I can say."

"But how terrible!" Muriel said, with a shudder. "Don't you see that the man-eater must be playing some part in it? That is why Abul was so afraid when he saw that I knew."

She arose to her feet, and caught Blake's ragged robe.

"You must do something, Mr. Blake," the tender-hearted girl went on. "I know that these two men deserve punishment, but not of the type that the rajah would give them. Even death is better than long-drawn torture. Oh, you must try and save them."

"That is what I am here to do," came the quiet response. "and to-night, by some means or other, I must get into the palace. I have found a native who is friendly, and he will help me—although I cannot rely on him, for at heart he is an arrant coward."

Muriel was silent for a moment, then she clapped her hands together.

"Oh, I think it could be managed," she broke out; "and you would not need to rely on anyone."

She went up to Blake and lowered her voice.

"The rajah is sending another gift this evening," she explained. "Abul told me to expect it to arrive about an hour after sunset. The messenger will go back to the palace as soon as he has delivered his gift."

She halted and looked at Blake.

"The sentinel on the palace gate will be expecting the messenger to return," she went on; "and if someone—someone bold enough, and clever enough, could make a prisoner of that messenger, there is no reason why he should not take his place."

Blake looked up, a glint in his eyes.

"Excellent, Miss Muriel," he said. "That is a scheme worth studying. Will this messenger be accompanied by anyone?"

"I shouldn't think so," Muriel returned. "You see, we have had the ceremonial visit this morning. The rajah takes good care to send his messenger through the main streets, so that the people may see how friendly he is with the British representative. But this other gift is more of a personal one to myself, and I should think that the one who brings it will come alone."

They plunged into an eager discussion, and at last reached a definite plan. Muriel was to receive the gift from the messenger, and was to detain him for a few moments. When he made his departure, she was to hurry to the roof at once, and show a light for a second or so.

"But you will be careful, Mr. Blake," Muriel urged; "you must take no risks."

"I will take no risks that I can avoid," said Blake, as he arose to his feet, "and now, I have one more request to make. I want a large piece of raw meat, the bigger the better. You can make it appear as a sort of gift to me."

Muriel had not the faintest idea why the detective should make such an extraordinary request, but she did not stop to ask idle questions. One of her servants were summoned, and returned presently with a great chunk of deer-flesh, wrapped in a sheet, which he handed to the disguised detective. Blake, with another low salaam and murmur of thanks, left Muriel, and followed the servant across the roof. The girl watched until the ragged figure crossed the courtyard beneath, finally vanishing through the big gateway.

"I hope he will succeed,' she murmured to herself; "but, oh, I am afraid. The odds against him are so many."

She spent the rest of the afternoon a prey to a hundred fears, and, when the messenger from the rajah was announced, Muriel was almost inclined to prevent the man from leaving, so that Blake might not be able to put his scheme into action.

She kept the messenger, a keen-eyed household servant of the palace, talking as long as she dared, but finally she had to let him go. As soon as the man left the chamber, Muriel darted up to the roof, an oil lamp in her hand. She held it aloft and swung it slowly once, twice, over her head.

A long-drawn cry came to her ears—the cry that a moslem priest gives from the minaret—but Muriel knew that it was no priestly voice that sounded.

Her signal had been seen and answered. The girl dropping on to her knees beside the deep chair, found a little prayer coming from her heart.

"May he prove successful," was the burden of her pleading.

The messenger, swinging along beside a high wall, had little fear of anything happening to him. He wore the blue livery of the rajah, and that was sufficient to protect him from any of the rogues and robbers who infested the lower quarters of the city.

He reached an angle of the wall and turned to his left. As he did so, there arose, almost at his feet, the shadowy figure of a ragged beggar. A bowl was thrust out at him, and the whining voice intoned:

"Alms, for the love of Allah, alms!"

"Out of my way, carrion," the rajah's servant cried. "I am in haste."

He stepped forward and knocked the begging bowl out of the man's hand. Instantly the crouching figure stooped lower, and a pair of wiry arms were suddenly wrapped around the servant's thighs. With one swing the man was lifted clean off his feet, and was sent backwards on to the hard roadway, the thud with which he struck the ground, knocking the senses out of him.

"Quick, sahib," a low voice whispered, and a door creaked in the wall. The beggar caught at the senseless servant, and with a powerful pull dragged him through the dark doorway, while the door clanged behind him. A moment later there was a spluttering of a match and a lamp was lighted. Blake, for it was the detective who had carried out the neat trick, promptly stooped and adjusted a bandage around the palace servant's eyes.

A gag followed, and then the man was hurriedly stripped of his blue robes and badge. Chandra Lal wrapped the ragged robe which Blake had discarded, around the gagged man; then a straw rope was produced, and the servant's hands and feet were tied tightly, and he was lifted on to a pile of carpets that stood in one corner of the chamber.

"He will be safe until morning," Chandra Lal whispered. "And by that time thou wilt have succeeded—or failed."

Blake had studied the features of the servant, and he drew forward a little leather bag. First, the straggling beard of the fakir was removed, then Blake adjusted over his upper lip a strip of black, soft hair, following this, by removing the heavy shaggy brows, and white unkempt wig. A close fitting wig of sleek hair was selected from the assortment that the leather bag contained. Chandra Lal, leaning back with the lamp between his hands, watched the swift transformation take place. At the end of it he drew a deep breath.

"Allah himself would not know thee," Chandra Lal breathed. "Thou art the twin-brother of the man we have just taken."

And, indeed, in the blue livery, and his face altered with the inimitable skill that he possessed, Blake had cast off all traces of his fakir disguise. He was the palace servant, sleek, well-fed, arrogant.

He stepped towards the door and opened it.

"You know what to do, Chandra Lal," he said quietly. "Go to the Temple of the Vine, and wait there for my assistant. When he comes, you will do as he demands."

Chandra Lal salaamed.

"I am the protector's slave," he said, "and may Allah aid the protector on this great task before him."

As Blake passed through the doorway he stooped and picked up a bulky package, which he slipped beneath the blue robe. In the street he took to the centre of it, and walked on boldly until he reached the high wall of the palace. Just before he came to the gates, a figure moved in the darkness beside the wall.

"Out of my way, dog?" said Blake, waving the figure aside. But a cunning eye might have noted that his hand, as it made the gesture, threw something into the lap of the huddled figure. Tinker clutched at the little bag that gave forth a musical tinkle, and the lad's eyes followed the upright one of his master as it turned through the gateway. there was a long pause, and Tinker rising to his feet shuffled past the gates, glancing inside as he did so. The door of the great guardroom was ajar, and the tall figure of a trooper was outlined in the flood of light. Tinker saw the blue robe just vanishing into the shadow, and a breath of relief came from the lad's lips.

He's got through the guard—and that's a good omen," he muttered. "Now it's time for me to make a move."

He turned into the main street of the city, and presently found himself in a dark, musty smelling courtyard. There was a fire burning in the centre, and around it were gathered a number of squatting forms, while behind them Tinker could see a row of horses standing against a wall.

"I am in search of Selim, the horse-dealer," Tinker said as he reached the fire.

A tall figure arose from the circle.

"Thou has brought the rest of the money?"

Tinker swung the little bag forward.

"It is here," he said.

Selim moved away from the fire, picking up a brand as he went. Reaching the wall the horse-dealer stopped for a moment while he counted the coins. Apparently the amount was correct, for he slipped them back into the bag and pocketed it.

"They are ready for thee," he said. "Five of my best horses, saddled and fed."

He began to move the steeds tethered to the wall, and presently he had rounded up five of them. Each saddled and bridled native fashion. Tinker swung into the saddle of the mount nearest to him, and Selim gave him the gathered bridles of the others.

"Salaam," the horse-dealer cried.

And Tinker replied:

"Salaam to thee."

He rode off through the dusk out of the yard and on towards the East Gate. The clatter of the horse's hoofs echoed and re-echoed, and long before he reached the gate, the guard had turned out to stop him.

"No mounted man can leave Kashopore without the permission of his Highness the rajah," the turbanned subahdar said. "Surely thou knowest that."

Tinker slipped from the saddle. He had been warned about this and had his plans ready.

"Where can I leave the horses until the morning?"

"Take them back to where they came from," was the reply.

"I bought them from a travelling horse-dealer," said Tinker, "and he has gone towards Delhi, so I cannot do as thou would'st have me."

Now as the reader may remember, there was accommodation for belated travellers who wish to come into Kashopore, but, naturally enough, the rajah had not thought of making similar arrangements for anyone wishing to go out. The subahdar, a rather dull-witted man, scratched his bearded chin thoughtfully.

"I will tie them to the wall here and await the morning," said Tinker cheerfully; "or perhaps there is room for them in the guard-room."

A growl went up at this.

"Our guard-room is no stable, impudent," the leader of the guard returned.

"Then what am I to do?"

Someone behind the leader ventured a suggestion. The night was rather chill and they were wasting time out there.

"Why not let him stable his horses outside in the dak-bungalow and let him remain within the city until morning," the trooper suggested. "After all, he will not venture to try any trickery upon us if his horses are taken from him."

And this was the plan finally agreed upon. The horses were walked through the gate and stabled in the empty shed behind the dak-bungalow that stood about fifty yards away from the gates.

"Come back in the morning at sunrise," said the subahdar. "Thy horses will be safe enough."

Tinker backed away.

"I call thy men to witness that thou art responsible if anything happens to my steeds," he returned as he wheeled and vanished into the darkness again.

The subahdar little dreamed that his action had been exactly anticipated by the brain of the keen man who had arranged the scheme. The horses were safely out of the city, and so, one strict law of the rajah's had already been broken. The means of escape were there and waiting, and now all that was left to do was to find the way.

In this case the more difficult task of the two.

CHAPTER 12
Rescued!

The palace of the rajah was something of a rabbit-warren, so many and devious were its passages and courts. Blake might easily have wasted the best part of the night in wandering about the place, but he had not neglected that detail. Chandra Lal had supplied him with close directions and he had also drawn a rough sketch, giving the position of the tower which Blake had to find.

Once inside the big palace the detective found it easy enough to avoid detection. He crossed one spacious court with a fountain in the centre, passed through an archway, and came into the wider inner court. There were subdued lights shining from some building on the left, and Blake, keeping below the balcony, drew near to a lighted doorway. Presently a servant came hurrying past him, bearing a silver salver on which a quantity of fruit was placed. Blake watched the man vanish into a door, and the fact that other servants laden with various dishes came and went through the door told Blake that it was the banqueting hall, and that his Highness was enjoying one of those interminable meals that the Eastern potentate think so necessary to his high dignity.

Blake went on and made a quiet examination of the various sides of the square. He found the place he was in search of at last—a strip of ornamental garden leading to a lily pond. At the end of the lily pond was little ornamental bridge of marble, which spanned a sluice-gate. A narrow channel of water ran beyond the bridge under a dark archway on which a tower had been built. According to Chandra Lal's instructions, this channel led out to the river, and was the only possible means of escape from the palace. Chandra Lal, however, had never been in the position to judge whether the possibility existed.

"I suppose he is right," Blake muttered, glancing down into the dark channel, "but it does not seem a very promising way."

He turned and glanced back into the centre of the courtyard, where the square bulk of the tower arose. The tower in which Carlac and Kew were held prisoners.

It was about fifty yards away, not a very long sprint for anyone to tackle. If he could get the men out they could make at once for the ornamental bridge and hide beneath it, then, each in their turn, could tackle the sluice-gate, climbing it and dropping into the deep channel beyond. Blake knew that Carlac was a powerful swimmer, and Kew—well, there was very little that that wrinkled man could not do when put to the test.

Blake made his way back to the strip of garden and, finding a seat, flung himself down to rest. He knew that he would have to wait until the inmates of the palace were at rest before making his attempt. An hour passed, and then the patient man heard the watch being changed, the clatter of swords and spurs echoed through the vaulted passages of the old palace, and finally came silence. Blake stepped out of his shelter and saw now that the lights had vanished from the building on the right. He crossed the courtyard and reached the gallery through which the passage from the tower to the main building ran. A carved marble pillar gave him an easy foothold, and with noiseless ease, he drew himself up on to the roof of the gallery. Keeping on the outer ledge, Blake crept forward until he was close to the tower. A narrow window was just above his head, a window which evidently served to light the rooms on the first floor.

Blake raised himself cautiously and leaned in through the open gap—for the windows in India are innocent of such modern adornments as glass.

There came to his nostrils the hot unmistakable twang of cat—that fetid scent which hangs about the great lion house in our Zoo. No one can mistake it—rank, evil stench as it is.

Blake's nerves were like set steel, yet he found himself withdrawing his head hurriedly with a quick catch of breath.

The tiger was in that very room.

Blake turned and cast another swift glance around him. The palace seemed as silent as the grave itself.

"I have no time to waste," he thought. "If the brute is there I must tackle it."

"From beneath his robes he drew the bulky package and unfolded the wrappings, the great chunk of raw deer flesh slipped into his hands.

"Here you are, my friend," the detective muttered. "A tit-bit for supper."

He reached out and placed the chunk of meat on the ledge. As he did so a great paw shot out suddenly from the darkness and the piece of raw meat vanished.

"By Jove, the brute must have been waiting just inside the window." came the startled thought. "That was as near an escape as I want."

The whole thing happened so swiftly that just for a moment Blake leaned against the wall of the tower, his heart drumming against his ribs. The stealthy beast inside had actually scented his presence at once. It had waited in the darkness; a grim, intent evil thing.

"Thank goodness it was the meat and not my arm that touched the ledge first," the plucky man muttered to himself. he drew nearer to the window and listened. Presently he heard coming from within the low gurgling purr of the brute at feed. Once he heard the crisp sound of the jaws as they met through some bone. He could almost picture the sleek brute squatting in the darkness, tearing at the flesh.

"I give you five minutes," Blake said grimly, "and you will never eat another meal again."

He waited in silence, listening intently. The moments seemed to drag past, then suddenly there came the first sound from the brute. A heavy thud, followed by the awful sound of claws striking wildly into the woodwork of the floor. The sharp crackling of splinters as they were torn up by the great claws, and, at last, thick throaty breathing.

Presently Blake heard another thud, and through the gap of the narrow window the lean head and shoulders of the tiger appeared. Dark though it was, Blake could see the foam-flecked jowl and the glaring evil eyes. And the great cat saw the lithe figure pressed flat against the wall of the tower, and, in one last desperate fury, it tried to reach him. The moments that followed were ones that Blake never forgot. He could not retire, for the brute strained half-way through the window. All he could do was to lean as far out over the gallery as he dared, pressing himself against the rounded wall of the tower at the same time.

And the claws struck again and again on the wall so close to him that the granite splinters sprayed on his tense cheek.

It seemed as though the cunning brute knew that here was the one who had tricked it at last, and all its dying energy was put into its furious effort to reach the strained figure. Just once would these claws have to fix into the arm, then Blake would be drawn into the merciless grip, and the foam-stained teeth would extract a grim vengeance.

But it was not to be. In the middle of a last furious struggle the great cat came to a halt, clawed high above its head for a moment, then came the death-rattle in the savage throat. the tiger sank down over the ledge, its fore paws, powerless now, hanging limply against the wall, the evil head between them.

Another moment passed before Blake ventured to move, and he did so warily, keeping his eye on the shadowy heap in the window. But the tiger gave no sign, and at last Blake stretched out his hand and touched it, The fur was still warm, but there was no sign of life in the sinewy body.

Blake ran his hand along the brute's flanks.

"I thought as much," he muttered, "you have been kept without food for days. Well, it was your life or mine, and I took the chance."

He pulled himself up into the gap and, stepping on to the motionless body of the great cat, lowered himself into the room.

A pocket torch came beneath his fingers, and he pressed the spring. As the round white light struck through the darkness another thought suddenly came to him.

"What if there was another tiger?"

There was just a possibility that the rajah might have turned out more than one of the grim beasts in the tower. Blake stood rigid and on the alert as he swing the light round. He saw now that the room was closed, the door in front of him being locked.

On the left, however, there was a narrow flight of steps leading up into another chamber. Blake stepped on boldly to the foot of the stairs, and climbed it. He was now on the second floor, and above him was the roof. The flight of steps caught his eye, but he noted that here the trapdoor was closed. The bolts were thrust into their sockets, but Blake drew them out, and the trap swung downward, revealing a glimpse of the starry sky above. A moment later Blake stepped out on to the broad roof of the tower, and looked at the little, round store. Over one ledge of the low wall a fragment of dark material was hanging, and as Blake crept up to the tower and listened, he heard heavy, laboured breathing—the breathing of an exhausted man plunged in deep sleep.

"Carlac!"

Out from the dusk came that whisper, and the ears of the sleeper heard. Carlac sat up, his nerves leaping.

"Carlac! Are you there?"

Again the voice! No dream this. With a struggled cry the big man drew himself to his feet, and peered over the wall—the wall over which he had so often looked in agony. He saw the figure standing below, and thought for a moment that it was a figment of his imagination.

"Who are you? Speak!"

And in quiet English came the reply:

"I am a friend, and I've come to get you out of this. Is Kew there?"

Carlac heard a soft tread by his side, and the hawk features of Kew slid past his shoulder to peer down.

"Come along; you have no time to waste!"

"But the tiger?"

"Is dead. I have poisoned it. Quick! Come down!"

The steady confident tones told the two wretches that the hour of their deliverance had indeed come. A sudden panic seized them both for the moment, steely-nerved rogues though they were.

"Don't leave me—don't leave me, Carlac!" Kew whispered, clutching at the broad arm of his companion. "I cannot move as quickly as you!"

They threw themselves down the open trapdoor and out through the door of the store on to the roof. Carlac peered hard into the brown, moustached face of the man who waited them, but the disguise was too clever, and his skill failed him.

"Come, you must follow me," said Blake, speaking in a low, distinct voice. "I need not tell you to be careful. The tiger is dead, but there are other sentinels just as quick-eared as he was."

He led the way down the narrow stairs, Kew and Carlac following obediently at his heels. When the reached the chamber on the first floor, the light from the electric torch revealed the great body of the dead animal wedged in the window. Kew drew back with a gasp of fear.

"You—you said that it—it was dead! he breathed.

Blake stepped up to the window, and, raising the striped tail, gave it a tug, then cast it aside.

"Does that satisfy you?" he asked slowly. There was no mockery in his voice. He realised that these men must have gone through some deadly torment that had sapped their courage, for Blake had also given Carlac and Kew full credit for nerves of steel.

He climbed through the window, and Carlac followed, helping Kew over the dead brute. Down the marble pillar they slid, reaching the courtyard. For a moment they waited in the shadows, then Blake gave his quick instructions. Carlac was the first to dart across the court, and as he had vanished beneath the bridge, Blake gave the word to Kew to follow. The professor started off but as he did so, there came a creak of a bolt, and a door in the building opposite opened, and there emerged a robed figure bearing a lantern and carrying with him a stone jar and a plate.

Kew caught the sight of the man, and in an instant knew what it meant. This was the rajah's servant who brought them their food nightly, passing up through the rooms on the other side of the tower to gain the roof.

Instantly his nerve, which had deserted him, returned to Kew then. With a lightning-like dart he was across the court, and as the man with the lantern turned to close the door behind him, Kew leaped, like a giant monkey, right on the broad, stooping back.

His fingers tightened around the throat, choking back the cry of alarm. So sure and deadly had been his aim that the swift pressure was sufficient. His tumbs were pressing on a certain spot in the man's neck, and beneath them his enemy went down in a heap on the tessellated floor of the porch. The lantern dropped to the ground, and Kew, bending forward turned out the light.

The whole incident happened in less time than it takes to tell, and as soon as his man was down, the professor arose and sped off across the court, to vanish below the bridge. A moment later and Blake was beside the two panting men.

His quick whispered commands were obeyed. Carlac and Kew scrambled over the sluice gate and vanished into the dark channel, and Blake followed.

A dozen strokes saw the detective beneath the black arch, and the strong current dragged him on and on for a long minute, then suddenly he saw the stars above his head again, in front of him loomed the stone steps of a ghat. He struck out for it, and as he drew near he saw the huge figure of Count Carlac scramble up out of the river, then turn to help the stunted figure of his companion.

Blake reached the steps and climbed them. Carlac and Kew were waiting for him as he reached the top.

"Follow me," said Blake; and, little dreaming whom it was that they obeyed, the two master criminals fell into step behind the lithe, active figure of the detective, and went on into the dark city, vanishing like wraiths into the shadows.

CHAPTER 13
The Last Trick

When the subahdar in charge of the East Gate guard had turned Tinker back into the city, after taking the youngster's horses away from him, and putting them into the empty shed in the dak-bungalow outside the gates, he thought that he had done a very clever thing, and had solved a very difficult problem.

In its way his idea was not a bad one, for it meant that Tinker would have to turn up again in the morning if he wanted his horses, and he would have to come to the East Gate to do that. If by any chance there was something wrong the guard would have been warned by that time. For in Kashopore the order was that no gates had to be opened in the morning until the sunrise gun sounded from the palace. When the rajah or his staff had any reason to prevent one from escaping, they put an effective check on this by simply omitting to fire the gun. In that case the guard stood to arms, and not a soul was allowed to enter or leave until word came direct from the palace.

So the subahdar was, perhaps, justified in his contentment with his plan. But he had reckoned without his Tinker.

The youngster himself could not get away from the city. But there was a companion of his who made short work of walls.

Tinker headed for a closed stall in one of the markets, and, stooping in the darkness, he lifted a loose flap. A wet muzzle was pressed against his hand, and Pedro came gliding out from beneath his hiding-place.

"Poor old man!" Blake's assistant murmured, patting the sagacious head. "You've had a pretty rotten time of it, stowed away there all these hours. But it's all right, and now you've got to make yourself useful."

He drew a book from his pocket, scrawled a note—he had practised the art of writing in the dark—and this is a much harder task that the average man would imagine, and the short note was soon finished. Tinker fastened the note to Pedro's broad collar, then, with the dog at his heels, the slim youngster punged into a labyrinth of side streets that presently came to an end, as did all other streets in the city, at the interminable wall. It was fifteen feet high, but at this particular spot someone had erected a sloping-roofed shed which rose to a height of about eight feet.

Tinker leaned down and put his arm round Pedro's neck.

"You've got to go home, old man, to the temple. Chandra Lal will be waiting there, and you must see that he finds this note. Do you understand?"

And, indeed, it seemed as though the dog did understand. Its heavy tail beat to and fro, and the moist tongue gave Tinker's fingers an affectionate lick. Tinker pointed to the shed.

"That's the way, Pedro," he whispered. "Go on! Just let me see if old age has stiffened you. Up, sonny!"

The bloodhound started forward, gathered its limbs beneath it, and with a splendid bound had reached the top of the crazy shed. The roof creaked to the dog's weight, but Pedro wasted no time. Another mighty effort saw it on the top of the four-feet wide parapet, and it vanished from Tinker's sight. The lad heard the scrambling of its feet as it went down head first for the great leap, that carred it on to the roadway, eighteen feet below.

A sharp voice rang out, and Tinker dodged back into the shadows. He knew that sentries were constantly moving to and fro along the wide parapet. There came to his ears the quick patter of feet, and presently the tall figure of a trooper was silhouetted against the dusky sky above him. The man was bending forward, peering into the roadway.

Tinker laughed softly to himself as he noted that the man's short carbine was poised and ready for use.

"Too late, old man!" the lad murmured. "If you can get a shot at Pedro now, you're a wonder!"

He crouched down, watching the sentry, until the man, realising the hopelessness of his task, turned away and resumed his steady patrol.

After all, it was only a dog, the sentry decided; no doubt one of the rapacious scavengers that haunted the streets of the old city. He would have liked to sent a bullet into its lean carcase; but it did not matter very much. How could the coming or going of a dog make any difference to the plans of his prince?

But had the sentry followed the lithe, black shape of the hound, he might have had cause to alter his decision. Pedro headed straight for the little Temple of the Vine, making his way through the narrow track of the paddy-field with an unerring accuracy that landed him in quick time at his destination.

Pedro pushed aside the heavy rug that hung across the doorway of the temple and slid inside. Chandra Lal was sleeping, stretched out on a pile of rugs. The lamp was burning dinly by his side, and he was snoring gently.

"Wow!"

Pedro went across to the sleeper and pressed his cold muzzle against Chandra Lal's cheek. The native came back to earth with a shout of fear. His alarm died down, however, when he recognised the great-thewed hound.

"Allah, but thou did'st frighten me!" the native muttered, sitting up and looking about him. "Where art thou, Tinker?"

Chandra Lal had leaped to the conclusion that the youngster was with the dog. But there was no response to his question, and presently Pedro thrust his head on to Chandra Lal's chest again. It was a significant hint, as much as to say, "Use your eyes, you fool!"

The piece of white paper sticking below the collar caught the man's attention, and he drew out the note. One of Chandra Lal's many accomplishments was the reading of the English language, a fact that Tinker was aware of.

"There are five horses in the stall behind the dak-bungalow at the East Gate. Go and steal them, and take them back to the Temple of the Vine. Then wait there until we all arrive."

The laconic message brought a quick smile to Chandra Lal's lips as he arose to his feet.

"There is no waste of words here," he muttered. "'Five horses—steal them.' Well, obedience is one of the virtues."

He yawned and stretched himself; then, picking up a robe, he wrapped it round his shoulders, and stepped out of the temple.

Pedro calmly settled himself in the warm place that Chandra Lal had lately occupied on the heap of rugs. The native grinned at the action.

"So thou art not inclined to follow me!" he said. "Well, I do not blame thee for that, wisest of dogs. The temple is the warmer place."

Chandra Lal knew his way about that district blindfolded, and he made for the East Gate by a short route through the fields, which brought him out exactly opposite the shed behind the belated travellers' bungalow.

The silent-footed man stepped into the shed and found the horses, counting them swiftly by moving along the wall to which they were tethered.

"Five is correct," said Chandra Lal, "and if that means one for each of us, then there are two others to join."

He loosened the ropes, and led the horses out through the wide gap that served as a doorway. The animals were evidently well trained, for they followed him quietly enough.

Chandra Lal plunged at once into the reeds, leading the horses behind him, The faint, rustling sound that he made was not more than what a fugitive wind might have caused, and the sentry on the gateway did not even hear it.

The long hours passed, and midnight came. Then the subahdar of the guard, half asleep on his hard bed, heard the noise of angry voices, accompanied by the deeper-toned ones of the sentry.

With a muttered word, the tall subahdar swung himself round and arose to his feet, his spurs clanking on the stone floor. The East Gate was beginning to prove itself a nuisance.

"What ails thee now?" the subahdar grumbled, as he stepped out of the guardroom.

He found that the sentry was standing in a group. There were four figures around him, and the foremost one was that of the youngster who owned the horses.

"There is trouble over the horses!" the sentry explained.

Tinker turned towards him, and rattled off a sentence in quick, voluble Hindustani.

"Thou canst prove that I am no liar!" he cried, mimicking perfectly the piping tone of the type he represented. "My master here swears that I have lost or sold the horses that he gave into my charge."

"I know that thou art a thief, and the son of a thief!" a deeper voice put in. "If my horses are not stolen, then where are they?"

The subahdar swung forward and looked at the speaker. He was dressed in a well-fitting robe, and the turban on his head was a silken one, finely embroidered. The face was brown, and a dark beard covered the lower part of it. Judging from his clothes, the man seemed a fairly well-to-do merchant—one of the type that made periodical visits to Kashopore, doing much business there.

Now, it was well known in Kashopore that his Highness the rajah, although in secret he might despise these men, knew that they meant added wealth and prosperity to his little State, and he therefore encouraged them to visit the town. The subahdar decided that this person was one that it was best to try to please, if possible.

He could not see much of his companions. They were standing in the shadow, swathed in dark robes. One of them was a giant of a man, while the other seemed a little, stunted creature.

"Thy syce speaks truth," said the subahdar. "Thy horses are safe enough! But it is the order of his Highness that no one may pass through these gates between sunset and sunrise. That ordinance thou must have knowledge of."

"This is my first visit to Kashopore," said Blake, for it was the detective who was playing the principal part in this last trick, "and thy orders are of the old kind. Kashopore must be asleep if it exists under such commands! In Delhi or the other great cities such an ordinance would bring scorn on its makers!"

The subahdar listened respectfully. Here was a man who had travelled far, who had visited all the great cities of the East. A personage of some importance, no doubt, and one of the very kind that his Higness wished to encourage.

"We find the order an irksome one," the leader of the guard admitted, "and many of us would be glad to have it otherwise. But we are but servants and must obey the law."

"True! But if my horses are safe, where are they?"

"In the stall behind the dak-bungalow."

Blake pretended to be surprised.

"But it means that they have passed through the gates!" he went on. "How could that happen?"

The subahdar flushed slightly, and fumbled with the hilt of his sword.

"It was the fault of thy syce!" he explained. "He had no place to stable the beasts, and I thought that they would be safer in the stall than were they to wander loose through the city."

"But surely that was against the law!" Blake persisted.

"Thy horse could not go without the rider," the rajah's soldier returned, "and I took care that he should remain here." It was a lame explanation, and the subahdar knew it.

"Well, I like this not, subahdar!" said Blake. "My horses are valuable, and I will have them brought back into the city! We will find some shelter for them until sunrise, which is not far distant now."

There was no getting out of that request, and at last the subahdar, armed with a lantern, opened the gates for the second time that night, and passed through with Blake at his heels. One by one the others followed, and the sentry, after a doubtful glance at them, let them go, contenting himself with a shrug of his shoulders as Tinker passed.

"It is no affair of mine!" he muttered. "The subahdar is in command."

Tinker felt his heart beginning to thump as he approached the bungalow.

"If that brown skunk hasn't come and pinched those horses, we're absolutely in the cart!" he thought.

It was the last link in the intricate chain that Blake had fashioned so carefully, and if it failed them all was lost!

The subahdar, striding ahead, reached the shed and held up his lantern.

"Let thine own eyes convince thee!" he said. "Thy horses are here, and safe until morning, when thous canst come and claim—— Allah, they have gone!"

The empty stall seemd to mock him. There was not so much as a shoe to be found!

"Now, by Allah, this is what I expected!" Blake broke out, pretending to leap into a fury. "I have been tricked—robbed! I feared as much!"

He turned to the subahdar with well-assumed rage.

"Thou art in this plot, with my thieving servant!" he went on. "But I will have the rajah's justice upon thee!"

The subahdar was pale to the lips now.

"I swear that I know nothing of this!" he stammered. "With my own hands I fastened up thy steeds——"

"Then where are they? Answer me that!"

Blake made a swift dart, and caught Tinker by the shoulder, shaking him violently.

"Thief and ingrate! Thou hast played this trick upon me—thou and this cunning soldier! Speak! I want the truth! To-morrow I seek the rajah, and place the whole history of this case before him!"

Something like a groan broke from the subadhar. He knew what to expect if he was brought in front of his merciless prince. Even if he could prove that he had not stolen the horses, he would yet be found guilty of breaking the orders of the guard by allowing the horses to go through.

"The subahdar is speaking the truth," Tinker broke out, in a snivelling whine. "Perhaps we can find the horses! They may only have strayed a little way.

It was only a straw, but the subahdar clutched at it.

"Yes, yes; that may be so!" he said eagerly. "Let us search!"

He led the way out of the stall, and held up his lantern. Where the low ditch of the paddy-field began was a great gap in the reeds, and on the soft mud were marks of hoofs.

"See! They are quite fresh!" the eager soldier continued. "We may find them——"

He came to a halt. His duty was to remain at the gate! For a moment he hesitated, then thrust the lantern into Blake's hand.

"Go and search for these accursed animals of thine!" he cried. "And if thou dost find them, in Allah's name mount and get on thy way! I have had enough of thee and thy servant this night!"

It was victory, most subtly gained; but Blake played the game to the end.

"And if I find them not, I will return!" he grumbled, as he took the lantern so eagerly extended towards him. "They are of value, and I am not going to lose their worth."

He moved off towards the reeds, and his companions spread out in a line, as though they meant to beat through the paddy-field in search of the missing animals. The subahdar waited until they had vanished into the field; then, with a grunt of relief, he turned and strode back to the gate, closing it tightly, and locking it.

"If these dogs return, do not admit them!" he growled. "And what is more, thou wilt swear that thou has never clapped eyes on them before! No one has passed through these gates—neither man nor beast! If they have their story to tell, so, too, must we have one prepared. It is only their word against ours, and, after all, we are the servants of the rajah. He will believe us."

The sentry chuckled in his beard.

"I will remember," he said.

But he was not to be troubled by the return of the men. Neither on that night, nor any other. And the miracle had happened, for Sexton Blake and his companions had been able to get out of the guarded city of Kashopore between sunset and sunrise, and, thanks to their ruse, no one would ever know how it was accomplished, for the subahdar, valuing his skin, was bound to keep silent.

The result was that on the following day, when the dead body of the tiger was discovered and the flight of the prisoners traced, the rajah and his servants were deceived. A messenger went hot-foot round the gates, to receive assurances from each one that no living thing had entered or left.

That meant that the two fugitives were still in the city, the rajah decided, and a house-to-house search was made.

Late in the afternoon, the fat butler at the Residency came hurrying into the study where Colonel Bryce and Vernon were at work.

"Your—your excellency will protect his servant?"

Bryce looked up.

"What is it?"

"Men from the palace have entered the house, and are searching in our quarters!" the butler went on. "They are armed, and one of his Highness's staff is with them!"

Vernon leaped to his feet, his eyes kindling with anger.

"I say, sir, that's a bit too thick!" he broke out. "The Residency is British territory, and these beggars have no right to be here without your permission!"

Bryce's jaw was like steel?, and there was a dangerous flash in his usually kindly eye. He stalked out of the room, followed by his aide-de-camp, the stout butler shuffling behind. In the courtyard, Bryce came on three or four men in the rajah's uniform, gathered round a well, down which one of their number was peering. Behind them stood a turbanned figure, whom Bryce recognised as being one of the captains of the palace guard.

"What is the meaning of this?" the old officer snapped out. "By whose orders do you come into my home?"

"It is his Highness's orders," came the brief reply. "Two prisoners have escaped from the palace and we are searching for them."

"Then order your men out of here at once or I will have them driven out," came the fierce return. "His Highness may search here when he cares to let me know, but not until then."

"There was that in the old officer's eye which made the searchers stop at once, and led by their captain they beat a swift retreat, followed by the grins of the Residency servants.

Colonel Bryce turned to Vernon.

"I will go across and see his Highness this evening," he went on quietly. "If prisoners have escaped, of course we will give every facility for a search to be made. But it must be carried out in a regular manner."

At eight o'clock that evening, the rajah, a sulky figure, was seated in his private room when Bryce's name was announced. For a moment the rajah hesitated, then nodded to his servant, and the tall, soldierly figure appeared, clicking his heels together and making a swift salute.

The rajah looked at Bryce from beneath ruffled brows.

"Then it seems that you are no longer my friend," he said in his excellent English. "To-day you insulted me through my servants."

"Your servants insulted me," said Bryce quietly. "and I simply pointed out to them how to carry out their duty."

He came nearer to the prince.

"If your Highness still desires to make a search in my home, it is open to you," the colonel went on; "but something has happened since your search-party called that makes me doubt whether it is worth your Highness's while continuing this search."

"What do you mean?"

Bryce slipped his hand into his pocket and drew out an envelope.

"This was handed to the British agent at Valghat, which, as your Highness knows is just beyond the border of Puljara. It was forwarded to me at once and reached Kashopore half an hour ago. Your Highness may care to read it."

The rajah took the opened letter, glanced at it for a moment, then his eyes hardened, and he read the long letter through from beginning to end. Bryce, watching the dark face, smiled inwardly at the varying emotions that appeared upon it.

For the letter was from Sexton Blake and was a brief report of what had happened. Blake had been careful not to give away the secret of his escape through the East Gate, nor did he mention the part that Muriel had played, but otherwise, the letter was a bare recital of the hard facts, that made a story worth reading.

"He entered my palace alone and unaided." It was the rajah's voice, and he was obviously talking to himself. "Through my guards and sentries—killed that fierce brute, and helped these wretches to escape! By Allah, but this is a man after my own heart."

Bryce leaned forward.

"No other man in the world would have dared so much," he put in; "I hardly believed the letter when I read it. I did not know that Blake was in India even—but someone in my household did know that."

"Thy daughter?"

It was a quick guess at the truth, and the honest old soldier nodded his head.

"Yes, Muriel told me this evening that she had met him, disguised as a fakir."

A look of enlightenment leaped into the rajah's eyes.

"Not the holy man who had taken up his abode at the Temple of the Vine?"

"Yes."

"Then by Allah I have been tricked with the others!" the ruler cried. "For I sent him food and offerings—and he is an Englishman!"

It seemed as though the sheer audacity of Blake's deed had dispelled all anger in the ruler's heart. But presently his brow clouded and he turned again to Bryce.

"Yet I doubt if these dogs that he saved were worthy of the sacrifice," he put in. "It is true that I broke your English law in taking them from their own country—but they are criminals and can never be ought else. Perhaps this man Blake may find out in the future that it would have been better for his peace and the peace of his country had he left them in my hands."

Bryce shook his head.

"I do not think so," he returned. "We British do not see with your eyes. To us torture of any living thing is hateful and impossible. Our vilest criminals may meet a swift doom, but it is our way to make it as merciful as possible. Blake remembered that I had promised him to do any service he wished, and the delivery of that letter into your hands was the result of that compact. I might not have brought it here had he not asked me to do so. But now you know the truth, and all that remains is to know what your Highness intends to do.

It was a question that much hung upon. Bryce, a diplomatist to the finger tips, knew that it was his duty to keep on friendly terms with this prince. Blake's letter had caused him a great deal of misgivings, and only his promise given to the detective made him take it to the rajah.

There was a silence, then as though he was casting something away from his shoulders, the ruler of Puljara arose.

"What I intend to do?" he repeated. "Why, cast it out of my mind, old friend. After all, the days those wretches spent on they tower is punishment enough. They will long remember the vengeance that followed their evil designs."

He crossed to Bryce and slipped his arm beneath the colonel's.

"And I will give orders to have thy quarters made ready for thee," he said. "From top to bottom will be changed, and all traces of what has happened, there will vanish."

His brown eyes smiled, and there was the old friendly glint in them.

"And if thy beautiful daughter should ask what has been amiss with me during these days, tell her that I was smitten by a fever—fever that comes from old, wild blood. But I have reached sanity again, and will be glad to welcome her and her fiancee. Perhaps it might happen that we could have a wedding at the palace. It would be a ceremony of great worth, and would put an end to the shadow that has existed so long between us."

He came to a halt and held out his hand suddenly, English fashion.

"We are friends again?"

Bryce caught the smooth brown hand.

"We are friends," he said.

. . . . . .

And there, so far as the reader is concerned, the case of the rajah's treasure-chest came to an end. But it had an aftermath that deserves a place.

On the express that thundered its long way from Puljara through the open plains down to the coast, late at night, the guard, chancing to lean out of his carriage thought he saw two figures fall from one of the first-class compartments. The hour was late, and there was no moon, and as the guard's compartment flashed past the spot its occupant could see no sign of the accident.

For a moment he hesitated. In official India there is a lot of enquiry which takes place when such an important thing as the mail train is brought to an unnecessary halt. Apart from that, this particular express happened to be an hour late, and at the portion of its journey, with a long flat plain in front of it, the engine-driver was trying to make up the lost time.

"I must have been dreaming," the half-caste guard decided; "and if I wasn't—well, I need not say that it happened before my eyes."

He was glad that he had decided thus, for when the train pulled up in the early morning and he walked along the line of carriages, there was no comment made by any of the occupants, yet each carriage had its human freightage.

From one of the carriages in the centre of the train a prosperous-looking merchant, followed by a slim youngster, emerged and crossed to the buffet.

Hot coffee tastes extraordinarily well at five in the morning, even although it be half sand.

Tinker sipped at his steaming cup then glanced at his master.

"You're not going to make any fuss, guv'nor?"

"No," Blake returned, "it would be of no use if I did. They chose their time very cleverly—and they may be anything from fifty to a hundred miles away by now."

He smoothed out a crumpled sheet of paper—the paper that he had found beneath his sleeping pillow when he awoke that morning to find that whereas four men had gone to sleep in the compartment on the previous night, there were only two left.

The message was characteristic, and was in Kew's small professional hand:

"We are taking French leave, having trespassed on your hospitality long enough. I have also ventured to borrow the two hundred-rupee notes that you had in your kit. The rajah forgot to supply us with any ready cash when we left the palace.

"And now a word on what has happened. We are not ungrateful, and yet, as you stand for just exactly the opposite to us, there cannot be any friendly feelings between us. But I have taken back a vow I had made—I meant to kill you after our failure with the treasure-chest.

"You know that I possess means of inflicting death that is certain and deadly. Perhaps you will believe that I could have found an opportunity of carrying out my vow.

"However, I take it back and we start once again, so far as I am concerned, with clean sheets. You, of course, will not see it in that light—in your eyes I am still a convict at large, and to be arrested at sight, if possible. But that is a risk I have run for years now, and it only adds a spice to life.

"We know that had we remained with you, your duty would have made you hand us over to the British police. We did not want to end our adventure in that very prosaic manner, so we take French leave.

"And the future to me will find us enemies as of old. Your skill against ours—and may the better man win.

"Adieu, or rather au revoir, for we are bound to meet again."

And beneath this extraordinary human document were scrawled the signatures of the two master criminals:

"Kew."

"Count Ivor Carlac."

"Perhaps it was the best way after all," Blake mused, "but it leaves their many crimes still unpunished. And until they do pay the penalty—we are, as Kew says—enemies."

Tinker smiled.

"And yet you saved them at the risk of your own life, guv'nor," he muttered. "That's the sort of thing that people wouldn't believe if you told them."

"I only thought of them as white men, men of my own race," said Blake quietly; "and the white man must always be upheld if the white man has to remain as rulers of the world."

A speech that went far to explain all that had happened.

THE END

273

SEXTON BLAKE AND TINKER *AND THE* LEAGUE OF CRIME.

MARCH 5TH 1945

THE CENTRAL CRIMINAL COURT OF THE OLD BAILEY, LONDON ~

JOHN LEAGUE, THE WORLD'S MOST NOTORIOUS CRIMINAL, WANTED BY THE POLICE OF EVERY CONTINENT, IS SENTENCED TO FIFTEEN YEARS' IMPRISONMENT.

Ten years ago, Sexton Blake, the famous Baker Street detective, was responsible for the bringing to justice of the arch-criminal, John League. League got fifteen years' hard labour, and when he heard this sentence the crook burst out in a wild tirade against Blake and finally he swore to have his life when he got out.

BUT AT DARTMOOR JOHN LEAGUE IS WATCHED VERY CAREFULLY ══ - REALISING THE WISDOM OF PLAYING A WAITING GAME, HE WORKS HARD AND WELL

The court was horrified at League's savage outburst, but it was not an uncommon thing to happen and he would be safe enough in Dartmoor prison. True, they kept an extra close watch on the cunning and ruthless prisoner while he worked with other prisoners in the quarries, but all the time League thought and planned a daring escape.

NIGHT AFTER NIGHT, YEAR IN, YEAR OUT, LEAGUE'S ONLY THOUGHTS ARE OF ESCAPE AND VENGEANCE

ESCAPE FROM DARTMOOR AND VENGEANCE ON SEXTON BLAKE.

LATE SUMMER 1955 ~
THE DAY FOR WHICH JOHN LEAGUE HAS BEEN WAITING TEN YEARS.

A WARDER, NEW TO DARTMOOR, UNWARILY TURNS HIS BACK.

To the warders League seemed a model prisoner. He worked well and obeyed his instructions implicitly, never for a moment did they suspect that he was merely waiting his chance and that he was watching their actions more keenly than they were watching his. One afternoon, in a lonely part of the quarry, the warder's attention strayed——

THE ROCK FLIES UNERRINGLY FROM LEAGUE'S HAND AND SENDS THE CARELESS WARDER TO THE GROUND SENSELESS — — LEAGUE'S LUCK HOLDS GOOD — — — HIS VICIOUS ACTION HAS BEEN UNOBSERVED — —

THIS IS WHERE I SAY FAREWELL TO DARTMOOR — NOW LET SEXTON BLAKE BEWARE!

THE NEXT DAY, JOHN LEAGUE DESCENDS FROM A RAILWAY CARRIAGE FIFTY MILES FROM DARTMOOR PRISON.

MORNING, SIR! ON A SHOOTING HOLIDAY? WE'RE NOTED FOR OUR PHEASANTS IN THESE PARTS!

I'M AFTER BIGGER GAME THAN PHEASANTS, PORTER!

League felled the warder with a lump of rock and after exchanging clothes, the crook made off into the mists of Dartmoor. Later he entered a train—slowed by the weather conditions. A well-dressed man, obviously out for a shooting holiday, sat alone in a compartment. He was easy meat for League in a dark tunnel.

SOUTHAMPTON — THREE WEEKS LATER. PASSENGERS ARE BOARDING THE QUEEN ELIZABETH, OUTWARD BOUND FOR NEW YORK — AND AMONGST THEM IS JOHN LEAGUE, TRAVELLING UNDER A FORGED PASSPORT.

I SAY, JUST A MOMENT!

YOU DROPPED YOUR NEWSPAPER, SIR!

THANK YOU, CONSTABLE.

GOOD-BYE, SEXTON BLAKE, WHEREVER YOU ARE! BUT DON'T THINK I'VE FORGOTTEN YOU — I'M COMING BACK!

League emerged at the next station with his travelling companion's clothes and possessions, and from then on the police lost track of him. True there were moments when the master criminal feared recapture, but he took care to cover his tracks and finally left the country with an assumed name and a forged passport.

MANY MONTHS AFTER LEAGUE'S ESCAPE — THE FAMOUS DETECTIVE IS SITTING IN HIS STUDY IN COMPANY WITH TINKER, HIS YOUNG ASSISTANT. SUDDENLY, THERE COMES A SOFT TAP AT THE DOOR — —

GOOD AFTERNOON, MR. BLAKE!

AH, COME IN, LEAGUE! I'VE BEEN EXPECTING YOU!

JOHN LEAGUE Newspaper Cuttings Notes Etc...

But he was not running away from Sexton Blake—he really did mean to get his revenge, and some months later he returned to keep his word. One afternoon Tinker answered a knock on the consulting-room door. Standing there, gun in hand, was John League, and in his burning eyes was all the pent-up fury and hatred of an embittered man.

The atmosphere was tense with danger, but not by so much as a flicker of an eyebrow did Blake betray unusual interest in his visitor. In fact, it was League who was unsteadied for a moment by his casual reception—but the master crook held the whip hand and coolly announced that he had come for his revenge—that he intended to kill Blake!

Unperturbed Blake sardonically introduced Tinker to John League, and his clever deduction about the material of League's overcoat betraying the fact that he had been in South America, clearly began to get the crook rattled. With a snarl of hate League leapt to his feet, his crooked finger hovering on the trigger of his automatic.

" Still the clever detective, eh ? " snarled the man, maddened by Blake's outward calm. Maybe he had expected Blake to break down and start whimpering in the face of certain death—any lesser man than the famous detective might well have done so. Even if he was to be deprived of that part of his revenge, League still meant to take Blake's life.

Backing towards the door, League raised the revolver. Sexton Blake rose from his chair, and Tinker gasped in horror. League's finger tightened on the trigger and at that moment there was a sudden turn of the handle and the door behind him opened. League shot a glance over his shoulder to see who it was, and instantly Blake's fist shot out!

The force of the blow sent the notorious criminal reeling clean out of the room and backwards down the stairs. The girl could not have walked in at a better moment—she had saved Sexton's life. The front door had been left open by League and she had walked straight in, for she needed help herself—from the very man who had attacked Blake.

Sexton Blake and Tinker ran after League, but at the top of the stairs they halted. One of League's men had left the car waiting outside and followed the girl into the building—and now he stood at the foot of the stairs with a tommy-gun. League ordered him not to shoot. For some reason the crook did not want the girl harmed.

League's leg was injured and his men carried him out to the waiting car. The notorious criminal was intent now on getting away before a passer-by chanced to notice what was happening and report to the police. And for his own reasons Blake was willing to let him go, for he feared the girl might be hurt if he tackled League there and then.

Back in his study Blake set to work to plan the downfall of the crook. First he set Scotland Yard on the trail of the car in which League had escaped—then he heard Joyce Standish's story, and an amazing tale it was. She had every reason to fear that her father, a scientist, may have come to some harm, for he had vanished.

According to Joyce the last man who had visited her father on the previous evening was John League, and Blake was sure that in some way the terrible criminal was responsible for the Professor's disappearance! The great detective decided to motor down to Joyce's home in Devon straight away. He hoped to find a clue there.

In a few minutes Tinker had Sexton Blake's special car ready and they were speeding on the way to Devon. They cleared London and many hours afterwards they flashed through the outskirts of Exeter and on into the heart of Devon. Near Morton Manor, Joyce's home, Tinker pointed out an old, ruined priory standing in its own grounds.

A baker's van stood at the gate, and Tinker realised that someone was living there in spite of its ruined appearance. Little did he guess it was John League and his gang who were there, and that at that very moment League was lying in bed, still injured from his fall, planning the next move in the crooked game he was playing.

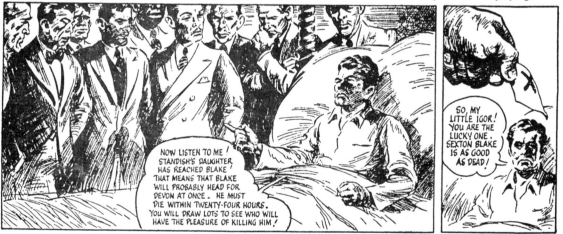

John League ordered all his gang to his bedside. They were the arch-criminals of a dozen different countries, and not one of them betrayed a glint of compassion when their master told them that Blake was probably on their trail and that he must die within twenty-four hours. They were to draw lots to decide who would do it !

The deed fell to "little" Igor! At that moment the telephone bell rang. It was another of League's men reporting Blake's arrival at Moreton Manor, and with a sardonic smile the master crook told Igor to go ahead. It seems as though Blake has played into League's hands by going down to Devon, for the crook's spies are everywhere.

But even if Blake had suspected that their arrival at the manor was known to League, he did not let it worry him. So long as a man like League was at large, organising crime, everyone in the country was in danger, and if the master crook really had kidnapped Professor Standish, then some of England's most vital secrets might be forced from him.

Sexton Blake and Tinker set to work in Professor Standish's study, hoping to find some clue as to why he should have been kidnapped. Joyce helped them, and it was some time before they found anything of interest, and then only Blake realised it might be a clue. The paper he found showed that the professor had bought a mine.

All three turned round at the sound of steps in the passage. Tinker and Joyce gasped in amazement, and "little" Igor lumbered into the room. He was massive! His frame seemed to fill the whole doorway. Then his ape-like hands reached towards Sexton Blake. With a quick turn and a sudden heave, the detective flung a large table in the monster's path!

Igor seemed surprised that anyone should resist him. He looked on people as flies, but the table had knocked him over and he felt annoyed and he threw Sexton Blake viciously aside. Tinker grabbed a brass candle-holder and crashed it down on the giant's head—but it might have been a roll of paper for all the difference it made. Igor grabbed Tinker.

He meant to throw Tinker out of the window because he had dared to strike him. The monster raised Tinker over his head and tensed himself for a great throw, but as he turned to the window he found himself looking into the mouth of an automatic held in Joyce's quivering hands. It was her father's and she had remembered where he kept it.

281

Igor stood and looked at her, his dull brain trying to cope with this new menace, and then with surprising speed he suddenly flung Tinker clean at Joyce. Luckily, Tinker fell short and the carpet was soft, but it was enough to make Joyce drop her automatic, but then Sexton Blake saw his chance and snatched up the deadly little weapon.

Blake's shot fired at close range was aimed deliberately to wing Igor, although the shock was enough to cause the sullen brute to fall back against the window and crash through it. Even that fall didn't finish Igor, and as he slunk away into the bushes Blake did not fire again—Igor would lead them to League's headquarters.

With the instinctive cunning of a trapped animal, Igor shot quick glances over his shoulder as he lumbered through the woodlands, but by expert tracking and exercising every care, Sexton Blake and Tinker were able to follow the monster until he was seen to enter an old ruined priory. Sexton Blake sent Tinker back for the car at once.

Meanwhile inside the priory League's men had been using force to extract information from Professor Standish—at last under extreme pressure, the clever scientist had broken down and revealed the location of the mine he had bought. That was enough for League, for he hoped to get plans of the mine by searching the professor's home, Moreton Manor.

The master criminal smiled grimly at the success of his plans—but then his smile suddenly changed to a look of horror as the injured Igor appeared in his room. He realised that Sexton Blake had got the upper hand, that he was sure to have trailed Igor and might be in the priory at that very moment. Now League was in danger !

Sexton Blake was thinking one move ahead of League all the time now. He knew how League would react to Igor's return—the house and the grounds would be searched, but there was one place where they would not think of looking, and that was OUTSIDE LEAGUE'S BEDROOM WINDOW! He climbed up a drain-pipe and grasped the sill.

Professor Standish was the only one who noticed Sexton Blake at the window. League was too busy directing his men in their search to think of his own bedroom, and when the master criminal went out with the others, leaving one of his men to guard the professor, Blake leaped into the room. A left hook knocked all argument out of the guard.

The man staggered back, crashed through the rotting balustrade and dropped down on to the stairs below. The noise brought League's men tearing to the spot and they were amazed to see Sexton Blake with the professor at the top of the stairs. There was now no way of escape—except the landing window just by their side.

The branch of a tree below the window offered a slim chance to Sexton Blake, but the professor was just about all in. He had stood much of League's devilry that day and now the elderly man was on the point of collapse, but Blake persuaded him to make the final effort and together they leapt from the window down on to the branch below.

Even as they swung down from the branch League and his men appeared up at the window with automatics levelled, and at that range they surely could not miss, but the drone of a car engine baulked them in their intentions. To shoot then would have given them away to whoever was passing. Actually it was Tinker with Sexton Blake's car.

When League saw who it was it was too late to start shooting, but League did not give in. He thought there was still time to get to that mine—to find out whatever secret it might hold, and to get away before Sexton Blake had time to find out what was going on. But first to Moreton Manor for the plans.

Joyce had stayed at the manor to continue to search for clues when Sexton Blake and Tinker had gone after Igor. Blake has not returned directly to the manor for Standish needed urgent attention by the village doctor, which meant a detour of some miles. This gave League's men time to get to the manor first. They overpowered Joyce.

When, at last, Sexton Blake and Professor Standish did return with Tinker to the manor, they found no sign of Joyce. League's men had turned the place upside down searching for plans of the mine. It was then that the professor revealed that the mine was being used by him, with the government's approval, for secret atomic experiments.

SO BLAKE TINKER AND THE PROFESSOR SET OUT WITH ALL SPEED FOR THE MINE WHICH IS IN A LONELY PART OF THE COUNTRY. THEY LEAVE THE CAR SOME DISTANCE FROM THE MINE ENTRANCE AND CREEP FORWARD CAUTIOUSLY

Sexton Blake guessed that League would lose no time in getting to the mine, so he phoned the police and then drove there himself. If League obtained the atomic secrets he would be sure to use them in waging the worst wave of crime ever known in history. They parked the car some distance from the mine and crept towards the entrance.

A FEW MOMENTS LATER, A RUSTLING NOISE IN THE DARKNESS BRINGS THE GUARD WHIPPING ROUND — HIS GUN RAISED. AND IN THE SAME INSTANT BLAKE SPRINGS FORWARD.

There was an armed guard on the opening to the mine shaft, and that meant that League was definitely in the mine. Sexton Blake stole forward as silently as a cat—the guard heard him at the last moment, but as he swung round with his gun Sexton Blake closed in and knocked him to the ground with a smashing straight right to the jaw.

The professor knew a secret entrance into the mine which would take them straight into the laboratory. There the professor's scientists were being threatened by League and his gang. The master crook was menacing them with an automatic and he gave them five minutes to live, unless they handed over all the details of their experiments.

There was a deathly quiet in the laboratory as the minutes ticked by; not one of the scientists made any attempt to do what League had ordered. Sexton Blake, Tinker and the professor watched the scene through the door, and then Blake and Tinker stepped into the laboratory, guns in hand. Instantly League dragged Joyce across in front of him.

League dared not shoot for fear of his own life, and using Joyce as his shield he had baulked Sexton Blake for a moment, but suddenly all eyes are riveted on Igor. The dull-witted monster had picked up a glass flask and was about to hurl it at Sexton Blake and Tinker—and that flask contained a super-high explosive!

287

But already Tinker had pressed the trigger of his automatic and shot Igor in the thigh. With an animal like grunt the giant man slowly crumpled and fell, dropping the deadly flask. Throwing himself forward, Tinker just caught it before it splintered on the ground and blasted them all to destruction.

Now the battle really was on. Ducking down behind the crates and tables in the laboratory, League and his men took cover. Sexton Blake and Tinker did likewise and exchanged shots with the crooks. It would have gone ill with Sexton Blake against such odds had not the police arrived at that moment.

BUT LEAGUE DOES NOT KNOW THAT THE TUNNEL COMES TO A DEAD END AT THE YAWNING OPENING TO A NEW SHAFT WHICH, THOUGH NOT COMPLETED, ~~ DROPS DEEP DOWN INTO THE BOWELS OF THE EARTH. NOW, FINDING HIMSELF TRAPPED ~ HE TURNS AT BAY ~~~

But League, the master criminal, had not given in. He still had an ace to play, for Joyce was his prisoner, and in the sudden confusion of the arrival of the police, he crept away with her down one of the old mine tunnels. Sexton Blake leapt across the laboratory and followed them, not daring to shoot for fear of hitting Joyce.

John League dragged Joyce along as fast as he could and then suddenly stopped aghast, his heart sinking, for the tunnel ended abruptly at the gaping hole of a new shaft. He was trapped, and he turned like a frightened rat towards Sexton Blake, with the professor's daughter held in front of him. He was still defiant!

Breathing hard, League swore he would jump to his death and take Joyce with him unless Blake guaranteed his freedom. Then Sexton Blake noticed the huge iron bucket suspended on a rope, part of the excavating machinery of the mine. The detective aimed carefully and severed the rope. The bucket swung down straight at League.

Sexton Blake leapt forward and pulled Joyce to safety when a piercing scream came from League as he was thrown into the gaping shaft hole. The master-criminal had met his end, and Joyce forgot the horror of the last few hours when she was reunited to her father. Sexton Blake had saved the world from the terrible ravages of John League.